Mercy Triumphs

A Contemporary Novel

BY JANA KELLEY

⇒ Endorsements ⇐

"I highly recommend this book that kept me wondering, *What's next?* after each chapter. In *Mercy Triumphs,* Jana Kelley weaves a story of God's mercy, set in Sudan, Kenya, Dubai, and the United States. Its relevance to current realities in our world makes it more than just a good story. It speaks to the plight of refugees who flee oppression in their home countries. It details the struggles and dangers of those who choose to leave Islam and follow Jesus Christ. It's transparent about the daily life of an American family living out their faith in North Africa and the surprising pain of leaving that hard life to return to America. Jana has lived and witnessed these realities and her words ring true on the page. In the end I came away challenged to continue boldly sharing the gospel, even when it is rejected, even when there may be persecution—because Jesus Christ is worth it all."

—SUSAN LAFFERTY, served 26 years in South Asia and Southeast Asia

"*Mercy Triumphs* will not disappoint. Jana Kelley once again weaves the dramatic impact that obedience to Christ makes on individuals and families. *Mercy Triumphs* takes us on a journey to look outside ourselves and to the needs of others."

—RUTH RIPKEN, missionary, speaker, and partner in *The Insanity of God*

"Jana's characters take us on an intense journey to belong, a journey the Western church would do well to undertake. Where, and to Whom, do you belong? I would highly recommend *Mercy Triumphs* for numerous reasons, but chief among these is the vital question of how faith is lived out in persecution—within one's own culture, peoples, and family. This book goes down some important paths as her characters seek to leave their culture and family behind, only to develop a deep hunger for the persecutors within their own family to become part of the family of God known through Jesus Christ."

—NIK RIPKEN, author of *The Insanity of God* and *The Insanity of Obedience*

"*Creative, captivating,* and *inspiring* are just a few words to describe Jana Kelley's third book in her true-to-life series about ministry on the missions field. *Mercy Triumphs* brings to a satisfying conclusion the stories of three women committed to Christ but who face overwhelming challenges in a Muslim society. I recommend this book, not only as an exciting and enjoyable read, but also because of the missiological insights presented throughout about evangelizing cross-culturally. Pastors, church staff, missionaries, and everyone of all ages in church congregations will be blessed, inspired, and helped by reading *Mercy Triumphs.*"

—DR. ROBIN DALE HADAWAY, professor of missions and dean of students, Midwestern Baptist Theological Seminary

"In *Mercy Triumphs*, Jana once again opens our eyes and hearts to the courage, struggles, sacrifices, and joys of following Christ—for both Westerners and Muslim background believers—with her story of a journey of learning to trust in our merciful God. Life in Sudan, Dubai, Kenya, and the USA are described in vivid detail, transporting the reader into those places with remarkable ease! The novel also provides sound biblical teaching and a fresh impetus to pray for those who pay a heavy price for following Jesus."

—NILANTHI SIM, friend and co-laborer in Christ

"God uses people whose hearts are surrendered to Him *wherever* they may be—a powerful lesson for each of us to learn, whether we are given opportunity to do so across the world or in our own backyard. As she has done so well before, Jana Kelley weaves a beautiful story based on real experiences and understanding that teaches truth, helps us learn about ourselves as well as the Muslim culture, and stirs our hearts. This heartwarming conclusion to her trilogy comes full circle and reminds us to never stop trusting or following God's leading in our lives—even when it doesn't quite meet with our expectations."

—JAMI BELEW, project manager, Women of Faith

"No one depicts the love of a missionary for those living in a closed country better than Jana Kelley. It is a difficult paradox to encourage those who lose home and family for the sake of Christ while knowing they themselves will never have to walk that lonely and difficult road. With this third book in the series, I could not turn the pages fast enough to find out what would happen to this Christian community in a dry and barren land. Once again Jana excellently weaves the story of how God reigns supreme in the hearts of believers, helping them to realize that God is on His throne and is in control of every situation, whether on behalf of the veteran missionary or the newly converted Muslim."

—KATHY HADAWAY, former missionary, adjunct missions professor,
Midwestern Baptist Theological Seminary

"What an encouragement to read a book that clearly shows God's hand working in different parts of this world simultaneously to accomplish His purpose! As a former missionary who struggled with having to unexpectedly return to the USA, this book stirred up so many memories of the same feelings of returning to my homeland that doesn't feel like home anymore. But God is faithful to use us anywhere He places us, as shown so well in *Mercy Triumphs*. I just hope this isn't the final book in this series. I'm sure there's more to the story yet to come!"

—JANA THOMPSON, former missionary in Europe

Other books by Jana Kelley

Side by Side

Door to Freedom

Mercy Triumphs

A Contemporary Novel

BY JANA KELLEY

NEW HOPE®
PUBLISHERS
Gospel-Centered. Missions-Driven.

Birmingham, Alabama

New Hope® Publishers
PO Box 12065
Birmingham, AL 35202-2065
NewHopePublishers.com
New Hope Publishers is a division of WMU®.

New Hope Publishers serves its authors as they express their views, which may
not express the views of the publisher.

This is a work of fiction. Although based on real-life events, the names, characters,
businesses, places, events, and incidents are either the product of the author's
imagination or used in a fictitious manner and are not intended to represent any
actual person or occurrence.

Library of Congress Cataloging-in-Publication Data

Names: Kelley, Jana, 1971- author.
Title: Mercy triumphs / by Jana Kelley.
Description: First edition. | Birmingham, Alabama : New Hope Publishers,
 [2017]
Identifiers: LCCN 2017012252| ISBN 9781625915283 (permabind) | ISBN
9781596699816 (Ebook)
Subjects: | GSAFD: Christian fiction.
Classification: LCC PS3611.E4427 M47 2017 | DDC 813/.6—dc23
LC record available at https://lccn.loc.gov/2017012252

ISBN-13: 978-1-62591-528-3

N184102 • 0817 • 2M1

❧ Dedication ❧

*Dedicated to the women who obey Jesus' command
to go (Matthew 28:19), even when the "go" looks
different from what they imagined.*

➳ Acknowledgments ⥲

Thank you to the Lord who shows us mercy. I am thankful to see the wonderful ways He draws people to Himself, and I am grateful for the opportunity to write about them.

To my husband, Kris, and our sons, Aaron, Seth, and Joel: you are my best advocates, and I am so thankful for you. To my extended family: thanks for encouraging me to keep writing.

A big thank you to my beta readers: Edward, Kathy, Mom, Robin, and Zanese. You put up with a lot of typos and crazy sentences when you read my early manuscript. Thanks for looking past the ugly to see the potential.

Thank you, Natalie Hanemann. Once again, I am indebted to you for your gifted insight.

Thank you, New Hope Publishers. I believe in the work you do and am thankful to be part of it.

To the readers of this book: thank you for taking the time to read. If you have followed this story from the beginning, thanks for sticking with me. If it is your first time to pick up a book like this, I hope you'll enjoy the story and take the time to soak in God's mercy. I am thankful for each of you.

⇒ Glossary ⇐

ARABIC WORDS

Abaya: robe-like covering worn by women

Aeeb: "not good manners," often used when talking to a child who is misbehaving

Ala keifik: "as you like"

Aleykum wassalaam: "and peace to you," response to "salaam aleykum"

Alhamdulillah: "Thanks be to God."

Allah: God

Allahu akbar: "God is the greatest."

Amreeka: America

Astaghfir Allah: "God, forgive us."

Aywa: "Yes."

Bakhoor: incense

Bi sura'a: "Do it quickly."

Bilakthar: "I miss you more," response to "mushtagiin."

Dirham: denomination of money used in Dubai

Habeebtee: "my dear," a term of endearment

Haboob: sandstorms common in North Sudan and other desert countries

Haj: pilgrimage to Mecca that all Muslims should take, title given to one who has taken the pilgrimage, one of the Five Pillars of Islam

Ibrahim: Abraham

'Tirmia: Jeremiah

'Illa 'irrahiim: "God is merciful."

Injil: New Testament

Innazaaha: integrity

Insha' Allah: "if Allah wills"

'Isha: evening prayers

Isa: Jesus

Jallabeeya: white robe worn by Northern Sudanese men

Kafir: infidel, a person who is not Muslim

Karkaday: hibiscus tea

Keffiyeh: checkered scarf worn by men in some Arab countries

La ilaha illa-llah, Muhammadu-rasulu-llah: "There is no god but Allah and Mohammed is his prophet," the Muslim statement of faith

Mahalabeeya: Sudanese rice pudding

Masha' Allah: "Thanks to God."

Niqaab: full-body covering worn by some Muslim women

Qur'an: holy book of Islam

Ramadan: month of fasting for Muslims

Sabah 'ilxayr: "Good morning."

Sabah 'innoor: "morning of light," response to "sabah 'ilxayr"

Salaam aleykum: "Peace be upon you," Arabic greeting

Salaam aleykum wa rahmatullahi wa barakatuh: "Peace to you and Allah's mercy and his blessing."

Shihada: the Muslim statement of faith

Shukran: "Thank you."

Subhia: Northern Sudanese bridal dance ceremony

Sura al-Imran: section of the Qur'an

Taba'an: "Of course."

Tarha: headscarf worn by Sudanese women

Tobe: traditional full-body scarf worn by married women in Sudan

Wa entee?: "And you?"

Zibeeb: raisin, also the word for the bruise on the forehead caused by bowing forcefully to the ground during prayer, a sign of piety

SWAHILI WORDS

Jambo: greeting

Matatu: minibus used as public transportation

Mercy triumphs over judgment.

—James 2:13

⮞ Chapter 1 ⮜
Khartoum, Sudan

Mia Weston closed her eyes and rubbed her right cheek, feeling the heat that emanated from the swollen area. She winced. The tooth had been hurting for quite some time, but she had no idea a cavity could escalate to an ordeal like this. She laid her head against the dentist's chair, expecting to feel the soft padding. Instead she felt a rough hard surface.

With her other hand, Mia reached back and pulled tree bark out of her hair. *What in the world?* She turned to look behind her and realized she was not in a dentist chair at all. She was sitting on the dusty ground, leaning against a giant tree. The dental equipment and x-ray screen that had filled her vision faded away, replaced by desert sand.

Then she remembered. She was in a village. In Sudan. Sudan was the worst place in the world to have a dental emergency. But she and Michael decided that with an abscessed tooth, there wasn't much else they could do. She was at the mercy of a dentist in Africa.

"*Salaam aleykum.*" The voice of the female dentist scraped like a tin can dragging across gravel. The old woman wore a white coat and carried a tray of stainless steel tools. As she approached, her lips spread into a giant grin.

Mia recoiled. The woman's teeth, the few that remained, were crooked and stained. One of them wobbled as if about to fall out. Suddenly, bits of gravel and sand began to fall onto Mia's face. She tried to brush them away, but they kept hitting her. And then it was no longer sand and gravel. Teeth were falling on her.

Mia opened her mouth to scream for help, but the only sound leaving her throat was a pathetic groan.

And then she opened her eyes. She was lying on her bed at home. Flies danced and hopped about on her face. She brushed them away, sat up straight, and looked around her. She was safe. Breathing a sigh of relief, she instinctively held a hand to her right cheek. It was not feverish or swollen. Another sigh of relief.

Mia remembered the pain she'd felt in her lower molar the day before when the family had gone out for ice cream. Perhaps she really did have a cavity.

The bedroom door flew open as Michael kicked it, trying not to spill the mugs of coffee in each hand.

"Good morning, beautiful," he said as he turned and attempted to kick the door shut. A little coffee splashed on the floor. "Oops."

Mia grinned. "That's OK, it's tile. And anyway, it's so dry here it'll evaporate in two minutes."

Michael handed her one of the mugs and then returned to his side of the bed. He arranged his pillow against the headboard and settled himself beside her.

"What's wrong with your cheek?"

"Oh." Mia hadn't realized she was still rubbing it. "Well, my tooth was hurting. But it's fine. I'm sure it's nothing."

"I bet we can find a dentist here you can go to."

"No way. I had this terrible dream, Michael. This old lady dentist was going to pull my tooth out. Her office was in the desert, and I had to sit against a tree. Then teeth were raining down on me, and the dentist had the most horrible teeth you ever saw . . ."

Michael threw his head back and laughed. Piqued by his flippant reaction, Mia frowned and took a sip of coffee. The pause afforded her a moment to think back over the words she'd just said to Michael.

I should be laughing too. It's just . . . it felt so real . . .

Michael looked at her and stopped laughing. "Are you upset?"

Mia smiled. "No. It was a crazy nightmare. I had another one earlier this week, the night we started talking about buying tickets for our trip to Texas this summer."

"Yeah . . ." Michael leaned his head against the wall and pondered. "I can't believe we've been living in Sudan for three years. It'll be good to spend some time at home before putting in our final year here."

Home. Mia thought about the word. Where was home anyway? Ever since Michael took the job as project coordinator for Kellar

Hope Foundation, their family had taken on the challenge of making Khartoum, Sudan, their home.

"It's already April. I can't believe we're going back in a month. Do you know how many times I've pleaded with God to tell us to go back to Texas?"

"Well, it's just for the summer. I still have a job here in Khartoum. Work at refugee camps is never finished."

"That's the best part." Mia sat up straight and crossed her legs. "We get to go enjoy all the good stuff like Mexican food and Walmart and don't have to say goodbye to our friends here. I'm not ready to leave Sudan for good yet; I just think a break is what we need."

Michael glanced at his watch. "Well, no break yet. I gotta go to work. Habiib told me there is a problem with our paperwork. We may have to leave Sudan sooner than we think."

He leaned over and kissed Mia on the cheek. She was relieved to notice her cheek didn't hurt when he did. She didn't have a cavity, but even if she did, she would absolutely not go to a dentist here in Africa. She could wait and go to one in Dallas.

Mia watched the door shut behind Michael. She closed her eyes and took a deep breath, silently thanking the Lord for a new day and asking for opportunities to be an encouragement to others. Sweat gathered along her hairline and a couple of flies flitted about on her arms, but she ignored both, relishing the quiet moment before the day started.

Wait a minute. Leave sooner than we think?

She jumped out of bed and ran to the front door, but Michael was already gone. Mia sighed. "Thanks a lot, Michael. Now I'm gonna be thinking about that for the rest of the day." She gulped the last bit of coffee from her mug and immediately grimaced at the mouthful of coffee grounds. The first thing she was going to buy this summer was a new drip coffee maker. Too bad Khartoum stores didn't carry them; she'd pay any price for a machine that didn't dump grounds into the carafe every time.

Mia picked bits of coffee grounds from her teeth as she walked to the kitchen to set her mug in the sink. She turned on the light switch in the kitchen, but the room remained dark. No electricity. If she wanted air-conditioning, or even ceiling fans, she was going to have to handle Bertha by herself.

"Mom, it's hot." Her ten-year-old stood in the doorway of the kitchen. Corey's dark hair, compliments of Michael, was already damp with sweat. The other two kids would be waking up any minute now. It was too hot to sleep late.

"I know. The electricity went off."

"Can Dad go deal with Bertha?"

"He's already gone to work. I'll do it." Mia twisted a curl of her hair around an index finger and smiled at her oldest son, trying not to look nervous.

"You?" Corey did not hide his surprise as he followed Mia to the front door.

The two stared through the glass pane at Bertha across the yard. She sat defiantly on a cement slab by the outer wall. An old dirty mass of metal and cogs and belts, Bertha was the generator, and she was a mean one. She was loud and dirty and greasy. Her main belt was exposed, which made standing close enough to start or stop the machine dangerous. But on the days she decided to work, she provided electricity for the Westons. So she was a necessary evil.

Michael purchased the used generator only a few months earlier because of frequent power cuts. The next time the electricity went off, Mia attempted to start the machine on her own. She'd been wearing a scarf tied loosely around her neck. It was windy that day and her scarf blew into the exposed belt. The belt caught Mia's scarf and yanked it right off. If the scarf had been wrapped tighter around Mia's neck . . . well, she didn't want to think about what could have happened. From then on, the generator took on a personality of its own, a mean one. The family named her Bertha, and Mia vowed to never mess with Bertha. And yet, here she was, about to do battle with the old metal monster again.

Just then Mia's cell phone rang. She breathed a sigh of relief. This early in the morning it had to be Michael. Maybe he would come home and deal with Bertha himself. The number on her phone screen was not Michael's, though he could be calling from an office phone.

"Hello?"

"Halimah?"

Mia's heart skipped. "Who is this?"

"Halimah?"

Mia punched the *end* button and stared at her phone. Her hand began to tremble.

"Who was it, Mom?"

"Nobody." Mia forced a smile and looked into Corey's eyes. She couldn't lie to him. "I mean . . . I don't know who it was."

"Wrong number?"

"Maybe." That wasn't a lie. There were other Halimahs in Khartoum. Just because a girl named Halimah had hidden in their home when her family tried to kill her didn't mean it was the same Halimah the caller was asking for, right?

How could anyone have gotten Mia's number anyway? And could they really prove Halimah had been in their home? There was no evidence. Mia glanced across the yard at the front gate. Were they calling from right outside? She pulled Corey away from the front door.

"Let's go see if Annie and Dylan are awake."

"I thought you liked it when we slept late."

"I do. But to tell you the truth, I don't really want to deal with Bertha today. I think we should go visit your friend Saleh and his mom. It's a school holiday today, so they'll be home."

Corey wrinkled his forehead. "But the whole neighborhood is out of power, so they won't have electricity either."

"Yes, but they have a nice new generator with a cover, so I am sure Saleh's mom has already turned hers on. Now hurry, go wake up your siblings, and I'll get some breakfast ready."

Corey disappeared into the children's shared bedroom. Mia dialed Michael's number. Then she hit *cancel*. What if their phones were being bugged again, like last year when the security police were keeping tabs on them? Should she risk telling Michael what had happened over the phone? No, it was better to wait.

She would take the kids to Hanaan's house to play with Saleh. That way she wouldn't be home if the caller came to the house. She couldn't run away every day, but until she had a chance to make a plan with Michael, this was the best she could come up with.

➤ Chapter 2 ⬅
Khartoum, Sudan

Mia sat on the veranda of her neighbor's home. Hanaan bustled around the kitchen, instructing her house-helper, Didi, on what to feed the children. While she waited, Mia replayed the phone call in her mind. The voice had been female. Definitely Sudanese. Kind of gruff with an effort to sound pleasant. It could have been a coincidence, a genuine wrong number. Mia hadn't noticed anyone watching their house when she and the kids walked to Hanaan's, so she had no reason to think anyone was looking for Halimah at their house. Mia was just paranoid.

Her mind shifted to the comment Michael made before leaving the house. Did he mean they may have to leave earlier in the summer, like in a week rather than a month . . . or did he mean leave before their final year was complete?

Hanaan emerged and settled herself in a chair opposite Mia. "The children will eat their snack inside and then they can play video games . . . I know." Hanaan held her hand up to stop Mia from protesting. "You don't want them to play war games; I have asked Saleh to choose a soccer or basketball game."

Mia smiled at her Sudanese friend. "*Shukran*. Thank you."

The ladies sipped their cinnamon-infused tea for a few amiable moments before Mia spoke again. "I'm going to miss you this summer. You know . . ." She was going to say that they might have to leave sooner than expected, but she remembered she didn't actually know what Michael meant by his comment. So she said, "You know I will," and then smiled.

Hanaan smiled, "*Bilakthar, habeebtee.* I will miss you more, my dear. Can you believe we have been friends for three years now?"

Mia could feel her body relax. Everything was going to be OK. Sitting with Hanaan made Mia feel normal again. Maybe she had simply been overwhelmed this morning and had overreacted. She looked across the

...etal coffee table at her Muslim friend and marveled at how two very different ladies had become good friends.

"Did I ever tell you why I came to your house the first day we met?"

"No, but your Arabic wasn't as good then. Maybe you didn't think you would be able to explain. But now your Arabic is good, *masha' Allah*. So tell me."

"Well . . ." Mia fidgeted with the cuticle of her fingernail. "When I first moved here, I felt so sad because I didn't have many friends. I wanted to meet Sudanese women, but I didn't know how. They don't leave their houses much."

"Yes, that's right." Hanaan adjusted the scarf that faithfully concealed her hair. "Traditional Muslim women do not leave their homes unless they are going to a wedding, a funeral, or visiting family. And they never go alone. Our family is a bit freer, but even so, I would never go out alone and do the things Western women do."

"Now remember, Hanaan, all Western women are not like the ones you see on TV."

"OK, yes, you are right. But you know, most Sudanese women assume you are just like those women."

"Yes, I know. And most American women think Muslim women hate Christians."

Hanaan nodded. "Yes."

"So how do we change these perceptions?" Mia wondered out loud.

"By doing this," Hanaan said, with one hand gestured toward the children inside and one hand toward herself. "Just look at us. Our children play together almost daily, and you and I visit at least once a week. This is how we do it. This is small, but this is something."

Hanaan grinned broadly as if she had spoken the most profound words of the decade, which Mia decided she had. This is exactly how they could fight the misperceptions flooding the media: one relationship at a time. "Yes, this is something."

"So, you didn't tell me why you came to my house that day."

"Oh. Well, I was sad because I didn't have Sudanese friends. So I told my American friend, and we prayed and asked God to provide a friend for me. And it was you, Hanaan. God provided you to be my friend."

"*Alhamdulillah*. Thanks be to Allah." Then, as she always did when Mia tried to talk about God or Jesus, Hanaan busied herself. This time it was to gather their empty tea glasses and the sugar bowl back onto a tray. Instead of calling for Didi to come retrieve the tray, she took it to the kitchen herself. "You just relax, Mia. I'll be right back."

Mia tried to push away the frustration welling in her heart. For three years she had been praying for and sharing with Hanaan about Jesus and about how He could forgive her sins. Because of Him she did not have to try to gain salvation through good works, like Islam taught. But to no avail. Hanaan remained Mia's closest Sudanese friend while simultaneously ignoring the truths Mia shared.

Mia sighed and looked out across the yard. The dusty green bushes by the back wall took a golden hue. She raised her gaze up to the cloudy sky and noticed an orange glow in the atmosphere. Though it was midmorning, the skies looked as if they were preparing for a magnificent sunset. This meant only one thing: a sandstorm was on its way, and from the looks of it, time was short.

Mia stood and walked to the front door, calling back to the kitchen. "Hanaan, I need to go home. A *haboob* is coming."

"What?" Her friend called from the back of the house.

"A *haboob*. I left the windows open in my house. I have to go home."

Hanaan's large frame filled the doorway of the kitchen. She glanced toward the front door, and her eyebrows arched. "Yes, of course, you should go home. Leave your children here if you like. They are having a good time."

Hanaan did not know how thankful Mia was for the offer. If anyone were at the house looking for Halimah when Mia returned, she did not want the children present. Mia walked across Hanaan's living room to the kitchen where the children gathered around the table, eating an assortment of snacks. The table seemed to strain under the weight of bananas, oranges, noodles, egg rolls, kebabs, cakes, and dried dates. The children chattered in a smorgasbord of Arabic, English, and giggles. Aladiin, Hanaan's oldest son, was not there, of course. The handsome teenager was too cool to hang out with young children. His brother, Saleh, however, was Corey's best friend. The ten-year-old pair laughed and pretended to shoot each other with their bananas-turned-handguns.

"*Aeeb, aeeb,*" Hanaan scolded. "Bad manners."

Annie, quiet and polite at seven years old, ignored the boys and concentrated on eating noodles without spilling the broth on her dress. Her blond curls bounced around her face, causing an extra hurdle as she worked to keep them from dipping into the steaming bowl.

Dylan tried to join the older boys. His five-year-old eyes danced as he watched the impromptu shoot out, and he grabbed an orange in his pudgy hand, winding back as if ready to launch it over the table. "I have a grenade," he squealed.

"No, Dylan." Mia grabbed his hand just in time. She looked at Hanaan with reluctance. "Maybe I should take Dylan with me."

"Don't be silly, *habeebtee.*" Hanaan walked to Dylan, plucked the orange out of his hand, and began to peel it. "I'm raising two boys myself, remember? Dylan is a joy." She smiled at the boy and handed him several orange segments. "Here you go, Dylan. This orange is very sweet. It is more fun to eat it than throw it."

Dylan smiled and stuffed two segments in his mouth. His cheeks puffed out and orange juice dribbled down his chin. Mia reached for a tissue on the table but Hanaan shooed her out the door before she could grab one.

"You need to hurry before the sand gets all through your house."

"You are right. I'm going. Children, I'll be back in a little bit. I have to go shut the windows at our house."

Mia hurried out the door and across the yard to the gate of the privacy wall surrounding Hanaan's house, just like every house in Khartoum. The air around her felt thick as she unlatched the metal lock and let herself out. Wind swirled the trash that littered the streets, forming mini garbage tornadoes. Sand pelted her face as she made her way down the dirt road to her own gate. She squinted down the street and saw that just beyond her neighborhood, a giant wall of brown sand was headed her way. It moved steadily, engulfing houses like a giant monster. No time to stand and gawk at the gargantuan billow of sand that would soon consume her own house.

A few minutes later, with the windows and doors shut, Mia stood just inside the front door and watched through the glass pane as the orange air turned brown and then black. She was in the belly of a giant *haboob* billowing in from the Sahara Desert. These desert phenomena frequented Khartoum, but usually on a smaller scale. The sky would turn orange for a day, or even several days, and sand would scatter across the city with no respect for décor . . . or newly cleaned floors. But this monstrous-sized *haboob* only happened every few years. Mia, in fact, had never seen one so severe. She held her breath as she stared outside into the darkness, hardly believing it could be midmorning.

Mia hoped her children were not scared. She hadn't realized the sandstorm would be so severe. Corey would comfort his younger siblings. She imagined him giving them an assuring word. "Don't worry; God is in control of all of this." Would Hanaan hear him?

The blackness continued for a few minutes. Mia couldn't see anything outside but could hear the sand pinging against the glass pane. Then, as if the shadow of the monster passed by, the black brightened to a dark brown and then the light came back. The sky glowed a pale orange. Mia surveyed the yard. The *haboob* had left its signature mark in its wake—brown dirt and dust. The grass, bushes, and trees were brown. They looked burned.

On the floor inside the house, Mia could see her own footprints in the layer of dust covering the once freshly mopped tiles. All shutting the windows had done was keep trash from blowing in. Dust and dirt had managed to fill the house and cover the furniture.

Three years ago an event like this would have sent Mia spiraling into despair. But Mia was three years stronger now. Three years tougher. And really, all she could think about was how this *haboob* reminded her of how lost her friend Hanaan was. Hanaan saw no need for Jesus, even though Mia had explained it to her many times. Layers and layers of traditions and habits covered Hanaan's heart so there was no green—no life—left in her. She was like the trees outside. They looked burned and dead on the outside. But Mia knew that somewhere underneath Hanaan's exterior was a heart longing to be filled with forgiveness and love—things only Jesus could offer.

Her house was a disaster now, but all Mia wanted to do was go back to Hanaan's and share with her one more time about Jesus. One more time before Mia was gone for the summer, especially if they were leaving sooner than planned. She stepped outside and locked the front door; cleanup could wait until later. Her teeth crunched against the sand in her mouth and her hair was covered in dust. Oh, well, everyone else's was too. Now was not the time to think about the mess. Now was the time to think about her friend's eternity.

⇒ Chapter 3 ⇐
Northern Kenya

H ow long have you been a translator at Kame Refugee Camp?"
"One year." Halimah noticed the man interviewing her had
hair like Michael Weston's. The thick black waves made him look Arab,
though he was most definitely from the West. Just like Michael and his
wife, Mia. Two years had passed since she'd seen them, and probably six
months since she'd heard from them. Did they still live in her hometown
of Khartoum? She should try to find a way to send them a message.
Would it be safe to send a text message? Surely no one could find her
here in Kenya.

"Ma'am?"

Halimah jumped. Her thoughts had taken her far away from this
stifling little room with its single metal table and two metal chairs. "Sorry.
What was the question?"

"Your full name. What is your full name?"

"Sara Danial."

"Your full name."

"That is my full name. Sara Danial." It wasn't really. Even after two
years of using the name, she still longed for someone to call her Halimah.
The name "Halimah" meant she was Arab, she was the daughter of a
wealthy Sudanese businessman, she was beautiful, she was a cherished
daughter, and she belonged. Sara Danial meant nothing.

"Sara Danial," the man repeated slowly as he filled in the form he was
processing.

The name, which she had chosen herself, was ambiguous enough that
no one could be for sure if she was Arab or from South Sudan. Was she
Muslim or Christian? No one could tell from her name alone. Choosing
a new name meant she had no family, and there was no "Danial" to be
her father. Halimah had chosen to follow Christ, and therefore she didn't
belong—not in the physical world.

"Home country?"

"Sudan."

The man looked up from the form and raised his eyebrows. "You don't look Sudanese."

"I'm not from the South."

"Where are you from?"

"Khartoum."

"Are you Arab?"

"Does it matter?"

The man set his pencil on the desk and leaned back in the rickety chair. "Look, you're going to get the job, don't worry about that. You are lucky, by the way. Not everyone is being offered a new job, and I know you've heard the rumors about this place closing down. I just have to fill out this form. The more information you can give me, the quicker we can get this done, and you can fly to Nairobi and far away from . . . this."

"This" was 100,000 men, women, and children who lived in mud and thatch houses lined up in uniform rows across the desert. "This" was limited movement, daily handouts, life at the mercy of humanitarian aid workers who volunteered for a season and then returned to their rich countries and free lives. Halimah could see it in the eyes of the women she translated for. Having escaped the horrors of war in their own countries, they would enter the camp with glowing hope for a better future. After months—sometimes years—of waiting, the glow turned to a dull gaze of resignation. "This," as the man had put it, was Kame. And Halimah was more than ready to get out.

Halimah acquiesced to the man's request and steadily gave him her information as best she could, though she never said her real name. She, like the refugees of Kame, was at the mercy of other people. She had gained the respect of the director of the aid organization she'd been working for in South Sudan. He had recommended she get out of Sudan. Though she was grateful to have been given papers and ferried across the border into Kenya, her standard of living had plummeted upon arrival at the vast refugee camp.

And now, Kame was closing down. It had begun as an effort to deal with the overflow of the bigger refugee camps. But lack of funding caused severe setbacks and now, finally, the end of Kame was probably only months away.

Perhaps this new job in Nairobi would be a better fit for her anyway. Though she was a new creation in Christ, she had to admit she still missed the comforts and benefits of being an upper-class Arab. Wasn't there some way she could be both? Her father would say absolutely not. That was why she had left home, not of her own volition, but beaten and bruised, running for her life. She was an infidel since she had left the Muslim faith. Infidels brought shame on their families.

If it hadn't been for Michael and Mia, Halimah didn't know where she might have ended up. A Khartoum prison, perhaps, or a "reeducation school," if she had survived at all. She sat quietly in her chair as she watched the man who looked like Michael complete the rest of the form and dramatically stamp "Approved" in red ink across his signature at the bottom.

"You have a couple days to say your goodbyes. Pack your things and be ready to leave Monday. There is a flight out of Loki in the afternoon, so you'll leave from here that morning. And good luck." The man stood and extended his hand.

Halimah shook his hand. Even after two years she was not accustomed to touching men who were not family members. She thanked the man and walked out of the room into the bright sun.

She should have gone directly into the camp to find the aid workers who needed her help translating English to Arabic. That was still her job, after all. Instead she headed to her cinder block room in the cloister of square buildings that made up the temporary housing for aid workers and volunteers.

She could hear the loud generator running, which meant her phone was getting a charge. That was good because Halimah had decided she would try to contact Michael and Mia. It might be dangerous, but she could really use some encouragement. The fact was, though moving to Nairobi was a step up, she was terrified to do it.

The noise from the generators made it difficult for Halimah to use her phone. She shut the door of her tiny room, lay on the bed, and covered her head with a pillow. Two phone numbers were burned in her memory. The number for Mansur, the pastor of her underground church in Khartoum, and the number for the Weston family. Mansur had changed his number several times since she left Khartoum. She figured the police in Khartoum hassled him for information on her or some other Arab who left Islam. He probably changed his number often. The Westons had the same number, however. As far as she knew anyway.

She dialed their number and then lay with the pillow over her head, waiting for an answer. A fly landed on her bare foot and tickled her as it crawled and hopped. She shook her foot, but didn't get up to swat it. She was concentrating too hard on who might answer the phone.

It rang a few times, and then a small voice answered. "*Salaam aleykum*, this is the Westons' house." Halimah's heart melted. It was the voice of a child. But it had been so long since she'd heard the voices of the Weston children, she couldn't be sure which one it was.

"*Aleykum wassalaam*. May I speak to Mia?"

"Yes. May I ask who is calling?" The voice on the other end of the phone sounded so polite and adult-like. Halimah concluded that it had to be Corey. She remembered when her brother Ali was the same age as Corey. His voice sounded the same way . . . so young and innocent, even when the words sounded so grown-up.

Halimah contemplated telling Corey who she was. It would be so nice to have a conversation with him before talking to Mia. She would like to hear how his friendship with his neighbor Saleh was coming along. Was he doing well in school? How were his siblings? But she reminded herself that she did not know who might be at their house at this moment, and announcing who she was would not be a good idea.

"I am . . . an old friend," Halimah replied. She wondered if Corey could recognize her voice. She spoke in English, however, and her accent had vastly improved since working as a translator. Corey probably didn't realize she spoke English so well now.

"OK, I will tell her. One moment."

Halimah waited as he called for his mom. Her heart began to beat heavily in her chest. It had been two years since she left the Westons' house and escaped to the south. So much had happened since then. But to keep the Weston family safe, she had only been in contact through email. And since she lived in a refugee camp, where the Internet connection was spotty at best, she didn't send them news much at all.

"*Salaam aleykum.*"

Halimah would recognize that voice anywhere. She suddenly remembered the first time she heard Mia speak to her. Almost three years ago, when sitting in the house of a stranger, she'd heard the words, "I love you, my sister." She remembered asking herself, "How can a stranger love me?" For the next several months she saw the answer to that question lived out by the Weston family as they nursed her back to health, discipled her, and helped her find a safe place to live.

Halimah skipped the polite greetings. "Mia, this is Sara." She hoped that Mia remembered the new name she had chosen for herself. It would be too dangerous for her to say her real name.

"Sara? Is it really you?"

Halimah couldn't help laughing. "Yes, it's me. How are you, my sister?"

"Oh, Sara, I am fine. How are you? And where are you? Are you safe?"

"I am . . . still far away." She did not reveal her location on the phone. She knew the tactics of the Sudanese police well. They could easily tap into phones. "Yes, I am safe. I just . . . wanted to hear your voice."

Suddenly the words spilled out. Without using names or locations, Halimah told Mia all about her sister, Rania, becoming "our sister in faith," about the work she was doing at the refugee camp, and about the opportunity to go to "a bigger city." She hoped Mia would understand she was talking about Nairobi. She told Mia how, even though the opportunity was a good one, and much better than living where she was now, she had a strange feeling in her spirit.

"Do you think the Holy Spirit is talking to me?" she asked Mia. "I know it is a great opportunity, but I just don't feel sure about it. Maybe it's not the right thing to do. But what else can I do?"

Mia listened to Halimah, just like she used to do when Halimah lived in her home. "Let's pray about it," she said. Halimah smiled. This is why she had called Mia. She missed having someone to pray with.

The ladies prayed over the phone. Mia, choosing her words carefully so if anyone were listening in, no information was given away, and Halimah praying a prayer of agreement in her heart. Peace filled Halimah and lifted her spirits, and when they were done, Halimah thanked her friend.

"I wish I had time to talk to you more. I want to hear all about your family. But this phone call has probably used all my credit, and I am afraid it will cut off soon. We will have to do this again another time, after I buy more credit for the phone."

"Don't worry. We are fine. We are praying for you all the time. Keep safe. And listen to that voice in your spirit, Sara. You are God's child now. You will recognize His voice when He speaks."

Halimah had recognized the Holy Spirit's voice one morning, long ago, when He told her, "Walk out of your house." She was beaten and cursed by her own father, and she should not have been able to escape. But when she heard the voice in her heart, she walked down the hall and out the front door, and no one stopped her.

This was the same voice. But why would the Holy Spirit tell her not to go to Nairobi? There was no future for her here at Kame. Surely God would want her to move to a better job, a better place. What choice did she have anyway? She'd already filled out the paperwork, and the plane would leave in two days. There was no going back.

Halimah pushed the pillow off her head. It toppled to the floor, and the fly that had been tickling her feet buzzed around the air and landed on the pillow. She sat on the edge of her bed, staring at the phone in her hand.

The man filling out her forms had told her she only had a couple of days to pack and say her goodbyes. A lot to do in 48 hours. She picked up a headscarf and headed out the door. She didn't know what she should do, but if she did decide to leave in two days, there were a lot of refugees she wanted to tell goodbye.

She walked along the eastern edge of the camp, where she did most of her work. Normally she only translated for one of the aid workers, but lately the aid organizations working in Kame were overloaded, and she was tasked with translating for several workers. Her days were long and full of sad stories.

Rumors swirled that some of the larger refugee camps were going to close, and as a result, refugees were flooding to Kame. Kame could not handle the influx of refugees; it was at capacity already. Then there were the rumors that Kame would soon be closing. It seemed like an impossible situation.

The Arab aristocrat side of Halimah's personality thought these Sudanese, Somali, and Eritrean refugees should quit relying on Kenya's compassion and just go back home. But the compassionate side of her, the side that had found life and mercy in Christ, listened to the horrible stories of these poor people and longed to help them find a solution.

Halimah was caught somewhere in the middle. She was not one of the refugees, but she was not a foreign aid worker either. Even the Kame Camp administrator had not known exactly how to classify her. They had finally settled on "local hire," even though she wasn't Kenyan either.

From her unique perspective, she could observe both sides. The Kenyan government had so far been generous to allow hundreds of thousands of refugees to live in their country while waiting for a solution to their own countries' various problems. But Kenya had its own problems to deal with and wanted to send people back home to repatriate them.

The refugees, on the other hand, fled terrible and unthinkable horrors in their home countries, and they desperately wanted to be resettled in a country that would allow them to begin a new life.

If neither repatriation nor resettlement were possible, the only other solution was to assimilate these people into Kenya itself. Was it possible? There were no jobs, and education and food were at the mercy of volunteers and donations.

As Halimah walked down the dirt road, she replayed the various scenarios in her head. She tried to think of a fourth solution, something no one had thought of that would solve this terrible crisis. But nothing came.

It didn't matter really. She was hired to simply translate for those who gathered data. Halimah walked along the edge of the dusty road. Recent rains had flooded the camp, and insufficient drainage left pools of stagnant water to breed mosquitoes. Mosquitoes meant malaria and dengue. Halimah had managed to avoid both of these diseases so far, but many refugees had died after falling ill with one of them. She hoped the aid workers would come fill these puddles with sand soon.

As she skirted the camp, she noticed a young woman sitting on the ground looking toward the lines of thatched huts. She was dark-skinned and too thin. The gaunt look in her eyes and the reddish tinge in the hair peeking out of her headscarf revealed malnutrition. She held a baby in her lap. Why would a mother sit in the sun with her baby and not at least sit in her makeshift house? Unless she'd had a fight with her husband or one of the other people living under the same roof.

"What are you doing?" Halimah called. But the woman didn't answer. Halimah walked closer to her. "*Salaam aleykum*. What are you doing? Why aren't you inside?"

"I don't live here," the woman said.

"Where are you from?"

"Torit."

"Then why did you come here? Go back home." It was, of course, a silly thing to say. Torit was in Sudan, several hundred kilometers away.

"I can't," the woman said. "My husband sent me here. He said we would die if we stayed there."

"What is so bad about Torit?"

"There is a drought. We have been living on nothing but mangoes."

Halimah looked out past the woman. The arid ground was endless behind her. In fact, Kame, the name of the camp, meant "arid" in Swahili. The closest town was many kilometers away. This woman would never make it.

"You should go to the main office, and talk to the people there. Tell them your story." Halimah pointed toward the camp. "Just pass Zone 5, and ask for the offices. Someone will help you find it."

"I am scared," the woman said. As if to accentuate her mother's fear, the baby began to cry. "They won't speak Arabic like you do. They won't understand me."

"I'll go with you," Halimah said. "Here, let me carry your bag." She picked up the small shoulder bag sitting on the ground beside the woman, and the two ladies walked back the way Halimah had come. She'd have to say goodbye to her friends later.

Rania watched Uncle Faisal stare at the giant painting. He had drilled a hole in the wall above the sofa just so he could display his niece's most recent masterpiece. The giant canvas dominated the small living room. Blues and purples and gold trim framed the red calligraphic words written in Qur'anic Arabic.

> *The servants of the Most Merciful are those who walk upon the earth easily, and when the ignorant address them, they say peace.*
> —The Qur'an 25:63

Rania would have preferred to spend her hours painting a Bible verse. She longed to paint 1 Timothy 2:5, "For there is one God and one mediator between God and mankind, the man Christ Jesus." But her professor was teaching the art students how to paint calligraphy, and every assignment was a verse from the Qur'an.

Why would it be anything else? She was attending the Arab Art School in Dubai, a Muslim country. As it was, she was risking ridicule by painting an obscure and rather benign verse compared to the other students. For such a large canvas, and for the amount of delicate work this project required, every student except Rania had chosen the *shihada*, the Muslim statement of faith: *La ilaha illa-llah, Muhammadu-rasulu-llah.* There is no god but Allah, Mohammed is his prophet.

Rania was a follower of *Isa*, Jesus. She had come to confess Him as Lord of her life back in Sudan. Only her mother and her sister, Halimah, knew about her secret belief. Halimah believed before Rania, but when their father found out, he beat Halimah and made plans to send her away. His anger grew so fierce that Halimah had to run for her life.

It had been almost three years now, but Rania could still feel the tears rolling down her cheeks and the painful thump of her heart beating against her ribcage. She could still see her hands trembling as she fumbled through her purse for the money she'd given Halimah just seconds before her sister, dressed in rags and limping from the beating, tiptoed out the front door.

Rania was not as brave as Halimah. She could not bring herself to tell her father that she too had experienced the forgiveness of *Isa*. But she had a second problem. She loved art, and just like following *Isa*, art did not fit into the "good Sudanese girl" mold that her father wanted for her. Mercifully, Mama pulled some strings and got Rania a spot at an art school in Dubai, even though she was only 17.

Rania lived with Uncle Faisal and Auntie Badria while taking classes at the nearby college on the outskirts of the city. Rania had gathered the courage to tell her mother that she believed in *Isa*. But she determined Uncle Faisal and Auntie Badria would never find out. She did not want her mother getting in trouble and, to be honest, she didn't want to get in trouble either.

"*Masha' Allah*, thanks to Allah. It is beautiful, Rania."

"Thank you, Uncle. I'm glad you like it." Rania had no trouble giving her uncle the art piece. She didn't want to keep it. The other students were probably selling their pieces for several hundred *dirham*, and she could too. But she didn't want money for a Qur'anic verse.

"The next piece must be for sale, Rania. You could send money home to your family, and they would be so proud. Or you could keep the money for yourself. I won't say a word." The man winked at Rania. "Well now, I must be on my way. Your auntie will be home in an hour. Tell her I've gone to the mosque. I'll be back later." Uncle Faisal smoothed his pristine white robe and adjusted his white turban.

Rania busied herself arranging her paintbrushes and tubes of paint and feigning interest in the orders of the colors until her uncle left, locking the door behind him. Rarely did Uncle Faisal and Auntie Badria leave her alone in their overpriced luxury apartment. Friday was the exception. During the time that Auntie visited an old Sudanese friend and Uncle went to the mosque, Rania had a bit of time to herself. With any luck, she'd have close to an hour.

As soon as the door lock clicked, Rania dialed a number on her cell phone. After two rings she heard her sister's voice.

"Hello?"

"Sara, is it you?" Rania felt uncomfortable calling her sister by a different name. But Halimah insisted they needed to use her new name for security reasons. Even though she was now safely outside Sudan, she still had to be careful. Her father's anger had not subsided yet. Maybe it never would.

"Yes, *habeebtee*, it's me. How are you doing in Dubai? How is school?"

"I'm doing fine. Uncle Faisal and Auntie Badria take good care of me. I think they spend too much money here though." Rania glanced around the salon as she talked. Her painting was free, but the other paintings on the walls were expensive. The gold frames and the giant vases in the entryway and corners of the room dripped of excessive spending. The furniture was more ornate than comfortable. A giant chandelier hung over the marble coffee table like a spaceship made of diamonds.

Like the other Sudanese families Rania had met in Dubai, Uncle Faisal and Auntie Badria spent money they didn't have to look a little better—appear a little richer—than the other Sudanese living around them.

Halimah laughed on the other end of the line. "Yes, that sounds like a true Sudanese couple. Well, I know you probably don't have much time, so let's talk about the Bible. Do you have any questions from what you have been reading this week?"

Rania had many questions. She read the Bible every chance she got. After her aunt and uncle went to sleep, she would pull out her Bible and try to understand what it said.

"I need to talk about something else today . . . Sara. I need to ask you what you think I should do. My studies at the art school will finish in a few months, and I don't know what to do next. If I go home to Khartoum, Father will have me married to Waliid right away. I know it is wrong to marry an unbeliever, but what if I don't have a choice?"

Halimah paused before she answered. "This is a difficult question. I don't have a good answer. We need to pray."

Rania sighed. "I thought you would say that. I know it is true, but it is so hard for me to just pray. Shouldn't I be doing more?"

"Yes, of course," Halimah said.

Relief came over Rania. "Good," she said. "What is it?"

"Trust."

"What?"

"Trust. You can pray, and you can trust. And while you are at it, you can pray for me too. I am going to get a new job in Nairobi. But I am feeling unsure about it. I think maybe the Holy Spirit is telling me it is not the right thing to do. I don't know if I should go."

"What are you going to do?"

"The same thing I told you to do. I want you to look up Jeremiah 29:11."

Rania went to her room and retrieved the Bible she kept carefully hidden under her mattress. She looked up the verse, using the book's table of contents. Then she read it to Halimah, "'For I know the plans I have for you,' declares the LORD, 'plans to prosper you and not to harm you, plans to give you hope and a future.'"

Halimah's voice was soft and confident over the phone. "God has a plan for us, Rania. He will not harm us. He will give us hope."

As the sisters continued to talk, Rania felt her confidence rising and peace filling her heart. If only Halimah could be with her in person right now. She longed to sit beside her sister and pour over Bible verses together. Before she was ready for it, an hour had passed, and it was time to say goodbye until the next Friday.

"Trust the Lord, Rania. He's worthy of that. Believe me."

Rania said goodbye and quickly hid her Bible just before she heard Auntie Badria turning the key in the lock.

"*Salaam aleykum*, Rania. I'm home."

"*Aleykum wassalaam*," Rania walked out of her bedroom. "How was Sit Abubakr today?"

"She was ornery as usual. She bought new salon furniture and the set looks lovely," Auntie eyed her own set of furniture in distaste.

Then she shook her head as if to dispel the jealous thoughts. "But I have better news than Sit Abubakr's furniture." Her eyes sparkled. "She has generously invited us to her home next week to read coffee grounds." Auntie placed her oversized leather purse on the coffee table and plopped on the sofa. Bending over she began to rub her swollen ankles.

Rania wanted to go back to her room and begin painting, but she read her auntie's nonverbal signals that it was time to sit and talk. Auntie Badria was kind enough, but her demeanor commanded obedience. Most of her friends, and even Uncle Faisal, acquiesced. Rania was no different.

She chose the carved wooden chair opposite her aunt and sat down, curling her feet up under her. It was the only chair she was allowed to put her bare feet on.

"Sit Abubakr reads the future in coffee grounds? I thought it was done with tea leaves."

"Well, here in Dubai, she has begun to do it with coffee grounds. She learned it from an Emirati, a native of Dubai. The other Sudanese ladies tell me she is quite good. She said she would read our futures for free."

"Wow, how did you manage that?" Rania watched her aunt continue to rub her ankles. The walk up two flights of stairs in high-heels had really done a number on her.

Auntie Badria stopped and looked up at Rania, smiling. "I invited her to your wedding."

Rania forced a smile, but it was weak. She didn't like to be reminded that she was still betrothed to Waliid. The thought of going back to Khartoum this summer worried her.

She hadn't heard a lot from her father, but she assumed he was planning for her wedding to be within the year. That's why she hadn't bothered to ask to speak to Father when she called home each week. She didn't want to talk about Waliid. The subject was depressing.

To Rania's surprise and relief, Auntie Badria stood up and began walking down the hallway leading to the bedrooms. "I am tired. I'm going to lie down for a few minutes. Oh, and Rania, your mother called on my phone while I was out. Your parents will be coming up for your graduation."

"Yes, Mama told me they will come and stay with us. That is wonderful." Rania tried to sound excited. This took great acting skills on her part because she was trying to appear calm these days, while also figuring out how she would escape her father's marriage plans. She had only a few months to work with.

"But Rania, you'll be happy to know they plan to come early. They will be here in four weeks."

Rania froze. Thankfully, Auntie Badria didn't notice the look of shock in her eyes. Her aunt turned and walked down the hall to her room and shut the door.

⋙ Chapter 5 ⋘
Khartoum, Sudan

M ichael, I got a strange phone call yesterday. It might have just been a wrong number, but the lady asked for Halimah."

Mia sat at the end of the bed, watching her husband rifle through the closet in search of a shirt.

"What did you say to her?"

"Nothing. I didn't know what to say. I just hung up."

Michael pulled a short-sleeved knit shirt off a hanger and put it on. Mia couldn't help but be envious. She had to wear long sleeves because women in Sudan weren't allowed to show their arms if they were modest women.

"OK, we just need to be careful. Don't answer calls from any unknown numbers."

"But don't you think it could have just been a wrong number?"

Michael shrugged. "Maybe." He didn't look convinced.

Mia looked down at the cell phone in her hand. Suddenly she felt like she was holding a time bomb. Would the lady try to call again? Was there any way she could track Mia's phone? They did it in the movies all the time. Mia turned her phone off and set it on the bed.

She thought about bringing up Michael's comment from the other morning about having to leave Sudan early. He'd said it with such nonchalance as he left for work, and she'd mulled it over in her mind the whole day. But he never mentioned it again. It was probably nothing. And anyways, they didn't need distractions today.

It was Friday, and they were meeting with Abbas and Widad, who believed in Jesus but had not told anyone except the Westons. The pesky fear of a phone call or a worrisome comment that she'd probably misunderstood was not going to rob her joy today.

A few hours later, the Westons were on the banks of the Nile River that cut right through the city of Khartoum.

Mia stretched her legs out across the picnic mat. There was no way to sit comfortably on the ground when wearing a long skirt. She looked across at Widad, who never seemed to shift around quite as much as Mia. Every few weeks their two families took a picnic and gathered on the banks of the Nile River. What was a normal Friday outing for most Sudanese was actually a discipleship meeting for these families.

Why did Widad believe in Jesus after just a few visits from Michael and Mia while Mia's neighbor Hanaan, after many conversations, remained resolute in her commitment to Islam?

Mia didn't know the answer to this question. But she enjoyed every minute spent with Widad and her husband Abbas because she was reminded how God could change the hearts of Muslims and draw them to Himself. She needed to be reminded often because sometimes it felt next to impossible to see how God was glorified at all in an Islamic country like Sudan.

Widad and Abbas began to learn about the love and forgiveness of Jesus through the New Testament that Abbas read several years earlier. Though they didn't tell anyone in their neighborhood of their beliefs, they had become the butt of neighborhood jokes.

"Abbas reads a Christian book and socializes with kafir, *infidels."*

"Don't buy from their store; you might accidentally buy a Christian spirit."

As a result, only strangers and desperate neighbors frequented Abbas's neighborhood store, and they barely made enough money to feed themselves and Yusra, their little girl. The products on the shelves of Abbas's little store slowly dwindled, but he had no money to restock.

"I know *Isa* loves us," Widad told Mia as the two ladies watched their husbands and children splashing and playing in the shallow bank of the Nile. "Yesterday, my aunt, who doesn't know about our new belief, visited me and brought me these bananas and the bread." Widad gestured toward her donation to the day's picnic. "*Isa* knew we needed food for today. He provided it. How could I ever turn my back on Him now?"

"What keeps you from getting angry with your neighbors for talking bad about you and Abbas?" Mia asked, shifting her position again. Her back hurt from trying to sit with her legs straight, so she shifted to a kneeling position, hoping her feet wouldn't fall asleep.

"Well," Widad said, "we read in the *Injil*, the New Testament, how *Isa* showed mercy to everyone He met. I think showing mercy is more important than judgment. It is not our place to judge."

Wise words for such a new believer. Mia looked back toward the river where her husband playfully splashed water on Corey, who screamed and splashed back. It wasn't too many months ago that the security police had arrested Michael and kept him overnight with no charge. They intimidated him and in the process scared Mia half to death. Mercy was not the first thought in her mind during those dreadful hours. Anger, fear, panic . . . yes. Mercy? Not so much.

But Michael and Mia were American. They could leave Sudan anytime they felt the pressure was too much. Abbas and Widad, on the other hand, were Sudanese citizens. They had no rights, they had no money, and they had no chance for a better life. Yet Widad was quick to offer mercy. The strength and faith of this woman reminded Mia of Halimah.

No time to think more about such deep things. The kids and fathers were making their way to the picnic mat. Black sand stuck to their wet legs and the edges of their rolled up trousers dripped from wading in a bit too deep. Yusra and Annie were the cleanest ones, having only waded ankle deep in the water. Annie plopped on the mat with a giant pout on her face.

"Mom, Dylan splashed me and got my dress wet." She pointed to her shoulder and the upper half of her dress. Water dripped from the drenched sleeve.

"Dylan," Mia turned to her youngest son whose face was already contorted into the defensive look of an innocent victim. "Why did you splash Annie when you know she doesn't have a change of clothes?"

"I was just trying to have fun."

"Upsetting your sister is not a good way to have fun, Dylan. Here, bring this towel over to her." Mia handed him a clean towel.

As the two families settled on the mat, Yusra began to sing. The others joined in. Mia smiled as she sang. Halimah used to sing the song often when she lived with them.

> Heaven for eternity!
> Jesus paid the debt for me!
> Daily walking in His love,
> Together we shall overcome.
> There is no punishment or hell,
> For me, and I will live to tell,
> His blood will cleanse all who believe.

Michael prayed a short prayer, asking God to help them understand the Scripture verses they were about to read. Then the adults and Corey opened their Bibles to 1 Peter. After doing so, Mia pulled out some coloring pictures and crayons from her bag for Yusra, Annie, and Dylan. Coloring didn't keep Dylan's attention for very long, but Yusra and Annie would be occupied the entire time.

The little group was finishing the study of 1 Peter with a discussion on chapter five. After reading it together, Michael asked the group what the passage said about God, and what the passage said about people. Then he asked what the passage might be saying to them as individuals.

"I feel like this whole book was written just for us," Abbas said. "Look here, it says we must be self-controlled and alert because the devil wants to attack us. I experience this every week when our neighbors make fun of us and laugh at how I am losing customers at our store. In this chapter I read how others throughout the world are undergoing similar trials." Abbas leaned back on his arms and looked out over the Nile waters. "Do you think there are others in Sudan who also believe?"

Mia caught Michael's eye. They both were thinking the same thing. Halimah. If only she were here to encourage this sweet family.

"Who are we going to meet with when your family goes to America? Three months is a long time for us to be . . . alone," Widad said.

"You have the Holy Spirit, and you know He is already speaking to you every day," Michael answered.

"Yes, of course," Abbas said. "But the Bible also says we should encourage one another and fellowship together. How can we do that if there is no one else who believes?"

Mia and Michael had been discussing this very thing on their way to pick up Abbas and his family. They talked about the possibility of introducing Abbas and Widad to Mansur.

Mansur was the pastor of a secret Christian church. He had been Halimah's pastor and was instrumental in discipling her and later helping her escape from her father. Perhaps it was a good time to introduce this young believing family to Mansur.

Mia was sure the pastor would agree to the connection, but she wasn't so sure about Abbas and Widad. Making connections between people in a country like Sudan was risky. One could never be sure who was being hired by the secret police to spy on others or who had a gossiping tongue and might say too much around others. Michael and Mia trusted both Mansur and Abbas, but would these men trust each other?

"You know," Michael began. "Mia and I will only be gone for a few months this summer. But you are right. You need fellowship. We happen to know a man who can help you. He is Sudanese, but he is a believer as well."

Abbas and Widad looked at each other in surprise and then turned back to Michael. "Really?" Abbas asked. "We're not alone?"

"Are you willing to meet him?" Mia knew Michael was asking the couple to take a huge risk. She couldn't help recalling the mess they had gotten Halimah into when they trusted the wrong person.

"Yes, we are," Widad answered immediately. "We need fellowship." Abbas nodded his head.

"OK then." Michael smiled. "I will contact him, and we will arrange for you to meet."

They returned to their discussion of 1 Peter. As always, both Michael and Mia struggled to get their ideas across in Arabic and to understand what the Sudanese couple was trying to explain. Despite the risk, Mia conceded it would be best for this couple to have a native Arabic speaker discipling them.

That night, after the kids were in bed and as Michael finished some paperwork to take in to the office, Mia read over the last chapter of 1 Peter again, focusing on verse nine.

"Standing firm in the faith, because you know that the family of believers throughout the world is undergoing the same kind of sufferings."

Mia thought of Halimah and of the young family they had just spent the day with. There were many others just like them: individuals and families who believed in Jesus despite risk and suffering—the kind of risk and suffering that Mia would probably never experience. These giants of the faith had a special bond that was deep. Mia thought they probably also had a special bond with Jesus Himself, who had suffered on their behalf.

She took a ballpoint pen and wrote in the margin of her Bible, *I am honored to know some of these.*

Her thoughts were interrupted when Michael returned to the bedroom and crawled into bed next to her.

"I'm worried about Abbas and Widad," he said.

"Why? They seemed to be doing well. I think it's a great idea for them to meet Mansur. He will be able to encourage them while we are gone this summer."

"I am worried about his store. If he loses his business, he'll have no way to take care of his family. He can't get help from his neighbors, they are the reason he's losing business. And it is only a matter of time before Yusra is going to be ridiculed and mistreated at school because of her parents. I just don't know what they should do."

Mia's happy feelings about connecting Abbas's family with an Arabic-speaking pastor suddenly vanished. Michael had a good point. She was happy this family had received salvation, but what would they do with no livelihood? If it was dangerous to send Yusra to school, what would she ever be able to do without an education?

Mia realized what Abbas and Widad had probably known all along—what she was just now coming to understand: in a place like Sudan, making the decision to follow Jesus came at an enormous price.

Only someone like Halimah could fully understand what Abbas and Widad were facing.

Perhaps it was coincidence that Halimah had just called Mia, but she preferred to think it was providential. The Lord knew Halimah needed encouragement, but He also knew Mia was going to need Halimah's help. She grabbed her cell phone from the bedside table and dialed her number. She could hear the phone ring twice and then a message in English announced that the phone number was no longer in service.

"Where are you going?" Michael asked as Mia jumped out of bed.

"Halimah's phone is not working anymore. I'm going to get my computer and send her an email. She said Internet is not good where she is, but I'm going to write her anyway and ask if she would write a note of encouragement for Widad. Wouldn't that be great?"

Mia didn't wait for an answer. She sat at the dining room table, opened her laptop, and wrote a short message, asking if Halimah would write a note of encouragement for "a new sister from your background."

⇒ Chapter 6 ⇐
Khartoum, Sudan

It was Saturday evening, and Mia was nervous. She always felt this way before hosting Sudanese guests. She knew some of the culturally appropriate things to do, like serving a glass of water upon arrival and waiting until later in the visit to serve tea because it meant the visit was almost over, and the host was ready for the guest to leave. But there seemed to be a measure of ambiguity on etiquette of the rest of the visit. When should she bring out the cookies and dates? Was her selection of finger foods appropriate?

She asked her house cleaner, Tzega, that morning if the box of cookies she chose was suitable to serve. Tzega said yes, but she, of course, was always polite. Would she really tell her employer if the cookies weren't the right ones to serve? And would her house cleaner even know what was appropriate? Tzega was Eritrean, and though she'd lived in Sudan for several years, she probably had no idea what finger foods an upper class Sudanese family would deem acceptable. Tzega mentioned they always ate popcorn in Eritrea. Popcorn. Interesting. Mia decided to pop a bowl of the salty snack just to add some variety.

Michael sauntered into the kitchen as Mia finished the preparations. He grabbed a handful of popcorn and sat in one of the kitchen chairs.

Mia slapped his hand. "Michael, that's for tonight."

He grinned and stuffed the popcorn into his mouth before she could object any further. "Popcorn? For tonight?" His voice was garbled as he spoke with his mouth full.

"Yes," she said, laughing. "So quit eating it."

"You remember when I said we might have to leave earlier than planned?"

Mia's heart beat harder in her chest. She thought of their "go" bags sitting at the ready with a change of clothes for each family member, basic toiletries, money, and passports. "What's going on?"

53

"I just meant we may have to leave a month or two before our contract is up. I thought about it after I got to work and realized I might have scared you. I meant to tell you, but then we got to talking about your strange phone call, and I forgot all about it. Sorry about that." He looked sheepishly at her, and then took another handful of popcorn.

"Oh, it's fine." Mia tried to sound casual. She wanted to be the calm and collected wife. But then she sighed. "OK, to be honest, you did scare me a little bit. How are things going at the office? I mean, I know things have been rocky in the past. Is the government still giving the foundation trouble?"

"Yes and no. The government is always looking for a reason to shut us down. But no, I don't think it is anything that will happen in the next year. The reason we might have to leave a couple months early is simply because of the way our permission papers work. Our visas will run out a few months earlier than we thought."

Mia shouldn't let these things send her emotions on a roller coaster ride. She should have known when Michael made the comment that it was nothing to be concerned about. She had been living in this situation for three years, after all. And things had been a lot worse in the past. Things were fine right now. She should enjoy it.

At eight in the evening, Habiib and his family arrived. Habiib was a colleague of Michael's. He was hired to help the foundation fill out paperwork for visas and various types of permits and permissions required to operate in Sudan.

The Sudanese man wore a solid white *jallabeeya* and a turban, perched loftily on his head. Mia remembered Halimah saying the bigger the turban, the more self-important the man wearing it felt. Habiib apparently thought well of himself.

Nahla, his wife, carried their one-year-old daughter on her hip and held the hand of their two-year-old son. Little Lamya wore a frilly pink dress and black patent leather shoes, while Hamid was dressed in what looked like newly purchased trousers with a matching shirt. Nahla herself wore a beautiful sky-blue *tobe*, the traditional full-body scarf worn by all married Sudanese ladies.

Mia cringed. As hard as she tried, she could never remember and follow all the Sudanese customs. She had been so preoccupied with what to serve the guests she had completely forgotten to dress up for the occasion. She was wearing the same skirt and blouse she'd been wearing all day—which meant she'd been sweating in it of course—and the kids were wearing shorts and T-shirts. Dressing up was an unspoken Sudanese sign of giving the other person honor. She hoped Habiib and Nahla had not noticed their casual attire.

Everyone—even the kids—exchanged greetings and handshakes. Then the adults settled in the salon. Lamya sat on Nahla's lap, but Corey offered to take Hamid to the children's room to play. He held out his hand to Hamid, who eagerly grabbed it, and they walked down the hall, with Dylan skipping along behind them.

"Annie, why don't you help me serve drinks?" Mia asked.

Annie smiled and nodded. She loved to help Mia when guests came and was growing more adept at carrying a tray of glasses.

After serving the water, Annie joined the children in the bedroom. Mia poured water in the kettle for serving tea later in the visit and then joined the adults.

"So, your family will be going to *Amreeka* this summer?" Habiib asked.

"Yes, just for three months. The children have not seen their grandparents in a long time," Michael said.

"Too bad you aren't leaving in April, the hottest month."

"Well, we need to wait for the children to get out of school first. So how much time do you need in order to get exit permits for our passports?"

"It depends. There is no way to know for sure how long it will take . . ." Habiib paused and then said casually, "But if you are willing to add on an . . . administrative fee, I think I can convince someone at the immigration office to expedite the process."

"No," Michael said. "No administrative fee. How long will it take you to get the permission for us to leave without a fee?"

Michael's voice was strong and determined. Mia thought he was overreacting to Habiib's simple suggestion. But the two men worked together in the office on a daily basis. Perhaps Michael knew what he was doing.

"Well—" Habiib looked at the remaining water in his glass and then paused again, drinking the last of it and sighing deeply. He sat the empty glass on the small table beside his chair. "I can try to get it done by the time you want to leave. But you know the immigration office is investigating all the aid organizations. They will want to take time to do an investigation on your family. A small gift would help to . . . what do you say in your language?" Habiib switched from Arabic to heavily accented English, "Greez da wheels."

Michael laughed. "Where did you learn that? Yes, Habiib, I know a gift would help things go faster, but I don't want to do that. It is not honest. In English, we call that a bribe."

Habiib sat up straight, and the grin that had been on his face disappeared. "Do not call it a bribe. It is an administrative fee."

Mia had not seen Habiib upset before. He appeared offended at Michael, as if he had insulted Habiib's character.

"OK," Michael conceded. "An 'administrative fee.' But I still cannot do it. Please get our exit permits for the normal price."

Habiib relaxed again. "Give me the money for the normal price tonight, and I will get the process started. Give me your passports as well. If they approve your request and are ready to put the stamp in them, I will not have to take more time to come get them from you later."

Mia did not like the idea of giving her family's passports to Habiib. She trusted him as much as anyone in Sudan, but she wasn't sure she trusted him with her passport. They had no choice, of course. Her family could not leave without permission from the immigration office, and in order to get it, they had to be willing to give the officers their passports.

Michael gave Habiib the money and the passports. Mia told herself everything would be OK.

Habiib seemed more relaxed after receiving the money and passports. Mia was skeptical. Why did he seem so satisfied? She hated being suspicious of Michael's colleague, but she couldn't shake the catch in her spirit.

"I've read *Sura al-Imran* again, and I have a question for you." Habiib changed the subject abruptly.

"Ah, have you been reading the *Qur'an* more?" Michael grinned. "I wish you would read the Bible instead."

Habiib laughed. "I am not as convinced as you that the Bible is true. You know it was corrupted, and you do not have the true translation."

"My friend, don't you think God is powerful enough to protect His own written Word? The Bible is not corrupted as you think it is. But what is your question from the passage of the *Qur'an*?"

"You said *Sura al-Imran* brings out important facts about *Isa*, whom you call Jesus."

"Yes, it does," Michael said. "It shows us that we can be 100 percent sure we can go to heaven."

"No one can be sure, my friend. It is not for us to know, only for Allah to know."

"When you go home tonight, read the *sura* again. You will see that *Isa* was sinless, and that He has power over death. Also, it says He is in heaven, near God. Where does the *Qur'an* say the prophet Mohammed is?" Michael spoke boldly, especially considering he was talking to the man who held the passports—the lifelines—of his family members.

"What do you mean?" Habiib asked.

"Well, Mohammed said he was only a warner, and he did not know where he or his followers would be in the hereafter."

"*Alhamdulillah*, Mohammed speaks the truth," Habiib said. He turned to his wife, "You see, this is why I like to talk to Michael and Mia, they talk about important things like this."

Nahla smiled in return. Mia noticed she seemed to listen with genuine interest. Mia tried not to think about the fact that Habiib had their passports. Instead she prayed in her heart that the Holy Spirit would speak to Nahla as she listened to the men talk.

Michael spoke next. "Do you know what *Isa* says? He says that He sits at the right hand of God. Now, you tell me: who would you rather follow? The one who says he does not know where he will be in the afterlife or the one who says He sits at the right hand of God?"

Habiib laughed. "Ah, you pose a difficult question, my friend."

"It is a question that is worth your consideration."

A ruckus in the hallway interrupted the conversation. The children tumbled into the room like toppling blocks.

"Is it time for snacks yet, Mom?" Dylan asked.

"Yes, I suppose it is." Mia smiled and rose to make tea in the kitchen. "Annie, why don't you come with me and get the cookies for you kids to eat?"

Annie followed her to the kitchen and took the plate of cookies Mia had prepared ahead of time. Nahla followed them and stood in the doorway with Lamya on her hip.

"Come in," Mia said, excited to have her Sudanese friend with her in the kitchen. In Sudan, the women always hung out together, but Mia, being American, never figured out how to fully fit in. Nahla joining her in the kitchen was a step forward.

"May I help?" she asked.

"I'm just putting the water on to boil," Mia said. "But we can sit in here and visit while we wait. She gestured toward the kitchen table and chairs.

Nahla nodded and they sat down. Lamya sat on Nahla's lap. "Do you believe the things Michael talks to Habiib about?"

"You mean about *Isa*?" Mia asked. "Yes, I do. I believe He is the way to heaven."

"There are seven ways to heaven." Nahla adjusted her *tobe* as she spoke.

"Seven ways?" Mia asked, thinking perhaps she had not heard correctly.

"Well, seven doors to heaven."

Mia resisted the urge to argue back. She wanted to tell her friend that this is not true. She wanted to say Jesus is the only way. But arguing was not the way to convince a Muslim of the truth. Only the Holy Spirit could convince a person.

"Tell me about these seven doors," Mia said.

"Well, they are each different. Some open to difficult paths. A bad person, for example, would have to take a long hard road to get to heaven. Our prophet Mohammed, peace be upon him, has the easiest path."

Mia didn't respond right away. She didn't believe what Nahla just told her. But saying so wouldn't help convince Nahla. She needed to ask a thought-provoking question or at least have a good response. But she hadn't heard anyone talk about this before and wasn't prepared.

Nahla must have taken the pause to mean she had the upper hand on the conversation because she sat up straight and spoke with more confidence.

"The *Qur'an* is a beautiful miracle. It came from heaven, you know."

Mia did know something. She knew that the book Nahla spoke of didn't come from heaven. But she didn't want to offend her friend needlessly. For the second time in the span of only a few minutes she was stumped for a response. But Nahla was not actually looking for a response; she'd made a statement, not asked a question.

Mia was relieved to hear the water in the kettle bubbling. She stood and began pouring water into teacups. The ladies returned to the salon with a tray of tea and snacks. Conversation remained around the differences in American and Sudanese culture, spurred on by the popcorn Mia served. Popcorn was apparently served by Eritreans but not by Sudanese. Mia tried not to be offended by Nahla's wrinkled nose and Habiib's humored look.

After Habiib and his family left, Michael got the kids in bed while Mia cleaned up the kitchen and washed the teacups and plates. When she was done, she found Michael sitting on the sofa in the living room going through some papers from his briefcase.

"No time to rest?" she asked, smiling.

Michael chuckled. He straightened the papers in his lap and returned them to his briefcase. "There's always work to be done. I just have a hard time leaving it, I guess. Hey, the popcorn was a nice touch tonight."

"*Ugh.*" Mia flopped on the couch beside him. "It was not. Apparently only Eritreans serve popcorn. Sudanese think it's weird. Did you see the looks on their faces?"

"Well, I liked it."

Mia laid her head on Michael's shoulder. "Thanks."

"While you and Nahla were in the kitchen, I mentioned to Habiib that the four of us could read the Bible together after the summer. Habiib didn't agree, but he didn't refuse either."

"I know Habiib is a friend of yours, but I'm nervous that he has our passports. I feel like he is in control and we aren't, you know? Do you think he's going to be honest with the money and use it to get our exit permits, or will he make up some reason to ask for more?"

Michael remained quiet for a few moments before he spoke. "I don't know, Mia. But we don't have a choice."

≈ Chapter 7 ≈
Nairobi, Kenya

Saying goodbye to Kame had been harder than Halimah anticipated. She did not miss the simple housing, loud generators, and shortage of food. But she missed the hurting people that she helped—the mothers desperate for safety for their children and the children in need of love. Kame offered the safety while Halimah offered the love. They seemed to be a good fit. But Halimah knew she couldn't stay in Kame forever. There was no future for her there. She decided to push against her uneasy spirit and take advantage of the opportunity.

She peered out the window of the 50-seat turboprop airplane. Her hands clenched the armrests, and she tried to ignore the butterflies in her stomach. Although she was raised in a wealthy family, she had never actually flown anywhere. Could this plane really take all these people up into the air?

Halimah's parents and brother flew to Saudi Arabia when they took the *haj* that every good Muslim should make at least once in their lifetime. She had been next on the list of family members to make the pilgrimage, but of course that was long ago. She wouldn't be going now. Her younger brother Ali had probably taken her place. Even when she escaped out of Sudan into Kenya she had not flown. She had instead traveled across countless miles of arid and semiarid land until she crossed the Sudan border into Kenya and eventually arrived at Kame.

She watched as the plane gained height over the small town of Loki and flew southwest. Before she knew it they were flying over the vast refugee camp that had been her home. The thatched roofs blended in to the dusty ground. The corrugated tin roofs, however, glinted in the sun, shooting flashes of light at her like Morse code that she learned about in high school in Khartoum. S.O.S. Save our souls.

Eventually the arid ground gave way to the savanna. Dots of green trees morphed into clumps of vegetation and gradually into fields of green. Halimah had never seen so much green at one time. She strained her eyes, hoping to see a giraffe or an elephant. Sudan used to have a lot of elephants and even rhinoceroses. But years of war scared them away into countries like Kenya and Uganda. Sudan's loss was their gain.

The plane was now too high in the air to see any animals. Fluffs of white clouds whisked by Halimah's window, blocking her view of the earth beneath. She leaned her head against the seat back and let her mind relax. Just for a few moments, while she was between worlds, she could let her thoughts take her back to a time before her life changed forever.

She was in high school and her sister Rania was just a small girl, maybe eight or nine years old. She'd been called Halimah back then—the pride of her father. But the memory rising to the surface of Halimah's mind was a time she had given her father one of her attitudes.

"Father, I want to go to the Sisters' school. They teach the students to speak English."

"*Habeebtee*, my dear, you do not need English to be successful. Arabic is the heavenly language, and the only one needed on earth."

"That's not true, Father," little Rania said. She did not realize she had stumbled upon her father and Halimah having a real argument. She sat on her father's lap and tugged at the sash on the giant turban that sat loftily on his head. "I hear you speak English when you talk to someone on the phone."

"No, my little darling, you are mistaken." Father pinched Rania's cheek. "I was using English words, but I was not speaking the language. I speak Arabic and only use English when I have to."

"And sometimes you have to, right, Father?" Halimah gestured toward her little sister. "Rania said it herself. She heard you. So why can't I study at the Sisters' school?"

"Because it is a Catholic school, Halimah. I do not want them filling your head with nonsense. And yes, yes, I know," he said, holding his hand up to stop the words that dangled on the tip of her tongue. "Many of your friends go there. But my daughter will not go to a Catholic school. You do not need their teachings, and you do not need English."

His words were final. And as if it would fix everything, he fished in his *jallabeeya* pocket and found several bills, enough to buy the two girls a fruit juice from the store at the end of the street. He handed the money to Halimah.

"Go," he said. "And, Halimah, I know they sell the perfume you like at that store, so go ahead and buy a new bottle for yourself." He smiled as if buying treats would cover any hurt feelings.

Father infuriated her. But she loved him. She loved him even now. Even after he had tried to kill her. He didn't understand, of course. If he truly understood the forgiveness she had found in *Isa*, he would believe too. Then he wouldn't have to kill her to restore his family honor. But he didn't believe . . . not yet anyway. She hoped he would read her copy of the Bible that he'd found in their house the day he confronted her. She missed him so much that her heart ached.

Halimah whispered the words of a verse that brought her comfort. "A father to the fatherless, a defender of widows, is God in his holy dwelling" (Psalm 68:5).

"That's from the Bible."

Halimah's eyes popped open. "Huh?"

The man sitting beside her greeted her surprise with a giant, toothy smile. Halimah had been so consumed by her own thoughts she had not noticed anyone around her.

She smiled nervously at him. He was probably Kenyan. She had worked with Kenyans at Kame, and even some Southern Sudanese. She had been around dark African people for more than two years now. But she still could not stifle the surge of prejudice welling up within her. Would *Isa* ever be able to banish those thoughts from her mind? She had looked down on black Africans her whole life. They were beneath her. She was Sudanese Arab, after all. She was allowed to look down on darker races.

If it showed on her face, the man didn't seem to notice her conflicting thoughts. He looked past Halimah and out her window. "Ah, Nairobi. My homeland." He smiled, and his giant pearly teeth were rivaled only by the bright shine in his eyes. "I have missed it."

They were getting closer to this man's home . . . and so much farther from her own.

The small plane landed in what Halimah heard the pilot say was the Jomo Kenyatta International Airport, which sounded like a big airport, but she didn't see any big planes.

"We are in a separate section," the man beside her said, as if hearing her thoughts. "This section is for United Nations planes and planes from the refugee camps like Kame. Don't worry; we are at the right airport."

Once they exited the plane and fetched their bags in a small arrival hall, Halimah was greeted by a second Kenyan man with a grin as big as her seatmate's on the plane. "Sara Danial?"

Halimah almost didn't answer but then realized he was talking to her. "Yes, that's me."

She rolled a suitcase behind her. It was small because she didn't own much. Her whole life fit into one bag: a few changes of clothes, some notebooks, two Bibles, and several commentaries.

"Please, follow me." The man turned and led her on a short brisk walk to the parking lot and then past many cars until they stopped beside a white van. A refreshing breeze brushed against Halimah, and she pulled her *tarha*, scarf, closer around her face. The air was several degrees cooler than the air in Kame, but it wasn't the temperature that impressed her. It was the freshness. Even here, in the parking lot of a giant airport . . . the air felt clean. Perhaps because it had just been delivered from the vast plains or perhaps the lush hills. Halimah didn't really know, but it hadn't come from sandy desert, and it felt wonderful.

The man took Halimah's suitcase, hoisting it into the back of the van. He then opened the side door for her and waited until she was comfortably seated before closing the door and going to the right side of the van. Strangely enough, that was where the steering wheel was.

"We will go to Nairobi via Mombasa Road, so if you are lucky, you may see something interesting out the left side of the car as we pass Nairobi National Park." He turned to look at Halimah in the back seat and beamed. "Nairobi is the only major city with a game park in it."

Halimah gasped as the man steered the van into the wrong lane of a huge roundabout on their way into Nairobi. The man glanced into the rearview mirror and broke into a friendly laugh. "Did I scare you? In Kenya we drive on the left side of the road, like the British do. Don't worry, I won't make us crash."

Halimah breathed a sigh of relief. But to keep her equilibrium from going crazy again, she looked out the side window rather than the front windshield.

Nairobi was busy and fast. Cars whizzed by at speeds she had never seen the vehicles in Khartoum go. Women walked alongside the road in brightly colored *batiks*, balancing baskets on their heads. Some had babies strapped to their backs. Men wore suits or trousers. No one was wearing a *jallabeeya*. Everyone was much darker than she was.

And the scenery was so . . . green. In Khartoum, the land was green for about 200 meters on either side of the Nile River. But after that, the desert took over again. Khartoum was mostly brown. Green was a color on a *tobe*, or the color of okra as it began to cook in Mama's cooking pot. But here in Kenya, green was the scenery. Halimah thought it was beautiful.

According to the driver, they were skirting the city and not actually going through the center of town. Halimah spent the entire time staring out the window. The driver pointed out when they were passing near the game park, but she didn't see any animals.

In an hour's time, they pulled up to a gate guarded by a man with a gun. He opened the gate and waved at the driver, who waved back as they pulled up the long driveway to a white building surrounded by a lush green lawn. In Khartoum, a gardener would have to water a lawn like that for hours a day to keep it looking so nice.

The driver retrieved Halimah's small suitcase from the van and led her up the steps of the building. The white walls and wooden shutters on the windows, reminiscent of British colonial days, reminded Halimah of old buildings in Khartoum, especially in the downtown area. A tall, skinny white lady who said her name was Jessica greeted her. Halimah could hear her mother say, "She looks homesick." Homesick and skinny were synonyms in Mama's vocabulary.

The homesick lady showed Halimah to her bedroom, which was upstairs and down a creaky wooden hallway. A slow moving ceiling fan sent cool air across Halimah's face. This time the air didn't feel refreshing. It felt cold and dank, like it had been sitting in the damp attic for several hours before the fan coaxed it down to sweep across her face.

Halimah looked at the sparse room. A single bed, a nightstand, a wardrobe, and a mirror that hung on the wall. Linens were neatly folded at the end of the bed. The unease that nagged her mind back in Kame returned. Maybe this was a mistake. She wished she could call Mia, but she had been using a phone supplied by Kame and had to return it before she left the camp. There was no one she could talk to. Halimah suddenly felt very alone.

Chapter 8
Nairobi, Kenya

The skinny lady didn't notice Halimah's wide eyes or the tear threatening to drip from her lashes and roll down her cheek. She remained in the doorway to Halimah's room and stared out the small window on the opposite wall.

"All your meals will be provided downstairs. There is a small local market within walking distance if you want to buy snacks. As long as you don't walk alone at night, this is a safe area." She handed Halimah the key to her bedroom. "Dinner will be at eight tonight, and we'll meet with the director tomorrow. You'll be working in the offices right here in the same building."

"Do you live here too?" Halimah asked. "Perhaps we could meet up for dinner."

"No, I don't live here. But you'll meet the others soon enough."

With that, the lady turned and walked back toward the staircase. The wooden floors complained.

After unpacking her belongings into the small cupboard in her bedroom, Halimah ventured out of the building and headed down the street toward where the lady said the market was. What was a Kenyan market like anyway?

"Hey, miss, what are you doing?"

Halimah turned back to see the guard from the front gate waving at her.

"I am going to the market."

"It is not open right now, lady. Only in the mornings. Tuesday is the only evening it is open. So you can go tomorrow evening if you like."

"Oh." Halimah turned and walked back toward the gate and the guardhouse, wondering why the homesick woman hadn't mentioned that detail. "Where were you when I passed by just now?"

The man grinned, his white teeth glowing. "I bent down to tie my shoe, so you didn't see me, and I didn't see you. Anyway, it's almost time for vespers, so you shouldn't go out. You should go to vespers; you can learn what Christians believe."

"I know what Christians believe," Halimah said.

"Oh? I thought you were Muslim." The guard pointed to her *tarha*.

"I always wear a scarf."

"Well, here in Kenya, only Muslims wear a scarf like that."

Halimah fingered the edge of her *tarha*. "Good evening." She sounded abrupt, but she wanted to get away from the guard and hide. As she walked briskly toward the giant white house, the guard called after her, "Don't forget vespers."

Halimah didn't stop until she'd reached her room and shut her creaky door. She looked into the mirror hanging on the wall beside the door. She had always worn a *tarha* in public. The guard was right though. She didn't have to wear a scarf in Kenya. She was free in Kenya. She was free in Christ. A smile appeared on her face. She took the *tarha* off, folded it, and placed it in one of the drawers of the cupboard. No more *tarhas*.

Vespers, Halimah discovered, was held on the front lawn. The mixture of African and white-skinned foreigners sitting in the plastic chairs seemed to be about even. She looked for the skinny lady, the only person she knew, but all of the faces belonged to strangers. Halimah felt exposed as she walked across the lawn and found an empty chair on the back row. To her surprise, no one seemed to notice her head was not covered. Soon she relaxed and enjoyed the music of the praise songs sung in English.

Halimah recognized two of the songs because Mia used to sing them to her kids back when Halimah lived with the Westons in Khartoum. She could remember enough of the words to sing along. The other songs were new to her, but they were beautiful, and Halimah closed her eyes, relishing the freedom of not wearing a scarf and of praising the Lord out in the open with no worries of repercussions.

After singing, a Kenyan stood in front of the group and read from the Bible. Halimah closed her eyes again, just like she'd done with the songs, letting the words wash over her. "It is for freedom that Christ has set us free. Stand firm, then, and do not let yourself be burdened again by a yoke of slavery" (Galatians 5:1).

At eight the next morning, Halimah was dressed and ready to meet the director. She had already eaten a breakfast of hot tea and toast. The cook tried to coax her into eating an egg and something he called stewed tomatoes, but she politely declined.

Before showing up for work, Halimah managed to find time to check email from an old desktop computer set up for the staff to use. She hadn't been able to check it much at Kame, so she didn't expect to have received anything, which made an email from Mia a nice surprise. If she couldn't call her friend, at least they could write each other.

Mia asked Halimah to write encouraging words for a believer in Sudan. Halimah smiled as she read. The Holy Spirit was moving in the hearts of people in her home country. Ideas for things to say flowed into her mind effortlessly. But she determined to write her friend back later. Today she needed to focus on her new job.

Not only had Halimah neglected to wear a *tarha* that morning, she'd also opted to wear a short-sleeved shirt that she normally only wore under a long-sleeved blouse. But after considering her new freedoms here in Kenya, she decided to experiment with new styles—ones she had previously only seen in magazines. The shirt she wore extended to just below her waist, and this would take some getting used to, as she had always made certain her shirts were long enough to completely cover her rear end.

Again, just like the night before, no one seemed to take notice that her hair and arms were visible or even that she wore trousers without a tunic. She'd never realized before how easy it was to move about without being encumbered by scarves and clothes.

The director's name was Mr. Smith. He wore a safari suit that looked shockingly similar to the clothes members of the National Intelligence and Security Services (NISS) in Khartoum wore. As she stood on the opposite side of Mr. Smith's desk, she mentally reminded herself that the director was not a part of the group her father surely paid to try to find her. This rhetoric in her head was helped along by the fact that Mr. Smith wore a ridiculous-looking safari hat to go along with his suit. He looked more like a hunter on an African safari than a humanitarian aid worker.

"So . . ." Mr. Smith thumbed through papers strewn across his massive wooden desk. "The folks at Kame tell me you are a clever young lady and will be a big help to us here in our Nairobi office. We are dealing with urban-based refugees, and we are seeking durable solutions to the areas of Nairobi affected by the influx of refugees. I know you are used to working as a translator, but we don't really need translators right now. I just need you to file papers for me. I wish I could say it was more exciting." He gave an apologetic shrug.

Halimah nodded and smiled. File papers? Was this why she had come all this way? She couldn't make a life for herself by alphabetizing folders. She was only in Kenya legally because the kind people at Kame had obtained her permission papers. But if all she could do was menial office tasks, where was her future? She would have to return to Sudan, maybe. What else could she do?

But she couldn't think of that right now. She had to keep her mind on the new job. Perhaps if she worked hard and showed them that they really needed her. . . . Thankfully, her English had improved vastly since living with the Westons and then working as a translator for over a year. That was something, right?

She spent the morning alphabetizing files of refugees who were seeking assistance or applying for refugee status. She could tell from the names on the tabs that most of the people were from South Sudan, Ethiopia, Eritrea, and a few from Uganda.

The files of Sudanese were especially interesting to her. She tried to focus on filing, but every once in a while she would open one of the folders and read the stories—horrible stories of people who were robbed, assaulted, or beaten. Halimah saw a side of her own people that she only realized existed when she started working with refugees.

The perpetrators of the horrible abuses were Sudanese Arab. So was she. Only, she was not like that at all. And neither was anyone she knew.

Her father would never do something like this. Her brother Abdu would never either. But these stories were true, and her own people had done these horrible things.

After the office closed at five, Halimah had a few hours before dinner. She decided to venture to the market since it was Tuesday. She grabbed her pocket purse and walked the long driveway toward the street. The guard, the same one as yesterday, met her at the gate. "*Jambo*," he said in Swahili.

"*Jambo*. The market is open today, right?"

"Yes." The guard laughed. "You can go today. And I see that you are not Muslim today. Have you become a Christian after vespers last night?"

Halimah couldn't help smiling back at him. His was the friendliest face she'd seen since arriving in Nairobi. "No, I was already a Christian before that. I just didn't wear my scarf today."

"I see that," said the guard. "You look very nice."

Halimah smiled at him, but then she lowered her eyes and hurried past him and down the road. Was he flirting with her? She usually didn't talk to single men unless circumstances required it. She was definitely not used to men telling her she looked nice. Was it because she didn't wear her *tarha* or perhaps because of her short sleeves?

It didn't matter so much now though, right? She was free in Christ. Deep inside, she had enjoyed the compliment even though it made her nervous. She hoped the guard's shift would be over before she returned so she wouldn't have to see him again.

The cool breeze out on the road was refreshing, not like the dank air inside the house she was living in. She would never get tired of the smell of greenery all around her. Before coming to Nairobi, she didn't know colors had a scent. And then there were the flowers, which bloomed everywhere. Even the weeds and wildflowers were beautiful.

Halimah picked her way alongside the road, trying to stay out of the traffic, which involved a lot of cars and *matatus*—minibuses used as public transportation. She was not the only pedestrian. Other people, as well as chickens and dogs, walked along the street. Halimah felt conspicuous at first, since she was wearing less than she usually did, but no one gave her a second glance, so she relaxed.

The market was a wonderful party of colors and smells. Three rows of buildings housed indoor clothing shops and a small grocery store. Makeshift stalls and fruit stands lined the sidewalks and parking lots, and young people walked up and down the streets hawking their wares, which included anything from watches to perfume to snacks. The scene reminded Halimah of the markets of Khartoum, where she loved to shop.

Halimah didn't have anything in particular she needed to buy. Her stomach would soon be full of beef stew and flatbread so she didn't need snacks, and she didn't have any friends to buy gifts for. But one of the indoor shops caught her eye. "Nairobi Fashion: Big Discount" the sign read. The clothes in the window looked stylish. Halimah decided to browse.

Twenty minutes later she left the shop with a new pair of trousers and a blouse. Since she was free in Christ, she might as well enjoy that freedom. The trousers fit tighter than any she had ever worn before, and the blouse just barely covered her waist. But the shade of blue in the blouse was what her mother always said looked beautiful against her skin. She told herself that as long as she didn't raise her arms, her blouse wouldn't lift up, and she would be all right.

Halimah meandered through the rest of the market area but didn't find anything else to buy. The pleasure of her clothing purchases had only lasted a few minutes before thoughts about her bleak future crept back into her mind. She wanted more than to just survive, but that's all that this new job was. Why had she been so determined to come to Nairobi at all?

She left the market and hurried back to the house, hoping to make it in time for vespers. Out of breath, she approached the front gate and saw a new guard at the post. Good.

The melody of voices singing praise songs filled the front drive as she made her way to the lawn and found an empty chair on the back row. As the attendees sang, Halimah bowed her head.

What do I do, Lord? I think I've made a mistake.

⇒ Chapter 9 ⇐
Dubai, UAE

Rania recognized the earthy scent of *bakhoor* that filled the room. The cushions and curtains of Sit Abubakr's salon were infused with the familiar Sudanese incense due to countless hours of burning the mixture of woodchips and oils over a live coal nestled in a clay holder.

Most Sudanese women living in Dubai switched over to electric incense burners and perfume-filled incense in the form of sticks or liquids. Sit Abubakr would have nothing of it. She continued to import authentic Sudanese incense to be burned over a live coal.

Rania and Auntie Badria sipped Turkish coffee from tiny demitasse cups decorated in gold filigree designs. Sit Abubakr sat like a happy hen in one of her throne-like chairs. She announced with pride that her husband imported the salon set from Abu Dhabi.

"Aren't you going to drink with us, Sit Abubakr?" Auntie Badria asked.

"Oh no, I have had too much coffee already today." She refused with a wave of her hand. "It's not good for my stomach. No, I *read* coffee more than I drink it now." She laughed as if she had just told a funny joke.

Rania preferred tea to coffee. And she didn't want to have her fortune read. She couldn't remember where exactly, but she did recall reading somewhere in the Bible that fortune-telling was wrong. The future belonged to God alone. People should not dabble in what did not belong to them.

Not that Rania had a choice in the matter. Auntie Badria had not asked for her opinion. She had insisted, and here they were. "It will be fun, Rania. I can't believe your mother never took you to have your tea leaves read in Khartoum."

So on the day that Auntie Badria told her it was time, Rania found herself in the backseat of a pink taxi. In Dubai the pink ones signaled a lady driver. Rania suggested they take the city bus, which was cheaper, but Auntie did not want Sit Abubakr to see them arrive in anything less than a pink taxi, even if it was expensive It was not Rania's place to force her opinion. It was her place to simply obey her aunt's wishes.

Rania sat with the two older ladies and tried to enjoy herself. She couldn't shake the unsettled feeling she had in her heart. Auntie Badria may just think that having her future read was a fun little pastime or a way to hold on to Sudanese culture, but Rania knew Sit Abubakr was tinkering with a world that did not belong to her.

Rania swished the thick liquid in her cup. What if she mixed up the grounds . . . could it be that easy to change her future? She glanced up at her aunt who was glaring at her. She quit swirling the cup and simply drank it.

When both ladies finished, Sit Abubakr instructed them to turn their cups upside down on their saucers.

"Do it carefully," she said. "And quickly. Turn and place. Yes, just like that, Rania. Good. Now we must wait for a few minutes for the coffee to dry. Rania, tell me about the wedding."

"I don't know much just yet. When Mother and Father come to visit, I'm sure I will learn more."

"Did you hear? They are coming next month and will stay with us." Auntie Badria was more excited about this than Rania. But Rania tried to at least appear excited. She was, in fact, looking forward to seeing her family because it had been a full year. But she was not excited at the idea that seeing her family meant plans were moving forward with the wedding.

Rania listened as the two older ladies talked excitedly about Rania's parents and about the wedding. Auntie Badria told Sit Abubakr all about Waliid and his family. This part interested Rania because she actually did not know much about her fiancé. She had hoped perhaps he would become interested in reading the Bible so they could follow *Isa* together.

That wasn't an impossible prospect. In fact, it had looked like a real possibility when she and Jamal had considered marriage. But then Jamal decided to remain Muslim and marry a devout young woman. That's when Father arranged for Waliid to come for dinner. It was the first time Rania had met her distant cousin.

He was tall with a big smile. He was not bad looking, but it was the *zibeeb* on his forehead that bothered her. This bluish bruise just above his eyebrows signified he was a devout Muslim who prayed often, pressing his forehead into the prayer rug every time he bowed to Allah. How could she, a follower of *Isa*, marry a strict follower of Islam?

As Rania wondered about her predicament, the women continued to chatter.

"You know," Sit Abubakr said. "This salon set, which my husband bought for me, is exquisite, don't you agree? I think Rania should have a set for her and Waliid. Perhaps her father could have one sent to Khartoum. He could take a look while he is here. My husband could take him to the store where he ordered them."

"How much did the set cost?" asked Auntie Badria.

"Oh, I think we got a good price. I don't know really. We bought it on credit."

Rania knew this was how most Sudanese families in Dubai kept up appearances of wealth. Most of them were heavily in debt.

"Well," said Auntie Badria. "I will be sure to tell him when he comes."

The older lady smiled and said, "OK, my friends. Would you like to peer into the future?" Without waiting for an answer, she leaned out of her throne chair and picked up Auntie Badria's cup and saucer. She flipped the cup right side up and examined the powdery contents that now stuck to the bottom and sides.

Auntie Badria sat at the edge of the chair in barely controlled excitement. Her hands rested on her knees, but her fingers silently tapped against them.

Sit Abubakr twisted and turned the cup thoughtfully. "I see the shape of a palm tree. This is good. This usually means some sort of wealth or good luck coming your way. And here is a flower. Ah, this definitely means happiness. Your coffee is telling you many good things are coming your way."

Auntie quit tapping her fingers and relaxed in her chair. "*Masha'*
Allah, thanks be to Allah. Perhaps the flower represents Rania's parents
who will be coming to our home. And I wonder . . . could the palm tree
mean that Faisal will get a raise?" Her fingers began to tap on her knees
again.

"It is not for me to say, Badria. I can only tell you what the coffee
grounds are telling me. But now . . ." Sit Abubakr looked at Rania. "It's
your turn. Are you ready?" She smiled.

Rania smiled back politely, though she did not want the woman to
look at her coffee cup. Oblivious, Sit Abubakr pulled the saucer toward
her. The cup jingled and wobbled, as if protesting for Rania's sake. The
older woman held the saucer and flipped the coffee cup right side up and
peered inside.

Rania sat on the edge of her seat just like her aunt had done. She
didn't mean to be interested in what the lady had to say about the coffee
grounds. But now that she was actually doing it, Rania couldn't help but
wonder what it would reveal.

"Probably something about your wedding," Auntie Badria whispered
to her.

"Shhh," the older woman said. "I have to concentrate."

The three women sat in silence as the soothsayer examined the
sediment in the bottom of Rania's cup. She seemed to be taking a long
time. Auntie Badria began to tap her fingers again.

Finally the woman spoke. "Well . . . the line could be a bow, which
would make sense because you are getting married and this represents an
engagement. But . . ."

"But?" Auntie drummed her fingers harder.

"Well, it's just that it looks more like an octopus, and that is a warning
signal."

"I think it must be a bow," Auntie said, leaning forward as if trying to
consult the reading.

"And I would tend to agree with you except . . ."

"Except what?" Auntie asked.

"Except there is also the shape of a black bird."

Rania didn't have to be told that a black bird represented something ominous. In Khartoum, if Mama saw a black bird perched on the top of an electric pole, she would gasp and begin to quote Qur'anic verses. "Something bad is going to happen, Rania." She would say. "*Astaghfir Allah*. God, forgive us."

"Are you sure it couldn't be something else?" Auntie asked.

The normally jolly Sit Abubakr frowned into the cup. Rania knew the lady was trying her best to find something other than bad symbols in her cup. She almost felt sorry for her. Finally the woman sighed and set the cup and saucer on the tray with a rattle and a clink. "I'm sorry," she said. "That's all I can find."

Shortly thereafter, Auntie and Rania said their goodbyes and hailed another expensive pink taxi. Auntie looked out the car window to make certain that Sit Abubakr had noticed the classy transportation they were in. Then she turned to Rania.

"Rania, *habeebtee*, I am so sorry. I can't believe I have invited that woman to your wedding."

"Auntie, it's OK. I don't really believe that stuff anyway. How can you see the future through coffee grounds?"

"You're probably right, *habeebtee*." Auntie peered out the window of the backseat in silence as the woman driver maneuvered through the heavy traffic of Dubai. "Still," she said, not willing to let the subject go. "I shouldn't have brought you."

"Auntie, don't worry. You meant well." Rania gave her aunt's hand a reassuring squeeze.

"You won't tell your mother about this during your weekly call, will you?"

"Not if you don't want me to."

"She doesn't need to know. It will only make her worry."

Auntie was worrying enough for everyone. "I won't tell her," Rania said.

Rania breathed a sigh of relief to be far away from Sit Abubakr's home. The whole aura of the place made her uneasy, like demons were lurking in the shadows. Why had those grim shapes appeared in her coffee cup? Rania reminded herself that she did not believe in reading coffee grounds or tea leaves. Only God knew the future.

Chapter 10

Khartoum, Sudan

Have you heard any updates on our exit visas?" Mia handed Michael a thermos of coffee.

"No, Habiib has been preoccupied with some new law that has come out about humanitarian aid organizations. He's trying to ensure that we are in compliance. I haven't wanted to bother him."

"If you don't push him a little, it will be us who lose out." Mia said the words in a mild tone but hoped Michael would pick up on the urgency. She helped Dylan put his backpack on his shoulders and then handed each of the three children their lunch boxes.

"I guess you're right. I'll try to find a time to talk with him." Michael grabbed his briefcase and walked toward the front door. "C'mon on, kids, don't want to be late for school." He stopped in the doorway, turning back to give Mia a kiss. "Have a good day, sweetie."

"I will if the electricity stays on."

Michael raised his eyebrows. "Have you tried starting Bertha lately? I greased her gears, so she should start smoothly."

Mia wrinkled her nose. "No, I haven't started Bertha. She's mean, and I don't like her."

Michael gave a mischievous grin. "If you don't push yourself a little, it will be you who loses out."

Mia laughed. "Just pray the electricity stays on, will you?"

"If I remember," Michael said, and winked at her. "Come on, kids, in the car."

Mia shut the metal gate after Michael and the kids pulled out of the driveway. She turned and gave Bertha a threatening look as she walked back to the house.

This was the first year for Dylan to attend school, and Mia was a free woman in the mornings. She had expected to have lots of time on her hands, but in reality, the mornings flew by, and it had taken her all year to figure out how to manage her time.

79

In the past, she might have met up with her friend Beth to visit a Sudanese family. But that was before their friendship fell apart and Beth moved to Casablanca. Even the name of the place sounded sophisticated, just like Beth. Mia missed having an American friend—someone who shared a similar background.

Tzega would be arriving soon to clean the house. Not wanting to appear lazy, Mia got a head start on clearing the breakfast dishes from the table and put a kettle of water on the stove to heat for washing dishes.

Her hands worked on the dishes and her mind worked on her worries. What if Habiib decided to keep the money and never turn in the passports to be processed? Would he do that? Where would that leave them?

Before her thoughts harassed her any further, the front gate squeaked, and she heard the soft tapping of Tzega's footsteps entering the house.

"*Sabah 'ilxayr*, good morning." She greeted Mia in Arabic, since that was the language they could both speak.

"*Sabah 'innoor*," Mia returned. Her worries skittered away and a smile replaced the lines on her face. "How is your family today?"

"They are fine, thank you."

"Any news on your father?" Mia tried not to ask too many times about Tzega's father, who had been arrested in Eritrea because he was the pastor of a Protestant church that was now illegal in the country.

"No news. It has been over a year. We still don't even know which prison he is in."

Mia thought of her own father back in Texas. She disliked the time difference, which complicated communication, but that was only an inconvenience. Tzega couldn't talk to her father because he was in prison. That was as different as Arabic and English.

"I still pray for your father every day." Mia gave Tzega a tentative side hug. She wasn't sure if it was the right thing to do. Did Eritrean women encourage each other with hugs?

"Thank you." Tzega smiled as she took the kettle off the stove top and filled the sink with hot water. Her hands smoothly grabbed dirty dishes and scrubbed them down with a sponge and dish soap.

When Mia left the kitchen, her mind had changed its course. She had no reason to be worried. Even if Habiib stole the money or the immigration officers refused their exit permits, Mia still had her husband and children with her, and she could pick up the phone and talk to her parents.

Settling herself in a plastic chair on the veranda, Mia surveyed the lime tree across the small yard near the wall. Miniature white flowers were beginning to disappear, being replaced by green bulbs, each at a different stage of becoming a golf ball-sized lime. Something fluttered in the branches, and dust, leftover from the giant *haboob,* released from the leaves and floated to the ground. Mia strained her eyes, peering through the limbs, and caught a flash of dazzling yellow as a bird flew out of its hiding place and across the sky above her. It soared to freedom, somewhere far beyond the walls that encircled Mia.

She stared into the sky for several moments, wondering what it would be like to fly over Khartoum like the yellow bird. She spread a map of Khartoum across the plastic table in front of her. The Blue Nile ran up from Ethiopia, and the White Nile ran up from Uganda. Right in the middle of Sudan's capitol, the rivers joined each other to become the Nile River that flowed to Egypt and then into the Mediterranean Sea. This convergence of two rivers into one divided Khartoum into three sister cities: Khartoum, Bahri, and Omdurman.

In her own way, Mia was the yellow bird gliding across Khartoum as she ran her fingers over the map. A pink highlighter marked her house as well as Hanaan's next door, the produce stands, the kids' school, and the international church that held English services. She traced her finger over the bridge to Bahri, the city to the northeast of Khartoum. A blue highlighter circled Abbas and Widad's house and store.

Mia traced her finger along the markings, praying for the people she knew who lived at each star or highlight. In the margin of the map, Mia wrote the names of Sudanese people whose house locations she did not know. Halimah was there, though Mia wrote her new name, "Sara," and so was her sister, Rania. Mia also drew a group of little stick figures representing the street children she often saw on the side of the road.

She didn't know their names, but they needed someone to pray for them. Well, she did know one of them. Mia would always remember Lily. How could she forget the little girl who threw a half-eaten orange at her car?

"Ma'am." Mia jumped, though Tzega's voice was soft.

"Oh, sorry, you startled me. I was just . . . praying." Mia tapped the map with her highlighter. "See, here is my neighborhood, and I've marked the houses of all the people I know. Where do you live, Tzega?"

The Eritrean woman looked at the map and then wrinkled her nose. "I don't know how to read a map." She said. "I live in Haj Yousef, near the main road."

"OK, maybe I can find it." Mia hadn't marked anything in that part of town. Haj Yousef was filled with refugees from both within and outside Sudan. Tzega was the only refugee Mia knew. "Here is Haj Yousef," she said, running her finger along a yellow line marking the main street. Do you live close to this road?"

Tzega wrinkled her nose again. "I don't know. Maybe."

Mia marked the area with a highlighter and wrote "Tzega" next to it. "I'm sorry, I don't even remember the names of your family members. What is your husband's name? And your kids?"

It wasn't that she didn't want to know their names, but they were Eritrean names, and just like Tzega's, they were difficult to spell and almost impossible to remember. "Here, you write them down for me." Mia handed her a pen and pointed to the highlighted spot on the map.

Tzega was meticulous as she wrote the name of her husband and two children. "Oh, and add the name of your father, I pray for him all the time as well. His name is Tesfalem, right? I do remember that one."

Mia twisted a lock of hair around her finger and watched Tzega write. She wrote the names in Latin script for Mia's sake since the Eritrean language was actually written using the ancient Ethiopian Ge'ez alphabet. She must have studied at least some English in her past to be able to write the names this way. Mia leaned over Tzega's written work and tried to read the words. "Wel-DEZ-gee, HEE-wot, Tze-gah-RAY-dah."

Tzega smiled in approval, and Mia realized there was so much about this beautiful lady she did not know. How long had she lived in Sudan?

Did her children get to go to school? How were they treated by the Sudanese government?

"You told me before that you could not live in Eritrea or Ethiopia because neither country would accept you. And you told me your father is in prison. Did your government force you to leave?"

Tzega's brow wrinkled, as if trying to find the Arabic words to express her thoughts. Mia wished they could speak in the heart language of at least one of them. But Arabic was the only common language between them.

"When we were married in Ethiopia," she said, "we thought our countries would accept the documents and let us live in either country. When we heard that the church my father pastored in Eritrea was having problems, my husband and I moved there to try to be a help to him and my mother. My husband got a job at first, but then more problems began. Government officials began coming to our house and asking us a lot of questions. Then my father disappeared, and we found out that he was arrested. My mother died the next year. She had malaria, but I think the stress of my father's arrest was too much for her. Afterward, we decided we should leave. But by then there was no way to do it through the airport. They had taken our documents."

"What did you do?"

"We had to leave by land. We had to pay a lot of money, and we had to leave at night." Tzega stared at the map, but her eyes betrayed that she was hundreds of miles away. Her voice wobbled as she continued. "When you leave quickly like that, you just leave with what you can carry in your hands. For a long time we did not have papers or documents of any kind here in Sudan. It was dangerous because they can arrest you if you don't have papers."

"How do they know?" Mia asked.

"The police drive into Haj Yousef in a truck. They stop when they see a group of Eritreans, and they ask for documentation. If we cannot show them any papers, they make us get in the truck, and they take us to jail. But we have papers now, we are registered as refugees, and we hope one day to leave Sudan."

"Where will you go?"

"Maybe Canada. It depends on who will take us."

Mia wanted to ask more questions, but Tzega kept glancing over her shoulder toward the inside of the house.

Of course. She wants to finish her work so she can get back home to her family.

"You can go back to working if you want," Mia said.

"I cannot iron the clothes because the power is out."

"Oh no," Mia looked up. The lifeless ceiling fan confirmed what Tzega said. The morning breeze must have kept her cool enough not to notice the blades had quit spinning. But now that she knew, she felt hot. "It's OK, no need to iron."

There really was a need to iron. Mia had washed several loads of laundry the day before. All their clothes had to be ironed in order to transform them from stiff and itchy to pliable and wearable. She tried not to think about the pile of crinkly clothes.

"I will mop instead," Tzega said and then disappeared back into the house. Mia had barely finished praying over Bahri when Tzega returned to the veranda. "There is no water."

"Of course," Mia said remembering the ground tank was hooked to an electric pump. Their water tank on the roof only worked if they remembered to pump water up to the roof, which, apparently, they had not remembered to do.

Michael's parting words now rattled in her head. "If you don't push yourself a little, it will be you who loses out."

Lord, I don't want to deal with Bertha. I want to sit here on the veranda and pray. I want electricity and ironed clothes and clean floors.

Tzega was now eyeing Bertha, but she didn't say a word. Tzega, who was a refugee and whose father was in prison. Mia winced. She had nothing to complain about.

"I am going to start Bertha."

"You are?"

"Yes. I am going to start the generator. Then you can iron the clothes and mop the floor."

Tzega smiled. "Thank you, ma'am."

Mia stood up from her comfortable spot. The plastic chair protested by dragging loudly against the tile. She took a deep breath. Her steps were deliberate if somewhat tentative as she made her way toward Bertha, her eyes boring a hole into the belly of the metal monster.

Standing in front of Bertha, Mia opened the fuel tap and turned the choke to the left. Then she made certain her blouse was not flapping in the breeze and she was standing as far away from the machine as possible. She turned the key and Bertha rumbled and complained, and the gears and belts began to spin. A grin spread across Mia's face.

"Take that, Bertha," Mia said in triumph. No one could hear her though, as Bertha rumbled like a train.

Mia marched back to the veranda and switched the lever on the electric box near the front door from "city" to "generator." The blades of the fan above her began to rotate and the lights flickered back on. She half expected Tzega to congratulate her for defeating Bertha in spite of her fear. But Tzega had no idea of the drama that had just played out in Mia's mind, and besides, neither one of them could hear each other because of the engine noise. Mia's reward would be clean floors and ironed clothes.

Mia wondered if anyone in Haj Yousef had a generator. Tzega and her family certainly did not have anything so luxurious. Did she even have running water at her house? She couldn't stop thinking about Haj Yousef. Maybe she should drive over to that part of town and pray for the people there.

≥ Chapter 11 ≤
Khartoum, Sudan

Michael left for work early the next day, taking a rickshaw and leaving the car with Mia so she could drive the children to school. This was unusual for him because he hated rickshaws. Mia wasn't fond of them either, but sometimes they didn't have any choice. These black two-person vehicles were driven by a motorcycle-type motor and were loud and always seemed a little unstable. They were open-air vehicles with zero safety features. Riding a rickshaw was like throwing a can out into the middle of a busy intersection and crossing one's fingers in hopes it didn't get smashed by an oncoming vehicle.

Mia decided that, since she had use of the car, today would be a good day to try to find Haj Yousef. She studied the map first to make sure she was confident of her directions.

"Why do you have your prayer map with you, Mommy?" Dylan asked as the kids piled into the SUV to go to school.

"Oh, I was just looking at it."

"You can't pray and drive, Mom," Corey said, throwing his backpack into the passenger seat and crawling in after it.

"Sure I can. I just can't look at the map and drive." Mia smiled. "OK, everyone buckled up?"

Dylan laughed. "Mommy, you are silly. There are no seatbelts in this car."

"You know, when we go to the States this summer, you'll all have to wear seatbelts."

"Awwwww, what?" Dylan sounded annoyed.

"And you'll have to sit in a booster seat, Dylan," Corey said.

"No way."

"Yes, you will. Won't he, Mom?"

"Well, yes, probably so. There are a lot of laws and rules in the States that, well, we just don't have here."

When they arrived at the children's school, Mia pulled to the side of the busy road and parked under a tree. The shoulder of the street was only dirt, and there were no lines to mark the parking spots. The small school the Weston children attended was surrounded by a brick wall. Star Friends, run by a group of Kenyans, was not registered as a Christian school, but it was taught by Christian teachers. Somehow they had managed to keep getting permission to stay open. Probably because there were still a large number of Christians from other countries who lived in Khartoum and also because the academic standard was high. Several wealthy Muslim families even sent their children to Star Friends because they wanted their children to learn English well.

The kids hopped out of the car, and Mia walked them to the green metal gate manned by Joseph, the second grade teacher. When he smiled, his teeth glowed like a row of pearls.

"Good morning, Mrs. Weston. Good morning, children."

"Good morning, Joseph." Mia waved to her children; all three had already run through the gate and into the school yard, backpacks bouncing on their backs like loose camel humps. Mia laughed. "Bye, kids. Have a great day."

Joseph shrugged. "What can I say? They love it here."

He was right. Who would have thought a place as sold out to Islam as Sudan would have a wonderful little school run by Christians and operated in English? It was just another one of Sudan's ironies.

Mia thanked Joseph and made her way back to the car. Cars drove by at an unnerving speed and Mia whispered a prayer as she backed out into traffic. She breathed a sigh of relief once she was safely in the flow of traffic steering her car toward Haj Yousef.

Traffic in Khartoum did not only consist of cars. Pedestrians, donkeys, sheep, and on occasion a train of camels heading to the camel market added an extra element of danger. Driving was not for the faint of heart. Luckily, Mia's father had taught her to drive a manual shift car from the time she was a teenager. If he had not, she would have had a hard time driving in Khartoum since no one drove an automatic.

Mia noticed several military tanks at one of the intersections, and when she crossed the bridge over the Nile, she saw more guards than usual. Sometimes, when there were rumors of an attack on the government, the military beefed up their presence around town. It wasn't completely unusual, so Mia kept driving.

She couldn't tell exactly when she had arrived in Haj Yousef. Dirt and sand and rows of square brown buildings lined the streets. Donkey carts, which were wooden flatbed affairs with two car tires, replaced automobiles. Mia was in one of the few motorized vehicles on the road except for rickshaws. It was as if she had stepped back in time about 50 years. This must be Haj Yousef.

Mia realized quickly that it would be impossible to find the road Tzega lived on. No wonder her house cleaner hadn't been able to read the map. This area of town was a maze of streets and single-story buildings with no distinguishable features. Everything was brown and covered in sand. She decided to simply stay on the main road, the only paved one, and pray for the area in general.

"Lord," she said out loud, since no one else was in the car, "I pray for the people who live here in Haj Yousef. I pray they will come to know You as their Savior and find forgiveness and love."

Mia noticed a black truck on her side of the road, facing her. It looked like a police truck, so she slowed down. As she passed, she saw police, guns slung over their shoulders, directing a group of men and women into the back of the truck. Mia kept driving, but soon the paved road ran out, and she was forced to turn around and head back. When she passed the place where the truck was, a sizeable crowd had gathered. By now the truck bed was loaded with at least ten people and two guards. The black vehicle pulled up onto the road in front of Mia, and since she was now going in the same direction as the truck, she was forced to drive behind it.

She could tell from their facial features, the high cheekbones and penetrating eyes, that the passengers in the back were from Eritrea or Ethiopia. They didn't look like thieves or any other kind of lawbreakers. This must be one of those police sweeps Tzega had told her about. Mia knew the only law they had likely broken was fleeing their home countries for fear of their lives and entering Sudan without proper paperwork.

Mia saw three women sitting in the bed of the truck with the men. Everyone except the guards looked frightened. Some stared out of the truck with frightened eyes and clenched jaws. Others lowered their heads as if trying to hide. Mia frowned. They probably had children waiting for them at home or bosses waiting for them at work. Tzega had explained these people would be put in a cell at the police station until they could produce some sort of legal identification. She didn't know what would happen to them if they didn't . . . or couldn't. She did not want to think about it. That was an insensitive reaction, but she could only bear so much heartbreak.

Mia had no choice but to keep following the police truck until they reached a larger road where she planned to turn in the opposite direction of the truck. She was growing increasingly uncomfortable driving behind it. The two guards in the back of the truck periodically turned and stared at her. Would they ask the driver to stop so they could request to see her identification?

Mia carried a copy of her passport in her purse, but Habiib had the original. What would she do if they asked for it? The truck began to slow down and Mia's stomach lurched. One of the two guards in the back jumped out of the truck. This was it: the arrest of Mia Weston. She tried to breathe normally. She whispered a prayer for courage.

Then the man banged on the back of the truck as if saying thank you to the driver, gave a big wave to his fellow guard, and turned and walked away down one of the nameless streets. The truck picked up speed again and Mia relaxed.

They were simply giving the guard a ride home. *No need to worry, Mia. And anyway, you are an American woman. They will not pick you up on the street and parade you through town in a truck.*

Mia felt a sting of injustice. Why was she protected while the men and women in the truck weren't? The only difference between her and them was the country they were born in, and no one had control of that.

She was thankful to have been born a citizen of the United States. But it wasn't fair that these people were suffering through no fault of their own.

At the next intersection, the police truck turned right and Mia turned left. Mercifully, left was the way she needed to turn to get home. She prayed silently for the refugees who had been picked up in the police sweep. Then she prayed for the policemen themselves. "Lord, help them to come to know You as well. I don't know how it would happen, but I know You are powerful enough to make it so."

Traffic seemed heavier than usual. The cars seemed to be driving faster than normal. As Mia neared the bridge back to Khartoum, she noticed there were few pedestrians on the road. Also odd. Then her cell phone began to ring, and against her better judgment, she held it to her ear with her shoulder and tried to listen as she drove.

"Mia, it's Michael. Where . . . you?"

"Michael, I can't hear you very well. You are cutting out. I'm across the bridge, why?"

". . . back now . . . can't be out . . . closed."

"What? I can't hear you. What is closed?"

"Bridge . . ." And then the line went dead.

Mia pulled the car to the dirt shoulder and put it in park. She tried to call Michael back, but the phone went to the automated Arabic message: "The number you are trying to call is not in service. Please try again later."

Mia remembered the last coup attempt. Bridges closed and, because everyone in Khartoum tried to call their relatives to check on their well-being, cell phone lines had been overloaded. It had happened on a Friday, a day off in Sudan, so her whole family had been at home at the time. Mia remembered Habiib eventually getting through to them on the phone and telling them to stay home and lie low.

That wasn't going to be the case today, if this was a coup. Michael was at work, the kids were at school, and Mia was across the bridge. Why had she thought driving over here to "prayer drive" was a good idea? Her photocopy of an American passport was not going to save her from crossfire during a coup attempt.

Since she couldn't get home, the second safest thing for her to do would be to get out of sight. Also impossible. She prayed for wisdom and racked her brain for an idea. She felt like a lightning rod in an electric storm.

The cell phone beeped. A message from Michael. *Thank You, Lord.* She opened it and read, *New bridge still open, drive fast.*

This was good. Something to work with. She wasn't sure how to get to the new bridge, but she had a general idea of the direction. Over here on this side of the Nile, paved roads were scarce. She figured if she stayed on the paved roads and navigated west, she'd eventually get to the right place.

Mia took the scarf that she kept in the car and covered her hair as best she could. She was already in a predicament by being a white woman all alone in a car far from home. But her blond curls made her stand out like the highlighted streets on her prayer map.

She put the vehicle in first gear, second gear, third gear . . . driving as quickly as she could toward where she thought the new bridge would be. It wasn't hard for her to drive fast, by now most of the people and vehicles were off the street. Mia bit her lip and concentrated on missing potholes, trying not to think about what would happen if she didn't make it to the bridge in time.

Five minutes later, which was record time in Khartoum, she made it to the new bridge. A tank was arriving from her left and guards posted themselves at the entrance to the bridge. The motion of her car speeding toward them made the guards stop and look toward her. She slowed down and peered at the guards. Her frantic expression pleaded with them. Two men, who looked to be in their twenties, motioned her through. She could hear their muffled yells through the glass, "*Bi sura'a, bi sura'a!* Quickly, quickly!"

The streets were empty on the other side of the bridge as well. Mia tried not to look about as she drove. She trained her eyes on the road, scanning for potholes. The children's school was not far away, and she decided the best option would be to head there. Steering with one hand

and punching buttons on her cell with the other, she managed to call the school's front desk. The phones, however, were still not working, and she received the same message she got when she tried to call Michael.

She tossed her cell phone in the passenger seat and focused on getting to the school safely. She'd have to worry about how to gain entrance later. Fortunately, her timing had been impeccable. When she parked the car and ran for the front gate, she saw Joseph peering over the top of the wall. He saw her and then his head disappeared as he jumped down from whatever he had been standing on and opened the gate to let her in.

"Mrs. Weston, what are you doing here?"

"There is a problem outside. I think a coup or something."

"Yes, there are bad things happening out there; you shouldn't be on the street. Stay here until things calm down. It won't be long." Joseph led her across the sandy school yard and into the front office. "We have moved all the children inside, and they will take their lunch break indoors today. Everything should be back to normal by this afternoon."

"But what if there was a coup? Things won't go back to normal then."

Joseph's pearly teeth appeared as he smiled. "This is Khartoum, Mrs. Weston. If it is a coup attempt, it will not be successful. Who in Sudan has the power to overthrow the government?"

Who indeed? The Khartoum regime owned tanks, aircraft, and artillery. The president had overthrown the government in a bloodless coup nearly 30 years ago. He knew a thing or two about how the opposition might think. He would never let a coup happen during his rule.

"No," Joseph continued, "they will find the perpetrators, punish them soundly, and by tomorrow it will be as if this never happened." Joseph's expression changed as he said the words. Dark creases appeared in his forehead as his brow furrowed for a moment. But then his smile returned. "But you can stay with Margaret until it's safe to go home."

Mia followed him across the school yard into the reception area where Margaret, a Kenyan like the other staff, smiled from behind her desk.

"Good morning, ma'am."

"Good morning, Margaret." Mia sat on a wooden bench against the wall. She took out her cell phone to send Michael a message. Perhaps a text would get through to him, even if a phone call would not.

Am at kids' school. All OK. You?

She waited for several long minutes before her phone beeped, and she saw his return message.

PTL. Am fine. Love you.

⇒ Chapter 12 ⇐
Nairobi, Kenya

Halimah filed papers in the downstairs office of the big white house for a full week and tried not to think about the possibility that coming to Kenya had been a mistake. She relished the fresh air, the vespers every evening, and the lush garden surrounding the house. But every night she sat alone on the edge of her bed and thought about how she missed her family in Khartoum. She remembered the words of her pastor, Mansur, who led the underground church she attended before getting caught.

"It will be a long time before you can return home, Halimah."

She would give up Kenya in a heartbeat to go back home and be with her family. But she wouldn't give up *Isa*. He was the true way to God, and she wouldn't deny the truth.

Since it was Tuesday, Halimah returned to the market. She had worn her new outfit twice the week before and loved the way it made her feel free. No more *tarha* to cover her head, no more *abaya* to cover her from neck to toe. And the most surprising thing to Halimah: no one appeared to think anything about it. No one except perhaps Jessica, the skinny lady who raised her eyebrows any time Halimah emerged with her new stylish clothes on. But what did that matter? Halimah's mother was right. The lady was probably homesick or unhappy since she was so skinny. What right did Jessica have to judge someone else?

Halimah had managed to ride to a shopping mall with some of her fellow office workers twice during the week. They caught a *matatu* in front of the house and rode the minibus into town. The ride had been crowded, but she felt safe. She used some of her paycheck to buy more clothes. The two shirts she bought had short sleeves, and the pair of trousers was tight. But it didn't matter anymore. She was free.

She even didn't mind the guard flirting with her anymore. He was nice actually. His name was Simon.

The other pedestrians walking along the road toward the market were Kenyan, but as she entered the market area she saw a woman in a *tobe*, just like Mama used to wear. And beside her was a man in a *jallabeeya*. Halimah couldn't take her eyes off the couple. She pretended to be interested in a small shop selling Kenyan crafts. She examined a woven basket with halfhearted interest and then fingered the small soapstone figurines arranged neatly on a table. All the while she kept her eye on the couple, who were several shops away, purchasing some fruit.

"Do you want anything from my shop?" The pudgy store owner didn't mask his irritation.

Halimah had been holding a soapstone elephant and staring off into the distance. "Hmm? Oh no, thank you." She set the figurine back on the table and walked toward the couple.

"*Salaam aleykum,*" she said as she approached them. In Khartoum, she never approached strangers in a market and just started a conversation. Perhaps she would do so to ask a price or directions, but never just to talk. But this couple dressed like they were from Sudan, and it had been so long since she had talked to a Sudanese Arab.

"*Aleykum wassalaam,*" the woman replied.

"Are you from Sudan?"

"*Aywa,* yes," the woman said. "*Wa entee?*"

"*Aywa,*" Halimah answered excitedly, feeling as if she were meeting an old friend. Even the way the woman said, "Yes, and you?" was spoken in a Khartoum accent. The woman looked to be around Mama's age.

"Have you been to the far side of the market yet? They sell Sudanese things. I have seen *karkaday* and coffee and other Sudanese drinks. They also sell *bakhoor* incense that will make your house smell just like Sudan, *masha' Allah.*"

"Are there many Sudanese who live here?"

"Yes, many live in this area. We live only about a mile down the road. There is a mosque just a few blocks away where we all go to pray. You are welcome to come with us."

"*Shukran,*" Halimah said. She wouldn't be going to the mosque, but she appreciated the invitation. She missed hearing a Sudanese Arab voice and the rough cadence of her own dialect. She hadn't realized until now how different the accents were between tribes. Sure she heard a lot of Arabic over the last two years. She had been a translator, after all. But the people she listened to were from Darfur and Ethiopia and Eritrea and South Sudan. This woman had the voice of an angel. Halimah wanted to follow the woman and her husband and ask questions. Any question would do. And she didn't care what the answers were, as long as they were spoken in her beloved Sudanese Arabic.

The woman and man began to walk away. "We have to go now. But it was nice to meet you. I hope we'll see each other again. You must come to our house for tea. Are you free this week?"

Halimah felt jittery with excitement. Of course she could make time for tea. Anything to spend time with someone from home. "Yes, I'm sure I will have time. I don't have a local number yet, but perhaps you could give me your phone number?"

"*Taba'an*, of course." The woman reached into her large handbag and fished out a pen and piece of paper. While she wrote, her husband watched Halimah with a look of curiosity that unnerved her. She looked at the ground.

Oblivious, the woman handed the paper to her. Halimah smiled at the lady, trying to ignore the husband. "*Shukran*."

"Call anytime, and we can have tea. Later, you can give me your number."

Feeling increasingly uncomfortable, Halimah stuffed the paper in her pocket and glanced behind her. "I think I better go now. Thank you again."

The husband placed his shopping bag on the ground by his feet and crossed his arms. He leered at Halimah. "What is your name?" he asked.

"Sara," she answered easily.

"What is your father's name?"

"Danial," she said, less convincingly.

The man's eyes seemed to bore into her face. She felt the heat of his glare burn her cheeks. "Sara Danial." It wasn't a question, but he said the name as if he were deciding whether or not to believe it. "Sara Danial . . . from where? You don't look Southern Sudanese. You must be from the North."

Halimah gulped. Khartoum was a big city, but not that big. Most Arabs knew, just from someone's father or grandfather's name, exactly what tribe and family any acquaintance was from. And he was right; she did not look like she was from any tribe other than an Arab one. Her skin was dark for an Arab, but not dark enough to be from a Southern Sudan tribe.

She glanced at her wrist as if she wore a watch, which she didn't. "I have to go now. I am probably late already."

"You seem familiar to me, Sara. I think I may know your father's family. Who is your grandfather?"

Halimah ignored the man, which was rude. She looked at the wife and attempted a smile. "I really must go. I will try to call you."

"Yes, you must come for tea."

Halimah nodded, but no sound came from her mouth because all the words stuck in her throat. She turned and began to walk away.

"Hey, girl." The man raised his voice. "Who is your grandfather?"

Halimah picked up her pace and willed herself not look back to see if she was being followed. She didn't slow her pace until she reached the guard post of the big white house. By then she was out of breath, and her heart thumped angrily in her chest.

"*Jambo*," Simon said. "Why the worried look on your face?"

Halimah forced her breathing to slow and did her best to look calm. "Oh, I was just walking fast," she said.

"Don't be scared. No one will bother you here. I am on duty."

Halimah smiled and thanked him as she walked through the gate that he held open for her. She took one final look behind her and saw nothing unusual. She was more thankful for the protection than Simon knew.

Dinner was a simple cafeteria-style affair with bread and soup, vegetables, and small portions of roasted chicken. As usual, Halimah ate with the other nine people who lived in the upstairs portion of the two-story house. One was the cook, one was the caretaker, and the other seven worked in the same office as Halimah.

"It's not a bad job," one of the ladies said to her as they ate at one end of the long wooden dining table. She was a young British girl, perhaps the same age as Halimah. Halimah wondered if she missed England, though she wasn't skinny like Jessica. "You'll be more comfortable here than you were in Kame, that's for sure. But the work is not as interesting. Shuffling papers is boring compared to hearing the stories of refugee families firsthand. But, if it weren't for us, there would be no Kame. So . . ." She shrugged and stuffed a spoonful of green beans into her mouth and chewed thoughtfully.

Later, in the lonely quietness of the African night, Halimah retreated to her room and cried. She couldn't help it. The voice of the woman in the market had made her more homesick than she had been in all her two years since leaving Khartoum. She had made so many big changes in her life. She had done all of it with God's grace. But when she heard a voice she didn't realize she missed, the deep longing for home filled every vein in her body.

But more than a sick feeling for home was the fear she felt when she replayed the man's voice. "Who is your father?" If she told him her father's name, he would probably have recognized it. She had been told before that her family had distinct features. She had always received the comment with pride. But today it scared her. She had been so stupid. She shouldn't meet other Sudanese people, not if she wanted to be safe.

Why had she done something as dangerous as introducing herself to an Arab couple from Khartoum? How widespread was the story of her conversion? Was it talked about enough so even distant friends might put together that she had escaped to a nearby country? Would there actually be people in Kenya who might be looking for her?

Halimah lay on her bed and covered her face with her hands.

"Have mercy on me, my God, have mercy on me, for in you I take refuge. I will take refuge in the shadow of your wings until the disaster has passed. I cry out to God Most High, to God, who vindicates me" (Psalm 57:1–2).

Just before dawn Halimah heard the call to prayer coming through her window. "*Allahu akbar. Allahu akbar.* Allah is the greatest. Allah is the greatest." It wasn't loud, like the mosque in her neighborhood in Khartoum, but the sound was enough to wake her. She rubbed her cheeks and felt the salt left by tears from the night before.

The verse she'd quoted over and over as she drifted to sleep came to her mind again, and as it did, she realized God had answered her prayer. He had been merciful to her, even before she'd gotten herself into the predicament with the couple at the market.

Because she did not have a local phone number, the couple had no way to get in touch with her. As long as she did not go to the market, she would not see them again. She breathed a sigh of relief. But the realization became more concrete in her mind as she rose from her bed and began to dress for the day. She was not really safe here in Kenya. If she lived within walking distance from a Sudanese community, there was a good chance she would be found.

Halimah recalled the catch in her spirit back at Kame. She was sure now it was the Holy Spirit who had been telling her not to come to Nairobi. But now that she was here, what was she to do?

Chapter 13
Dubai, UAE

Rania sat in the back of the sedan and listened to her uncle and his colleague from work talk and laugh. Mr. Rashid talked about work some, but mostly he told jokes. Uncle Faisal was a systems analyst and his colleague Rashid was an accountant. Rania figured they told each other jokes because there was nothing interesting about their jobs.

"You know," Rashid said from the passenger seat, "a Saidi and his son moved to Cairo one day."

Uncle Faisal laughed from the driver's seat. "Another Saidi joke? Give the Egyptians a break."

"No, no, listen. This man and his son went to Cairo so his son could go to school."

"And what happened?"

"Well, the son went to school, and when he came home, he said, 'Father, they taught us to count today, and I was the only one who could count to 100. Is that because I am Saidi?' And his father replied, 'No, my son, it is because you are so smart.'

"The next day his son returned home and said, 'Father, today we learned the alphabet, and I was the only one who already knew it. Is that because I am Saidi?' To which his father replied, 'No, son, it is because you are so smart.'

"And the third day the son returned home to say, 'Father, today we were measured, and I was the tallest in the class. Is that because I am Saidi?' And his father said, 'No, my son, it is because you are already 30 years old.'"

The two men laughed, and Rania couldn't help smiling from the back seat. Arabs loved to tell jokes on villagers from Upper Egypt, called Saidi. Rania thought they were funny, but Mama always said jokes were for the men.

Uncle Faisal and Rashid seldom talked to Rania, which was fine with her. She put in her ear buds and listened to music all the way to the art school. She wanted to listen to Christian music, but Uncle always looked through her music selections, so she had to keep it to Arab pop music. Still, it was better than listening to the men.

When they arrived at the school, Rania thanked her uncle and stepped out of the car. It was nine in the morning. Her class did not actually begin until 9:30, but she had padded the time a little when giving her uncle her schedule. This allowed her time to go to the student store or see an advisor. But since she didn't have anything she needed to do on this day, she enjoyed a few moments without her aunt and uncle poking their noses into all of her business.

Rania took a long route to get to her first class. She enjoyed the exercise. It felt good to walk farther than simply from her bedroom to the kitchen.

Souad met her in the hallway. "*Sabah 'ilxayr*, Rania."

"*Sabah 'innoor,* Souad. How are you today?"

"I am good. Except I am so curious as to why the professor told us to bring our portfolios. Aren't you wondering the same thing?"

"I didn't think much of it. Maybe he just wants us to work on them in class."

Souad shook her head. "I think it's more than that. I spent a lot of time last night organizing mine. Did you?"

"Well, no. I'm just glad I remembered to bring it."

Souad opened the door to the classroom, and the girls entered and found empty seats near the front.

Ten minutes into class, Rania's cell phone beeped to notify her of a new message. Her art professor glared at her.

"May I remind you that all phones must be put on silent before class begins? We cannot have interruptions nor can we afford to have creativity stifled by technology."

The man waved his paintbrush like a wand, as if he would cast a spell on Rania's book bag. Professor Mustafa, a well-known artist from Morocco, was famous partly for his teaching and partly for his eccentricity. No one could deny his magical ability to draw out excellence in his students.

That's why Rania endeavored to please him, and why she was mortified to have her phone be the one to garner his negative attention today.

"Please pardon me, professor." She bent down to fish her phone out of the bag and turn it on silent.

Professor Mustafa brushed away her apology with his paintbrush and stepped behind his podium to assume a lecture position. "We'll not be painting today. I have someone to introduce to you. For some of you, he will be a great asset. For others, he will only be a dream you try to catch. But for all of you, his attention to your artwork will be a worthy goal." He continued to wave his paintbrush, this time as if he were conducting an orchestra. "And now I present to you the one and only Khalid Ali."

Souad leaned over to whisper in her ear. "*The* Khalid Ali?"

Rania shrugged. "I guess so. Who is he?"

Souad's eyes widened. "Only the most coveted art dealer in Dubai. I can't believe you've never heard of him."

A tall figure rose from the front row and joined Professor Mustafa on the stage. Khalid Ali was thin and—Rania felt guilty for thinking so—handsome. He dressed in Western clothes, though his features and of course his name suggested he was from an Arab country. When he spoke, Rania knew he was an Emirati.

"*Salaam aleykum wa rahmatullahi wa barakatuh*, peace be on you and the mercy of Allah and his blessing. My name is Khalid Ali, and I am eager to look at your work. I am always in the market for original art, and the Arab Art School produces some of the best artists of all. I will be here all day, so if you don't get a chance to talk to me during class, be sure to stay late, or come back in the afternoon so I may talk to you."

The students began to fumble for their portfolios until Professor Mustafa silenced the room with a wave of his paintbrush.

"Enough noise. You may leave now unless I call your name. Those of you who are not called may arrange to return and meet with Khalid Ali after class. The following are the students who may stay and show their portfolios first."

The professor read ten names, including both Souad and Rania. The students who were not called tried to mask their disappointment while gathering their portfolios and departing. Souad's eyes twinkled. Her eyes were the only way Rania could see how her classmate felt. Souad wore the *niqaab*, the black head covering that revealed only her eyes.

Khalid Ali sat down at a table on the stage, and the professor sat beside him. Professor Mustafa announced he would call the names of the ten students one at a time, and each one would have the opportunity to show his or her portfolio to the art dealer.

Souad tapped her foot against the leg of her chair as they waited. "I'm so nervous, Rania. Are you?"

Rania shook her head. "Not really. I'm going back to Sudan soon. I guess I won't have a need to sell my artwork in a few months. It doesn't matter what he thinks of my work."

"Then why come to Dubai to study art at all?"

"Long story." Rania didn't want to say any more about the subject. She retrieved her phone to check the message that had come during class.

This is Sara. This is my new number. Praying all is well.

Souad's eyes widened. "Good message?"

Rania smiled. "Yes. From my sister. I miss her, and it is always good to receive a message from her."

Souad nodded. "Yes, it is always good to hear from family. I guess you must miss all your family in Sudan."

Rania did not explain that her sister was no longer living in Sudan. Someone like Souad, someone who wore the *niqaab*, would not understand Rania and Halimah.

"Rania." The professor called from the stage.

Rania grabbed her portfolio, and Souad patted her arm as if to wish her good luck. Rania felt more nervous to stand in front of her professor than this supposedly famous art dealer. As much as she loved to paint, she tried to keep her ambition tightly tethered. No need to dream when she already knew those dreams would not come true.

She lowered her gaze when she approached the table. Professor Mustafa introduced her to Khalid Ali, and she nodded her head politely. Then she opened her portfolio and pushed it across the table toward the men.

Khalid Ali nodded as he looked through the samples. "Yes, yes. These are beautiful. She is gifted, Mustafa. You have done well."

The professor sat tall in his chair. Khalid Ali's compliment puffed him up like a peacock.

Khalid Ali looked straight at Rania. "You are a promising artist. Please take one of my business cards, and feel free to contact me when you have a piece to sell. I buy only originals, and I promise to offer you a generous payment." The man closed her portfolio and pushed it back toward Rania.

"*Shukran*," Rania said. She took her portfolio and walked off the stage just as she heard the professor calling Souad's name. She smiled at her classmate and nodded. "You'll be great," she whispered as they passed each other. Souad's eyes darted from Rania up to the desk where the two men sat waiting.

Rania's class schedule for the day was full, but after her last one, she still had half an hour before Uncle Faisal and Mr. Rashid came to pick her up. She sat on a bench in the hallway, took out her phone, and dialed the new number.

"Sara? Is this Sara?"

"Rania. I am so glad you got my message. I just got this number and I was hoping it worked. You are the first person I sent a message to."

"I'm so glad to hear from you. How is Nairobi?"

"Lonely."

Rania sighed. "I wish I were lonely. The only time I am truly alone is on Friday when Uncle and Auntie lock me in the apartment."

"They lock you in?"

"They don't want me to run away, I guess. But it's OK because that's when you and I can talk freely. Anyway, guess what Auntie did last week? She took me to have my fortune read, and now she is convinced something terrible is going to happen to me. She is even more superstitious than Mama."

"I wish she could know about *Isa*. Have you ever said anything to her about Him?"

"Sara, you have been out of the Arab world for too long. You have forgotten what it's like. Of course I have not said anything to her."

"I have not forgotten, Rania, *habeebtee*. Not a day goes by that I don't think about what it's like. I'm the one disowned from the family, remember?" Rania could hear the prickle in Halimah's voice.

"I know. I'm sorry."

"And even though there could be consequences, you cannot withhold the truth from Auntie when you know you have the solution she needs."

"I'll have to think about it, Sara. Pray for me?"

"Of course." Halimah's voice softened.

"Auntie scared me half to death when she told me Father and Mama were coming to Dubai in just four weeks. Thankfully the plan has changed. I don't think they will come until I am finished with school. I hope they don't. I am afraid if Father comes earlier, he'll decide to take me back to Khartoum right away and marry me off to Waliid."

"Sounds like we have several things to pray about. Let's pray that you can finish school and also that you'll have a chance to share with Auntie."

⇒ Chapter 14 ⇐
Khartoum, Sudan

The attempted coup had been thwarted. Just as Joseph had predicted, the military quickly arrested all of the guilty parties, and by the end of the work day, the city had returned to normal . . . just as if nothing had happened.

Mia had waited in the school office until the staff at Star Friends announced it was safe to return home. By then Michael had found a ride to the school and joined the family there.

Even though businesses and schools were open as usual the next day, Michael hesitated to leave.

"Are you sure you are OK here at the house, Mia?"

"I'm fine. Why do you ask?"

"I'm just worried about you. Please don't go driving across the bridge again, at least without letting me know ahead of time."

Mia stopped clearing the breakfast dishes off the table and gave her husband a hug. "You are worried about me. Honey, I'm fine."

"And don't answer the phone if you don't recognize the number."

"That only happened once. I'll be fine."

After Michael and the kids left, Mia sat on the veranda with her Bible and prayer map. She began praying for the residents of Haj Yousef, but her thoughts kept wandering to her summer plans. If they were going to Texas for the summer, she had a lot to do.

She needed to clean the dusty suitcases before they could pack them, and she wanted to organize the children's toys and clothes too so she could get rid of things they'd outgrown. Also, she wanted to plan a surprise anniversary party for her parents, who had been married for 40 years.

Mia squeezed her eyes shut. "Lord, please be with Tzega's family and provide them a way to get to Canada, if that's your plan."

Dusty, broken toys danced in her head. Today would be a good day to sort through the kids' room. Maybe she could pray as she worked. Mia closed her map and headed back into the house.

By the time Tzega arrived, Mia had sorted the toys into several piles. The ones she knew the kids no longer wanted, she put into a large plastic bag so Tzega could take them home to her own children. She put a second pile of toys into a box to ask the kids about later. She returned the third pile to the toy box and bookshelves.

I should feel relieved to get a big job out of the way. Why do I just feel more stressed?

Mia brushed away a stray curl with the back of her hand and surveyed the bedroom.

Maybe the stress of the past few days is getting to me. Maybe I was exaggerating when I told Michael I was fine.

She glanced at her wristwatch. She had arranged to visit Hanaan for a cooking lesson at ten in the morning. Maybe a visit would distract her. She might as well go now. Hanaan wouldn't mind if she were a little early.

Mia pulled an *abaya* over her clothes and draped a *tarha* around her shoulders.

"Tzega, I am going to visit Hanaan. You can just lock the door when you are finished working."

"OK, ma'am."

Mia was right. As soon as she arrived at Hanaan's house and her friend treated her to splendid Arab hospitality, she forgot the stress of the past few days and submerged herself into the cooking lesson.

"I think you should come to my house sometime so I can teach you to cook American food," Mia said as she measured out two plastic cups of dried rice and poured them into a large saucepan.

Hanaan scrunched her nose. "Does America have its own food? You eat a lot of potatoes, right?" She shook her head. "Your food tastes too strange."

Mia wondered if Hanaan ever considered the fact that Mia might feel the same way about Sudanese food.

"*Mahalabeeya* is a good dish to cook for breakfast, and you can even have it for a snack. It is good when served warm or cold, either one." Hanaan used her teacher voice as she added twice as much water as rice to the saucepan, plunked two large cinnamon sticks and a few cardamom pods in the water, and placed the pan on her stove top.

"When do we add the raisins and peanuts?" Mia asked. Those had been her contribution to the lesson.

"That will come later, after the rice is cooked," Hanaan replied. "We don't want the peanuts to be mushy, only soft."

Hanaan poured the peanuts onto a platter and began sorting through the pile. "Here, you do the same with the raisins," she said to Mia. "These are local foods, so they are not cleaned very well. We'll need to pick out the pebbles and twigs." Hanaan raked her fingers through the legumes, inspecting them with a critical eye. "See?" She pulled out a tiny pebble and set it to the side. "After cleaning these, we'll rinse them in water and set them aside to add later."

Mia mimicked her actions with her own tray of raisins. They worked in silence for a few minutes before Hanaan spoke again.

"Mia, do you believe in three gods?"

"No. Why did you ask?"

"My husband says that Christians believe in what you call the Trinity, and it is really three gods."

"No, we don't believe in three gods. We believe in one God who has three ways of revealing Himself. Perhaps that is what your husband is talking about."

"What do you mean by three ways to reveal Himself?"

Mia had no idea how to answer. The Trinity was just something she had always believed.

Oh, Lord, please help me.

"Well, it's sort of like water. Water can be liquid, like what we drink, or solid, like ice, right?" Hanaan nodded so Mia continued. "But water can also turn to steam and be a vapor. But it's all water." Hanaan looked confused. "Well, it's hard to describe really. But we don't believe in three gods."

"Good, I'm glad to hear that. I don't really understand what you mean about the water, and I know my husband won't think it makes any sense. But I will believe you. You worship only one God. That is good."

Mia pondered the discussion for the rest of the day. That evening, after the kids were in bed, Mia wanted to talk to Michael about her conversation. But when she saw him shuffling through papers from his briefcase and spreading them out across the dining room table, she crawled in bed to read a book instead. An hour later she fell asleep.

Sometime in the middle of the night a noise woke her. She opened her eyes and saw Michael standing at the door looking at her.

"What is it?" She asked, propping herself up on her elbow.

He looked shaken and his expression intense. "We have to leave in an hour."

Mia sat up straighter. "Leave for where?"

"The States."

Was he kidding her? From the look on his face, he was not. Mia didn't have time to ask why. She jumped out of bed and stood in the middle of the room, trying to think clearly. The "go" bags already had all their important documents (minus their passports of course) and a change of clothes for each family member. She needed to pack their Bibles, toiletries, more clothes, her journal . . . where was the big suitcase?

Mia ran from the master bedroom across the house to the guest room. The suitcase was stored under the guest bed, still waiting to be washed. She fished the suitcase out from under the bed but as she stood, she was startled to see Michael lying in the guest bed.

"What are you doing?" she yelled. "We only have an hour to pack, and you are lying on the bed!"

The room around her brightened, and she heard Michael answer her. "What do you mean?"

Mia sat up. She was in their bedroom, and Michael was lying in bed beside her looking bewildered. She turned and looked at her bedside clock. 5:00 a.m.

Groaning, she laid her head back on the pillow. "Never mind. I was dreaming . . . again."

Michael patted her hand and then got out of bed. "I'll go start the coffee. I can't go back to sleep now; you scared me half to death."

"Well you did too . . . in my dream."

A few minutes later, Mia met Michael in the kitchen, and they sat at the table to drink their coffee.

"You told me we had to leave Sudan in one hour. It felt so real."

"Are you feeling stressed?"

Mia shrugged. "It's Sudan. I'm always a little stressed. But I guess it's more than usual. The weird phone call, having to give up our passports and Habiib pressing for a bribe, the attempted coup. . . . I'm ready for a break."

Michael reached across the table and placed his hand gently on Mia's cheek. "I know, sweetheart. Just a few more weeks. We'll be headed to the States before you know it."

"Unless Habiib can't get our exit permits in time. . . . Did you ask him about it?"

"I did. He said it was still in process."

"Do you think we should reconsider his offer?"

Michael raised his eyebrows. "For a bribe?"

"Well, what if it really is just an administrative fee? We could be sure to get our exit permits and leave on time. I really need this break."

Michael shook his head. "It just doesn't feel right. On the other hand, he did seem to think it would be a genuine miracle for us to get the paperwork done in time. I don't know, Mia. Let's think about it."

"Thank you." Mia smiled at her husband.

"I have an idea that might help you feel better in the meantime. I think we should go camping this coming weekend. You need to get away from the city; I think that would help you feel better."

"You don't have time to take the weekend off."

"I'll make it work." Michael's eyes twinkled. "Besides, the Meroë pyramids are not far from the camping sites. I think it would be fun to go see them. And, honestly, I could use a break too."

❧ Chapter 15 ❦
Nairobi, Kenya

Mr. Smith closed the office for the day, due to a visit he was making to Kame and some of the other refugee camps. Halimah welcomed the opportunity to sleep late, but she really didn't want a day with nothing to do but feel homesick and worry about the Sudanese couple she'd met the day before. She wanted to explore the area—maybe try catching a *matatu* on her own—but she couldn't risk meeting another Sudanese person.

After breakfast she sat on the front steps of the big white house, looking out over the garden. Birds of paradise, carnations, lilies, and orchids bloomed effortlessly, and every free spot of soil was covered in ferns, moss, and grasses. Even the places where the gardener neglected to weed bloomed with wildflowers just as beautifully as the cultivated flowers. Halimah nestled a cup of hot tea in her hands, felt its warmth, and watched the steam rise into the fresh morning air.

Halimah looked up and smiled at Jessica, who was walking up the driveway toward her. They had not talked much since the day Halimah arrived when Jessica had shown Halimah to her room. Jessica intimidated her, but she couldn't very well ignore someone who was walking right toward her.

"*Jambo*," Halimah said with a smile.

"*Jambo*, Sara. What are you doing today?"

"Nothing, really. Maybe go shopping somewhere."

Jessica eyed Halimah's outfit: a pair of mid-length shorts and a tank top. "I think you have enough new clothes. Why don't you come with me today? I'm going to the game park."

Halimah shook her head. "No, thanks. I'm scared of big animals."

Jessica threw her head back and laughed. Even though she was too skinny, she was pretty, especially when she smiled. "You won't be with the animals, Sara. We just drive by and look at them. Come on, it will be fun. It's my favorite place to go."

"OK, I'll go." Halimah felt somewhat reluctant, but surely it was better than sitting around all day. She changed into jeans and, at Jessica's request, put a button-up shirt over her tank top. Then she met Jessica at her car, an old Land Rover.

The ladies drove in silence for the first few kilometers as they skirted the business district and then headed a few more kilometers south. Halimah was surprised when she saw the entrance sign.

"Nairobi National Park," she read out loud. "Are we here already?"

"Yes, isn't it crazy? A game reserve practically in the middle of town." Jessica paid at the front gate and then drove the vehicle down the dirt road right out into the grassy plains. "Now look behind us," she said.

Halimah turned to look out the back of the vehicle and saw tall buildings in the distance. The business district. So close, yet here they were driving through the plains of Africa as if there were no hint of civilization for kilometers. Halimah turned back to the front. "Is this safe?"

Jessica smiled. "As long as we stay in the vehicle." She seemed to know which turns to take, and within five minutes they spotted a herd of wildebeest. A few more kilometers down the road they spotted an elephant in the distance. "If we are lucky, we'll see giraffes. But if not, we can see one later. I know some of the staff, and they have a mother and baby giraffe we can feed on our way out."

Halimah looked at Jessica. "How do you know the staff?"

Jessica smiled. "I've lived in Nairobi all my life." She took her eyes off the bumpy path just long enough to look at Halimah and laugh at her wide-eyed surprise. "What? Did you think I hadn't lived here long?"

Halimah shrugged. "You are a humanitarian aid worker. I assumed you were just here for a short time. Most of them are. And, honestly, I thought you were probably homesick."

Jessica smirked. "Nairobi *is* my home. Why did you think I was homesick?"

"Because you are so skinny. My mother says people who are skinny are not happy, so I thought maybe you were homesick."

"'Don't judge a book by its cover.' You know what that means?"

Halimah looked out the window and thought. "Hmmm, I guess don't make a decision based on appearance only?"

"Right," Jessica said. "I grew up in Nairobi, and even though my passport says I'm from the United States, I don't know much about living there. My parents were missionaries, so I used to work with them. When they retired and moved back to Mississippi, I stayed here. I've been working with Mr. Smith for five years."

"You never wanted to go home . . . be with your family?"

"Yeah, sure. Sometimes I do. I did go back to get my college degree. I had a great job offer there too. Coulda made a lot of money."

"What made you come back? I know you probably don't make a lot of money here."

"What made me come back?" Jessica tapped the steering wheel with her fingertips as she thought. "The opportunity to serve others, I guess, and not myself."

The words stuck with Halimah throughout the day. They continued to drive and talk about everything from their families to what they studied in college, but Halimah couldn't shake Jessica's comment. After driving the length of the park, the ladies returned to the front gate and parked. Jessica took Halimah into the front office and introduced her to the staff. Then they were ushered to a partitioned section outside. The structure housed several wild animals. Jessica led her up a flight of bamboo steps to a platform looking down over an enclosure that held a mother and baby giraffe.

"Come look," Jessica said, leaning over the bamboo railing. Halimah eyed her with suspicion. She was not about to lean down and get close to a wild animal. She shook her head. Jessica smiled. "It's a giraffe. It won't hurt you. Come on."

Halimah took two tentative steps toward the railing and then she saw the giraffe. The majestic animal moved with elegance as it sauntered across the enclosure. Its eyes, like giant cow eyes, were laced with enormous eyelashes and looked almost sad. Mesmerized, Halimah walked the rest of the way to Jessica, joining her at the railing.

"Amazing," she whispered. "I have never seen an animal bigger than a camel. She is so beautiful." Halimah looked down and saw the baby, too small to reach up to the platform but still tall. The baby was grazing from the leaves of a small acacia tree. The mother, however, looked to the ladies to see if they had any treats. Jessica smiled and grabbed a fresh branch from the table on the platform.

"These are for feeding the mother," she said. "Watch."

To Halimah's amazement, the mother giraffe began walking toward them. Halimah held her breath and stood frozen beside Jessica. She watched as the mother, in slow motion, lowered her long neck until her head reached down to their level. The giraffe opened its mouth and something like a large wet snake slithered toward her. Halimah gasped.

"Shhhh." Jessica put her free hand to her lips. "Don't scare her. It's just her tongue." The mother giraffe grabbed the branch with her tongue, drew it to her mouth, and then raised her head back up to her full height. Jessica smiled as she watched the creature chew on the branch and leaves. "They never cease to amaze me, these creatures. Do you know that giraffes eat about 29 kilos of vegetation every day?"

"God's creation is amazing."

"I guess that's part of what I love so much about Kenya. So much of God's creation to see. Sure, there are a lot of bad things, but there is so much good too."

"I love Sudan, my home, like you love Kenya. I wish I could go back."

"Perhaps you won't be able to go back, but you could have a touch of it."

"How?"

"What about your sister? Didn't you say you have a sister in Dubai? You could go see her. It's not Sudan, I know ... but ... better than nothing maybe?"

"I would love to see her again. We could encourage each other ..."

"Exactly. But"—Jessica gestured at Halimah's clothes—"you'll have to get different clothes. I don't think the folks in Dubai will look too highly on you wearing tight pants and tank tops."

Suddenly feeling self-conscious, Halimah buttoned up her outer shirt. "Oh, am I dressing immodestly?"

"Immodestly, no. Lots of ladies wear what you are wearing. But I know you come from a conservative culture. I'm just surprised you changed so quickly."

"Are you 'judging a book by its cover'?"

Jessica laughed. "Ah. Good one, Sara. You got me. Except in this case I would say I'm not. I know your heart is to help people, especially Sudanese, and most especially your family. I just think you are getting distracted by the freedom that Kenya offers you."

"I do enjoy being free to think and do as I please. I've never had that before."

"You can use your freedom to clothe yourself in the character of Christ, not fancy clothes. Does that make sense?" Jessica shrugged. "I guess what I mean is, don't let your freedom become a stumbling block . . . to you or to anyone else." She turned back toward the giraffe. "Anyway, shall we feed the giraffe one more time before I take you home? Come on, your turn." She took a second branch off the table and handed it to Halimah.

Halimah took the branch and held it out for the giraffe. She summoned all her courage to stand still while the enormous animal walked toward her, lowered its head, and scooped the branch out of her hand with its long tongue.

"Ewwww. I have giraffe spit on my hand," Halimah said, laughing.

An hour later, Jessica dropped Halimah off at the front gate to the large house. "Sorry I made you miss lunch," she said.

"Oh, it's no problem. Tea will be served in an hour and besides, I can miss a meal. I'm not skinny like you."

"You mean homesick, right?"

Halimah grinned. "Right." She waved goodbye to her new friend and walked to the house.

Evening vespers were canceled since the office was closed, but Halimah decided to sit alone in the lawn anyway and read her Bible. It felt wonderful to read the Word of God so freely, with no fear of repercussions. She opened to Galatians. "It is for freedom that Christ has set us free" (5:1).

She was free to read the Bible in public. She was free to wear what she wanted. So why had Jessica made the comment about her clothes? She kept reading the chapter until she got to verse 13. "You, my brothers and sisters, were called to be free. But do not use your freedom to indulge the flesh; rather, serve one another humbly in love."

Maybe that's what Jessica meant when she said she could have stayed in her home country and earned a lot of money. She was free to do so, but rather than practice freedom for her own sake, she returned to Kenya to serve others.

"Lord, I came to Kenya for my own sake. I know I did. I was tired of seeing thousands of people losing hope. I was tired of the refugee camp and scared because it was closing. What should I do now? I can't go home. I can't stay here. Am I going to become a refugee too?" Halimah prayed out loud with eyes shut tight. She desperately wanted to hear from the Lord. She'd been so distracted lately by work, her new life in a big city, and—she was ashamed to admit—new clothes.

The word that came to Halimah was *mercy*. In a way she never experienced as a Muslim, she felt the love of God envelop her like the embrace of a parent. She was single and fatherless in a strange land, yet she was home.

A second word came to Halimah's mind. *Family*. God was pursuing her family. Halimah knew this because Rania believed too. Maybe God wanted to use them to continue to share the fantastic news of complete forgiveness through *Isa*. She didn't know how He could do it, but she believed He had the power to do it.

Halimah was overcome with the need to talk to Rania. Her younger sister was Halimah's only link to her family. But it was Wednesday, and Rania said it was not safe to call her any other time besides their normal Friday calls. Rania had, however, called from the Arab Art School before, so perhaps there really were other times they could talk. Maybe just a short text. Halimah fished her phone out of her pocket and tapped in a short message. *This is Sara. Can you talk?*

She lay down in the lawn, feeling the lush grass against the back of her neck. Now if she could just talk to her sister, it would be perfect.

Halimah waited on the grass until the sun began to lower in the sky, but there was no reply from Rania. She tried to push away her disappointment, but she really needed someone to talk to . . . someone who really knew her. Mia would listen. But Halimah felt guilty for not taking Mia's advice the last time they talked on the phone. Mia told her to listen to the voice in her heart, the Holy Spirit. She hadn't done so, and now she was in a mess. Halimah considered sending Rania a second message but thought better of it. The first had been risky enough.

After a few more minutes on the lawn, Halimah walked back into the big house. Dinner was at eight, so Halimah had time to take a shower. After her trip to the National Park, she felt the need to bathe, paying special attention to her hand that had been the recipient of giraffe saliva.

She surveyed her wardrobe. Somehow her new, tight fitting clothes didn't seem appropriate anymore. She'd purchased them on a whim really, and she realized the freedom she enjoyed most was a free heart, not the freedom to wear stylish clothing.

And though she knew no one should "judge a book by its cover," she did not want to be a stumbling block to anyone either. She pulled a long tunic from the bottom of the drawer and smoothed out the wrinkles. It was more modest than what she'd been wearing lately but would look nice with a pair of trousers.

She joined the others downstairs for dinner. The cook had prepared grilled chicken and vegetable kebabs. Halimah enjoyed the delicious food, even though it was so different from the stews and breads she was used to in Sudan. After everyone got a plate, the cook—a large Kenyan man with a commanding voice—led a prayer of thanksgiving. Halimah bowed her head and said her own prayer.

Learning how to please You is hard for me. I still have so much to learn.

Halimah didn't feel like talking much during dinner. All she could think of were those two words: *family* and *mercy*. The others at the table carried on a lively conversation, but Halimah finished her food quickly and excused herself.

In her room, she retrieved her Bible from the nightstand and reread the verses from Galatians. She sat on the edge of her bed and squeezed her eyes shut, trying to ignore the fact that she felt cold and lonely.

Lord, many times in the past two years I have felt You speaking to me. I really need to hear You tonight. I need to know what I am supposed to do now.

⇒ Chapter 16 ⇐
Dubai, UAE

Rania had taken to painting in the living room. Auntie Badria was not keen on the arrangement, but Uncle Faisal insisted because, he said, he loved to watch his niece work. Rania thought Uncle Faisal was acting a little creepy when he just sat there and watched her, as if he were watching television. He would smoke his water pipe, always burning apple-flavored tobacco. She could hear the bubbles when he inhaled, and the sweet smoke that filled the room when he exhaled made her dizzy.

Auntie Badria refused to open the windows because she wanted to run the air-conditioner all the time. So the living room filled with smoke, and Rania continued to try to concentrate on her artwork while Uncle Faisal smiled and nodded and Auntie Badria fussed about the kitchen making coffee.

"What project are you working on now, Rania?" the old man asked, adjusting himself in his chair, as if getting comfortable for a movie.

"Today I am beginning an abstract piece. It will be of a Sudanese bride dancing."

"You mean a *subhia*?" he asked.

"Yes, I want to bring in Sudanese culture. None of my classmates will have anything like it. They come from Gulf Arab countries mostly." She tapped the end of a paintbrush against her chin thoughtfully. "I think I'll have a pretty unique idea."

"I don't think you should paint a *subhia*, Rania. That is an event for women only, and your teacher is a man."

"Now don't you tell Rania what to do. She should have the freedom to be the artist she wants to be. Isn't that why she is here?" Auntie Badria was always within earshot—not wanting to miss any drama going on in the house.

Uncle Faisal took a long draw out of the water pipe and Rania prepared herself for a fog of apple smoke. Then he shrugged. "*Ala keifik*, as you like." He shrugged as if to say, "It's on you if you fail the assignment."

Rania turned back to her easel and adjusted the canvas. How did he think she was going to be able to paint while she was also performing for him as if on stage? Suddenly her phone on the coffee table beeped.

"What's that?" Uncle Faisal asked.

"Just my phone, Uncle. Don't worry. I'll check it later."

"I'll check it for you," he said, and reached for the phone.

Rania clenched her jaw and forced herself to open a tube of paint. She would not jump for the phone, even though he was invading her privacy. She stood with her back to him, staring at the canvas. The message was probably from one of her classmates—maybe Souad—asking about the assignment. Rania was known as one of the better art students, so she sometimes offered tips or suggestions to the other students.

"It's from someone named Sara," Uncle Faisal said.

Rania gasped and dropped her paintbrush. It bounced twice and rolled under a salon chair. Uncle Faisal didn't notice her reaction. He was staring at the phone. "It has a strange number, definitely not from Dubai. But I don't recognize it. Where is this Sara from?"

Rania turned to face her uncle. "The art students come from many different countries." Rania choked on the words. Uncle Faisal looked at Rania's expression and furrowed his brow.

"Well, where is *this* art student from?"

Rania was a terrible liar. She couldn't weave together stories like her friend Maysoon in Khartoum who had managed to become a hip-hop singer without her family ever knowing. "Sara is not an art student, Uncle."

"I knew it," Uncle Faisal stood up, holding the mouthpiece of the water pipe in one hand and shaking Rania's phone at her with the other. "Sara is a code name for a boy, isn't it? Who is this boy?"

"*Astaghfir Allah.*" Auntie Badria came running into the salon from the kitchen, hands over her head as if the sky were falling. "Rania is secretly seeing a boy. What will we do? This is terrible. This must be the bad fortune Sit Abubakr saw in the coffee reading. Rania, what have you done? You are already engaged."

"What? No, I'm not seeing a boy. Sara is not a boy."

Uncle Faisal angrily punched buttons on her phone and began to read all the messages on her phone while Auntie Badria sobbed.

"What did we do wrong, Faisal? Why is this happening to us?"

Rania sighed. This had to stop.

"Sara is Halimah, my sister."

The announcement floated in the air between the three of them. Uncle Faisal stopped pushing buttons and stared at Rania. Auntie Badria stopped crying and her hands dropped from her head and hung limp at her sides. Both of them looked at Rania as if she were a ghost. Rania said a silent prayer for wisdom.

"You know: Halimah, who left two years ago."

Auntie Badria was the first to find her voice. "Yes, Rania. We know who Halimah is. But how did you find her? And where is she?"

"She is . . . not in Sudan."

To Rania's surprise, Uncle Faisal and Auntie Badria, after their initial shock, did not appear to be angry like she thought they would be. This was, after all, much better news than they originally thought.

There was no conversation at dinner that night. Both adults ate quietly and seemed contemplative. Several times Rania caught them looking at each other, communicating something she didn't understand.

Even more surprising than their reaction was the fact that Uncle Faisal gave the phone back to her. He didn't forbid her from calling Halimah or anything of the sort. She wondered if perhaps the news of Halimah becoming an infidel, a traitor to Islam, had never reached them over here in Dubai.

It was midnight by the time they turned off the television and headed to bed. In a city that almost never sleeps, midnight was early for

Uncle Faisal. The shocking afternoon must have worn him out. Rania cleaned up her paint supplies and carried them back to her bedroom. As she propped her canvas up on her desk, Auntie Badria came and stood in the doorway.

"We are glad to hear that Halimah is OK," she said. Her face was calm and her eyes soft. She was not lying.

"Thank you," Rania said.

"We are worried about her. She cannot just live alone. We think she should come live here with us, at least until your father will take her back."

"Father will not take her back, Auntie. He has disowned her."

"Maybe one day, when his anger has subsided."

Rania shook her head. Did Auntie not even know her own culture? Her own religion? Forgiveness or "anger subsiding" was not even a part of who they were as people.

"Auntie, that won't happen."

"Well, we think she should come here. She will be safe here. At least until we can find a more permanent solution. Uncle says you can call her and tell her." She handed Rania two crisp bills. "Uncle says to buy some extra minutes for your phone so you can call long distance . . . you know, to wherever she is."

"Auntie, if she comes, what will you tell Father and Mama?"

The woman shrugged. "If they don't ask, we have nothing to say, right?"

Rania smiled. "Goodnight, Auntie. Sleep well."

Rania waited until her aunt closed the door and her footsteps faded down the hallway. She would buy extra minutes for her phone in the morning on her way to class. A text would have to do for now. And anyway, Halimah was surely already asleep.

Sorry delayed reply. All is good. Normal call on Friday. Can't wait. Exciting news.

Rania hit *send*. She didn't want to get her hopes up. Right now, more than anything in the world, she wanted Halimah to come be with her in

Dubai. But it was hard for her to believe Uncle Faisal and Auntie Badria were telling the truth that they would protect Halimah. And how could they find a solution for Halimah in a month's time, before her parents came? And would her aunt and uncle keep Halimah's presence in their lives a secret?

Rania pulled her Bible out from its hiding place under her mattress. She held it with reverence. This book was the only tangible thing that represented her new life in Christ. It was the Word of God. And surely He had a word for her.

Time seemed to stand still whenever Rania read the Bible. At two in the morning she stopped to look at the clock on her desk and decided she'd better get some sleep. She had class early in the morning.

She grabbed her phone and sent one more text. A verse that stuck in her mind from her readings. She left the reference off, hoping if Uncle Faisal read her texts again, he wouldn't realize she was quoting from the Bible.

Perhaps this will encourage you, Sara. Rania hid her Bible again and flipped off her bedroom light.

⇒ Chapter 17 ⇐
Nubian Desert, Sudan

A s the car left the city of Khartoum and the square buildings disappeared from the shoulders of the road, Mia's body began to relax. The sand began to claim the shoulders and parts of the edges of the tarmac and the square mud-brick houses moved farther away from the road, collecting into little villages dotting the desert on either side. The farther from town the Weston family traveled, the less frequent the villages appeared.

Mia couldn't fully relax yet, however. They still had to pass one or two police checkpoints to get to their destination. They were prepared with copies of each passport and a letter of permission to travel that they had obtained from the Khartoum police office.

Police checkpoints were identified by an object blocking the road. It could be a wooden box or a metal gate of some sort. In this case it was a broken plastic chair. A shipping container on the side of the road, converted into a makeshift police station, confirmed this spot was the checkpoint. Men in military uniform saw the vehicle approaching and stepped toward the blockade, guns slung over their shoulders.

Unable to tame their curiosity at a car full of foreigners so far outside of town, several men gathered around the driver's window. Michael handed them the paperwork. They thumbed through the papers, as if trying to find something wrong with them—something to enable them to keep the car from passing through. Mia held her breath. They had never actually been turned away, though others had. Mia hoped it wouldn't be them this time.

Mia whispered a prayer and immediately wondered if it was OK to ask God for help on something like a police checkpoint. She wondered if God would listen to her plea for help. She hadn't exactly been spending time in prayer or reading her Bible the past few days. She silently promised God she would spend some time with Him out in the desert if He would just get them through the checkpoint.

The guard in charge nodded his head and pulled the plastic chair out from the middle of the road, waving the car through. Mia breathed a sigh of relief.

As Mia's shoulders relaxed, she peered out the window. Nothing between them and the pyramids except desert. As far as her eyes could see there was brown sand. Short acacia trees dotted the landscape, along with herds of goats nibbling on the tiny leaves from the barbed branches. Then the ground became a giant field of desert melons: baseball-sized gourds scattered about the sand, almost indistinguishable from the sand around them.

Villages appeared like mirages. The square dwellings were camou-flaged against the vast sandy surroundings. The only reason a passerby would even notice the cloisters of houses was because in each village there was one brightly colored building, the only one with real paint on it. If one were to drive by at nighttime, which was not advisable in the desert, the village mosque would be the only one using electric light. It was square, like every other structure, but the minaret stood tall like a flagpole staking its claim. *This village belongs to Allah.*

Mia scoured a village as they sped by. She pointed out the window.

"Look, Michael. Right there on the edge, with its gate facing out to the sea of sand. That's the one I'd live in."

Michael grinned. "You do this at every village."

Mia twisted a blond curl around her finger. "I just like to imagine. . . . It is so peaceful out here. No traffic, no men leering at me, no secret police or government officials questioning people at your office, and my cell phone doesn't even work out here, so no creepy phone calls. Look, I can even wear a T-shirt with short sleeves and a pair of jeans. I am free. I know all the stress is waiting for me back in Khartoum and will be there when we return tomorrow. But somehow, leaving it, even if only for 24 hours, makes me feel free."

After three hours of driving, Michael pointed out the window to his right.

"Look, kids, the pyramids."

"Are we in Egypt?" Annie asked.

"No, honey. These are Sudanese pyramids."

"It felt like we drove all the way to Egypt," Annie said. She wasn't as excited as Dylan, who was bouncing in his seat.

"Pyramids, cool!"

"These are called the Meroë pyramids, kids." Michael pulled off the road and drove through the sand in the direction of the structures that looked like skinny cousins to the ones in Egypt. "This is an ancient Nubian necropolis."

Corey looked confused. "A what?"

"A cemetery," Michael said. "This one belonged to the royalty of the kingdom of Kush."

"Are they old?" Dylan asked, pressing his face to the window to get a better look.

"Yes, very old," Michael said.

Michael stopped the vehicle just in front of a simple metal fence that surrounded the pyramids. The family got out of the vehicle and stretched. From where she stood, Mia could see pyramids emerging out of the sandy hills in the distance.

Just in front of the metal fence, some of the villagers from the area assembled a makeshift market by spreading out their souvenirs on woven mats in the sand. Their wares ranged from homemade traditional musical instruments to handmade wooden bowls to painted gourds. Mia bent down to examine a tiny model of a pyramid. She smiled at the little boy who squatted beside the mat. Like the others, he looked skinny, and his clothes were simple and worn.

Suddenly, all her problems, as big as they were, seemed trivial. This little boy may not even know where his next meal was coming from. He may not even go to school. And here she was, worrying about not getting to go home for the summer. She smiled at the boy and promised to return when they were finished at the pyramids.

Michael paid the entrance fee at the guardhouse and the family made their way toward the pyramids. The three kids ran ahead while Mia and Michael walked. Mia wanted to reach out and hold Michael's hand, but the villagers at the makeshift market were watching, and displays of affection were taboo. So they just walked beside each other.

Mia studied the pyramids rising up to the sky like stone trees, narrow and tall.

"Why are some of them missing their tops?" Mia asked.

"They have been blown off by grave robbers seeking gold."

"No kidding? That's crazy. Did they find any?"

Michael shrugged. "I don't know. An Italian explorer named Giuseppe Ferlini did the most damage. He decapitated about 40 of them in the 1800s."

"Too bad. How do you know all of this, Mr. Tour Guide?"

"I read about it in a book on Sudan that I found at the office. Interesting stuff actually. Look." Michael pointed to one of the pyramids closest to them. "Sudan's Department of Antiquities has worked to have some of the pyramids restored, like this one. But you can see they don't look the same. The new bricks at the top are not rugged and sand blasted like their ancient counterparts."

"Are we allowed to just walk right up to them and touch them?" Mia was watching their kids who had now reached the first pyramid.

"Yes. Apparently the guard doesn't mind, so long as we don't do any damage."

They walked along in silence for a few minutes as they made their way across the sand. Then Michael spoke.

"I thought about what you said. Maybe it would be all right to offer some extra money for Habiib to get our exit permits. I mean, if we don't, the alternative is we don't get to go for the summer and . . . well, I just think our family could use a vacation."

"Really? You are willing to pay the bribe?"

"Wait a minute. I thought you said that's what you wanted. Why are you suddenly accusing me?"

"Sorry. I just thought you sounded so adamant about not paying extra when you talked to Habiib."

"I was. But now I'm rethinking it. I mean, Habiib is my friend, but I'm not sure we can trust him to come through with the exit permits unless we agree to what he suggested."

"No one would fault us, right? I mean, people pay extra fees all the time."

"No. No one would fault us."

Somehow Michael's tone didn't comfort her, and he didn't sound like he believed his own words.

When they arrived at the first pyramid, Annie and Dylan were already finished looking at it and were running to the second one, about 30 yards away. Corey had entered into a chamber on the first one, and Mia could hear the hollow sound of his voice bouncing on the walls inside.

"Wow, Mom, come look."

"Hang on, Corey, I'm coming." Mia ran her hand across the side of the pyramid. "I can't believe I'm touching something so old."

"Mom, what does this say?" Corey's voice echoed.

Mia peered inside the doorway and found Corey tracing his fingers across hieroglyphics chiseled into the wall.

"I don't know. What do you think?"

"It says that a great king was buried here."

"Yes, it very well could say that. Come on, let's catch up with your brother and sister and check out the other pyramids."

An hour passed quickly, and by then all five Westons were tired and ready to head to the camping location. After they exited the wire fence, Mia stopped to look at the little boy's merchandise again.

Her interest made every other seller call to her and even pull on her arm to coax her to their spot. Pleasing everyone was impossible so Mia decided to just buy from the one boy.

Corey chose a small pyramid model, Annie chose a beaded bracelet, and Dylan chose a wooden bowl.

"Are you sure you want a wooden bowl, Dylan?"

"Yes, I like it."

Mia bargained with the little boy for a good price, and as she did so, she felt tension returning to her shoulders. She paid more than the items were worth, but she told herself that at least she helped this boy out, and perhaps his family would be able to use the money toward buying more food.

Mia had started a ruckus among the other sellers by buying from only one boy. Michael herded the family back to the car, and they quickly jumped in and drove away with the villagers still calling to them to come buy something.

After 30 minutes, Michael pulled the car off the road again, this time driving through the sand toward an enormous hill made of giant boulders piled on each other. The top of the rocky formation was hundreds of feet high, and when they drove around behind it and parked, the road was completely blocked from view. It appeared as if they were the only ones in the whole desert.

A single tall acacia tree grew out of the ground behind the mass of boulders. Michael parked in its dappled shade. At four in the afternoon, the sun beat down as if it were midday.

"This is where we'll be camping." Michael hopped out of the car and Mia and the kids followed.

Corey shaded his eyes from the sun as he gazed to the top of the rocks. "Wow, Dad. That looks fun. Will you climb with me?"

Michael tousled his son's hair. "Sure, son, let's go."

"Bet I can beat you!" Corey called over his shoulder as he ran toward the base of the rocks.

Mia laughed at the two as they stumbled over the rocks and the soft sand.

"Mom, come climb with me and Dylan," Annie called as she made her way to the small rocks closer to the bottom.

"You guys go ahead," she replied. "I want to sit and relax for a little."

Mia took her journal and Bible and walked several yards away where there was a lone boulder jutting out of the ground. She crawled on top and sat down facing the endless desert. After a few moments, she began to write.

I will always love the desert. Yes, it is the desert that sends sand and dust into every crevice of my home. But here, relaxing in the desert, I am overcome by its beauty. The desert is peace. Yes, it is heat and danger and barrenness. But the desert is beauty at its core. How can both extremes be present in one expanse of land? That's the mystery of the desert.

Mia gazed out at the expanse and sadness gripped her heart.

She whispered, "Lord, I'm sorry I have not spent time with You like I should. You have given me plenty of time each morning, and I've used it for other things. Sitting here, enjoying the beauty of Your creation, I'm somehow finally hearing Your voice again. I've missed it."

⇒ Chapter 18 ⇐
Nubian Desert, Sudan

"M om, Mom!" Corey's voice sounded so tiny, swallowed by the vastness of the open space.

Mia stopped praying and turned around. Behind her, Corey was halfway up the giant rocks. He stood tall, waving so she could see him.

Mia waved back. She wanted to yell, "Why don't you come down now, where it's safe?" But she caught herself and instead smiled and called as loudly as she could, "Wow, great job." She gave a thumbs-up and then walked back toward the campsite.

Michael had already cleared a spot for their campfire and was spreading out a mat.

"I thought you were hiking with Corey. It's kind of dangerous for him to go alone, don't you think?"

Michael kept working. "He's fine, Mia. He's just being a boy."

Annie and Dylan played on the lower rocks near the campsite. Mia was glad they weren't trying to do anything too dangerous. Worrying about one child was enough.

Mia busied herself unpacking the dinner supplies from the car. Hot dogs, potato chips, and homemade cookies.

"This was a great idea, Michael. I'm glad you suggested we come out here this weekend. Maybe we will get to camp this summer in Texas."

"I don't know, Mia." Michael stuffed crumpled newspaper underneath the arrangement of wooden logs. "I am going to be enjoying the air-conditioning so much this summer, I don't know that I'm going to want to be sleeping on the ground with the mosquitos in the Texas heat."

Mia shaded her eyes from the sun with one hand and wiped sweat off her brow with the other. "Hmmm, air-conditioning sounds really good right about now."

Michael lit the newspaper and monitored the impromptu kindling until small bits of the logs began to catch flame, building momentum with each passing minute.

"Fire!" Dylan called as he ran up to join Michael. "Great job, Dad. Mom, can I have a hot dog?"

"Well, I guess it's about time to start dinner, huh? All right, let me get the hot dogs out of the ice chest. Annie, can you hear me? Why don't you call for Corey and get him to come down? It's almost time to cook dinner."

After dinner the kids helped Michael and Mia lay the sleeping bags on mats around the fire. They spent the evening singing songs until Dylan and Annie began to yawn.

"Time for bed, everyone," Michael said. "Let's have a prayer to finish off this day. Corey, will you pray?"

"Thank You, God, for a great day. Thank You for the pyramids and the desert, for dinner, and for fun on the rocks. Help us sleep well tonight. I know we will because we can trust You, and You will keep us safe. Amen."

Mia's favorite part of camping out was lying in her sleeping bag late at night after everyone else was asleep. She didn't have to worry about Dylan running off into the desert, about Corey falling off a giant boulder, or about Annie getting sand in her eyes for the umpteenth time. She lay on her back and stared at the stars. Diamonds on black velvet. Her hand reached off the woven mat and fingered the sand. Countless grains of sand. Countless stars in the sky. Yet God knew them all. Billions of people on the earth, yet God knew each one. She believed this when she relaxed here in the quiet desert. It was easy to believe when troubles were far away. Mia drifted into a peaceful sleep.

The first bit of morning light touched the horizon in the distance behind the acacia tree. Moments later the sky began to brighten. Mia didn't want to pull her head from the covers, but she didn't want to miss the sunrise either. She poked her head out of the sleeping bag like a shy turtle.

Light gradually filled in the dark places in the distance and the vast expanse of sand turned from black to gray to yellowish-brown. Before long, a tiny sliver of bright orange peeked over the horizon. Rays of yellow hit the clouds, as if the sun were reaching out to pull itself up into the sky.

Mia stretched, her muscles tight and a bit sore from a night lying on the hard sand. She pulled her sleeping bag open and let the cool morning air brush against her arms and face. She glanced at her watch. It was six in the morning.

Grabbing her Bible and notebook from the mat, Mia made her way to the rock where she'd sat the afternoon before. In the morning light she wrote in her journal again.

I woke up this morning with the words of Corey's prayer in my mind. "We can trust You, and You will keep us safe." I realize now I've had it all wrong. I've forgotten that it is not about trusting Habiib for the exit permits. It is about trusting You.

Mia stared at the horizon. She couldn't help but wonder. . . . What was happening back in Khartoum while they were away? Anything could have happened. Rebels from the south, or from the west or east for that matter, could have attacked the city. The president could have announced all Americans must leave the country immediately. Kellar Hope Foundation could be closed down.

Whatever happens, Lord, I will trust You. That goes for the exit permits, the strange phone call, and even Hanaan. I've been wanting so badly for her to understand the meaning of forgiveness in Christ, and I've forgotten that You want it even more than I do. I trust You with all of this, Lord.

Any of the things Mia mentioned in her prayer could go terribly wrong. It was completely within the realm of possibility. This was Sudan, after all. Crazy things happened. But somehow, out in the vast landscape where it looked as if they were camping on Mars, it didn't matter. They were in another dimension. A peaceful one.

At ten in the morning, before the sun became unbearable, the Westons loaded the car to head back to Khartoum. A donkey sauntered up to the campsite and began scouring the ground for a shrub to nibble on. Two young boys followed soon after. They stood under the acacia tree and watched everything the Westons did. Michael gathered the leftovers from breakfast and handed the boys a bag of goodies along with two bottles of water.

"*Shukran*," one of the boys said. Then they eagerly looked through the bag together. But they didn't leave. Watching an American family pack their car was probably the most entertainment they'd had all week.

By now the sun was inching into the sky, and the temperature had gone from chilly to sweltering. Mia could already feel the burn on her arms. They waved to the two little boys and Michael steered the car toward the other side of the rocks, to the road that would take them home. The children, exhausted from the trip, fell asleep within the first 30 minutes.

After driving in silence for a while, Michael spoke. "So, I've been thinking about our conversation regarding the extra money, you know . . . the bribe. Last night I prayed about it, and I don't think we should do it." He reached over and took Mia's hand. "Are you mad?"

Mia squeezed his hand. "I don't think we should do it either."

"You know this means Habiib may not come through for us, and we may not get to go to the States?"

Mia nodded. "I know. But this morning I realized we've been focusing on Habiib and whether we trust him or not. We should be focusing on trusting God instead."

"What if we don't get the exit permits?"

"Let's just keep praying for a miracle."

Michael nodded. "I'll call Habiib when we get home."

*Y*ou, my brothers and sisters, were called to be free. But do not use
your freedom to indulge the flesh; rather, serve one another humbly
in love.

Halimah stared at the text on her phone. She hadn't told Rania about
the passage she was studying. Was it just coincidence that her sister chose
to send her the same verse?

She read the verse again. Strange how the words, first penned long ago,
pointed so precisely to her own life. Somehow she had gotten sidetracked
by the appeal of freedom. No, she decided, it wasn't coincidence. In spite
of her "indulging in the flesh," God showed mercy to her by using Jessica
and Rania to reach out and touch her heart.

Halimah slipped out of bed and knelt on the floor. The wooden slats
were cold and felt damp against her legs. The bed creaked as she propped
her elbows on it and bowed her head.

"Lord, I have been using my freedom in *Isa* for selfish things. Please
forgive me. I want to serve others in love. Please show me how. Whatever
it is, I am willing to do it."

Her prayer was short and simple, but Halimah felt a burden lifted
from her heart. She felt forgiveness like she'd never felt when she was
a Muslim. A smile spread across Halimah's face, and as she dressed for
work, she sang a song she used to sing back in Khartoum, before her faith
in *Isa* had been discovered:

Heaven for eternity!
Jesus paid the debt for me!
Daily walking in His love,
Together we shall overcome.
There is no punishment or hell,
For me, and I will live to tell,
His blood will cleanse all who believe.

As soon as she finished eating breakfast, Halimah typed an email to Mia. She included a letter for Mia's friend. Halimah had never met this "sister" from Mia's email, but she knew they had one thing in common: *Isa*.

Dear Sister in *Isa*,

Wonderful to hear about your faith. I know it's not easy to accept the truth when everybody around you is blind. I say that because I have a story similar to yours.

I am from a Muslim background. After I accepted *Isa* as my Savior, my life totally changed. I was persecuted and nearly beaten to death, but the God we trust is faithful, and He will remain faithful forever. He didn't promise us an easy life. He said, "They will persecute you for My name."

My own father told me I am not his daughter—I am the devil's daughter. My mother said I brought shame to the family, and everybody around me told me how horrible I was for becoming Christian. But in my heart I knew they were wrong. They don't know God. That is why they say all these things about Him and me.

He gave us a relationship with Him and eternal life after. I love the freedom I have in Him, and I still remember the peace that came to my heart after I accepted *Isa*. He promised us that no one will take this peace from us. They can hurt our flesh, but our soul and spirit are saved. What a wonderful promise. When I told others about that, they were angry, but they didn't hurt my soul.

I still have peace in my heart, and I am praying for you as I write this letter. Remember our God is stronger than any human, and He loves you more than anybody else, even your own family. They do all this to you because they don't know Him, and I pray they will come to know Him one day soon. He let all this happen to you because He loves you, and He has a good plan for you. Your life is with Him, and that is what is important.

Pray and rejoice and ask Him to strengthen your faith more and more and to use you as a witness to them. Forgive them too because they don't know. I knew after I accepted the Lord that I would face persecution, but I wasn't sure when and what it was going to feel like. When it happened it helped me understand all the beatings and the suffering that *Isa* went through to set us free from sin. It was painful, but it made me praise Him and trust Him more, and I know you do too.

Keep your eyes on *Isa*. He loves you and will take good care of you.

—Your sister in *Isa*

As she wrote words of encouragement, Halimah found her own heart being refreshed. It was as if the practice of writing out words to encourage someone else ended up encouraging her as well.

She could hardly wait for Jessica to arrive for work. Halimah wanted to tell her about the verse and how she was beginning to understand what Jessica meant when she talked about putting others first. Sitting on the front steps, she watched impatiently as various staff members arrived. Each one greeted her and she returned the greetings, but only halfheartedly. Her focus was on the arrival of Jessica's vehicle.

She looked down the driveway at the guardhouse and thought about Simon. She had flirted with him and felt ashamed. She should not have done that, even though his attention made her feel good. She didn't want to do it, but she had to make changes in her life to match the things she read in God's Word.

Taking a deep breath, Halimah walked the length of the driveway. She hoped Simon was not on duty. Perhaps her willingness to apologize was enough. But as she neared the guardhouse, she saw Simon step out into the driveway.

"*Jambo*, Sara," he said with a big grin.

"*Jambo*, Simon." Halimah stopped walking and stood awkwardly for a few seconds before she began talking again. "I want to say I am sorry to you for being too friendly. I come from a strict family and flirting is not allowed. Even though I am no longer Muslim, I still do not want to use my freedom selfishly. You are my brother in Christ, and I should be respectful."

Halimah looked down at her feet as she talked. She knew her words were awkward, and she did not want to look at Simon's reaction. But he didn't say anything, so she looked up at his face. Wrinkles spread across his forehead, and his eyes looked as if he were humored by her apology.

"Ummm, it's OK. I flirt with everyone." His face broke out into a big smile again.

Halimah couldn't help laughing. "OK, that's up to you. But I am not going to do it anymore."

She turned to walk back to the big white building. Simon called after her. "Hey, my sister in Christ, don't forget to go to vespers tonight."

Simon reminded her of her little brother Ali. She suddenly wanted to protect him, not flirt with him.

"All right, I will go. And you don't forget that not all girls you flirt with are good girls. You be careful."

Simon gave his big smile again. "I will."

Halimah walked slowly back up the drive, musing about what just happened. Jessica was right, the Bible verse she'd read had much more to do with Halimah than she originally thought. Somehow, in obeying the verse, she felt even freer than before. She wondered what other changes God wanted her to make.

When Jessica's white jeep finally pulled up the driveway and parked, Halimah stood up to greet her friend.

"*Jambo*," Halimah said as Jessica stepped out of the car. "I read a verse from the Bible this morning that I just have to share with you. It is about serving others rather than looking out for ourselves, just like you talked about yesterday. I think I understand now what you were saying. It's, wait a minute, let me look . . ." Halimah thumbed through the pages of her Bible as she stood by Jessica's car. She smiled and put her finger on the verse. "Yes, here it is. Galatians 5:13."

"I can't really talk right now, Sara." Jessica's voice sounded flat. Surprised by the tone, Halimah looked up from her Bible and realized that her friend's cheeks were wet and her eyes red.

"What's wrong?"

"Nothing." Jessica retrieved her purse from the car and shut the door. She began walking toward the building and Halimah called after her.

"Was it something I said? I was just so excited about what I found."

Jessica stopped and waited for Halimah to catch up. "It's not you, Sara. Mr. Smith returned from visiting the refugee camps. It seems as though the rumors are true. The smaller camps like Kame will be closing soon."

"What does that mean for us? Do we have jobs?"

"I'm not worried about that," Jessica reached in her bag for a tissue and wiped her eyes. "I feel terrible for the refugees. Where will they go now?"

Halimah was ashamed. Of course. The refugees. Here she was worrying about her own job when thousands of people were simply hoping to stay alive another day.

"You're right. That's terrible."

"Look," Jessica said. "Don't say anything to anyone yet. Mr. Smith will need to make a plan and then let everyone know. I just happen to know because we are good friends. We've worked together a long time."

Jessica wiped her eyes one more time, then adjusted the bag on her shoulder and walked up the steps to the house. Halimah stood on the bottom step and watched her new friend.

Mr. Smith didn't talk about the impending change to the staff in the office that day, as far as Halimah knew. Jessica herself kept busy, and when they saw each other at lunch Jessica was back to her old self. Halimah guessed she was trying to stay positive for the sake of all the office staff. But she couldn't help wondering what would become of her own job. And what would she do if she didn't have it any more?

⇒ Chapter 20 ⇐
Dubai, UAE

"Did you call Halimah?" Uncle Faisal stood in the entryway to the apartment, wrapping his white turban on top of his head. With the turban and the white robe-like *jallabeeya* on, he looked like a typical Sudanese man. If he had worn a red and white-checkered *keffiyeh* on his head instead, he might look like an Emirati because of his lighter skin, narrow nose, and piercing eyes. But Uncle Faisal was proud of his heritage, and he always dressed the part.

"Not yet, Uncle. I will send her a message about it today." Rania didn't want to tell her uncle any more than she had to. She didn't want to tell him that they talked every week because Halimah was discipling her. She didn't want to tell him that Halimah was in Kenya. She didn't want to tell more than he already knew until she could be sure of his motives.

Uncle grunted. "But your aunt told you Halimah should come stay with us?"

"Yes, Uncle. She told me."

"Then it is settled." This was not a question. Uncle tucked in the end of the turban and turned his head, checking his work in the mirror.

"I don't know if she will come," Rania said. What she meant was that she didn't know if it was safe for her to come, but she kept it to herself.

Uncle turned to Rania. "If she comes here, I will not have to tell your father that you have been keeping a secret from him." He took one last look in the mirror and then opened the front door. "Call her," he said, and then he closed and locked the front door behind him.

Rania stood in the salon staring at the shut door. What did he mean? When Auntie had talked to her the night before, Rania felt comforted. Now she sensed a veiled threat.

She waited a few minutes after Uncle left to make sure he hadn't forgotten anything that would make him come back. Then she grabbed her cell phone and sat down on one of the salon chairs.

First, she memorized Halimah's phone number, then she deleted it and all messages associated with it from her phone. She also deleted the call log. Although Rania had never been sneaky, she knew many of her friends back in Khartoum did this all this time. Usually they were hiding secret boyfriends from their fathers. Rania never had a secret boyfriend. She never tried to hide anything from her parents until she'd decided to believe in *Isa*.

Alone in the apartment, Rania felt free to pray out loud. "Oh *Isa*, let there come a day in Sudan when we don't have to hide what we believe. May believers like Halimah and me be free to live safely in our own homes and also follow what is true."

Surely this was the Lord's will: to have His followers living in peace. She hoped one day it would be the new reality.

Rania punched the memorized number into her phone and let it ring. She had only been able to talk a few minutes at a time with Halimah since her sister had moved to Nairobi and worked in the office during the day. She was thankful to have any time at all but craved more time with her.

"Sara? Hello, it's me. Can you talk?"

"Hi, Rania. I can take a short break from work. I don't think Mr. Smith will mind. Thank you for sending the Bible verse. I was hoping you'd be able to talk earlier in the day yesterday. Did you get my message?"

"Yes, unfortunately, so did Uncle. He took my phone from me and eventually figured out it was you." Rania told her sister all about the day before and how she'd been forced to tell them who "Sara" was when they thought she had a secret boyfriend. "I'm so sorry."

"No, don't worry, *habeebtee*. You did what you had to do."

"But now Uncle wants you to come here, and I am not sure if he is telling the truth or not."

"What do you mean?"

"He says you will be safe if you come here. Then today he told me if you did not come here, he would be forced to tell Father that I know where you are. I don't know what to do."

"Well, maybe I should come. I can't stay in Nairobi much longer. Mr. Smith says they are going to close the office soon. He will try to find new locations for the staff, but I am sure the others who have been here much longer than I will have priority."

"But Sara, what if Uncle Faisal is not telling the truth? What if it is a trap just to get you here?"

"I don't think we have a choice, Rania. If I come, I may be in trouble. But if I don't, then you are in trouble. I will not be responsible for you getting in trouble. I'll make arrangements to come as soon as I can."

"How can you be so calm?"

"Because I believe God is working in our family. The verse you sent me last night in your text was just what I have been reading over the past few days. God used that verse to point me in the right direction. And you know what else? I think He wants more members of our family to hear the truth about *Isa*. At this point it is up to you and me. We have to trust that God will give us the wisdom to know how to do this, and I think also we should trust Him to protect us."

"But you were beaten, Halimah. Father beat you. That doesn't seem like you were protected."

"Oh, but I was, Rania. I could have been hurt much worse. In fact, it was a miracle that I did not have serious injuries. God protected me. And besides, if it weren't for what happened, other families in the neighborhood may not have heard about me, about my testimony. Because of what I went through, many people heard. Think about it: would you have taken the time to read the book I left you, the Gospel of John, if I had not been beaten for having a Bible?"

"No."

"Exactly. You see? God is working. We have to be willing to join Him and work with Him on His terms, even if they don't make sense to us. I'll make arrangements to come. We'll trust the results to God."

Rania and Halimah ended their phone call in prayer. Rania knew she should not be so worried, but she could not control her feelings. So when the house phone rang, just minutes after saying goodbye to Halimah, she jumped like a child caught stealing sweets.

Rania tried to calm herself. She wasn't doing anything wrong. She was sitting in the apartment on a Friday, locked in by her relatives like she was every week. No reason to be alarmed by a phone call, even though it was unusual to receive a call on the house phone.

"*Salaam aleykum*," Rania spoke into the receiver.

"*Aleykum wassalaam*, is Badria home?"

"No, she is out. She will return in an hour or so."

"Rania, is that you? This is Auntie Fareeda, I'm calling from Khartoum."

"Auntie, how are you?"

"I am fine. How are you? Oh, I am so glad to hear your voice. I have missed you and Halimah. Your parents never come to visit us anymore. I know we live far away, but one would think they could make a visit now and then. We are family after all. But the only time we see them is when we come to Khartoum, like now. I know Halimah is gone and you are studying art in Dubai. Oh, that is wonderful, Rania. I wish I could have continued to study after high school. But of course I got married. Not that marriage is bad. I hear you are getting married soon."

When the chattering stopped for the woman to take a breath, Rania jumped in. "Would you like me to take a message?" In any other situation, Rania would relish a conversation with sweet Auntie Fareeda. But she already felt she was in over her head. She didn't want to get in trouble for using the house phone.

"Well, actually there is no reason to give a message to Badria. In fact, don't tell her I called. I will call her back on a different day." She paused, and Rania thought perhaps the call had been disconnected because Auntie Fareeda never paused when there was an opportunity to speak. But then her aunt began again, this time in a whisper. "I heard . . . your sister had been reading a book. Do you know anything about that?"

This must be a test. Rania didn't want to lie.

"Should I know something?"

"Well . . ." Auntie Fareeda's voice wavered as if she could not decide whether or not to continue. "I can't say much now, but you see, I have a Christian friend. Well . . . had. My husband won't let me have those kinds of friends anymore. But before that, I learned about their holy book. I think there are some good things in there. I heard rumors Halimah was reading that sort of book."

"Why don't you ask my parents?" Stupid question, Rania knew.

"Oh, your parents don't want to talk about it. Your father is still angry. Listen, I should probably go now. Let me give you my cell phone number. I would love to talk to you again sometime."

Auntie Fareeda gave the number to Rania, who wrote it down. After they hung up, Rania thought better of it and memorized the number instead. She tore the paper up and threw it in the trash.

⇒ Chapter 21 ⇐
Khartoum, Sudan

Mia smiled as she read the email on her computer screen. She hadn't been sure if Halimah had even received the email she wrote to her after visiting with Widad. She read the message with eagerness.

Dear Mia,

I am in Nairobi now. It is different for me, and I miss my family so much. I wish I could just go back home to Sudan, but I know God does not want me to right now. Please pray for me.

My uncle has invited me to join my sister in Dubai, but I cannot stay for long there because my parents will find me. Please, if you know of a place for me, help me to find a safe place to go.

With this email, I am including a letter for your friend. I hope it will encourage her to stay strong in her decision to follow *Isa*.

All love forever,
Sara

"What's that look on your face?"

Mia turned to see Michael standing in the doorway, briefcase in hand. He walked over to the dining table where Mia sat and looked over her shoulder at the laptop computer screen. "Wow, an email from Halimah? How did she manage that?"

"This email must have come in while we were camping over the weekend. She moved to Nairobi. Now she is thinking of going to Dubai but she doesn't know if it will be safe for very long. She's asking for help. Is there anything we can do?"

"Well, she can't come back here, obviously. We don't have offices in Nairobi. I'm not sure if we can do anything."

"I hate not being able to help her, Michael. She has nowhere to go and no family she can trust to look out for her. I can't just write back and say, 'Nope, sorry.'"

Michael patted her on the shoulder. "All right, I'll give it some thought. Maybe there is something she could do at one of Kellar Hope Foundation's offices somewhere. But right now I've got to go or I'll be late. Come on, kids. Time for school."

"I've got the kids this morning, Michael. Hanaan and I are taking them to school and then joining Corey and Saleh's class for a field trip. We'll go in Hanaan's car."

"Even better, I'll be early to work. That will give me time to talk to Habiib about the exit permits." Michael kissed her and then headed out the front door. "Bye, kids, see you at dinner."

Mia wondered what Habiib would say when Michael gave him the final no about paying a bribe.

Mia bowed her head. "Lord, we don't trust Habiib, but we do trust You. Please help us get the exit permits so we can go home this summer."

She read the email from Halimah again. Focusing on others seemed to help her stop obsessing about her own problems. Besides, how could her situation compare to Halimah's? At least she still had a family to go home to.

Mia opened a fresh page on her computer and began an email to Halimah.

Dear Sara,

First of all, your English is improving so much. You sound like a fluent speaker. Second of all, please know we pray for you often, and we will do all we can to help you find a solution for where you should go.

Thank you for sending a beautiful letter of encouragement for my friend. I will bring it to her, and I know she will be strengthened by your words to her.

I miss our time together, but I know the Lord is watching over you.

With love,
Mia

Mia shut down her computer and returned to her bedroom to dress for the day. All the while she couldn't get Halimah's email out of her mind.

"Lord, Halimah is Your daughter. She has no earthly family to care for her and no place to go. Please help her, and please show us what we can do to help her."

Mia tried not to, but sometimes she was filled with anger at Halimah's father. How could he beat her and disown her? All she did was decide to believe something different from what he did. Halimah had explained her father's actions to Mia when she lived with the Westons.

"My decision has brought shame on my family, and my father must do anything he can to restore honor. Honor is a very important thing for an Arab Muslim."

It still didn't make sense to Mia, but it was clear enough for her to be convinced that coming back home to Khartoum was not a good solution for Halimah. She would definitely need to find a different place to live. But Mia couldn't think about it now. Hanaan would arrive with Saleh and their driver at any moment, and she had to be ready to go.

When the driver rang the bell at the front gate, Mia and the kids were already sitting on the front steps waiting. This was Mia's first field trip with the school. Corey's teacher had arranged a visit to a local potter.

Annie and Dylan pouted all the way to school because they wanted to go too, sensing that the presence of both moms must mean the trip was important.

"You'll have just as much fun in your own classes today. Besides, the trip to the potter will be long, and the school bus doesn't have air conditioning."

Mia's words seemed to satisfy Annie, but Dylan's lower lip was still protruding when they unloaded and walked through the gate and into the school yard.

"Good morning, Joseph," Mia said to the teacher at the gate.

"*Sabah 'ilxayr,*" Hanaan said as she walked in behind Mia.

Joseph gave his usual big smile. "I hope you have a lovely trip to the potter today."

The kids ran to the playground to find their friends. Corey and Saleh held hands as they went. Mia made a mental note to tell Corey that in America, boys their age didn't hold hands, and he should probably only do so with his Sudanese friends.

"Let's sit here to wait." Hanaan pointed to a wooden bench under a pair of palm trees in the side school yard.

The women sat and watched the school children running back and forth, playing hopscotch, or kicking a soccer ball. The school was small, with a little more than 100 children in all. All of the classes and the office were housed in a large old home built in the 1950s.

Mia had been looking forward to the field trip not only because she wanted to see what a Sudanese pottery looked like, but because she figured that today held many opportunities to share Bible stories with Hanaan.

No time like the present. Mia jumped right in. "You know, the Bible talks about pottery."

"Really?" Hanaan's voice sounded mildly interested.

"Yes, I was reading this morning about the prophet Jeremiah." Hanaan's face was blank. "Oh, I think you might know him as 'Tirmia.' Anyway, God told the prophet Jeremiah to go to the potter's house and he would receive a message from God. So Jeremiah went. He watched a potter make a pot out of clay, but the pot was marred, so the potter formed a new pot instead."

Hanaan didn't respond, so Mia kept talking. "Well, see, this shows God can do anything. We are like clay in His hand."

"What was the message God gave him?"

"Well, actually the message was that He was planning a disaster against the people unless they repented . . . but the point is, we are like clay and He is our maker."

"What do you mean by 'the people'? Who were they?"

Mia didn't want to answer the question. "The people" were the people of Judah, the Israelites. The Israelites were not the people she wanted to bring up with her Muslim friend. Bringing up the Jews with a Muslim was asking for a rant on how terrible they thought the Jews were.

"Well, that's not the point really . . ."

"It seems like that is the point."

Ugh. She needed to get out of this conversation; it was going nowhere. Well, it was going nowhere good. "Oh, look at Corey and Saleh; they are playing with the soccer ball. Saleh has taught Corey so much about soccer. I know Corey really appreciates it."

Ms. Vivian, the fifth grade teacher, was a tall Kenyan woman who was funny and kind but also demanded the attention and respect of her students. She was the perfect personality for the rowdy bunch that made up the fifth grade. Ms. Vivian wore a traditional Kenyan *batik* dress and tied her hair back in a matching scarf.

Ms. Vivian lined the fifth-graders against the outer wall of the school yard and led them in a silly song while waiting for the driver to bring the bus around to the front gate. Like Mary Poppins, she seemed to be able to control the unruly group, and when the driver popped his head inside the gate to signify he was ready, the class marched out in orderly fashion and boarded the bus.

Hanaan stood. "Let's go. We'll follow in my car. It will be more comfortable."

Mia agreed. She did not want to be on a hot bus without air-conditioning. Besides, maybe they would have a chance to talk some more.

They followed the bus across the bridge toward Omdurman, one of the three sister-cities making up greater Khartoum. In Omdurman, the roads were rife with potholes and the shops along the streets were single-story square buildings. The occasional multiple-story building jutted up from the rooftops like a tower.

As they neared the neighborhood known for its pottery, donkey carts piled with fresh clay slowed the traffic as the animals lumbered down the road, pulling their heavy loads. Rows of mud bricks lay on the sides of the road, baking in the sun.

"Look," Mia said, pointing out the car window. "They make bricks with the same clay they make pots out of."

The driver parked the school bus on the side of the road next to a small square building surrounded by clay pots. Hanaan's driver pulled their car up next to the bus. The students piled out of the bus while Ms. Vivian went into the building. A few moments later she emerged with a man whom she introduced as the potter.

The man was in his sixties and said that his own father had started the pottery business and passed it down to him. He led the group through the various rooms, explaining how the clay was mixed in giant mixers and then shaped on potter wheels.

In the main room he let the students and chaperones watch the potters at work. There were ten potter wheels, and they hummed steadily while the men ran their hands up and down the spinning lumps of clay. The gray mud swelled and contracted at the command of their fingers and palms until the blobs magically formed into flowerpots 18 to 20 inches tall. Mia had at least ten similar pots at home.

"Now come. I'll show you where we bake the pots."

Mia and Hanaan followed the students and listened to the potter's explanations. Mia saw spiritual application in just about everything, but she kept it to herself. She didn't want to overwhelm Hanaan.

On the way back to the school, however, Mia couldn't help trying to share Scripture one more time. "That was so interesting. As I watched the potter I thought about how the Book of Isaiah says God is the potter and we are the clay. He gets to decide what to do with us, His creations. It asks somewhere else if the clay can say to the potter, 'What are you making?'"

"I see what you mean. Allah can shape us as He wills. Yes, I agree."

"You do?" Mia was shocked. Hanaan hardly ever agreed with her on spiritual matters. She smiled and enjoyed the rest of the ride to the school in silence.

Mia watched the traffic increase and the buildings become more modern as they crossed the bridge headed toward Star Friends. She thought on the verse she'd read that morning in 1 Corinthians. "But we have this treasure in jars of clay to show that this all-surpassing power is from God and not from us."

"Thank You, Lord," Mia prayed in her heart. "Thank You that any wisdom Hanaan gets from what I say comes because You speak to her, not because of me. I will continue showing her God's love, even if she never believes."

Mia and Michael sat with Abbas on metal chairs in the dirty little courtyard of his humble home. Since the weather was getting increasingly hot as summer approached, the families decided not to meet on the banks of the Nile.

Instead of splashing in the river water, the children played on the dirt road outside the gate. Corey, Annie, and Dylan enjoyed playing with Yusra and her friends. This time, however, it was just the four of them.

"The neighborhood children have quit playing with Yusra," Abbas said. "I suppose their parents have forbidden them from doing so."

Mia hadn't wanted to mention it, but when they parked their car in front of Abbas's little neighborhood shop, she noticed the supplies had dwindled down to a couple of bags of sugar and some canned goods. Hardly worth opening his store anymore. It was as if Abbas's family was slowly being erased from the neighborhood.

Widad emerged from the kitchen with a tray of tea glasses in one hand and a kettle of steaming water in the other. She poured hot water in a slow stream over a small sieve of tea leaves she held above each tea cup. The dark liquid trickled out and mixed with the sugar in the bottom of the cups. When each cup was full, she placed a fresh sprig of mint on top and served the tea.

"I have something to read to you," Mia said. She took a piece of paper out of her purse and unfolded it. "I know someone else who is Sudanese and who is a follower of Jesus. I asked her to write you a note of encouragement."

Abbas and Widad listened eagerly as Mia read the words of the email from Halimah. When she had finished, she looked up at the couple and saw Widad's eyes fill with tears. Mia grabbed her hand and squeezed it.

Then she folded the letter up and placed it in her hand. Widad held it to her heart.

"I am so sorry for the problems your family has because of following *Isa*," Michael said.

"Oh no." Abbas reached out as if to stop Michael from speaking. "It is an honor. When we read of the things that happened to His followers in the Bible, we feel so honored to be allowed to suffer for *Isa's* name. Please don't feel sorry for us."

"I have spoken with our friend Mansur. He is a pastor, and he will understand a lot of what you are going through. He is out of town right now, but I gave him your number, and he will call you as soon as he returns. He will be a big help to you." Michael took an envelope out of his pocket and handed it to Abbas. "This is a gift from our family."

Abbas took the envelope with a quizzical look on his face. "What is this?"

"You have been so kind to us, you and Widad. We are so grateful for your friendship, and we hope this will help you, at least this summer while we are away."

The amount of money they agreed to give Abbas and Widad was only a temporary solution. Mia hoped Mansur would have ideas to help Abbas support his family, now that his store was failing.

Abbas and Widad thanked Michael and Mia. Then Widad left the courtyard and appeared a few minutes later with two large bags of candy.

"These are for you."

Mia reluctantly took the bags from Widad. They had probably come from their store. She wanted to insist they keep them and try to sell them, but it would insult the hospitality offered. Instead she took the bags and said, "*Shukran.*"

Mia was quiet as they drove home after saying goodbye to Abbas, Widad, and Yusra. She thought about Halimah and the letter she'd written. What must it be like to not know a single soul from your country who believed the same way you did? She wished the two ladies could meet. They did not know each other, but they had more in common than Mia would ever have with either one of them. Both were persecuted for their faith in Jesus. One was exiled and unable to return home. One was persecuted, yet had no resources to escape. Both were daughters of the King and shared in a special grace from the Lord that Mia did not fully understand.

As they neared their house, Michael broke the silence. "You know, we are supposed to leave for the States in a week, and we still don't have our exit permits. I think we need to prepare for the inevitable."

"I know." Mia glanced in the backseat to see if the kids were listening. The younger two had fallen asleep, and Corey had put his earbuds in and was listening to music on his MP3 player. Mia could see his lips moving as he sang along with the song. She turned back to Michael. "I haven't wanted to think about it, but you're right. We've gotta face the facts."

Spending a summer in Khartoum took a good amount of mental preparation. The days were long and hot, and since so many people left for the summer, those who stayed behind were not only hot and sweaty, they were bored too. Mia hadn't yet told the children that there was a chance they wouldn't be going back to the US. She couldn't bear to see their disappointed faces when they realized they wouldn't get to see their grandparents.

"Every day Habiib reminds me that extra money would guarantee permission for us to leave," Michael said. "But I still think we are doing the right thing."

"I do too. And I try not to be angry with Habiib, but it's hard. I just need to keep focused on God and His plan and not on people or things."

As they pulled in and parked in their driveway, Michael's phone rang. He spoke in Arabic and then hung up. "That was Habiib. He wants to meet me at the office."

"On a Friday? The office is closed."

"I know, I guess he just wants to meet in front of it."

"That seems strange. Do you think he has information on that new law he was investigating? If he wants to meet you on Friday, it can't be good."

Michael nodded. "I know, I was thinking the same thing. I think we need to prepare ourselves. . . . It could be bad news."

"Will you help me get the kids inside first?"

Annie woke up on her own when they arrived, but Dylan snored softly on his sister's lap. Michael carried him to his bed and then gave Mia a kiss and left.

"Annie, Corey, want to play a game?" Mia was exhausted as she always was after making a cross-cultural visit, but she needed a distraction. Something to keep her thoughts from constructing crazy scenarios of why Habiib wanted to meet with Michael. A game of dominoes would keep her mind off the strange request.

⇒ Chapter 22 ⇐
Khartoum, Sudan

Mia's phone rang.

"I'm holding our passports in my hand."

"He didn't get the exit permits did he? He gave the passports back without the permits?" Mia willed her voice to sound calm.

"Mia, he got the permits. They are stamped in our passports. We can go home after all." Mia could hear the excitement in Michael's voice. It must be true.

"Oh, Michael, I can't believe it."

"Time to start packing. Oh, and one other thing. Habiib wants to take us out on a boat trip before we go."

"A boat trip? Before we go? Michael, we can't. We have a lot to do to get ready to leave."

"I know, honey, but we can't say no to this. Habiib got us the exit permits even when we insisted we wouldn't pay the bribe. We can't turn down this invitation."

Michael was right, but Mia couldn't help being miffed with Habiib for taking up her valuable time that way.

So two days before the Westons' departure, they loaded the car with snacks, drinks, their kids, and Habiib's family. Mia tried to make the best of it. She was, in fact, mildly interested in where they were going. Habiib said they were taking a boat ride at the Sixth Cataract, but Mia had no idea what it was and was interested to find out.

On the way, Habiib sat in the front passenger seat next to Michael. Mia and Nahla sat in the back seat with baby Lamya on Nahla's lap. Little Hamid wanted to sit with the big kids, so all four piled into the very back of the vehicle.

Habiib fancied himself a tour guide as he explained the Sixth Cataract to Michael and Mia. "The Nile River crosses the borders of multiple African countries. The river has several areas of shallow water called cataracts. One of them is in Egypt and the other five are in Sudan. The Sixth Cataract is at Sabaloka, where we are going."

Mia wanted to ask Habiib how far outside of Khartoum Sabaloka was, but she thought better. The last time she'd been on a trip with Habiib was to visit Nahla when Lamya was born. She had returned to the village to deliver, and Mia had gone to visit her. That trip proved to be much farther away and took much longer than expected. She told herself that it was better not to have expectations. *Just enjoy the experience, Mia.*

She was thankful they had packed snacks for the trip. She brought sandwiches, boiled eggs, packaged cookies, and thermoses of ice water. She had wanted to bring popcorn since it was an easy snack to make but decided not to. She did not want a repeat of the looks Habiib and Nahla made when she served them popcorn at her house.

They drove through the busy city streets until the houses began to dwindle and finally disappear while the road continued into the desert. The desert was beautiful . . . haunting. As they sped along the tarmac road, flat sand extended like a golden sea for miles on either side and ahead. An occasional thorny bush and sometimes dark black rocks were the only things breaking up the vast monotony of the desert.

Then, out of nowhere, a man in a white *jallabeeya* and turban would appear, walking alongside the road. *Where did he come from, and where was he going? In the middle of all the sand and dust, how did he keep his white robe so clean?* Sometimes a camel or a donkey could be seen nibbling what few leaves they could find on the thorn bushes.

Mia never tired of looking out over the desert, its quirky scenes, and the little villages dotting the landscape, sometimes in the distance and sometimes close to the road. The only colors were the white Toyota single cab trucks parked outside some of the houses and the pastel colored mosques with their accompanying minarets reaching toward the sky.

Mia looked at the little villages and imagined what it would be like to live there. The government would never give them permission to live outside of Khartoum, but it didn't stop her from imagining. What would it be like to live in a square mud house with no electricity, market day only once a week, no running water, and no telephone service?

Habiib instructed Michael to turn the car off the road to the left and head out into the desert. Mia felt a lump in her throat. What was Habiib doing? Could it be that he was tricking them? Taking them off somewhere so they would get lost? No, that was ridiculous. Habiib was a good friend.

They drove in the sand for what felt like a long time until they came upon a makeshift gate made of wood. A man stood beside the gate wearing a *jallabeeya* and a turban. His clothes were not white but were rather dirty and old looking. The man had only one leg, and he had a little broken chair that sat lopsided beside him. There was no fence to go along with the gate, so the barrier simply stood in the vast expanse of open desert on either side.

Habiib instructed Michael to stop the car and then he hopped out and spoke with the one-legged man. The man nodded and then he let the wooden pole, weighted on the other end by a huge boulder tied to it, rise. He held tightly to a rope tied to his end of the pole so he could pull it back down to shut the gate after the car passed through. On the other side of the gate was more sand, but Mia could see a village appear in the hazy distance. She breathed a little easier now that she knew Habiib was not leading them out to their demise.

Huge boulders appeared, looking like rocky creatures rising out of the sand. As they drove into the village, which was no more than a collection of mud-brick houses, they had to drive around and in between huge rocks. Some houses were built up against the larger rocks, perhaps using them as one of the walls.

On the other side of the village was more rock than sand, then gardens, and beyond that was the Sixth Cataract of the Nile River. As instructed by Habiib, Michael parked the car next to a banana tree grove. They piled out of the car and made their way to the water's edge.

Habiib spoke with two local men who were reclining on wooden beds. Rope was wound around the frames to create a sort of stiff hammock. One of the men sat up on his hammock-like bed and nodded toward the water. He was the owner of a boat, and he agreed to take the group on a tour of the river. At ten in the morning it was already over 100 degrees. Mia opened the ice chest in the back of the vehicle and handed individual water bottles to each person. Thankfully, the boat was shaded and a light breeze blew off the water as the boatman expertly navigated his craft upstream.

Plantations of bananas and fields of corn grew close to the edge of the river, and the ground between was covered in trees and brush. From branches overhanging the water, Mia noticed hundreds of wicker balls hanging like Christmas tree ornaments.

"What are those?" Mia asked Habiib.

"They are weaver bird nests," he replied, sounding authoritative. "I have studied a lot about birds. You know, I've even led a bird watching safari. People travel from far away to see the birds of Sudan, Kenya, and Uganda. I am even a member of a birding group in Khartoum."

"There is a bird watching group in Khartoum?" Michael asked in surprise.

"Yes, it is a group of foreigners, you know, people like you. They like to go on trips to photograph birds. I found this interesting, so I went to translate for them."

This was a side of Habiib that Mia had not seen. She found it easy to be frustrated with Habiib, but she reminded herself she really should be more patient.

They traveled upstream about half an hour. The muffled roar of the boat motor in the water was the only sound. Even the children were transfixed by the beauty of the Nile River. Mia leaned over the edge and let her fingers skim the top of the water.

"Crocodiles have been seen in these waters," the boat driver said.

Mia yanked her hand out of the water and looked at Michael. "Is he serious?"

Michael shrugged.

"Kids," Mia said, trying to talk over the roar of the motor without sounding panicky, "don't put your hands in the water."

Mia spent the rest of the ride scanning the still pools of water along the edge of the river where the rocks jutted out and created mini-lagoons. Some of the rocks looked shockingly like crocodile heads poking up for air.

Eventually the boatman turned the boat around and headed back to the rocks where their journey had begun. Back on land, they rented a little shaded area to sit and have lunch. Several men had gathered, and they stood around watching the two families. Nahla didn't seem to care, but of course, they weren't staring at Nahla. They were staring at Mia and her kids.

Mia was used to being the odd person in an outing. It happened often in Sudan. But these men acted strange. She couldn't quite put her finger on it, but she got an eerie feeling about them.

"Who are those guys?" Mia whispered to Michael when she got a chance.

"I don't know. We'll just stick close to Habiib and Nahla, and it should be fine."

After eating lunch they cleaned up and put the thermoses back in the vehicles. Just past where the car was parked, the rocks piled up high above the ground and the kids wanted to climb them. Mia walked part of the way up the base of the rocks, just high enough to see the river and part of the village and the vast desert beyond.

Habiib had been right. Sabaloka was a beautiful place. From the beauty of the desert to the tiny intricate ball-shaped nests of the yellow weaver birds, God's amazing creative work shouted His glory.

As she made her way down the rocks, she saw Michael and Habiib talking to the men who had been watching them earlier. Something seemed odd about the mood of the group, but Mia told herself she was just being paranoid.

"*Salaam aleykum*," she said as she walked up and nodded at the four men and Habiib as she stood beside Michael.

"*Aleykum wassalaam*," said one of the men. He seemed friendly enough. Mia smiled at him. Why weren't Michael and Habiib smiling? "Are you American?" The man asked Mia in English.

"Yes." She looked at Michael, who stared intently at his shoes.

Habiib tried to change the subject, mentioning something about a new hotel being built in Khartoum. She didn't get the whole thing because he was rattling off in Arabic, like he was talking as fast as he could.

The other three men seemed mildly interested, but they reverted their attention to the first man when he continued talking to Mia in English.

"What do you think of the bombing?"

"What bombing?" Had she missed something?

"The bombing. When your president bombed innocent people in Khartoum."

Mia felt sick to her stomach. Had this happened today while they'd been relaxing on the boat? She looked at Michael for answers. He was still looking down. His hand wrapped around her wrist, not in support, but as if he were going to pull her away. She opened her mouth to answer the man, with what words, she didn't know. But Michael turned and pulled her with him toward the car. She could hear Habiib, his voice tense, speaking to the men in Arabic.

The man speaking English yelled in Mia's direction. "Your president killed innocent people in Sudan. That's what your country does."

Michael maintained his firm grip on Mia's wrist and guided her on a brisk walk to the car. "Don't say anything, Mia. Don't look back. Just get in the car. I'll get the kids."

The engine was running and Nahla was already in the car. Lamya had fallen asleep in her arms. Mia crawled in and Michael shut the door behind her. He tapped on the window and motioned for her to lock the doors.

Nahla smiled at Mia. "She was so tired," she said, rubbing her cheek against her baby girl's curly head. Mia took a deep breath, trying to calm her heart rate. She smiled back.

Mia stared at her lap, afraid to look outside. She jumped when she heard someone trying to open the car door. It was Michael and the four children. She unlocked the doors, and as she opened her side, noise of the kids' laughter and chatter filled her ears.

She leaned to the side and didn't complain when they accidently kicked her arm while trying to crawl over her seat and into the back. They could kick her as much as they needed for all she cared. She just wanted to get everyone safely in the car and drive away.

Michael climbed into the driver's seat and then turned back toward Mia.

"You OK?"

"Michael, did we bomb Khartoum?" The words were supposed to be whispered, but they came out in squeaky lumps. She thought she might burst into tears.

"Let's just get out of here first," he said. He rolled down the window and called Habiib's name. The man waved and walked to the car. The four men followed but stopped just short of the car as Habiib got in and shut the door.

"You can drive away now," he said. He waved at the men, who did not wave back.

They drove through the village and past the one-legged gate guard in silence. Mia sat in a daze. When they were back on the paved road and speeding along toward Khartoum, Michael spoke.

"The bombing was a long time ago, Mia. Those men just wanted to pick a fight."

"You shouldn't have told them you are American," Habiib scolded her. "They were not good men."

Mia wanted to defend herself. *I was just trying to be friendly*. But Michael spoke instead. "She didn't know, Habiib. This is not her fault." His voice was stern and strong.

Habiib shrugged. "Don't worry, they didn't even have their facts straight. The bomb didn't kill anyone."

Michael explained. "Back in the late 90s, when the United States was trying to defeat bin Laden, they had intel that a pharmaceutical plant in Khartoum was making nerve gas. The US bombed the plant but no proof was found of the nerve gas."

"But why did those men say the bomb killed innocent people?"

"Well, the bomb didn't, but the explosion did destroy the plant that supplied medicines for many diseases in Sudan. So, some would say the bomb did kill thousands eventually."

"Oh." Mia's voice was small.

Habiib's voice boomed, commanding all sad feelings to go away. "But never mind those men. They are stupid. *Alhamdulillah* we had a good day on the Nile River. A good day and good friends. *Masha' Allah*. And, *insha' Allah* they will not come to the airport."

"What do you mean?" Michael asked.

"Well, they were very mad. I told them not to worry, that your family was leaving. Then they said they would come to the airport to stop you."

"What?" Michael swerved, and Mia grasped the door. She wasn't sure if her heart skipped a beat from Michael's driving or Habiib's announcement.

"No, no, don't worry, my friend." Habiib brushed away Michael's reaction with a flick of his hand. "Those men were just angry, that's all. They won't cause problems at the airport . . . *insha' Allah*."

⇒ Chapter 23 ⇐
Nairobi, Kenya

Halimah spent the weekend praying. When a group of staff members invited her to join them on a trip to the beautiful Ngong Hills south of the city, she refused. Her need to find God's will was more pressing in her heart than the need to relax. This time around, Halimah wanted to be sure she was making the move God wanted her to make.

On Monday morning, Halimah felt confident. She wore linen slacks and a blue tunic: a power combination. She knew that Mr. Smith had arrived in his office downstairs because his safari hat hung on the rack in the hallway. Halimah tapped lightly on the partially open door.

"Good morning, sir," she said.

Mr. Smith stood with his back to her, flipping through papers and folders stacked haphazardly on a side table. "Hmm?" He turned toward the door, each hand holding a file. "Oh, yes, good morning, Sara. Are you here to help me organize these files?" His voice was hopeful.

"Yes, I can help you, sir. But first, may I speak with you about . . . an important matter?"

Mr. Smith stood still for a moment, as if trying to comprehend what could be more important than the mess on his side table, but then he refocused on the moment and smiled. "Well of course, Sara. Come in, have a seat." He gestured toward the wooden chair on the opposite side of his desk. "Monday mornings are a bit hairy for me. You'll have to excuse my behavior." He set the files down and folded his hands together on the desk.

Halimah sat on the edge of the chair, not willing to relax. She needed to concentrate, to make sure she got the English right. "I've just had an opportunity come to me," she said. Then she explained about her relatives in Dubai and their desire for her to join them there. When she had finished, Mr. Smith turned to his computer and began to type.

Halimah stared at him, waiting for a response. Was he ignoring her, or simply telling her by his actions that he did not approve?

Still staring at the computer screen, he said, "Looks like for the time being Sudanese citizens do not need entry visas to get into Dubai." He looked at Halimah, pushing his glasses back up on his nose. "That may not last long because Sudan's politics are so unpredictable. The president, as you know, has a warrant out for his arrest from the International Criminal Courts, and he is making things difficult for his citizens. If you want to go to Dubai, I'd suggest you do it soon. Jessica can help you with purchasing a ticket. I assume you have some money?"

"Yes sir, I've saved up. I think I have enough for a one-way ticket."

Halimah had been meticulous about saving the little bit she earned at Kame refugee camp as well as in Nairobi. Except for her season of buying clothes in the market, she had not had a reason to spend money on anything.

She thought of the pocket purse of money she kept hidden under her mattress. That's how Haboba used to keep her money. *Just because your grandmother does it that way doesn't mean you should.* She could hear her mother's voice scolding her. But it didn't matter now. She would only have a few bills left after giving the rest of it to Jessica to buy the ticket.

Halimah couldn't help but feel excited. She had not seen Rania for over two years. Had her younger sister changed after moving to Dubai? The thought of her aunt and uncle made her feel nervous. She'd tried to sound confident and strong for Rania while on the phone, but deep in her heart, she wondered if her uncle really was setting a trap to catch her and send her home to Khartoum.

The day before Halimah's departure she made the rounds at the office to say goodbye to each person. She thanked the chef for his delicious meals and the staff for their hospitality and welcoming attitudes toward her. She shook Mr. Smith's hand and thanked him for giving her a job, even if only for a short time. It was most difficult to say goodbye to Jessica. She hugged her new friend and promised to stay in touch.

On Saturday morning, Halimah woke up and read her Arabic Bible like she did every morning.

"Because of the LORD's great love we are not consumed, for his compassions never fail. They are new every morning; great is your faithfulness" (Lamentations 3:22–23).

"Oh Lord, thank You for renewing Your compassion, Your mercy, every morning. You are faithful even when I am not. I trust You to guide my steps, even though I don't know where they are taking me."

She closed her Bible, placed it in her handbag, and walked down the creaky staircase one last time. She would not miss the cold dank air of the upstairs rooms.

Within the hour, Halimah sat in the back seat of the same van that brought her to the big white house on her first day in Nairobi. She turned to look at the house as the driver guided the van down the driveway and turned left toward the airport. She stared until the trees blocked the view.

At the airport, Halimah checked in and received her boarding pass. The large waiting room made her feel small. When a uniformed worker announced the flight to Dubai, Halimah gladly followed the crowd to the gate.

Walking toward the plane Halimah felt like a pro, having just flown to Nairobi a short time ago. But once she boarded the plane, the inside looked different. For starters, the cabin was much larger than the cabin on the plane she flew out of Loki. As she stood in the aisle of the plane, waiting on the man in front of her to fit his carry-on into an overhead compartment, she saw what must have been more than a hundred passenger seats. She hadn't known so many people could fit on one plane.

Next, Halimah struggled to find her seat, as she had to decipher the code on her ticket. The flight from Loki had not been so complicated. A friendly Kenyan lady with a *batik* scarf tied in her hair helped Halimah locate her seat.

Once buckled in, Halimah was relieved to see that the nice woman who had been so helpful happened to be assigned to the seat next to her. She had been afraid she would have to sit next to a man, and she didn't want to do that on a trip to the Middle East. She didn't want anyone asking her questions about what she was doing—especially not a man.

The enormous engine rumbled as the plane backed away from the terminal. Halimah felt as if she were in the belly of a monster as it flexed its muscles and lumbered down the runway. But then the wings seemed to catch hold of the air, and in moments the plane lifted up and began a smooth glide like a giant bird.

Halimah laid her head against the headrest and closed her eyes. Perhaps it was rude not to speak to the lady who sat beside her as she seemed to be ready for conversation. But Halimah wanted to sit quietly and try to wrap her mind around what was happening: she was on her way back into a Muslim country.

It should have frightened her but it didn't. Instead, peace filled her heart. She was following the Holy Spirit's direction. She knew this because she recognized His voice. What happened once she got to Dubai was in God's hands, and she trusted Him.

Uncle Faisal, Auntie Badria, and Rania welcomed Halimah at the arrival hall with a flourish of kisses and hugs and *alhamdulillahs*. Uncle Faisal took Halimah's suitcase and walked out to the sidewalk and toward his car. The three women walked behind, though not as quickly because Auntie Badria was wearing high heels and couldn't keep up the pace.

Dubai in real life was just like the Dubai in Halimah's imagination. Buildings rose into the sky as high as she could see, one after another. Smooth roads were filled with sleek cars zooming to important places. On the way to their apartment from the airport, Uncle chose a longer route so Halimah could see the Burj Khalifa—the tallest skyscraper in the entire world and the pride of Dubai. Halimah thought surely the tip of the building pierced into heaven itself.

Auntie handed her a brochure of Dubai that showed the Palm Islands—man-made islands resembling the fronds of palm trees. Rows of deluxe houses were built on these long narrow islands and purchased by the richest Arabs and foreigners. Halimah had only read about wealth such as this and had never dreamed she would get to see it.

Uncle Faisal and Auntie Badria babbled all the way home, leaving no chance at all for Halimah and Rania to catch up with each other. Halimah squeezed Rania's hand and smiled at her. They would have their chance later, when their relatives had gone to sleep. Halimah could hardly wait. She did notice, however, a strange look in Rania's eyes that she could not decipher. Everything seemed to be going fine so far. What was Rania worried about?

⇒ Chapter 24 ⇐

Dubai, UAE

Rania smiled back at Halimah as they sat side by side in the back seat of Uncle Faisal's car. That morning she had tried to act as calmly as she could. When Auntie asked her why she was fidgeting so much at breakfast, she said it was because she was excited about Halimah's arrival. This was true, of course, but that's not why she was fidgeting.

Rania had been the last one to bed the night before. After saying goodnight to her aunt and uncle and promising to have the extra bed in her bedroom made and ready for Halimah's arrival the next day, she had gone to her room and closed the door. Too excited to sleep, she'd begun working on the secret painting she hid from Uncle. But a few minutes later she had bumped her jar of rinsing water, so she tiptoed to the kitchen to get a towel to clean her mess.

That's when she saw Uncle Faisal's phone in the salon. She wouldn't have noticed it at all—way over on the far side of the room—except it had just received a message and the screen lit up in the dark. On a whim she tiptoed to the coffee table where it lay and saw the message was from Father.

Rania gulped. She stared at the phone for a few seconds, trying to decide what to do. Should she open the message to see what Father had said? If she did, Uncle would know she had been messing with his phone. Uncle Faisal said he and Father rarely talked. So he was lying. What else was he lying about?

Perhaps, even after all of their kindness, they really had set a trap to get Halimah back. How could she have been so careless in telling them about her sister?

She had hardly slept at all that night. After cleaning her spill in the bedroom, she carefully covered the painting and crawled into bed. She spent the hours in darkness, alternating between sleep and prayer.

In spite of the mess she had created, Rania was glad to see her sister. Halimah had believed in *Isa* longer than she and perhaps would have wisdom to offer in this situation. She dreaded telling Halimah, however, and when she saw her sister emerge from the arrival terminal, all smiles, her heart broke. She watched Halimah embrace their aunt and uncle and couldn't help thinking her beloved sister was walking into an ambush.

The ride home was long and tedious. Uncle Faisal and Auntie Badria chattered happily . . . almost too happily. They touted all the wealth of Dubai as if it were their own. What was their angle? Halimah didn't seem concerned, but she didn't know what Rania had seen on their uncle's phone.

Rania felt the warmth of Halimah's hand when she reached over and squeezed Rania's as if reassuring her. Halimah smiled, and Rania gained strength from her sister. It had been so long—too long—since she'd felt the peaceful courage that emanated from Halimah's presence.

She remembered the words Halimah said to her on their last phone conversation. "You see, God is working. We have to be able to join Him and work with Him on His terms."

At the apartment, Uncle Faisal and Auntie Badria gave Halimah a warm reception. The four of them sat in the salon and chatted amiably for two hours before the older couple excused themselves and went to bed. The evening had been exhausting and terrifying to Rania.

She was pleased to see they did not press Halimah for answers about where she had been living or what she had been doing. They never mentioned her decision to leave Islam. All of this should have made Rania feel better about the situation, but it only made her feel worse.

"What's wrong, *habeebtee*?" Halimah asked.

The girls were lying in their beds in Rania's room. The lights were off and the apartment was silent. Rania had missed the days when they shared a room back in Khartoum. She wished things were as simple as they were back then.

"You remember celebrating *Eid al-Adha* back in Khartoum?" Rania asked.

"Of course. We celebrated the Festival of Sacrifice every year. How could I forget?"

"Well, you know how Father would buy a sheep the week before? We kept the sheep in the courtyard and fed it so well every day. Then, early in the morning on the festival day, a man would come to the house and slit the throat of the sheep."

"Yes, Rania, every Muslim family in Sudan does it to commemorate how Allah provided a ram so *Ibrahim* would not have to sacrifice his son. Why is that bothering you right now?"

"Well, I wonder if that's what Uncle and Auntie are doing to you right now. You know, just keeping you until Father gets here."

"To do what? To slit my throat?"

"Well, I don't know, Halimah. But it is strange to me that they are being nice to you and aren't even asking questions. I'm just suspicious, that's all. The night before you arrived, I saw a text on Uncle Faisal's phone. It was from Father."

"What did it say?"

"Well, I don't know. I didn't open it. But Uncle Faisal said they don't talk. So why was he getting a message?"

"Maybe they are just arranging their arrival times. You said they were coming for your graduation, right? Which we need to talk about because I need to not be here when they arrive. We have what? A month?"

"I feel like I am the only one who is worried here. What if they are coming sooner than we think, and Uncle is just not telling us?"

"Rania, I had a lot of time in Kenya to think about my decisions and to think about the Lord. He is so wonderful, you know? So full of mercy. He will not forsake us."

"Well, there is something else. On Friday, when I was here alone, the house phone rang, which it hardly ever does. I answered, and it was Auntie Fareeda."

"Bashir's mom?" Halimah had not heard any news from Auntie Fareeda since before Halimah was disowned by her family. The last she heard was when their cousin Bashir was being sent to an Islamic school because the family thought he was demon-possessed. It was the same school they might have sent Halimah to, if she had not escaped instead.

"Yes. I tried to take a message, but then she kept talking about you and the book you read and well, you know how much she talks. It made me so nervous. What she talked about was dangerous."

Rania could hear the covers shuffle as Halimah sat up in her bed. "Wait, you mean Auntie Fareeda is asking about the book I read? The Bible?"

"Yes."

"Rania, that's wonderful."

"No, Halimah, it is dangerous."

Halimah lay back down. "Rania, remember when we were younger and I would tell you stories while we were in bed at night?"

Rania smiled into the darkness. "Yes, I miss those days."

"Well, let me tell you a story. Did you know that our great grandfather was from Yemen?"

Rania snuggled under her covers and smiled. This was just like old times. For a moment she could forget the troubles that tied knots in her stomach. "No. I didn't know," she said.

"Well, he was," Halimah said. Her voice settled into the familiar cadence of a well-seasoned storyteller. "He came to Sudan and married a young woman. They lived in the desert where he raised camels. He became wealthy and owned a lot of camels. When he became tired of living a nomadic life, he moved to a village and hired a man to take care of his camels.

"One day this man lost two of the camels, and after searching for many days, he could not find them. This man was poor and could not afford to pay for the loss of property. He gave his daughter to our great grandfather in marriage as payment for the camels that he could never find. This new wife, his second wife, bore him many children, but she eventually ran away, abandoning her husband and children.

"By then our great grandfather was very old. His son, our grandfather, took care of the children, along with his own children. One of these children is Uncle Asim, who we have always thought of as our Father's brother."

"Uncle Asim? So he's not our real uncle?"

"Well, technically he is our great uncle. Anyway, as you know, he married Auntie Fareeda. You were so young back then, but I remember when they got married."

"I never knew that stuff about our grandparents."

"So you see, Rania, God was working all along in our family. Even way back to Yemen, when He brought our great-grandfather to Sudan. I believe He has a plan to bring our family to *Isa*. But it may take a long time, and it may be difficult. This is why I am so happy Auntie Fareeda has asked you questions. Perhaps she is ready to hear more about our belief. Do you have a way to contact her again?"

"Actually, yes. She gave me her number."

"Let's call her now."

"Now? Are you crazy? No, Halimah. Not now. Let's wait until Friday. We'll have some time alone on Friday when both Auntie and Uncle are gone at the same time."

⇒ Chapter 25 ⇐
Khartoum, Sudan

Two days after the trip to Sabaloka, Mia watched as the Nile River zigzagged across the brown background of Khartoum like a giant snake. The plane was high enough now to look at the city from above like looking down on the map she used for prayer.

The wheels were off the ground. No one had stopped them at the airport. The exit permits were valid. This was really happening. Mia breathed a sigh of relief and turned her attention to Dylan who was beaming with excitement.

"That was cool, Mom. We were going so fast." He grabbed the armrests and looked up at Mia. "What was that?"

"Just the wheels going up into the plane after takeoff."

"Oh, OK." Dylan turned back to the window, mesmerized by the view below.

Mia laid her head back on the seat and closed her eyes. Wheels up. They were home free. Just a short layover in Amsterdam and the next stop was Dallas/Fort Worth. She was more than ready for this break.

The last days in Khartoum had been a flurry of activity. Michael was busier than ever at work, trying to get projects wrapped up and his summer work turned over to a colleague at the office. Mia pretty much had to pack everyone's bags by herself. Before a long trip, it was customary to make visits to each Sudanese friend's home, so Mia took the kids to visit Hanaan, and the family had visited Abbas and his family.

"Is Mansur back in town yet?" Abbas had asked.

"No," Michael replied. "But he will contact you as soon as he returns. He is eager to meet you."

The evening before their departure, Michael insisted they make one last visit.

"Michael, visiting Habiib makes me nervous," Mia said. "Besides, we already spent an entire day with him when we went to Sabaloka."

"We have to do it, Mia. We have to keep this relationship on good terms."

Mia sighed. "I know it's true. It's just . . . he was so adamant about the bribe. What if he is bitter about you not giving it to him? What if he tells us these are fake exit permits in our passports?"

Michael raised his eyebrows. "Fake exit permits?"

Mia sighed. "I know it sounds ridiculous, but I really need this break, and I am scared something is going to happen to mess it up."

In the end, they made the visit. Mia was thankful they had because as they were leaving his house, Habiib said to Michael, "When you come back from America, let's make a plan to meet together to talk more about the Bible. I want Nahla to hear it too."

"Why are you so interested?" Michael asked.

"Because you have *innazaaha*."

Neither Mia nor Michael knew the word he had used, but they agreed to meet with Habiib and Nahla as soon as the summer was over. When they got home, Mia looked up the word in their Arabic/English dictionary and found the meaning: integrity.

The Dallas/Fort Worth baggage claim area in the international terminal was a giant room full of conveyor belts. Countless pieces of luggage sat on the moving belts or gathered in huddles on the floor, waiting for their owners to find them.

Michael and Corey found the conveyor belt that would deliver the luggage from their flight. Mia stood to the side with the younger two and the carry-on luggage. She looked around her at all of the people: a variety of skin tones and nationalities. There were countless white faces; she hadn't seen so many in one spot in years. Her heart fluttered in excitement. Surely out of this many people she would know one or two of them. She looked around expectantly but couldn't find a single person whom she knew.

At first Mia resisted the urge to say hello to the lady nearest her. She was wearing short cutoffs and was munching on a bag of Funyuns. Her eyes were glued to her phone, but then she suddenly looked up at Mia and smiled, saying something Mia didn't quite catch. Mia smiled back. A connection.

Two white faces in a crowd. Surely they had a lot in common. Mia said hi back and was delighted that the lady responded. Then she saw the wire connecting the lady's phone to her ear. She was talking to someone on her phone. Oh well. There would be other people to talk to. And so many of them spoke English. Even their accents sounded familiar . . . like home. This was fantastic.

"Mommy, how much longer?" Dylan tugged on Mia's long skirt.

"Not much longer, honey. I know you are tired. After we get our luggage and go through customs, we'll get to see Grandma and Grandpa."

Dylan sprawled on the floor and laid his head against a backpack. "Wake me up when it's time."

Mia opened her mouth to tell Dylan not to lie on the floor, but she glanced down and saw that the floor was cleaner than her own floors back in Sudan, and Dylan laid on those all the time. So she didn't say anything.

Annie hugged a stuffed bunny and watched the people all around. Her hair was a mess of tangled curls, though Mia had tried to comb it out during the flight. They would just have to wait for a good hair washing and some de-tangler. Annie's eyes were bloodshot from the long trip.

"You doing OK, sweetie?" Mia ran her hand over Annie's curls.

"Yes, ma'am." Annie smiled and tiptoed to whisper in Mia's ears. "There are so many fat people."

Mia glanced around. There did seem to be a high percentage of overweight people around.

"*Shhh*," Mia raised her finger to her lips. "Remember, most people here speak English, so they will understand what we are saying."

"Oh," Annie said in surprise. She hugged her bunny and watched the other passengers in silence.

Mia watched the people too. Everyone she saw looked almost familiar, as if she should know them. The tall man over there looked like her uncle and the lady over there looked like a former Sunday School teacher.

Michael and Corey loaded all the bags on two carts: five suitcases and five carry-ons. Mia breathed a sigh of relief. All their bags had made it. Michael waved for Mia to come push a cart. They were heavy, and Corey, even at ten, could not manage to maneuver it around the other people.

The immigration officer took the customs form from Michael. "Anything to declare?" he asked.

"No, sir."

"No animal products or food items?"

"No, sir."

Mia was glad they had not tried to bring raw coffee beans or tribal daggers or animal skin anything, which all had been suggested by Michael as souvenirs. Now they could sail on through customs and not be delayed filling out extra forms or explaining the contents of their luggage. All she wanted to do was see her parents and then go to sleep in a real bed.

The officer flipped through the stack of passports Michael handed him and then eyed the family. Mia's gaze drifted to the poster of a giant American flag on the wall behind the man. The stripes were candy-red, and the stars were as white as the crisp *jallabeeyas* that Sudanese men wore to the mosque on Fridays.

"What is your reason for living in Sudan?" The officer asked.

"I am the project manager for Kellar Hope Foundation, an aid organization."

"I don't know how to say this really, were you treated well?"

Michael grinned. "For the most part. Most Sudanese Arabs are hospitable."

Mia's mind flashed back to Michael's arrest. Her ears heard the screaming sermons of the imam preaching against Americans. She recalled the distrust they felt when they had given Habiib their passports, and she felt the betrayal of the employee who had spied on them and reported to the secret police. She felt the tension of the day she received a telephone call asking for Halimah. Mia gulped and tried to remain calm.

The officer closed the passports and smiled at Michael. "I'm glad to hear that. Welcome home."

"Welcome home." The words echoed in her ears, and an unexpected and intense feeling of pride swelled in her chest. The land of the free and the home of the brave. As they passed the immigration stands and wheeled their luggage carts into the arrival area, the sign they passed in the hallway pierced her heart. The United States of America. She was home.

At the front of the small crowd awaiting passengers stood her mother and father. Mia left her cart and ran to hug her mother. She was home. No one would arrest Michael. No one would spy on her any more. No more sneaking around to disciple believers. No more hiding her Bibles in closets. She was free. Tears ran down her cheeks, but she couldn't stop smiling.

After hugs and laughs and tears from the entire family, Mia's father suggested they move the welcome party to the parking lot where they could load the luggage.

"We borrowed the church van so we could all fit," Mia's mom said.

As they drove to her parents' house on the outskirts of Dallas, Mia gazed out the window. She tried to listen to her mother's update on all of her church friends, but her mind was distracted by the scenery. The streets were clean. All the cars stayed in their lanes. The van sped along the freeway smoothly, as if hovering in the air.

As they drove into the suburbs, Mia did not see any donkeys or goats walking alongside the road, or even people for that matter. It hadn't seemed strange to her before Sudan. But it did now.

⇒ Chapter 26 ⇐
Dallas, Texas

Mia lay in bed as long as she could stand. But she'd been awake for at least an hour, trying not to move around too much and wake Michael, who did not seem bothered at all by jet lag.

She glanced toward the window of her parents' guest room, hoping to see the beginnings of a sunrise. Pitch black. It must be the middle of the night.

Mia sighed and rolled out of bed. She tiptoed to the kitchen and was surprised to see a figure sitting at the kitchen table.

"Mom. I didn't expect to see you up. What time is it?"

The older woman smiled. "Good morning dear. It's five o'clock. I usually get up about this time." She gestured with her chin, "Gotta make your father his coffee. He'll be up here before too long." She chuckled. "I can't sleep past five any more. You just wait; you'll be the same way when you're my age."

Mia smiled and joined her mother at the table. "Thanks for letting us stay with you this summer. I know it's a lot to have all of us living in the same house."

Her mother reached across the table and squeezed her hand. "Of course, dear. You know you are always welcome to stay with us. It gives us a chance to spend time with our grandkids. Who, by the way, have grown so much."

Mia heard the coffeemaker give its final sputter of steam and coffee into the pot, and she stood to pour herself a cup.

"Nancy called last night after you and Michael had already gone to bed. She wants to see you today. She is driving a nice new car, a BMW I think."

Mia winced.

"Now Mia, she's your best friend. You know you'll have to call her back."

Best friend. What did that mean anyway? Nancy had only emailed her a couple of times when Mia's family first moved to Sudan almost four years ago. Could Nancy really be considered her best friend?

"I'll call her eventually, Mom. I have a lot to do today."

"Nonsense. Michael will need to go to the Kellar Hope Foundation office, and I'll have the kids with me. You can even use my car to go meet Nancy. Though you'll have to wait until after ten. She has yoga class at the gym."

Yoga class. A best friend who takes yoga class at the gym and bought a new car. At this point, her closest friends were Sudanese. She thought of Widad, who lived in a house with a dirt floor and would never have enough money for a car or even a yoga class. She would only have enough extra money to buy a soda for her daughter every once in a while.

Still, it would be good to see Nancy again.

Mia didn't have to borrow her mother's car because Nancy called right after yoga class to say she would swing by to pick Mia up in her new convertible. "We'll go for a smoothie," Nancy said.

"A smoothie?" Mia asked.

Nancy laughed. "Yes, they are the best. And healthy for you too."

Mia hung up the phone with one hand, twisting a stray curl of hair around her finger with the other. "Since when does Nancy drink smoothies? She sounds like a health nut."

"Did you say something, dear?" Mia's mother had begun bustling about the kitchen, mixing batter for pancakes.

"Hmmm? Oh, no. It's nothing." Mia stood over the kitchen table, idly thumbing through the morning's paper her mother had left open to the sports page. Football. That meant soccer in Sudan. Her friends in Khartoum wouldn't have any idea what American football was.

Just then, all three children appeared in the kitchen. They were still wearing their clothes from the day before. They had fallen asleep on the way home from the airport and slept all night.

"Good morning, kids. My goodness this is the latest I've ever seen you three sleep. The trip must have really worn you out," Mia said.

The kids settled in chairs around the table and Mia's mom poured them orange juice. "Grandma is so happy to have you at my house. We are going to have so much fun today."

Before long, the table was set with plates and a large platter of steaming pancakes.

"Wow, Mom. These look great. Kids, don't these look delicious?"

"Yes, ma'am," Corey said. "Grandma, I've missed your pancakes."

Mia put a pancake on each of the kids' plates and helped Dylan put syrup on his, even though he scowled at her.

"I'm almost six, Mommy. I can do my own syrup."

"Yes, I know you can sweetie, but we want to have enough syrup left for everyone."

Just then they heard a car honk twice, one long honk and one short one. Mia smiled. She would recognize that honk anywhere. "Nancy is here. Kids, do what Grandma says. I'll be back in a couple of hours."

"Yes, ma'am," they said in chorus.

"I'll make sure they get bathed. I have new clothes for each of them."

"New clothes?" Annie's eyes widened.

Of course, her mother was thinking ahead. Her kids were in good hands. Mia kissed the top of Annie's curly head as she grabbed her purse and headed out the door.

"Thanks, Mom."

"Of course, dear. I've been waiting years for this." Her mother was happy as a hen with her chicks.

Mia stepped out into the bright Texas morning. The summer sky was a cloudless blue canvas. She shaded her eyes to look at Nancy's car as she made her way down the walkway. The cobalt blue body of the car matched the convertible top. She wondered why Nancy didn't have the top down. The weather was perfect.

Mia opened the passenger door and slipped in, instantly feeling the cool of the air conditioner, followed by a huge hug from her friend.

"Mia, I can't believe it's been so long. Oh my gosh, I've missed you so much." Nancy continued hugging her. "I still can't believe you went to Africa. I'm so glad you are back."

She finally let go and settled back in the driver's seat. Mia laughed. "I missed you too, Nancy. Nice car by the way."

Nancy smiled, rubbing her hands across the sleek dashboard. "Thanks. Bill bought it for me."

"Wow, he still loves you, huh?" Mia meant it as a joke.

"Yeah, well, that's what he wants me to think," Nancy said. Mia noticed a glint of sadness in her friend's eye.

"Don't be silly, Nancy. Bill is crazy about you."

"Yeah, crazy about me," Nancy said flatly. "But enough about husbands. Let's go get a smoothie. There's this great new place I want to take you to."

The bleak look in Nancy's eye disappeared. She revved the engine and smiled again as she drove down the road, a little too fast for a residential area.

Mia eyed the screen on the dashboard that looked like a small television. "Good grief, it's got all sorts of information on here. Time, date, temperature . . ."

"It's a GPS too if I need it."

"Wow. Really nice, Nancy. Hey, it says it's only 92 degrees. Why aren't we driving with the top down?"

Nancy raised her eyebrows and gave Mia a concerned look. "That's why. Because it's 92 degrees. Are you crazy?" She shook her head in dismay. "You are crazy. You've been in the desert too long."

They both laughed. So what if Nancy hadn't emailed her? It was hard to keep up a friendship long distance. But now that they were back together, it was like slipping into a worn-in pair of jeans: comfortable and cozy.

They arrived at Lean Green Smoothie Shop a few minutes later. Mia eyed the sign, unimpressed by its claim to nutritious drinks.

"'Your health is our wealth,' what does that even mean?"

"Oh c'mon, you'll see. They are yummy." Nancy killed the engine and hopped out of the car. She was clad in yoga pants and an exercise top. She looked fantastic of course, as always. But Mia was shocked by her attire. Was she really going to wear those clothes in public?

Mia glanced down at her own clothes. She wore blue jeans and her only good shirt that wasn't long-sleeved. It was a plain red shirt she'd purchased on the Internet and had sent to her mother's house so she'd have something fresh to wear her first week in the States. It had cap sleeves, which she hadn't worn in ages. She always had to cover her arms in Sudan. In fact, she felt scandalous with so much arm showing. But now, looking at her friend in skintight clothes, she felt matronly.

Oblivious, Nancy locked the door of her convertible and led the way. "C'mon, it's like a furnace out here."

The cashier was a young man with stylish glasses and a trendy haircut. He was flirtatious, Mia noted. Though she reminded herself he was only being friendly and that it had been three years since any person of the opposite gender, besides Michael, had paid her any attention.

"He's not being inappropriate; he's just being friendly." She repeated to herself.

Mia looked at the menu posted on the wall behind the cashier. So many choices. To her relief, Nancy ordered first.

"I'd like a large skinny Vegan Apple Kale, and can you add an herbal bonus?"

"Are you speaking English?" Mia's brow wrinkled. She squinted and looked again at the options. Where to start? They all looked so good. Except for what Nancy ordered, which didn't sound good at all.

Nancy laughed. "Let me order for you. I'll start you off on something mild." She glanced over the menu and then ordered Mia a large Greek Yogurt and Strawberry Delight.

The cashier punched some buttons on the register. "Do you want a bonus with that?"

"Ummm . . ." Mia hated to continue acting like she didn't know what was going on, but the pictures and all the words were blurring together. "What do you recommend?"

"An herbal bonus, a probiotic bonus, a skinny bonus . . . it's up to you really."

Nancy mercifully stepped in front of Mia and handed the cashier her credit card. "She doesn't want a bonus."

Mia watched as the cashier slid the credit card through the machine. "We can't use credit cards in Sudan. I don't even know if I remember how to use one," Mia said as they slipped into a booth and waited on their smoothies.

"Why can't you use credit cards?"

"Well . . . you know, the sanctions against Sudan." By the look on Nancy's face, she definitely didn't know what Mia was referring to. Mia shook her head. "Never mind. Tell me about your smoothie. I didn't understand half of what you said. What's an herbal bonus?"

"Oh it's just an addition to the smoothie. It provides a lot of extra vitamins to help promote defense against nitrosative stress."

"Goodness, Nancy. I know we are both speaking English here, but I still only understand about half of what you say."

Nancy laughed. "Don't worry about it. You can taste mine when it comes and see what you think."

A bell on the front door jingled and Nancy looked up and grinned. "There's Marsha. You remember her, right? From Sunday School? I asked her to join us. She's been eager to see you."

Marsha waved from across the room. She looked like Nancy's twin yoga sister. Her form-fitting clothes were almost identical. She made a quick order at the register and then slipped into the booth beside Mia, giving her a side hug.

"Mia, it's so good to see you again. Welcome home. I know you must be so glad to be back."

"It is good to be back," Mia said, smiling. The young man from the register arrived with a tray and three smoothies. Conversation paused as the three friends organized drinks, straws, and napkins.

"So, how was your trip to Africa?" Marsha sipped her green tea smoothie.

"Her trip? Marsha, it wasn't a trip. She *moved* there." Nancy laughed. "She has been living there for years."

"Whatever," Marsha rolled her eyes and then looked back at Mia. "How was it?"

"I don't really know how to answer the question." Mia searched for words. Scenes from Sudan flashed across her mind. The peaceful Nile, the mysterious pyramids, and the dirty streets of Khartoum. A woman beaten by her own father because she chose to leave Islam. A giant dust storm. The beauty in the eyes of a poor man who baptized his poor wife because both of them had just received the riches of new life in Christ. Each scene was so extreme. Impossible information to share flippantly to a general question.

"It was good." Mia finally said, knowing the answer was insufficient.

"I'm so glad," Marsha said. "It's nice to have you back."

"Tell her about circumcision, Mia. This is crazy, Marsha, you won't believe it."

Mia felt a little awkward sharing this information without giving the full context of the culture of Islam. "Well, in Sudan, all the Muslim girls are circumcised."

Marsha stopped, mid-sip. The green concoction from her smoothie hovered halfway up the straw and then descended back into the cup. "What on earth? What do y'all mean? I've never heard of such a thing."

"Well, I guess I hadn't either before moving to Sudan. But actually, more than 200 million girls worldwide are circumcised. It's a huge problem really, because it causes so many health issues."

Marsha shivered. "I can't believe people would do that. I didn't realize Africans were so uneducated. Don't they love their children? How could they do that to them?"

"Yes, of course they love their children. And there are many well-educated Sudanese people. This is just part of their culture. I do believe this is something that should change, but it just can't happen overnight."

Marsha leaned across the table. "How many people did you convert?"

Mia raised an eyebrow. "Ummm, well . . . if you mean how many became Christians . . . it's not that simple really . . . but I guess two."

Marsha did her mid-sip pause again and then asked, "Two?"

The words Mia was certain her friends wanted to say floated in the air between them: *How come you were there for three years and only two people became Christians?* Nancy broke the awkward pause. "Well, aren't we glad those two people believed?"

Marsha smiled. "Yes, we are. Good job, Mia."

Mia curled a lock of hair around her finger, trying to distract herself from crying. Maybe she was just tired. It was a long trip from Sudan and her fatigue was so much more than just physical.

"Tell me how you've been, Marsha," Mia said. She wanted to say, "How many people did *you* lead to the Lord in the last year, *Marsha*?" but she settled for listening to Marsha's story about the new house she and her husband were having built. As her friend droned on about the difficulty of choosing just the right knobs for her kitchen cabinets, Mia thought of Widad, who worried about where to find her family's next meal.

When the conversation moved to their children, Mia relaxed. Here was a subject they could all relate to. She was shocked to hear how tall Nancy's oldest son had grown and how Marsha's twin daughters were already in sixth grade. She couldn't help laughing as she talked about Dylan's latest antics and was proud to brag on Corey's and Annie's aptitudes for Arabic.

In spite of their obvious differences, Mia had to admit it felt good to spend the morning with her friends. And after seeing that no one stared at the two women in yoga pants, she wondered if she too would look good in them. Maybe she would join a gym for the summer.

Nancy drove Mia back to her parents' home. "Sorry about Marsha. She doesn't really understand what you've been doing."

"Oh, I know. It's fine. It's still great to see her. And you too, Nancy. I have really missed you."

"Yeah, I've missed you too. Sorry I didn't write you much. I'm just not good at writing emails. I'm glad you have a friend though. Your mom told me you had a good friend there who is a nurse. Works with Michael, I think?"

"Beth. Yes well, we kind of had a falling out. Then she moved away."

"You? Mia Weston? You had a falling out? I didn't think people like you did that."

"Nancy, I am normal, and I have normal problems."

Nancy laughed. "I love you, Mia. But you are not normal. No one who chooses to live in a place like Sudan is normal."

"Hey, we like Sudan." Mia laughed too.

When Mia returned home, she thought about what Nancy said. What did she mean she didn't think people like Mia "did that"? Did what? Had friendship problems? She hadn't planned on losing a friend, it just happened.

Beth and Mia had been close friends until Mia started speaking more frequently about Jesus to her Muslim friends. The more she did it, the more excited she got about the opportunities and about how open so many Sudanese were to talking about the Bible. But all the while, Beth grew more agitated. She finally wrote a letter of complaint to Michael's boss. Since then, they had not been friends.

Mia remembered the stab in her heart, the feeling of betrayal. It was painful when Mia was hurt by an unbeliever, but she had never felt as hurt as when she felt attacked by a sister in Christ. In the end Beth left and Mia remained in Sudan. But she'd never found a friend as close as Beth had been. Honestly, she hadn't tried.

⇒ Chapter 27 ⇐
Dallas, Texas

Mia's dad was reading the paper in his recliner when she walked in the door.

"Hi, Dad. Where's everyone else?" She set her purse on the entryway table and walked to the living room to give her father a kiss on the head.

"Michael went to Kellar Hope's office and your mother walked the kids down to the park."

"Wow. I wasn't gone very long." Mia sat on the couch and looked across the room at the man who'd scared her half to death by having a stroke the year before. He looked as healthy as ever now, all kicked back in his chair like he'd done ever since she could remember. "Dad?"

"Hmmm?" His voice was muffled behind the copy of *The Dallas Morning News*.

"I've missed you."

The paper wall between them disappeared, and Mia's father dropped his arms, crinkling the newsprint in his lap. "Well, darlin', we have missed you something awful. We are so proud of you and Michael, but I tell you what, after my, uh . . . episode last year . . . I was wondering if I was gonna get to see my grandkids again or not. I sure am glad I did."

Mia smiled. "Me too."

The house phone interrupted the father-daughter conversation. Mia's father answered, then held the handset out for Mia.

"It's Nancy. Weren't you just with her?"

Mia laughed and took the phone. It was just like high school again.

"Hello?" The connection crackled over the line, but Mia didn't care because this was America, and no one was tapping her parents' phone.

"Mia, I'm going home to shower and then I'm going to the store. Why don't you come with me? It'll be fun."

"Nah, I'm gonna stay here and talk with Dad."

"Sure, I understand. Do you need me to pick up anything for you?"

Mia walked into the kitchen and checked the shopping list her mother had hung on the refrigerator with a strawberry-shaped magnet.

"Looks like we need sliced cheese and orange juice."

"Sure thing. What kind of cheese do you want?"

"Oh, just sliced."

"You want the real stuff, right? Not the cheese-food stuff."

Mia chuckled. "Right, get some real cheese. Thanks."

"Colby or Monterey or Swiss? Or something else?"

"Ummm, can you just get cheddar?"

"Sure, just plain cheddar or mixed?"

"Good grief, just plain I guess."

"OK. Lite or regular?"

"Nancy, just cheese. Just sliced cheese. I don't care. The stuff I get in Khartoum isn't even refrigerated, so I'm not picky."

Pause. "OK, Mia. Got it."

Mia sighed. She needed to be more patient. She just wasn't used to all the choices. "Thanks, Nancy. Oh, and don't forget the orange juice."

"Orange juice, right. The real stuff right?"

"Just orange juice, Nancy."

"Right, but there's orange-flavored juice and fresh orange juice."

"Good grief, the fresh I guess."

"Perfect. Pulp or no pulp?"

"What does that even mean?" Were there this many choices before she went to Sudan? She didn't remember shopping being so difficult. "Surprise me."

"Got it. OK. Anything else?"

"Are you kidding me? No, that's enough decision-making for today."

Nancy laughed. "Of course. You haven't been to the grocery store yet, have you? Come with me, it'll be fun."

Mia walked back to the living room. Her father's head leaned back against the headrest, and his eyes were closed. His breathing was heavy, as if he'd fallen asleep.

"OK, I'll go."

"I'll pick you up in 20 minutes."

This is a good idea, Mia told herself. She could go to the store and watch Nancy shop. All she had to do was choose a gallon of orange juice and some cheese. The rest was up to Nancy.

How was she ever going to survive an actual grocery shopping trip on her own? Mia was thankful they would be splitting their time between her parents and Michael's parents. She wouldn't have to actually make a real grocery shopping list and buy things like cleaning supplies. Cheese and orange juice were taxing enough.

Nancy was true to her word, and 20 minutes later Mia heard the car honk. Mia winced and looked at her dad. He opened his eyes and spoke in a sleepy voice. "Nancy here?"

"Sorry. I don't know why she does that."

He smiled. "She did it in high school too."

"She did? I didn't remember. I guess I didn't notice when I was a teenager. If Mom comes home before I do, tell her I'll be back soon. I'm going to the store."

Mia's dad nodded and closed his eyes again. Mia slipped out the front door and waved at Nancy before she honked again.

At the store the aisles were packed from front to back with what seemed to Mia like a million varieties of every item to choose from. It was like Christmas on steroids. Except, of course, none of it was free. But still, it was available: right there at her fingertips.

"Oh, look. Nancy, wait. There's duct tape. I need to buy several rolls to bring back. Here, take these two, and I'll get three more."

"What can you possibly need with five rolls of duct tape?"

"Well . . ." Mia paused to think. "I'm not sure really. But if we get over there and need it, at least we'll have it. This stuff is so useful." Even the tape had options to choose from: wide, narrow, various colors, and even patterns. Mia stuck with the standard silvery color but did choose one pink roll just for fun. "Oh, and gauze, can we get some sterilized gauze? Did you know most of the pharmacies in Khartoum don't even stock the stuff?"

"Are you planning on having injuries more serious than Band-Aids?"

"Well, no, but you can't be too careful. Let me just get several packets of various sizes. I promise that's it. We'll go to the grocery side for your groceries next."

"It's fine." Nancy brushed off the comment with a smile. "It's fun to shop with you. Everything is so exciting. Marsha and I always complain about having to grocery shop, but you give me a new perspective on the whole thing."

"And you know what the best part is? We aren't getting hit on by men at the fruit section." Nancy raised one eyebrow and looked at Mia. "I mean it. The men who run the fruit stands in Khartoum always try to hit on me, and I hate it. I always walk away feeling so . . . I don't know . . . violated, I guess. I bet when we go choose some apples and bananas over there no one will even give us a look. It feels so free to be. . . . hmmmm what is it? Anonymous."

"Anonymous?"

"Yeah, I feel like I can come in here and shop and talk to you and no one is staring at me. No one is talking about me. No one is critiquing what I buy. Anonymous. It feels good."

Nancy shrugged. "Well, I don't really get it, but I'm glad it makes you happy. Can we get my groceries now?"

Mia smiled. "Yes, as long as you help me get the orange juice and cheese. I may not be ready for something so complicated."

Mia sat on the back porch of her parents' house holding a large glass of sweet iced tea. She laid her head against the tall back of the wooden rocking chair and closed her eyes. It was good to be back in Texas. Two weeks had sailed by, and Mia felt herself relaxing more and more with each passing day.

"Mom? You comin' out here?" She called out, hoping it was loud enough to penetrate the glass door that kept the air-conditioning inside and the mosquitoes outside.

Mia remembered when she was a teenager. She and her mother would sit on the porch with their iced tea and talk about everything from boys to Mia's favorite classes to the latest styles in clothes. Mom had been there for her through the roller coaster ride called high school and then through her college years when she'd come home once a month to get a good home-cooked meal, lots of hugs from Dad, and a heart-to-heart on the back porch with Mom.

She heard the back door open, and to her surprise she saw Michael instead of her mom. His tall frame filled the door, and the look on his face dampened the happiness of a sunny afternoon.

"Michael, what's wrong? Where's Mom?" She jumped up from her chair, sloshing her ice tea on the porch. Ever since her dad's stroke the year before, she'd felt like her parents were ticking time bombs, ready to drop with some illness at any moment.

"It's not your mom, she's fine. Actually, she's watching the kids because we need to talk." He sat in the rocking chair meant for her mom and motioned for her to sit back down, which she did. "We can't go back to Sudan."

Mia stared at him. "What are you talking about?"

Michael sat on the edge of the rocker. "The situation in Sudan has deteriorated. The government is finally doing what they have threatened to do for several years now. They have closed down three humanitarian organizations in the time since we left. Habiib says Kellar Hope Foundation is next on the list and will be receiving notification soon. Probably next week."

Mia felt her mouth go dry. "Can we appeal? Surely there is something we can do." She refused to believe there was no recourse. A tear made its way down Mia's cheek.

"Mia, there is nothing we can do. Remember, this is Sudan we are talking about. Dr. Kellar says he will let me go back to Khartoum to pack our things. It'll have to be soon, though, before they cancel my work visa." He cleared his voice a couple of times, trying to keep his own emotions in check. "Dr. Kellar says I have a job here in Dallas in the home office, and after I return from Sudan, I can start work here."

So that was it. No fanfare. No goodbye parties. No closure at all. Their time in Sudan was over. End of story.

Decisions had to be made fast. So fast, in fact, that Mia felt her head spinning. That same day Michael booked a round trip ticket to Khartoum. He would be leaving in three days. Mia emailed the children's school to withdraw them. She jotted down the items she wanted Michael to bring back in his suitcase. Only two things. She wanted the framed picture of Hanaan and her that she'd recently displayed on their bookshelf, and she wanted the drawing that hung over their couch. It was a beautiful depiction of a Nubian-style door that was just cracked open, with light shining through.

She remembered when Rania gave the drawing to her. Rania: the younger sister of her dear friend Halimah, who had given up everything to follow Jesus. At the time, Mia had been reminded of a verse from the Bible. "A great door for effective work has opened to me, and there are many who oppose me" (1 Corinthians 16:9). The Lord had opened the door for her family to live in Sudan. It was hard to believe He was closing it now. Mia felt numb.

The day Michael left to return to Khartoum, Mia handed him the list, which still had only two items on it. He looked at it and raised his eyebrows. "That's it? That's all you want me to bring back?"

"Well, maybe my recipe book and my extra Bible. You can sell everything else. I told the kids to make lists too. Most of their toys are filthy with Sudanese dust, but they hold a lot of memories for them. I think it's worth it."

Michael shrugged. "OK, if that's all you want. I'm kind of surprised. I thought you'd think of at least a suitcase worth of things."

"Don't worry. I'm sure the kids' lists will fill the suitcases up just fine."

The fact was Mia wanted all of her stuff. She wanted all of it, and she wanted to move back to Sudan.

Michael left for the airport and Mia cried. Not because he was leaving her. She would see him in a week. She cried because this was it.

The Westons were not going back to Sudan. Up to now it had felt like one of those strange dreams she eventually woke up from. But watching her father drive Michael out of the driveway and toward the airport made her realize this was no dream. Michael was going back to close up their house . . . and their life. Sudan was over.

She would never get to say goodbye to Abbas and Widad. Would they even understand the reason or would they think Mia had gone home to "rich America" and decided she didn't want to return? She wanted to share the love of Jesus with Hanaan just one more time. And there was Tzega. She would lose her job as their house cleaner, which didn't seem fair. Mia felt like a traitor.

She watched the car until it turned the corner and went out of sight. A million things she should have told him. A million things she would have done if she'd known she wasn't going back.

I should have told him to bring the gold-colored teakettle. It would remind me of Sudan. I should have told him to buy as many tribal daggers as he wanted.

After Michael left, Mia didn't feel like doing anything. If she was a traitor, she might as well be a lazy one. She lay on her mother's couch and watched game shows on television. After lunch, she took the kids to the nearby park and sat at a picnic table in the shade while her kids played.

"Mommy, push me," Dylan called from the swing set.

"Get Corey to," she called back. *I'm a traitor, and I'm a lousy mom.*

If the Lord had given the Westons so many opportunities in Sudan, why was He pulling them out now? Maybe she had not been good enough, and God had sidelined her.

Mia could have melted into a puddle of tears right there at the picnic table. It wouldn't be the first time the kids had seen her break down. But there were joggers and walkers in the park. She didn't want to make a scene.

As she sat stewing, watching Corey try to push Dylan hard enough to satisfy him, a lady with two small children walked up to the swing set. There was one swing left, so the lady put her toddler in the swing and pushed him while holding the baby on her hip. The lady wore a headscarf tight around her head. It reminded Mia of Hanaan. She remembered Hanaan's words: *Every strand of hair showing is one more burning coal in hell for a woman.*

For the first time in several days, Mia was distracted and thinking about something other than her own problems. She was thinking about this woman, who was definitely a minority in a Texas suburb. How many Muslims lived here anyway? Did this woman feel alone? Mia summoned the energy to pull herself up off the picnic bench and walk to the swings.

On a whim, she decided to try Arabic. "*Salaam aleykum,*" she said.

The woman looked at her with eyebrows raised. "*Aleykum wassalaam.*" Then she broke into a big smile. "You speak Arabic." Her accent was heavy.

"Oh, only a little," Mia said. "I live . . . well . . . I used to live in Sudan. Where are you from?"

"I am from Jordan, but we live here now."

Mia continued talking with the lady until her baby began to cry and she had to go. They didn't exchange numbers, but Mia learned the lady's name was Amal. She whispered a prayer for Amal and wondered if they would get to meet up again someday here at the park.

A little spark of hope fluttered in Mia's heart. It gave her pep in her step as she walked toward Dylan's swing. "You can go play on the monkey bars, Corey. I'll push Dylan."

Chapter 28
Dubai, UAE

Halimah and Rania were never alone in the apartment. Uncle Faisal and Auntie Badria either stayed home or took the girls along with them wherever they went. Rania offered to take Halimah to class with her.

"No," Auntie Badria said in a matter-of-fact tone. "I need Halimah to come shopping with me."

Halimah looked forward to Friday. Rania explained Friday was the one day they were certain to be alone. But on Friday, Auntie insisted the girls join her on a visit. They did not return to the apartment until after midnight.

The girls excused themselves and went to Rania's room. They waited until the lights in the salon went off and they heard the master bedroom door shut.

Then Rania whispered to Halimah, "I have a plan."

"What?"

Rania held her finger to her lips and tiptoed to the door. She slowly turned the lock and then pressed her ear to the door to check for any sounds in the hallway. When she was satisfied, she nodded.

"So what's your plan?" Halimah asked.

"This." Rania pulled the white sheet off of an easel in a dramatic display. Halimah saw the beautiful art piece, and despite being deeply impressed by Rania's ability, she couldn't help but make a sarcastic remark.

"What? You're going to paint us out of Dubai?"

"No." Rania sighed in frustration. "We are going to sell this. I already have a buyer. We just have to figure out how to get this to the Mall of the Emirates."

Halimah eyed the painting with skepticism. "How are we going to transport this huge painting there?"

"We don't have to take it like this. I'll remove the canvas from the frame, and we'll roll it up."

"And how are we going to get permission to go there?"

"Uncle and Auntie seem keen on keeping you occupied until our parents come. Why don't you tell them you want to see a big shopping mall? The Mall of the Emirates is Uncle Faisal's favorite. I am sure he will take us there. You won't believe this mall, Halimah. It's the most amazing thing. Of course, we can't afford anything in there, but it's fun to go anyway."

"If you sell this painting, which you've painstakingly hidden from Uncle, he'll make you send the money back to Father."

Rania smiled. "I have a plan for that too. He won't know I have it."

The next morning, while drinking a glass of tea, Halimah mentioned the mall to Uncle Faisal.

"Of course you need to see a mall in Dubai. And today is Saturday. It's a good day for us to go as a family." He grinned and looked at his wife. "Don't you think so, Badria? Don't you think we should take Halimah to a mall? How about the Mall of the Emirates? That's a nice one. It is one of the largest shopping malls in the world."

Uncle Faisal did not want to bother with driving, so after everyone dressed, they hailed a taxi and took off toward the Mall of the Emirates. The vehicle sped along Sheikh Zayed Road. Halimah should have been admiring the beautiful buildings along the way, but she was thinking about Uncle Faisal.

Since arriving, he had played the role of gracious host with conviction. He appeared to be enjoying the fact that his nieces lived with him. He had Auntie Badria make them all tea in the evenings. He joked and laughed during meals. He scoured the Sudanese community newsletter to look for events they could attend together, and—like today—he took them to iconic locations around Dubai. Was he genuinely enjoying them?

Or was he keeping them distracted until Father could get away from his work in Khartoum and come fetch his infidel daughters?

Infidels. That's what they were. Did Uncle know it? He knew Halimah and Rania were different. He knew Halimah had—at least at one point in the past—rejected Islam. He knew Rania wanted to be an artist and her family had allowed her to postpone her wedding. But if he believed they were infidels, why was he being so nice to them?

The taxi dropped the family off at the front of the vast retail complex. As they entered, the marble floors and glass ceilings made Halimah feel as though she were stepping through an entrance into a different world. She had never seen any place so clean, so big, so luxurious. Escalators looked as if they were suspended in midair, and the railings boasted intricate designs. Giant palm trees, three stories high, grew up from the ground floor, and a fountain gurgled happily in the midst of shoppers. The shops appeared to be mostly expensive name brand stores, and the workers, in tidy uniforms, were people from other countries like the Philippines and India.

In fact, the mall looked like a giant deluxe melting pot of every nation in the world. Halimah saw Westerners, Africans, Arabs, Indians, and countless Asians. Uncle Faisal must have been right when he said that more than 80 percent of people in Dubai were foreign-born.

"I want you to see something," Uncle Faisal said, almost giddy.

The women followed as he led them on a long walk to the west end of the mall. Auntie Badria asked to stop at several shops, but Uncle insisted they would do so later. Finally they arrived at an enormous glass window, several stories high.

Halimah peered through the panes and saw a giant picture of a winterscape in Europe, only it was not a picture. This was an actual indoor ski slope. The ground was covered in fresh piles of snow, and the people inside were bundled up in coats and hats and gloves. Some of them carried skis and snowboards.

"What's this?" asked Halimah, eyes wide.

"A ski slope, *masha' Allah,*" Uncle said, chest held high as if he were the one who invented it. "It is the first indoor ski resort in the Middle East."

They stood by the glass panes and gazed over the scene for a long time, as if watching television. Halimah imagined Rania would have tried to talk Uncle Faisal into paying for her to ski if she hadn't had a giant painting strapped to her leg under her *abaya*.

"I'm tired," Auntie Badria complained.

"We just got here." Uncle Faisal rolled his eyes.

"You made us walk a mile to get here, Faisal. Why didn't you have the taxi drop us off at a closer door? Anyway, too late, I'm already tired. Let's get some coffee."

Rania jumped into the conversation. "Halimah and I don't really want coffee. I'd like to show her the art shops. We'll meet you for lunch at the level one food court, say in about an hour?"

Rania grabbed Halimah's hand and walked off before Uncle Faisal had a chance to argue. "Don't be late." He called after them like a father trying to maintain control of his two unruly daughters.

Rania's brisk walk was hampered by the expensive splint on her left leg. Halimah almost started to laugh, but she noticed the intent look on her sister's face and opted to be helpful rather than funny. When they'd walked a good distance away, Rania veered off to a public toilet where she removed the rolled up painting from under her *abaya*. Then they continued walking down the hallway and up one of the fancy escalators.

"Where is this art shop?" Halimah asked.

"Well, it's not actually an art shop here. We are meeting a man who owns an art shop in another part of town. Obviously we can't get to his place without looking suspicious to Uncle and Auntie, so he agreed to meet us here. In fact, here is the place." Rania pointed to a coffee shop up ahead.

"How do you know this is not the same one Uncle Faisal is taking Auntie to?"

"We'll just have to be quick."

They entered the shop and Rania greeted a lanky man with thick-rimmed glasses and a V-neck T-shirt. His sharp features looked Emirati, but he dressed like some American hipster.

"Ah, Rania. How good to see you." He stood, but did not shake her hand. He nodded politely to Halimah. "I am Khalid Ali." Then he turned his attention back to Rania. "Do you have the piece for me?"

"Yes," Rania said. She unrolled the painting and held it for the man, who gasped and reached to take the canvas from her.

"Amazing," he said. His eyes ran eagerly over the entire picture, from edge to edge, from top to bottom. "Hmmm . . . yes . . ." he repeated as he did so. Then he rolled up the canvas and sat it on the table. "And the price?"

Rania handed him a slip of paper, which he unfolded. Halimah anticipated his eyebrows rising and his lip curling in a display of disgust. Isn't that how everyone bargained? Halimah watched many a time how her own mother fussed and complained about the terrible quality of some item, only to get a good deal and go home to brag about what a wonderful purchase she had made.

The man, however, made no reaction except to nod his head and pull out his billfold. He handed Rania the amount in cash.

"*Shukran*," Rania said.

The man nodded and smiled. "Always a pleasure to do business with students from the Arab Art School. And you are said to be one of the best."

Rania grinned and lowered her gaze. Then she grabbed Halimah's hand and they exited the shop.

"How much did you get?" Halimah asked.

"Enough to get us out of here," Rania said. "C'mon let's go. We still have some time before we have to meet for lunch."

The sisters window-shopped, laughing and talking, acting as if meandering the floors of one of the grander malls in the world was the most normal thing for them to do. Rania had visibly relaxed now that she was no longer hiding the painting. Halimah wondered if she regretted parting with such a beautiful picture. It would be stretched back out onto a wooden frame and displayed in a shop across town. Some Arab would buy it and hang it in their home and never even give a thought to the hours of tedious work Rania had put into it. She thought about asking Rania how she felt, but when she saw how happy her younger sister acted, she decided to leave the subject alone.

They met Uncle Faisal and Auntie Badria right on time. After lunch they spent the afternoon walking through the mall, stopping for snacks, and even sitting patiently at a table so Uncle Faisal could try the melon-flavored tobacco in a shisha bar.

Halimah was ready to go home after dinner, but Uncle Faisal was just getting started. When the sun set Uncle was irritated with Auntie Badria for taking so long at one of the *abaya* shops and making them miss the chance to watch the sun cast golden rays across the majestic Dubai skyline. She cheered him up by suggesting they quickly drive to the Dubai Fountain where they would walk along the man-made lake near the Burj Khalifa tower. "If we hurry, we can get there in time for the light and water show."

"Ah yes." Uncle perked up. "Halimah, you must see this spectacle. You know, the Dubai Fountain is the world's largest performing fountain system."

Halimah wanted to roll her eyes like a teenager. If she heard one more superlative about Dubai, she might scream. She decided that this glitzy, ostentatious city was fake . . . almost plastic. Where was the dirt? Where was the sweat? The dirt was covered in cement and the sweat was covered in perfume.

Still, the sale of Rania's artwork could not be considered a success unless they made it through the entire evening without arousing suspicion. So Halimah smiled and said, "I can hardly wait, Uncle."

The following Friday Uncle Faisal and Auntie Badria got their wires crossed and left the girls at home alone. Halimah was sure it had been a mistake by the look in Uncle Faisal's eyes when he realized Auntie had already left to visit her Sudanese friends and he was late for Friday prayers at the mosque.

"I will be back soon," he said to them before he left. "Don't go anywhere while I am gone."

Halimah wondered how he thought they would be able to go anywhere since he locked the door from the outside. She looked at her sister as if to ask her, but Rania just shrugged and said, "He does that every week. Well, I mean, before you got here."

"I can't believe he locks you in."

Rania shrugged again. "What can I say to him? It's just his way."

Halimah shook her head in disbelief. "Well, we can do a lot without leaving. How long do we have?"

"I usually have an hour or two alone; but who knows what they'll do today? We better work quickly. We should try to buy tickets to get out of here."

"Rania, we have no place to go. I think we should pray and wait for the Lord. And while we wait, we should call Auntie Fareeda."

Rania sighed. Trusting God was hard. "OK," she said. "I have her number memorized. We'll call her from my phone and then delete it from the call log."

She dialed the number and waited while it rang. Halimah could hear Auntie Fareeda's reaction when she heard Rania's voice. It made her laugh because, just like Rania had said, their aunt talked so much that Rania hardly had a chance to say anything. When the woman took a breath, Rania jumped in. "I have an answer to your question about Halimah."

Rania smiled and handed the phone to Halimah. "Auntie Fareeda, I hear you have some questions for me."

Her aunt's voice was salve to a heart that had missed family for a long time. Halimah would have listened to any and everything Auntie Fareeda cared to say, just to hear her voice. But time was short, so she kept control of the conversation.

"I know that you are genuinely seeking Allah and that you want to know the truth. I found a loving and forgiving God in the book I was reading. And yes, Auntie, it is the Bible, the holy book of followers of *Isa*. If you are willing, I would like to tell you about it."

To her surprise, Auntie Fareeda agreed and remained quiet as she listened to Halimah tell her about believing in *Isa* as the only way to God and about forgiveness because of *Isa's* death and Resurrection.

"Would you like to pray right now and ask *Isa* to forgive you and be your Savior, Auntie? It means you will be a follower of *Isa* and no longer follow Mohammed. But it also means that you will have a relationship with God, and He will send His Holy Spirit to help you."

"Yes, Halimah, I want to," Auntie Fareeda said in a soft, earnest voice. Halimah told her what to say, and the woman prayed over the phone. Halimah's heart felt like it would burst with joy. There was hope for her family.

When they had prayed, Halimah told her aunt she had to go. "OK, Halimah. But call me again, and next time I will have a pen and paper. I want to write down everything you tell me. There is so much I need to learn."

"Auntie, don't tell anyone just yet about what you have done. You need wisdom from God to know when to talk to your husband or anyone else."

"Yes, Halimah, that is good advice. I will not tell anyone. But I want to talk to you and Rania more. I will look forward to the next time."

"Halimah, wake up."

Halimah felt Rania patting her on the shoulder. She opened her eyes and stared at Rania in confusion. "What's wrong? What time is it?" She looked around the room, trying to remember where she was.

"You need to wake up," Rania whispered. "It's Saturday morning, and I just heard Auntie on the phone. She was talking to Father." Rania mouthed the last word, not even wanting the sound of her whispered voice to say it. "I heard her say something about them coming in two weeks, which is not far away at all. What are we going to do?"

Halimah sat up in bed and rubbed her eyes. "Well," she said, "I can think of two things we can do. First, I will write an email to Mia again, maybe she can help. You remember her, right? She is the American lady in Khartoum who gave you my phone number after I escaped."

"I remember. I hope she can help. What's the second thing?"

"Have you ever fasted as a follower of *Isa*?"

"No. Isn't fasting what we do . . . or did . . . during *Ramadan*? I thought it was a Muslim thing."

"Fasting can be done by Christians too. But it's different. You know that Muslims fast to gain favor with Allah and because it is one of the Five Pillars of Islam. Well, as Christians, we can fast to seek God. It's not about gaining His favor because He loves us already, but it's about seeking His will. And we definitely need to do that. We need God's wisdom."

≫ Chapter 29 ≪
Dallas, Texas

If Mia was going to have to live in America, she might as well live like an American. She would get rid of her long skirts and buy something cute. She could join the gym. Nancy offered to bring her as a guest to her yoga class. The same one Marsha went to. Mia even purchased exercise clothes and a matching pair of tennis shoes.

Nancy honked when she pulled up to Mia's parents' house and Mia winced. They weren't teenagers anymore. She really needed to ask Nancy to quit honking. There were other people in this neighborhood after all.

"I'm gone, Mom," she hollered up the steps to where her mother and the kids were watching Saturday morning cartoons. Then she grabbed her purse and ran out the door. She had decided to wear her exercise clothes to the gym like Nancy did, only Mia hadn't worn such a little amount of clothing since the day in Khartoum when she'd worn a pair of shorts in her front yard, not realizing that Habiib would come in the front gate and see her. But this was the United States. No one cared here.

However, as Mia walked to Nancy's car, she felt exposed. What was she thinking wearing skin-tight pants and a flimsy T-shirt in public like this? Plus, her hair was falling down around her shoulders and blowing in the breeze. She never let her hair down in Sudan; it was too provocative. She was relieved to hide in the passenger seat of Nancy's car.

"Morning," Nancy said. "You look adorable."

"I feel like a loose woman." Mia pulled at her yoga pants, trying to make them stretch.

"Don't do that." Nancy slapped at her hand. "They fit you great. You look fabulous. Really."

Mia curled a strand of hair around her finger and frowned. "People shouldn't dress like this in public."

Nancy laughed and put her car in drive. "You'll get used to it."

Marsha met them at the gym. She came running up and gave Mia a bear hug. "I heard you aren't going back to Africa." She pulled away and held Mia's hands in hers. "I know you must be so relieved. You know . . ." she leaned in close, as if sharing a secret. "Maybe the Lord just wanted to know that you were *willing* to go back. Now that He knows you are willing, He will let you stay." She smiled brightly.

"Maybe," Mia choked out the words. "Y'all go ahead to class. I've gotta go to the bathroom. I'll meet you there." Mia turned and walked to the ladies' room as quickly as she could. She stood at the sink and splashed cold water on her face.

A few moments later Nancy opened the door and peeked in. "You OK?" Mia had just washed away a flood of tears, but a new barrage of them trickled down her cheeks. "She just doesn't get it, Mia."

"I *wanted* to go back, Nancy. And, no, I am *not* relieved. My life has been ripped away from me."

"But you can have a life here."

"I don't want a life here," Mia groaned. She sounded like a spoiled child, but she didn't care. "I can't do this right now, Nancy. Tell Marsha I'll see her at church on Sunday."

"You don't have a car."

"I'll call Mom."

"Mia—" Nancy started to speak and then stopped and shook her head.

"What Nancy? I know you want to say something."

"It's just . . . you seem so willing to adapt to Sudanese culture for the sake of sharing the love of Jesus there. Why aren't you willing to do the same here?"

Mia grabbed her purse and brushed past Nancy without a word. She left the gym and stood on the sidewalk outside, wondering what to do next. She called her mother and then sat on the curb to wait.

In Sudan I'd be able to hail down a rickshaw or even one of those decrepit taxis. It's ridiculous how this town doesn't have public transportation.

Michael returned from Khartoum bringing two suitcases brimming with sand-encrusted toys from the kids' room and the two pictures Mia had requested. She'd had the good sense to email him after he left and ask him to bring her teakettle and two tribal daggers.

Mia unwrapped the drawing from Rania and traced her fingers along the sides of the depiction of a door. What did the Lord mean by pulling them out of Sudan? Was He truly in control of all things or had something slipped His notice?

It didn't matter now. The Sudanese government had canceled their work visas. Michael had sold or given away all their belongings, which hadn't taken long because the Kellar Hope office had supplied their furnishings. The Sudanese staff that was working at the office would sell all the foundation's assets and close the office for good within a couple of weeks.

"Abbas and Widad wanted to send a gift for the kids," Michael told Mia. "But it was a bird. I tried to describe international travel to them, but Widad still didn't grasp what sorts of things could be brought on a plane."

"Sweet Widad," Mia said. "What did you do with the bird?"

"I gave it to Habiib. He was happy to bring it home for his own children. Oh, and here is a gift from Hanaan."

Mia opened the typical black plastic bag and found homemade incense and a beautiful silk *tobe*. At the bottom of the bag was a note.

Dear Mia,

I am so sad to hear the news that you will not come back. May Allah bless you and your children. I want you to know I cherish all the conversations we had. Please pray for me. The things you shared with me about your beliefs are things I think about a lot, and they make me want to know even more. Thank you for always showing me love.

—Hanaan

Mia's eyes filled with tears while she folded the letter and placed it in her Bible to remind her how the Lord often worked in ways she couldn't see. She was glad the Lord hadn't let her give up on talking about Jesus around Hanaan.

Following Michael's return from Sudan, he took the week off. He spent the first day perusing car magazines and websites for car lots. The second day, he and Mia chose two cars to buy. On day three, Michael announced it was time for apartment hunting.

"We need to find a place halfway between your parents' home and Kellar Hope Foundation," he said.

"We need to find a place that is big enough for our family and is in a good school district," Mia added.

Eventually, they found an apartment that met both sets of criteria and even had a pool, which made the kids happy.

Now that the Westons were living in America, not just visiting, Mia had different shopping priorities. She purchased a pair of capris and several short-sleeved blouses. She found a sale on curtains and splurged to buy a set for the kitchen of their new apartment. The sunny yellow color added cheer and made her smile. This is where she spent the first half-hour of each morning—reading her Bible and drinking her coffee.

Over the next few days, Mia distracted herself by unpacking all the things they'd put in storage during their time away. She poured herself into decorating her new home and everything looked so . . . American . . . except for Rania's drawing that hung on the wall behind the sofa. Every day it reminded her how far away she was from her life in Sudan.

"Mom, can you pick up the kids for Sunday School tomorrow?" Mia twisted a curl of hair around her finger nervously. There was a long pause. She had guessed this would not be easy. While they were living with Mia's parents it had been easy to send the kids off with her mother to attend Sunday School. Michael and Mia had used Sunday mornings to relax before heading to the late service at Grace Community Church.

"Mia, I think you and Michael should attend Sunday School."

"It's just . . . kind of hard right now, Mom. We're dealing with a lot of stuff."

"I know you are. But you need a community."

Mia sighed. "Fine, Mom. We'll take them ourselves."

"And go to Sunday School?"

"I don't know. Maybe."

She said goodbye and hung up the phone, then looked at Michael, who was sitting at the kitchen table with the kids, eating a bowl of cereal.

"Sounds like we need to go to Sunday School," he said, gulping the last spoonful and wiping his mouth with a napkin.

"Yay! Mom and Dad are going to Sunday School with us," Corey said.

"Why didn't you go before?" Annie asked. Her golden curls bounced around the bow in her hair as she looked from Michael to Mia.

"That's a hard one to answer, princess," Michael said. "Your mom and I have been pretty tired. We needed some time to rest. But now we are ready, so in the morning, we'll all go together as a family. But today is Saturday, so who wants to go to the park?"

The three kids yelled "Me!" in unison. They quickly brought their cereal bowls to the kitchen sink and then hurried to their rooms to find their shoes. Mia waited until they were out of earshot before she spoke.

"Nice save, Michael. We've never really talked about it. Now that I stop to think about it, why haven't we gone to Sunday School?"

Michael shrugged. "It's just one more big jump from Sudan to America. Maybe we've been pacing ourselves. I don't think it was wrong to rest, to wait until the church service and worship corporately, but I think your mom is right. It's probably time we actually join the church and not just attend."

"I guess you're right. I'm nervous. I don't feel like I can relate."

"We'll go to the couples class so we can go together."

Mia smiled. "I'd like that."

Chapter 30
Dallas, Texas

On Sunday morning the Westons loaded into Michael's car and headed toward Grace Community.

Michael wore a long-sleeved dress shirt and a tie.

"You look handsome in your American clothes, dear."

Michael smiled. "You look pretty good yourself."

Mia looked down at her dry-clean-only dress and her heels. It was easy to look clean and neat in a land with central air-conditioning. Mia had even started wearing makeup again, which she never did in Sudan since it melted right off her face.

"I'm glad you are coming to Sunday School," Dylan said as he buckled himself into a booster seat in the back of the sedan. "You can talk to my teacher Mrs. Carnegie. She says I tell stories that aren't true."

"Dylan, what have you been talking about in class?" Michael asked.

"We are learning about Bible stories, like Moses and Noah."

"Yes, I know that. But what are *you* talking about in class?"

"Just stuff. Mrs. Carnegie says I need to remember what is real and what is make-believe. But one time she said I was telling make-believe stories when I was telling a real one."

"What story were you telling?"

"I told about going inside a pyramid. Mrs. Carnegie was kind of mad because all the kids asked me questions and I just told them all about it. Do you think she was mad because I went inside a pyramid without an adult?"

"She probably just doesn't know that you really did go to a pyramid. She thinks you were making it up."

Dylan rolled his eyes, "But, Daddy, everyone has been to the pyramids."

Michael laughed. "No, Dylan. Not everyone has been to the pyramids. I bet most people don't even know that Sudan has pyramids. Most people think of Egypt."

"I have some pictures we took when we were there," Mia said. "Probably even a picture of you inside one. Why don't I print some out and let you take them next Sunday? You could show them to Mrs. Carnegie, and maybe she'll let you show them to the class."

"Yes, let's do that." Dylan smiled.

"Mom," Annie said, "I was crying last week because a girl in my class got mad at me when I spoke Arabic to her. She said I was making fun of her. I just forgot, Mom. She is African American, but I forgot, and my mind told me she was Sudanese. So I started talking to her in Arabic."

"What did she do?" Mia asked.

"She told the teacher I was being mean. But I don't think I was because I don't even know why it's mean. I was just trying to be her friend."

Mia glanced at Michael. This was so hard. She wanted to make everything easy, at least for her kids. She just wanted to go back to Sudan where, oddly enough, things suddenly seemed simpler.

She was thankful that Michael spoke up first. "It just takes a while for all of us to get used to things here. We have to be patient with ourselves and with others."

Michael parked the car near the children's wing of the church building, and they walked together through the double doors held open by two greeters.

"Well, good morning Weston family. Long time, no see. Good to have you home!" The tall man holding one of the doors was Mr. Collins. He'd been working in the children's Sunday School department for years. "Let's see here," he said, digging in his trouser pocket. "I believe I have a little something for each of you. . . . ahhh, here they are." He pulled out three pieces of candy and handed them out to the children. They smiled and thanked him before walking inside and nearly disappearing into the packed hallway.

Children and parents bustled around, calling greetings to each other and signing in to the various classrooms.

"Why don't you take Corey, and I'll take the younger two," Michael suggested.

Mia nodded and turned to try to keep up with Corey who was already darting down to the far end of the wing where the older children's classes were located.

"This is my class, Mom. See you afterward," Corey said, slipping through the door and high-fiving one of the boys who had already arrived. The lady standing at the door, who Mia guessed was the teacher, reached out her hand and smiled.

"You must be Corey's mom. I'm Amanda. It's so nice to meet you. We have so enjoyed having Corey in our class. He is a great kid."

Mia shook her hand and smiled. "Thank you. It's nice to meet you too." Mia stood at the doorway and talked to Amanda until Michael finished signing Annie and Dylan in to their Sunday School classes. Then she thanked Amanda, and they made their way to the adult wing to attend the couples class.

Mia had forgotten how friendly everyone was at church. Of course everyone had been friendly when they attended services the past few weeks, but they had never stayed around long enough to really get into conversations. But in Sunday School, the couples greeted them and made sure they had coffee, donuts, and a good place to sit.

Mia leaned over to Michael and whispered in his ear. "Texans can be just about as hospitable as Arabs."

"Michael and Mia Weston!" Nancy laughed in delight as she made her way down the row of chairs and plopped herself next to Mia. "Oh, I am so excited you are here. Marsha and her husband will be coming too. And I'll save a seat right here for Bill." Nancy put her purse on the seat beside her and leaned over to Mia. "Things are going better with him, Mia. He's even coming to church every Sunday now."

Mia gave her friend's hand a squeeze. "I'm so glad."

"Hey, I'm taking Marsha's and my kids to the Dallas Zoo tomorrow. Why don't you let me take yours? They would have a blast."

"Wow, that would be great. That would give me some time to finish getting settled in the apartment and do some shopping."

"Perfect. Drop them off in the morning, and I'll bring them back in the afternoon."

Nancy put her arm around Mia and gave her a side hug. Mia smiled. Maybe she could really enjoy being here. Joy was possible again.

After church and lunch out with Mia's parents, the Westons returned to the apartment to rest. As Mia lay on the sofa flipping through channels on TV, she began to think about Halimah, who was also having to learn to live in new places. Had she decided to move to Dubai?

Mia took her laptop from the kitchen counter and turned it on. Perhaps Halimah had been able to email her. Mia scanned her inbox. No email from Halimah. Mia spotted an email address she didn't recognize. The subject line said "Tzega." Could it be from her former house helper? She had left her email address with Tzega when they left, just in case Tzega needed to contact her about a problem with the house. And, of course, Michael had met her on his return trip in order to pay her and tell her they would not be coming back.

But Mia hadn't really expected Tzega to contact her. She was pretty sure Tzega didn't know how to use a computer. She must have had someone take her to an internet café and help her. Maybe her husband? Mia opened the email.

Der Mia,

My fater now wit Jesus. Ples pray for us. Ples also pray for prison gards. They do not no ower Jesus. Thank yo.

—Tzega

Mia stared at the computer screen. Even with the misspelled words, the message was clear. Dazed, Mia searched the words *Eritrean pastors* on the Internet. She wanted more information. The search brought up numerous news articles about imprisoned pastors. Mia didn't see the name of Tzega's father, but, according to the articles, hundreds had been arrested by the Eritrean government. Tzega's father was unknown to the world, yet Tzega's family had suffered so much for the name of Christ.

"I should be there," Mia said out loud. How could she sit in her comfortable American home on her comfortable American sofa, in her cute American clothes, when people in Africa were literally dying for their faith? The least she could do was be there for Tzega. Tzega had lost her job because Mia didn't come back, and now she had lost her father.

Mia shut her laptop and put it in the bottom drawer of the dresser in her bedroom. No more email. She couldn't bear any more bad news. She wouldn't check her email anymore. Her heart couldn't take it.

On Monday morning Mia planned to go shopping. It was just a simple trip to the grocery store. Mia made a list, and all she had to do was buy the items written on the paper. There was nothing unusual on the list, just the normal things anyone would buy for their family.

Two weeks had gone by since Mia had made a proper shopping trip because she had become lazy and relied on her mother, Michael, or sometimes Nancy to pick up things while they were out.

But today was the day she was going to shed her longing for Sudan and embrace her new life in America.

After she waved goodbye to Michael as he left for work, then dropped the kids off at Nancy's, she drove to the grocery store. She pulled into a parking spot that apparently some other lady had her eye on, because the lady honked and yelled at her as she drove by. Then she left her purse in the car, and after having walked halfway to the store, had to turn around and go back to get it.

Once inside the store, she retrieved a shopping cart from the front of the store and pulled out her list. Every item seemed to have five to ten options. Cheese crackers. Do you want giant size, regular size? Cheddar cheese or white cheese? Rainbow colored or original colored? Detergent. Do you want scented or original? Powder or liquid or tablets? Whitening or stain guard or recommended by skin doctors or original? Frozen chicken or fresh? Bones or boneless? Free range or organic or farm raised? She started to get dizzy. In Sudan she wouldn't have this many choices, and it wouldn't take nearly so long.

She pushed her cart down the aisle toward the frozen section. This part of the store was so cold it was a miracle snow didn't fall from the ceiling. She wondered how much the electric bill was. Then she wondered how many poor Sudanese families could be fed with the extra money if the store would just use less air-conditioning. Didn't they know people in other countries were struggling just to find their next meal?

By the time Mia got to the checkout counter, she was mad at everyone. She found herself looking into the shopping carts of the others in line and counting up the wasteful items. Candy bars? *Frivolous.* Magazine? *Ridiculous.* Toys? *Why?* The kids in Africa have to make their own toys out of trash.

Mia was a ball of nerves when she arrived at the apartment complex. As she pulled into her parking spot, she remembered the lady who honked and yelled at her. Why had that lady gotten so worked up over a place to park when people were dying in Sudan? Mia could feel heat emanating from her face and anger filling her heart.

As she opened her trunk, she saw her mother walking toward her.

"Mom, good morning. What are you doing here?"

"I just came for a visit because I could. We haven't had you living so close in such a long time." Her mother smiled and began to gather some of the grocery bags from Mia's trunk.

"Why don't you come in for a glass of tea? Let's unload this stuff and then we can visit."

They unloaded the groceries, and Mia's mom helped her organize them in the kitchen. Then Mia made them each a large glass of iced tea and they sat at the kitchen table. It wasn't Mom's back porch, but it was good enough. The window off the kitchen looked out over a small garden and let in enough sun to brighten the room.

"How are the kids doing with the idea of not going back to Sudan?"

Mia took a sip of tea. "Better, I think. Once school starts it will take some getting used to, I'm sure."

"How about Michael?"

"Oh, he loves his job. He's helping the foundation come up with ways to be more intentional about sharing Christ and is talking about adding a division that gives out Bibles in various countries. Sounds exciting, right?"

"And how about you?"

"Me? Well, you know. I just miss Sudan. I wish I had a chance to say goodbye. I worry about all my friends there who won't hear any more about Jesus because we aren't there."

"You think you are the only one who can tell them?"

"Well, technically no. But in some cases I am the only Christian they know. And then what about Abbas and Widad? We met with them all the time to disciple them, and they are really hurting right now because their neighbors and friends are deserting them. What will they do now that we are gone? And people here, Mom, they just don't understand. Marsha talks about all sorts of things that don't matter, and I just want to grab her by the shoulders and say, 'Marsha, people in Sudan are dying without Jesus, so what does it matter what color your floor rug is?'"

"This is more than just about a rug, Mia. What's really wrong?"

Mia sighed and looked outside. "I just got some news about Tzega. Her dad died in prison. I just can't reconcile in my mind how this can be fair. I feel so helpless. I should have been there for her."

Mia let the tears flow freely, and her mother listened as Mia poured out everything in her heart. It had been a long time since Mia felt close to her mother. She never would have guessed that now, when she struggled for someone to understand, it would be her own mother, the one who hadn't even wanted them to move to Sudan in the first place.

"Mia, God is merciful," her mother said as she gave Mia a long hug. "He will take care of you, and He will take care of those you left in Sudan."

God is merciful. What a strange thing to say. Muslims said it all the time: *'illa 'irrahiim*. She had always felt the words were tossed around like an excuse. Hanaan had used it several times when Mia asked her, "Do you think you will go to heaven?"

But this was different. These were words from her mother's mouth. And they were true. God is merciful. Even when she couldn't see it in the circumstances around her.

"You are trying to deal with things in your own strength, Mia. God has strength and rest and peace to offer you, but you have to be willing to let go."

"That's the thing, Mom. I don't want to let go. God sent us to Sudan to show Jesus' love, and so we did. Why would He take away those friendships and opportunities now? Did we do something wrong?"

"Mia, God called you to go there and you obeyed. Now He has called you to come here. After all you have been through with Him, are you going to disobey Him now?"

"But what about our work there? What about Abbas and Widad? What about Hanaan? And . . ." A tear streamed down Mia's cheek. "What about Tzega?"

"It never was *your* work, Mia. It was—it is—God's work."

Mom was right again. It wasn't Mia's work. And therefore it wasn't hers to hold.

"I want to show you something." Mia pulled a map out from her Bible on the counter. She spread it out on the kitchen table and ran her fingers across the highlighted areas of the neighborhoods where she had driven and prayed during her time in Khartoum. "This is my prayer map, Mom." She pointed to the names she had written in the margin. "Tesfalem" was highlighted with the note "with Jesus" that she had added since receiving the email from Tzega.

She watched as her mom looked at the map with interest. She placed her hand at each highlighted area, smiling. "Since I've never been to Sudan, I like getting to see what your old home and neighborhood look like."

Mia sniffled and then smiled. "It's much less hot and dusty this way."

Her mom smiled and gave Mia a hug. "You're going to be fine, Mia. God is in control. He's with you here in Texas, and He's still in control in Sudan. His mercy never fails."

⇒ Chapter 31 ⇐
Dallas, Texas

Sundance Square in downtown Fort Worth offered family friendly entertainment on a warm summer Saturday. Historic buildings lined redbrick streets. Signs painted on the windowpanes or hanging outside doors advertised boutiques, art galleries, coffee shops, and restaurants. The plaza offered live music in the evenings. But in the daytime, one feature in particular attracted families with children.

The splash pads began at nine in the morning, so the Westons drove over from Dallas early and were sitting at a nearby umbrella table ten minutes beforehand. Corey was not sure if he was too cool for the splash pads or not, so he brought a library book to read just in case. The younger two, however, were clad in swim shorts and shirts and slathered in sun lotion. Michael had offered to pick up coffees at a nearby coffee shop, and now he and Mia sat together and watched Dylan and Annie do cartwheels and somersaults on the rubber padding of the splash pads.

"Wouldn't it have been great to have something like this in Khartoum?" Mia asked.

"We had Child City," Michael answered with a sly grin on his face.

Mia laughed. "Oh, Child City. You mean the park with the broken swings and the dangerous minicoaster and the old Ferris wheel which would fail even a half-hearted safety inspection?"

"But remember all the fun the kids had there? Once we got over the fact that it was dirty and dangerous, it was really pretty entertaining."

Annie and Dylan squealed as spouts of water began to shoot in the air from various points around the splash pads. They ran from hole to hole laughing. Dylan tried to guess which one would spit out water while Annie tried to guess which one wouldn't. After only a few minutes of fake-reading his book, Corey left it on his chair and joined his siblings and a few other children whose parents were looking for a free Saturday morning activity.

"You know, the other day Mom asked me a question and it really made me think about my attitude toward God. 'After all you have been through with Him, are you going to disobey Him now?' That's what she asked. I have been pushing against the Lord, even though He clearly brought us here."

"It's a hard transition," Michael said.

"What about you? Do you want to be here?"

"At first I didn't. I wasn't sure that the home office really had a place for me. I mean, my old position was already filled."

Mia winced. "Yeah, and you didn't have a lot of support from home either. Sorry, Michael, I haven't been myself lately."

Michael reached over and gave her shoulder a squeeze. "It's OK, Mia. We've all been dealing with the move in our own ways. I haven't been myself either. I mean, I even checked all the phones at work for wire taps, and I know I've been pretty impatient with everyone."

"Well, what changed it for you?"

"The opportunities I see here. I think God is working here just like He is in Sudan. When Dr. Kellar asked me to develop a department that distributes Bibles and helps believers, I felt pretty overwhelmed. What do I know about stuff like that? But then I got an idea."

"Oh?"

"Remember the letter Halimah wrote to Widad to encourage her in her faith?"

"I remember. It really helped Widad to know there was someone else with a similar background."

"Right. Well, Halimah is someone who knows how to help believers. She needs a place to go, right? What if we ask Dr. Kellar to invite her and her sister Rania here to help with the work?"

"Here? You think Dr. Kellar would go for it?"

"I don't know for sure, but I put together a pretty convincing proposal."

"I don't know if they could even get visas to enter the United States. Could they maybe get some sort of refugee status?"

"You are asking all the same questions I've been asking myself. But this morning I read a verse in the Bible that set my heart at ease." Michael pulled a piece of paper from his pocket and read his messy handwriting. "*Psalm 77:14: You are the God who performs miracles.* This statement was true about God back when the psalm was written, but it is also true for us today. We saw many miracles in Sudan, you know? I think God still wants to perform miracles, even here in America."

Mia thought about how Michael reading the Scripture and applying it to their lives was a miracle. He only began truly reading and applying the Bible since moving to Sudan. Both of them had only begun seeing the Bible as relevant since Sudan.

So yes, God was indeed the God who performed miracles. She had trusted Him in so many situations in Sudan. Now Michael was challenging her to trust God again, but this time in Texas. Was God big enough to overcome the impossibilities of getting these two young Arab girls into the United States?

"I think it's a great idea," Mia said. "I could help too. Maybe figure out where they could live, help them get used to life in America."

"You'd be the one to do it." Michael grinned. "You've been learning that yourself."

"If you feel like this idea is from God, there's got to be a way for it to work. You said it already: He is a God who performs miracles."

Mia's heart danced with excitement at the possibility of Michael's idea. God showed His mercy again. She hadn't gone through all the pain of reentry for nothing. Perhaps the Lord was using all of it to prepare her for what He had next. And yes, it was bigger than Sudan, although Sudan was part of it. He was still using her to reach others with His love. In Sudan, in the United States . . . the location was semantics really.

Mia sipped the last of her coffee and her mind whirled at top speed. But it wasn't the caffeine. Mia realized she wasn't sidelined or out of the game at all. In fact, she never had been.

Mia sat on a park bench and looked out over the water. The blue sky, reflected by the crystal water of the pond before her, looked like a painting. The cotton-ball clouds were as white as freshly bleached *jallabeeyas*. A little family of ducks huddled in the shade under a tree nearby. The grass around her and growing up the hill beyond the pond was greener than anything she ever remembered seeing in Sudan.

She looked down at the journal in her lap and read over the verse written at the top of the page.

Have mercy on me, my God, have mercy on me, for in you I take refuge. I will take refuge in the shadow of your wings until the disaster has passed. I cry out to God Most High, to God, who vindicates me.

—Psalm 57:1–2

Taking her pen, she wrote an entry just under the verses:

I am seeing the importance of trusting God and of not being in control— letting go of many things. It's OK for things to be confusing and out of my control. It's OK to not know the answers—not be able to figure it all out.

Jesus Christ is the pure sacrifice. I don't have to be perfect before I enter His presence, before I present myself to Him as a sacrifice.

Jesus is my pure and perfect sacrifice. I can give myself today . . . now.

It's not about Sudan. It's about the world. God has bigger plans than what I had imagined.

Mia looked up at the scenery again and smiled. Texas had its own unique beauty. The same God who had created the grand desert in Sudan also created the vibrant colors of Texas. He loved them equally because He loved the people who lived in them equally. And so should she.

Nancy approached from behind. "Hey, Mia, what's up with meeting at the park?" Mia turned and looked at her friend. A good friend who stuck around even when Mia was unkind in return.

Nancy wore her workout clothes and carried a bottle of water. Her name-brand sunglasses covered her eyes and made her look like a giant bug. In spite of that she still looked attractive. Mia would never wear workout clothes in public again, but she decided a great pair of sunglasses was not a terrible idea, and maybe she should buy some too.

"Hey, friend," Mia said, giving Nancy a hug as she sat down next to her. "Where's Marsha?"

"She's coming," Nancy said. "She's in the car finishing up a call with the contractor who is building her kitchen cabinets. She was afraid to say anything about it to you."

When Marsha joined them, Mia sat up straight and smiled at her. "Marsha, how is the progress in your kitchen?"

Marsha glanced at Nancy with a questioning look. "Oh, fine. No biggie, you know."

"No, it is a big deal. I know you have great taste. I'd love to see your house sometime. And actually, maybe you could give me some tips on what to look for in a new house. You know, Michael and I are looking to buy."

Marsha lifted her own pair of name-brand sunglasses and looked at Mia. "Really? I'd love to. I have a great real estate agent I could introduce you to. And I could work on a list of do's and don'ts."

Mia smiled. "That would be great. Thanks, Marsha. Now, I guess you are wondering why I wanted to meet at the park." Both ladies nodded. "Well," Mia said, standing up and facing them. "Look around you. See how many ladies come out here to walk? What if we came out and walked, but prayed as well. A prayerwalk. We might even get to meet some of these ladies."

Nancy and Marsha looked around the pond. The jogging track was busy with moms pushing strollers and other ladies jogging or walking.

"I don't know, Mia." Marsha looked hesitant. "These ladies don't look like they want anyone stopping them to talk."

"Then we'll just pray for them as we see them. We have to start somewhere."

"I like the gym better," Marsha said.

Nancy jumped in. "Hey, why not both? Marsha and I will start praying for the ladies in the class at the gym, and Mia and I can walk here at the park. Mia can show me how to do this prayerwalking thing. Once I learn how to do it, I'll teach you, Marsha. I think Mia is on to something: God has big plans for the ladies in this city."

"Sure, I can do that," Marsha said. "You know, Mia, I thought sharing Jesus with others was more like passing out Bibles, holding some sort of big meeting, or knocking on the doors of strangers. But you're talking about meeting people we run across in our daily lives and praying for them or serving them. I never realized I could be doing something like that too. I mean, right here where I live."

Mia nodded. "Yeah, it took going all the way to Africa for me to learn how I could do the same things right here too. I am learning that wherever we are, people need Jesus."

After stopping for a smoothie with Marsha and Nancy, Mia drove home. On the way, she thought about the conversation she'd had with her two friends.

A new chapter was beginning. The Sudan chapter was over, at least the chapter that involved the Westons living there. Mia hadn't wanted the chapter to end but she couldn't change that. Funny thing was she wouldn't want to now. Nancy and Marsha were just starting to learn how to be a light for Jesus, right there in their own lives, and Mia had so much to offer in the way of helping them. But Mia had a lot to learn from those two ladies too.

Mia pulled into the apartment complex with an hour to spare before her mom would be bringing the kids home from baking cookies at her house. It was the perfect amount of time for a nap. As she walked down the sidewalk toward the apartment, her phone beeped. She checked the text message: Michael was asking her to check their email. Her heart beat hard against her rib cage. The last time she used her computer, she had found the email from Tzega. What could have happened now? She opened the apartment door and flipped on the light. She glanced at the verse she'd posted on one of the kitchen cabinet doors.

They will have no fear of bad news; their hearts are steadfast, trusting in the LORD.

—Psalm 112:7

Mia quoted the verse to herself as she walked to her bedroom and opened the bottom drawer of her dresser. She stared at the laptop. *They will have no fear of bad news; their hearts are steadfast, trusting in the Lord.*

Mia took a deep breath and pulled her laptop out of the drawer. She turned it on and opened her email. She immediately saw the email Michael referred to. It was from "Sara." Mia smiled. Halimah had written them. They knew she had been trying to leave Kenya, but didn't know for sure what had happened in the end.

Dear Michael and Mia,

I am in Dubai with my sister. We are happy to be reunited. But now we see it is no longer safe to stay here. We are unsure where to go, but my parents are coming in just two weeks so we must find a new place to live. Please pray that we will have wisdom to know what to do.

We both yearn for our home country and our family, but we do not think the Lord wants us to return there right now. But where does He want us to go? We have to leave quickly. Please pray for us.

Pray also for our uncle and auntie here in Dubai. They are caught up in trying to look wealthy for their friends and family. They have a lot of debt, and it makes them stressed. They need to hear about *Isa* so they can have peace.

Thank you my brother and sister,
Sara

Mia called Michael at the office.

"Don't worry," he said. "The plan is already in motion. I have received approval from the office, and Kellar Hope Foundation has extended an invitation to Halimah and Rania."

"Oh honey, I am so relieved. How soon can they get here?"

"Well, as soon as they can get tickets they can come. Dr. Kellar has connections and can get them here as visitors first, and then they will apply for a longer term visa. It will be limited, but Dr. Kellar told me there is a definite possibility he would be able to offer a work contract to both of them."

Mia emailed Halimah several times throughout the week to arrange details for travel. Every time she hit *send* on an email, she prayed that Halimah's uncle would not discover her email account. In spite of his tight grip on Halimah and Rania, he had not thought about the possibility of them communicating with anyone over the Internet. This was, of course, a miracle.

Mia could hardly wait for the two young ladies to arrive. She counted down the days. She made welcome signs with the children. She recounted down the days in case she'd made a mistake the first time.

The kids were almost as ecstatic as Mia. Corey remembered Halimah well. "She taught me a lot of Arabic," he said. "I hope she will teach me more." Annie remembered how she liked having another girl in the house. Dylan remembered how much he loved having Halimah sleep in their room with them.

When Halimah first came to live with the Westons in Khartoum, she had not wanted to sleep alone. Mia did not understand Sudanese culture as well back then. She did not realize most Sudanese girls would be scared to sleep alone, and to them it was much better to share a room. Mia had taken extra effort to provide Halimah with a room to herself, but it didn't take long for Halimah to pull the mattress off her bed and drag it to the children's room.

"Will she bring her mattress into my room again, Mommy?" Dylan asked.

"Not this time, sweetie. Her sister is coming with her. She won't be alone."

Mia hadn't told the kids anything about the risk that Halimah and Rania were taking. Michael and Mia had done all they could from their end, but now it was up to Halimah and Rania. Mia prayed that God would make a way for them to be able to leave their aunt and uncle's house.

⮬ Chapter 32 ⮪
Dubai, UAE

I can't believe we are going to America, Halimah. Did you ever imagine? The invitation to work with your friends in Texas is . . . more than I ever dreamed of. We will be free to follow *Isa,* and we will be free to call Auntie Fareeda whenever we want." Rania put the last folded blouse into her suitcase and shut it. She turned to look across the room at her sister, who was supposed to be finishing her packing as well. But Halimah just sat there on her bed, staring at the floor. "Halimah, what's wrong? This is an amazing opportunity. Why do you look so concerned?"

"There is something we have to do."

"I know, I know. I will make sure I have cleaned out the closets completely and that I haven't left a Bible or anything here. There isn't anything left to hide. I mean, Uncle already took away my phone and computer. I'm just glad we got the tickets before he did."

"No, Rania." Halimah picked up her own copy of the Bible and thumbed through the pages thoughtfully before looking up at her sister. "We have to tell Uncle Faisal and Auntie Badria."

"Yes, we agreed already. We'll work on a note together and we'll leave it on the dining table before going. We are lucky they left us alone again today. I guess neither Auntie nor Uncle wanted to give up their Friday schedule to stay here and guard us. This really is the perfect time for us to slip away without making a scene. But we need to hurry; we don't have long."

"Rania. We have to tell them about *Isa.*"

"In the note?"

"No, in person."

"What? Halimah, what you are saying is crazy. Father and Mama are on their way any day now. If we tell Uncle Faisal and Auntie Badria about *Isa* and that we believe in Him, they'll lock us in this room until Father comes. And don't you think they won't."

"But Rania, if they don't hear the truth from us, who will they hear it from? I think this is what God wants us to do. I think we need to trust Him with what happens after that. Do not forget what *Isa* has said, 'Do not be afraid of those who kill the body but cannot kill the soul.' Rania, we have so much more than they do."

Rania's mind flashed back to a day two years earlier. Halimah was bruised after a beating from their father and older brother. Her hair was raggedly cut short and she wore an old house dress because all of her stylish clothes had been burned. Halimah's last words to Rania before she walked out the door that day echoed in her mind. "Rania, don't worry about me. *Isa* is taking care of me. Remember, you must get the book that is hidden and read it. It is the best news you will ever read about."

Halimah had been right back then, and in spite of how crazy it sounded, Halimah was right today as well.

"All right, we will tell them. But they won't let us leave, Halimah. You know that, right?"

"I have an idea." Halimah held up a key and said, "I found an extra door key. Come on, let's get our bags downstairs. The taxi will be here any minute."

Halimah didn't tell Rania what her plan was, and Rania had the feeling her older sister was putting on her best acting skills to keep a calm demeanor.

The pink taxi the young women ordered arrived, and they loaded their suitcases into the trunk. Then Halimah convinced the driver to park in the side parking lot and wait for them. She handed the lady a handful of bills and said, "I will pay you the rest when we come back."

Then they went back up to the apartment to wait. Rania felt it was the longest 15 minutes of her life. But then, when she heard her uncle's footsteps in the hallway, she wished it had been longer.

Rania and Halimah stood together by the door when Uncle Faisal and Auntie Badria walked in.

"Hello Uncle, Auntie," Halimah began bravely. Rania forced a little smile. Halimah continued talking before the couple had a chance to respond or go their separate ways: Uncle to his chair to light his water pipe and Auntie to the kitchen to make him tea. "Rania and I have something we want to tell you. This is dear to our hearts, and I ask for you to hear us out before you respond. Please, will you sit down?" Halimah gestured toward the ornate dining table just inside the front door.

Confused, Uncle Faisal and Auntie Badria pulled out the carved dining chairs and sat down. Rania, for one, was too nervous to sit, and when she looked over to Halimah, she noticed her sister was too. Halimah stood beside a chair opposite the table from the couple, but she simply grabbed the back of the chair instead of sitting in it.

"We want you to know that we both believe in *Isa*, but we want to tell you why. *Isa* is the only way to know for sure your sins are fully forgiven. We can see how you are diligent to pray and to give to the poor and to attend the mosque."

This was not entirely true. Rania had not seen much religious activity from the couple for the whole year she had lived with them. Except for Uncle Faisal's weekly trip to the mosque, the couple didn't show much piety. But Halimah was speaking to them in a respectful way, the way a young person should.

"We know you do these things so one day, *insha' Allah*, God will forgive you. But what if you do many good things but never enough to outweigh the bad? We are all human. We can never conquer all the sin in our lives.

"But *Isa* lived a sinless life. You know that, Uncle. You believe what the *Qur'an* says about Him, I know you do. Did you know that because He was sinless, He was the perfect one to take the punishment for our sins? He is the Son of God, and He is the only one who can forgive us. We believe it, Uncle. We believe *Isa*, Auntie."

Rania looked at her aunt and uncle. They sat stunned in their chairs, as if they had just seen a ghost. Suddenly she was not afraid of them anymore. She saw them for what they were—lost souls who were seeking peace and love and finding neither one. They were in need of forgiveness. In need of *Isa*. Rania's heart ached for them.

"I see," Uncle said. A vein popped out on his forehead. He was obviously trying to restrain himself. He stood, a little too quickly, and his chair fell backward on the floor behind him.

"Please, Uncle," Halimah held her hand forward and Rania thought at first she was trying to stop him from coming toward her. But then she saw Halimah was pointing to the table and to the small book she'd left there. "Please, I am giving you this book. It is a Bible. Please read it before you decide if we are right or wrong. Don't just take our word for it."

"Never," Uncle Faisal yelled. Rania thought the vein on his forehead might pop. She'd only seen this much anger one time before. The night Halimah told Father she was a Christian. But Uncle Faisal did not act in the same way. Instead, he turned and stormed down the hall toward the master bedroom.

Auntie Badria, however, stood calmly. She reached her hand out and touched the Bible with a sort of reverence that surprised Rania. Her fingers gently wrapped around the book and she pulled it toward herself, looking at it almost as if she were gauging whether it was going to burn her or bless her.

Every nerve within Rania told her to make a run for it. But Halimah was still standing behind the chair, watching their aunt. Rania wanted to grab her sister's arm and go. But she waited for Halimah's next move.

"What is it, Auntie?"

"Could it be?"

Rania heard their uncle in the bedroom. He was yelling. Was he on the phone? Maybe calling their father? Rania grabbed Halimah's hand. "We have to go," she whispered.

Halimah wouldn't budge. "What is it, Auntie?"

Auntie Badria looked up at the two young ladies. "Last night I prayed 'isha prayers, evening prayers, which I never do. Afterward I prayed for you, Rania, because of the message you received from Sit Abubakr's coffee reading. I asked Allah for a sign. Could this be it?"

"Yes, Auntie, I believe it is. And you must not ignore a sign from God." Halimah's words were steady and strong.

The older woman picked up the book and held it to her chest. She opened her mouth as if to say something, but then they heard Uncle Faisal yelling again. This time he was calling for Auntie Badria.

The woman stood quietly, still clutching the Bible. She opened a drawer in the ornate china cabinet against the wall and slipped the book inside. Then she walked away, down the hall toward her husband.

"Now," Halimah whispered to Rania. The two slipped out the front door and ran to the elevator. It felt to Rania like the doors would never open, but they eventually did, and then the girls ran to the parking lot. To Rania's amazement, the pink taxi was still waiting there, just as they'd requested.

She didn't want to look out the window for fear she would see Uncle Faisal running after them, screaming for the driver to stop. But the taxi pulled into traffic, and before she knew it they were on their way to the airport.

Rania held Halimah's hand in the back of the taxi. She repeatedly glanced out the back window to look for Uncle Faisal's car. They had made it out of the apartment and into the taxi, but what about when they arrived at the airport? Would Uncle know to look for them there?

"Don't worry. Everything will be OK." Halimah's voice calmed Rania. She wanted to ask her sister what they would do if Uncle Faisal got to them before they could get on the airplane, but she didn't want to speak in front of the driver.

At the airport, Rania looked over her shoulder. She scanned the crowds of people on the sidewalk. She watched every car that pulled up to the curb behind their taxi as she waited for Halimah to fumble through her purse to get the money to pay the rest of the taxi bill.

At the check-in counter, Halimah calmly handed the man in uniform their tickets and passports. That's when it occurred to Rania that she was still a teenager and that they may not allow her to travel without her father's presence.

When she flew from Khartoum to Dubai, her father was there to give his consent. What about here in Dubai, did it matter? She squeezed her eyes shut and prayed for a miracle.

⇒ Chapter 33 ⇐
Dallas, Texas

On the day Halimah and Rania were to arrive, Michael helped Mia make a pallet on the floor of the boys' room for Annie. Then they put fresh sheets on the twin beds in Annie's room.

"You know," Mia said as she fluffed a pillow and placed it on one of the beds. "One thing that made adjusting back to America so difficult for me was that I thought it was all about Sudan. You know what I mean? I was just so caught up with life in Sudan. Everything was always about Sudan. So when I didn't have it anymore, I wasn't sure what to do."

"What about now?" Michael asked as he smoothed out the bedspread on one of the beds.

"Now I realize that actually, it is all about God and His glory. Initially, I thought I was part of Sudan's story. But actually, Sudan is a part of my story. And my story is part of God's grand story. Once I was able to let go and allow God to write the story, it became more wonderful than I could ever have written on my own."

Michael nodded. "Several years ago, God wanted us to be willing to be a light for Him in Sudan. Now, even though it's not what we expected, He wants us to be a light for Him here in the United States. It's different from what we thought it would be."

Mia nodded. "But it's good."

Michael put his hands on his hips and surveyed the room. "Well, looks good. Need anything else?"

"No," Mia said, rearranging a precarious stack of Annie's stuffed animals so they wouldn't fall off her dresser. She stared at a pink unicorn teetering on the edge. "Do you think they'll come?"

"I hope so."

"We haven't heard from them in two days. What if they were caught?"

"There's only one way to find out," Michael said. Then he walked across the room and placed his hands on Mia's shoulders. "Honey, we have to trust that the Lord is helping them."

Mia sighed. "I know. I'm just worried." She shook her head as if dispelling any negative thoughts, then she smiled at Michael. "You're right. I need to trust."

Michael nodded, satisfied. "All right then, I'm taking the kids to your parents' house and then I'll be back to pick you up so we can head to the airport."

Just then Annie appeared in the doorway to her room. "I'm ready to go, Daddy." She held a book bag with her name embroidered on the front. "Grandma is taking us to the library. See? She gave me my own book bag." Annie held it up for Michael to see.

"Let me go see if Corey and Dylan are ready," Mia said, walking toward the boys' room.

She helped the boys find their book bags, also given to them by their grandmother, with their names embroidered on the front.

"Have fun with Grandma and when you get back, Miss Halimah and Miss Rania will be here." Mia hoped it was true.

When Michael and the kids were gone, Mia took her map of Khartoum and spread it out on the table. Her fingers traced the streets as she prayed. Then she folded the map and pushed it to the side. She spread out a new map her mother had given her. "I thought you might want to mark the places you pray for on this map too," she said.

Mia spread out her colored highlighters and pens. She marked their apartment complex, her parents' house, the gym, Grace Community Church, and just kept going.

The more she highlighted, the more she prayed. And when she was done, she looked over her work and saw that, though much of the map was marked, there were still many unmarked streets. It was definitely time for some prayerdriving.

In the margin of the map, Mia wrote the names of friends and acquaintances, the children's Sunday School teachers, and even Amal, the lady she met at the park.

Mia looked out the kitchen window. Past the sunny yellow curtains and the glass window was a world that needed the light of Jesus' love.

Just as she had learned to show mercy to Muslims overseas, she had received mercy from her own friends in Texas. Muslims often used the phrase "God is merciful," and Mia heard it many times in Sudan. But she now knew from her own experience God was merciful. And mercy triumphs over judgment.

"You ready to go?" Michael had opened the front door and stood in the entrance of the apartment. "I just dropped the kids off at your mom's and I've got the car running. We'll be late if we don't beat the traffic."

"Yep, I'm ready."

They left the suburbs and headed toward Dallas/Fort Worth International Airport. If they had been able to get away, Halimah and Rania would arrive on a direct flight from Dubai in an hour. What shape would they be in? Mia knew it had been tricky to arrange leaving their uncle's house. The last email they'd received, two days earlier, was the arrival information. But the email was short and the wording cryptic. Were they afraid their uncle had been investigating Rania's computer?

After finding a parking spot and the building for international arrivals, they waited impatiently for the sisters to appear. So this is what it felt like to stand on the receiving side and wait for a loved one to arrive. She imagined her mother and father standing—maybe in that very spot—waiting for them to walk through the doors just a few months earlier. Had they felt as excited as she did now?

Mia glanced at the clock on the left wall. "It's been a long time, Michael. It seems like most of the passengers have come through."

"Maybe their luggage got lost."

They waited. Mia's legs were getting tired, but she dared not walk away to find a place to sit. Her eyes were glued to the automatic glass doors. Each time they opened they squeaked, and she caught her breath and looked. But it squeaked and out came an older couple. Then it squeaked and out walked a businessman, then a family. Every time, it was someone other than Halimah and Rania.

Michael looked around the room. "I wonder if there is an information desk nearby. Perhaps we could explain that we need someone to go inside and look for them. What if they are confused and got lost?"

Mia didn't want to ask the other question: *What if they never got on the flight?*

Refusing to leave their spot in front of the doors, they looked around the room for a desk or a sign that said *information*. All Mia saw was a coffee shop, a public telephone, and a newspaper stand. The doors squeaked again and two young ladies walked through the entryway, each pulling a suitcase and looking around. It took only a second for Mia to recognize them.

Mia hadn't expected to cry, but she didn't try to stop the tears. She ran to the girls and embraced them.

"Welcome to Texas," she said. "Let's get your bags and go home."

On the way to the apartment, the girls filled Michael and Mia in on their last few days in Dubai. Conversation was a mixture of Arabic and English. Every few minutes Mia reached back and squeezed Halimah's hand, just to remind herself that this was really happening.

As the traffic died down and the car exited the freeway and headed toward the suburbs, Halimah and Rania slowed down the conversation. They must have been exhausted from the trip. They stared out the window at the skyline disappearing in the distance and then at the rolling cotton field that separated the city from the towns on the outskirts. How different this must look from Dubai.

Mia had mixed feelings about Halimah and Rania coming to the United States. This country was not what they probably imagined it would be. Even though they were allowed to be followers of Jesus without fear of being punished, other equally difficult challenges would face them. But this time Mia wasn't worried. She had learned that God was always faithful. And He was merciful.

A new chapter for Halimah and Rania. And a new chapter for Mia as well. Mia could hardly wait to see what God had in store.

What will they do when persecution strikes close to home?

Door to Freedom, the sequel to *Side by Side*, unlocks the mysterious Muslim world of the Sudanese Arabs. In this dusty, Islamic country, Rania, the daughter of a wealthy Sudanese Arab, seeks to find the reason for her sister's sudden disappearance. Mia, an American mom recently emboldened to share her faith, holds some of the answers. Both women quickly discover they must choose their own door to freedom— God's sovereignty or the security of man.

NEW HOPE®
P U B L I S H E R S
Gospel-Centered. Missions-Driven.

For more information, including where to purchase, please visit **NewHopePublishers.com**.

ADO 2.0

Programmer's Reference

David Sussman
Alex Homer

Wrox Press Ltd.®

ADO 2.0 *Programmer's Reference*

© 1998 Wrox Press

Published by Wrox Press Ltd. 30 Lincoln Road, Olton, Birmingham, B27 6PA.

Printed in USA

ISBN 1-861001-83-5

ADO 2.0

Introduction

This book provides a concise and yet comprehensive guide to the ways ADO 2.0 can be used in all kinds of applications. It demonstrates the use of ADO in both Web applications written using ASP, and in compiled applications written using Visual Basic and other languages. It also includes a reference section for fast access to detailed lists of the properties, methods and events available in ADO.

What Is ADO?

So, what is ADO? If you are new to data access programming with Microsoft technologies, you may not yet be aware of ADO, although it's hard not to have come across it if you've had anything at all to do with the Internet. ADO stands for **Active Data Objects** (sometimes called ActiveX Data Objects).

ADO is a set of ActiveX controls that provide programmatic access to Microsoft's latest underlying data access technologies. This can be through almost any programming or scripting language, as long as it can instantiate and use ActiveX controls—which are effectively COM objects.

ADO is based on an underlying data access technology called **OLE-DB**. This is a defined set of interfaces that all data sources can implement through special drivers (or **providers**), and thereby expose their data content in a uniform way. OLE-DB relies on a low-level **Application Programming Interface** (API) designed for use with languages like C++. ADO wraps these interfaces into ActiveX/COM objects that can be used in a far wider range of languages.

In other words, ADO gives us a standard way of managing data from all kinds of data stores, not just relational databases. In Chapter 1, we'll expand on these concepts to show you just how useful this whole approach is when building data management applications.

The ever-increasing role and importance of the Internet in application development has also driven the design concepts of ADO. It provides a range of ways that remote data access can be achieved over the Internet, using a Web browser, or through custom applications written in a range of programming languages.

This book covers the broad outlines and purpose of ADO, as the Microsoft data access technology of the future. It also describes the new features that are included in version 2.0 of ADO, as provided with the latest versions of the Microsoft development platforms and operating systems.

What Is This Book About?

This book is about ADO, and particularly the new features available in ADO version 2.0. It covers the advanced ADO topics as well as the new features added in the latest version, and acts as a vital reference on syntax and semantics for working with ADO.

It also explains how ADO fits into the whole Microsoft **Distributed interNet Applications** (DNA) picture for distributed data-oriented applications, and describes the advantages of ADO over other existing Microsoft data access technologies.

Finally, it shows how ADO interfaces with the core OLE-DB data access driver model to provide connectivity with a whole range of data stores. This can include messaging systems, text files, and specific non-standard data formats as well as the more usual relational databases.

This book is a reference guide for the ADO programmer, and primarily aimed at demonstrating and explaining the features of ADO 2.0, and the ways that they can be used. As such, it isn't a beginner's guide—though if you have programmed any data-access applications in the past, you'll be able to use it to get up to speed with ADO.

In particular, the book is aimed at the application developer who already uses Microsoft's data access methods in applications, but wants to take full advantage of the new features of ADO 2.0. It includes all the information required for any reasonably experienced developer to start using ADO within their Web pages and distributed applications. Finally, it is ideal for all existing ADO users, to bring them up to date quickly with version 2.0.

In this book, we've avoided discussion of ASP and data handling programming in components — with the exception of the techniques directly connected with using ADO. As a result, the examples are concise, and designed to demonstrate ADO techniques rather than to build entire applications. However, we do provide pointers to other sources of information to indicate the kind of things that can be achieved.

The book offers users an easy-to-follow tutorial and reference to ADO, by splitting the whole topic into neat and intuitive segments. This also makes it easier to find specific information later as you come to use ADO in real-world applications. To help out, a comprehensive quick reference section is also included. It lists the properties, methods and events of each of the ADO objects, together with other useful information.

The segmentation of the book looks like this:

- Introduction to ADO, and what's new in ADO 2.0
- Connecting to data stores, including a discussion of driver technologies
- The **Command** object, and ways of executing queries against a data store
- **Recordsets** and **Cursors**, and how they are used to retrieve data from a data store
- Collections of objects, including **Fields** and **Errors**
- Remote Data Access, showing how ADO can be used in Web-based applications
- Data shaping, events, and offline usage
- Examination of ADO performance, comparing cursor and locking types

ADO has been available for some time in various versions, and is installed with a whole range of other applications or development environments. The most common version before the arrival of ADO 2.0 was version 1.5. This was provided with the Windows NT4 Option Pack, Visual InterDev, and many version 5 Microsoft programming languages.

Version 2.0 of ADO is included with the new version 6.0 of Visual Studio, which consists of Visual InterDev, C++, Visual Basic, and J++ together with a host of other development tools and a cut-down version of SQL Server. It will also be included with Microsoft Office 2000, and Windows NT5, although by this time it is likely to be version 2.1, with added features.

In the meantime, if you don't have version 2.0 of ADO, you can download it from the Microsoft Data Access site at: http://www.microsoft.com/data/mdac2.htm.

We provide the source code for the samples that you'll see in this book on our Web site, and you can even run some of them directly from there to save installing them on your own machine. The main samples menu page for this book is at http://webdev.wrox.co.uk/books/1835/. This site also contains a range of other resources and reference material that you might find useful, including other books that demonstrate ADO applications.

To run the samples yourself, and build applications that use ADO 2.0, you will require only your usual preferred development tools. To build Web-based or Intranet-based applications that use ASP, this will be just a Web server and a client browser. The Web server will need to have ADO 2.0 installed, and will probably be running Internet Information Server 4 from the NT4 Option Pack. For the remote data access examples in Chapter 7, the browser should be Internet Explorer 4 or higher.

To build compiled applications which don't use the Internet or your own Intranet, but rely on communication over a traditional LAN, you'll need just your own choice of programming language development tool. This will also be required if you want to build custom business components for Internet or Intranet-based applications.

ADO is a language-neutral topic — in other words it can be used in any programming language that supports the instantiation of ActiveX/COM objects. This includes Visual Basic, C++, Delphi, Java, J++, and of course scripting languages such as JavaScript, JScript, and VBScript — as used in client-side browser and server-side ASP programming.

As such, we've provided some guidance as to how the ADO objects can be accessed in various languages in Chapter 2. We then use either a generic syntax, or the most appropriate language, for each part of the ADO object model. This means that you can use the information within your own favorite language, or the language that you deem to be best suited to the task in hand.

In some chapters, we show how ADO can be used in components. The fundamental principles are the same as in scripting, so the chapters demonstrate just the differences, i.e. the way objects are declared and instantiated, and the way the properties, methods and events are referenced.

Conventions

We have used a number of different styles of text and layout in the book to help differentiate between the different kinds of information. Here are examples of the styles we use and an explanation of what they mean:

Advice, hints, or background information comes in this type of font.

> **Important pieces of information come in boxes like this**

- **Important Words** are in a bold type font
- Words that appear on the screen in menus like <u>F</u>ile or <u>W</u>indow are in a similar font to the one that you see on screen
- Keys that you press on the keyboard, like *Ctrl* and *Enter*, are in italics

Code has several fonts. If it's a word that we're talking about in the text, for example, when discussing the **For...Next** loop, it's in a bold font. If it's a block of code that you can type in as a program and run, then it's also in a gray box:

```
objRec.Open "authors", objConn, adOpenKeyset, adLockOptimistic, _
        (adCmdTable OR adAsyncFetch
```

 Sometimes you'll see code in a mixture of styles, like this:

```
<OBJECT CLASSID="clsid:BD96C556-65A3-11D0-983A-00C04FC29E33"
        ID="dsoBookList" HEIGHT=0 WIDTH=0>
  <PARAM NAME="Server" VALUE="http://www.yourserver.com">
  <PARAM NAME="Connect" VALUE="SERVER="http://dataserver.com;
                              DRIVER={SQL Server};DATABASE=yourdb;
                              UID=anon;PWD=">
  <PARAM NAME="SQL" VALUE="SELECT * FROM BookList">
</OBJECT>
```

 The code with a white background is code we've already looked at and that we don't wish to examine further. Note also that we use ADO 2 and ADO 2.0 interchangeably.

What Is ADO?

ActiveX Data Objects (ADO) and OLEDB, its underlying technology, are going to play a big part in the future of data access. Microsoft has unequivocally committed their future to it, and quite rightly so. The paperless office has yet to appear, but the amount of data being stored on computer systems is increasing every day. The rate at which the Web is expanding shows this quite clearly, and that's just the public face of data. There's much more data that is hidden from general view.

In this chapter we are going to look at the terms and technology behind ADO. This isn't actually required if you need to start coding straight away, but like any form of learning, your understanding will be better if you have a good foundation.

To give you that good grounding, there are several important topics we will discuss in this chapter:

- What we mean by data
- What we mean by a data store
- How ADO fits with existing data access strategies
- Data access in the client/server world

Because ADO is so central to Microsoft's data access strategy it is important to understand why it came about and what sort of a future it has.

What is Data?

In a spare few minutes open up Explorer and have a look around your hard disk. Make a little note of how many separate pieces of information you've got; databases, documents, spreadsheets, email messages, HTML and ASP documents, and so on. Quite a lot, eh? They are all data, albeit stored in different forms. This might seem obvious, but traditionally data has only been thought of as information that is stored in a database. To build a business application the data had to be in a database. Whilst that might be true for a large proportion of existing data, why should the remaining data be excluded? In fact, as computers get more powerful, the concept of 'data' is starting to include multimedia items, such as music and video, as well as the more normal document-based data.

So, by data we mean any piece of information, whatever its contents. Whether it's your address book, your monthly expenses spreadsheet, or a pleading letter to the IRS, it's all data.

What Are Data Stores?

Knowing what we consider data to be might make a Data Store obvious – it's somewhere where data is kept. However, there is much more to Data Stores than you first might think. Instead of looking at your hard disk, let's look at mine this time, and see what I've got installed:

- **Databases**: Both Access and SQL Server, which we consider to be traditional data stores. I have everything from accounts and invoicing to sample databases for books.

- **Spreadsheets**: Financial data with year end figures for my tax returns and bills.

- **Mail and News**: I use Outlook and Outlook Express to handle my mail and Internet news.

- **Documents**: This is the largest proportion of data on my machine, containing all of my personal letters and documents, and chapters for books (including this one).

- **Graphics**: Screen dumps and pictures for books.

- **Internet**: HTML and ASP pages, containing samples and applications.

- **Reference Material**: Including MSDN and encyclopedias.

So that's the actual data, but how is it stored? Well, the databases are self-contained, so they are their own data store. The reference material is, by and large, stored in its own format, so that could be considered a data store. The mail and news hold data on their own as well, so they are also a data store. Everything else is stored as files, and therefore the file system itself becomes a data store. OK, the data it stores is in a myriad of formats, but it's all stored in the same way – folders and documents.

You could even include my CD-ROM drive and tape backup unit. The CD-ROM uses the standard documents and folders format, so this could be considered part of the file system data store, but the tape backup has its own format, and could therefore be considered a data store too.

There are also numerous other data stores, from mainframe file systems to databases and mail. As the enterprise gets bigger we also need to include user account databases, and other machines attached to the network, such as printers and scanners. They might not all be data stores themselves, but as items of data they'll be in a data store somewhere - such as NT5.0's Active Directory Service Interfaces.

About Universal Data Access

Universal Data Access (UDA) is Microsoft's strategy for dealing with all of this data. It's aimed at providing high performance access to a variety of data sources. The cynical amongst you might think it's another attempt to shoehorn in another Microsoft technology, but let's look at the modern business.

To be a successful business you have to be flexible, to adapt to change. How do you know when to change? There's no simple rule here, but most companies make decisions by asking a few questions. How much can we sell? How much are we selling? How much are our competitors selling? What does research show customers want? Those sorts of questions can be answered by figures, and where do the figures come from? That's right, data. But we've already seen that data is stored in many different ways, and there is no single way of accessing them all.

So with UDA we are looking at an easy-to-use methodology that is intended to allow access to multiple sources of data with a single method. Build in high performance and support for existing data access methods, and you're on your way to something that could make a real difference, because you don't have to spend the time and resources you would need to bundle together all of your data into a single data source. Let's have a look at how UDA streamlines your data access.

When building an application you can make sure it uses ADO for its data access, and ADO will talk to all of the data sources required. This means that programming is made easier, since only one technology needs to be learnt. As ADO will give fast, transparent access to many different data sources, there's no reason to use any other method.

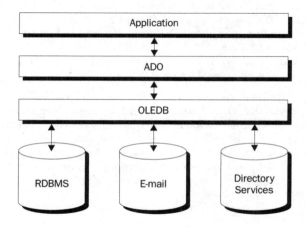

You can clearly see what Microsoft are aiming for when you look at the three main design goals for the Data Access Components:

- Meeting the key customer requirements, such as performance, reliability, and broad industry support.

- Giving access to the widest range of data sources, through a common interface.

- Providing an easy migration path for existing data access technologies.

So far, the components seem to be meeting these admirably.

This method contrasts with Oracle who, naturally, are pushing Universal Server, where all of the data will be stored under one central data store. The ultimate aim is the same – broader access to data, but the Oracle approach initially involves more data conversion and translation as the data is imported to the store. From that point on, however, your data is easier to access.

Neither of these two methods is clearly the best, as your choice of data access method depends very much upon your business needs and legacy computer systems.

Existing Technologies

Before we explain why ADO came about, let's take a quick look at some existing technologies and see how they fit into the picture.

- **DBLib:** This is the underlying technology for connecting to SQL Server, and is primarily designed for C, but is often used in Visual Basic. Because it is specific to SQL Server, it is extremely fast and functional. For this very reason, however, it doesn't allow access to any other source of data.

- **ODBC:** Open DataBase Connectivity, was the first step on the road to a universal data access strategy. It was designed by Microsoft and other DBMS vendors as a cross-platform, database-independent method, using API calls. Although it was designed for multi-database use, it was very often only used on a single database, and from a programmer's point of view, was complex to use.

- **DAO:** The Data Access Objects were introduced with Microsoft Access, and provided a strict hierarchical set of objects for manipulating data in Jet and other ISAM databases. These objects were available with Visual Basic and quickly became the most used data access method for Visual Basic programs. DAO also had the advantage of being able to sit on top of ODBC, thus allowing it to communicate with many different databases, although, because the technology is optimized for use with JET, this is quite slow.

- **RDO:** Intended as the successor to DAO for Visual Basic programmers, Remote Data Objects is a thin layer that sits on top of ODBC, allowing better access to server databases, such as SQL Server. This brought the flexibility of ODBC with a much easier programming model, but, like DAO, it has a strictly hierarchical programming model.

- **ODBCDirect:** An extension to DAO, which combines DAO and RDO. It allows programmers to use the DAO programming model, but access ODBC data sources without having the Jet database loaded.

- **JDBC:** Java Database Connectivity was designed by Microsoft as another DBMS neutral API, especially for use in Java applications.

The problems with these technologies are very simple. Both DBLib and ODBC are low-level API's and therefore are complex to use for many programmers. Both DAO and RDO offer the user another interface to ODBC, but this introduces another layer of code to go through, and performance can drop. All of these technologies also suffer from a very strict and hierarchical object model, which adds extra overhead to both programming and execution.

They are also more or less constrained by providing access to relational databases, although Microsoft Excel and simple text documents could also be used as data sources when using ODBC. ODBC drivers have also been produced for object oriented and hierarchical databases, which allow the data to be accessed in a way similar to a relational database.

What is OLEDB?

OLEDB is designed to be the successor to ODBC, but you might be asking why we need a successor? Well, there are three main trends at the moment. The first, fairly obviously, is the Internet. The second is an increasing amount of data being stored in a non-relational form, and the third is Microsoft's desire for a COM world, where all object usage is handled through their Component Object Model.

The Internet brings a range of new challenges to standard data access because of its distributed nature. Applications are now being written on a truly global scale, and you can no longer guarantee that the data you are accessing is stored on your local network. This means that the way you access data has to be carefully considered, as well as the type of data you access. The new business opportunity of e-commerce has meant that selling becomes a whole new ball game – you can now have an application that shows pictures of your products, plays music, and even videos, all running over the Web. The Web is also more distributed (and often less reliable) than conventional networks, so your data access method has to take this into account. You can't, for example, assume that your client and server remain connected at all times during an application – in the stateless nature of the Web this doesn't make sense.

So OLEDB is a technology designed to solve some of these problems, and over time it will gradually replace ODBC as the central data access method. Even so, new versions of ODBC are supplied with ADO 2.0, and ODBC will continue to be developed and supported. 'Along with the new version 3.5 of ODBC, OLEDB is now the guts of the new data access strategy.'

11

Why ADO?

OLEDB is a COM based set of object oriented interfaces, and thus for a large proportion of the programming community it is too complex to use, or does not map onto their particular programming language, especially scripting languages. ADO is the higher level model that most people will use. It equates fairly well to the DAO level, where you create an object, and call its methods and properties. Being an ActiveX component means it can be used from any language that supports COM – including Visual Basic, VBA, scripting languages, VC++ and VJ++.

So now our diagram looks even more enticing:

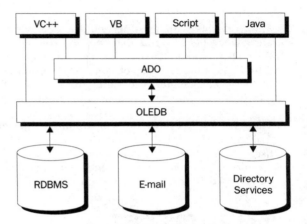

We have various languages, all with the ability to use a central data access strategy. Some languages can talk directly to OLEDB – as well as talking to the easier ADO – although we'll only be looking at the ADO layer in this book.

ADO also increases the speed and ease of development by introducing an object model that allows data to be retrieved from a data source with as little as one line of code. And this line of code can be switched between languages with minimal changes.

Another pressing need for ADO is the increasing use of the Web as an application medium. Conventional applications are generally connected via a Local Area Network to their data store. They can open a connection to the data, and keep that connection open throughout the life of the program. Consequently, the data store knows who is connecting. Many applications also process data on the client – perhaps a set of records that the user is browsing through or updating. Since the client is connected to the server, or source of the data, there's no trouble updating the data.

On the Web however, the native mechanism is stateless. There's no permanent connection between client and server. If you think about the way the Web works for a second, you'll realize why this is a problem:

1. You request a Web page in your browser.
2. The Web server receives the request, runs any server-side script, and sends the page back to you.

That's it. As soon as this is over the Web server forgets about you. Admittedly with ASP you can store some sort of session state, but it's not very sophisticated. Even with session data each request to a page is essentially a separate program. How then, with this disconnected network, do you provide a system that allows data to be updated on the client and sent back to the server? This is where ADO comes in, with disconnected recordsets. They allow the recordset to be disassociated from the server, and then re-associated at a later date. Any updates can be saved in the client copy, and the server can be updated at a later date. Add this to the fact that you can save these disconnected recordsets locally, you can have an application that lets the user change records, and any time later, update the central set of records.

The use of client-side data manipulation also allows you to sort data, find records, and generally manage recordsets without resorting to a trip back to the server. Although this idea primarily fits with the nature of the Web, it can work just as well for the standard type of applications running on a LAN, and can reduce network traffic.

Data Providers and Data Consumers

OLEDB introduces two new terms that help to explain how OLEDB and ADO fit together a little more clearly. A **Data Consumer** is something that uses, or consumes, data. Strictly speaking, ADO is actually a consumer, because it uses data provided by OLEDB.

A **Data Provider** is something that, unsurprisingly, provides data. This isn't the physical source of the data, but the OLEDB mechanism that connects us to the physical data store. The provider may get the data directly from the data store, or it may go through a third party product, such as ODBC, to get to the data store. It can even use other data sources and provide added value along the way – the MSDataShape provider is an example of this. This means that you can immediately start using ADO to access existing data stores that support ODBC, even if there isn't an OLEDB provider available for them yet.

The initial set of OLEDB providers supplied with ADO 2.0 are:

- **Jet 3.51**, for Microsoft Access databases. This allows access to standard Access databases, including linked tables.

- **Directory Services**, for resource data stored, such as Active Directory. This will become more important when NT5.0 is available, as the Directory Service in NT5.0 will allow access to user information, as well as network devices.

- **Index Server**, for Microsoft Index Server. This will be particularly useful as Web sites grow, as the indexed data will be available.

- **Site Server Search**, for Microsoft Site Server. Again for use with Web sites, especially large complex sites, where Site Server is used to maintain them.

- **ODBC Drivers**, for existing ODBC Drivers. This ensures that legacy data is not omitted as part of the drive forward.

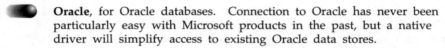

Oracle, for Oracle databases. Connection to Oracle has never been particularly easy with Microsoft products in the past, but a native driver will simplify access to existing Oracle data stores.

SQL Server, for Microsoft SQL Server, to allow access to data stored in SQL Server.

Data Shape, for hierarchical recordsets This allows creation of master/ detail type recordsets, which allow drilling down into detailed data.

Persisted Recordset, for locally saved recordsets. This isn't strictly a data provider, but acts as one for recordsets that have been saved locally.

This is just the list of standard providers supplied by Microsoft; other vendors are actively creating their own. ISG for example, provide an OLEDB provider that allows connection to multiple data stores at the same time. Oracle provide an OLEDB provider, which they claim is better than the Microsoft one, and most other database suppliers have OLEDB providers for their databases.

OLEDB also provides a few other services, such as a query processor and a cursor engine, so these can be used at the client. There are two reasons for this. The first is that it frees the actual provider from providing the service, so that the service can be smaller, and secondly it makes it available as a client service. This means that cursor handling can be provided locally, which is an important point of disconnected recordsets and Remote Data Services.

Distributed Internet Applications

Distributed interNet Applications, or DNA, is the architectural strategy that Microsoft are defining as the ideal way to write distributed, n-tier, client-server applications. One of the interesting things about this strategy is that it's really just a set of ideas and suggestions, rather than a complex, locked-in solution. It's not a new idea, but there are now some really good tools that make creating this type of application, not only a reality, but also a relatively easy reality.

The basic premise is that you partition your application into at least three tiers. The first is the user interface tier – this is what the user sees, and could be a Web page or another type of application, written in any language. The second tier is where the business rules or processes lie – these determine where the data comes from, what rules apply to the data, and how it should be returned to the user interface. The third tier is the data layer – the actual source of the data.

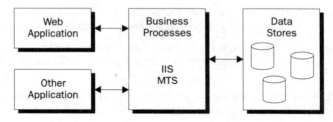

The great thing about DNA is that it aims to be language independent, since it all hinges around COM (and COM+ when that arrives with NT5.0). COM is the Component Object Model that allows easy object creation and re-use. Any component that supports COM will fit into this picture, so you can write your application in ASP and JavaScript, Visual Basic, VC++, VJ++ , Delphi, or any language that supports COM. Likewise, your business components can be in any language, so you can program in whatever environment you feel happy. There's no need to learn a new language.

In the Business Processes tier you see that IIS and MTS are mentioned. IIS supplies the connection from Web applications to components, which could be stand-alone components or MTS components. The great advantage of MTS is that it makes your middle tier suddenly very easy to manage – you can just create a component and install it into MTS. Now it suddenly becomes available to all applications that can call COM objects, without having to worry about the nasty registration process that you had to do previously. You can access the components on remote machines using DCOM. You also get the added advantage of transaction processing and easy scalability, without having to program it in yourself. The user interface can then be built in any language that supports COM.

> *If you'd like to learn more about MTS and its use in DNA applications, take a look at MTS MSMQ with Visual Basic and ASP from Wrox Press, ISBN 1-861001-46-0.*

ADO 2.0 Availability

The Microsoft Data Access Components are available as a separate download from the Microsoft Web site, at www.microsoft.com/data, as well as being supplied with Visual Studio 6. Future versions of ADO are to be supplied with Internet Explorer 5, which ships with ADO 2.1, and Microsoft Office 2000. These future versions will allow greater support for XML, especially with the ability to transfer and save recordsets as pure XML data, and bind HTML elements to XML data.

ADO 2.0 New Features

ADO 2.0 has a host of new features that make programming easier. This section is not going to cover them thoroughly, as they will be dealt with in more detail in the later chapters.

Events

Not only does ADO 2.0 now support asynchronous operations, but also event notification. You can now open connections and recordsets asynchronously, allowing fast response time to user requests. This allows you to get control back in your program as soon as you have issued the command. The connection or opening of the recordset can proceed in background.

For Connections, you can be notified when the connection starts and ends, when a command executes, and when transactions start, end and abort.

For Recordsets, you can be notified when a recordset is fetched (or the progress as it is being fetched), whether certain actions will change the contents of fields or rows, and whether actions will change the current record.

A useful feature from within some of the event procedures is the ability to cancel the action that caused the event to be raised. Some events are raised just before the action actually takes place, so you can see why it is happening and decide whether or not to allow it to continue. This is particularly useful when users have the ability to submit their own queries, or alter data.

VC++ Extensions

There is a new interface in ADO 2.0 allowing C++ users to retrieve data into native C and C++ data types. This makes using ADO 2.0 much easier as well as increasing performance, as previously data had to be returned via variants.

Hierarchical Cursors and Data Shaping

The easiest way to understand what this is about is to imagine the TreeView control, or Windows Explorer. A hierarchical cursor allows you to define child recordsets for a field in the parent recordset. ADO 2.0 supports the access of these programmatically, and new visual controls in Visual Basic 6.0 can bind directly to these recordsets.

This is quite useful for those master/detail scenarios, and particularly for Web sites that are backed by a database and need to supply two sets of related information. Very often they have a list from which you pick an option, and then when your request is submitted, they return another set of data from a database. If the data set is not too large, this could be supplied as a single, shaped, recordset which you wouldn't have to return back to the server.

Hierarchical recordsets and data shaping are explored in more detail in Chapter 8.

DataFactory Customization

ADO 2.0 allows the overriding of the default DataFactory connection or command by use of a customization file and a handler. This allows you to customize the parameters of the DataFactory to restrict access on a user-by-user basis when writing custom business objects.

Although this is not the most technical solution, it does help in getting around some of the security problems that are inherently tied-up with RDS.

Recordset Creation

Creating a new recordset is now as easy as appending field objects to the recordset's fields collection. The recordset behaves as a normal recordset and allows data to be inserted into it from any data source.

One use of this is a situation where you need to pass custom data between the tiers in an n-tier client server system. The use of ADO 2.0 recordsets allows this data to be marshaled between the tiers easily, without the need for any custom code.

Recordset Persistence

Persistence of recordsets allows you to save recordset data – and metadata – as a file. Later on, you can use the saved file to re-create a recordset. The file format can be an internal format or Extensible Markup Language (XML). XML will be supported in ADO 2.1, to be shipped with Office 2000 and IE5.

You could use this for remote or travelling users, allowing them to disconnect from the central store, and continue to process records offline. This is covered in more detail in Chapter 8.

There is also a new method, `GetString`, that instantly converts a recordset into XML, HTML, or a character delimited format. This will allow very quick HTML table creation. The XML format of this will be supported in ADO 2.1.

Index Support for Find, Sort and Filter

ADO 2.0 allows the creation of internal indexes to optimize the use of `Find`, `Sort` and `Filter`. In previous versions of ADO, it was often quicker to recreate the recordset than to `Filter` it or `Sort` it, and this slowness was sometimes a problem when using disconnected recordsets at the client. The new optimization will allow quicker manipulation without resorting to the server.

ADO for J++

Available in conjunction with Visual J++ version 6, you can now access ADO directly with Java. There's a set of classes pre-built to allow easy access to the ADO 2.0 features, as well as native type support.

Support for Visual Studio Analyzer

ADO submits events to Visual Studio Analyzer to help examine performance. This is particularly useful if you feel that your application has some performance problems, as you can use the Analyzer statistics to produce performance information.

Conflict Resolution for Client Cursors

Support for resolving record conflicts has been added to functions like **Resync** and **Update** when used with client side cursors. Although client-side cursors can reduce network traffic and give better performance for some user situations, changing data locally means that you have to resolve any conflicts when other users have also changed the data. ADO 2.0 has additional support for these situations.

Security Enhancements

The ActiveX security model has been brought to ADO 2.0 to allow integration with the Internet Explorer Security Levels and Zones. RDS and ADO objects are marked as either 'safe' or 'unsafe' depending upon the security model in place.

Of course, this will really only affect those situations where you are using recordsets on the client.

ADO Examples

Since this is primarily a reference book, it seems sensible to give you a few documented samples of code, so that you can see what's possible and how some of the components fit together. You can use this as a sort of "table of contents" to the rest of the book, where the various aspects are covered in more detail. The next chapter goes into the language specifics in more detail, so we'll use Visual Basic here because it's easy to read and understand.

Example 1

The following section of Visual Basic code creates a connection to SQL Server, opens a recordset, and then adds some details from the recordset to a listbox:

```
' Define two object variables
' The object model is discussed in Chapter 2
Dim objConn      As New ADODB.Connection
Dim objRec       As New ADODB.Recordset

' Open a connection to the pubs database using the SQL Server OLEDB Provider
' Connection strings are discussed in Chapter 2
' The Connection object is discussed in Chapter 3
objConn.Open "Provider=SQLOLEDB; Data Source=Tigger; " & _
             "Initial Catalog=pubs; User Id=sa; Password="

' Open a recordset on the 'authors' table
' The Recordset is discussed in Chapter 5
objRec.Open "authors", objConn, adOpenForwardOnly, adLockReadOnly, adCmdTable

' Loop whilst we haven't reached the end of the recordset
' The EOF property is set to True when we reach the end
While Not objRec.EOF
    ' Add the names to the listbox, using the default Fields collection
    ' The Fields collection is discussed in Chapter 6
    List1.AddItem objRec("au_fname") & " " & objRec("au_lname")
    ' Move to the next record
```

```
      objRec.MoveNext
Wend

' Close the objects
objRec.Close
objConn.Close

' Release the memory associated with the objects
Set objRec = Nothing
Set objConn = Nothing
```

Example 2

This example runs a SQL statement and doesn't expect a set of records to be returned.

```
' Define the object variable
Dim objConn      As New ADODB.Connection

' Open a connection to the pubs database using the OLEDB Provider for ODBC
objConn.Open "DSN=pubs"

' Run a SQL UPDATE statement to update book prices by 10%
objConn.Execute "UPDATE titles SET price = price * 1.10"

' close the connection
objConn.Close

' Release the memory associate with the objects
Set objConn = Nothing
```

Example 3

This example runs a stored query in Access, passing in some parameters.

```
' Declare the object variables
' The Command object is discussed in Chapter 4
' The Parameter object is discussed in Chapter 6
Dim objConn      As New ADODB.Connection
Dim objCmd       As New ADODB.Command
Dim objRec       As ADODB.Recordset
Dim objParm      As ADODB.Parameter

' Open a connection to an Access pubs database using the Access OLEDB provider
objConn.Open "Provider=Microsoft.Jet.OLEDB.3.51; " & _
             "Data Source=C:\temp\pubs.mdb"

' Create a new Parameter
Set objParm = objCmd.CreateParameter("RequiredState", adChar, _
                                     adParamInput, 2, "CA")

' Add the parameter to the Parameters collection of the Command object
objCmd.Parameters.Append objParm

' Set the active connection of the command to the open connection object
objCmd.ActiveConnection = objConn

' Set the name of the stored query that is to be run
objCmd.CommandText = "qryAuthorsBooksByState"

' Set the type of command (Access stored queries appear as tables)
objCmd.CommandType = adCmdTable
```

```
' Run the stored query and set the recordset which it returns
Set objRec = objCmd.Execute

' Loop through the recordset, adding the items to a listbox
While Not objRec.EOF
    List1.AddItem objRec("au_fname") & " " & objRec("au_lname") & _
                  ": " & objRec("title")
    objRec.MoveNext
Wend

' Close the recordset and connection
objRec.Close
objConn.Close

' Reclaim the memory from the objects
Set objRec = Nothing
Set objCmd = Nothing
Set objConn = Nothing
```

Example 4

This example uses the Fields collection of the recordset to loop through all of the fields in a recordset, printing out the details in the debug window:

```
' Declare the object variables
Dim objRec      As New ADODB.Recordset
Dim objFld      As ADODB.Field

' Open a recordset on the 'authors' table using the OLEDB Driver for ODBC
' without using a connection
objRec.Open "authors", "DSN=pubs", _
            adOpenForwardOnly, adLockReadOnly, adCmdTable

' Loop through the Fields collection printing the name of each Field
' The Fields collection is discussed in Chapter 6
For Each objFld In objRec.Fields
    Debug.Print objFld.Name; vbTab;
Next
Debug.Print

' Loop through the records in the recordset
While Not objRec.EOF
    ' Loop through the fields, this time printing out the Value of each field
    For Each objFld In objRec.Fields
        Debug.Print objFld.Value; vbTab;
    Next
    Debug.Print
    objRec.MoveNext
Wend

' Close the recordset and release the memory
objRec.Close
Set objRec = Nothing
Set objFld = Nothing
```

ADO in Visual Basic 6

Although this is an ADO book, it seems a good opportunity to briefly show two of the new features in Visual Basic 6 that rely on ADO. We're not going to look at these in detail, but just to give you a little glimpse of what's possible.

Data Environment

The data environment makes database programming so much neater within Visual Basic, since you have a central place to keep all of your data store connection details:

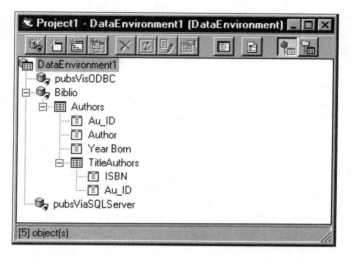

This diagram shows three connections – one to the SQL Server pubs database, via the OLEDB Provider for ODBC, one to the Access database **Biblio.mdb**, and one to the pubs database via the SQL Server OLEDB provider. The Biblio connection has two commands added to it – one to the Authors table, and a sub-command, to the TitleAuthors table. This sub-command idea is one of the really cool things about the Data Environment and it goes hand-in-hand with the new Hierarchical FlexGrid:

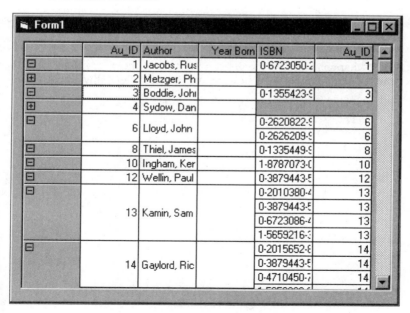

You can see that this grid shows the detail from the AuthorTable and from the TitleAuthor table, and gives you the ability to expand items in the grid, to show the sub-items. Achieving this took less than thirty seconds, as all you have to do is set the data environment, draw the grid on the form and set two properties.

There are many other new features in Visual Basic 6 that greatly increase productivity and make code easier to maintain, including a host of new data-bound controls aimed at taking advantage of ADO.

Summary

So far we've explored the principles of data access, and the new range of problems created by the increasing variety and location of data and users. We've taken a bird's eye view of the significance of ADO, and its advantages, and briefly looked at the other data access technologies it builds on, replaces or complements. We then moved on to take a closer look at the new features of ADO 2.0. In particular, we've considered:

- Data and data stores
- The existing technologies for accessing data, and Microsoft's new scheme to streamline data access, UDA
- What OLEDB and ADO 2.0 are, and how they tie in with each other
- The distinction between data providers and data consumers, and Microsoft's Distributed interNet Applications framework for client/server solutions
- The many new features of ADO 2.0, including events, improved access from VC++, data shaping, and new recordset capabilities

In the next chapter, we'll be moving on to discuss the much expanded ADO object model, and demonstrate how to use its new flexibility and power.

The ADO Object Model

Like all other data access technologies from Microsoft, ADO has a distinct object model. This defines the objects that comprise the model, and their hierarchy. That is, which objects belong to other objects, and in which order they need to be instantiated. If you've done any database programming before, you'll probably be familiar with the general layout of these objects, as they lean heavily on the lessons learnt from DAO and RDO. So although ADO has a good object model, it is not as strict as the previous incarnations, giving the programmer a great deal more flexibility, and reducing development time. For example, you can create a recordset of data with a single line of code.

This has been achieved by flattening the object model. It's still shown as a hierarchy, with a single object at the top, but some of the lower objects can exist on their own, and the higher level objects are built behind the scenes. This means that a programmer can use the object most suitable for a particular task, without having to create a lot of objects that aren't really required in your program. If ADO requires these objects, then it creates them and uses them without you needing to know they are there.

The Object Model

There are three main objects within ADO: the **Connection**, the **Command**, and the **Recordset**. The object model in its strictest sense shows a hierarchical relationship between the **Connection** object and the **Command** and **Recordset** objects, but these can exist independently of a Connection.

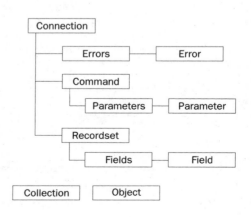

The **Error**, **Parameter**, and **Field** objects, though, do exist within a hierarchy, but only as part of a Collection.

There is also another collection that can belong to more than one object. Each of the objects shown to the right has its own **Properties** collection. This defines the extended details of the particular object.

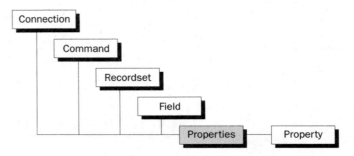

The following sections just give a brief overview of what the various objects are and how they can be used.

The Connection Object

The Connection is actually the hub of ADO, as it provides the methods that allow us to connect to a data store. Although it appears at the top of the object model, it is not necessary to create a Connection before creating a Recordset or a Command. What this means is that you can actually create recordsets or run commands with a single line of code. For example:

```
objRec.Open "authors", "DSN=pubs", adOpenStatic, adLockReadOnly, adCmdTable
```

This creates a recordset on the **authors** table from the pubs database, based on the ODBC Data Source Name **pubs**. Although this example is using a Recordset, it actually creates a Connection underneath, so you can then create a separate Connection object from the one that ADO created for you:

```
Set objConn = objRec.ActiveConnection
```

This sort of mix and match approach to connection creation frees the programmer from a rigid structure and allows the code to be written in a way that is naturally easier.

Although this looks simple, every time you use a connection string to establish a connection to a data store you create a new connection. If you are going to be running several commands or creating several recordsets, then you are recommended to create a Connection object directly:

```
objConn.Open "DSN=pubs"
```

or

```
objConn.Open "Provider=SQLOLEDB; Data Source=Piglet; Initial Catalog=pubs; User
Id=sa; Password="
```

You can then use this Connection throughout your code, without worrying about the number of connections you are creating. Not only is this more efficient, but it's faster too, since once a connection to a data store is established, it can be reused.

Once you have decided upon the provider, the properties of the Connection object allow you to see what kinds of facilities are available from the data provider. For example, picking the SQL Server provider allows you to see some the properties for that provider, even before the connection is opened:

```
objConn.Provider = "SQLOLEDB"
For Each objProp in objConn.Properties
    Print objProp.Nama
Next
```

Since ADO is designed to run against different data stores, you can examine the Properties collection of the connection to check to see whether a particular function is supported before you call it. This is particularly useful when using ADO as part of a development or query tool that gives the user the ability to connect to different data stores.

The Connection object isn't just about connecting to, and holding information about, a data store. Using a connection you can actually run commands and create recordsets. For example:

```
objConn.Execute "UPDATE titles SET price = price * 1.10"
```

This would run a SQL UPDATE query. Alternatively, to run a command and return a recordset:

```
Set objRec = objConn.Execute ("SELECT * FROM authors")
```

So, not only can you use a Recordset to connect to a data store, but you can use a Connection to create recordsets. It's all part of the 'code as you want' strategy.

The Connection is also where all of the errors are stored, if any occur during your ADO operations. Although you might think this breaks the flexibility, it gives a central place to find error information. Since the **Recordset** and **Command** objects have a connection underneath, it is extremely simple to get access to this error information without creating a Connection.

The Command Object

The Command object is designed more to run single commands, especially those that require parameters. This is an important point, because the use of stored queries and procedures is a great way both to improve speed, and segment your application.

Like the Connection object, the Command object can be used to run action queries that don't return a recordset, as well as creating recordsets. Unlike the Connection however, you'll need a couple more lines of code, as you cannot specify the command text in the same line:

```
objCmd.CommandText = "UPDATE titles SET price = price * 1.10"
objCmd.CommandType = adCmdText
objCmd.Execute
```

To return a Recordset you use a similar style:

```
Set objRec = objCmd.Execute
```

The greatest difference in command execution comes when using the **Parameters** collection, as this allows you to use stored procedures and queries that are saved on the data store. This removes the SQL code from your program, making it faster and more maintainable. Using stored procedures you can have SQL statements that are in a compiled form, and perform a set of actions using the values you supply as parameters.

With a Command, if the data provider supports this facility, you can also save the command details for execution at a later date. Once you've finished with your connection, the saved commands are automatically deleted. This is known as a prepared statement. You can also use a command object more than once, and on different providers if you require. Just change the **ActiveConnection** property of the command to point to the new connection and re-run the command.

Another feature allows you to turn the command into a method of the Connection, allowing you to build up a connection object that contains many new methods. This is quite useful in client-server scenarios, as you could attach different commands to the connection depending upon the privilege of the user. This is explained in more detail in Chapter 4.

The Recordset Object

The **Recordset** object is probably the most used object, and consequently has more properties and methods than the other objects. Like the Command object, a Recordset can exist on its own or attached to a Connection:

```
objRec.Open "authors", "DSN=pubs", adOpenStatic, adLockReadOnly, adCmdTable
```

This opens a recordset using a new connection. To use an existing connection you simply substitute the connection string for a connection object:

```
objRec.Open "authors", objConn, adOpenStatic, adLockReadOnly, adCmdTable
```

If you are creating several recordsets then this is the preferred method, since the connection to the data store doesn't have to be established each time you create the recordset.

Another important point about recordsets is that it's the only way to specify the recordset's cursor type and lock type. The **Execute** method of the Connection and Command objects, both give you the default cursor type, which is a read-only, forward-only cursor (often referred to as a **firehose** cursor).

You use recordsets to examine and manipulate data from the data store. The Recordset gives you facilities to move about through the records, find records, sort records in a particular order, and update records. You can do updating in two modes; either directly, where the changes are sent back to the data store as they are made, or in batches, where the changes are saved locally and then sent back to the data store in one go.

In client/server applications, you can also pass recordsets between the business logic tier and the user interface tier, where they can be manipulated locally. This saves database resources, which can be critical on large-scale applications, as well as minimizing network traffic. These recordsets are called disconnected recordsets.

The Fields Collection

The Fields collection identifies each field in a recordset, and there are two ways in which this can be used. The first is with existing recordsets, where you can examine each field, see its type, check its name, etc. This is quite useful when you are unsure of exactly what the recordset contains, and can be useful in scripting when showing tables dynamically. Using the **Fields** collection allows you to find the name of each field. For example, in ASP script you could do this:

```
Response.Write "<TABLE>"
For Each fldF In objRec.Fields
  Response.Write "<TR><TD>" & fldF.Name & "</TD></TR>"
Next
Response.Write "</TABLE>"
```

This creates an HTML table showing which fields are in a recordset. In fact, using a similar method, you could easily create a simple script routine that accepts any recordset and builds an HTML table from it. You could use the Fields collection to supply the table header, showing the column names, and the recordset to fill in the details of the table.

The second method is if you wish to create a recordset manually. So far we've only talked about data coming from a data store, but there might be occasions where you need a recordset of data, but no provider exists for that data store. For example, imagine you wanted to provide a recordset of keys and values from the registry. There's no OLEDB provider for the registry, but you could read the values yourself, and construct your own recordset:

```
objRec.CursorLocation = adUseClient
objRec.Fields.Append "Key", adVarChar, 50, adFldFixed
objRec.Fields.Append "Value", adVarChar, 50, adFldFixed
```

You now have two fields in the recordset, so you could look through the registry keys adding items to the recordset.

You can also use this method to create a single recordset combining selected fields from two other recordsets.

The Errors Collection

The **Errors** collection holds all of the errors when a data provider generates an error, or returns warnings, in response to some failure. This is provided as a collection because a failure can generate more that one error. For example, the following statement generates two errors because **X** and **Y** are unknown columns.

```
objConn.Open "DSN=pubs"
Set objRec = objConn.Execute "SELECT X, Y FROM authors"
```

You could check the errors by looping through the collection:

```
For Each objErr In objConn.Errors
  Print objErr.Description
Next
```

If you haven't got a predefined connection object you can use the
ActiveConnection property of the Command or Recordset:

```
objRec.Open "SELECT X, Y FROM authors", "DSN=pubs", _
            adOpenStatic, adLockReadOnly, adCmdTable

For Each objErr In objRec.ActiveConnection.Errors
  Print objErr.Description
Next
```

As with the Fields collection, you could easily build a simple routine that
centralizes error handling.

The Parameters Collection

The **Parameters** collection is unique to the **Command** object and allows you to
pass parameters into stored queries and procedures. One of the great advantages
of stored procedures is their ability to accept parameters and then act upon
them, so there is a collection especially for handling parameters.

Parameters contain several pieces of information, including:

- **Name**, which is the name they are defined as in the stored procedure
- **Type**, which identifies the type of data the parameter stores
- **Size**, to identify the size of the data
- **Direction**, to specify whether the parameter is an input parameter, an output parameter, both, or a return value
- **Value**, which is the actual parameter value

When using parameters you have two options. Firstly you can ask the data
provider to fetch the parameters from the data source, and the Parameters
collection will be filled in automatically for you:

```
objCmd.Parameters.Refresh
```

The downside of this is that it requires a trip to the server, which may cause
your program to perform poorly, especially if you do this often. However it's a
great way of finding out what ADO expects your parameters to be, and is very
useful during development.

The second option is to add the parameters to the collection manually, like so:

```
Set objParm = objCmd.CreateParameter ("ID", adInteger, adParamInput, 8, 147)
```

This creates an input parameter called `ID`, which is an integer (length 8), and has a value of 147. Once created, the parameter can be appended to the parameters collection:

```
objCmd.Parameters.Append objParm
```

Despite the fact that it's better to manually append parameters, using Refresh can be very useful during debugging to determine what type and size the provider expects a certain parameter to be. Another good use is to use Refresh when you first connect to the data store, and cache the parameters details locally, perhaps in an array, or in a user collection. This sort of approach allows you to write generic routines that process stored procedures. There's an example of this when we look at parameters in more detail.

The Properties Collection

The Properties collection contains provider-specific information about the object. For a Connection it contains a large amount of information about the facilities that the provider supports, such as the maximum number of columns in a SELECT statement, or what sort of outer join capabilities are supported. For a recordset, there's just as much information, ranging from the current locking level to the asynchronous capabilities supported by the provider.

You can examine or set individual values by just using their name to index into the collection. For example:

```
Print objConn.Properties("Max Columns in Select")
```

To examine all of the properties you can use a simple loop:

```
For Each objProp In objConn.Properties
   Print objProp.Name
Next
```

For much of the time you will probably never use this collection, unless you are writing an application that supports multiple data providers, in which case you may need to query the provider to examine what it supports.

Language Differences

One of the things we've tried to do with this book is make it relatively language-independent. As ADO can be used by any programming language that supports COM, the subject of which language to show samples in becomes quite a sticky one. So, to give this the widest possible audience, we've stuck with a pseudo-code type style. For example, in the examples that show something being printed we've just used `Print`. You can then substitute the command for your language of choice.

The different methods for languages are shown overleaf:

Language	Method	Notes
Visual Basic	`Debug.Print   "message"`	Prints the text to the debug window
	`MsgBox   "message"`	Pops up a window with the text
ASP & VBScript	`Response.Write   "message"`	Returns the text to the browser
ASP & JavaScript	`Response.Write   ("message");`	Returns the text to the browser
VBScript	`document.write   "message"`	Inserts message into the html document
	`MsgBox   "message"`	Pops up a window with the text
JavaScript	`document.write   ("message");`	Inserts message into the html document
	`alert   ("message");`	Pops up a window with the text

Although we've tried to keep this language-independent, most of the samples we've used show a Visual Basic/VBScript style, because this is where we see the greatest market for ADO usage as being. However, this should be easily translated into your favorite language.

Creating Objects

Creating the ADO objects is one area where pseudo-code doesn't really work too well. There are significant differences between Visual Basic and VBScript for example, so we've covered these in more detail, in the three languages where ADO is going to have most impact. This isn't intended as a full explanation of all of the objects and how they are used in each language, but more to show the major differences between the languages.

Visual Basic

Before you can create an ADO object in Visual Basic you must make sure you have a reference to the ADO library set. From the Project menu select References, and then pick ActiveX Data Objects 2.0 Library. Once selected there are two ways to create objects. The first, is probably the most often used:

```
Dim objRec As New ADODB.Recordset
```

This creates and instantiates the object immediately. If you want to create the object but not instantiate it you can do this:

```
Dim objRec As ADODB.Recordset
```

When you need to instantiate the object you can then do this:

```
Set objRec = New ADODB.recordset
```

This gives early binding and allows Visual Basic to provide tooltips on the functions. The second method is the older style, using late binding, and is less used these days:

```
Dim objRec As Object

Set objRec = CreateObject("ADODB.Recordset")
```

Using the methods and properties is extremely simple. For example:

```
objRec.Cursorlocation = adUseClient
objConn.Open "authors", objConn, adOpenKeyset, _
            adLockOptimistic, adCmdTable
```

The **ad** constants are automatically available to you in Visual Basic once you have referenced the ADO library.

Looping through a recordset is just a question of using the **MoveNext** method and checking the **EOF** property:

```
While Not objRec.EOF
   Debug.Print objRec("field_name")
   objRec.MoveNext
Wend
```

VBScript

Creating the objects in VBScript is different from Visual Basic because VBScript doesn't have variable types or support for a type library, although it does use the Visual Basic syntax for assigning object variables using **Set**. Therefore there's no need to define the variables, although for completeness it's always best to.

```
Dim objRec
Set objRec = Server.CreateObject("ADODB.Recordset")
```

This creates a connection object in ASP script code.

Using the object follows the same procedure as for Visual Basic:

```
objRec.Cursorlocation = adUseClient
objConn.Open "authors", objConn, adOpenKeyset, _
            adLockOptimistic, adCmdTable
```

The only difference here is that the constants are not automatically available, as scripting languages do not have access to the type library and its constants. There are two options available to you. The first is to use the values that these constants represent, but this means your code is sprinkled with various numbers. For example, using this method the above statement would read:

```
objRec.Cursorlocation = 3
objConn.Open "authors", objConn, 1, 3, 2
```

This makes your code hard to read, and therefore less maintainable. The second option is to include the constants in your ASP script, which means you can use the constant names instead of their values. You can include them using the following line:

```
<!-- #INCLUDE FILE="adovbs.inc"-->
```

This file is installed in the default directory of **Program Files\Common Files\System\ADO**, and can be moved to your local ASP directory or referenced from a central virtual directory.

> *To learn more about ASP you should try Beginning Active Server Pages 2.0 (ISBN1-861001-34-7) or Professional Active Server Pages 2.0 (ISBN 1-861001-26-6), both from Wrox Press.*

Looping through recordsets in VBScript is exactly the same as in Visual Basic:

```
While Not objRec.EOF
  Response.Write objRec("field_name")
  objRec.MoveNext
Wend
```

Jscript

JScript has a different syntax to VBScript, although much of the object usage is similar. The major thing to watch for is that JScript is case-sensitive. If you were using JScript you would use:

```
var objRec = Server.CreateObject("ADODB.Recordset");
```

Use of the methods and properties is the same too:

```
objRec.Cursorlocation = adUseClient;
objConn.Open ("authors", objConn, adOpenKeyset, adLockOptimistic, adCmdTable);
```

To loop through a recordset in JScript you would use:

```
while (!objRec.EOF)
{
  Response.Write (objRec("field_name"));
  objRec.MoveNext();
}
```

Visual J++

Visual J++ is Microsoft's version of the Java language, and is a much more object-oriented language than either of the scripting languages, but looks similar in structure to JScript. To use ADO within J++ you must import the ADO library:

```
import com.ms.wfc.data.*;
```

Creating an object follows this syntax:

```
Connection objConn = new Connection();
Recordset objRec = new Recordset();
```

Opening and looping through a recordset is not much different from JScript in layout, although the actual commands are different. The following shows the Java native types feature in ADO 2.0:

```
objConn.open ("DSN=pubs");
objRec.open ("author", objConn,
             AdoEnums.CursorType.DYNAMIC,
             AdoEnums.LockType.OPTIMISTIC,
             AdoEnums.CommandType.TABLE);

while (!objRec.getEOF())
{
    System.out.println (objRec.getFields().getItem(field_number).getString());
    objRec.moveNext();
}
```

Visual C++

To use ADO within C++ you must import the ADO library:

```
#import "c:\program files\common files\system\ado\msado15.dll" \
    no_namespace \
    rename( "EOF", "adoEOF" )
```

You must make sure the file path points to the location of your version of the ADO DLL. The **no_namespace** keyword is added so that you don't have to scope the ADO names. The **EOF** property has to be renamed due to an unfortunate name collision with the **EOF** constant defined in the Standard C library.

Creating an object follows this syntax:

```
_ConnectionPtr          pConnection;
pConnection.CreateInstance( __uuidof( Connection ) );
_RecordsetPtr           pRecordSet;
pRecordSet.CreateInstance( __uuidof( Recordset ) );
```

Opening and looping through a recordset is not much different from J++ in layout, although the actual commands are different:

```
pConnection->Open( "DSN=travelDB", "", "", -1 );

pRecordSet->Open( "Packages", pConnection.GetInterfacePtr(),
        adOpenDynamic,
        adLockOptimistic,
        adCmdTable );

_variant_t      theValue;
```

```
while ( !pRecordSet->adoEOF )
{
    theValue = pRecordSet->GetFields()->GetItem( fieldNumber )->Value;
    printf( "%s\n", (char *)_bstr_t( theValue ) );
    pRecordSet->MoveNext();
}
```

OLEDB Providers

We've already mentioned that ADO can connect to many different data providers, and this is due to OLEDB. Remember that ADO is just a layer that sits on top of OLEDB to hide the complexity, so it seems sensible to look at some of these data providers in more detail. We need to see what differences there are between them, for although most of the ADO usage will be the same, OLEDB Providers don't always support the same facilities. This is natural, because some of them are fundamentally very different. Most of the relational database providers, for example, will provide similar facilities, but other providers might not work in the same way.

When you install the data access components you are supplied with the following OLEDB providers:

Driver	Description
MSDASQL	ODBC, which allows connection to existing ODBC data sources, either via a System DSN or from dynamically provided connection details.
Microsoft.Jet. SQLOLEDB.3.51	Jet, for connecting to Microsoft Access databases.
SQLOLEDB	SQL Server, for connecting to Microsoft SQL Server.
MSDAORA	Oracle, for connecting to Oracle databases.
MSIDXS	Index Server, for connecting to Microsoft Index Server
ADSDSOObject	Active Directory Services, for connecting to Directory Service agents.
MSDataShape	Data Shape, for hierarchical recordsets.
MSPersist	Persist, for locally saved recordsets.
MSDAOSP	Simple Provider, for creating your own providers for simple text data.

These are just the defaults supplied, some of which may not appear, depending upon your installation options.

You can find out which providers are available on your system by creating a new Data Link. This is similar to an ODBC DSN, but for OLEDB connections you can create one in any directory simply by right mouse clicking (or from the File menu) in Explorer, picking New, and selecting Microsoft Data Link. This creates a file with a UDL extension, and you can then view the properties. From the Provider tab you can see the available providers:

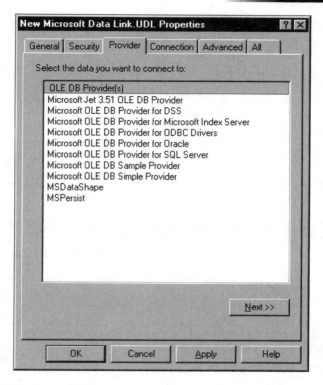

In fact, using the Data Link is a good way to create connection strings if you are unfamiliar with them. You can create a Data Link file, filling in the details on screen, and then examine the UDL file (which is what the data link file is stored as) in notepad.

Connection Strings

One of the major differences between providers is in the connection string, as different providers require different information to connect you to the data store.

ADO only recognizes four arguments in the connection string, and passes all others onto the provider. The main one you are interested in is **Provider**, which identifies the OLEDB provider to be used. The second one is **File Name**, which can be used to point to an existing Data Link file. If you use this option then you can omit the **Provider**, since the Data Link file contains this information. The other two are for Remote Data Services, and are covered in detail in Chapter 7.

ODBC

The OLEDB Provider for ODBC is the default provider, so if you don't specify which one to use, this is what you'll get. For the ODBC provider you have three choices: to use an existing ODBC Data Source Name, a DSN-less connection string, or an ODBC File DSN.

For a DSN based connection, simply specify the data source name:

```
Provider=MSDASQL; DSN=data_source_name
```

For a DSN-less connection, the connection string varies with the database you are connecting to. It follows the same conventions as an ODBC connection string – you can see the parameters in the ODBC applet in the Control Panel. There is one important option which is the same for all ODBC connections, as it specifies the ODBC driver to use:

```
Provider=MSDASQL; Driver=
```

The name of the driver is the same name that is shown when you create a new DSN from the Control panel. Your list of drivers may differ from this:

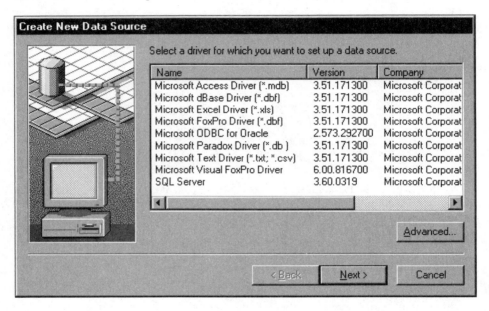

You should enclose the driver name in braces. For example, to connect to Microsoft Access, your connect string would start like this:

```
Provider=MSDASQL; Driver={Microsoft Access Driver (*.mdb)}
```

You then have to specify the Access database:

```
Provider=MSDASQL; Driver={Microsoft Access Driver (*.mdb)}; DBQ=C:\mdb_name.mdb
```

To connect to SQL Server you need to supply a little more information:

- **Server** is the name of the SQL Server
- **Database** is the database name
- **UID** is the SQL Server user ID
- **PWD** is the password for the SQL Server user ID

For example:

```
Provider=MSDASQL; Driver={SQL Server}; Server=Tigger; Database=pubs; UID=sa;
PWD=
```

Jet

When using the Jet driver you only need to specify the database name:

```
Provider=Microsoft.Jet.SQLOLEDB.3.51; Data Source=C:\mdb_name.mdb
```

If you have a system database you can use the **Properties** collection to set this before opening the connection , but you must specify the provider first:

```
objConn.Provider = " Microsoft.Jet.SQLOLEDB.3.51"
objConn.Properties("Jet OLEDB:System database") = "C:\system_db_name"
objConn.Open "Data Source=C:\pubs\pubs.mdb"
```

A database password is also set in this way:

```
objConn.Properties("Jet OLEDB:Database Password") = "LetMeIn"
```

SQL Server

As SQL Server can contain multiple databases you need an extra parameter:

```
Provider=SQLOLEDB; Data Source=server_name; Initial Catalog=database_name; User
Id=user_id; Password=user_password
```

For example:

```
Provider=SQLOLEDB; Data Source=Tigger; Initial Catalog=pubs; User Id=sa;
Password=
```

Index Server

For Index Server you only need to specify the provider name, unless you have multiple catalogs in use under Index Server. In this case you use the **Data Source** to specify the required catalog:

```
Provider=MSIDXS; Data Source=catalog_name
```

Asynchronous Processing

Asynchronous processing is one of the new features in ADO 2, and allows commands to be executed at the same time as other commands. This is particularly useful if creating very large recordsets, or running a query that may take a long time, as you can continue with another task, and let ADO tell you when the command has finished. You can also cancel a long running command if you wish. Events can also be used when certain actions are about to happen or when they have happened.

Note: Scripting languages do not support events.

Events

Only the **Recordset** and **Connection** support events, and there are generally two types of events – those that are called before an operation starts, a **Will** event, and those that are called after it has completed, a **Complete** event. There are a few other events that are called after an event has completed, but they are not part of the **Will** and **Complete** event pairs.

A **Will** event is called just before the action starts. You then have a chance to examine the details of the action, and cancel the action if you decide that you do not want it to run. The **Complete** event is called just after the action completes, whether or not it was cancelled. If it was cancelled, then the **Errors** collection is filled with details of why it was cancelled.

The **Will** events generally have an argument, **adStatus**, indicating the status of the event. You can set this argument to **adStatusCancel** before the method ends, to cancel the action that caused the event. For example, suppose a connection generated a **WillConnect** event; setting **adStatus** to **adStatusCancel** will cancel the connection. The **ConnectComplete** event will then be called, with a status indicating that the connection failed.

The nature of events means that there can be several **Will** events that could result from a single action. Although all of these will be called, there is no guaranteed order in which this will happen.

Event Pairings

The way the **Will** and **Complete** events are generated can often be confusing, especially in terms of what happens when you wish to cancel an event. The action triggers the **Will** event, which has it's own event procedure. This code runs, and then the action itself is run. After the action is finished, the **Complete** event is triggered, which runs its event procedure. Once that has completed, execution will continue at the line after the action. The following diagram shows this using Connection events, when opening a connection:

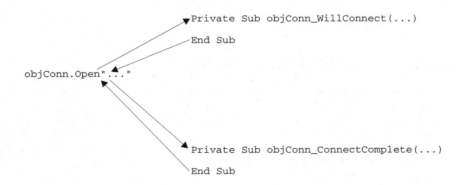

In the **WillConnect** event procedure we can decide whether we want this action (that is the **objConn.Open**) to take place or not. The event procedure has a parameter called **adStatus**, which we can use. If we set this to **adStatusCancel** before the event procedure finishes, then the action is cancelled. The **ConnectComplete** event still runs, but with its parameters indicating an error. For example:

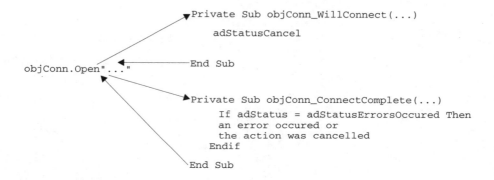

```
                              Private Sub objConn_WillConnect(...)

                                  adStatusCancel

objConn.Open"..."           End Sub


                              Private Sub objConn_ConnectComplete(...)
                                  If adStatus = adStatusErrorsOccured Then
                                  an error occured or
                                  the action was cancelled
                              Endif

                              End Sub
```

The important thing to note is that the **ConnectComplete** event is still generated, but the connection does not actually take place.

Some actions may generate more than one event, so what happens here? Well the **Will** event is always generated before its associated **Complete** event, but where there are two **Will** events, the order in which they are generated is not guaranteed. If you cancel the action from within an event procedure, and this happens to run as the first event procedure, then the second set of event procedures (both the **Will** and the **Complete**) are never generated. For example, imagine a recordset, where you have events to detect when fields and records change:

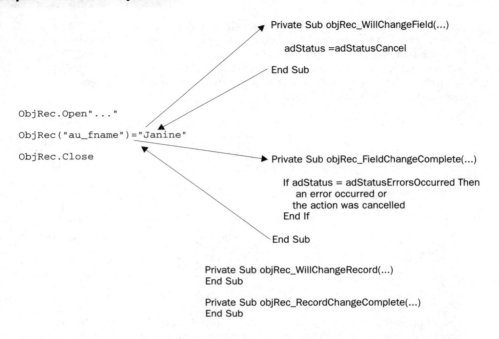

```
Private Sub objRec_WillChangeField(...)

    adStatus =adStatusCancel

End Sub
```

```
ObjRec.Open"..."
ObjRec("au_fname")="Janine"
ObjRec.Close
```

```
Private Sub objRec_FieldChangeComplete(...)

    If adStatus = adStatusErrorsOccurred Then
        an error occurred or
        the action was cancelled
    End If

End Sub
```

```
Private Sub objRec_WillChangeRecord(...)
End Sub
```

```
Private Sub objRec_RecordChangeComplete(...)
End Sub
```

Here the action has been canceled in the **WillChangeField** event procedure. The **FieldChangeComplete** event procedure runs, but indicates that an error occurred, and the actual action, that of setting the field value is not executed. The **WillChangeRecord** and **RecordChangeComplete** event procedures are not run.

Although these diagrams use Visual Basic, it's the order of events that's important.

Visual Basic

To use events within Visual Basic you declare a variable using the **WithEvents** keyword. This must be a module level variable, as **WithEvent**s is invalid within procedures:

```
Private WithEvents objRec As ADODB.Recordset
```

Note that the **New** keyword is omitted when using this syntax, because you can't instantiate objects at the same time as declaring the variable with events. You have to do this separately:

```
Set objRec = New ADODB.Recordset
```

Once you have declared the variable, the object will appear in the objects list in the code combo, and a list of events in the event combo:

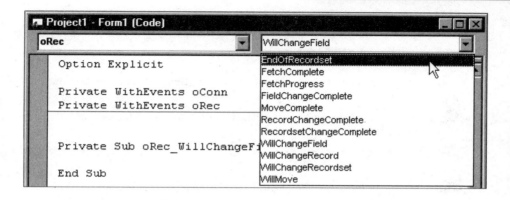

Visual J++

The procedure is a little more complex in J++, but still pretty easy. Firstly you must declare an event handler variable – this one's for a connection

```
ConnectionEventHandler evtConnHandler =
    new ConnectionEventHandler(this, "onConnectComplete")
```

The handler variable is called **evtConnHandler**, and the procedure we are creating is **"onConnectComplete"**. This can be any name you choose, but it's best to stick to the standard names. Next you need to add that handler to the connection:

```
objConn.addOnConnectComplete(evtConnHandler)
```

This links our piece of handler code to the **ConnectComplete** event. At the end of your program you need to remove the event handler:

```
objConn.removeOnConnectComplete(evtConnHandler)
```

All you have to do now is write the actual handler itself:

```
public void onConnectComplete (Object sender,
                               ConnectionEvent e)
{
    if (e.adStatus = AdoEnums.EventStatus.ERRORSOCCURRED)
        System.out.println("Connection failed");
    else
        System.out.println("Connection succeeded");
    return;
}
```

This is the code that is run when the event is generated. For more details of this you should consult the J++ documentation.

Connection Events

There are nine connection events:

- **BeginTransComplete** is called after a **BeginTrans** method has completed.

- **CommitTransComplete** is called after a **CommitTrans** method has completed.

- **RollbackTransComplete** is called after a **RollbackTrans** method has completed.

- **WillConnect** is called just before a connection is established.

- **ConnectComplete** is called after a connection is established.

- **Disconnect** is called after a connection has disconnected.

- **WillExecute** is called before an **Execute** method is run.

- **ExecuteComplete** is called after an **Execute** method has completed.

- **InfoMessage** is called when the provider returns information messages.

An example of the **Complete** events could be to indicate to the user the status of their connection.

The individual events for a Connection are discussed in more detail in Chapter 3.

Recordset Events

The recordset has a couple more events than the connection:

- **FetchProgress**, is called periodically during an asynchronous recordset creation.

- **FetchComplete** is called when the recordset has been fully populated with its records.

- **WillChangeField** is called before an action causes a field to change.

    FieldChangeComplete is called after an action caused a field to change.

- **WillMove** is called before an action causes the current record to change.

- **MoveComplete** is called after an action caused the current record to change.

- **EndOfRecordset** is called when there is an attempt to move beyond the end of the recordset.

- **WillChangeRecord** is called before an action causes the data in the current record to change.

- **RecordChangeComplete** is called after an action caused the data in the current record to change.

- **WillChangeRecordset** is called before an action causes the recordset to change (such as a filter).

- **RecordsetChangeComplete** is called after an action caused the recordset to change.

The Will events can be used to notify the user that an action may change data, or may change the underlying records in the recordset.

One thing to watch in Visual Basic 6 is when using the new ADO Data Control, as this automatically updates records when using the video style buttons to move around the records. If you change a field, then the **WillChangeField** event is called, and if the value is not correct you can cancel the action. However, what gets cancelled is the **Update**, not the move. It's not a major problem, but something to bear in mind.

The individual events for a Recordset are discussed in more detail in Chapter 6.

Object Usage

One thing that confuses some people is when to use which object. After all, the **Connection**, **Command**, and **Recordset** can all return a recordset of data. There are only a few hard and fast rules, but in general here's what you should do:

- If you only ever need to run queries that don't return a recordset, and those queries are not stored procedures with parameters, then use the **Connection** object and the **Execute** method.

- If you need to use stored procedures with output parameters then you must use the **Command** object.

- If you need to specify the cursor type or lock type, then you must use a **Recordset** object.

- If you are creating only one or two recordsets of data, then you can use the **Recordset** directly, passing in a connection string.

- If you are creating three or more recordsets, then create a **Connection** object first, then the **Recordset** objects. Remember that each time you connect to a data store with a connection string, a new connection is opened.

Summary

OK. In this chapter, we looked at ADO 2.0's flexible object model, and discussed its most important objects - the **Connection**, **Command** and **Recordset** objects. We also covered its several collections: **Field**, **Errors**, **Parameters** and **Properties**. We then covered how to create and instantiate all of these objects quickly and easily in a range of languages and from a number of OLEDB providers. Finally we discussed asynchronous processing in ADO 2.0 and covered its most important appplication, in the concept of **Events**. In the next four chapters of the books, we'll move on to look at these objects in considerably more depth, and cover their properties and methods. We'll begin, in the next chapter, with the **Connection** object.

Chapter

3

The Connection Object

The Connection object is what connects the consumer to the provider. That is, it's the link between the program and the data. You've already seen that the flat model of ADO means that Connection objects don't need to be explicitly created, and that you can pass a Connection String directly to a Command or a Recordset object. However, creating a Connection object is worthwhile if you are going to be getting data from the data source more than once, because the connection won't have to be established each time.

Connection Pooling

Following the newsgroups in the early days of ADO, there was a lot of talk about connection pooling, and whether the benefits really are worthwhile. One of the most time-consuming operations you can perform is to connect to a data store, so anything that can speed this up is defined as 'a good thing'.

Connection Pooling means that ADO will not actually destroy connection objects unless it really needs to. This is dictated by a timeout value, so if the connection hasn't been reused within this time, it is destroyed. So, if you open a connection, perform some data access, and then close the connection, from your point of view, the connection is closed. But underneath, OLEDB keeps the connection in a pool, ready for it to be used again. If you then decide that you need to open the same connection again, you will be given a Connection object from the pool of connections, and ADO doesn't actually have to perform all of the expensive data store stuff again. You may not necessarily get your original object back, but may get one that matches the same connection details. In fact, existing objects will be given to anyone who requests them, so this is even better in a multi-user system.

One important point to note about connection pooling is that connections will only be reused if they match the exact connection details. So on multi-user systems, if you specify the same data store, but different user names and passwords, then you will create a new connection, rather than having one reused from the pool. This may seem a disadvantage, but pooling must be done this way to avoid breaking security – it just wouldn't be right to reuse a connection if the user details differed.

You might not think that connection pooling can make a big difference, but you can easily see this as you can turn pooling on and off. Consider this piece of code, using the Microsoft OLEDB Provider for SQL Server:

```
sConn = "Provider=SQLOLEDB; Server=Tigger; " & _
        "Database=Pubs; User Id=sa; Password=;"
For iLoop = 1 To 1000
    oConn.Open sConn
    oConn.Close
Next
```

On my system (P166 96Mb Memory NT Server 4.0) this runs in 1973 milliseconds. However, if I turn off connection pooling it takes 2073 milliseconds. Now admittedly that's not a lot of difference, and you're unlikely to perform this sort of Open/Close in this manner anyway, but you can see there is a difference. If you have a busy web site, with lots of data access and many users, it's clear that connection pooling can provide a big performance benefit.

Although you probably wouldn't want to, you can turn off connection pooling by adding `OLE DB Services = -2` to the end of the connection string, or by setting the Connection objects Properties entry of the same name:

```
sConn = " . . .; OLE DB Services = -2"
```

or

```
oConn.Properties("OLE DB Services") = -2
```

This property takes values from the DBPROPS_OS constants (see Appendix F). If you've already flicked to the back to find the constant with a value of -2, you'll notice there isn't one. There is, however, a constant to turn connection pooling on, so, to turn it off you have to use some binary arithmetic. Take the value for turning on connection pooling and perform a logical NOT operation on it. DBPROPVAL_OS_RESOURCEPOOLING has a value of 1 so:

```
        DBPROPVAL_OS_RESOURCEPOOLING = 00000001
NOT     DBPROPVAL_OS_RESOURCEPOOLING = 11111110
```

and this equals -2.

If you're using an include file containing these constants then you can use this format:

```
oConn.Properties("OLE DB Services") = DBPROPVAL_OS_ENABLEALL AND _
                    (NOT DBPROPVAL_OS_RESOURCEPOOLING)
```

This says we want all services enabled, apart from resource pooling. This sort of bit masking is how many of the Properties are used.

The Properties collection is discussed in more detail in Chapter 6 and Appendix C

For ODBC Connections, the Control Panel applet controls connection pooling.

50

Connection Methods

BeginTrans

Begins a new transaction

```
Long  =  Connection.BeginTrans
```

A transaction provides atomicity to a series of data changes to a recordset (or recordsets) within a connection, allowing all of the changes to take place at once, or not at all. Once a transaction has been started, any changes to a recordset attached to the Connection object are cached until the transaction is completed or abandoned. At that stage all of the changes will either be written to the underlying data store (if the transaction is Committed) or discarded (if the transaction is Aborted).

The return value indicates the level of nested transactions. This will be 1 for a top-level transaction, and will be incremented by 1 for each subsequent transaction. You can ignore this value if you don't need to keep track of transaction levels.

Not all providers support transactions, and calling this method against a provider that does not support transactions will generate an error. To check that transactions are supported you can check the **Transaction DDL** property of the Connection object's Properties object. For example:

```
iSupported = oConn.Properties("Transaction DDL")
If iSupported = DBPROPVAL_TC_ALL Then
  ' transactions are fully supported
   oConn.BeginTrans
End If
```

DBPROPVAL_TC_AL has a value of 8. The constants are explained in more detail in Appendix F, and the Properties collection in Appendix C.

Nested Transactions

Nested transactions allow you to have transactions within transactions, and allow you to segment your work in a more controlled manner. For example, consider the following situation:

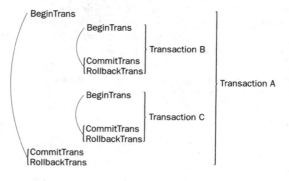

Transaction A starts, which is the first transaction, and no changes made within this transaction will be visible outside of the transaction, unless dirty reads are being used. Then transaction B starts, and the nesting level is now two. The changes in B are not visible to transaction A, until B commits or rolls back. At this stage A can see the changes, but processes outside of A cannot. The same happens with C – its changes will not be visible to A until C commits or rolls back. Once A commits, then all of the changes, that is those in A, B and C, are visible to other processes. If A rolls back its changes, it does not roll back any changes committed by B or C.

The use of the connection attributes to force transactions to automatically start on commit and rollback can have serious consequences when nesting transactions. This is because every time you commit or rollback a transaction, a new one is automatically started. Imagine some code like this:

```
' start first transaction
objConn.BeginTrans

' start nested transaction
objConn.BeginTrans

' do some processing

' commit nested transaction
objConn.CommitTrans
```

If auto transaction mode is in place, then as soon as this nested transaction is committed, another nested transaction is started. You don't have a way to commit a transaction without it starting another, so you can never get back to the first transaction.

You might never use nested transactions, but it's good to be aware that this problem can arise.

Cancel

Cancels the execution of a pending, asynchronous **Execute** or **Open** operation.

Connection.Cancel

This is particularly useful when writing applications that allow a user to specify connection details, or when users explicitly log on to a connection. If, after a certain delay, the connection has not been established, you can inform the user and offer the option of canceling the connection attempt. For example, in Visual Basic you could open the connection asynchronously, and offer the user a Cancel button, which would call this method.

Calling Cancel will return a run-time error if **adRunAsync** was not used as one of the *Options* on the **Execute** or **Open** operation.

Close

Closes an open connection and any dependant objects.

Connection.Close

Closing a connection does not remove it from memory, and you can change its settings and reopen it. You must set the object variable to **Nothing** to free the object from memory. For example:

```
objConn.Close
Set objConn = Nothing
```

If you want to ensure you don't get an error when trying to close a connection that is not open, you can do this:

```
If objConn.State = adStateOpen Then
  objConn.Close
End If
Set objConn = Nothing
```

The **Close** method closes any Recordset objects associated with the connection. If you have any Command objects associated with the connection, they will persist, but the **ActiveConnection** parameter will be cleared, thus disassociating the command with a connection, producing a disconnected recordset.

Any pending changes in Recordset objects associated with the connection will be rolled back. If a transaction is in progress, then using **Close** will generate an error. Transactions will be automatically rolled back if a Connection object falls out of scope, and no error is generated.

CommitTrans

Saves any pending changes and ends the current transaction.

Connection.CommitTrans

All changes made since the previous **BeginTrans** will be written to the data store. This only affects the most recently opened transaction, and you must resolve lower level transactions before resolving higher level ones. So, if you are nesting transactions, you cannot start two transactions and then Commit or Abort the outer transaction without first Committing or Aborting the inner transaction.

If the **Attributes** property of the Connection object is set to **adXactCommitRetaining** then the provider automatically starts a new transaction after this call.

Execute

Executes the query, SQL statement, stored procedure, or provider specific text.

```
Set Recordset = Connection.Execute(CommandText,
[RecordsAffected], [Options])
```

Name	Type	Description	Default
CommandText	String	Contains the SQL statement, table name, stored procedure name, or provider specific text to execute.	
RecordsAffected	Long	A variable into which the provider returns the number of records that the operation affected (Optional).	
Options	Long	A value that indicates how the provider should interpret the **CommandText** argument (Optional).	-1

Options can be one or more of the **CommandTypeEnum** constants:

adCmdText, for a SQL string

adCmdTable, for a table name

adCmdTableDirect, for a table name

adCmdStoredProc, for a stored procedure name

adCmdFile, for a saved recordset

adCmdUnknown, for an unknown command type

adAsyncExecute, for asynchronous execution

adAsyncFetch, for asynchronous fetching

adAsyncFetchNonBlocking, for asynchronous fetching that does not block

adExecuteNoRecords, for a non-row returning command

More details of these options can be found under the **CommandType** property.

A new Recordset object is returned, even if it is not used. If the command did not return any rows then the recordset will be empty. If you specify the **adCmdExecuteNoRecords** option, then a null recordset is returned. The Recordset object returned is always a forward-only, read-only (often called a firehose) cursor. You can get different cursor types by using the **Open** method of the Recordset object.

You can use this method with or without some arguments, and with or without it returning a recordset. For example, to return a recordset you could use this syntax:

```
strCommandText = "SELECT * FROM authors"
Set objRec = objConn.Execute (strCommandText, , adCmdText)
```

If your command does not return any rows, then you should include the **adExecuteNoRecords** option, as this can improve performance:

```
strCommandText = "UPDATE titles SET price = price * 1.10"
objConn.Execute (strCommandText, , adCmdText And adCmdExecuteNorecords)
```

If you want to find out how many records were affected by the command then you can use the *RecordsAffected* argument, passing in a variable. This is especially useful for action queries, where a recordset is not returned:

```
strCommandText = "UPDATE titles SET Price = Price * 1.10"
objConn.Execute strCommandText, lngRecs, adCmdText
Print lngRecs & " were updated."
```

To have the command executed asynchronously you can also add one of the asynchronous flags to the *Options* argument. For example:

```
objConn.Execute strCommandText, lngRecs, adCmdText And adAsyncExecute
```

An **ExecuteComplete** event will be raised when this operation finishes. This happens even if the command is executed synchronously, but is more useful when asynchronous operations are in use.

Open

Opens a connection to a data source, so that commands can be executed against it.

Connection.Open(*ConnectionString, UserID, Password, Options*)

Name	Type	Description	Default
ConnectionString	String	The connection information.	
UserID	String	The user name to use when connecting.	
Password	String	The user password to use when connecting.	
Options	Integer	Extra connection options.	-1

Options can be one of the **ConnectOptionEnum** constants. At the moment the only constant is **adAsyncConnect**, which indicates the connection should be made asynchronously.

The **ConnectionString** property inherits the value from the *ConnectString* argument.

Values passed in the *UserID* and *Password* arguments override similar values passed in the *ConnectionString* argument.

Some typical connection strings are shown below. For the ODBC Provider connecting to an Access database you would use:

```
Driver={Microsoft Access Driver (*.mdb)}; DBQ=database_file
```

The DBQ argument points to the physical path name of the Access database. To connect to SQL Server, again using ODBC, you would use:

```
Driver={SQL Server}; Server=server_name; Database=database_name; UID=user_name;
PWD=user_password
```

Switching over to the native OLEDB drivers, connecting to Access would be like this:

```
Provider=Micrsoft.Jet.OLEDB.3.51; Data Source=database_file
```

For SQL Server, using the native driver, it would be:

```
Provider=SQLOLEDB; Data Source=server_name; Initial Catalog=database_name; User
Id=user_name; Password=user_password
```

More details of the different connection strings that can be used can be found under the **ConnectString** property, as well as in Chapter 2.

OpenSchema

Obtains database schema information from the provider.

```
Recordset = Connection.OpenSchema(QueryType, [Criteria],
[SchemaID])
```

Name	Type	Description	Default
QueryType	Schema Enum	The type of schema query to run.	
Criteria (Optional)	Variant	An array of query constraints for each Schema option.	
SchemaID (Optional)	Variant	The GUID for a provider specific schema query not defined by the OLEDB specification.	

Each value of **SchemaEnum** has a specific set of criteria values, and as this list is large, it's included in Appendix F.

This method is most useful for obtaining table and procedure names from a data store. For example

```
Set oRec = oConn.OpenSchema(adSchemaTables)
While Not oRec.EOF
    Print oRec("TABLE_NAME")
    Print oRec("TABLE_TYPE")
    oRec.MoveNext
Wend
```

Note that the Visual Basic quick tips show the arguments for **OpenSchema** as *Schema, Restrictions* and *SchemaID*. These are the same as above, but just named differently.

The various Schemas are examined in detail in Appendix D.

RollbackTrans

Cancels any changes made during the current transaction and ends the transaction.

```
Connection.RollbackTrans
```

All changes made since the previous **BeginTrans** will be cancelled. This only affects the most recently opened transaction, and like **CommitTrans**, you must resolve lower level transactions before resolving higher level ones.

If the **Attributes** property of the Connection object is set to **adXactCommitAbort** then the provider automatically starts a new transaction after this call.

Connection Properties

Attributes

Indicates the transactional facilities of a Connection object.

```
Long = Connection.Attributes
Connection.Attributes = Long
```

The value can be one or more of the **adXactAttributeEnum** constants:

- **adXactCommitRetaining,** to ensure that new transactions are automatically started after a **CommitTrans**

- **adXactAbortRetaining** to ensure that new transactions are started after a **RollbackTrans**

- A combination of both to indicate that new transactions are automatically started after an existing transaction is finished

Note that not all providers support this property.

You can combine the two by **AND**ing them together:

```
oConn.Attributes = adXactCommitRetaining And adXactAbortRetaining
```

Beware of automatic transaction enlistment when using nested transactions, as this can lead to problems committing the higher level transactions. For more details of this see the Nested Transactions section, under **BeginTrans**.

CommandTimeout

Indicates how long, in seconds, to wait while executing a command before terminating the command and generating an error. The default is 30.

```
Long  =  Connection.CommandTimeout
Connection.CommandTimeout  =  Long
```

An error is generated and the command cancelled if the timeout period is reached before the command completes execution. Setting this property to 0 will force the provider to wait indefinitely.

For example, the following will ensure that an error is generated if the command doesn't complete within 10 seconds:

```
oConn.CommandTimeout = 10
```

This value is not inherited by a Command object's **CommandTimeout** property.

ConnectionString

Contains the details used to create a connection to a data source.

```
String = Connection.ConnectionString
Connection.ConnectionString = String
```

ADO supports only four arguments in the connection string, and all other arguments are ignored by ADO and passed directly to the provider:

- *Provider=* identifies the name of the provider
- *File Name=* identifies the name of the provider specific file containing connection information (for example a UDL file)
- *Remote Provider=* is the name of a provider that should be used when opening a client-side connection (This only applies to RDS)
- *Remote Server=* is the path name of the server that should be used when opening a client-side connection (This only applies to RDS)

The connection string may be changed by the provider after the connection is established, as it fills in some of its own details.

You cannot pass both the *Provider* and *FileName* arguments. This is because using a *FileName* means that ADO will load the provider, since the provider details will be stored within this file.

Some examples of various connection strings are shown below:

For the ODBC provider connecting to Microsoft Access:

```
Driver={Microsoft Access Driver (*.mdb)}; DBQ=C:\ADO\Database.mdb
```

For the ODBC provider connecting to Microsoft SQL Server:

```
Driver={SQL Server}; Server=server_name; Database=database_name; UID=user_name;
PWD=password
```

You can also use an existing DSN:

```
DSN=pubs
```

The pros and cons of using a DSN versus a full ODBC connect string are discussed in Chapter 9.

Notice that you can omit the *Provider* option when using the OLEDB provider for ODBC as this is the default.

For the OLEDB provider for ODBC using an ODBC Data Source Name:

```
DSN=data_source_name
```

For the OLEDB provider connecting to Microsoft Access:

```
Provider=Microsoft.Jet.OLEDB.3.51; Data Source=C:\ADO\Database.mdb
```

For the OLEDB provider connecting to Microsoft SQL Server:

```
Provider=SQLOLEDB; Data Source=server_name; Initial Catalog=database_name; User
Id=user_name; Password=user_password
```

For example, to connect to a SQL Server using the OLEDB provider you would do something like this:

```
oConn.ConnectionString = "Provider=SQLOLEDB; Data Source=TIGGER; Initial
Catalog=pubs; User Id=davids; Password=bouncy"
oConn.Open
```

If, when you open a connection, you pass the connection details into the *ConnectionString* argument, then the `ConnectionString` property will be filled in with these details.

For more information on Connection strings, refer to Chapter 2.

ConnectionTimeout

Indicates how long, in seconds, to wait whilst trying to establish a connection before aborting the attempt and generating an error. The default is 15 seconds.

Long = *Connection*.ConnectionTimeout
Connection.ConnectionTimeout = *Long*

An error is generated and the connection cancelled if the timeout period is reached before the connection opens. Setting this property to 0 will force the provider to wait indefinitely.

You cannot set this property once the connection has been established.

CursorLocation

Sets or returns the location of the cursor engine.

```
CursorLocationEnum = Connection.CursorLocation
Connection.CursorLocation = CursorLocationEnum
```

This can be set to one of the following values:

- **adUseClient**, to use a client side cursor
- **adUseClientBatch**, to use a client side cursor. This is included for backward compatibility only, and **adUseClient** should be used instead
- **adUseServer**, to use a server side cursor
- **adUseNone**, to indicate no cursor services are used. This is included for backward compatibility and should not be used

A disconnected recordset can only be achieved by setting this to **adUseClient**. The use of disconnected recordsets is discussed in more detail in Chapter 8.

A Recordset created against the Connection will inherit the value you have set.

Changing this property has no effect on existing connections.

The performance issues surrounding various cursor types are discussed in Chapter 9.

DefaultDatabase

Indicates the default database for a Connection object.

```
String = Connection.DefaultDatabase
Connection.DefaultDatabase = String
```

You can access objects in other databases by fully qualifying the objects, if the data source or provider supports this.

For example, using Microsoft SQL Server, you can create two recordsets on different databases:

```
objConn.DefaultDatabase="pubs"

objRec.Open "authors", objConn, _
                adOpenKeyset, adLockReadOnly, adCmdTable

objRec1.Open "Sales.dbo.Orders", objConn, _
                adOpenKeyset, adLockReadOnly, adCmdTable
```

The first uses the **authors** table from the **pubs** database, and the second uses the **Orders** table in the **Sales** database. This is just an example, and the Sales database is not installed with SQL Server.

IsolationLevel

Indicates the level of transaction isolation for a Connection object.

```
IsolationLevelEnum = Connection.IsolationLevel
Connection.IsolationLevel = IsolationLevelEnum
```

The Isolation Level allows you to define how other transactions interact with yours, and whether they can see your changes and vice versa.

This value only comes into effect when you call the **BeginTrans** method. The provider may return the next greater level of isolation if the requested level is not available.

The value can be one of the **IsolationLevelEnum** constants:

- **adXactUnspecified**, which indicates that the provider is using a different isolation level to the one you specified, but that it cannot determine what this isolation level is.

- **adXactChaos**, which indicates that a higher level transaction has control over the records. This means that you cannot overwrite any pending changes from another user.

- **adXactBrowse** or **adXactReadUncommitted**, which allows you to view uncommitted changes in another transaction. You should be careful when using this value, as the changes in another transaction have not been committed. They could therefore be rolled back, leaving you with invalid values.

- **adXactCursorStability** or **adXactReadCommitted** (the default), which indicates that you can only view changes in other transactions once they have been committed. This guarantees the state of the data. However, new records and deleted records will be reflected in your recordset.

- **adXactRepeatableRead**, which doesn't allow you to see changes made from other transactions unless you re-query the recordset. This allows you to see new records that might have been added to your recordset.

- **adXactIsolated** or **adXactSerializable**, which indicates that transactions are completely isolated from each other. This means that all concurrent transactions will produce the same effect as if each transaction was executed one after the other. With this mode there is no possibility of reading incorrect data.

Mode

Indicates the available permissions for modifying data in a Connection object.

```
ConnectModeEnum = Connection.Mode
Connection.Mode = ConnectModeEnum
```

The value can be one of the **ConnectModeEnum** constants:

- **adModeUnknown**, which is the default, to say that permissions cannot be determined, or they haven't been set yet

- **adModeRead**, for read-only permissions

- **adModeWrite**, for write-only permissions

- **adModeReadWrite**, for read/write permissions

- **adModeShareDenyRead**, for preventing other users from opening a connection with read permissions

- **adModeShareDenyWrite**, for preventing other users from opening a connection with write permissions

- **adModeShareExclusive**, for preventing other users from opening a connection

- **adModeShareDenyNone**, for preventing other users from opening a connection with any permissions

You can use this to set or return the provider access permission for the current connection.

You cannot set this property on open connections.

Provider

Indicates the name of the provider for a Connection object.

```
String = Connection.Provider
Connection.Provider = String
```

This property can also be set by the contents of the **ConnectionString** property.

Note that specifying the provider in more than one place can have unpredictable results. Microsoft doesn't actually specify what 'unpredictable' means in this case, but it's probably best to only set this on one place.

If no provider is specified the default is MSDASQL, the Microsoft OLE DB Provider for ODBC.

The supplied providers are:

- **MSDASQL**, for ODBC

- **MSIDXS**, for Index Server

- **ADSDSOObject**, for Active Directory Services

- **Microsoft.Jet.OLEDB.3.51**, for Microsoft Jet databases

- **SQLOLEDB**, for SQL Server

- **MSDAORA**, for Oracle
- **MSDataShape**, for the Microsoft Data Shape with hierarchical recordsets. This provider is discussed in more detail in Chapter 8.

The various Provider and **ConnectionString** options are discussed in more detail under the **ConnectionString** property, as well as in Chapter 2.

State

Describes whether the Connection object is open or closed.

*Long = Connection.*State

This will be one of the following **ObjectStateEnum** constants:

- **adStateOpen** for an open connection
- **adStateClosed** for a closed connection

You can use the State property to ensure that you don't generate errors when closing a connection. For example:

```
If objConn.State = adStateOpen Then
    objConn.Close
End If
```

Version

Indicates the ADO version number.

*String = Connection.*Version

The version number of the provider can be obtained from the Properties collection.

Connection Events

Connection Events are a big new feature of ADO 2, and they can be quickly summarized as follows:

- **BeginTransComplete**, is raised after a transaction has begun
- **CommitTransComplete**, is raised after a transaction has been Committed
- **ConnectComplete**, is raised after the connection has been established
- **Disconnect**, is raised after a connection ends
- **ExecuteComplete**, is raised after an Execute command has completed
- **InfoMessage**, is raised when the provider returns extra information

- **RollbackTransComplete**, is raised after a transaction has been Rolled back

- **WillConnect**, is raised just before the connection is established

- **WillExecute**, is raised just before a command is executed.

These events work in both synchronous and asynchronous modes.

All events will have a bi-directional parameter, **adStatus**, to indicate the status of the event. This is of type **EventStatusEnum** and can be one of the following constants:

- **adStatusOK**, to indicate that the action that caused the event was successful.

- **adStatusErrorsOccurred**, to indicate that errors or warnings occurred, in which case the Errors collection should be checked.

- **adStatusCantDeny**. On a **Will** event this indicates that you cannot cancel the action that generated the event, on a **Complete** event it indicates that the action was cancelled.

- **adStatusUnwantedEvent**, which indicates that the reason the event was generated should no longer generate events.

On a **Will** event, assuming **adStatusCantDeny** is not set, before the procedure exits you can set **adStatus** to **adStatusCancel** to cancel the action that caused this event. For example, assume that you have moved from one record to the next – this will raise a **WillMove** event. If you decide that you do not wish to move to another record, you can set **adStatus** to **adStatusCancel**, and the **Move** action will be cancelled. This allows you to perhaps cancel actions where the data is incorrect.

One thing to watch for when using **Will** events is implicit method calls. For example, taking the above **Move**, if the current record has been edited, then ADO implicitly calls **Update**. In this case you might get more than one **Will** event. We discuss this in more detail in Chapter 8.

If you no longer wish to receive events for a particular action, then before the procedure exits you can set **adStatus** to **adStatusUnwantedEvent**, and they will no longer be generated.

BeginTransComplete

Fired after a **BeginTrans** operation finishes executing.

```
BeginTransComplete(TransactionLevel, pError, adStatus,
pConnection)
```

Name	Type	Description
TransactionLevel	Long	Contains the new transaction level of the **BeginTrans** that caused the event.
pError	Error	An Error object that describes the error that occurred if **adStatus** is **adStatusErrorsOccurred**. Otherwise it is not set.
adStatus	EventStatusEnum	Identifies the status of the message.
pConnection	Connection	The Connection object upon which the **BeginTrans** was executed.

You can use this to trigger other operations that are dependent upon the transaction having been started. For example, you might like to build a transaction monitoring system, and you could log the start of the transaction in this event.

CommitTransComplete

Fired after a **CommitTrans** operation finishes executing.

```
CommitTransComplete(pError, adStatus, pConnection)
```

Name	Type	Description
pError	Error	An Error object that describes the error that occurred if **adStatus** is **adStatusErrorsOccurred**. Otherwise it is not set.
adStatus	EventStatusEnum	Identifies the status of the message.
pConnection	Connection	The Connection object upon which the **CommitTrans** was executed.

You can use this to trigger other operations that are dependent upon the transaction having been completed successfully, such as updating log files or an audit trail.

ConnectComplete

Fired after a connection starts.

ConnectComplete(*pError*, *adStatus*, *pConnection*)

Name	Type	Description
pError	Error	An Error object that describes the error that occurred, if **adStatus** is **adStatusErrorsOccurred**. Otherwise it is not set.
adStatus	EventStatusEnum	Identifies the status of the message.
pConnection	Connection	The Connection object for which this event applies.

You can use the **ConnectComplete** event to examine the details of the connection and whether it completed successfully. For example:

```
Private Sub oConn_ConnectComplete(ByVal pError As ADODB.Error, adStatus As
ADODB.EventStatusEnum, ByVal pConnection As ADODB.Connection)

    Select Case adStatus
    Case adStatusErrorsOccurred
        Print "Errors occurred whilst attempting to connect."
        Print "Connection String is: " & pConnection.ConnectionString
        Print "Error description: " & pError.Description
    Case adStatusOK
        Print "Connection sucessful."
    End Select

End Sub
```

Disconnect

Fired after a connection ends.

Disconnect(*adStatus*, *pConnection*)

Name	Type	Description
adStatus	EventStatusEnum	Identifies the status of the message.
pConnection	Connection	The Connection object for which this event applies.

You can use this to examine whether the disconnection was successful. You can also use it to track users as they log onto and off from data sources. It can also be useful to alert users when a connection drops unexpectedly.

ExecuteComplete

Fired after a command has finished executing.

```
ExecuteComplete(RecordsAffected, pError, adStatus, pCommand,
pRecordset, pConnection)
```

Name	Type	Description
RecordsAffected	Long	A Long variable into which the provider returns the number of records that the operation affected.
pError	Error	An Error object that describes the error that occurred if **adStatus** is **adStatusErrorsOccurred**. Otherwise it is not set.
adStatus	EventStatusEnum	Identifies the status of the message.
pCommand	Command	The Command object for which this event applies. This may not be set if a Command object was not used.
pRecordset	Recordset	The Recordset object upon which the **Execute** was run. This may be empty if a non-recordset returning command was run, such as an action query.
pConnection	Connection	The Connection object upon which the **Execute** was run.

This allows you to examine whether the command completed successfully, and how many records it affected. You can use this instead of the *RecordsAffected* argument of the **Execute** method. For example:

```
Private Sub oConn_ExecuteComplete(ByVal RecordsAffected As Long, ByVal pError
As ADODB.Error, adStatus As ADODB.EventStatusEnum, ByVal pCommand As
ADODB.Command, ByVal pRecordset As ADODB.Recordset, ByVal pConnection As
ADODB.Connection)

    If adStatus = adStatusOK Then
        Print RecordsAffected & " records were affected by this command."
    End If

End Sub
```

InfoMessage

Fired whenever a **ConnectionEvent** operation completes successfully and additional information is returned by the provider.

InfoMessage(*pError, adStatus, pConnection*)

Name	Type	Description
pError	Error	An Error object that describes the error that occurred if **adStatus** is **adStatusErrorsOccurred**. Otherwise it is not set.
adStatus	EventStatusEnum	Identifies the status of the message.
pConnection	Connection	The Connection object upon which the command was executed.

The parameters define what type of information message this is. This is particularly useful when dealing with ODBC data sources, especially to SQL Server, as it returns informational messages, and could be used to log these in an audit trail.

For example, you could connect to the **pubs** database on SQL server with this connect string:

```
Driver={SQL Server}; Server=Tigger; Database=pubs; UID=sa; PWD=
```

and then put this code into the **InfoMessage** event:

```
Debug.Print pError.Description
For Each pError In pConnection.Errors
    Debug.Print pError.Description
Next
```

On my server that gives the following:

```
[Microsoft][ODBC SQL Server Driver][SQL Server]Changed database context to
'master'.
    [Microsoft][ODBC SQL Server Driver][SQL Server]Changed database context to
'master'.
    [Microsoft][ODBC SQL Server Driver][SQL Server]Changed language setting to
'us_english'.
    [Microsoft][ODBC SQL Server Driver][SQL Server]Changed database context to
'pubs'.
```

In general this event can be used to track connection messages, or actions on the connection that return SQL_SUCCESS_WITH_INFO.

RollbackTransComplete

Fired after a `RollbackTrans` operation has finished executing.

`RollbackTransComplete(pError, adStatus, pConnection)`

Name	Type	Description
pError	Error	An Error object that describes the error that occurred if `adStatus` is `adStatusErrorsOccurred`. Otherwise it is not set.
adStatus	EventStatusEnum	Identifies the status of the message.
pConnection	Connection	The Connection object upon which the `RollbackTrans` was executed.

You can use this to trigger other operations that depend upon the transaction having failed, such as log files. For example:

```
Private Sub oConn_RollbackTransComplete(ByVal pError As ADODB.Error, adStatus
As ADODB.EventStatusEnum, ByVal pConnection As ADODB.Connection)

    Print "Transaction was rolled back. Changes have not been saved."

End Sub
```

This could be extremely useful in nightly batch jobs.

WillConnect

Fired before a connection starts, indicating that the connection is about to take place.

`WillConnect(ConnectionString, UserID, Password, Options, adStatus, pConnection)`

Name	Type	Description
ConnectionString	String	The connection information.
UserID	String	The user name to use when connecting.
Password	String	The user password to use when connecting.
Options	Long	Extra connection options, as passed into the Connection objects `Open` method.
adStatus	EventStatusEnum	Identifies the status of the message.
pConnection	Connection	The Connection object for which this event applies.

The parameters supplied can be changed before the method returns – for instance, if the user has specified certain connection attributes, but you wish to change them. As an example, imagine an application that allowed the user to specify connection details. You could prevent them connecting as a certain user, but allow connection as another:

```
Private Sub oConn_WillConnect(ConnectionString As String, UserID As String,
Password As String, Options As Long, adStatus As ADODB.EventStatusEnum, ByVal
pConnection As ADODB.Connection)

    If adStatus = adStatusOK Then
        Select Case UserID
        Case "sa"
            Print "Connection as system administrator not allowed."
            adStatus = adStatusCancel
        Case "Guest"
            UserID = "GuestUser"
        End Select
    End If

End Sub
```

This stops the user trying to connect as **sa** and cancels the connection attempt. If a user tries to connect as **Guest** then the user id is changed to **GuestUser** and connection proceeds. This allows you to have a set of real user details that are hidden, whilst exposing a viewable set of user details.

WillExecute

Fired before a pending command executes on the connection.

WillExecute(*Source, CursorType, LockType, Options, adStatus, pCommand, pRecordset, pConnection*)

Name	Type	Description
Source	String	The SQL command or stored procedure name.
CursorType	CursorTypeEnum	The type of cursor for the recordset that will be opened. If set to **adOpenUnspecified** it cannot be changed.
LockType	LockTypeEnum	The lock type for the recordset that will be opened. If set to **adOpenUnspecified** it cannot be changed.
Options	Long	The options that can be used to execute the command or open the recordset, as passed into the *Options* argument.
adStatus	EventStatusEnum	Identifies the status of the message.

Name	Type	Description
pCommand	Command	The Command object for which this event applies. This may be empty if a Command object was not being used.
pRecordset	Recordset	The Recordset object for which this event applies. If the **Execute** command didn't return a recordset, then this will be an empty Recordset object.
pConnection	Connection	The Connection object for which this event applies.

The execution parameters can be modified in this procedure, as it is called before the command executes.

This is particularly useful when building user-query type applications where the user has the ability to set details of the connection, as it allows you to examine the parameters and modify them if necessary. For example:

```
Private Sub oConn_WillExecute(Source As String, CursorType As
ADODB.CursorTypeEnum, LockType As ADODB.LockTypeEnum, Options As Long, adStatus
As ADODB.EventStatusEnum, ByVal pCommand As ADODB.Command, ByVal pRecordset As
ADODB.Recordset, ByVal pConnection As ADODB.Connection)

    If Source = "SalaryDetails" Then
        Print "Nice try, but you're not allowed to look at these"
        adStatus = adStatusCancel
    End If

End Sub
```

This cancels the event if someone tries to connect to the **SalaryDetails** table.

You can also use this to protect against ad-hoc insertions and deletions.

Connection Collections

The collections are discussed in depth in Chapter 6.

Errors

Contains all of the Error objects created in response to a single failure involving the provider.

*Connection.***Errors**

The Errors collection is cleared when another ADO operation generates an error.

Each Error object represents a specific provider error, not an ADO error, as ADO errors generate run-time errors.

The Errors collection may contain warnings as well as errors, so the **Clear** method should be used before certain operations to ensure that the warnings are relevant to the most recent operation. Use this for the **Resync**, **UpdateBatch** and **CancelBatch** methods or the **Filter** property on a Recordset object, and the **Open** method on a Connection object.

You should be aware that when using custom business objects in MTS, the errors are not passed back, as MTS just returns a generic Automation Error number. If this is required, you should devise a method of passing errors back, such as converting them into an array.

Properties

Contains all of the **Property** objects for a **Connection** object.

Properties = *Connection*.*Properties*

The Properties collection is discussed in more detail in Chapter 6 and a full list of the properties available is in Appendix C.

The Command Object

Although the Connection object allows the execution of commands against a data store, the Command object has greater functionality and flexibility, and can improve connection performance by avoiding continual reference to default values. The Command object is not actually required to be supported by the provider, but where it is supported, it proves not only useful, but essential in certain areas.

> When using stored procedures or stored queries that accept parameters you must use a Command object. One of the collections that the command object contains is the Parameters collection, which allows the passing of parameters into and out of stored procedures, as well as allowing a recordset to be passed back.

Command Methods

Cancel

Cancels execution of a pending Execute call.

Command.Cancel

A run time error will be generated if the **adExecuteAsync** option was not used with the Execute call. This is particularly useful when allowing users to submit their own queries, as these can often have long execution times, and you may wish to provide them with a Cancel button on the screen.

CreateParameter

Creates a new Parameter object.

```
Set Parameter = Command.CreateParameter([Name], [Type],
[Direction], [Size], [Value])
```

All of the method's arguments are optional.

Name	Type	Description
Name	String	The name of the parameter.
Type	DataTypeEnum	The data type of the parameter. Default is `adEmpty`
Direction	ParameterDirection Enum	The direction of the parameter. Default is `adParamInput`
Size	Long	The maximum length of the parameter value in characters or bytes. Default is 0
Value	Variant	The value for the parameter.

`ParameterDirectionEnum` can be one of the following constants:

- `adParamUnknown,` to indicate that the direction of the parameter is unknown.

- `adParamInput`, to indicate that the parameter is an input parameter to the command.

- `adParamOutput`, to indicate that the parameter is an output parameter from the command.

- `adParamInputOutput`, to indicate that the parameter is both an input to and output from the command.

- `adParamReturnValue`, to indicate that the parameter is a return value from the command.

The `DataTypeEnum` list is quite large, and is included in Appendix F.

You use `CreateParameter` to create parameters to pass to stored procedures or stored queries. There are two ways of using `CreateParameter`. The first is with all of the parameters, and the second is without any parameters. For example, the following two sets of code are logically equivalent ways of assigning specific values to a parameter object's properties:

```
Set oParm = oCmd.CreateParameter ("ID", adInteger, adParamInput, 8, 123 )
```

and

```
Set oParm = oCmd.CreateParameter
oParm.Name = "ID"
oParm.Type = adInteger
oParm.Direction = adParamInput
oParm.Size = 8
oParm.Value = 123
```

Note that this does not add the parameter to the Parameters collection of the command object concerned. For this you must use the **Append** method. For example:

```
oCmd.Parameters.Append oParm
```

Multiple parameter objects can be appended to the same command object. However, if you attempt to append a parameter object which does not have a specific value assigned to at least one of its properties, an error will be generated.

Execute

Executes the query, SQL statement, or stored procedure specified in the **CommandText** property.

```
[Set Recordset = ]Command.Execute([RecordsAffected],
[Parameters], [Options])
```

Name	Type	Description
RecordsAffected	Long	A Long variable into which the provider returns the number of records that the operation affected.
Parameters	Variant	An array of parameter values passed with a SQL statement. Output parameters will not return correct values if passed here.
Options	Long	A value that indicates how the provider should interpret the **CommandText** property of the Command object. Default is -1

RecordsAffected can be used to determine how many records were affected by the command executing. For example:

```
oCmd.CommandText = "UPDATE titles SET royalty = royalty * 1.10"
oCmd.Execute lngRecs
Print "Number of records affected by command: "
Print lngRecs
```

Parameter values passed in the *Parameters* argument will override any values in a command's Parameters collection. For example:

```
oCmd.Parameters.Refresh
oCmd.Parameters("FirstParm") = "abc"
oCmd.Execute , Array("def")
```

This command will use **def** as the value for the **FirstParm** parameter instead of the value supplied in the Parameters collection.

Options can be one of the following constants:

- **adCmdText**, to indicate that the command text is to be interpreted as a text command, such as a SQL statement.

- **adCmdTable**, to indicate that the command text is to be interpreted as the name of a table.

- **adCmdTableDirect**, to indicate that the command text is to be interpreted directly as a table name. This enhanced some internal options to provide speed options.

- **adCmdStoredProc**, to indicate that the command text should be interpreted as the name of a stored procedure or query.

- **adCmdUnknown**, to indicate that the nature of the command text is unknown.

For asynchronous operation you can add **adAsyncExecute** to the *Options* argument to make the command execute asynchronously, and **adAsyncFetch** or **adAsyncFetchNonBlocking** to make the recordset be returned asynchronously:

```
oCom.Execute  , , adCmdTable Or adAsyncExecute Or adAsyncFetch
```

> Note that early versions of the ADO documentation state that the asynchronous flags are adFetchAsync **and** adExecuteAsync. **These are both incorrect.**

Command Properties

ActiveConnection

Indicates the Connection object to which the command object currently belongs.

```
Set  Connection = Command.ActiveConnection
Set  Command.ActiveConnection = Connection
Command.ActiveConnection = String
String = Command.ActiveConnection
```

This can be a valid Connection object or a **ConnectionString**, and must be set before the **Execute** method is called otherwise an error will occur.

There is a subtle difference between using an extant Connection object and a connection string when setting the **ActiveConnection** property. For example, consider the following lines of code:

```
oConn.Open "Provider=Microsoft.Jet.OLEDB.3,51; _
             Data Source=C:\ADO\ADOTest.mdb"
Set oCmd.ActiveConnection = oConn

oCmd.ActiveConnection="Provider=Microsoft.Jet.OLEDB.3,51; _
             Data Source=C:\ADO\ADOTest.mdb"
```

Although both lines appear to do the same thing, the first line uses an existing connection object, whereas the second will create a new connection. Connection pooling, however, may reuse an existing connection if it can speed up the connection in this second case.

In Visual Basic, if you set this value to *Nothing* then the Command is disassociated from the connection, but the Command object remains active. However, the Parameters collection will be cleared if the provider supplied the parameters (i.e. with a **Refresh** method call). If the parameters were manually created then they are left intact. This could be useful if you have several commands with parameters that are the same.

CommandText

Contains the text of a command to be issued against a data provider.

String = *Command*.CommandText
Command.CommandText = *String*

This can be a SQL Statement, a table name, a stored procedure name, or a provider-specific command, and the default is an empty string.

If you set the **Prepared** property of the Command object to **True,** then the command will be compiled and stored by the provider before executing. This temporary stored procedure is retained for the duration of the connection. If you are using the SQL Server provider, this may create a temporary stored procedure for you if you have the **Use Procedure for Prepare** property in the Connection Properties collection. This is particularly useful when the same command is to be executed several times, but with different parameters.

For example, to set the command text to a SQL string, you can do the following:

```
oCmd.CommandText = "SELECT * FROM authors WHERE state = 'CA'"
```

If you need to pass parameters into a stored procedure in SQL Server, there are two ways. You can use the Parameters object, or you can pass the stored procedure and its arguments as a text command:

```
oCmd.CommandText = "usp_Foo 'abc', 123"
oCmd.CommandType = adCmdStoredProc
oCmd.Execute
```

This method is sometimes quicker to code than using the Parameters collection, although you obviously have no way to use output parameters with this method. You could also use the alternative method of the Parameters argument:

```
oCmd.CommandText = "usp_Foo"
oCmd.CommandType = adCmdStoredProc
oCmd.Execute , Array("abc", 123)
```

CommandTimeout

Indicates how long, in seconds, to wait while executing a command before terminating the command and generating an error.

```
Long = Command.CommandTimeout
Command.CommandTimeout = Long
```

An error will be generated if the timeout value is reached before the command completes execution, and the command will be cancelled. If you are using Visual Basic, then the **ExecuteComplete** event will be fired when the error is generated, and you can check the *pError* argument to detect the error.

This property bears no relation to the Connection object's **CommandTimeout** property.

CommandType

Indicates the type of Command object.

```
CommandTypeEnum = Command.CommandType
Command.CommandType = CommandTypeEnum
```

You should use this property to optimize the processing of the command. For example, if you know that your command will not return any data, you should use the **adExecuteNoRecords** in conjunction with **adCmdText** or **adCmdStoredProc**:

```
oCom.CommandType = adCmdStoredProc + adExecuteNorecords
```

The reason for doing this is that it informs the provider beforehand, what sort of command you will be executing. The provider can therefore jump directly to its internal code, which allows an increase in performance.

The distinction between **adCmdTable** and **adCmdTableDirect** is quite subtle. Imagine the following:

```
oComm.CommandText = "authors"
oComm.CommandType = adCmdTable
```

This actually sends **SELECT * FROM authors** to the provider, whereas using **adCmdTableDirect** only sends **authors** to the provider.
The performance implications of these options are discussed in Chapter 9.

Name

Indicates the name of the Command object.

String = *Command*.Name
Command.Name = *String*

In many cases you probably won't use this, but it could be used to uniquely identify a command object in a collection of commands. For example, imagine an application that allows users to build up a number of commands. You could store these in a collection and use Names to identify them. Think about the query window in SQL Server — you could build quite a good emulation of this using ADO to connect to multiple data sources, and using a collection to store various command objects.

One rarely noted feature is that if you name a Command and then associate the command with a Connection object, the Connection object inherits a method corresponding to the name of the Command.

For example, suppose you have a User and a Manager, both of whom need to look at the Employee details, and the manager is allowed to see the salaries, whereas the user is not. You have decided to use stored procedures to encapsulate all of your SQL logic, so you have two possibilities. The first is to build a single SQL statement to return the employee details, and have it check whether the user is a manager or a user. Your user then calls a business object which fetches the data for you:

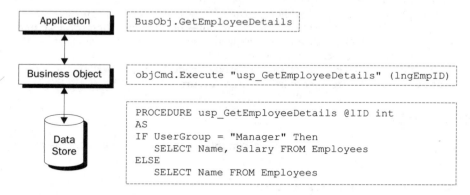

The trouble with this is that you now have a business rule built into the SQL, making it harder to maintain. You also have to work out details such as how to get the group the user is in, etc. Although this isn't particularly complex, here's a better situation:

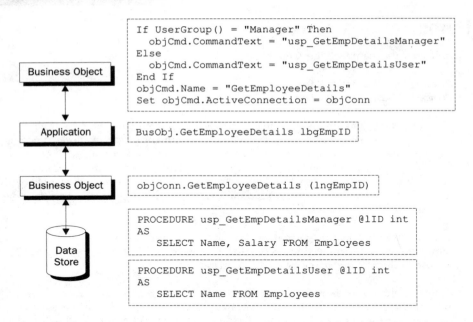

```
If UserGroup() = "Manager" Then
   objCmd.CommandText = "usp_GetEmpDetailsManager"
Else
   objCmd.CommandText = "usp_GetEmpDetailsUser"
End If
objCmd.Name = "GetEmployeeDetails"
Set objCmd.ActiveConnection = objConn
```

```
BusObj.GetEmployeeDetails lbgEmpID
```

```
objConn.GetEmployeeDetails (lngEmpID)
```

```
PROCEDURE usp_GetEmpDetailsManager @lID int
AS
    SELECT Name, Salary FROM Employees
```

```
PROCEDURE usp_GetEmpDetailsUser @lID int
AS
    SELECT Name FROM Employees
```

In this situation the application calls a business object first, perhaps when it starts, which establishes the role: user or manager. This sets the appropriate stored procedure, and attaches the command as a method of the connection. Later on, the application can simply call the business object, which calls this new method. Since the method is one of two stored procedures, the correct stored procedure is run. Although this seems like more code, it actually simplifies some of the programming. It puts the business logic in a component, where it is easily reused, and it's made the stored procedures simpler — these will now run faster since there is no run time decision to make.

Using this method you must set the **Name** property before setting the **ActiveConnection,** otherwise an error occurs.

Prepared

Indicates whether or not to save a compiled version of a command before execution.

```
Boolean = Command.Prepared
Command.Prepared = Boolean
```

The default value of the property is False. It can be set to the value **True** when the command is to be repeated several times. Although the compilation process will slow for the first execution of the command, subsequent executions will be quicker since the command text does not have to be parsed.

If you're using the SQL Server provider and you set the **Use Procedure for Prepare** property of the Connection object to **True,** then a temporary stored procedure will be created for prepared commands. Generally, you should only prepare commands if they will be executed more than three times.

If you are creating prepared commands against SQL Server and not disconnecting, then you should ensure that tempdb has enough space to accommodate the stored procedures.

State

Describes whether the Command object is open, closed, or currently processing a command.

```
Command.State = Long
```

State can be one of the following constants:

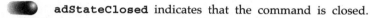 **adStateClosed** indicates that the command is closed.

adStateOpen indicates that the command is open.

adStateExecuting indicates that the command is currently executing.

adStateFetching indicates that the command is currently fetching records.

Using the **State** property allows you to detect the current open-state of the command. For example, to detect if the Command is still executing an asynchronous query you could use this line:

```
If oCmd.State = adStateExecuting Then
    command is still executing
End If
```

Command Collections

Parameters

Contains all of the Parameter objects for a Command object.

```
Parameters = Command.Parameters
```

The Parameters collection is most often used when passing arguments to stored procedures or queries. Parameter objects are appended to this collection by use of the **Append** method:

```
Set oParm = oCmd.CreateParameter (. . .)
oCmd.Append oParm
```

You can enumerate the objects in this collection by use of the **For Each...Next** command:

```
For Each oParm In oCmd.Parameters
    Print oParm.Name
Next
```

You can use the **Refresh** method to get the provider to fill in the Parameters collection for you.

The Parameters collection is discussed more fully in Chapter 6.

Properties

Contains all of the Property objects for a Command object.

Properties = *Command.*Properties

Parameter Object

The parameter object comprises all of the information for a single parameter to be used in a stored procedure or query, and is only really used in conjunction with the Command object and its associated Parameters collection.

Parameter Methods

AppendChunk

Appends data to a large or binary **Parameter** object.

*Parameter.*AppendChunk(*Data*)

Name	Type	Description
Data	Variant	The data to be appended to the parameter.

The first call after an edit writes data to the field, overwriting any existing data. Subsequent calls add to existing data.

This is most often used for putting images into tables. There's a full discussion of using images and **AppendChunk** at the end of Chapter 6.

This is functionally equivalent to the **AppendChunk** method of the Field object, and works in the same way. The only difference is you are dealing with a different base object.

Parameter Properties

Attributes

Indicates one or more characteristics of a **Parameter** object.

```
ParameterAttributesEnum = Parameter.Attributes
Parameter.Attributes = ParameterAttributesEnum
```

This can be one of the *ParameterAttributesEnum* values:

- **adParamSigned**, to indicate that the parameter will accept signed values. This is the default.

- **adParamNullable**, to indicate that the parameter will accept null values.

- **adParamLong**, to indicate that the parameter accepts long data, such as binary data.

You can combine these together by using a logical **Or** statement:

```
objParam.Attributes = adParamNullable Or adParamLong
```

Setting **adParamLong** doesn't appear to be compulsory for binary data. A SQL Server stored procedure with a parameter of type image will accept long data without this set.

Direction

Indicates whether the **Parameter** object represents an input parameter, an output parameter, or both, or if the parameter is a return value from a stored procedure.

```
ParameterDirectionEnum = Parameter.Direction
Parameter.Direction = ParameterDirectionEnum
```

ParameterDirectionEnum can be one of the following values:

- **adParamUnknown**, to indicate that the direction of the parameter is not known.

- **adParamInput**, to indicate that the parameter is to pass information to the stored procedure or query.

- **adParamOutput**, to indicate that the parameter is to return information from the stored procedure or query.

- **adParamInputOutput**, to indicate that the parameter can be used to pass information to, and return information from, a stored procedure or query.

- **adParamReturnValue**, to indicate that the parameter will contain the return value of the stored procedure or query.

In SQL Server you would declare an output parameter by appending OUTPUT to the parameter declaration. For example, the following SQL code creates a stored procedure with input and output parameters, and return values.

```
CREATE PROCEDURE usp_GetValues
    @PubID      char(4),            ' indicates an input parameter
    @Value      integer    OUTPUT   ' indicates an output parameter
AS
BEGIN
    . . . .
RETURN 123                          ' indicates the return value
```

The return value is always the first parameter in the Parameters collection, and is named RETURN_VALUE. If creating parameters, you would create the return value first:

```
objCommand.CreateParameter  ("RETURN_VALUE", adVarInteger, _
                            adParamReturnValue, 0, lngRetVal)
```

The return value should be declared as a long integer. If you use **Refresh**, then a return value parameter is always created, irrespective of whether the command returns a value.

You can also set this property by using the *Direction* argument of the **CreateParameter** method of the Command object.

Microsoft Access does not have output parameters or return values.

Name

Indicates the name of the **Parameter** object.

```
String = Parameter.Name
Parameter.Name = String
```

This just identifies the parameter name in the Parameters collection, and doesn't have to be the same as the name of the parameter as defined in the stored procedure or query — but it makes sense to keep these the same. This makes the code more readable and easier to maintain.

You can also set this property by using the *Name* argument of the **CreateParameter** method of the Command object.

NumericScale

Indicates the scale of numeric values for the **Parameter** object.

```
Byte = Parameter.NumericScale
Parameter.NumericScale = Byte
```

The numeric scale indicates how many digits are to the right of the decimal place.

Precision

Indicates the degree of precision for numeric values in the **Parameter** object.

```
Byte = Parameter.Precision
Parameter.Precision = Byte
```

The precision indicates the maximum number of digits that are used to represent a numeric value.

Size

Indicates the maximum size, in bytes or characters, of a **Parameter** object.

```
Long = Parameter.Size
Parameter.Size = Long
```

There are a couple of things to watch out for when using this property. The first is that you must always set the Size for variable length parameters, such as character strings or binary data, otherwise an error will be generated.

The second is that for binary data you have to be quite specific about the size of the parameter. For example, if a SQL Server stored procedure has a parameter of type **image**, and you refresh the parameters, the size of this parameter is returned as **2147483647**. If you create the parameters yourself and use this size, and then **AppendChunk** to add the data to the parameter there are no problems, but creating the parameter with the actual size of the binary data doesn't work. That's because this is the maximum size of the parameter, not its actual size.

Type

Indicates the data type of the **Parameter** object.

```
DataTypeEnum = Parameter.Type
Parameter.Type = DataTypeEnum
```

A full list of the **DataTypeEnum** values is shown in Appendix E, but the table below shows the SQL Server provider and Access provider data types and what they map to. A blank space means there is no direct mapping between the two database types.

SQL Server	Access	Enum Value
binary	Binary	adVarBinary
varbinary		adVarBinary
char	Text	adVarChar
varchar		adVarChar
datetime		adDBTimeStamp

SQL Server	Access	Enum Value
smalldatetime		adDBTimeStamp
float	Single	adSingle
real		adSingle
int	Long Integer	adInteger
smallint	Integer	adSmallInt
tinyint	Byte	adUnsignedTinyInt
money	Currency	adCurrency
smallmoney		adCurrency
bit	Yes/No	adBoolean
timestamp		atVarBinary
text	Memo	adVarChar
image	OLE Object	adVarBinary
	Double	adDouble
	Date/Time	adDate
	Replication ID	adGUID
	Value	adEmpty

One interesting and often confusing thing to note is that date parameters in SQL Server don't map to the obvious **adDate** datatype, but rather to the **adDBTimeStamp** data type, and the **timestamp** maps to **adVarBinary**. This can often cause the command to fail if the parameters are of the wrong type.

If you wish to create your parameters using the **CreateParameter** method, but are having trouble matching datatypes or sizes, then the simplest fix is to temporarily call the **Refresh** method, and examine the Parameters collection. You can do this in VBScript by looping through the collection, or by using the Locals window in Visual Basic. You can then copy the values that ADO has used, and amend your code accordingly. Don't forget to remove the **Refresh** once you've sorted out your parameters, as leaving it in will cause a performance penalty.

Data Types are discussed indepth in Appendix D.

Value

Indicates the value assigned to the **Parameter** object.

```
Variant = Parameter.Value
Parameter.Value = Variant
```

This is the default property and can be omitted if desired.

For a parameter holding binary data, you can use this as well as using the AppendChunk method. For example:

```
objRec.Parameters("@Logo").Value = varChunk
```

There's a full description of how to use binary data at the end of Chapter 8.

Parameters Collection

When dealing with stored procedures or queries that accept arguments, you have two options:

- Use the Execute method of the Command object, passing in the parameters as an array of values into the second argument of this method.
- Use the Parameters collection of the Command object.

In many cases the former is acceptable (and is in fact easier to code), but the one restriction of this is that you can't return any values from your stored procedure. For example, assume you have a stored procedure like this:

```
CREATE PROCEDURE usp_AuthorsByState
    @RequiredState    char(2)
    @ID               integer    OUTPUT
AS
BEGIN
    SELECT *
    FROM    authors
    WHERE   state = @RequiredState

    SELECT @ID=123

    RETURN 456
END
```

This procedure does three things:

- It returns a recordset using one of the parameters to restrict the rows that are returned
- It sets the output parameter to an arbitrary value
- It returns another arbitrary value

While the output value and return value are falsely constructed, it illustrates a common technique to return information from a stored procedure.

If you wish to call this stored procedure you use code like this:

```
objCmdText = "usp_AuthorsByState"
objCmdType = adCmdStoredProc
Set objRec = objCmd.Execute (, Array("CA", lngID))
```

This simply calls the procedure passing in two arguments — CA, to filter the recordset, and lngID (a long integer) to be used as the output parameter. This works fine, except that lngID is never filled in with the output value, and there's also no way to access the return value. So while this method is extremely easy to use, it doesn't give you the functionality that the Parameters collection does.

The Parameters collection contains a Parameter object for each Parameter in a stored procedure, including the return value if the procedure has one. It only has one property and four methods.

Parameters Methods

Append

Appends a **Parameter** object to the **Parameters** collection.

Parameters.Append(*Object*)

Name	Type	Description
Object	Parameter	The Parameter object to be appended to the collection.

Parameters are created using the **CreateParameter** method, and you must set the **Type** property before calling this method. For example:

```
Set objParam = objCmd.CreateParameter
objParam.Name = "Name"
objParam.Type = adVarChar
objParam.Direction = adParamInput
objParam.Size = 25
objCmd.Parameters.Append objParam
```

Although more cumbersome to use than the **Refresh** method to build a parameter list, this method is much more efficient, as it minimizes the number of calls to be made to the provider.

You can combine the **Append** and **CreateParameter** methods into a single statement:

```
oCmd.Paramters.Append oCmd.CreateParameter ( . . .)
```

Delete

Deletes a **Parameter** object from the **Parameters** collection.

Parameters.Delete(*Index*)

Name	Type	Description
Index	Variant	The number or name of the Parameter to remove from the collection.

You must use the **Parameter** object's index or its **Name** when deleting a parameter. You cannot use an object variable.

Refresh

Updates the **Parameter** objects in the **Parameters** collection.

Parameters.Refresh

This has the impact of querying the data provider for details of the parameters. You can then access the parameters by name or ordinal number by indexing into the collection. For example:

```
oCmd.Parameters.Refresh
oCmd.Parameters(0).Value = 1
oCmd.Parameters("FirstName") = "Janine"
```

You should use this method only when you are willing to accept the performance hit of the provider requerying the data source for the parameter details. This is especially important if the same set of parameters is used frequently.

You can actually use this method quite effectively by querying the provider for the parameters once, say, at the start of the program. You could then copy the parameter details into a global variable, perhaps an array or a collection, or even a fabricated recordset, where it can be used many times during the program. The advantage with this method is that you don't have to keep repeating CreateParameter calls, and you can create a generic piece of code to run a command. Also, you can change the stored procedure without having to change the code that runs the command. The disadvantage is, of course, the delay as the program starts whilst the parameters are read in. However, you may consider this delay worthwhile.

The performance issues regarding Refresh are discussed in Chapter 9.

Parameters Properties

Count

Indicates the number of **Parameter** objects in the **Parameters** collection.

Long = *Parameters*.Count

You can use the Visual Basic or VBScript **For Each...Next** command to iterate through the parameters collection without using the **Count** property.

Item

Allows indexing into the **Parameters** collection to reference a specific **Parameter** object.

```
Parameter  =  Parameters.Item(Index)
```

Name	Type	Description
Index	Variant	The number of name of the parameter in the collection

This is the default property and can be omitted. For example, the following lines are identical:

```
objRec.Parameters.Item(1)
```

```
objRec.Parameters(1)
```

```
objRec.Parameters("@FirstName")
```

Retrieving Output Parameters

The ability to return information from stored procedures in parameters is extremely useful, but there are some points you should be aware of. The first is whether output parameters are supported at all by the provider — Access doesn't support them. The second is at what stage the output parameters are available, and for this there are two choices:

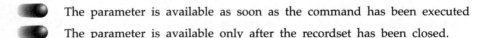 The parameter is available as soon as the command has been executed

The parameter is available only after the recordset has been closed.

This latter option is the one you have to watch for, because ADO will only read the parameter values from the provider once. This means that if you try and read the parameter before you have closed the recordset, close the recordset, and then try and read the parameter value again, the value may not be available.

You can check to see which of the modes your provider supports, by examining the **Output Parameter Availability** custom property for the connection. This will return one of the three **DBPROPVAL_OA** constant values:

DBPROPVAL_OA_ATEXECUTE, to indicate the parameters are available after the command has been executed. This has a value of 2.

DBPROPVAL_OA_ATROWRELEASE, to indicate that the parameters are available after the recordset has been closed. This has a value of 4.

DBPROPVAL_OA_NOTSUPPORTED, to indicate that output parameters are not supported. This has a value of 1.

You could check these values with code like this:

```
Set objCmd.ActiveConnection = objConn

objCmd.CommandText = "usp_ProcedureWithOutputParam"
objCmd.CommandType = adCmdStoredProc
objCmd.Parameters.Append objCmd.CreateParameter("ReturnValue", _
                                adInteger, adParameterReturnValue)
Set objRec = objCmd.Execute

intParamAvail = objConn.Properties("Output Parameter Availability")
if intParamAvail = 4 Then
    ' parameter not available until recordset is closed
    objRec.Close
End If
intRV = objCmd.Parameters("ReturnValue")
```

This isn't a problem with commands that do not return recordsets, as there is no recordset to close.

The Recordset Object

The recordset is really the heart of ADO, since data is what it's all about. The recordset contains all of the columns and rows returned from a specific action.

Recordset Methods

AddNew

Creates a new record for an updateable Recordset object.

Recordset.AddNew([*FieldList*], [*Values*])

Name	Type	Description
FieldList	Variant	A single name or an array of names or ordinal positions of the fields in the new record.
Values	Variant	A single value or an array of values for the fields in the new record. If *FieldList* is an array *Values* must also be an array with the same number of elements.

You can use **AddNew** in two ways. The first is without any arguments, and places the current record pointer on the new record. You can then set the details for the new record and save the changes with **Update** if using immediate update mode,or **UpdateBatch**, if using batch update mode.

The second method uses the arguments, allowing you to pass in an array of fields and values. For example, the following line adds a new record filling in one field:

```
objRec.AddNew "author", "Jan Lloyd"
```

The following line adds one record, but fills in two fields:

```
objRec.AddNew Array("author", "year born"), Array("Jan Lloyd", 1969)
```

If you are using this method and batch update mode is not being used, then the changes are effective immediately – that is, there is no need to perform the **Update** method. If using batch update mode, however, you must still call the **UpdateBatch** method to update the data source.

When using the Array method, you must ensure that both arrays contain the same number of arguments, and that the details of the arrays are in the correct order. The array method is also particularly good when fabricating recordsets.

You can only use **AddNew** when the recordset supports addition of new records. You can check this by examining the **Supports** property:

```
If objRec.Supports(adAddNew) Then
    ' recordset supports additions
End If
```

Cancel

Cancels execution of a pending asynchronous Open operation.

Recordset.Cancel

This is particularly useful when allowing users to submit queries, as it gives them an opportunity to cancel the query if they feel it is taking too long.

If the recordset was not opened asynchronously then an error will be generated.

CancelBatch

Cancels a pending batch update when in batch update mode.

Recordset.CancelBatch([*AffectRecords*])

Name	Type	Description
AffectRecords	AffectEnum	Determines how many records will be affected. Defaults to **adAffectAll**

The **AffectEnum** values can be one of the following constants:

- **adAffectCurrent**, to only cancel updates for the current record.
- **adAffectGroup**, to only cancel updates for records that match the current **Filter**, which must be set before using this option.
- **adAffectAll**, to cancel all pending updates, even those not shown due to a **Filter**.
- **adAffectAllChapters**, to cancel all pending updates in child (chapter) recordsets, when using shaped data.

You should be careful of using **adAffectGroup**, because it's possible to miss canceling some pending changes to records that do not match the current filter.

You should always check the Errors collection after performing this method, since there may have been an underlying conflict, such as a record having been deleted. Conflict resolution is discussed in more detail in Chapter 8.

It's always sensible to set the current record position to a known record before this call, as the current record can be left in an unknown position.

CancelUpdate

Cancels any changes made to the current record, or to a new record prior to calling the Update method.

Recordset.`CancelUpdate`

This is used when in normal update mode, and cancels changes to the current record.

You can use this to cancel the addition of a new record, in which case the current record becomes the record you were on before adding the new record.

Clone

Creates a duplicate Recordset object from an existing Recordset object.

`Set` *Recordset_Clone* `=` *Recordset.*`Clone([`*LockType*`])`

Name	Type	Description
LockType	LockTypeEnum	The lock type to create the new recordset. Defaults to **adLockUnspecified**

In this case **LockTypeEnum** is a subset of the full list of constants, and should be one of:

 adLockUnspecified, to indicate that the cloned recordset should have the same lock type as the original recordset.

 adLockReadOnly, to indicate that the cloned recordset should be read only.

It's important to note that this doesn't create two independent recordsets. Rather, it creates two recordset objects, both pointing to the same recordset. The advantage of this is that it allows you to change the current record in the clone, whilst keeping the current record the same in the original recordset copy.

Cloning recordsets is often more efficient than creating a new recordset with the same request criteria since another trip to the server is not made.

Cloning is only allowed on bookmarkable recordsets, in which case the bookmarks are valid in all clones. You can use the **Supports** method to determine if bookmarks are supported in the recordset:

```
If objRec.Supports(adBookmark) Then
    Set objRecClone = objRec.Clone
End If
```

If you make any changes to a recordset, then those changes will be visible in all clones until the time you **Requery** the original recordset. At that stage the clones will no longer be synchronized with the original recordset.

Close

Closes the Recordset object and any dependent objects.

Recordset.Close

You should beware of closing the recordset when changes are in place, as the following will occur:

 When in batch update mode, changes will be lost.

 When in immediate update mode, an error will be generated.

Closing a recordset does not free all of its resources from memory, and you should set its object variable to **Nothing** to achieve this:

```
Set objRec = Nothing
```

To be absolutely sure that you protect against errors, you can also check to see whether the recordset is open before closing it:

```
If objRec.State = adStateOpen Then
    objRec.Close
    Set objRec = Nothing
End If
```

CompareBookmarks

Compares two bookmarks and returns an indication of the relative values.

CompareEnum = *Recordset*.CompareBookmarks(*Bookmark1*, *Bookmark2*)

Name	Type	Description
Bookmark1	Variant	The bookmark for the first row to be compared.
Bookmark2	Variant	The bookmark for the second row to be compared.

CompareEnum will be one of the following constants:

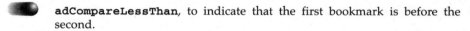 **adCompareLessThan**, to indicate that the first bookmark is before the second.

adCompareEqual, to indicate that the bookmarks are equal.

adCompareGreaterThan, to indicate that the first bookmark is after the second.

adCompareNotEqual, to indicate that the bookmarks are not equal, and not ordered.

adCompareNotComparable, to indicate that it is not possible to compare the two bookmarks.

This is really only applicable for comparing bookmarks from the same recordset or its clones. Even if two recordsets were created in exactly the same way, their bookmarks are not guaranteed to be the same.

Bookmarks are comparable across sorts and filters.

Note that this compares the actual bookmarks, not the values in the records to which those bookmarks point to.

Delete

Deletes the current record or group of records.

Recordset.Delete([*AffectRecords*])

Name	Type	Description
AffectRecords	AffectEnum	A value that determines how many records this method will affect. Default is **adAffectCurrent**

AffectEnum can be one of the following constants:

adAffectAllChapters, to delete all chapters associated with the record or group of records.

adAffectCurrent, to delete only the current record.

adAffectGroup, to delete only records that affect the current **Filter**.

Remember that when in batch update mode, the records are only marked for deletion, and are not removed from the data store until **UpdateBatch** is called.

Find

Searches the Recordset for a record that matches the specified criteria.

```
Recordset.Find(Criteria, [SkipRecords], [SearchDirection],
[Start])
```

Name	Type	Description
Criteria	String	The statement that specifies the column name, comparison operator, and value to user for the search. Only one criteria is supported, and multiple values by use of OR or AND will generate an error.
SkipRecords	Long	The offset from the current row, or *Start* bookmark, from where the search should begin. Defaults to 0.
SearchDirection	SearchDirectionEnum	Indicates the direction of the search. Default is **adSearchForward**
Start	Variant	The bookmark for the record from which the operation should begin.

SearchDirectionEnum can be one of the following constants:

- **adSearchForward**, to search forward in the recordset.
- **adSearchBackward**, to search backward in the recordset.

Start can be a valid bookmark, or one of the **BookmarkEnum** constants:

- **adBookmarkCurrent**, to start the search on the current record.
- **adBookmarkFirst**, to start the search from the first record.
- **adBookmarkLast**, to start the search from the last record.

Criteria follows the basic form of a SQL WHERE clause. For example:

```
state = 'CA'
```

```
age = 13
```

```
au_lname LIKE 'S*'
```

If **Criteria** is met the current record is positioned on the found record, otherwise the current record is set on the end of the recordset (and EOF is set).

For example:

```
objRec.Find "au_lname = 'Lloyd'"
If objRec.EOF Then
   Print "Record was not found"
End If
```

You can use a criteria to search for values that are less than, equal to, greater than, or like a particular value. For example:

```
objRec.Find "Price < 14.99"
objRec.Find "Price > 14.99"
objRec.Find "au_lname Like 'L*'"
```

The latter will find all values of **au_lname** that start with **L**.

Only single search values are allowed. Using multiple search values with AND or OR generates an error. For example:

```
objRec.Find "au_lname = 'Lloyd' And au_fname = 'Janine'"
```

This is invalid and will generate an error. This is one area where the direct migration from DAO to ADO will cause problems.

If you do need to use multiple criteria values, then your only choice is to create a new recordset, or use a **Filter**, which does accept multiple values.

GetRows

Retrieves multiple records of a Recordset object into an array.

Variant = Recordset.GetRows([Rows], [Start], [Fields])

Name	Type	Description
Rows	Long	Indicates how many records to retrieve. The default indicates that all remaining rows in the recordset should be fetched. **adGetRowsRest** is default.
Start	Variant	The bookmark for the record from which the operation should begin.
Fields	Variant	A single field name, an ordinal position, an array of field names, or an array of ordinal values representing the fields that should be fetched.

Start can be a valid bookmark, or one of the **BookmarkEnum** constants:

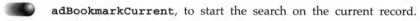 **adBookmarkCurrent**, to start the search on the current record.

adBookmarkFirst, to start the search from the first record.

adBookmarkLast, to start the search from the last record.

The columns are placed into the first dimension of the array, and the rows placed into the second. For example:

```
varRec = objRec.GetRows
intCols = UBound(varRec, 1)
intRows = UBound(varRec, 2)

For intRow = 0 To intRows
  For intCol = 0 To intCols
    Print varRec(intCol, intRow)
  Next
Next
```

Although this is not the obvious way around, this column/row order has been used to allow backward compatibility with DAO and RDO. Any values that do not make sense to store in an array, such as chapters or images, are given empty values.

For *Fields*, you can specify either a single field name, or an array of fields to be returned. For example:

```
varRec = objRec.GetRows (, , "au_lname")
```

or

```
varRec = objRec.GetRows (, , Array("au_lname", "au_fname"))
```

If using the latter method, then the order in which the columns are placed in the array dictates the order they are returned in.

After you call **GetRows,** the next unread record becomes the current record, or **EOF** is set if there are no more records.

When dealing with a large recordset you may find that calling **GetRows** several times with a smaller number of records is more efficient than calling it once to retrieve all records. For example, if calling **GetRows** on a table with 1,000 records, it might be quicker to call it 10 times using 100 as the number of rows to retrieve, rather than retrieving all rows at once. This is examined in more detail in Chapter 9.

GetString

Returns a Recordset as a string.

String = Recordset.GetString([StringFormat], [NumRows], [ColumnDelimeter], [RowDelimeter], [NullExpr])

Name	Type	Description
StringFormat	StringFormatEnum	The format in which the recordset should be returned. Default is `adClipString`.

Name	Type	Description
NumRows	Long	The number of rows in the recordset to return. All rows will be returned if this is not specified, or if it is greater than the number of rows in the recordset. Default is -1.
ColumnDelimeter	String	The delimiter to use between columns. Defaults to the TAB character.
RowDelimeter	String	The delimiter to use between rows. Defaults to the CARRIAGE RETURN character.
NullExpr	String	Expression to use in place of NULL value. Defaults to an empty string.

The only valid value for **StringFormatEnum** is **adClipString**, although we are promised HTML and XML support for later versions. Even without the HTML version, you can use this method to quickly build an HTML table in an ASP page:

```
NBSPACE = chr(160)
Set objConn = Server.CreateObject("ADODB.Connection")
Set objRec = Server.CreateObject("ADODB.Recordset")

objConn.Open "Provider=SQLOLEDB; Data Source=Tigger; " & _
             "Initial Catalog=pubs; User ID=sa; Password="

objRec.Open "authors", objConn, _
            adOpenForwardOnly, adLockReadOnly, adCmdTable

Response.Write "<TABLE BORDER=1><TR><TD>"
Response.Write objRec.GetString (adClipString, -1, _
                                 "</TD><TD>", _
                                 "</TD></TR><TR><TD>", _
                                 NBSPACE)
Response.Write "</TD></TR></TABLE>"

objRec.Close
objConn.Close
Set objRec = Nothing
Set objConn = Nothing
```

This saves having to loop through the fields collection to manually build the table.

Only row data is saved to the string, not schema data. You cannot, therefore, re-open a recordset from this string.

Move

Moves the position of the current record in a Recordset.

Recordset.Move(*NumRecords, [Start]*)

Name	Type	Description
NumRecords	Long	The number of records the current record position moves.
Start	Variant	The bookmark for the record from which the operation should begin.

Start can be a valid bookmark, or one of the **BookmarkEnum** constants:

 **adBookmarkCurrent**, to start the search on the current record.

adBookmarkFirst, to start the search from the first record.

adBookmarkLast, to start the search from the last record.

You can supply a negative number for *NumRecords* to move backwards in the recordset. For example, to move backwards three records you could do this:

```
objRec.Move -3
```

You should be aware that forward-only recordsets will not allow moving backwards, and may not allow moving forwards by any number other than 1. You can use the **Supports** method to check for this:

```
If objRec.Supports(adMovePrevious) Then
    objRec.Move -3
End If
```

If you move past the beginning or end of the recordset, then you will be positioned on **BOF** or **EOF,** and the properties set accordingly. A subsequent call to **Move** beyond the start or end of the recordset will generate an error, as will trying to **Move** in an empty recordset.

If the current record has been changed, and **Update** not called, then a move will implicitly call **Update**. You should call **CancelUpdate** before calling **Move** if you do not wish to keep the changes.

MoveFirst

Moves the position of the current record to the first record in the Recordset.

Recordset.MoveFirst

This moves to the first non-deleted row in the recordset, and sets **BOF** if all rows are deleted.

You should receive an error when using this on a forward-only recordset. Some providers may allow this, and implement it by resubmitting the command. For example, the OLEDB Driver for ODBC allows MoveFirst when talking to SQL Server, even though the supports method indicates that it is not supported:

```
objRec.Open "authors", "DSN=pubs", _
        adOpenForwardOnly, adLockOptimistic, adCmdTable
```

```
' The following line works
objRec.MoveFirst

If oRec.Supports(adMovePrevious) Then
    ' This code doesn't get executed
End If
```

This could have serious consequences on performance if the command you are running takes a long time.

If the current record has been changed, and **Update** not called, then a **MoveFirst** will implicitly call **Update**. You should call **CancelUpdate** before calling **MoveFirst** if you do not wish to keep the changes.

MoveLast

Moves the position of the current record to the last record in the Recordset.

Recordset.MoveLast

This moves to the last non-deleted row in the recordset, and sets **EOF** if all rows are deleted.

You will receive an error when using this on a forward-only recordset, since they only allow movement by one record at a time. Unlike **MoveFirst**, for example, using an ODBC connection doesn't allow this, returning an error that indicates that moving backwards is not supported. This seems an odd message when trying to move to the end of the recordset, but it's a single error message to indicate that moving using bookmarks is not supported.

If the current record has been changed, and **Update** not called, then a **MoveLast** will implicitly call **Update**. You should call **CancelUpdate** before calling **MoveLast** if you do not wish to keep the changes.

MoveNext

Moves the position of the current record to the next record in the Recordset.

Recordset.MoveNext

If you try to move past the last record in a recordset, then the **EOF** property is set. Subsequent calls to **MoveNext** will generate an error.

If the current record has been changed, and **Update** not called, then a **MoveNext** will implicitly call **Update**. You should call **CancelUpdate** before calling **MoveNext** if you do not wish to keep the changes.

MovePrevious

Moves the position of the current record to the previous record in the Recordset.

Recordset.MovePrevious

If you try to move past the first record in a recordset, then the BOF property is set. Subsequent calls to MovePrevious will generate an error.

You can use the Supports method to check whether MovePrevious can be used on the recordset:

```
If objRec.Supports(adMovePrevious) Then
    objRec.MovePrevious
End If
```

If the current record has been changed, and Update not called, then a MovePrevious will implicitly call Update. You should call CancelUpdate before calling MovePrevious if you do not wish to keep the changes.

NextRecordset

Clears the current Recordset object and returns the next Recordset by advancing through a series of commands.

Set   Recordset = Recordset.NextRecordset([RecordsAffected])

Name	Type	Description
RecordsAffected	Variant	A Long variable into which the provider returns the number of records that the operation affected.

RecordsAffected is only meaningful for a non row-returning recordset.

This can be useful if you only wish to build up a set of SQL statements and send it to the provider in one go. However, not all of the data may be returned to the client in a single batch, and may require a trip to the server for each recordset. Each SQL command will be executed when the NextRecordset command is issued. Issuing a Close on the recordset will close the recordset without executing any outstanding commands..

You could use this for returning separate lists to be used in combo boxes. For example, imagine the following code that creates a stored procedure:

```
CREATE PROCEDURE usp_ListBoxes
AS
BEGIN
    SELECT * FROM authors
    SELECT * FROM titles
END
```

Opening a recordset on this stored procedure would return the first command in the series. Once you've finished with the data from that recordset, you could issue a NextRecordset command to execute the next command. For example:

```
objRec.Open "usp_ListBoxes", objConn, _
            adOpenForwardOnly, adLockReadOnly, adCmdStoredProc

Set objRecAuth = objRec.NextRecordset
```

Notice that the above example returns the next recordset into a new recordset variable. You can also use the same variable:

```
Set objRec = objRec.NextRecordset
```

The next recordset can be returned in several states:

- As a closed recordset, but with records. You can open the recordset and proceed as normal.

- As a closed recordset (with no records), for a non row-returning recordset.

- As an empty recordset (with no records), where both **BOF** and **EOF** will be set.

You should therefore check the **State** property and the **BOF** and **EOF** properties to determine the status of the recordset. When there are no more recordsets, the recordset object will be set to **Nothing**.

When using immediate update mode, a call to **NextRecordset** will generate an error if editing is in progress, so you should ensure that you have updated or cancelled the changes.

Closing the recordset will terminate any further pending commands.

Not all providers support multiple recordsets, so you should consult your provider documentation.

Open

Opens a Recordset.

```
Recordset.Open([Source], [ActiveConnection], [CursorType],
[LockType], [Options])
```

Name	Type	Description
Source	Variant	A valid Command object, a SQL statement, a table name, a stored procedure, or the file name of a persisted recordset.
ActiveConnection	Variant	A valid Connection object or a connection string to identify the connection to use.
CursorType	CursorTypeEnum	The type of cursor the provider should use when opening the recordset. This may be changed by the provider if the cursor type is not supported. Default is **adOpenUnspecified**.

Name	Type	Description
LockType	LockTypeEnum	The type of locking (concurrency) that the provider should use when opening the recordset. Default is `adLockUnspecified`.
Options	Long	A value that indicates how the provider should interpret the *Source* argument if it represents something other than a Command object or a persisted recordset. Default is `adCmdText`

`CursorTypeEnum` can be one of the following constants:

- `adOpenForwardOnly`, for a recordset that only allows forward movement.
- `adOpenKeyset`, for a keyset-type cursor.
- `adOpenDynamic`, for a dynamic-type cursor.
- `adOpenStatic` for a static-type cursor.

These are covered in more detail under the `CursorType` property.

`LockTypeEnum` can be one of the following constants:

- `adLockReadOnly`, for a read-only recordset.
- `adLockPessimistic`, for pessimistic locking.
- `adLockOptimisitic`, for optimistic locking.
- `adLockBatchOptimistic`, for batch optimistic locking.

These are covered in more detail under the `LockType` property.

Options can be one or more of the following constants:

- `adCmdText`, to indicate that the command is a textual command.
- `adCmdTable`, to indicate that the command is a table name.
- `adCmdStoredProcedure`, to indicate that the command is a stored procedure.
- `adCmdUnknown`, to indicate that the command type is unknown.
- `adCmdFile`, to indicate that the command is a saved recordset.
- `adCmdTableDirect`, to indicate that the command is a table.
- `adAsyncFetch`, to fetch the records asynchronously.
- `adAsyncFetchNonBlocking`, to fetch the records asynchronously, but without blocking the return.

108

The first six of these are discussed in more detail in Chapter 4, under the **CommandType** property.

For asynchronous usage, you should use a client-side cursor (**CursorType** = **adUseClient**) and use a logical **OR** to add the option. For example:

```
objRec.Open "authors", objConn, adOpenKeyset, adLockOptimistic, _
            (adCmdTable OR adAsyncFetch)
```

You can then use the **State** property or the **FetchComplete** event to determine when the recordset has been fully populated.

The difference between **adAsyncFetch** and **adAsyncFetchNonBlocking** is what happens when you request a record that has not yet been fetched. With **adAsyncFetch** your operation will wait until that record is available, whereas with **adAsyncFetchNonBlocking** you will be placed on EOF.

If you set **ActiveConnection** to a connection string, a new connection to the data store will be created, whether or not an active connection exists with the same details. To ensure the best performance when opening several recordsets, use an existing connection object. You can also use a valid Command object as the source, in which case you should not supply an **ActiveConnection**.

Requery

Updates the data in a Recordset object by re-executing the query on which the object is based.

*Recordset.*Requery([*Options*])

Name	Type	Description
Options	Long	Indicates the options to use when requerying the recordset. Default is -1.

This is equivalent to issuing a Close and Open. Since you cannot change the settings of the recordset, setting Options is merely an optimization issue to help ADO. The exception to this is if you add either of the asynchronous flags, **adAsyncFetch** or **adAsyncFetchNonBlocking**.

You cannot **Requery** a recordset whilst editing an existing record, or adding a new one, without generating an error.

When using client-side cursors, you can only issue **Resync** against a non read-only recordset, and not a **Requery**.

Resync

Refreshes the data in the current Recordset object from the underlying database.

*Recordset.*Resync([*AffectRecords}*, [*ResyncValues]*])

Name	Type	Description
AffectRecords	AffectEnum	Determines how many records will be affected. Default is **adAffectAll**.
ResyncValues	ResyncEnum	Specifies whether underlying values are overwritten. Default is **adResyncAllValues**.

AffectEnum can be one of the following constants:

- **adAffectCurrent**, to refresh just the current row.
- **adAffectGroup**, to refresh all records in the current Filter.
- **adAffectAll** to refresh all records in the recordset.

ResyncEnum can be one of the following constants:

- **adResyncAllValues**, to refresh all of the value properties, effectively overwriting any pending updates.
- **adResyncUnderlyingValues**, to refresh only the **UnderlyingValue** property.

Using **adResyncUnderlyingValues** allows you to repopulate the **UnderlyingValue** property without discarding any changes or the **OriginalValue** property. This is particularly useful for investigating optimistic update conflicts, and is discussed in more detail in Chapter 8.

Unlike the **Requery** method the **Resync** method does not re-execute the underlying command.

Save

Saves the Recordset to a file.

Recordset.Save(FileName, [PersistFormat])

Name	Type	Description
FileName	String	The complete path name of the file where the recordset should be saved.
PersistFormat	PersistFormatEnum	The format in which the recordset should be saved. Default is **adPersistADTG**

Currently **PersistFormatEnum** can only be **adPersistADTG**, which is a proprietary format. However, future versions are expected to allow **adPersistXML** (to save the recordset as an XML data file) and **adPersistHTML** (to save the recordset as an HTML file).

110

Using **Save** means the following actions will apply:

- Only records in the current **Filter** are saved.

- If the recordset is being fetched asynchronously then the **Save** will block until all records are fetched.

- The current row becomes the first row once the save is complete.

FileName should only be used for the initial save. Subsequent saves on the same recordset will automatically use the same file. A different filename can be supplied to save to a separate file.

You cannot use **Save** from a script executed by Microsoft Internet Explorer, since this violates security restrictions.

Supports

Determines whether a specified Recordset object supports particular functionality.

Boolean = Recordset.Supports(CursorOptions)

Name	Type	Description
CursorOptions	CursorOptionEnum	One or more values to identify what functionality is supported.

CursorOptionsEnum can be one or more of the following constants:

- **adAddNew**, to indicate the recordset supports addition of new records, via **AddNew.**

- **adApproxPosition**, to indicate that the recordset supports absolute position, via **AbsolutePosition** and **AbsolutePage.**

- **adBookmark**, to indicate that the recordset supports bookmarks, via **Bookmark.**

- **adDelete**, to indicate that the recordset supports record deletion, via **Delete.**

- **adFind**, to indicate that the recordset supports the finding of records, via **Find.**

- **adHoldRecords**, to indicate that changes to the recordset will remain if you fetch more records.

- **adMovePrevious**, to indicate that the recordset supports movement backwards, via **MoveFirst, MovePrevious, Move** or **GetRows.**

- **adNotify**, to indicate that the recordset supports notifications, and will return events.

- **adResync**, to indicate that the recordset allows the underlying data to be refreshed with **Resync.**

adUpdate, to indicate that the recordset allows records to be updated with **Update.**

 adUpdateBatch, to indicate that the recordset allows records to be updated with **UpdateBatch.**

You can use this to test what features a recordset has available:

```
If objRec.Supports(adUpdate) Then
    ' recordset may be updateable
End If
```

Note that just because the recordset supports a particular feature, the underlying data may make this unavailable, and this may result in errors from the provider. For example, a recordset based on a view where only certain columns are updateable will support **adUpdate**, but certain columns may not allow this.

Update

Saves any changes made to the current Recordset object.

*Recordset.***Update(***[Fields],   [Values]***)**

Name	Type	Description
Fields	Variant	A single name or **Variant** array representing the names or ordinal positions of the fields to be modified.
Values	Variant	A single name or **Variant** array representing the values for the fields in the new record.

You can update fields in three ways. Firstly by assigning values to fields and then calling the **Update** method:

```
objRec("au_lname").Value = "Lloyd"
objRec("au_fname").Value = "Janine"
objRec.Update
```

Secondly you can pass a single field name with a single value:

```
objRec.Update "au_lname", "Lloyd"
```

Thirdly, by passing multiple field names and multiple values:

```
objRec.Update Array("au_lname", "au_fname"), Array("Lloyd", "Janine")
```

The three methods are interchangeable. There's little difference between the methods unless updating multiple fields, in which case you should use methods one or three. Each **Update** issues a command to the server, so the fewer updates you do, the more efficient your code is.

Using any of the **Move** methods when editing a record will implicitly call **Update.**

UpdateBatch

Writes all pending batch updates to disk.

Recordset.UpdateBatch([*AffectRecords*])

Name	Type	Description
AffectRecords	AffectEnum	Determines how many records will be affected by **adAffectAll**.

AffectEnum can be one of the following constants:

- **adAffectCurrent**, to refresh just the current row.
- **adAffectGroup**, to refresh all records in the current Filter.
- **adAffectAll** to refresh all records in the recordset.

Using **UpdateBatch** allows changes to be cached until such time as you request the underlying data store to be updated. Caching starts when opening a recordset with **adLockBatchOptimistic**.

A failure to update will cause the Errors collection to be populated, and you can use the **Filter** property to see which records failed. This could be because of a conflict between a change made by you and a change made by another user. This is discussed in more detail in Chapter 8.

Recordset Properties

AbsolutePage

Specifies in which page the current record resides.

```
PositionEnum = Recordset.AbsolutePage
Long = Recordset.AbsolutePage
Recordset.AbsolutePage = PositionEnum
Recordset.AbsolutePage = Long
```

PositionEnum can be a valid page number, or one of the following constants:

- **adPosBOF**, to indicate, or position, the current record pointer at the beginning of the recordset.
- **adPosEOF**, to indicate, or position, the current record pointer at the end of the recordset.
- **adPosUnknown**, to indicate that the current page is unknown. This could be because the recordset is empty, the provider does not support this property, or it cannot identify the current page.

When setting this value, the current record is the first record in the current page. So setting this to 1 sets the first page, and thus, the record pointer to the first record in the recordset. This is used in conjunction with the **PageSize** property.

AbsolutePosition

Specifies the ordinal position of a Recordset object's current record.

```
PositionEnum  =  Recordset.AbsolutePosition
Recordset.AbsolutePosition  =  PositionEnum
```

PositionEnum can be a valid record number, or one of the following constants:

- **adPosBOF**, to indicate, or position, the current record pointer at the beginning of the recordset.

- **adPosEOF**, to indicate, or position, the current record pointer at the end of the recordset.

- **adPosUnknown**, to indicate that the current position is unknown. This could be because the recordset is empty, the provider does not support this property, or it cannot identify the current position.

You cannot use the absolute position to uniquely identify a record, since this value changes as records are added and deleted. Of course, if your recordset does not allow additions or deletions, then you could use **AbsolutePosition** to point to a record through the life of the recordset. However, bookmarks are the recommended way to perform this action.

ActiveCommand

Indicates the Command object that created the associated Recordset object.

```
Set Command  =  Recordset.ActiveCommand
```

When the recordset was created from a command, you can use this property to access the commands properties and parameters. For example:

```
objRec.Open "authors", "DSN=pubs", _
             adOpenForwardOnly, adLockOptimistic, adCmdTable
Print objRec.ActiveCommand.CommandText
```

This is particularly useful when you have only been supplied with the recordset, such as in the Visual Basic 6 Data Environment.

This property will be Null if the recordset was not created from a command.

ActiveConnection

Indicates to which Connection object the specified Recordset object currently belongs.

```
Set  Variant = Recordset.ActiveConnection
Set  Recordset.ActiveConnection = Variant
Recordset.ActiveConnection = String
```

As indicated, you can set this to a valid connection object or to a connection string, in which case a connection object may supersede the property.

This property will inherit the value from the **ActiveConnection** argument of an **Open** command, or from the **Source** property of a Command.

You can disassociate a recordset from a connection by setting this property to *Nothing*. The recordset remains valid, and can be reconnected to any connection object at a later date.

BOF

Indicates whether the current record is before the first record in a Recordset object.

```
Boolean = Recordset.BOF
```

This will also be True if the recordset is empty.

Bookmark

Returns a bookmark that uniquely identifies the current record in a Recordset object, or sets the current record to the record identified by a valid bookmark.

```
Variant = Recordset.Bookmark
Recordset.Bookmark = Variant
```

Using **Clone** on a recordset gives two recordsets with interchangeable bookmarks. However, bookmarks from different recordsets are not interchangeable, even if the recordsets were created from the same source or command.

You can use this property to temporarily store the position in the recordset, allowing you to return to it at a later date. For example:

```
varBkmk = objRec.Bookmark

' some processing that changes the current record

objRec.Bookmark = varBkmk
```

This is actually quite useful when using the **Find** method, since this positions you at EOF if the record you are searching for was not found:

```
varBkmk = objRec.Bookmark

objRec.Find "au_lname = 'Lloyd'"
If objRec.EOF Then
  Print "Record not found - moving back to last record"
  objRec.Bkmk = varBkmk
End If
```

Bookmarks are generally only supported on keyset and static cursors, although some providers may support them on dynamic cursors. You should check the **adBookmark** value of the **Supports** method to verify this.

CacheSize

Indicates the number of records from a Recordset object that are cached locally in memory. This defaults to 1.

```
Long = Recordset.CacheSize
Recordset.CacheSize = Long
```

The cache size affects how many records from the recordset are held locally, and this can have an effect on performance and memory usage. When a recordset is first opened, only the number of records defined by **CacheSize** are fetched locally, and the remaining records are not fetched until required. Moving to a record not in the current cache means the provider then fetches another cache of records. So, the larger the cache, the more efficient your recordset, but also the more memory it uses. In practice, ADO is pretty efficient at managing the cache.

An important point to note is that records in the cache do not reflect underlying changes made by other users, until **Resync** is issued.

You can change the cache size during the life of a recordset, but the new size only becomes effective when the next cache of data is retrieved. A cache size of 0 is not allowed and generates an error.

An undocumented feature, which is not supported, is that a negative cache size causes records to be fetched backwards from the current row, rather than forwards.

CursorLocation

Sets or returns the location of the cursor engine.

```
CursorLocationEnum = Recordset.CursorLocation
Recordset.CursorLocation = CursorLocationEnum
```

CursorLocationEnum can be one of the following constants:

 adUseClient, to specify the Microsoft Client cursor.

 adUseServer, to specify the cursor support supplied by the data provider, assuming it supports server-based cursors.

116

Server-side cursors often support better concurrency than client-side cursors, because it's the actual provider that is handling the concurrency control.

Client-side cursors should be used when creating disconnecting recordsets, or when opening recordsets with multiple results sets. This is because they are not supported by server-side cursors.

CursorType

Indicates the type of cursor used in a Recordset object.

```
CursorTypeEnum = Recordset.CursorType
Recordset.CursorType = CursorTypeEnum
```

CursorTypeEnum can be one of the following constants:

- **adOpenForwardOnly**, for a recordset that only allows forward movement, one record at a time. It is therefore not possible to use anything other than **MoveNext** or **Move** with a value of 1. Bookmarks are also not supported on this cursor type, since absolute position is not a requirement.

- **adOpenKeyset**, for a keyset-type cursor. This gives you a set of records for which the data is up-to-date with the underlying data, but the number of records may not be, as additions and deletions are not visible to the cursor. Movement is supported both forwards and backwards.

- **adOpenDynamic**, for a dynamic-type cursor, where both the underlying data and records are visible to the cursor. Movement is supported both forwards and backwards.

- **adOpenStatic** for a static-type cursor, where the data is fixed at the time the cursor is created. Movement is supported both forwards and backwards.

The Microsoft Access provider does not support dynamic cursors, and a keyset cursor is used instead. For this reason you should really query the **CursorType** property after the recordset has been opened, to see what type the provider has used. The cursor types requested and supported by the main providers are included in Chapter 9.

DataMember

Specifies the name of the data member to retrieve from the object referenced by the DataSource property.

```
String = Recordset.DataMember
Recordset.DataMember = String
```

Used to create data-bound controls in Visual Basic 6 using the Data Environment.

The **DataMember** identifies the object in the **DataSource** that will supply the recordset.

DataSource

Specifies an object containing data to be represented as a Recordset object.

```
Set  Object = Recordset.DataSourceSet
Set  Recordset.DataSource = Object
```

It is used to create data-bound controls in Visual Basic 6 using the Data Environment.

The **DataSource** identifies the object in the Data Environment to which the **DataMember** belongs.

EditMode

Indicates the editing status of the current record.

```
EditModeEnum = Recordset.EditMode
```

EditModeEnum will be one of the following constants:

- **adEditNone**, to indicate that the current record has no edits in progress.
- **adEditInProgress**, to indicate that the current record is being edited.
- **adEditAdd** to indicate that the current record is being added, that is, it's a new record.
- **adEditDelete**, to indicate the current record has been deleted.

You could use this in an interactive application that allows users to edit and move around records. Since moving around records intrinsically calls **Update**, you may want to offer the user the option of canceling or saving their changes before moving the record. For example, imagine a section of Visual Basic code that runs when a 'Next Record' button is pressed:

```
If objRec.EditMode = adEditInProgress Then
    strMsg = "The current record has changed. " & _
             "Would you like to save the changes?"
    If MsgBox (strMsg, vbYesNo) = vbNo Then
        objRec.CancelUpdate
    End If
End If
objRec.MoveNext
```

This simply checks the edit mode before moving to another record.

EOF

Indicates whether the current record is after the last record in a Recordset object.

```
Boolean = Recordset.EOF
```

This will also be **True** if the recordset is empty.

Filter

Indicates a filter for data in the Recordset

```
Variant = Recordset.Filter
Recordset.Filter = Variant
```

The **Filter** property can be set to a valid filter string, an array of bookmarks, or one of the following **FilterGroupEnum** constants:

- **adFilterNone**, which removes any current filter, and shows all records.
- **adFilterPendingRecords**, for batch update mode, which shows only records that have been changed but not yet sent to the server.
- **adFilterAffectedRecords**, which shows only records affected by the last **Delete**, **Resync**, **UpdateBatch**, or **CancelBatch**.
- **adFilterFetchedRecords**, which shows records in the current cache.
- **adFilterPredicate**, which shows deleted records.
- **adFilterConflictingRecords**, which shows records that caused a conflict during the last batch update attempt.

You can use an array of Bookmarks to filter with. This small section of Visual Basic code shows an example of this:

```
Dim avarBkmk(5)

avarBkmk(0) = objRec.Bookmark

' some more processing

avarBkmk(1) = objRec.Bookmark

objRec.Filter = avarBkmk
```

This can be quite useful when allowing users to select multiple records from a list.

Using a normal string to filter with follows much the same syntax as a SQL WHERE clause, as the following examples show:

```
objRec.Filter "au_lname = 'Lloyd'""
objRec.Filter "au_lname Like 'L*'"
objRec.Filter "Price > 10.99 And Price < 15.99"
objRec.filter "InvoiceDate > #04/04/98#"
```

You'll notice that multiple conditions are allowed here, unlike the `Find` command. When using date fields, you have to use the VBA syntax, surrounding the date with # symbols.

Once the `Filter` has been set, you are placed on the first record in the newly filtered recordset.

To cancel a filter you can either use an empty string ("") or use `adFilterNone`.

LockType

Indicates the type of locks placed on records during editing.

```
LockTypeEnum = Recordset.LockType
Recordset.LockType = LockTypeEnum
```

`LockTypeEnum` can be one of the following constants:

- `adLockReadOnly`, for a read-only recordset, where the provider does no locking and the data cannot be changed.
- `adLockPessimistic`, for pessimistic locking, where the provider attempts to lock edited records at the data source.
- `adLockOptimistic`, for optimistic locking, where the provider locks records on a row by row basis, when `Update` is called.
- `adLockBatchOptimistic`, for batch update mode, where locking occurs when `UpdateBatch` is called.

You cannot use pessimistic locking on client side cursors.

The locking method you choose is really going to depend upon the application. Since pessimistic locking locks the record as you start editing, you don't have to worry about a conflict with another user's changes. However, this implies a permanent connection to the data store, which may be either impractical, or impossible.

Using optimistic locking gives you better resource management, but you then have to cater for conflicts, as the lock doesn't actually occur until you try to `Update` the record. This means that someone else might have changed the record between the time you started editing it and the time you went to `Update` it. Since ADO doesn't know which copy is correct it generates an error, which can be trapped.

Although batch locking can be used with server-based cursors, it's more useful with client cursors and disconnected recordsets. This allows changes to multiple records before committing them to the data store in a single batch.

MarshalOptions

Indicates which records are to be marshaled back to the server.

```
MarshalOptionsEnum  =  Recordset.MarshalOptions
Recordset.MarshalOptions  =  MarshalOptionsEnum
```

MarshalOptionsEnum can be one of the following constants:

 adMarshalAll, to send all rows back to the server, which is the default.

 adMarshalModifiedOnly, to send back to the server only those rows that have changed.

This property is only applicable when using disconnected, client-side recordsets. By marshalling only the changed records, you can greatly improve performance (if only a few records are modified locally), as less data needs to be sent back to the client.

You can use this quite effectively when using an n-tier client/server architecture, using a business object on the server to supply recordsets. These can be modified locally, and only the changed records sent back to the business record for updating. This is covered in more detail in Chapter 8.

MaxRecords

Indicates the maximum number of records to return to a Recordset object from a query.

```
Long  =  Recordset.MaxRecords
Recordset.MaxRecords  =  Long
```

You can only set this property before the recordset is open. It defaults to 0, which indicates all records should be returned.

This is quite useful for applications that allow users to submit queries, since you can limit their set of records if it is too big.

PageCount

Indicates how many pages of data the Recordset object contains.

```
Long  =  Recordset.PageCount
```

The recordset will consist of **PageCount** number of pages, each containing **PageSize** records. If the **PageSize** is not set then **PageCount** will be –1.

It allows you to quickly move to the last page in a recordset:

```
objRec.AbsolutePage = objRec.PageSize
```

This positions you on the first record in the last page.

Not all providers support this property.

PageSize

Indicates how many records constitute one page in the Recordset.

```
Long = Recordset.PageSize
Recordset.PageSize = Long
```

You can use this to change the number of records in a current page. For example, imagine a Web application that shows search results from Microsoft Index Server. You could allow the user to page through these records, and to specify how many records should be seen in each page.

The page size doesn't correspond to the cache size. The cache is a way of managing the transfer of a number of records from the server to the client, whereas the page size is merely a logical structure that can be used for display usage. It allows you to neatly access a group of records which are next to each other in the recordset.

Not all providers support **PageSize**.

RecordCount

Indicates the current number of records in the Recordset object.

```
Long = Recordset.RecordCount
```

If the Recordset object supports approximate positioning, this will contain the exact number of records in the Recordset, even if the recordset is being fetched asynchronously and not all records have been fetched. Accessing the record count before the recordset is fully populated will give an incorrect value.

If the recordset does not support approximate positioning, it must be fully populated before an accurate **RecordCount** value can be returned. The best way to achieve this is to use **MoveLast** to move to the last record in the recordset before using **RecordCount**.

Sort

Specifies one or more field names the Recordset is sorted on, and the direction of the sort.

```
String = Recordset.Sort
Recordset.Sort = String
```

122

The sort string should be a comma-separated list of columns to dictate the sort order, each optionally followed by the sort direction. For example:

```
objRec.Sort = "au_lname ASC, au_fname DESC"
```

*Note that the sort order is **ASC** for ascending and **DESC** for descending. The ADO Help File is wrong.*

If using client-side cursors (`CursorLocation = adUseClient`), then a temporary index will be created for each field in the `Sort`. You can also force the creation of local indexes by setting the `Optimize` property of the `Fields Properties` collection. For example:

```
objRec("au_lname").Properties("Optimize") = True
```

This will create a local index, which will speed up sorting and searching.

Source

Indicates the command or SQL command for the data in a Recordset object.

```
String = Recordset.Source
Recordset.Source = String
Set Recordset.Source = Variant
```

This is useful for identifying the actual command text used to create the recordset, especially if it was created from a `Command` object.

State

Gives the state of the recordset in both synchronous and asynchronous mode. Indicates whether the recordset is open, closed, or whether it is executing an asynchronous operation.

```
ObjectStateEnum = Recordset.State
```

`ObjectStateEnum` can be one or more of the following constants:

- `adStateClosed`, indicating that the recordset is closed.
- `adStateOpen`, indicating that the recordset is open.
- `adStateConnecting`, indicating that the recordset is currently connecting to the data store.
- `adStateExecuting`, indicating that the recordset is currently executing a command.
- `adStateFetching`, indicating that the recordset is currently fetching records.

When the recordset is opened asynchronously, you should use logical operations to test these values. For example:

```
If (objRec.State And adStateFetching) = adStateFetching Then
   Print "Recordset is still fetching records"
End If
```

A positive test for **adStateExecuting** and **adStateFetching** implies **adStateOpen**, but you cannot test for this alone.

Status

Indicates the status of the current record with respect to match updates or other bulk operations.

RecordStatusEnum = *Recordset.*Status

Since **RecordStatusEnum** is quite long it's not been included here again, and can be one or more of the constants shown in Appendix F.

StayInSync

Indicates, in a hierarchical Recordset object, whether a reference to the child row should change when the parent record changes.

Boolean = *Recordset.*StayInSync
*Recordset.*StayInSync = *Boolean*

The default for this is True, and if set to False, a reference to a child recordset will remain pointing to the old recordset, even though the parent record may have changed.

Hierarchical recordsets are covered in more detail in Chapter 8, when looking at Data Shaping.

Note that the ADO Help File for this method is incorrect.

Recordset Events

ADO 2 supports notifications, which allows providers to notify the application when certain events occur. To use events you have to register your application to receive them. This, along with event ordering, is covered in Chapter 2.

Event Status

All events have a bi-directional parameter, **adStatus**, to indicate the status of the event. This is of type **EventStatusEnum,** and can be one of the following constants:

- **adStatusOK**, to indicate that the action that caused the event was successful.

- **adStatusErrorsOccured**, to indicate that errors or warnings occurred, in which case the Errors collection should be checked.

- **adStatusCantDeny**, to indicate that you cannot cancel the **Will** event, and when **Complete** events occur, indicates that the action was cancelled.

- **adStatusUnwantedEvent**, which indicates that the reason the event was generated should no longer generate events.

On a **Will** event – assuming **adStatusCantDeny** is not set – you can set **adStatus** to **adStatusCancel** in order to cancel the action that caused this event. This must be done before the procedure exits. For example, assume that you have moved from one record to the next – this will raise a **WillMove** event. If you decide that you do not wish to move to another record, you can set **adStatus** to **adStatusCancel**, and the **Move** action will be cancelled. This allows you to perhaps cancel actions where the data is incorrect.

One thing to watch for when using **Will** events is implicit method calls. Taking the above Move as an example, if the current record has been edited, then ADO implicitly calls **Update**. In this case you might get more than one **Will** event.

If you no longer wish to receive events for a particular action, then before the procedure exits you can set **adStatus** to **adStatusUnwantedEvent**, and they will no longer be generated.

Events cannot be used in scripting languages.

EndOfRecordset

Fired when there is an attempt to move to a row past the end of the Recordset.

```
EndOfRecordset(fMoreData, adStatus, pRecordset)
```

Name	Type	Description
fMoreData	Boolean	Set to **True** if it is possible to append more data to **pRecordset** while processing this event.
adStatus	EventStatusEnum	Identifies the status of the message.
pRecordset	Recordset	A reference to the Recordset object for which this event applies.

While in this method, more records can be retrieved from the data store and appended to the end of the recordset. If you wish to do this, you should set the parameter *fMoreData* to **True**. After returning from this procedure, a subsequent **MoveNext** will allow access to the newly added records. This can be useful if you wish to provide your own paging scheme, as you can read in the next batch of records when the user attempts to move past the end of the current page of records.

FetchComplete

Fired after all the records in an asynchronous operation have been retrieved into the Recordset.

`FetchComplete(pError, adStatus, pRecordset)`

Name	Type	Description
pError	Error	An Error object that describes the error that occurred if *adStatus* is `adStatusErrorsOccurred`. Otherwise it is not set.
adStatus	EventStatusEnum	Identifies the status of the message.
pRecordset	Recordset	A reference to the Recordset object for which the records were retrieved.

This is most useful when the recordset is being fetched asynchronously, as it saves having to periodically check the State of the recordset.

FetchProgress

Fired periodically during an asynchronous operation, to report how many rows have been retrieved so far.

`FetchProgress(Progress, MaxProgress, adStatus, pRecordset)`

Name	Type	Description
Progress	Long	The number of records that have currently been retrieved.
MaxProgress	Long	The maximum number of records expected to be retrieved.
adStatus	EventStatusEnum	Identifies the status of the message.
pRecordset	Recordset	A reference to the Recordset object for which the records are being retrieved.

MaxProgess may not contain the total number of records to be fetched if the recordset type does not support this.

This would be used for updating status indicators on user screens.

FieldChangeComplete

Fired after the value of one or more Field object has been changed.

FieldChangeComplete(*cFields, Fields, pError, adStatus, pRecordset*)

Name	Type	Description
cFields	Long	The number of Field objects in *Fields*.
Fields	Variant	An array of Field objects with pending changes.
pError	Error	Describes the error that occurred if *adStatus* is `adStatusErrorsOccurred`, otherwise it is not set.
adStatus	EventStatusEnum	Identifies the status of the message.
pRecordset	Recordset	A reference to the Recordset object for which this event applies.

You can use this to update status indicators, or to trigger other actions that are dependent upon some fields being changed.

MoveComplete

Fired after the current position in the Recordset changes.

MoveComplete(*adReason, pError, adStatus, pRecordset*)

Name	Type	Description
adReason	EventReasonEnum	The reason for the event.
pError	Error	An **Error** object that describes the error that occurred if *adStatus* is `adStatusErrorsOccurred`. Otherwise it is not set.
adStatus	EventStatusEnum	Identifies the status of the message.
pRecordset	Recordset	The Recordset object for which this event applies.

`adReason` will be a subset of the `EventReasonEnum` constants:

- `adRsnMoveFirst`, when a `MoveFirst` is issued.
- `adRsnMoveLast`, when a `MoveLast` is issued.
- `adRsnMoveNext`, when a `MoveNext` is issued.
- `adRsnMovePrevious`, when a `MovePrevious` is issued.
- `adRsnMove`, when a `Move` is issued
- `adRsnRequery`, when a `Requery` is issued, or a `Filter` is set.

A value of **adRsnMove** could also be generated by setting the **AbsolutePage** or **AbsolutePosition** properties, setting a **Bookmark**, or adding a new record with **AddNew**. Additionally, this value is generated when the recordset is opened.

These could also be generated when a child recordset has events and the parent recordset moves.

RecordChangeComplete

Fired after one or more records change in the local recordset.

```
RecordChangeComplete(adReason, cRecords, pError, adStatus,
pRecordset)
```

Name	Type	Description
adReason	EventReasonEnum	Specifies the reason for the event.
cRecords	Long	The number of records changing.
pError	Error	An Error object that describes the error that occurred if *adStatus* is **adStatusErrorsOccurred**. Otherwise it is not set.
adStatus	EventStatusEnum	Identifies the status of the message.
pRecordset	Recordset	The Recordset object for which this event applies, containing only the changed rows.

adReason will be a subset of the **EventReasonEnum** constants:

- **adRsnAddNew**, when an **AddNew** is issued.
- **adRsnDelete**, when a **Delete** is issued.
- **adRsnUpdate**, when an **Update** is issued.
- **adRsnUndoUpdate**, when an **Update** is cancelled, with **CancelUpdate** or **CancelBatch**.
- **adRsnUndoAddNew**, when an **AddNew** is cancelled, with **CancelUpdate** or **CancelBatch**.
- **dRsnUndoDelete**, when a **Delete** is cancelled, with **CancelUpdate** or **CancelBatch**.
- **adRsnFirstChange**, when the record is changed for the first time.

You could use this event for the creation of an audit trail, or triggering other actions that are dependant upon the data having changed.

RecordsetChangeComplete

Fired after the **Recordset** has changed.

```
RecordsetChangeComplete(adReason, pError, adStatus,
pRecordset)
```

Name	Type	Description
adReason	EventReasonEnum	Specifies the reason for the event.
pError	Error	An Error object that describes the error that occurred if *adStatus* is `adStatusErrorsOccurred`. Otherwise it is not set.
adStatus	EventStatusEnum	Identifies the status of the message.
pRecordset	Recordset	The Recordset object for which this event applies.

`adReason` will be a subset of the `EventReasonEnum` constants:

- `adRsnRequery`, when a `Requery` is issued.
- `adRsnReSynch`, when a `Resync` is issued.
- `adRsnClose`, when a `Close` is issued.
- `adRsnOpen.`, when an `Open` is issued.

WillChangeField

Fired before a pending operation changes the value of one or more Field objects.

```
WillChangeField(cFields, Fields, adStatus, pRecordset)
```

Name	Type	Description
cFields	Long	The number of **Field** objects in *Fields*.
Fields	Variant	An array of Field objects with pending changes.
adStatus	EventStatusEnum	Identifies the status of the message.
pRecordset	Recordset	The Recordset object for which this event applies.

This can be useful for validating user input.

This can occur due to the following Recordset operations: `Value`, and `Update` with field and value array parameters.

WillChangeRecord

Fired before one or more rows in the Recordset change.

WillChangeRecord(*adReason*, *cRecords*, *adStatus*, *pRecordset*)

Name	Type	Description
adReason	EventReasonEnum	Specifies the reason for the event.
cRecords	Long	The number of records changing.
adStatus	EventStatusEnum	Identifies the status of the message.
pRecordset	Recordset	The Recordset object for which this event applies.

adReason will be a subset of the EventReasonEnum constants:

- adRsnAddNew, when an AddNew is issued.
- adRsnDelete, when a Delete is issued.
- adRsnUpdate, when an Update is issued.
- adRsnUndoUpdate, when an Update is cancelled, with CancelUpdate or CancelBatch.
- adRsnUndoAddNew, when an AddNew is cancelled, with CancelUpdate or CancelBatch.
- adRsnUndoDelete, when a Delete is cancelled, with CancelUpdate or CancelBatch.
- adRsnFirstChange, when the record is changed for the first time.

You could use this when actions might change the record, and can be used in parallel with WillChangeField.

WillChangeRecordset

Fired before a pending operation changes the Recordset.

WillChangeRecordset(*adReason*, *adStatus*, *pRecordset*)

Name	Type	Description
adReason	EventReasonEnum	Specifies the reason for the event.
adStatus	EventStatusEnum	Identifies the status of the message.
pRecordset	Recordset	The Recordset object for which this event applies.

adReason will be a subset of the **EventReasonEnum** constants:

- **adRsnReQuery**, when a **Requery** is issued.
- **adRsnReSynch**, when a **Resync** is issued.
- **adRsnClose**, when a **Close** is issued.
- **adRsnOpen.**, when an **Open** is issued.

You can use this to identify when an action would cause the underlying set of records to change.

WillMove

Fired before a pending operation changes the current position in the Recordset.

WillMove(*adReason, adStatus, pRecordset*)

Name	Type	Description
adReason	EventReasonEnum	The reason for the event.
adStatus	EventStatusEnum	Identifies the status of the message.
pRecordset	Recordset	The Recordset object for which this event applies.

adReason will be a subset of the **EventReasonEnum** constants:

- **adRsnMoveFirst**, when a **MoveFirst** is issued.
- **adRsnMoveLast**, when a **MoveLast** is issued.
- **adRsnMoveNext**, when a **MoveNext** is issued.
- **adRsnMovePrevious**, when a **MovePrevious** is issued.
- **adRsnMove**, when a **Move** is issued, or **AbsolutePage** or **AbsolutePosition** is set, the current record is moved by setting the **Bookmark**, an **AddNew** is issued, or the recordset was opened.
- **adRsnReQuery**, when a **ReQuery** is issued, or a **Filter** is set.

This allows you to identify when an action will cause the current record to change.

Recordset Collections

Fields

The Fields collection contains zero or more Field objects, each representing a field in the recordset.

Recordset.Fields

You can enumerate the Fields collection to access each Field object individually:

```
For Each objField in objRec.Fields
    Print "Field name is " & objField.Name
Next
```

The Fields collection is discussed in more detail in Chapter 6.

Properties

The Properties collection contains Property objects, each representing an extended property supplied by the provider for the recordset.

Recordset.Properties

You can enumerate the Properties collection to access each Property object individually:

```
For Each objProp in objRec.Properties
    Print "property name is " & objProp.Name
Next
```

The Properties collection is discussed in more detail in Appendix C.

Collections

You can use ADO without resorting to any of the Collections, but there are certain facilities that won't be available unless you do. We have already covered the Parameters collection in Chapter 4, so now we'll look at the other three: Errors, Fields, and Properties. To finish up this chapter there is a section on using images with ADO.

When considering collections you need to look at two things:

 The Collection itself

 The objects of which the collection comprises

Typically, you'll find the collections and objects are sensibly named, where the collection is the plural and the object the singular:

Object	Collection
Error	Errors
Field	Fields
Parameter	Parameters
Property	Properties

Error Object

The **Error** object is used to hold all of the details pertaining to a single error (or warning) from an OLEDB provider, and therefore contains only data access errors. It is used in conjunction with the **Errors** collection, which in turn belongs to the **Connection** object. This means that to access the errors you have to refer to the connection on which they were generated. So, if you have an explicit connection object you would refer to this in order to access the first error in the collection:

```
objConn.Errors(0).Description
```

If, for example, you had a Recordset object without an explicit connection, then you can use the **ActiveConnection** property of the recordset to get access to the errors:

```
objRec.ActiveConnection.Errors(0).Description
```

Since the Error object contains a single error, and the provider can return multiple errors, you should really enumerate the collection to see all of the possible errors. In Visual Basic, for example, you would do this:

```
Dim objErr As ADODB.Error

For Each objErr in objConn.Errors
    Print "Error: " & objErr.Description
Next
```

Error Methods

The Error object has no methods.

Error Properties

Description

A description string associated with the error.

String = *Error*.Description

Since this is the default property, it can be omitted if required. The following two lines of code, for example, are equivalent:

```
Print objConn.Errors(0).Description
```

```
Print objConn.Errors(0)
```

HelpContext

Indicates the ContextID in the help file for the associated error, if one exists.

Long = *Error*.HelpContext

You can use this property if you wish to integrate your application with the standard Windows help system. Do this by calling the Help functions, then using the **HelpContext** to identify the ID number of the help description.

This will be zero if no further help is available.

HelpFile

Indicates the name of the help file, if one exists.

```
String = Error.HelpFile
```

Use this in conjunction with the **HelpContext** property when interacting with the Windows help system.

NativeError

Indicates the provider-specific error code for the associated error.

```
Long = Error.NativeError
```

This is useful for identifying errors produced, say, in stored procedures. The Native error will be the underlying error code. So, if an error was generated in the data stored, this is the error that is returned in this property. This is generally more useful than the ADO error number because it indicates the root of the problem, and since it is in the syntax of the provider, it also makes tracking the error down in the provider documentation easier.

Number

Indicates the number that uniquely identifies an Error object.

```
Long = Error.Number
```

This is a unique ADO number that corresponds to the error condition. For example, many database related errors will generate their own error number, which gets stored in the **NativeError** property, and the ADO Number property will probably get set to -2147217900 or -2147467259, both of which indicate an underlying object caused the error.

A full list of the error numbers is included in Appendix G.

Source

Indicates the name of the object or application that originally generated the error.

```
String = Error.Source
```

This could come from the class name of an object, the provider, or ADO. For example, ADO errors will be in the form:

ADODB.*ObjectName*

where *ObjectName* is the ADO object that generated the error. You'll notice that in the errors shown in the example section, the Source doesn't follow this form because those errors were generated by the provider.

SQLState

Indicates the SQL state for a given Error object.

String = *Error*.SQLState

This will contain the 5-character SQL error code if the error occurred during a SQL command. If the error doesn't have a specific state then this may be blank. You should consult your provider's SQL documentation for a list of these error codes.

The SQL State error codes are defined by the SQL Access Group and the X/ Open group, and are a standard for SQL error messages.

Errors Collection

The Errors collection contains zero or more Error objects, each representing a single error from the provider.

Errors Collection Methods

Clear

Removes all of the Error objects from the Errors collection.

Errors.Clear

This is automatically called when an error occurs, so that the new error information can be entered. ADO does this clearing, rather than the provider, enabling the provider to supply multiple errors details in response to a single error condition. There's no way to stop this happening, so if you need to keep error information you can store it in a custom collection, or custom recordset.

You might think that this is a bit superfluous if the Errors collection is cleared automatically, but there are some actions that cause the Errors collection to be filled with warning information. This specifically affects the **Resync**, **UpdateBatch**, and **CancelBatch** methods of the recordset, where records may have been deleted at the source whilst you were editing them.

Another case of this arises from miscellaneous warnings from the provider. For example, look at the following lines of code:

```
Dim objRec As New ADODB.Recordset
objRec.Open "authors", "DSN=pubs", _
            adOpenDynamic, adLockOptimistic, adCmdTable
```

This may appear fairly innocuous, but running this actually fills in an Error in the Errors collection of the **ActiveConnection** property of the recordset:

```
Description:    [Microsoft][ODBC SQL Server Driver]Cursor concurrency changed
HelpContext:    0
HelpFile:
```

```
NativeError:    0
Number:     0
Source:     Microsoft OLE DB Provider for ODBC Drivers
SQLState:    01S02
```

There's nothing wrong here, it's just that when you create a Recordset object, the cursor type is initially **adForwardOnly.** But here we have requested a different type, so the provider kindly tells us that it has changed it. These warnings are dependent upon the provider and data store.

Refresh

Updates the Error objects with information from the provider.

Errors.Refresh

You can use this to ensure that the Errors collection contains the latest set of error information from the provider.

Errors Collection Properties

Count

Indicates the number of Error objects in the Errors collection.

Long = Errors.Count

You can use the Visual Basic or VBScript **For Each...Next** command to iterate through the parameters collection without using the **Count** property. For example:

```
For Each objErr In objConn.Errors
    . . .
Next
```

Item

Allows indexing into the Errors collection to reference a specific Error object.

Error = Errors.Item(*Index*)

Name	Type	Description
Index	Variant	The number of the error in the collection. Zero based.

This is the default property and can be omitted. For example, both of the following lines are identical:

```
oConn.Errors.Item(1)
```

```
oConn.Errors(1)
```

Error Examples

The following piece of Visual Basic code shows a good way to list all of the errors in the Errors collection:

```vb
Public Sub ErrorTest()

    ' set the error handling on
    On Error GoTo ShowErrors

    ' declare a new command object and an error object
    Dim objCmd    As New ADODB.Command
    Dim objErr    As ADODB.Error

    ' set the command and run it
    objCmd.ActiveConnection = "DSN=pubs"
    objCmd.CommandText = "UPDATE pub_info SET pub_id='1111' " & _
                        "WHERE pub_id='9999'"
    objCmd.CommandType = adCmdText
    objCmd.Execute

    Exit Sub

ShowErrors:
    ' loop through the errors
    For Each objErr In objCmd.ActiveConnection.Errors
        Debug.Print "Description:"; vbTab; objErr.Description
        Debug.Print "HelpContext:"; vbTab; objErr.HelpContext
        Debug.Print "HelpFile:"; vbTab; objErr.HelpFile
        Debug.Print "NativeError:"; vbTab; objErr.NativeError
        Debug.Print "Number:"; vbTab; objErr.Number
        Debug.Print "Source:"; vbTab; objErr.Source
        Debug.Print "SQLState:"; vbTab; objErr.SQLState
    Next

End Sub
```

This uses the pubs databases, and tries to run a SQL statement that violates referential integrity. If you run this command using different OLEDB providers and data stores, you get similar, but not quite identical, results:

OLEDB Provider for ODBC to SQL Server

```
Description:    [Microsoft][ODBC SQL Server Driver][SQL Server]UPDATE statement
conflicted with COLUMN FOREIGN KEY constraint 'FK__pub_info__pub_id__2AEA69DC'.
The conflict occurred in database 'pubs', table 'publishers', column 'pub_id'
HelpContext:    0
HelpFile:
NativeError:    547
Number:    -2147217900
Source:    Microsoft OLE DB Provider for ODBC Drivers
SQLState:    23000

Description:    [Microsoft][ODBC SQL Server Driver][SQL Server]Command has been
aborted.
HelpContext:    0
HelpFile:
NativeError:    3621
Number:    -2147217900
Source:    Microsoft OLE DB Provider for ODBC Drivers
SQLState:    01000
```

Using the OLEDB provider for ODBC connected to SQL Server, you will notice that you get two errors generated. The first is an error indicating the exact nature of the error, and the second indicates that the command has been aborted. You can clearly see the SQL Server error numbers and descriptions.

You can also see that the ADO error **Number** is the same – this corresponds to 'The command contained one or more errors', so it's important you use the **NativeError** property to identify the exact problem.

A full list of ADO error numbers and descriptions is included in Appendix G.

OLEDB Provider for ODBC to Access

```
Description:     [Microsoft][ODBC Microsoft Access 97 Driver] You can't add or
change a record because a related record is required in table 'publishers'.
HelpContext:    0
HelpFile:
NativeError:    -1613
Number:    -2147217900
Source:    Microsoft OLE DB Provider for ODBC Drivers
SQLState:    23000
```

Using the OLEDB provider for ODBC connecting to an Access database with the same structure, you only get one error – the actual error that occurred. The Access ODBC driver doesn't send an extra error back.

SQL Server Provider

```
Description:
HelpContext:    0
HelpFile:
NativeError:    547
Number:    -2147217900
Source:
SQLState:    23000

Description:
HelpContext:    0
HelpFile:
NativeError:    3621
Number:    -2147217900
Source:
SQLState:    01000
```

Using the native OLEDB driver for SQL Server we still get two errors, but far less information because the Description and Source properties don't get filled in.

Jet Provider

```
Description:    You can't add or change a record because a related record is
required in table 'publishers'.
HelpContext:    5003000
HelpFile:
NativeError:    -535037517
Number:    -2147467259
Source:    Microsoft JET Database Engine
SQLState:    3201
```

For the OLEDB provider for Jet we only get one error, but we do get a full description of it. Notice that the ADO error number is slightly different – this corresponds to 'Unspecified error'. Also notice that the **NativeError** property returns a different error number than for the ODBC case, although both of these error numbers correspond to 'Application-defined or object-defined error'.

Field Object

The Field object represents a single column or field in a recordset. When you create a recordset, each row consists of a Fields collection, which contains zero or more Field objects.

Although Field objects can exist on their own, they are really only useful when used in conjunction with a Recordset object. Unless you are creating your own recordsets, where you create fields, you'll generally be dealing with an existing Field object. You can reference these in two ways. The first is by directly accessing the Field through the Fields collection:

```
objRec.Fields(0).Type
```

or

```
objRec.Fields("FirstName").Type
```

Alternatively you can use a Field object:

```
Dim objFld As ADODB.Field

Set objFld = objRec.Fields("FirstName")
```

The two methods are functionally equivalent, although using a Field object is more efficient (and therefore faster) if you are going to be referencing several properties or methods of a single field.

Field Methods

AppendChunk

Appends data to a large or binary Field object.

Field.AppendChunk(*Data*)

Name	Type	Description
Data	Variant	The data to be appended to the object.

The first call to **AppendChunk** after an **Edit** call writes data to the field, overwriting any existing data in the buffer. Subsequent calls add to existing data.

This is most often used when dealing with images or large text fields stored in databases. A full discussion of this is included at the end of this chapter.

GetChunk

Returns all or a portion of the contents of a large or binary Field object.

Variant = *Field*.GetChunk(*Length*)

Name	Type	Description
Length	Long	The number of bytes or characters to be retrieved.

The first call returns data starting from the start of the field. Subsequent calls start where the last call left off.

Like **AppendChunk**, this is most often used with images, and a full discussion is included at the end of the chapter.

Field Properties

ActualSize

Indicates the actual length of a field's value.

Long = *Field*.ActualSize
Field.ActualSize = *Long*

You should use this property when you need to set or find out how long a field actually is, rather than how long it can be, which is contained in the **DefinedSize** property. For fixed length data types these two properties will be the same, but they may be different for variable length data.

Attributes

Indicates one or more characteristics of a Field object.

Long = *Field*.Attributes

This will be one of the following **FieldAttributeEnum** values:

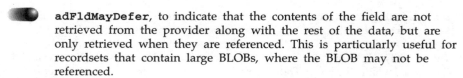

adFldMayDefer, to indicate that the contents of the field are not retrieved from the provider along with the rest of the data, but are only retrieved when they are referenced. This is particularly useful for recordsets that contain large BLOBs, where the BLOB may not be referenced.

adFldUpdatable, to indicate that the field can be updated.

- **adFldUnknownUpdatable**, to indicate that the provider doesn't know whether the field can be updated.

- **adFldFixed**, to indicate that the field contains fixed length data.

- **adFldIsNullable**, to indicate that Null values can be used when writing to the field.

- **adFldMayBeNull**, to indicate that the field may contain a Null value when you read from the field.

- **adFldLong**, to indicate that **AppendChunk** and **GetChunk** can be used on the field, since it contains long binary data.

- **adFldRowID**, to indicate that the field contains a RowID that cannot be updated. This doesn't indicate the Access AutoNumber or SQL Server IDENTITY fields, but rather an internal row number field, which is unique across the database. Oracle has these natively whereas many other data stores don't.

- **adFldRowVersion**, to indicate a field that uniquely identifies the version of the row, such as a SQL Timestamp field.

- **adFldCacheDeferred** to indicate that the values for this field will be cached once it has been read for the first time, and reading the value again will read from the cache.

Since this property is an enumerated type its value may not directly match one of the above constants. To check that a value is set you should use a procedure like this:

```
If (Field.Attribute And ad_constant) = ad_constant Then
   Print "field supports that attribute"
End If
```

For example, to check to see if a field might contain Null values:

```
Set objField = objRec.Fields("field_that_might_be_null")
If (objField.Attributes And adFldMayBeNull) = adFldMayBeNull Then
   Print "Field may contain a null"
End If
```

Note that this field is read/write when fabricating your own recordsets, and becomes read-only once this fabricated recordset is opened.

DataFormat

Identifies the format the data should be displayed in.

```
Set  DataFormatObject  =  Field.DataFormat
Set  Field.DataFormat  =  DataFormatObject
```

This is only useful when used in conjunction with Visual Basic 6 or Visual J++ 6, which include the new **DataFormat** object. This object contains several properties to identify the type of data the object holds, and the way in which it should be displayed. For example, in Visual Basic 6 you could do this:

```
Set txtDate.DataFormat = objRec.Fields("InvoiceDate").DataFormat
```

For more information on this you should consult the Visual Basic 6 or Visual J++ 6 documentation.

DefinedSize

Indicates the defined size of the Field object.

Long = *Field*.DefinedSize

For variable width fields this indicates the maximum width of the field, as opposed to the **ActualSize** property which identifies the actual size. For example, a SQL Server column declared as varchar(20) would have a **DefinedSize** of 20, irrespective of the actual size of the text it contains.

Note that this field is read/write when fabricating your own recordsets, and becomes read-only once this fabricated recordset is opened.

Name

Indicates the name of the Field object.

String = *Field*.Name

This is a necessary field when creating your own Field objects to add to the Fields collection, perhaps when creating a new recordset.

It is also useful when dynamically creating tables in ASP Script code, or filling grids manually in Visual Basic. For example, in ASP you could create a table header using the **Name** property:

```
Response.Write "<TABLE><THEAD><TR>"
For Each objField In objRec.Fields
  Response.Write "<TD>" & objField.Name & "</TD>"
Next
Response.Write "</TR></THEAD>"
```

You could then go on to create the rest of the table using the values from the recordset.

Note that this field is read/write when fabricating your own recordsets, and becomes read-only once this fabricated recordset is opened.

NumericScale

Indicates the scale of numeric values for the Field object.

Byte = *Field*.NumericScale

This identifies how many digits are stored to the right of the decimal place for numeric data.

145

Note that this field is read/write when fabricating your own recordsets, and becomes read-only once this fabricated recordset is opened.

OriginalValue

Indicates the value of a Field object that existed in the record before any changes were made.

Variant = Field.OriginalValue

The original value is the value stored in the field before any changes were saved to the provider. This is what allows the provider to simply return to the original value when you do a **Cancel** or **CancelUpdate** method call. For example:

```
' Assume when read that the field contains a value of 10.99
Set objField = objRec.Fields("Price")
objField.Value = 15.99
Print objField.OriginalValue      ' Prints 10.99
Print objField.Value              ' Prints 15.99
objRec.Cancel
Print objField.Value              ' Prints 10.99
```

Precision

Indicates the degree of precision for numeric values in the Field object.

Byte = Field.Precision

The precision is the maximum number of digits that will be used.

Note that this field is read/write when fabricating your own recordsets, and becomes read-only once this fabricated recordset is opened.

Type

Indicates the data type of the Field object.

DataTypeEnum = Field.Type

This can be one of the **DataTypeEnum** values, such as **adInteger** or **adVarChar**. Since this list is quite long, we've included it in Appendix F. Not all providers support all data types, but when fabricating recordsets you should be able to use all types, and the provider will convert any types it doesn't support into an equivalent supported type.

Note that this field is read/write when fabricating your own recordsets, and becomes read-only once this fabricated recordset is opened.

UnderlyingValue

Indicates a Field object's current value in the database.

Variant = *Field*.UnderlyingValue

The underlying value differs from the original value, as this property holds the current value of the field as stored in the database. This would, for example, hold the value if another user changed the value of a field. So if you call the **Resync** method, your fields will get repopulated with values from the **UnderlyingValue** property. This is particularly useful when dealing with conflicts between values that you have changed and values that other users have changed. We examine conflict resolution in more detail in Chapter 8.

Value

Indicates the value assigned to the Field object.

Variant = *Field*.Value
Field.Value = *Variant*

This indicates the current value of the field, and may not reflect the value stored in the database. The difference between the three value fields is quite simple:

- **Value** contains the current value of the field in your current recordset. So if you've made any changes to the field, they will be reflected in the **Value**.

- **OriginalValue** contains the value of the field as it was before you made any changes.

- **UnderlyingValue** contains the value of the field, as stored in the database, which might include changes made by other users.

This is the default property of a field and can be omitted if required. For example, the following two lines of code are functionally equivalent:

```
objRec("FirstName").Value
```

```
objRec("FirstName")
```

Field Collections

Properties

Contains all of the Property objects for a Field object.

Field.Properties

The Properties collection contains all of the properties that are associated with a particular field. This is discussed in more detail in Appendix C.

147

Fields Collection

The **Fields** collection contains zero or more **Field** objects. In existing recordsets there will be one Field object for each column in the recordset. When creating new recordsets, you append Field objects to the Fields collection.

This is the default collection of the Recordset object, and can be omitted if desired. For example, the following two lines are functionally equivalent:

```
objRec.Fields("FirstName")
```

```
objRec("FirstName")
```

Fields Methods

Append

Appends a Field object to the Fields collection.

Fields.Append(*Name, Type,* [*DefinedSize*], [*Attrib*])

Name	Type	Description
Name	String	The name of a new field object.
Type	DataTypeEnum	The data type of the new field. Default is **adEmpty**
DefinedSize	Long	The defined size in characters or bytes of the new field. The default value is derived from *Type,* and is 0
Attrib	FieldAttributeEnum	The attributes for the new field. The default value is **adFldDefault**, and if empty will be derived from *Type*. Default is **adFldDefault**

You must set the **CursorLocation** property to **adUseClient** before calling this method, because you cannot append fields to an existing recordset created from a data store.

This is quite useful for those situations where you would like some data to be processed as a recordset, but it is not in a data store, and there is no provider for accessing it. You could create a recordset and append your own fields to it. For example:

```
Dim objRec   As New ADODB.Recordset

objRec.CursorLocation = adUseClient
objRec.Fields.Append "Name", adVarChar, 25, adFldMayBeNull
objRec.Fields.Append "Age", adInteger, 8, adFldFixed
```

Calling this method for an open Recordset or a Recordset where the **ActiveConnection** property has been set will generate a run-time error. This applies even if the recordset has been disconnected from a data store.

Delete

Deletes a Field object from the Fields collection.

Fields.Delete(*Index*)

Name	Type	Description
Index	Variant	The name or index number of the Field object to delete.

You can use this to delete fields that you have added to your own recordset. For example:

```
objRec.Fields.Delete("Age")
```

You cannot use this method on an open recordset.

Refresh

Updates the Field objects in the Fields collection.

Fields.Refresh

Using this method has no visible effect. You should use the **Requery** method to retrieve changes, or the **MoveFirst** method if the Recordset does not support bookmarks.

Fields Properties

Count

Indicates the number of Field objects in the Fields collection.

Long = *Fields*.Count

In Visual Basic or VBScript you can use the **For Each...Next** command to iterate through the fields collection without referring to the **Count** property.

Item

Allows indexing into the Fields collection to reference a specific Field object.

Field = *Fields*.Item(*Index*)

Name	Type	Description
Index	Variant	The name or index number of the item in the collection.

This is the default property and can be omitted. For example, the following lines are equivalent:

```
objRec.Fields.Item(1)
```

```
objRec.Fields(1)
```

```
objRec.Fields("FirstName")
```

```
objRec.Fields.Item("FirstName")
```

Since **Fields** is the default collection this can also be omitted:

```
objRec("FirstName")
```

Property Object

The Property object contains the attributes of a single property, for any of the following objects:

- Connection
- Command
- Recordset
- Field

Each of these objects contains a Properties collection, which contain zero or more Property objects. It's important to realize that these do not contain the standard properties for an object, but rather the extended, or provider-specific properties.

A detailed list of properties is included in Appendix C.

Property Methods

The Property object has no methods.

Property Properties

Attributes

Indicates one or more characteristics of a Property object.

Long = Property.Attributes

The Attributes can be one or more of the `PropertyAttributesEnum` values:

- `adPropNotSupported`, to indicate that the provider does not support the property.

- `adPropRequired`, to indicate that before the data source is initialized, this property must be specified.

- `adPropOptional`, to indicate that before the data source is initialized, this property does not have to be specified.

- `adPropRead`, to indicate that the property can be read by the user.

- `adPropWrite`, to indicate that the property can be set by the user.

For example, before you connect to SQL Server you can examine the `Attributes` of the `User ID` property in the Properties collection:

```
Print objConn.Properties("User ID").Attributes
```

This gives a value of **1537**, which is a combination of some of the above constants:

Attribute	Value
adPropRequired	1
adPropRead	512
adPropWrite	1025
	1537

You don't have to worry about the numbers because you can test the attributes using the constants:

```
intAttr = objConn.Properties("User ID").Attributes
If (intAttr And adPropRequired) = adPropRequired Then
    ' Property is required
End If
```

Name

Indicates the name of the Property object.

String = *Property*.Name

This is the name by which the provider knows the property.

Type

Indicates the data type of the Property object.

DataTypeEnum = *Property*.Type

For example, the **User ID** property of a connection has a value of **adBStr**, which indicates a string.

The list of constants for **DataTypeEnum** is quite large, and is included in Appendix F.

Value

Indicates the value assigned to the Property object.

```
Variant = Property.Value
Property.Value = Variant
```

Some properties may be read-only, and do not allow you to set the Value, so you should check the Attributes beforehand:

```
intAttr = objConn.Properties("property_name").Attributes
If (intAttr And adPropWrite) = adPropWrite Then
  objConn.Properties("property_name").Value = some_value
End If
```

This is the default property and can be omitted if desired.

Properties Collection

The Properties collection contains zero or more Property objects, to indicate the extended properties of the applicable object. You can examine all of the properties by enumerating through the collection. For example:

```
For Each objProp In objConn.Properties
  Print objProp.Name
Next
```

This is a particularly good way to find out which extended properties are supported by a provider.

Properties Methods

Refresh

Updates the Property objects in the Properties collection with the details from the provider.

```
Properties.Refresh
```

This is required because by default the provider is the OLEDB Provider for ODBC. So, if you have set the **Provider** property to point to a different provider, you will need to **Refresh** the properties to ensure that they are applicable to the changed provider.

Properties Properties

Count

Indicates the number of Property objects in the Properties collection.

Long = *Properties*.Count

You can use the Visual Basic or VBScript **For Each...Next** command to iterate through the parameters collection without using the **Count** property.

Item

Allows indexing into the Properties collection to reference a specific Property object.

Property = *Properties*.Item(*Index*)

Name	Type	Description
Index	Variant	

This is the default property and can be omitted. For example, the following lines are equivalent:

```
object.Properties.Item(1)
```

```
object.Properties(1)
```

```
object.Properties("property_name")
```

Using Images with ADO

This can be one of the most confusing aspects of using databases, as it never seems quite as intuitive as it should be. Although many people say that storing images in databases isn't the most efficient use of the storage, and it can be slow, there are times when you need to do this, such as when you have legacy data or if a third party supplies your data to you.

I think a preferable solution is to store the images on disc as files, and just store the file name in the database.

Images and Parameters

There are a few simple rules to follow when using images with parameters.

- If reading and writing images from disc, then you should read into, and write from, a Byte array.

- The ADO Parameter **Type** should be **adVarBinary**.

- The ADO Parameter **Length** should be the maximum size of the binary data. For a SQL Server **image** or an Access OLE Object parameter this is 2,147,483,647.

- Either set the Value property directly, or use **GetChunk** and **AppendChunk** to get the image data into your ADO Parameter.

One thing to watch out for when dealing with images using stored procedures in SQL Server is that your procedure cache might not be big enough to allow the use of large images. In this case you'll get error 701, and you should consult the SQL Server documentation for details of how to increase this cache.

Here are a few examples to show how this works.

Storing Images using Parameters

The following shows how you could read an image from a file and store it in a SQL Server database, by using a stored procedure. This procedure was created as shown:

```
CREATE PROCEDURE usp_UpdateLogo
        @PubID     char(4),
        @Logo      image
AS
        UPDATE     pub_info
        SET        logo = @Logo
        WHERE      pub_id = @PubID
```

This simply updates the **logo** field for the publisher id supplied.

The code to call this procedure from Visual Basic could look like this:

```
Dim objConn      As New ADODB.Connection
Dim objCmd       As New ADODB.Command
Dim bytChunk()   As Byte
Dim varChunk     As Variant

' open bitmap file
Open "c:\temp\wrox.bmp" For Binary As #1

' resize the byte array, read in the data space, and close it.
ReDim bytChunk(LOF(1))
Get #1, , bytChunk()
varChunk = StrConv(bytChunk, vbUnicode)
Erase bytChunk
Close #1

' connect to data store
objConn.Open "Provider=SQLOLEDB; Data Source=Tigger; " & _
            "Initial Catalog=pubs; User ID=sa; Password="
```

```
' set up command
With objCmd
    .ActiveConnection = objConn
    .CommandText = "usp_UpdateLogo"
    .CommandType = adCmdStoredProc

    ' create the parameters
    .Parameters.Append .CreateParameter("@PubID", adVarChar, _
                                        adParamInput, 4, "9918")
    .Parameters.Append .CreateParameter("@Logo", adVarBinary, _
                                        adParamInput, 2147483647)

    ' set the parameter value
    ' use either this command, which is commented out
    ' .Parameters("@Logo").Value = varChunk

    ' or this one
    .Parameters("@Logo").AppendChunk varChunk

    ' now run the command
    .Execute
End With

objConn.Close

Set objCmd = Nothing
Set objConn = Nothing
```

Smaller Chunks

You may find that reading the whole image file into memory at once is wasteful of resources, especially considering how large images can be. You can break this down into smaller chunks, and use **AppendChunk** to append chunks of the image into the parameter. The Visual Basic code from above would be modified like this:

```
Dim objConn        As New ADODB.Connection
Dim objCmd         As New ADODB.Command
Dim bytChunk(512)  As Byte                  ' Note the size
Dim varChunk       As Variant

' open bitmap file
Open "c:\temp\chunks.bmp" For Binary As #1

' connect to data store
objConn.Open "Provider=SQLOLEDB; Data Source=Tigger; " & _
             "Initial Catalog=pubs; User ID=sa; Password="

' set up command
With objCmd
    .ActiveConnection = objConn
    .CommandText = "usp_UpdateLogo"
    .CommandType = adCmdStoredProc

    ' create the parameters
    .Parameters.Append .CreateParameter("@PubID", adVarChar, _
                                        adParamInput, 4, "9918")
    .Parameters.Append .CreateParameter("@Logo", adVarBinary, _
                                        adParamInput, 2147483647)

    ' continue reading from file whilst we haven't hit EOF
    While Not EOF(1)
        ' Read in a small chunk. The amount read is determined
        ' by the size of the byte array we are reading into
        Get #1, , bytChunk()
```

```
            ' Append the smaller array to the parameter
          .Parameters("@Logo").AppendChunk bytChunk()
      Wend

      ' run the command
      .Execute
End With

objConn.Close
Close #1

Set objCmd = Nothing
Set objConn = Nothing
```

This performs exactly the same action, only using a small chunk of memory to repeatedly read in from the image file. You may find this marginally slower, but it is more efficient on memory.

Retrieving Images using Parameters

Retrieving images using parameters should be possible, but seems to generate run-time errors whatever is tried. Even using **Refresh** to get the provider to fill in the parameter details leads us to improperly defined parameters. I have therefore put this down to an undocumented 'feature'.

If you need to extract images from a stored procedure, then return a recordset.

Images and Fields

Using images with fields is very similar to that of Parameters, only you have the extra **GetChunk** method to read the binary data.

Storing Images in Fields

To store images directly into fields quite simply requires a call to the **AppendChunk** method. The following Visual Basic code shows this:

```
Dim objConn     As New ADODB.Connection
Dim objCmd      As New ADODB.Command
Dim objRec      As ADODB.Recordset
Dim bytChunk()  As Byte

' open bitmap file
Open "c:\temp\single.bmp" For Binary As #1

' resize the byte array, read in the data, and close it.
ReDim bytChunk(LOF(1))
Get #1, , bytChunk()
Close #1

' open the connection
objConn.Open "Provider=SQLOLEDB; Data Source=Tigger; " & _
             "Initial Catalog=pubs; User ID=sa; Password="

With objCmd
    ' set the commmand properties
    .ActiveConnection = objConn
    .CommandText = "usp_FetchLogo"
    .CommandType = adCmdStoredProc
```

```
                 ' create the parameters
               .Parameters.Append .CreateParameter("@PubID", adVarChar, _
                                               adParamInput, 4, "9918")

               ' create and open a new recordset
               Set objRec = New ADODB.Recordset
               objRec.Open objCmd, , adOpenDynamic, adLockOptimistic, adCmdStoredProc
          End With

     ' update the logo field, passing in the image
     objRec("logo").AppendChunk (bytChunk)
     objRec.Update

     objRec.Close
     objConn.Close

     Set objRec = Nothing
     Set objConn = Nothing
```

Smaller Chunks

To use a smaller chunk size to conserve the memory resources on the client is
quite simple too.

```
     Dim objConn        As New ADODB.Connection
     Dim objCmd         As New ADODB.Command
     Dim objRec         As ADODB.Recordset
     Dim bytChunk(512)  As Byte                        ' note the size

     ' open the connection
     objConn.Open "Provider=SQLOLEDB; Data Source=Tigger; " & _
                  "Initial Catalog=pubs; User ID=sa; Password="

     With objCmd
          ' set the command properties
          .ActiveConnection = objConn
          .CommandText = "usp_FetchLogo"
          .CommandType = adCmdStoredProc

          ' create the parameters
          .Parameters.Append .CreateParameter("@PubID", adVarChar, _
                                          adParamInput, 4, "9918")

          ' create and open the recordset
          Set objRec = New ADODB.Recordset
          objRec.Open objCmd, , adOpenDynamic, adLockOptimistic, adCmdStoredProc
     End With

     ' open bitmap file
     Open "c:\temp\chunks.bmp" For Binary As #1

     ' whilst we haven't reached the end of the image file
     While Not EOF(1)
          ' Read in a small chunk. The amount read is determined
          ' by the size of the byte array we are reading into
          Get #1, , bytChunk()

          ' append this small array to the field
          objRec("logo").AppendChunk (bytChunk)
     Wend
     Close #1

     ' update the field
     objRec.Update
```

```
objRec.Close
objConn.Close

Set objRec = Nothing
Set objConn = Nothing
```

Retrieving Images from Fields

Retrieving images from fields is extremely simple, using the Value of the field, or the **GetChunk** method. This Visual Basic code shows how it can be done:

```
Dim objConn     As New ADODB.Connection
Dim objCmd      As New ADODB.Command
Dim objRec      As ADODB.Recordset
Dim bytChunk()  As Byte

' open the connection
objConn.Open "Provider=SQLOLEDB; Data Source=Tigger; " & _
             "Initial Catalog=pubs; User ID=sa; Password="

With objCmd
    ' set up the command
    .ActiveConnection = objConn
    .CommandText = "usp_FetchLogo"
    .CommandType = adCmdStoredProc

    ' create the parameters
    .Parameters.Append .CreateParameter("@PubID", adVarChar, _
                                        adParamInput, 4, "9918")

    ' now run the command
    Set objRec = objCmd.Execute
End With

' extract the logo into a variable
bytChunk = objRec("logo")

' store the image to a file and load it into a picture box
' Note: Visual Basic has no method to accept the image directly
'       from the variable so you have to save it to disk first
Open "c:\temp\image.bmp" For Binary As #1
Put #1, , bytChunk()
Close #1
Picture1.Picture = LoadPicture("c:\temp\image.bmp")

objRec.Close
objConn.Close

Set objRec = Nothing
Set objConn = Nothing
```

This used a command object and parameters, but you could equally use just a recordset and return a whole set of records with images.

The same sort of procedure is just as simple in ASP to push an image to the browser:

```
<!-- #INCLUDE FILE="adovbs.inc" -->
<%

    ' turn on buffering and set the mime type
    Response.Buffer = True
    Response.ContentType = "image/bmp"
```

```
    Dim objConn
    Dim objCmd
    Dim objRec
    Dim bytChunk

    Set objConn = Server.CreateObject("ADODB.Connection")
    Set objCmd = Server.CreateObject("ADODB.Command")
    Set objRec = Server.CreateObject("ADODB.Recordset")

    ' open the connection
    objConn.Open "Provider=SQLOLEDB; Data Source=Tigger; " & _
                 "Initial Catalog=pubs; User ID=sa; Password="

    ' set the command details
    objCmd.ActiveConnection = objConn
    objCmd.CommandText = "usp_FetchLogo"
    objCmd.CommandType = adCmdStoredProc

    objCmd.Parameters.Append objCmd.CreateParameter("@PubID", adVarChar, _
                                        adParamInput, 4, "9918")

    ' run the command and extract the logo
    Set objRec = objCmd.Execute
    bytChunk = objRec("logo")

    ' write iamge to the browser
    Response.BinaryWrite bytChunk
    Response.End
%>
```

Small Chunks

One of the disadvantages of using the above method is that for a large image it requires a large amount of memory on the client, and is not particularly efficient. If you think about how large images can get, then there seems little point in clogging up the user machine with a large amount of dynamic storage.

To alleviate this problem you can use **GetChunks** and limit the amount it reads. For example, the above Visual Basic code rewritten would be like this:

```
    Dim objConn     As New ADODB.Connection
    Dim objCmd      As New ADODB.Command
    Dim objRec      As ADODB.Recordset
    Dim bytChunk()  As Byte
    Dim varChunk    As Variant

    ' open the connection
    objConn.Open "Provider=SQLOLEDB; Data Source=Tigger; " & _
                 "Initial Catalog=pubs; User ID=sa; Password="

    With objCmd
        ' set up the command
        .ActiveConnection = objConn
        .CommandText = "usp_FetchLogo"
        .CommandType = adCmdStoredProc

        ' create the parameters
        .Parameters.Append .CreateParameter("@PubID", adVarChar, _
                                        adParamInput, 4, "9918")

        ' now run the command
        Set objRec = objCmd.Execute
    End With
```

159

```
' open the output file
Open "c:\temp\dest\barf.bmp" For Binary As #1

' read in the first chunk
varChunk = objRec("logo").GetChunk(512)

' GetChunk returns Null if there is no more data
While Not IsNull(varChunk)
    ' convert the data to a byte array and write it to the file
    bytChunk = varChunk
    Put #1, , bytChunk()

    ' read in the next chunk
    varChunk = objRec("logo").GetChunk(512)
Wend

' close the file and load the picture
Close #1
Picture1.Picture = LoadPicture("c:\temp\dest\barf.bmp")

objRec.Close
objConn.Close

Set objRec = Nothing
Set objConn = Nothing
```

You might think that this is much slower, but the delay is hardly noticeable.

Remote Data Access and ADO

In the previous chapters, we've been looking at ADO from an application-neutral and language-neutral perspective. We've taken advantage of the fact that the basic principles of using ADO are the same, irrespective of the type of application you are building or the programming language you use to build it. This is intentional, and is one of the core concepts of ADO itself. You can use it in a whole range of ways, with any language that can instantiate and use COM objects.

However, there is one specific application of ADO that is a core part of the technology. **Remote Data Access** is intended to broaden the appeal of ADO in scenarios where the client and server are disconnected—in the sense that there is no permanent physical connection between them. This is very much the case with Internet-based applications, where (until the new HTTP proposals are universally supported), the client and server cannot maintain state between connections. Each request from a single client is entirely separate from all other requests before and after the current one, and the server and client must create state artificially.

In this chapter, we'll look at what we mean by **disconnected applications** and **state** in more detail. We'll also see how one particular aspect of Remote Data Access, the Microsoft **Remote Data Service** (RDS), is such an important new technology. This chapter covers:

- An overview of what Remote Data Access is all about
- A look at the different kinds of remote data access technologies
- How we can implement remote data access in a Web page
- How we can bind data to HTML controls in a Web page
- Ways of creating remote recordsets directly using RDS and ADO

To begin, we look at the background and future of Remote Data Access as a whole, the current implementation of XML data remoting, and RDS. It's important to understand the concepts before we go on to look at its use in more detail.

What Is Remote Data Access?

Remote Data Access provides an opportunity to create applications that will appear to a client over the Internet (and more particularly over the Web) to work in much the same way as traditional client-server applications do over a local area network (LAN). In this section of the chapter, we'll look at why this is more difficult to achieve than you might at first assume, and how we can get round the problems.

Applications That Work Over the Internet

In a traditional LAN-based environment, a client logs on to a server by identifying itself to that server. The server then authenticates the client using their username and password (or through another method such as a smart-card or fingerprint recognition). However it's done, the result is that the server identifies the client as a valid user, and can then maintain a connection between itself and that client over the network. When data is sent to the server from the client, the server can automatically identify that particular client, and then send the appropriate data back to it.

This connection is effectively a permanent link between client and server during the time that the client is logged on. It provides **state**, in that the client and server can identify each other through the protocols supported by the network that connects them.

Once an application is moved to the Internet, or more specifically to the Web, this process fails. The HTTP protocol is **stateless**, in that it cannot automatically identify the client to the server. Once the server has created the return page and sent it back to the client, it effectively 'forgets' about that client. Instead, we have to rely on special extra layers within the application to handle this. It can be done in a range of ways — such as with ASP sessions or certificates, through custom techniques that use cookies, or by adding identification information to the request as part of the query string or the content of a form submission.

The Windows DNA Architecture

Just maintaining state is not enough, however. This book is about working with data from a data source, such as a relational database, and our data management applications may have to work over the Internet. ADO is specifically designed to be a part of the Windows **Distributed interNet Applications** (DNA) architecture. This is a Microsoft design methodology aimed at creating applications that will work in a disconnected and stateless environment like the Internet.

> *In this book, we aren't specifically covering DNA, or the provision of state in distributed applications. For more information about these topics, look out for Professional ASP 2.0 Programming (ISBN 1-861001-26-6) and Professional MTS/MSMQ Programming (ISBN 1-861001-46-0) from Wrox.*

164

So, we've discovered that building Web-based applications that handle data requires different techniques to traditional client-server applications on a LAN. Remote Data Access provides ways to recreate the LAN-based environment out on the Internet, in line with the DNA methodology. We'll look at the techniques it provides in more detail next.

Disconnected Data Management

The following diagram shows three data management scenarios. The first is the traditional client-server LAN-based environment, but here we are using ADO to provide the connection between the application (which carries out the processing tasks on the data) and the data store itself. In this case, the application and the user interface communicate directly. They could both be client-based, or the application components could be distributed between the client and the server. However, the point is that the various parts of the application communicate directly using the LAN. This automatically provides **state**:

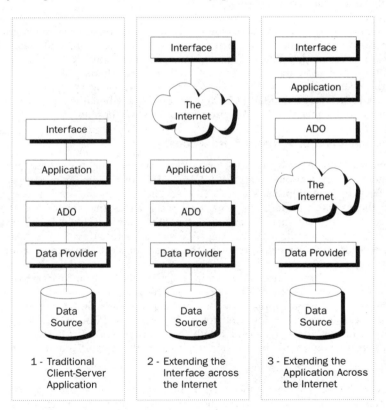

In the second section of the diagram, we move the user interface for the application out across the Internet. By using a Web browser or a custom application, we can communicate with a server-based application using the HTTP protocol of the Web. The application might be implemented using Active Server Pages, custom components; or it might be a more traditional CGI or

ISAPI application written in any of a range of languages. This is the common scenario for Web-based data management applications today. In effect, all we've done is introduce a remote-control feature that allows users on the 'net to work with the application on the server.

> *Active Server Pages (ASP), the Common Gateway Interface (CGI), and the Internet Server Application Programming Interface (ISAPI) are all ways to interface with the Web server and provide a server-based application that can communicate with a browser or other remote Web-based interface.*

The third section of the previous diagram shows how Remote Data Access can extend the *application* itself across the Internet, rather than just the *interface*. What it does is move the data manipulation tasks, and hence the data itself, out to the client. Now, ADO communicates with the back-end data store across the 'net. We've effectively moved the entire application out to the client, leaving only the data store on the server.

This is very much the way that some traditional client-server data management applications work. When you open a form to work with data in, say, Microsoft Access, a copy of the data is transferred across the network to your machine from the server. You then manipulate it using your client-side application, and save the changes back to the server again over the network. Remote Data Access allows a very similar technique to be used when the network is the Internet and the client is a Web browser or custom application.

The Pros and Cons of Remote Data Access

So, Remote Data Access provides us with an opportunity to extend our data management applications over the Internet. This overcomes a major problem with the currently popular scenario (the second one in our earlier diagram), where the remote interface must pass requests across the network to the server each time a different task is carried out on the data, or when a different view of the data is required. Remote Data Access can help to avoid the heavy network traffic that arises from even the most simple data manipulation tasks.

For example, a remote user is viewing a list of clients from a database and wishes to sort the list in a different order. The traditional method of using ADO with ASP or a custom application on the server means that the entire recordset must be transferred over the Web for each sort. Using Remote Data Access however, the recordset is cached locally and can be sorted, filtered, and viewed in a range of ways with no further requests to the server and no network traffic.

However, this has to be balanced with the requirements of the application. The customer list may contain several thousands of records. If the client is searching for a single record, it makes more sense to use the traditional technique of building a recordset containing just this record on the server with ADO and sending it to the client as a pure HTML page, rather than sending the whole set of records over the Internet. In many applications, you will need to consider a mixture of techniques, depending on the way the data will be used.

One of the factors that will affect the decision you make is the level of support for RDS in the various browsers. At present, only Internet Explorer 4 and above fully support RDS.

Using ADO on the Client

So far, this may seem just an interesting extension of the connectivity technologies provided by ADO. However, it provides us with an opportunity to provide more interactive and responsive applications, compared to the more usual Web-based data handling scenarios. As well as reducing the number of round-trips to the server, it allows us to access data programmatically while it is cached on the client.

The following diagram shows the impact of this in more detail. What we've achieved is to move the ADO programming interface from the server out onto the client, while leaving the original OLE-DB data provider interface on the server. In effect what this means is that, instead of creating the recordset with ADO and working with it on the server, we can now create it on the client as a cached local recordset and work with it there:

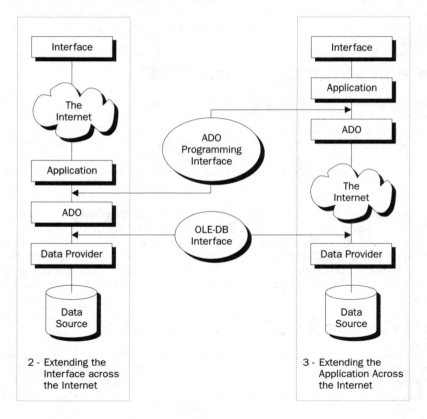

2 - Extending the Interface across the Internet

3 - Extending the Application Across the Internet

So, your ADO programming skills aren't wasted when you start using Remote Data Access methods. With a few minor exceptions (mainly due to the fact that the recordset is disconnected from the server), ADO techniques work exactly the same way on the client as they do on the server. The main difference is that the operations affect only the client recordset. As we'll see, however, Remote Data Service (RDS) allows these updates to be flushed back to the source data store, by submitting all the changes in one operation.

Remote Data Access Technologies

The technologies that implement remote data access are still maturing, and change with almost monotonous regularity. The topic is also made more complex by the fact that its very nature involves two separated platforms—your data server and the client browser or application. In fact, the whole concept of Remote Data Access in the Microsoft world is gradually evolving into two separate areas, the **Remote Data Service** (RDS) and **XML Data Remoting**.

We'll look at the concepts and the basic implementation of both of these in this section of the chapter. They are too complex to cover in their entirety, and this is not the topic at which this book is aimed. However, it is easier to appreciate the future directions of remote data access when you understand the basic issues.

The Remote Data Service (RDS)

Having looked earlier at an overview of what remote data access is designed to achieve, we'll take a more detailed view of how it's implemented in RDS. The major limitation is that, once we move the 'working parts' out from the server to the client, we rely on a far more specific environment to be in place there. What this means at present is that only custom Windows applications, and/or Microsoft Internet Explorer 4 (or higher) browser, can be used as the client with RDS.

Things are also made more complex by the fact that there are two versions of RDS in common use. The version that is supplied with Internet Explorer 4 is V1.5, while Internet Explorer 5 and Visual Studio 6 contain V2.0. To get round this problem, the V2.0 Data Access Software Development Kit (available from http://www.microsoft.com/data/mdac2.htm) provides tools that you can use to distribute the V2.0 client-side component files automatically to users who access your data via IE4.

Inside Remote Data Service

RDS takes advantage of several COM-based objects that are distributed between the client and the server. The version 2.0 client components are included with Internet Explorer 5, and with the latest releases of the client-side development environments like Microsoft Visual InterDev, Visual Basic and Visual C++. The server-side objects will also be provided with Internet Information Server through Windows NT5. However, at the time of writing, the NT4 Option Pack only contained version 1.5 of the components, and you need to download the version 2.0 components from http://www.microsoft.com/data/mdac2.htm.

The RDS Object Structure

The following diagram shows how the main objects used by RDS are distributed between the client and the server. On the server, a connection is made to the data store through an OLE-DB provider, or through a combined ODBC/OLE-DB driver (which will allow a connection to be made to a data store that only provides an ODBC interface).

The provider or driver supplies data to either the special RDS `DataFactory` object or to a custom component running on the server. The `DataFactory` object provides a default method of marshaling the data into a form suitable for transmission across the Internet.

The data is then passed to the Web server software and out across the Internet to the RDS `DataSpace` object on the client. This object implements the connection to the `DataFactory` object or custom component through a proxy and stub (the normal COM/DCOM communication method), handles marshaling of the data across the network, and recreates it as a recordset on the client.

Once received by the client, the recordset is cached locally and passed to the client-side `DataControl` object. Finally, if required, the **Data Binding Agent** object takes the data and binds it to controls on the client. This last step is usually specific to a Web page, where the client is a browser or a custom application that hosts an instance of the browser interface. The bound controls on the page then reflect the data content from the recordset. This is not mandatory, as script or other objects within the page can use the data directly, rather than binding it to controls in the page:

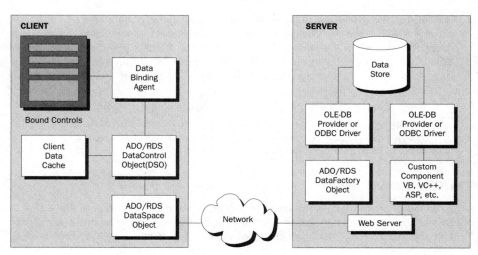

If the bound controls allow updating of the data (i.e. they are HTML **INPUT**, **SELECT**, **TEXTAREA**, etc. controls), the updates are stored in the locally cached recordset on the client. The `DataControl` object can then pass the updates back to the server on command, and the `DataFactory` object (or custom component) can update the source data.

Updating the Source Data with RDS

RDS allows the source data to be updated on the client using the same kind of approach as in a traditional LAN-based application. The user can make multiple changes to the recordset that is cached locally on their machine, then submit all the changes back to the server where the source data is updated with all the changes in one operation.

The RDS data source object provides a method **SubmitChanges**, which marshals the changed records into a recordset, and sends it back to the **DataFactory** object on the server. This automatically updates the original source data with the changes. However, this remote access capability introduces some major concerns with regard to data security.

Data Security with RDS

When a data management application is entirely server-based, the client only sends instructions on how the data should be manipulated. It never sees the data source directly, or the connection information. This is all hidden inside an ASP page, a custom component, or whichever other technique you use to communicate with the data source from your server-based application.

With RDS, however, the client is effectively communicating directly with the data source. This means that the data source connection information is moved from the server to the client. The instance of ADO running on the client can connect to the data store and manipulate the source data directly. The result is that you reveal the connection information to the user, and may risk them using this information to access the data store in ways that were not intended.

It's imperative, therefore, to use the capabilities of your data store to limit access to the contents. The usual methods are to set relevant permissions for users for each data source and each object within that data source (i.e. for each table, field, view, procedure, etc.). The techniques for doing so depend on the data store you use, and are outside the scope of this book.

> If you use SQL Server or Oracle integrated security with RDS in an Intranet scenario, no connection username and password need be revealed to the client. You can also use custom components in place of the default **DataFactory** object to limit client access to a data store.

The DataFactory Handler

In version 2.0 of RDS, some new capabilities have been added to the **DataFactory** object to control the access that clients have to the source data. A text INI file named msdfmap.ini is placed in your Winnt (or Windows) folder when version 2.0 of the Microsoft Data Access Components (MDAC) are installed. This defines the settings that are applied to the **DataFactory** when it is instantiated by a client connection.

The default settings depend on the option you choose when you install the components, and can be set to provide no access at all until you edit the file. Alternatively, you can set it up to allow free access to all connections, and then edit it once installation is complete and you are ready to deploy your application.

> *The file **msdfmap.ini** is the configuration file for the default **DataFactory** handler, named **MSDFMAP.Handler**. This is used unless you specify a different custom handler, which is done by setting the **Handler** property of the **DataControl** object or **Recordset** object. The RDS documentation contains details of how this can be done.*

The Future - XML Data Remoting

While passing data in the form of marshaled recordsets across the Web using RDS is a neat trick, the future of data transport lies in **Extensible Markup Language** (XML). If we are going to realize the dreams of truly universal data access across disparate platforms and operating systems, we have to use a data format that is independent of the platform itself. It would also be nice if the standard was set and maintained by an independent industry body, as it is then more likely to have universal support. Both of these conditions rule out RDS.

XML — a text-based format for describing data — is moving more and more into the mainstream. Microsoft provide several data source objects that can handle XML-formatted data with Internet Explorer 4 and 5. Netscape have also announced that the next version of Navigator will provide support for XML in line with evolving standards. In the meantime, the World Wide Web Consortium (W3C) have ratified version 1.0 of XML, and are working on several other proposed standards to describe the way data can be defined within XML.

Microsoft Internet Explorer 5 and XML

At the time of writing, Internet Explorer 5 was still in beta, but it already supports XML in many useful ways. The browser itself is an XML data source object, and can expose XML-formatted data directly to code in the page, or to the **Data Binding Agent** that binds the data to HTML controls in the page. The current implementation revolves around the new HTML element `<XML>...</XML>`.

> *Note that `<XML>` is an HTML element, **not** an XML element. It defines a section in an HTML document that **contains** XML, and is not itself part of that XML data.*

The `<XML>` element can be used to create a **data island**, where the XML is embedded in the HTML page. This is an example of an inline XML data island:

```
.. HTML code here ..
<XML ID="mydata">
.. the XML formatted data goes here ..
.. this is an XML data island within a HTML page ..
</XML>
.. more HTML code here ..
```

171

If the XML data is in a separate file, we can use a **SRC** attribute within the **<XML>** tag to link to it, as in the next section of code:

```
.. HTML code here ..
<XML ID="mydata" SRC="/data/myxmldata.xml"></XML>
.. more HTML code here ..
```

Once the page has loaded, together with the content of any linked XML files, the data described by XML is exposed to ADO as a recordset. This can be used on the client in almost exactly the same way as the recordset exposed by the RDS **DataControl** object that we looked at earlier. However, XML data can also be manipulated using **Extensible Stylesheet Language** (XSL). This is another of the W3C standards currently under development, and it is implemented in Internet Explorer 5.

> *For more information about XML and XSL, look out for the Wrox Press books:*
>
> *Professional Stylesheets(ISBN 1-861001-65-7) and Professional XML Applications (ISBN 1-861001-52-5). You can also find more information about XML support in Internet Explorer, and some useful tools and examples, from the Microsoft XML site at* **http://www.microsoft.com/xml/**

Implementing Remote Data Access

The simplest way to implement Remote Data Access on the client is to use a **Data Source Object** (DSO) specifically designed for this task. The specification for a DSO is open, and they can be implemented as a variety of languages. Several are either supplied with Internet Explorer and other programming environments, or can be downloaded from the Internet directly. The Internet Explorer Client SDK lists some of these objects and provides more information. We'll look at the popular ones next, then move on to see how they can be used.

Data Source Objects

We can implement Remote Data Access by instantiating a Data Source Object on a Web page in Internet Explorer 4 or higher. The connection is made, and the data is fetched across the network and cached on the client. At this point it can be bound to controls on the page, or manipulated using ADO.

At the time of writing, the following DSOs were freely available, either as part of the IE4/5 installation or as a separate download:

 The **Remote Data Service Control**, commonly known as the ADC/RDS control.

The **Tabular Data Control** (TDC), sometimes referred to as the Text Data Control.

The **JDBC Applet Control**, a Java applet providing an alternative to the ActiveX RDS control.

The **XML Data Source Control**, both as a Java applet and a C++
ActiveX Control.

 The **MSHTML Data Source**, implemented internally by Internet Explorer
itself.

Also on the way is a new XML Data Source Object from Microsoft, written in
C++, which is designed to be used both on the server and the client. And, as
we saw earlier in this chapter, Internet Explorer 5 is itself a Data Source Object,
in that it can expose XML-formatted data directly as a recordset on the client.
This data may come across the network from a separate file on the server, or as
a data island within the current page.

Instantiating Data Source Objects

Because each DSO is different, both in their implementation and in the type of
data they are designed to access, the way that each one is instantiated varies a
great deal. We'll briefly look at each one listed above. The example code shows
only a selection of the most useful property settings for each control. A full list
of the properties exposed by the RDS and TDC controls, together with all the
methods and events, is provided in Appendix B.

The Remote Data Service Control

The **Remote Data Service Control** is designed to connect to a data store through
an OLE-DB or ODBC driver. It was originally named the Advanced Data
Control (ADC) and is sometimes referred to as the ADC/RDS control in order
to avoid confusion over the use of RDS as a *control name* and RDS as a
technology. It can be used to update the source data on the server, and is
automatically installed with Internet Explorer 4 and higher:

```
<OBJECT CLASSID="clsid:BD96C556-65A3-11D0-983A-00C04FC29E33"
        ID="dsoBookList" HEIGHT=0 WIDTH=0>
  <PARAM NAME="Server" VALUE="http://www.yourserver.com">
  <PARAM NAME="Connect" VALUE="DSN=pubs;UID=anon;PWD=">
  <PARAM NAME="SQL" VALUE="SELECT * FROM BookList">
</OBJECT>
```

The code above creates the RDS object and instantiates it. It connects to the
server specified in the first **PARAM** element, and to the data store specified in
the second **PARAM** element. It then executes the SQL statement specified in the
third **PARAM** element, and retrieves the data into a locally-cached recordset.

Note that the database can be on a different machine from the Web server, and
in this case you would specify the server name in the **Connect** property as
well. In fact, to achieve this, the easiest way is to use a full connection string
instead of a DSN. For example, in the following code, the control gets its data
from a SQL Server database on a machine named **dataserver.com**:

```
<OBJECT CLASSID="clsid:BD96C556-65A3-11D0-983A-00C04FC29E33"
        ID="dsoBookList" HEIGHT=0 WIDTH=0>
  <PARAM NAME="Server" VALUE="http://www.yourserver.com">
  <PARAM NAME="Connect" VALUE="SERVER="http://dataserver.com;
                      DRIVER={SQL Server};DATABASE=yourdb;
                      UID=anon;PWD=">
  <PARAM NAME="SQL" VALUE="SELECT * FROM BookList">
</OBJECT>
```

173

Note that, on Windows NT4, you can't use Integrated security in the database if it is on a different server to the Web server. This problem will go away with NT5 and the new Active Directory Service. See Appendix B for a full list of the properties, methods, and events for this control.

The Tabular Data Control

The **Tabular Data Control** (TDC), sometimes referred to as the **Text Data Control**, is designed to expose a delimited text file as a recordset, and allow data binding and ADO to be used with the text data. It cannot be used to update the source data on the server. The TDC is automatically installed with Internet Explorer 4 and higher.

```
<OBJECT CLASSID="clsid:333C7BC4-460F-11D0-BC04-0080C7055A83"
        ID="dsoBookList" WIDTH=0 HEIGHT=0>
  <PARAM NAME="DataURL" VALUE="/data/booklist.txt">
  <PARAM NAME="FieldDelim" VALUE=";">
  <PARAM NAME="UseHeader" VALUE="true">
  <PARAM NAME="Sort" VALUE="tCategory; -dReleasedate">
  <PARAM NAME="Filter" VALUE="tCode=16-1*" >
  <PARAM NAME="EscapeChar" VALUE="\">
</OBJECT>
```

The code above creates the TDC object and instantiates it. It connects to the text file specified in the **DataURL** property and caches it as a recordset locally on the client. The next two **PARAM** elements specify that each line in the file uses a comma as the field delimiter (**FieldDelim**), and that the first line in the file is a definition of the field names and types (**UseHeader**). The default field delimiter, if not specified, is a comma. The default record delimiter is a carriage return, but it can be changed if required by setting the optional **RowDelim** property.

Of the remaining parameters, the **Sort** property specifies the sorting order of the records. In our example, records are sorted by category ascending then by release date descending (the minus sign appended to the start of the field name indicates descending sort order). The **Filter** property shown above specifies that only records in which the book code field value starts with '**16-1**' will be included. Finally the **EscapeChar** property specifies a character that can be used to 'escape' any characters within a field that are the same as the field delimiter. In the example above, we could use '**XML\; The Future For Data**' as a value in a field, and prevent the control treating the backslash as a field delimiter.

A simple data file for use with the code shown above might look like this:

```
tCode:String;tCategory:String;dReleaseDate:Date;tTitle:String;nSales:Int
16-041;HTML;1998-03-07;Instant HTML;127853
16-048;Scripting;1998-04-21;Instant JavaScript;375298
16-105;ASP;1998-05-10;Instant Active Server Pages;297311
... etc. ...
```

See Appendix B for a full list of the properties and methods for this control.

The JDBC Applet Control

The **JDBC Applet Control** provides an alternative to the ActiveX control structure of the ADC/RDS object, and is implemented as a Java applet. This allows browsers other than Internet Explorer to be used with your remote data applications. It connects to a data store through an ODBC driver – via a client-side DSN previously set up in **Control Panel** – and can be used to update the source data on the server. However, this requirement for an existing DSN prevents a 'hands-off' automatic download and install of the applet in a page, as happens with most other Java applets.

The control and information on using it can be downloaded from Microsoft's Web site at http://www.microsoft.com/gallery/samples/author/datasrc//JDBCapplet/JDBC.htm

```
<APPLET CODE="JDC.class" NAME="dsoBookList" ID="dsoBookList" WIDTH=0 HEIGHT=0>
    <PARAM NAME="cabbase" VALUE=
    "http://www.microsoft.com/gallery/samples/author/datasrc/jdbcapplet/jdc.cab">
    <PARAM NAME="dbURL" VALUE="jdbc:odbc:Books">
    <PARAM NAME="showUI" VALUE=false>
    <PARAM NAME="sqlStatement" VALUE="SELECT * FROM BookList">
    <PARAM NAME="user" VALUE="anon">
    <PARAM NAME="password" VALUE="">
    <PARAM NAME="allowInsert" VALUE="true">
    <PARAM NAME="allowDelete" VALUE="true">
    <PARAM NAME="allowUpdate" VALUE="false">
</APPLET>
```

Since a value for the **cabbase** parameter is provided, which specifies the location of the code for the applet, it will be downloaded if not already installed on the client machine. The remaining parameters define the properties to be set when the control is instantiated.

The **dbURL** property identifies the ODBC data source name (DSN) to use to connect to the database, and the **showUI** property specifies that the control should not display a user interface. The **sqlStatement** property is set to a SQL string that will extract the data from the database. The **user** and **password** properties can be set to the details of the account required to access the data, if this information is not provided by the DSN. As the control is running on the client machine, this DSN is a **File DSN** previously set up in the user's **ODBC** dialog available from **Control Panel**.

The remaining properties define how the data exposed by the control can be used, by controlling whether the code in the page can insert new records, or delete or update existing records.

The XML Data Source Control

The **XML Data Source Control** is available as a Java applet or a C++ ActiveX Control, and both can be downloaded as a complete package (including samples) from http://www.microsoft.com/xml/parser/xmlinst.exe. These DSOs provide read-only access to a client-based or server-based file that holds data in XML format. They allow data binding and ADO to be used to view the data.

175

The code to instantiate the Java Applet uses the normal `<APPLET>` element:

```
<APPLET CODE="com.ms.xml.dso.XMLDSO.class"
        ID="dsoBookList" WIDTH=0 HEIGHT=0 MAYSCRIPT=true>
   <PARAM NAME="URL" VALUE="booklist.xml">
</APPLET>
```

The `CODE` attribute specifies the package in which the code is implemented, which is defined in the user's Registry. Once instantiated, the control loads an XML-format data file from the location specified in the `URL` parameter, parses it, and makes the data available as a locally-cached recordset.

The C++ DSO is instantiated using script. The following is a sample in JavaScript. It creates the object, then sets the `url` property to the XML file that we want to parse and display:

```
<SCRIPT LANGUAGE="JavaScript">
   dsoBookList = new ActiveXObject("msxml");
   dsoBookList.url = "booklist.xml";
</SCRIPT>
```

A simple XML-format data file might look like this:

```
<?xml version="1.0"?>
<BOOKLIST>
 <ITEM>
  <CODE>16-041</CODE>
  <CATEGORY>HTML</CATEGORY >
  <RELEASE_DATE>1998-03-07</RELEASE_DATE>
  <TITLE>Instant HTML</TITLE >
  <SALES>127853</SALES >
 </ITEM>
 <ITEM>
  <CODE>16-048</CODE>
  <CATEGORY>Scripting</CATEGORY >
  <RELEASE_DATE>1998-04-21</RELEASE_DATE>
  <TITLE>Instant JavaScript</TITLE >
  <SALES>375298</SALES >
 </ITEM>
 <ITEM>
  <CODE>16-105</CODE>
  <CATEGORY>ASP</CATEGORY >
  <RELEASE_DATE>1998-05-10</RELEASE_DATE>
  <TITLE>Instant Active Server Pages</TITLE >
  <SALES>297311</SALES >
 </ITEM>
</BOOKLIST>
```

This screenshot shows the result of using the Java XML DSO in conjunction with some data-bound controls on the page. We'll be looking at the techniques for data binding later in this chapter.

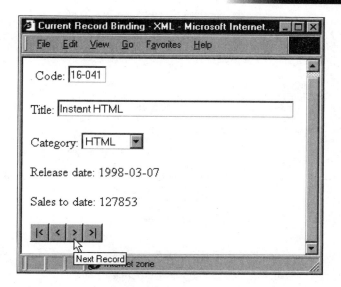

The MSHTML Data Source Object

The **MSHTML Data Source** is implemented internally by Internet Explorer itself, being part of the browser. It allows the contents of a client- or server-based Web page to be exposed as a read-only recordset, used with data binding, and manipulated with ADO. To instantiate the data control just requires the **DATA** attribute of an **<OBJECT>** element to be set to the URL of the HTML page containing the data:

```
<OBJECT ID="dsoBookList" DATA="/data/booklist.htm" HEIGHT=0 WIDTH=0>
</OBJECT>
```

Once the control is instantiated, it loads the page defined in the **DATA** attribute and exposes it as a locally-cached recordset. The values that form the content of the records are identified by their **ID** attribute in the source Web page. It doesn't matter what the actual elements that hold the data are, as long as they have both opening and closing tags. Their **ID** attribute value defines the field that they hold data for.

In other words, the following two HTML elements define a single field recordset with two records. Each record would hold the title of a book:

```
<H3 ID="BookTitle">Instant JavaScript</H3>
<SPAN ID="BookTitle">Instant Active Server Pages</SPAN>
```

However, it's usually more useful to use the same type of element for each value for a particular field. A simple data file for use with the MSHTML control might look like this:

```
<HTML>
 <BODY>
  <SPAN ID="CODE">16-041</SPAN>
  <SPAN ID="CATEGORY">HTML</SPAN>
  <SPAN ID="RELEASE_DATE">1998-03-07</SPAN>
  <SPAN ID="TITLE">Instant HTML</SPAN>
```

177

```
    <SPAN ID="SALES">127853</SPAN>
    <SPAN ID="CODE">16-048</SPAN>
    <SPAN ID="CATEGORY">Scripting</SPAN>
    <SPAN ID="RELEASE_DATE">1998-04-21</SPAN>
    <SPAN ID="TITLE">Instant JavaScript</SPAN>
    <SPAN ID="SALES">375298</SPAN>
    <SPAN ID="CODE">16-105</SPAN>
    <SPAN ID="CATEGORY">ASP</SPAN>
    <SPAN ID="RELEASE_DATE">1998-05-10</SPAN>
    <SPAN ID="TITLE">Instant Active Server Pages</SPAN>
    <SPAN ID="SALES">297311</SPAN>
  </BODY>
</HTML>
```

The great thing with this technique is that we can include HTML in the page to make it look OK on other browsers, or when loaded directly into IE. This extra code has no effect on the data control, and any formatting inside the elements that define the field values just becomes part of the field value:

```
<HTML>
 <BODY>
  Code Number: <SPAN ID="CODE"><I>16-041</I></SPAN><BR>
  Category: <SPAN ID="CATEGORY">HTML</SPAN><BR>
  Released Date: <SPAN ID="RELEASE_DATE">1998-03-07</SPAN><BR>
  Title: <SPAN ID="TITLE"><B>Instant HTML</B></SPAN><BR>
  Sales: <SPAN ID="SALES">127853</SPAN><P>
  Code Number: <SPAN ID="CODE"><I>16-048</I></SPAN><BR>
  Category: <SPAN ID="CATEGORY">Scripting</SPAN><BR>
  Released Date: <SPAN ID="RELEASE_DATE">1998-04-21</SPAN><BR>
  Title: <SPAN ID="TITLE"><B>Instant JavaScript</B></SPAN><BR>
  Sales: <SPAN ID="SALES">375298</SPAN><P>
  Code Number: <SPAN ID="CODE"><I>16-105</I></SPAN><BR>
  Category: <SPAN ID="CATEGORY">ASP</SPAN><BR>
  Released Date: <SPAN ID="RELEASE_DATE">1998-05-10</SPAN><BR>
  Title: <SPAN ID="TITLE"><B>Instant Active Server Pages</B></SPAN><BR>
  Sales: <SPAN ID="SALES">297311</SPAN><P>
  </BODY>
</HTML>
```

The next screenshot shows the result of using the MSHTML DSO in conjunction with a data-bound HTML table in the page. We'll be looking at the techniques for data binding later in this chapter:

178

Other Data Source Objects

Microsoft provides a new Data Source Object with Internet Explorer 5, a **Universal XML DSO** written in C++. This can be instantiated on both the server and the client, and is used to build the kind of XML-based applications we discussed earlier in this chapter.

At present the technology is still developing, but the new XML DSO provides a host of opportunities to build platform-independent applications. If the communication between the server and client is pure XML, in a universally agreed format, then any suitably equipped client will be able to communicate freely with any XML compliant server-based DSO.

Binding a DSO to HTML Controls

Once the data has been retrieved and cached locally, we can use it to populate HTML controls in a Web page (a process called **data binding**), or we can work with it directly using ADO code within the page. In fact, even when using data binding, we'll often still implement ADO code in the page. This is particularly the case when we want to update the data and submit the changes back to the server.

Data binding uses the **Data Binding Agent** object that is part of Internet Explorer 4 and higher. When programming in a language like Visual Basic or C++, the special controls that are part of that environment are used to implement data binding instead.

The Web-based Data Binding Agent can provide two types of data binding, either **tabular** data binding or **single record** data binding (often called **current record data binding**). All DSO controls can take part in tabular data binding or single/current record data binding. We'll briefly summarize the HTML controls that are used in Web pages next, then go on to look at the two types of data binding where they can be used.

Controls that can be bound to a DSO recognize special HTML attributes that provide the connection information they need. These are:

- **DATASRC** - the **ID** of the DSO that will supply the data, prefixed by a '#' hash character.

- **DATAFLD** - the name of the field in the DSO's recordset to bind this control to.

- **DATAFORMATAS** - Either **'TEXT'** (the default if omitted) to display the field value as plain text, or **'HTML'** to specify that the browser should render any HTML content within the value.

179

The full list of controls that can participate in data binding in Internet Explorer 4 and onwards is:

HTML Element	Bound property	Update data?	Tabular binding?	Display as HTML?
A	href	No	No	No
APPLET	param	Yes	No	No
BUTTON	innerText *and* innerHTML	No	No	Yes
DIV	innerText *and* innerHTML	No	No	Yes
FRAME	src	No	No	No
IFRAME	src	No	No	No
IMG	src	No	No	No
INPUT TYPE=CHECKBOX	checked	Yes	No	No
INPUT TYPE=HIDDEN	value	Yes	No	No
INPUT TYPE=LABEL	value	Yes	No	No
INPUT TYPE=PASSWORD	value	Yes	No	No
INPUT TYPE=RADIO	checked	Yes	No	No
INPUT TYPE=TEXT	value	Yes	No	No
LABEL	innerText *and* innerHTML	No	No	Yes
MARQUEE	innerText *and* innerHTML	No	No	Yes
OBJECT	param	Yes	No	No
SELECT	*text of selected* option	Yes	No	No
SPAN	innerText *and* innerHTML	No	No	Yes
TABLE	*none*	No	Yes	No
TEXTAREA	value	Yes	No	No

So, as an example, we could bind a **SPAN** element to the value in a field named **tTitle**, which is in a recordset exposed by a DSO that has the **ID** of **dsoBookList**, using:

```
<SPAN DATASRC="#dsoBookList" DATAFLD="tTitle"></SPAN>
```

The value of the **tTitle** field in the current record in the recordset would then be displayed in the page within the **SPAN** element as plain text (the default). If the **tTitle** field contains HTML formatting within the value, we can cause the browser to render it as such using:

```
<SPAN DATASRC="#dsoBookList" DATAFLD="tTitle DATAFORMATAS="HTML"></SPAN>
```

We can also use client-side script to set up or change the bindings once the page has loaded, by changing the `dataSrc`, `dataFld` and `dataFormatAs` properties of the appropriate elements. To remove the bindings, set the properties to an empty string. To change the binding of elements within a bound table, we must remove the binding of the table first (in the `<TABLE>` tag), change the bindings of the elements in the table, and then reset the binding of the table.

Tabular Data Binding

Tabular data binding depends on the ability of the `<TABLE>` element to repeat the contents of the `<TBODY>` section once for each record. It's important to recognize that the use of the word *tabular* – in the sense of the way the data is bound to controls – is entirely unconnected with the name of the Tabular Data Control.

The data source object is identified within the opening `<TABLE>` tag, and the column or field name for each bound control is identified within each table cell. Note that the `<TD>` element itself does not take part in the data binding process. Instead, a bound element is placed within each cell. This could be a `<SPAN>` or a `<DIV>` element, or one of the other HTML controls. For example:

```
...
'definition of a DSO named dsoBookList is elsewhere in the page ...
...
<TABLE DATASRC="#dsoBookList">
 <THEAD>
  <TR>
   <TH>Code</TH>
   <TH>Category</TH>
   <TH>Release Date</TH>
   <TH>Title</TH>
   <TH>Sales</TH>
  </TR>
 </THEAD>
 <TBODY>
  <TR>
   <TD><SPAN DATAFLD="tCode"></SPAN></TD>
   <TD><I><SPAN DATAFLD="tCategory"></I></SPAN></TD>
   <TD><SPAN DATAFLD="dReleaseDate"></SPAN></TD>
   <TD><B><SPAN DATAFLD="tTitle"></SPAN></B></TD>
   <TD><SPAN DATAFLD="nSales"></SPAN></TD>
  </TR>
 </TBODY>
</TABLE>
...
```

Table Paging with Tabular Data Binding

ADO recordsets support paging, as we discovered in Chapter 5 when we looked at the `Recordset` object. When tabular data binding is used, the `<TABLE>` element is bound to the DSO that provides the source recordset, and displays the records in that recordset. The DSO properties are exposed through the bound `<TABLE>` element, and this includes the `dataPageSize` property. In IE4 and above, this property is mapped to the `DATAPAGESIZE` attribute of the table as well:

DATAPAGESIZE - sets the maximum number of records that will be displayed within the body of a table.

By setting this attribute in the opening HTML **<TABLE>** tag, we can create a table that displays only a specified number of records:

```
<TABLE DATASRC="#dsoBookList" DATAPAGESIZE=10>
```

Then, we can move through the recordset by using the **nextPage** and **previousPage** methods. The bound table also exposes the **recordNumber** property of the underlying data set for each element within the table.

Single Record Data Binding

Tabular display is fine for displaying data, but for editing it we really need to be able to display the values from one record at a time within HTML controls. This is particularly true if we want to allow the user to update the source data.

As soon as a recordset is created by a DSO, the first record becomes the **current record**, in exactly the same way as when we create a recordset using ADO directly (if the recordset is empty, the **EOF** and **BOF** properties are both **True** at this point). We can display the values from the current record in any of the bindable HTML elements listed earlier by setting their **DATASRC** and **DATAFLD** properties. For example:

```
...
'definition of a DSO named dsoBookList is elsewhere in the page ...
...
Code: <INPUT TYPE="TEXT" DATASRC="#dsoBookList" DATAFLD="tCode" SIZE=6><P>
Title: <INPUT TYPE="TEXT" DATASRC="#dsoBookList" DATAFLD="tTitle" SIZE=20><P>
Category: <SELECT DATASRC="#dsoBookList" DATAFLD="tTitle" SIZE=1>
           <OPTION>HTML
           <OPTION>Scripting
           <OPTION>ASP
        </SELECT><P>
Release date: <SPAN DATASRC="#dsoBookList" DATAFLD="dReleaseDate"><P>
Sales to date: <SPAN DATASRC="#dsoBookList" DATAFLD="nSales"><P>
...
```

This produces the page we first saw earlier in this chapter, and the screenshot is repeated here. The buttons at the bottom of the page allow users to move around the recordset, and they work by calling the appropriate **move** methods of the underlying recordset object—as described below.

182

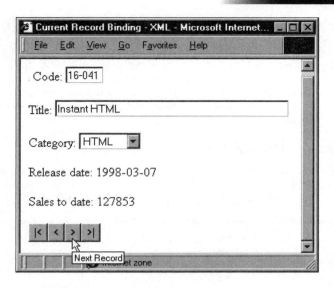

Moving Around and Updating the Data

If we display a single record, we need a way to move to another record. We also need a way to update the source data (if this is appropriate, depending on the DSO we are using) by adding, deleting and editing records. And we will probably also need to cancel updates, and refresh the data displayed in the controls at some stage. All these tasks are accomplished using the standard methods of the DSO that are exposed via ADO. The most common methods are:

Method	Description
`move, moveFirst, moveLast, moveNext, movePrevious`	Move the current record pointer within the cached recordset.
`cancelUpdate`	Cancels all changes made to cached records.
`refresh`	Re-queries the data source and reloads the recordset data cache.
`delete`	Removes the current record from the cached recordset.
`addNew`	Adds a new record to the cached recordset.
`submitChanges`	Updates the source data with all the changes made to the cached recordset.

To move to the next record, as shown in the previous screenshot, we can use a normal HTML **BUTTON** control to call the exposed methods of the DSO:

```
<button onclick="dsoBookList.recordset.MoveNext()"> &gt; </button>
```

See Appendix A for a full list of the properties, methods and events for the ADO **recordset** *object.*

Events Raised by Internet Explorer 4/5 and the RDS DSO

Both a DSO embedded within the page, and the browser itself, raise events that can be trapped and used in script on the client. We'll look at these events briefly next. They can be divided into two groups: those raised by the browser or the controls on the page (when the user navigates to another page or edits the data in the HTML controls), and those raised by a DSO as the user edits the data it exposes.

Events Raised by HTML Elements and the Browser

When a page containing a DSO is unloaded, or when the user edits the data in HTML controls that are bound to a DSO, various events are raised. Some can be cancelled by returning the value **false** from the event handler routine:

Event	Cancel?	Description
onbeforeupdate	Yes	Occurs before the data in the control is passed to the DSO.
onafterupdate	No	Occurs after the data in the control has been passed to the DSO.
onerrorupdate	Yes	Occurs if an error prevents the data being passed to the DSO.
onbeforeunload	No	Occurs before the current page is unloaded.

The **onbeforeunload** is raised by the **window** object, while the remainder are raised by the HTML controls on the page. With the exception of the **onbeforeunload** event, all events bubble up through the document hierarchy. So, we can display a message when the user changes the value in a control with:

```
<INPUT ID="txtTitle" DATASRC="#dsoBookList" DATAFLD="tTitle">
...
<SCRIPT LANGUAGE="JavaScript">
function txtTitle.onbeforeupdate() {
  return confirm("Are you sure you want to change this value ?");
}
</SCRIPT>
```

Events Raised by the RDS Data Source Object

The RDS Data Source Object itself raises events as various actions take place. Most are concerned with indicating the current state of the DSO as it loads the data. However, the first two are fired when the 'current record' changes as the user moves through the recordset. This could be done by clicking on a tabular data-bound table, or when the code in a page that uses single-record data binding calls one of the recordset **move** methods:

Event	Cancel?	Description
onrowenter	No	Occurs for a record when it becomes the current one during navigating the recordset.
onrowexit	Yes	Occurs for a record before another record becomes the current one during navigating the recordset.
ondataavailable	No	Occurs periodically while data is arriving from the data source.
ondatasetcomplete	No	Occurs when all the data has arrived from the data source.
ondatasetchanged	No	Occurs when the data set changes, such as when a filter is applied.
onreadystatechange	No	Occurs when the **readyState** property of the DSO changes.

Only the **onrowexit** event can be canceled by returning **false** from the event handler routine. All events bubble up through the document hierarchy. It's usual to take advantage of the **ondatasetcomplete** event for any script that you want to run once the data has arrived:

```
<INPUT ID="txtStatus" VALUE="Initializing, please wait ...">
...
<SCRIPT LANGUAGE="JavaScript">
function dsoBookList.ondatasetcomplete() {
  txtStatus.value = "Data arrived OK";
}
</SCRIPT>
```

Manipulating Data Directly with ADO

It's important to realize that each data source object is itself a **DataControl** object, and as such is an OLE-DB **data provider**. This has to be the case for ADO to be able to access the data exposed by the DSOs—remember that ADO is a way of communicating with an OLE-DB data provider (or an ODBC driver that exposes an OLE-DB interface).

The only difference here is that the data store is now a locally-cached recordset, and so the **DataControl** object or DSO takes the place of the server-side OLE-DB data provider. In fact, ADO continues this terminology by referring to bound controls on a Web page as **data consumers**.

Filling a SELECT List

Each DSO exposes the cached recordset to code running on the client through its **recordset** property. We can create a reference to this and work with the contents of the recordset. So, once we've got the data into a client-side cached recordset, we can use it just like we would in ADO on the server. For example we can use it to populate a **<SELECT>** list by iterating through the recordset. Note that we do it in the **ondatasetcomplete** event handler, where we know that the data has arrived:

185

```
<OBJECT CLASSID="clsid:333C7BC4-460F-11D0-BC04-0080C7055A83"
        ID="dsoBookList" WIDTH=0 HEIGHT=0>
  <PARAM NAME="DataURL" VALUE="booklist.txt">
  <PARAM NAME="FieldDelim" VALUE=";">
  <PARAM NAME="UseHeader" VALUE="true">
</OBJECT>

<INPUT TYPE="HIDDEN" DATASRC="#dsoBookList" DATAFLD="tTitle">

<SELECT ID="MyList" SIZE=1>
  <OPTION>Initializing ... please wait ...
</SELECT>

<SCRIPT LANGUAGE="JavaScript">
function dsoBookList.ondatasetcomplete() {
  objListBox = document.all("MyList");              // get reference to SELECT
list
  objListBox.options[0].text = "Select a book..."; // change current OPTION
text
  recBooks = document.dsoBookList.recordset;        // the DSO's recordset
  while (!recBooks.EOF) {                            // add titles to SELECT list
    strTitle = '' + recBooks("tTitle");
    objListBox.options.length += 1;
    objListBox.options[objListBox.options.length - 1].text =
recBooks("tTitle");      recBooks.MoveNext();
  }
}
</SCRIPT>
```

Here's the result, showing the list box contents after the **ondatasetcomplete**
event has fired, and the values have been inserted into the list by creating new
<OPTION> elements within it:

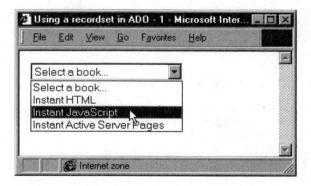

*In some circumstances, the RDS control can fail to initiate the data transfer
from server to client as there are no bound controls on the page. You can get
round this by placing a **HIDDEN**-type control on the page and binding it to
one field in the recordset, for example:*

```
<INPUT TYPE="HIDDEN" DATASRC="#dsoBookList" DATAFLD="tTitle">
```

Using the Recordset with Internet Explorer Dynamic HTML

As another example of using the recordset directly, we can create output in the page using Dynamic HTML—here to place values from the records into a **<H3>** heading element previously defined in the page:

```
<OBJECT CLASSID="clsid:333C7BC4-460F-11D0-BC04-0080C7055A83"
         ID="dsoBookList" WIDTH=0 HEIGHT=0>
  <PARAM NAME="DataURL" VALUE="booklist.txt">
  <PARAM NAME="FieldDelim" VALUE=";">
  <PARAM NAME="UseHeader" VALUE="true">
</OBJECT>

<INPUT TYPE="HIDDEN" DATASRC="#dsoBookList" DATAFLD="tTitle">

<H3 ID="MyHeading">Initializing, please wait ...</H3>

<SCRIPT LANGUAGE="JavaScript">
var strList = 'List of books:<P>';

function dsoBookList.ondatasetcomplete() {
  recBooks = document.dsoBookList.recordset;      // the DSO's recordset
  while (!recBooks.EOF) {                          // add titles to strList
string
    strTitle = '' + recBooks("tTitle") + '<BR>';
    strList += strTitle;
    recBooks.MoveNext();
  }
  document.all("MyHeading").innerHTML = strList; // put string into H3 element
}
</SCRIPT>
```

Both of these examples use similar code to get a reference to the client-side ADO recordset object, and then iterate through it extracting values from the records. You can use the values in more creative ways of course, and these two simple examples are designed just to show the basic technique.

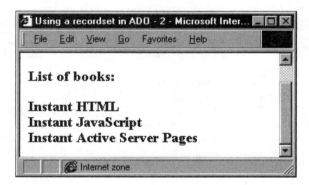

The samples for this book contain several examples that use the various DSOs we've discussed. You can download the samples, and even run some of them directly, from our Web site at http://webdev.wrox.co.uk/books/1835/

187

Creating Remote Recordsets Directly with RDS

So far, we've used data source objects to implement Remote Data Access through ADO. However, this isn't the only technique. With RDS, we can create instances of the objects lower down the hierarchy directly, and then use them to implement a more customized form of remote data access.

Using the RDS Object Hierarchy

Each DSO is itself a **DataControl** object, and when we instantiate a DSO on the page, it automatically creates instances of the **DataSpace** and **DataFactory** objects that perform the data transfer from server to client. Following is the diagram we used earlier in the chapter when we first looked at RDS:

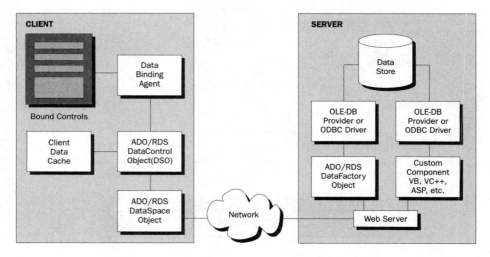

However, there are often times when we want to use a custom component on the server that supplies our recordset, rather than querying the data store directly through the default **DataFactory** object. This provides ways to reduce the security risks inherent in RDS, because we can structure the object to control how and when updates are applied to the source data. It also allows us to 'hide' the data store from prying eyes more effectively than exposing the original table would.

There are two basic techniques for retrieving a recordset directly:

- Using a SQL statement or query directly against the **DataFactory** object

- Using a custom business component on the server that returns a recordset

We'll look at each of these techniques in turn. In each case, we still use a **DataControl** object to store the recordset returned from the server, and a **DataSpace** object to make the connection to the server. However, what differs is the way that these are declared in the client-side page.

Using the DataFactory Object Directly

The **DataFactory** object provides a method named **Query**, which accepts a connection string and a SQL query string. It returns a recordset that is automatically passed to the client over the network, and which can then be assigned to the **SourceRecordset** property of a client-side **DataControl** object:

```
<!-- this is the normal RDS DataControl object with no parameters set -->
<OBJECT ID="dsoDataControl"
        CLASSID="clsid:BD96C556-65A3-11D0-983A-00C04FC29E33">
</OBJECT>

<!-- this is the client-side RDS DataSpace object -->
<OBJECT ID="dspDataSpace"
        CLASSID="CLSID:BD96C556-65A3-11D0-983A-00C04FC29E36">
</OBJECT>

<SCRIPT LANGUAGE="JavaScript">

   // first we create a DataFactory object, specifying the server to use:
   myDataFactory = dspDataSpace.CreateObject("RDSServer.DataFactory",
                                         "http://servername.com");
   // now we create a recordset from the DataFactory using its Query method:
   myRecordset = myDataFactory.Query("DSN=yourdsn;UID=username;PWD=password;",
                                "Select * From TableName");

   // finally, assign the returned recordset to the DataControl object:
   dsoDataControl.SourceRecordset = myRecordset;

</SCRIPT>
```

Although we've shown a Web-based connection here, by specifying the URL of the server, the **DataFactory** *object can also be instantiated using RPC protocols, by specifying the UNC address of the server in the form* *machinename (i.e.* *SUNSPOT).*

Using a Custom Business Component

We can create a custom business component that is a COM object, and which returns a recordset, then install and register it on the server. We can then pass the recordset it creates on to the client as a disconnected recordset for use with ADO or data binding on the client.

The custom component can provide a method that returns a recordset object. If required, the method can also accept parameters that define the contents of the recordset, for example a SQL statement, or application-specific values such as a record identifier key or other selection criteria. It's also possible to use a server-side custom business object that accepts a recordset passed in by reference as a parameter to a method within the object. It can then marshal this recordset ready to pass it to the client.

The important point is that the custom object must provide a recordset that specifies the **adUseClient** value for the **CursorLocation** property. (In previous versions of ADO, this property was called **adUseClientBatch;** this constant name is still supported, and is automatically mapped to the **adUseClient** value).

You can also use this technique to invoke any method of any business object, as long as it returns automation-compatible data types. This allows invocation of remote components through the HTTP protocol with DCOM.

In a Visual Basic component, we might use a function like this to create the recordset:

```
Public Function GetRecs(parameter1, parameter2, ... etc.) As Object

  Dim objConn As New ADODB.Connection
  Dim objRecs As New ADODB.Recordset

  'assuming that parameter1 contains a valid connection string:
  objConn.Open parameter1

  'set the correct cursor location before opening the recordset:
  objRecs.CursorLocation = adUseClient

  'use the 'Unspecified' values for the remaining parameters to make sure
  'that an ADO/R remote recordset is created. We'll assume that the second
  'parameter sent to the function contains a valid SQL query string:
  objRecs.Open parameter2, objConn, adOpenUnspecified, adLockUnspecified, _
                                                       adCmdUnspecified

  Set GetRecs = objRecs

End Function
```

In the client Web page, we can create an instance of the business object on the server, and then call this function directly to return the recordset. Then it's just a matter of assigning the recordset to the **SourceRecordset** property of a client-side **DataControl** object:

```
<!-- this is the normal RDS DataControl object with no parameters set -->
<OBJECT ID="dsoDataControl"
        CLASSID="clsid:BD96C556-65A3-11D0-983A-00C04FC29E33">
</OBJECT>

<!-- this is the client-side RDS DataSpace object -->
<OBJECT ID="dspDataSpace"
        CLASSID="CLSID:BD96C556-65A3-11D0-983A-00C04FC29E36">
</OBJECT>

<SCRIPT LANGUAGE="JavaScript">

  // first we create a DataFactory object, specifying the server to use:
  myCustomObject = dspDataSpace.CreateObject("MyObject.ClassName",
                                         "http://servername.com");
  // now we create a recordset from the custom object using a custom method:
  myRecordset = myCustomObject.GetRecs("parameter1, parameter2, ... etc.");

  // finally, assign the returned recordset to the DataControl object:
  dsoDataControl.SourceRecordset = myRecordset;

</SCRIPT>
```

Security Settings for Custom Business Objects

Custom components that are created by the client-side **DataSpace** object's **CreateObject** method require security settings to be enabled on the server that hosts the custom component. The easiest way to achieve this is to use a simple text file with the **.reg** extension, and run it on the server against the **regedit** program. This merges the new keys into the registry. The file we need looks like this:

```
REGEDIT4
[HKEY_CLASSES_ROOT\CLSID\{your_component_guid}\Implemented
Categories\{7DD95801-9882-11CF-9FA9-00AA006C42C4}]
[HKEY_CLASSES_ROOT\CLSID\{your_component_guid}\Implemented
Categories\{7DD95802-9882-11CF-9FA9-00AA006C42C4}]
[HKEY_LOCAL_MACHINE\System\CurrentControlSet\Services\W3SVC\
Parameters\ADCLaunch\your_component_class_string]
```

The first line tells **regedit** that this is a valid **.reg** file. The next two entries (which should each be on one line, not wrapped like the code above) enable the Safe for Scripting setting, and the third line allows IIS to instantiate the component on the server. Place the file on the server machine, then double-click it to merge the values into the registry. Remember to back up the Registry first before making any changes to it.

Passing Updates Back to the Data Store

Many **DataControl** objects (in the form of a DSO in the client-side page) can flush changes to the records back to the server, and on to the data store. This is done simply by calling the **SubmitChanges** method of the **DataControl** (DSO) object:

```
<SCRIPT LANGUAGE="JavaScript">
  function updateData() {
    dsoDataControl.SubmitChanges();
  }
</SCRIPT>
```

However, when we create the **DataSpace** and **DataFactory** objects ourselves (as shown earlier in this section of the chapter), we can flush changes to the records back to the server, and on to the data store, by simply calling the **SubmitChanges** method of the **DataFactory** object instead. In this case, we also have to provide the connection information, and a reference to the recordset (here obtained directly from the DSO's **recordset** property):

```
<SCRIPT LANGUAGE="JavaScript">
  function updateData() {
    // myDataFactory is a global variable, set when we fetched the recordset
    myDataFactory.SubmitChanges("DSN=yourdsn;UID=username;PWD=password;",
                                dsoDataControl.recordset);
  }
</SCRIPT>
```

If we are using a custom business component to carry out the creation of the recordset on the server, we have to do a little more work. The first step is to provide a method within the component that will accept a recordset, and then call the **UpdateBatch** method of the recordset object. In our example, we provide a parameter to allow us to send the connection string to the component, as well as the parameter that passes the updates to the recordset. This recordset parameter is defined as being of type **ADOR.Recordset**:

```
Public Sub UpdateRecs(strConnect As String, objRecs As ADOR.Recordset)

    'first we have to set the active connection property of the recordset
    'to a valid data store connection, so that the disconnected recordset
    'can be re-connected to that data store:
    objRecs.ActiveConnection = strConnect

    'now we an update the source data:
    objRecs.UpdateBatch

End Sub
```

The ADOR object library is a subset of the ADO library, and is specifically designed for use with RDS and the manipulation of remote recordsets.

In the Web page, we call this method and pass in the recordset that is attached to the client-side **DataControl** object:

```
<SCRIPT LANGUAGE="JavaScript">

function updateData() {
    // get a reference to the client-side recordset:
    objRs = dsoDataControl.recordset;

    // tell the recordset to only send back changed records:
    objRs.MarshalOptions = 1;    // adMarshalModifiedOnly

    // then call the method in our custom business component:
    // myCustomObject is a global variable, set when we fetched the recordset
    myCustomObject.UpdateRecs(objRs);
}

</SCRIPT>
```

Creating an Empty Client-side Recordset

It's possible to create empty recordsets on the client using ADO, and then attach them to a DSO **DataControl** object on the page, or directly to a **DataFactory** object. This means that we can deal with any remote data, or return parameters of any method calls, as long as it is formatted into a recordset. Each ADO recordset consists of a set of fields, and each field has four properties that you must set in code. These are the field name, the field type, the field size, and a Boolean value that specifies if the field will accept null values.

Defining and Creating the Recordset

The recordset is created by calling the **CreateRecordset** method of the **DataControl** (or **DataFactory**) object, and providing it with a pre-filled structure of values that define the recordset. The recordset definition is made up of a variant-type array of field definitions, each of which is itself a variant-type array of field shape specifications:

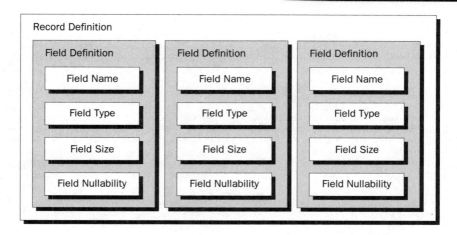

Providing we've already instantiated a **DataControl** object on our page, the
following code can be used to create a simple recordset like that shown above.
You'll notice we've switched to VBScript here. The **CreateRecordset** method
requires a variant-type array of variant-type arrays, and JavaScript has some
problems creating these in the exact format required by the method:

```
<SCRIPT LANGUAGE="VBScript">
Sub createNewRecordset()
    ' first define the individual fields:
    Dim arrField1(3)
    Dim arrField2(3)
    Dim arrField3(3)

    ' define field 1 shape
    arrField1(0) = "kBookCode"      ' field name, to hold book code string
    arrField1(1) = CInt(129)        ' field type (adChar)
    arrField1(2) = CInt(4)          ' field size 4 characters
    arrField1(3) = False            ' field cannot contain null

    ' define field 2 shape
    arrField2(0) = "dReleaseDate"   ' field name, to hold release date
    arrField2(1) = CInt(135)        ' field type (adDBTimeStamp)
    arrField2(2) = CInt(-1)         ' field size default for TimeStamp
    arrField2(3) = True             ' field can contain null

    ' define field 3 shape
    arrField3(0) = "tTitle"         ' field name, to hold book title
    arrField3(1) = CInt(129)        ' field type (adChar)
    arrField3(2) = CInt(50)         ' field size 50 characters
    arrField3(3) = False            ' field cannot contain null

    ' define and fill array holding the record definition:
    Dim arrRecord(2)
    arrRecord(0) = arrField1
    arrRecord(1) = arrField2
    arrRecord(2) = arrField3

    ' now create empty recordset using the current DataControl object:
    Set objRecordset = dsoDataControl.CreateRecordset(arrRecord)
    ...
```

Filling and Using the New Recordset

Once we've created the recordset, we can use ordinary ADO techniques to fill it with values, and then assign it to the **RecordSource** property of a **DataControl** DSO object:

```
' add new records and fill in the values:
objRecordset.AddNew
objRecordset.Fields("kBookCode") = "1797"
objRecordset.Fields("dReleaseDate") = "1998-09-01 00:00:00"
objRecordset.Fields("tTitle") = "Professional Web Administration"
objRecordset.Update
...
... // etc.
...
' now connect the new recordset to the DataControl object:
dsoDataControl.SourceRecordset = objRecordset

End Sub
</SCRIPT>
```

The samples for this book contain an example that uses the various RDS/ADO techniques to access a data store, and we also provide the Visual Basic source files to build a simple custom business object. You can download the samples from http://webdev.wrox.co.uk/books/1835/. The next screenshot shows what it looks like when you run it. The bottom half of the page contains a bound table, and the buttons in the top half of the page demonstrate how the recordset for this table can be created using the **DataFactory** object, a custom business component, and by creating a new local recordset:

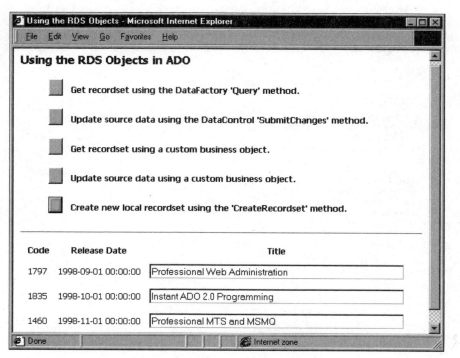

Asynchronous Data Retrieval

By default, the `DataControl` object fetches records from the server in asynchronous mode. In other words, control returns to the browser or client application immediately, instead of when all the records are available on the client. This is why we used the `ondatasetcomplete` event to run client-side code that accessed the recordset.

This behavior occurs because, by default, the `DataControl` object's `FetchOptions` property is set to `adFetchAsync` (3) and the `ExecuteOptions` property is set to `adExecAsync` (2). To cause the records to be fetched synchronously, in which case the browser will appear to 'hang' until the records have arrived, we can set the `FetchOptions` property to `adFetchUpFront` (1) and the `ExecuteOptions` property to `adExecSync` (1).

One useful technique is to use `FetchOptions = adcFetchBackground` (2), which allows the client-side code to start working with the records as soon as the first batch has arrived. When the client-side code accesses a record that has not been fetched, the `DataControl` object automatically fetches the appropriate batch from the server. However, bear in mind that this does not provide a truly disconnected recordset, as only part of it may be cached on the client.

The RDS DSO also provides an event named `onreadystatechanged`. This is fired periodically as data is being fetched from the server, and we can query the `ReadyState` property to check current progress. This property returns: `adcReadyStateLoaded` (2) when the query is still executing on the server and no rows have been fetched, `adcReadyStateInteractive` (3) once the first batch of rows have been fetched, and `adcReadyStateComplete` (4) when all rows have been fetched. Note that if an error occurs, the property still returns `adcReadyStateComplete`.

Using the ADO and RDS Named Constants in Script

Remember that script code does not have access to the ADO constant definitions. However, they are all available in files that are installed with the MS Data Access Components. For server-side programming, the files are `adovbs.inc` (VBScript) and `adojavas.inc` (JScript), which are installed by default in your \Program Files\Common Files\System\ado\ folder. For client-side programming, the files are `adcvbs.inc` (VBScript) and `adcjavas.inc` (JScript), which are installed by default in your \Program Files\Common Files\System\msdac\ folder.

You can paste the individual constant declarations you want from the file into a page. If you are using them on the server, you can include the complete file in a page by copying it to a folder on your Web site and using the ASP Server-Side Include instruction:

```
<!-- #include virtual="vpath_to_file/adcvbs.inc" -->
```

or

```
<!-- #include virtual="vpath_to_file/adcjavas.inc" -->
```

Summary

In this chapter, we've looked at a range of techniques that provide **Remote Data Access** for working with data over the Web. The two main areas are the use of **XML-formatted data**, which is the future for all remote data access, and **Remote Data Service** (RDS) which currently provides disconnected data management directly.

While XML is the future, it is only just starting to appear in a workable form in current software. For this reason, we've concentrated mainly on the second option—RDS. This provides a range of ways that we can move recordsets from server to client over the Web, and then pass updates back to the server where they can be used to update the data store.

We also spent some time looking at other techniques for sending data to the client, such as in the form of text files to the **Tabular Data Control**, and HTML pages to the **MSHTML Browser Control**. Neither of these can handle updates of the source data on the server, however.

And, because all these technologies revolve around caching and exposing a 'real' ADO recordset on the client, our ADO skills can be used to manipulate the data there, saving regular round-trips to the server each time the user wants to see the data displayed in a different way.

Overall, this chapter covered:

- An overview of what remote data access is all about
- A look at the different kinds of remote data access technologies
- How we can implement remote data access in a Web page
- How we can bind data to HTML controls in a Web page
- Ways of creating remote recordsets directly using RDS and ADO

In the next chapter, we'll clear up a few of the loose ends that we haven't had the space to include in previous chapters. This includes the concepts of data-shaping, or hierarchical recordsets, saving recordsets locally on the client, resolving conflicts when updating records, and indexing.

Chapter

8

Data Shaping and Recordsets

So far all of the chapters have been fairly self contained, but there are still a few topics that need mentioning. Some just don't fit neatly into the other sections of the book, and some apply to more than one section, so we've placed them here.

In this chapter we are going to cover:

- Data Shaping, and how to create hierarchical recordsets
- The use of autonumber and identity fields, and how to access the last added record
- Recordset persistence, and how to save recordsets locally
- Fabricating your own recordsets
- Conflict resolution when working offline
- Indexing

Data Shaping

Data shaping is one of the new features in ADO 2.0, so you might not know anything about it. The easiest way to understand data shaping is to use another term that is often used — hierarchical recordsets. Think about all of those times that you've had master and detail recordsets. Publishers and books are a good example. The easiest way to imagine this is to think of the Explorer, or a TreeView control.

With previous data access technologies, you would have to use two recordsets, or do a SQL JOIN which has an inherent overhead, but data shaping allows a column of your master recordset to contain a recordset of its own — that of the child recordset. These child recordsets are often called Chapters, and the data type of the column would be **adChapter**.

Data shaping will make the creation of XML documents much easier, due to the natural hierarchical nature, and with version 2.1 of ADO, you'll have the ability to save recordsets as XML. It would be great if, when you saved a hierarchical recordset in XML format, it automatically created a full structure, including the child recordsets.

When thinking about data shaping you must be clear in your mind about the difference between hierarchical recordsets and hierarchical databases. Hierarchical recordsets are standard recordsets, but with the data represented as a hierarchy, with parent and child details. A hierarchical database, such as IBM IMS/DB, actually stores data in a hierarchical format. What we are talking about here is the representation of the data in a recordset, and not the way it is physically stored.

There are two important things to know if you want to use data shaping:

 You have to use the **MSDataShape** provider.

 You have to use a special data shape language, which is a superset of SQL

If you've got Visual Basic 6 then there's a really quick way to produce your shape commands using the Data Environment Designer. You'll see an example of this later in the chapter. It is worth looking at the syntax though, as it's not always convenient to load Visual Basic just to create a shaped recordset, (unless you're developing a Visual Basic application, of course!).

The Shape Language

The shape command has its own formal grammar, which we won't list here (it's included in the ADO 2.0 documentation), but we will go through the way you use this command. In general, your shape command will look something like this:

```
SHAPE {parent_command} [[AS] table_alias]
APPEND ({child_command} [[AS] child_table_alias]
      RELATE parent_column TO child_column) [[AS] column_name
```

This defines the parent and the child, and how they relate. The command is a SQL command. If we take the **pubs** database, the sample database supplied with SQL Server, and show an example for publishers and titles:

```
SHAPE {SELECT * FROM publishers} AS publishers
APPEND ({SELECT * FROM titles} AS titles
      RELATE pub_id TO pub_id) AS titles
```

So, the first line is the parent — this will be a list of publishers:

```
SHAPE {SELECT * FROM publishers} AS publishers
```

For each publisher we want a list of titles, so we APPEND a query that lists the titles:

```
APPEND ({SELECT * FROM titles} AS titles
```

Now we identify how the two commands are linked together. This is the primary key in the parent table and the foreign key in the child table.

```
RELATE pub_id TO pub_id) AS titles
```

The alias used here is what the new column will be called. The shape provider creates this new column on the parent, and for each entry, this column contains a recordset of its own. What we end up with is a recordset structure like this:

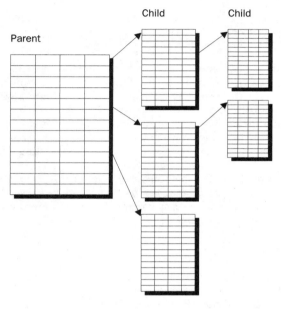

Here's a simple piece of VB code that prints this out — you'll need to change the connect string to point to your server for this:

```
Dim objConn      As New ADODB.Connection
Dim objRec       As New ADODB.Recordset
Dim objRecTitle  As ADODB.Recordset
Dim strShape     As String

' use the data shape provider,
' with SQL Server as the source of the data
objConn.Provider = "MSDataShape"
objConn.Open "Data Provider=SQLOLEDB; Data Source=Tigger; " & _
            "Initial Catalog=pubs; User Id=sa; Password="

' define our shape string and open the recordset
strShape = "SHAPE {SELECT * FROM publishers} AS publishers" & _
           " APPEND ({SELECT * FROM titles}  AS titles" & _
           " RELATE pub_id TO pub_id) AS titles"
objRec.Open strShape, objConn

' loop through the parent records
While Not objRec.EOF
    Debug.Print objRec("pub_name")
```

```
     ' set the recordset for the child
     ' records and loop through them
     Set objRecTitle = objRec("titles").Value
     While Not objRecTitle.EOF
         Debug.Print vbTab; objRecTitle("title")
         objRecTitle.MoveNext
     Wend
     objRec.MoveNext
  Wend

  objRec.Close
  objConn.Close
  Set objRec = Nothing
  Set objConn = Nothing
  Set objRecTitle = Nothing
```

The first thing to notice about this is that the Provider is **MSDataShape**, and we use **Data Provider** to point to the OLEDB provider which actually supplies the data. So the actual OLEDB Provider is **MSDataShape**, but this provider is really just a proxy — its job is to get the data from somewhere else and shape it. This means we have to tell the data shape provider where we want the actual data to come from, and this is the **Data Provider**. This means that the data shape provider can take data from any existing OLEDB provider.

The shape command becomes the source of our recordset, and we can loop through this as normal. Notice that we use a second recordset to point to the child recordset, which is stored as a column in the first recordset. The **Value** of this column is the child recordset. This produces the following output:

New Moon Books
   You Can Combat Computer Stress!
   Is Anger the Enemy?
   Life Without Fear
   Prolonged Data Deprivation: Four Case Studies
   Emotional Security: A New Algorithm
Binnet & Hardley
   Silicon Valley Gastronomic Treats
   The Gourmet Microwave
   The Psychology of Computer Cooking
   Computer Phobic AND Non-Phobic Individuals: Behavior Variations
   Onions, Leeks, and Garlic: Cooking Secrets of the Mediterranean
   Fifty Years in Buckingham Palace Kitchens
   Sushi, Anyone?
Algodata Infosystems
   The Busy Executive's Database Guide
   Cooking with Computers: Surreptitious Balance Sheets
   Straight Talk About Computers
   But Is It User Friendly?
   Secrets of Silicon Valley
   Net Etiquette
Five Lakes Publishing
Ramona Publishers
GGG&G
Scootney Books
Lucerne Publishing

Notice that some records don't have child records. In this case an empty recordset is created.

You don't have to use another Recordset object if you don't want to, as the child recordset can be accessed directly:

```
objRec("titles").Value.Fields("title")
```

Multiple Children

In the above example we saw publishers and titles, but a parent recordset is not restricted to only one child recordset. For example, the publishers also have employees, and we may wish to include this information in our data schema:

```
SHAPE {SELECT * FROM  publishers}  AS publishers
APPEND ({SELECT * FROM  titles}  AS titles
        RELATE pub_id TO pub_id) AS titles,
       ({SELECT * FROM employee}  AS employees
        RELATE pub_id TO pub_id) AS employees
```

This follows the same rules as the above example, but we are appending two commands. The parent is **publishers**, to which we **APPEND** two select queries (separated by a comma), giving them names of **titles** and **employees**. The syntax for these is the same, indicating the relationship of the parent to the child:

```
SHAPE {parent_command} [[AS] table_alias]
APPEND ({child_command_1} [[AS] child_table_1_alias]
        RELATE parent_column TO child_column_1) [[AS] column_name_1 ,
       {child_command_2} [[AS] child_table_2_alias]
        RELATE parent_column TO child_column_2) [[AS] column_name_2
```

Your recordset would now have two extra columns, which you could use in the same way as above:

```
Set objRecTitles = objRec("titles").Value
Set objRecEmps = objRec("employees").Value
```

Grandchildren

Data shaping doesn't have to be limited to sets of data one level deep. Each of the child records can have its own child. For example, suppose we wanted to add the sales for each title, showing the date purchased and the number sold. The shape command now becomes:

```
SHAPE {SELECT * FROM publishers}  AS publishers
APPEND (( SHAPE {SELECT * FROM titles}  AS titles
        APPEND ({SELECT * FROM sales}  AS sales
        RELATE title_id TO title_id) AS sales) AS titles
       RELATE pub_id TO pub_id) AS titles
```

This just adds another **APPEND** and **RELATE** command to relate the new child table to its parent. So now you could change your code accordingly. Add a new variable declaration:

```
Dim objRecSales As ADODB.Recordset
```

And then add the loop to print the sales:

```
Debug.Print vbTab; objRecTitle("title")
Set objRecSales = objRecTitle("sales").Value
While Not objRecSales.EOF
    Debug.Print vbTab; vbTab; objRecSales("ord_date"); vbTab;
objRecSales("qty")
    objRecSales.MoveNext
Wend
objRecTitle.MoveNext
```

What you now see is this:

Binnet & Hardley
  Silicon Valley Gastronomic Treats
    12/12/93   10
  The Gourmet Microwave
    14/09/94   25
    14/09/94   15
  The Psychology of Computer Cooking
  Computer Phobic AND Non-Phobic Individuals: Behavior Variations
    29/05/93   20
  Onions, Leeks, and Garlic: Cooking Secrets of the Mediterranean
    15/06/92   40

The SQL statement is not limited to just SELECT *, and you can use almost any SQL statement you like. The only restriction is that you have to have matching columns in the parent and child selects, but this is not different from a normal SQL join or sub-query. The examples above have shown the parent and child columns with the same name, but they can be different names, as long as they provide a relationship between the two tables.

Summarizing with Shapes

The data shape language also has a way to produce summary information, allowing your parent to hold summary details, while the children hold the individual details. This is really useful for those management information systems drill down situations, where you show a total, and then you can drill-down into the details. For example, imagine that you wanted to find out the total sales of books for each type of book, as well as being able to see the total sales for the books.

For this type of data shape, you need to use a different form of the shaping language:

```
SHAPE {parent_command} [[AS] table_alias]
COMPUTE aggregate_filed_list
BY group_field_list
```

For example, you could construct a shape command like this:

```
SHAPE {SELECT * FROM titles}  AS TitlesSales
COMPUTE TitlesSales, SUM(TitlesSales.ytd_sales) AS NumberSold
BY type
```

The first line is familiar — you are creating a shape, and it's to be called **TitlesSales**. You want to sum the **ytd_sales** column of this shape, grouping on the **type** column. Your parent recordset will contain 3 columns:

- **type**, which is the column we grouped on

- **NumberSold**, which is the column we summed

- **TitlesSales**, which is the child recordset

The parent recordset contains the SQL statement from the first line, and, as a result of this, everything in the **titles** table.

You could access the result with code like this:

```
While Not objRec.EOF
    Debug.Print objRec("type"); vbTab; objRec("NumberSold")

    Set objRecAuth = objRec("titlessales").Value
    While Not objRecAuth.EOF
        Debug.Print vbTab; objRecAuth("title"); vbTab; objRecAuth("ytd_sales")
        objRecAuth.MoveNext
    Wend
    objRec.MoveNext
Wend
```

And the results it produces would be like this:

```
business      30788
    The Busy Executive's Database Guide    4095
    Cooking with Computers: Surreptitious Balance Sheets    3876
    You Can Combat Computer Stress!    18722
    Straight Talk About Computers    4095
mod_cook      24278
    Silicon Valley Gastronomic Treats    2032
    The Gourmet Microwave    22246
```

Stored Procedures

As well as using select queries in your shape commands you can use stored procedures. For example, imagine two stored procedures:

```
CREATE PROCEDURE usp_Publishers
AS
    SELECT *
    FROM   publishers
```

and

```
CREATE PROCEDURE usp_TitlesByPubID
    @PubID char(4)
AS
    SELECT *
    FROM   titles
    WHERE  pub_id = @PubID
```

The first just returns all publishers, and the second returns all titles for a given publisher. You could create a shape command to use these two as follows:

```
SHAPE {{CALL dbo.usp_AllPublishers }} AS PubsByCountry
APPEND ({{{CALL dbo.usp_TitlesByPubID( ?) }} AS TitlesByPubID
RELATE pub_id TO PARAMETER 0) AS TitlesByPubID
```

Notice that instead of the select commands we previously had, there is now a call to the stored procedure. The stored procedure for the child takes a parameter, but since this is to be filled in by the parent, we **RELATE** the **pub_id** field to this parameter. The shape command processor automatically takes care of filling in this parameter for each child recordset. While this might look cool, you should be aware that this can have a detrimental effect on performance, as the child stored procedure is executed each time it is referenced. If you have stored procedures that are children, then all parameters must participate in the relationship.

If you wanted the parent stored procedure to accept an argument, such as the country, then it could be written like this:

```
CREATE PROCEDURE usp_PublishersByCountry
    @Country varchar(30)
AS
    SELECT *
    FROM    publishers
    WHERE   country = @Country
```

The shape command would now become:

```
SHAPE {{CALL dbo.usp_PublishersByCountry( ?) }} AS PubsByCountry
APPEND ({{{CALL dbo.usp_TitlesByPubID( ?) }} AS TitlesByPubID
RELATE pub_id TO PARAMETER 0) AS TitlesByPubID
```

You can pass parameters into this command in three ways. The first is to add it in manually:

```
SHAPE {{CALL dbo.usp_PublishersByCountry('USA') }} AS PubsByCountry
APPEND ({{{CALL dbo.usp_TitlesByPubID( ?) }} AS TitlesByPubID
RELATE pub_id TO PARAMETER 0) AS TitlesByPubID
```

The second is to create a Command object and use the Parameters collection:

```
objCmd.CommandText = strShape
objCmd.Parameters.Append objCmd.CreateParameter("@Country", _
                                adVarChar, adParamInput, 30, "USA")
Set objRec = objCmd.Execute
```

The third is again to use a Command object, but this time pass the parameter into the Execute method:

```
objCmd.CommandText = strShape
Set objRec = objCmd.Execute  (, Array("USA"))
```

You can pass in multiple parameters using any of these methods.

Updating Shaped Recordsets

Using data shaping doesn't mean that your recordsets behave any differently from normal recordsets. Assuming that your recordset allows updating, then you can treat shaped recordsets as you would normally: adding, updating, and deleting records. For example:

```
Set objRecTitles = objRec("titles").Value
objRecTitles("qty") = objrecTitles("qty") + 1
objRecTitles.Update
```

This sets a recordset to point to the child recordset, and then updates a value. Changing the relating field in the parent recordset means that the child recordset may become orphaned. Likewise, changing the relating field in the child recordset will stop it being related to the parent.

Data Shaping in Visual Basic 6

Having shown you the hard way to create shape commands, you won't be surprised to find that Visual Basic 6 has a quick (and rather cool) way to do this, as part of its Data Environment. To create a data shape command you first add a Command to the Data Environment. I created a connection to the **pubs** database, then added a command, pointing to the **publishers** table. You can do this by selecting the connection, right-mouse clicking, and selecting Add Command:

Then you add a Child Command (right mouse click on the existing command), which in this case will be the **titles** table. With child commands you have to specify the relationship:

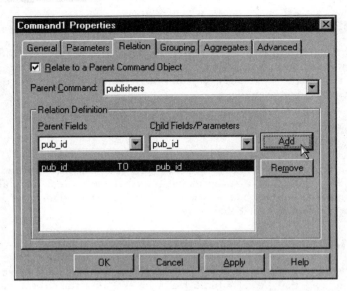

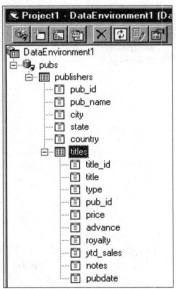

Once the child command has been added, you'll see it appear under its parent:

If you then right-mouse click on the parent, you can pick Hierarchy Info... from the menu to see the shape command:

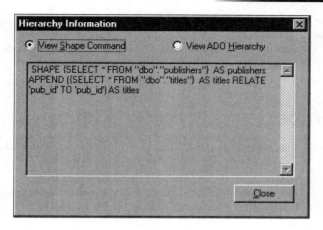

Simple eh? Another great thing about VB6 is that it has a grid, the Hierarchical FlexGrid, that binds directly to hierarchical recordsets, allowing you to drill down to the child data.

Of course, if you haven't got Visual Basic 6 you'll have to do it manually.

Why Data Shaping?

All of this might seem very smart, but what's the real use, especially when you can achieve the same result by joining the tables together? Well, imagine a parent recordset that has a hundred rows, and ten columns. It has a child recordset containing ten rows per parent row. Now look at a normal join:

```
SELECT * FROM parent, child
WHERE parent.id = child.id
```

For each child row, there will also be a parent row containing ten columns. Those ten parent columns will be the same for each of the childrens' ten rows. That's an awful lot of wasted network traffic and data handling.

If you use data shaping, then the parent row is only included once, so instead of one thousand rows we only have one hundred. Overall, it's smaller, easier to manage, and produces less network traffic when marshaled over the internet as a disconnected recordset. However, you should be aware of the way that data shaping actually works.

When you create a simple relation, such as between publishers and titles say, then both tables will be fetched before the hierarchy is created. A new field is added to the parent recordset — which is a pointer to the child recordset — and when that child is referenced, a filter is applied to the child recordset. This means that all child recordsets are initially fetched, so if the child recordsets are large you might find this slower than a normally joined recordset. This concept is examined in more detail in Chapter 9.

When using a parameter based hierarchy, this process does not happen, as the data for the child recordsets is not initially fetched. When the child recordset is referenced, the parameter query is executed with the parameter details from the parent. This means that there will be a trip back to the server to fetch data every time a new child recordset is required.

AutoNumber and Identity Fields

The following question is probably one of the most frequently asked questions about ADO, and it's of especial concern to people converting from DAO:

 When using AutoNumber and Identity fields, how do you add a new record, and then get the key value for the newly added row?

Unfortunately there's not always a simple answer; it depends on the provider you are using, as well as items like the cursor location, type, and locking method.

ADO states that when adding a new record, when you then **Update** that record, the cursor is placed on the newly added record. This is exactly what you need, but the identity or autonumber value may not be available. For example, code such as this may not produce the desired result:

```
objRec.AddNew
objRec("field_name") = "field_value"
objRec.Update

Print objRec("ID")
```

This assumes that ID is an automatically incrementing field.

Server-Side Cursors

Server-side cursors (using **CursorLocation = adUseServer**) are where you are going to have most success with the code above, because the cursor has more of a dynamic relationship with the server and the data.

Using the OLEDB Driver for Jet, you have no problems, since this works with all cursor and locking types (except for read only, of course). The newly inserted value is immediately available for use after the **Update**.

With the provider for SQL Server, you have more of a problem, since only keyset cursors work, and only then when you use pessimistic or optimistic locking. Using batch optimistic locking does not work.

The same result applies when using the OLEDB driver for ODBC, even when connecting to Access.

So if you need this facility, the general rule is to use a cursor type of **adOpenKeyset**, and a lock type of **adLockPessimistic** or **adLockOptimistic**. When using the OLEDB driver for Jet, then it doesn't matter which cursor type you choose, because Access gives you a keyset cursor anyway, whichever one you request.

Client-Side Cursors

Using client-side cursors prove to be more of a problem, and Microsoft is actively working on a way to get over this. If you think about the way client-side cursors work, then you'll realize why this is a problem. When you use client-side cursors, the connection with the recordset is read into a local cache, and the server data is only updated when required. Although you have access to the newly created row, the identity and autonumber fields are created at the server. If the data has not been sent back to the server, then the ID value will not have been updated. There is no way, therefore, that you can get hold of this value.

Of course, you can always batch update the server, and then Requery the data, but this might not match your requirements, and it seems to destroy some of the advantages of working with client-side cursors.

Using @@IDENTITY

With SQL Server, you have the notion of IDENTITY fields. These are standard auto-incrementing fields, but there is also a global value that represents the latest IDENTITY value added. So, using this you can obtain the value you need. For example, in a stored procedure you could do this:

```
CREATE PROCEDURE usp_AddAuthor
    @sAuLName    varchar(25),
    @sAuFName    varchar(25)
AS
BEGIN
    INSERT INTO authors (au_lname, au_fname)
    VALUES (@sAuLName, @sAUFName)

    RETURN @@IDENTITY
END
```

This adds a new record and then returns the **Identity** field just used. You could then run this stored procedure using a Command object, and access the return value through the Parameters collection. You can also use this method when running straight SQL queries.

Because the server handles this facility, you can use this with any type of cursor and location.

One thing to watch when running this method is that @@IDENTITY is a global variable, and represents the last IDENTITY value updated, irrespective of the table. So if you have an INSERT trigger on a table, and the table the trigger inserts into has an identity field, then @@IDENTITY will reflect this value, rather than the one you intended.

Recordset Persistence

The new **Save** method of recordsets allows data to be saved to a local, binary file, and then re-opened with the **Open** method. The great point about this is that it suddenly opens up the world of roving users. You now have the opportunity to provide the same application to both connected and disconnected users, and an easy way for them to switch states.

Imagine a sales situation where sales people occasionally take their laptops on the road with them. You could provide a Work Offline option that saves their data locally. On the road the application can open these persisted recordsets, and work on them as normal. When the user connects back online, the master copy of the data can be updated with the offline data.

Here's some Visual Basic code that could do this.

```
objRec.Save "c:\temp\OfflineData.dat"

' disconnect from connection and close connection
Set m_objRec.ActiveConnection = Nothing
objRec.Close
objConn.Close

' now re open in offline mode
objRec.Open "c:\temp\OfflineData.dat"
```

This could be executed when the user wishes to work offline. The recordset is saved locally, the connection and recordset closed, and then the local recordset opened. The user would be disconnected from the server and could continue as normal, although only the saved data would be available. Any new information, or information not saved, would only become available once the connection to the server was re-established.

To get back online, you could do this:

```
' reconnect to the data source
strConn = "Provider=Microsoft.Jet.OLEDB.3.51; " & _
          "Data Source=C:\temp\pubs.mdb"
objRec.ActiveConnection = strConn

' update the master table with the offline changes
objRec.UpdateBatch
```

This connects the recordset to a connection and then uses **UpdateBatch** to update the master copy of the records with the local copy. See the section on Conflict Resolution for more details of this.

You can see that this makes writing offline applications no different from writing an online application. You could have a simple flag that is set when the application is offline to indicate that the saved copies of the recordset are opened when the application starts.

A small sample application showing these techniques is available from the Wrox Press web site, at webdev.wrox.co.uk/books/1835.

At the moment, the only format for persistence is a proprietary, binary format. This is ADTG (datagram) format, which is the same format that disconnected recordsets are marshaled in. XML is expected to be supported in ADO version 2.1, which will ship with IE5 and Office 2000. This has a particular impact on web developers since it will allow transfer of recordsets from the server to the client in XML format, where they can then be bound to data controls, thus alleviating the need for client-side data binding objects.

Creating Recordsets

Creating recordsets actually has some very interesting uses, some of which have nothing to do with databases or large stores of data. Consider the following:

- You have a source of data for which there is no OLEDB provider, but you want to provide a consistent access to this data for your programmers. You could create a component that reads this data in, and then creates a recordset, which is exposed to the caller of the component.

- You are creating a multi-tier client/server application that needs to pass data around from tier to tier, but don't want it to be bound up creating arrays and odd structures. You could create a recordset with the data in and have this passed around. This does, however, rely on having ADO installed on the client.

- You are using Microsoft Message Queue Server, and need to pass data in the messages. The body of an MSMQ message must be a string of data, or an object that can persist its data, and ADO 2 can do this. If you think back to the roving users, instead of them connecting back to the server to update the data, you could actually have this data passed to and fro as a message, where it can be dealt with when the server is free.

Creating a recordset is simply a matter of appending fields to an empty recordset that is not connected to a data source. For example, in Visual Basic this could be done with the following code:

```
Dim objRec        As New ADODB.Recordset

objRec.Fields.Append "OrderNumber", adVarChar, 10
objRec.Fields.Append "OrderDate", adVarChar, 20
```

This just creates a recordset with two fields, both holding text data, which can be null. At this stage you have a closed recordset, so you can open it, and then add data as though it were a recordset created from a data source.

Conflict Resolution

Using client-side cursors and disconnected recordsets is great, especially with the ability to amend records, and then send them back to the server to update the master copy of the database. One thing you have to consider, however, is how to resolve conflicts between changes to the data you've made, and any changes that might have happened due to other users.

If you think back to the offline code, we used **UpdateBatch** to update the master records, and this will generate errors if any of the records conflicted with underlying recordset changes. There are two ways to investigate this problem:

 Have error trapping in the routine that calls **UpdateBatch**. You can then filter the recordset using **adFilterConflictingRecords** to see which records caused the problem.

 Use the recordset events, and place some code in the **RecordChangeComplete** event. If errors are generated by conflicts, then the recordset will already be filtered for you.

If you choose the latter approach, then your code could look like this:

```
Dim objFld      As ADODB.Field

If adStatus = adStatusErrorsOccurred Then
    Print cRecords & " caused errors.:"
    For Each objFld In pRecordset.Fields
        Debug.Print "Name"; vbTab; objFld.Name
        Debug.Print "Value"; vbTab; objFld.Value
        Debug.Print "UV"; vbTab; objFld.UnderlyingValue
        Debug.Print "OV"; vbTab; objFld.OriginalValue
    Next
End If
```

The argument **adStatus** indicates that an error occurred, and **cRecords** identifies the number of records that failed. The recordset, **pRecordset**, is the recordset filtered to show only those conflicting records.

Indexing

ADO 2.0 has introduced the concept of local indexing, for client cursors, and although it's fairly rudimentary at the moment, it can still be quite useful. This is achieved using one of the dynamic properties of the Field object, called **Optimize**. The way it works is that you decide which field you want to index, and then set the **Optimize** property to **True**. For example:

```
Set objField = objRec("au_lname")
objField.Properties("Optimize") = True
```

You don't have to use a separate Field object, as you can just access the properties directly from the recordset's field:

```
objRec("au_lname").Properties("Optimize") = True
```

This creates a local index, which will improve sorting and finding records. Setting the property to **False** will delete the index.

Future versions of ADO are expected to provide an **Indexes** collection and **Index** objects to help us manage, and give us greater control over, local indexes. This is in discussion at the moment, and plans for this have yet to be finalized.

Summary

This chapter has covered some interesting areas, especially those of new records and resolving conflicts. As you can see, ADO is not perfect in these areas, but there are sound reasons why this is so, and we can only expect this to get better. Certainly the issue of new records and the Identity/Autonumber issue is being discussed by Microsoft, and additional features may make it into the next version.

Data shaping is a great feature, and can certainly help to provide a neat structure for hierarchical data. This is especially useful for client side situations, where a permanent connection to the data source is not available, such as a data bound web page.

This is really the end of the main discussion regarding ADO, but there's still one very important area that has yet to be discussed — performance. That's where the next chapter takes us.

Chapter

Performance

This chapter will look at one of the most critical issues for all data store programmers – that of performance. Microsoft stated that one of their goals for ADO was achieving the best performance possible, but during testing, and in the early stages of its release, the newsgroups contained several messages regarding poor performance. What we plan to do here is show you whether or not those criticisms were justified.

Most of the performance statistics were generated using a Test Tool, built especially for this purpose in Visual Basic 5. The source code for this tool is available from the Wrox Press web site, at **webdev.wrox.co.uk/books/1835**, along with a test Access database, some SQL Scripts for creating the test database in SQL Server, and an Access database for logging the results.

This tool is provided as is, with no warranty of its fitness for purpose. You can use it as is, or extend it in your own environment. For obvious reasons we can't guarantee the same results on your systems. At the end of this chapter you'll see how this tool works, but we won't look to cover it in depth. It's sole purpose is to run various queries under various conditions, and time them. Not all of the tests were carried out using this tool, and we created several tools just for test purposes. Some of these are also available on the Web site.

The tests were run on a Pentium 166 Toshiba Satellite Pro 460CDT, with 64Mb memory and 2Gb EIDE disk, running NT Workstation 4. All tests were run on this machine, so those involving client cursors don't have the added network lag to contend with. Although this is less realistic, it ensures that only the difference between cursor types is tested, and not the network. This is important because network traffic can vary widely from situation to situation, and it's unlikely that my three machines, all within 10 feet of each other would ever give any kind of useful indication. It would therefore be wrong for me to say 'these timings take into account network usage', when this is quite clearly not the case. So, when running the tests yourself, make sure you allow for this.

We've tried to explain why some of the tests give the results that they do, although in some cases this is not possible, simply because we don't know what OLEDB and the providers are actually doing underneath. It would be nice to have these details explained, but as an ADO programmer it's not really necessary. As long as we know which mechanisms to use to give us best performance, and have a way of testing that, we should be relatively happy.

Cursor Type, Location, Locking

Three questions that both beginning and experienced users often ask are:

- What's the best cursor type to use?
- Should I use server-side or client-side cursors?
- What locking scheme should I use?

Like many design questions the answer is always the same: it depends. The cursor type and location that you choose will not only affect performance, but also the functionality. So, whilst in some cases it's easy to establish a particular cursor type as the fastest, it may not be the type to suit your particular business needs.

OLEDB Driver for Jet

The chart below shows the results from opening and closing a table, using the OLEDB Driver for Access. The code used in this test is simple:

```
objRec.Open "table_name", objConn
objRec.Close
```

This is the only bit of the code that was timed, with the various locking modes and cursor types being added to the **Open** command. This was run 10 times (that is we did the Open/Close ten times), and the average taken. All of the tests were done this way, taking an average, to ensure that the first run didn't distort the results because of data not being cached. Times are given in milliseconds, so the lower the number, the better.

Server-Side Cursors

The following figures were produced using server-side cursors, with a table holding 100 rows.

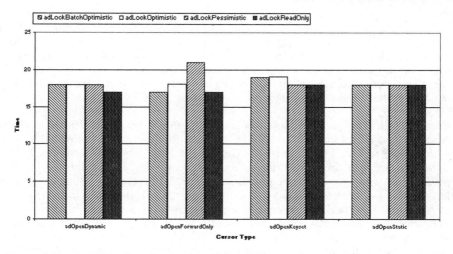

You might wonder why there is so little difference between the cursor types, unless you recall that, when using server-side cursors, Access only supports static cursors. No matter what cursor type you request, Access will always return a static cursor. You might think that larger tables would have an impact, but the times are almost exactly the same, even for a table of the same type with 100,000 records!

The lack of difference in speed when using larger tables is because, if you are using server-side cursors, only the first batch of data is read into the recordset. Consequently, it doesn't matter how many records there are when you open the table. And that's an important point. This test is essentially just opening and closing the table, without reading any data in.

Client-Side Cursors

The following chart shows the speed using client-side cursors, with the test table holding 100 rows.

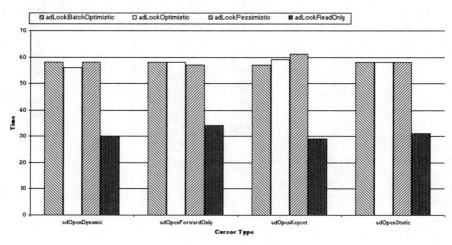

You can see that client-side cursors are much slower than server-side ones, as much as three times slower in some cases. Relatively, however, cursors with no locking, are faster than the other cursor types. Client-side cursors are inherently slower because they actually copy the data into a cache on the local machine, using the memory and disk space if necessary. This is why they are named client-side cursors, because the cursor facility is located in the central OLEDB handler, rather than being provided by the data store.

Comparing locking cursors, you can see that using a read-only cursor is almost twice as fast as the other two locking types, optimistic and pessimistic, between which there is very little difference. The graphs also suggest that there's little difference between the cursor types. You might wonder at this, but if you realize that when locking is required, the OLEDB Provider for Jet only supports keyset cursors. Therefore, whatever cursor type you request, you'll always get a keyset back. The **Errors** collection of the Connection may well have a warning indicating that the cursor type is different from that requested, although this will depend upon the provider. For read-only access, you should get what you ask for, except that Jet doesn't support dynamic cursors, providing instead a static cursor.

The reasons for the time differences between read-only and updateable locking should be fairly clear. With read-only cursors, Jet can stream out the data, without having to keep track of the records, as it knows that no changes will ever take place. This is obviously going to be faster than trying to keep track of the changes. The fact that, for updateable cursors, the cursor type has to be changed can be ignored, because you can see that for a keyset cursor the timings are approximately the same.

So have a look at the same test with 1000 rows:

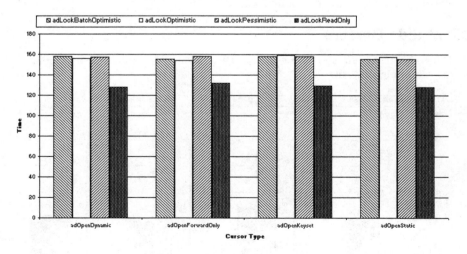

Again, not much difference between the locking types, although the difference in speed between read-only access and read/write is not as marked. The overall times have increased, reflecting that much more data is being pushed to the client, as compared to the server-side cursors, where there was little difference.

With 50,000 records, the result looks like this:

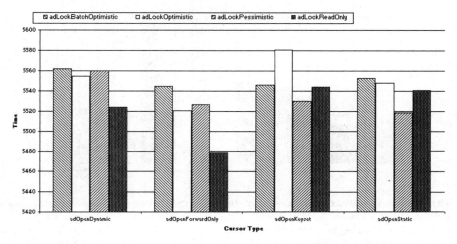

Now we see some more interesting results, with a much greater variation between the various cursor types and locking mechanisms. Again, the average times have increased to reflect the amount of data.

Since Access is using the same cursor types, this must be due purely to the amount of data, but remember, this is just opening and closing the recordset. We're not fetching any data. What's particularly interesting is that for keyset and static cursors, pessimistic locking is now faster than read-only mode. We're not entirely sure why this is so.

OLEDB Driver for SQL Server

The same tests for SQL Server show remarkably different results. Again, these are comprised of opening and closing a recordset 10 times, then taking the average figure.

Server-Side Cursors

SQL Server provides full support for server-side cursors, a fact that can be easily identified by using SQL Trace when running queries, since instead of just returning the data, it performs an **sp_cursoropen** on the requested data.

> *SQL Trace is a tool supplied with SQL Server that allows you to monitor requests being made to SQL Server.* **sp_cursoropen** *is an in-built stored procedure in SQL Server that creates a server side cursor, and provides cursor management.*

The following figure shows the results for a table of 100 rows.

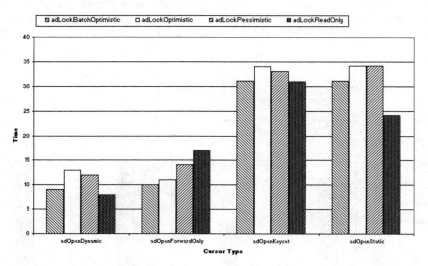

This shows a dramatic improvement in performance when using dynamic and forward-only cursors. This is because both keyset and static cursors require a copy of the data to be put into `tempdb` in the SQL Server before the cursor is created. In fact, a keyset cursor only puts the keys and the first buffer full of data into temporary storage. If you use SQL Trace you'll spot a lot more activity for keyset and static cursors. You can see how this has a marked effect as the number of rows increase. For a table with 1000 rows, the change is significant.

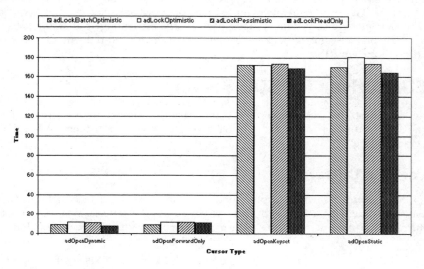

Wow! The figures for dynamic and forward-only are extremely close to the results for 100 rows, as they are for 50,000 rows, but keyset and static cursors have to cope with this huge data overhead. Not only does this affect the speed at which the cursor is opened, but also the performance of SQL Server. Consider an application using server-side cursors to open static cursors. Now imagine the same application with 10 users, or 20. A temporary table will be created for each user. The available space in `tempdb` is decreased and other actions that require temporary space will have less room to work with.

Client-Side Cursors

So how does this compare with client-side cursors, given that all the client-side cursor types were slower in Jet? For the initial test of 100 rows we get the following figures:

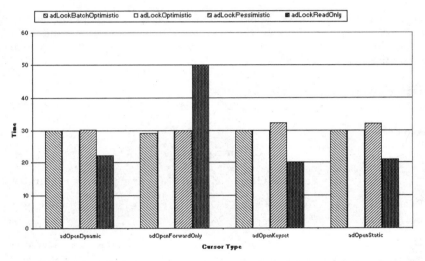

These seem to bear out what we know about client cursors. Overall, the performance is close for all cursor types and lock types, and this remains so as we scale table up to 50,000 rows. On the other hand, the overall speed is slower than server-based dynamic and forward-only cursors (as expected) because all of the data is returned to the client.

> *If you want to learn more about SQL Server cursor types and how they are used, then by far the best description can be found in Inside Microsoft SQL Server 6.5, published by MSPress, ISBN 1-57231-331-5. In fact, this book is full of extremely useful information for the SQL Server developer.*

OLEDB Driver for ODBC

For ODBC, the tests show similar results for the cursor types, locations, and locking mechanisms. We'll be contrasting the OLEDB Driver for ODBC against the native driver later in this chapter.

Cursor Summary

Despite the figures you've seen so far, it's not always possible to use the faster method because this may not meet your needs. Although server-side cursors are quicker to open, they don't always provide the same functionality that client-side cursors do, and cannot be used if you need to disconnect your recordsets. In the n-tier world of client-server development you may well be using disconnected recordsets to pass data between the various tiers in your application, so you'll have to use client cursors. If this is the case, then you want to minimize the amount of data being passed around.

With locking, you can see that in most cases read-only mode is faster, as you would expect. Use this to your advantage if you are just providing data browsing capabilities.

You've seen that the cursor type you actually get might not be the one you requested – this depends upon the provider, the cursor location, and the locking mechanism used. The following tables describe the cursor type that you receive according to these conditions.

OLEDB Provider for SQL Server

adUseServer

		Cursor type requested			
		Forward-Only	Keyset	Dynamic	Static
Lock Type	Read-Only	Forward-Only	Dynamic	Dynamic	Static
	Pessimistic	Forward-Only	Dynamic	Dynamic	Dynamic
	Optimistic	Forward-Only	Dynamic	Dynamic	Dynamic
	BatchOptimistic	Forward-Only	Dynamic	Dynamic	Dynamic

adUseClient

		Cursor type requested			
		Forward-Only	Keyset	Dynamic	Static
Lock Type	Read-Only	Static	Static	Static	Static
	Pessimistic	Static	Static	Static	Static
	Optimistic	Static	Static	Static	Static
	BatchOptimistic	Static	Static	Static	Static

OLEDB Provider for Jet

adUseServer

Cursor type requested

		Forward-Only	Keyset	Dynamic	Static
Lock Type	Read-Only	Forward-Only	Keyset	Static	Static
	Pessimistic	Keyset	Keyset	Keyset	Keyset
	Optimistic	Keyset	Keyset	Keyset	Keyset
	BatchOptimistic	Keyset	Keyset	Keyset	Keyset

adUseClient

Cursor type requested

		Forward-Only	Keyset	Dynamic	Static
Lock Type	Read-Only	Static	Static	Static	Static
	Pessimistic	Static	Static	Static	Static
	Optimistic	Static	Static	Static	Static
	BatchOptimistic	Static	Static	Static	Static

OLEDB Provider for ODBC with SQL Server

adUseServer

Cursor type requested

		Forward-Only	Keyset	Dynamic	Static
Lock Type	Read-Only	Forward-Only	Static	Dynamic	Static
	Pessimistic	Forward-Only	Static	Dynamic	Static
	Optimistic	Forward-Only	Static	Dynamic	Static
	BatchOptimistic	Forward-Only	Static	Dynamic	Static

adUseClient

Cursor type requested

		Forward-Only	Keyset	Dynamic	Static
Lock Type	Read-Only	Static	Static	Static	Static
	Pessimistic	Static	Static	Static	Static
	Optimistic	Static	Static	Static	Static
	BatchOptimistic	Static	Static	Static	Static

OLEDB Provider for ODBC with Access

adUseServer

Cursor type requested

		Forward-Only	Keyset	Dynamic	Static
Lock Type	Read-Only	Forward-Only	Keyset	Keyset	Static
	Pessimistic	Forward-Only	Keyset	Keyset	Keyset
	Optimistic	Forward-Only	Keyset	Keyset	Keyset
	BatchOptimistic	Forward-Only	Keyset	Keyset	Keyset

adUseClient

Cursor type requested

		Forward-Only	Keyset	Dynamic	Static
Lock Type	Read-Only	Static	Static	Static	Static
	Pessimistic	Static	Static	Static	Static
	Optimistic	Static	Static	Static	Static
	BatchOptimistic	Static	Static	Static	Static

Moving through Records

Since you very rarely just open and close a recordset, we need to look at moving through records, where the cursor type and mode can also have an impact on performance. The opening and closing of the recordset were not included as part of the timing, so this just includes the movement, and because we are comparing movement methods we will only consider one cursor and lock type.

There are two main ways of getting at the data in a recordset. The first is to use **MoveNext** to move from one end of the recordset to the other, and the second is to **GetRows** to read the data into an array. **GetRows** can also be used to fetch a smaller number of rows, and then repeating this operation until the whole recordset is read, although this method, called GetRows (chunked) in the graph, is less common. Consider a table of 10,000 rows:

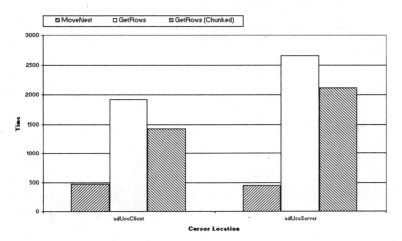

Here you can see that **MoveNext** is clearly the fastest method, but that using **GetRows** with small chunks is faster than trying to retrieve all of the records into an array at once. These results were obtained using SQL Server.

Command and Recordset Options

ADO 2 has introduced **adCmdTableDirect** as one of the options when specifying the command type, to indicate that this tells the provider to return all rows from the table named in **CommandText**. The documentation states that using this will cause some internal code to work differently, but does it make any performance difference?

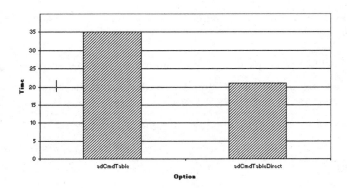

Well it seems so. This test, using SQL Server, was the open/close test using a client-side cursor. With a server-side cursor there was a less marked difference between the two, but the new option does make a difference.

Another new option is **adExecuteNoRecords**, which tells ADO that an action query will not return any records. To test this, the following code was used without the option set:

```
strSQL = "UPDATE tblOneThousand SET TextField = TextField"
Set oRec = oConn.Execute(strSQL, , adCmdText)
```

and compared against code with the extra option added in:

```
Set oRec = oConn.Execute(strSQL, , adCmdText + adExecuteNoRecords)
```

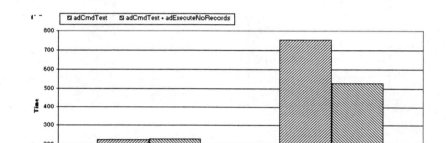

This shows that for Access **adExecuteNoRecords** makes very little difference, but does have a marked effect when using SQL Server. Whilst this test might not be a command that you perform frequently, it does show that this new option can speed up action queries.

Stored Procedure or Direct SQL?

Many people often put SQL statements directly into their programs for a couple of reasons:

 They feel it keeps everything required to run the program together.

 They are unsure about stored procedures and the benefits they can bring.

228

However, using stored procedures not only allows you to alter them without affecting your program, but brings the performance advantage of compiled SQL. When you run SQL statements they are parsed by SQL Server, and then executed, the SQL engine has to carry this every time the statement is used. When you create a stored procedure, the SQL is converted into a compiled form, eliminating this step when the procedure is run. Additionally, stored procedures are placed into a procedure cache, which is an in-memory store of the compiled SQL, improving performance even more.

You can bring the stored procedure benefit to straight SQL text strings, by setting the **Prepared** property of the **Command** object before execution, but this is only useful if you intend to run the command several times. With **Prepared** set to True, the first time the command is run, a temporary stored procedure is created, and subsequent runs of the command will use the stored procedure. So the first run will be slower, but later runs quicker.

The following graph shows the difference between a SQL statement and a stored procedure. The SQL in both cases was:

```
SELECT * FROM tblOneThousand
```

The SQL was run using the Connection object's Execute method, 10 times in a row. This process was repeated three times.

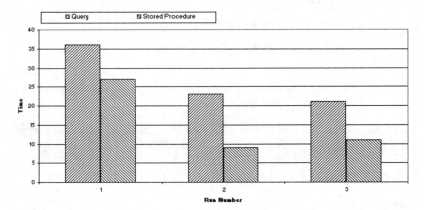

As you can see in each case the stored procedure is quicker. Notice that on the first run it is quicker because the SQL statements do not have to be compiled. On the second run the SQL statement has improved because the data is now in the data cache, but the stored procedure has improved too, probably because of the procedure cache. Continual runs of this narrowed the performance gap between queries and stored procedures considerably.

Parameters

When I started using ADO I had a lot of trouble using Parameters, partly because of the data types. I then discovered **Refresh** and used this during development to print out details of what the parameters should be. If you use SQL Trace when connecting to SQL Server, you can clearly see that using **Refresh** can have a big overhead as it makes a trip back to the server to get the parameters. However, I did wonder what the speed difference was between the following three methods:

- Using the **Parameters** collection.
- Using the **Parameters** argument of the Command's **Execute** method.
- Using direct SQL.

The following test used the pubs database supplied with SQL Server. The stored procedure contains the following commands:

```
CREATE PROCEDURE usp_SalesTest
    @iQty        int,
    @sPayTerms   varchar(12)
AS
    SELECT    *
    FROM      sales
    WHERE     qty = @iQty
    OR        payterms = @sPayTerms
```

The parameters to be searched for will be **20** for the quantity and **Net 60** for the payment terms.

A Command object was created for all three tests, giving us three sections of code. For the direct SQL statement it was:

```
oCmd.CommandText = "SELECT * FROM sales WHERE qty=60 OR payterms='Net 60'"
oCmd.CommandType = adCmdText
Set oRec = oCmd.Execute
```

Passing the parameters into the **Execute** method it was:

```
oCmd.CommandText = "usp_SalesTest"
oCmd.CommandType = adCmdStoredProc
Set oRec = oCmd.Execute(, Array(20, "Net 60"))
```

And to create **Parameters**:

```
oCmd.CommandText = "usp_SalesTest"
oCmd.CommandType = adCmdStoredProc
oCmd.Parameters.Append oCmd.CreateParameter("@iQty", adInteger, _
                            adParamInput, 8, 20)
oCmd.Parameters.Append oCmd.CreateParameter("@sPayTerms", adVarChar, _
                            adParamInput, 12, "Net 60")
Set oRec = oCmd.Execute
```

Again these were run 10 times and the average taken, and each set of runs executed three times:

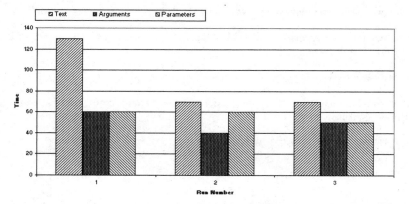

You can see that a stored procedure is faster than the text method. However, the difference between using parameters or passing the arguments into the **Execute** method isn't very large. The **Parameter** method has the advantage of making the parameters explicit, and of course you have to use this method if you require output parameters.

Native Providers and the ODBC Provider

ADO 2 has brought us native OLEDB providers for SQL Server and Access, and we were curious to see whether they really did improve performance by removing the ODBC layer. Let's first compare connection opening, using the following connection strings:

For the native OLEDB provider for SQL Server, SQLOLEDB, we used the connection string:

```
Provider=SQLOLEDB; Data Source=Piglet; Initial Catalog=pubs;
                  User Id=sa; Password=
```

For the OLDB provider for ODBC, connecting to SQL Server, the connect string was:

```
Driver={SQL Server}; Server=Piglet; Database=pubs; UID=sa; PWD=
```

For the OLDB provider for ODBC, connecting to SQL Server via a DSN, the connect string was:

```
DSN=pubs
```

For Microsoft Access, using the OLEDB provider for Jet, the connection string was:

```
Provider=Microsoft.Jet.OLEDB.3.51; Data Source=c:\temp\pubs.mdb
```

For Microsoft Access, using the OLEDB provider for ODBC, the connection string was:

```
Driver={Microsoft Access Driver (*.mdb)}; DBQ=c:\temp\pubs.mdb
```

For Microsoft Access, using the OLEDB provider for ODBC, via a DSN, the connection string was:

```
DSN=AccessPubs
```

Both of the DSNs were set up as system DSNs. These connection strings gave the times as follows:

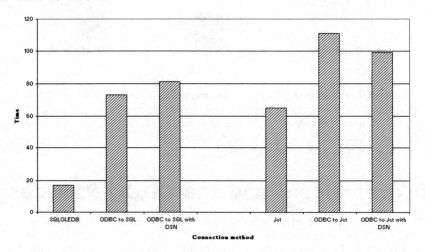

This shows that the native providers do connect more quickly. Using a DSN is interesting, because when you do this, your registry is searched for the connection details, and will most likely cause extra reading of the disc. This is an added overhead that you could skip by using the connection details directly in the connection string. Interestingly enough, the DSN connection to Jet seemed to work quicker than the ODBC connection string method.

So if connecting is quicker using the native providers, what about moving through the records? For 1000 records using client-side cursors we get the following:

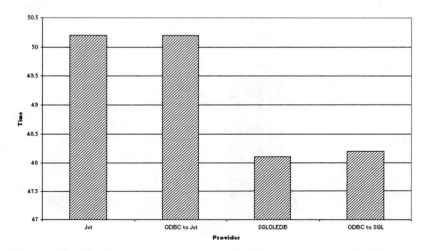

There's clearly not much difference between the ODBC and native drivers. For server-side cursors it's a different matter though:

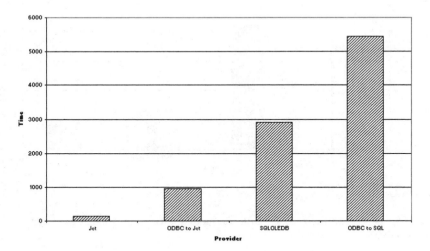

Here, the native drivers, Jet and SQLOLEDB are considerably quicker.

ADO and DAO

On the ADO newsgroup there has been the occasional claim that ADO is not as fast as DAO. This is an important point, considering the amount of existing DAO code, and the fact that Microsoft has stated that future versions of DAO will only be bug fixes. Let's try the connection open/close test:

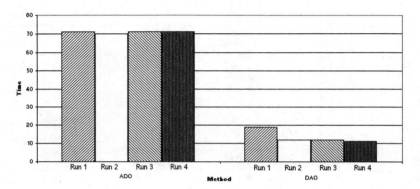

This clearly proves that the kvetchers have a point. Connecting to an Access database via ADO is definitely slower. How about opening recordsets:

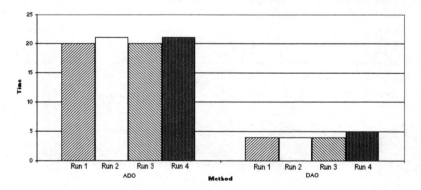

A similar story.

So ADO is slower than DAO, but we have to consider some other factors. A bit of plea bargaining, if you like:

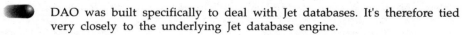

DAO was built specifically to deal with Jet databases. It's therefore tied very closely to the underlying Jet database engine.

ADO is designed for heterogeneous use, supporting different data stores. It's got a better object model, has better support for certain database features, and is easier to program.

Whilst that's hardly a case that will tie up a grand jury, bear those two points in mind. If you want to code for the future, then use ADO. It's not unrealistic to expect that performance in future versions of the OLEDB driver for Jet will improve.

However, if you have a lot of legacy code, or you know that you will only ever deal with an Access database, and these small speed considerations are important, then use DAO. But bear in mind its future.

Connection Pooling

Recently, the subject of connection pooling was brought up on the ADO newsgroup. The documentation states that to free a connection you should set the connection variable to **Nothing**. However, the question arose as to whether this cleared the connection from the pool of connections, and therefore had a detrimental effect on performance. So, using the Open/Close method again, using SQL Server, we'll try it with and without clearing the memory, and see if that has an impact. For the first test, the code was as follows:

```
objConn.Open sConn
objConn.Close
```

And for the second:

```
objConn.Open sConn
objConn.Close
Set objConn = Nothing
```

The figures were as follows:

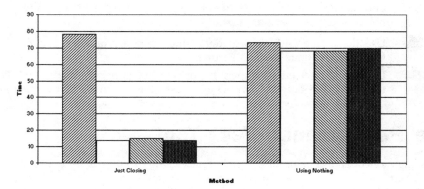

Once again the open/close was run 10 times, and then each batch four times. The figures above clearly show that, after the first time, just closing the recordset is considerably faster, whereas setting the connection object variable to **Nothing** produces very similar figures for all four batches. But does this really answer the question about connection pooling? Setting the object variable to nothing deallocates the COM object, so it could be just the creation of the COM object that is time consuming. If you run SQL Trace whilst testing this, you'll see that for the first test only one connection is made. However for the second connection, there are ten connections in a row, and ten disconnections.

In fact, if you put the two pieces of code on two separate command buttons and watch SQL Trace as you press them you'll see that for the first code, where we just open and close the recordset, SQL Trace just shows a connection without a disconnection. Pressing the button again doesn't show another connection because the first is still active and held in the pool. If you don't press a button for 60 seconds you'll see the disconnection. With the second command button, where we set the object variable to **Nothing**, each time you press the button you get both a connection and a disconnection.

This seems to indicate that setting the variable to **Nothing** does clear the connection from the pool.

Performance Summary

The first thing to remember is that these figures only show certain traits, under certain circumstances, so don't rely on them. Perform your own analysis, using your own data and see what results you achieve. You can use this chapter as a guideline for some of the criteria to test.

Having said that, there are some key points we've established from these tests:

- When opening recordsets, server-side cursors are generally quicker than client-side cursors, because less data is initially being transferred.

- If you need to use disconnected recordsets then you'll have to use client-side cursors. In this case, keep the amount of data transferred to a minimum.

- If using SQL Server and server-side cursors, then dynamic or forward-only are more efficient when selecting data. This is because the data is not copied into **tempdb** first.

- Use the native OLEDB providers, since they are quicker, and have more functionality than the ODBC ones.

- Use the correct cursor types. If you are not going to change any data then use read-only cursors. Don't waste the resources of the data store.

The Performance Test Tool

As mentioned at the beginning of this chapter, this tool is intended to help you do your own performance tests. It started as a few small routines to help decide a few issues, and grew into the program available from our website. We considered expanding this into a large test suite and supply it as a fully finished program, but then decided that – as a programmer – this is probably not what you really want, so we've decided to give it away as it stands. Bear in mind that it's far from a complete product, has little or no error handling, and some options that won't work under all conditions. Having said that, it does perform basic tests fairly well.

The opening screen allows you to connect to a data store:

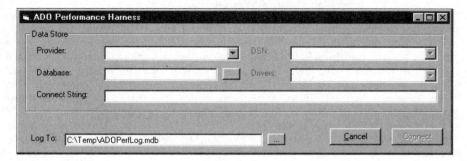

Here you can pick a provider, and if using ODBC, pick a DSN or a driver. The **Connect String** box will supply some default values, and you should overwrite these with your specific values before connecting. The **Log To** box allows you to pick the database to log timings to. Currently this is an Access database, but there's no reason why you couldn't convert the code to use another database.

Once you've connected you get to the main timing screen:

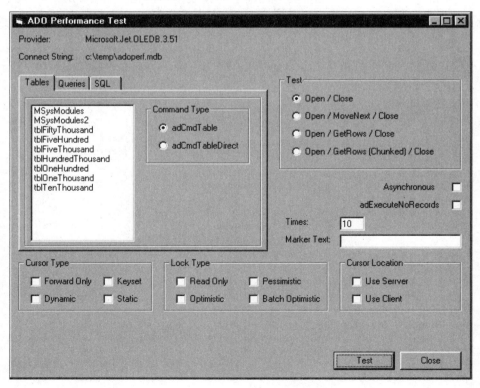

The tab control allows you to select from tables, queries, or your own SQL text. To the right you pick which test you want to run, but remember that some of these may not be suitable for SQL queries that don't return recordsets. Below this you can select whether records are to be returned. The asynchronous option isn't implemented, and was added to give you the opportunity to supply this. You can specify the number of times that the test is run, and add some marker text (to be written to the logging database) so that you can identify individual tests. At the bottom of the screen you can pick the cursor type, lock type, and cursor location. At least one of each of these must be picked to run a test, and you can pick more options to allow several tests to be compared.

The logging database just consists of one simple table into which the results are written. The graphs in this chapter were produced by pulling the figures from this table into Excel; it's often easier to appreciate the performance differences in visual form, so you may wish to consider doing the same.

Summary

In this chapter, we've shown you the results of our experimentation with the various options available in ADO 2.0. In particular, we've looked at the performance implications of using different data providers, as well as the often significant differences given by the various cursor types and locking options. In finishing, we discussed the VB tool we ran the tests with, and encouraged you to download it from the samples page for this book on our website, www.webdev.wrox.co.uk, for your own use and customization.

With this consideration of the performance implications of ADO 2.0, our discussion of ADO is complete. The appendices following this chapter are intended to provide a reference for using ADO 2.0; the documentation Microsoft supply is not quite complete, and wherever possible we have tried to include undocumented features.

ADO Object Summary

Microsoft ActiveX Data Objects 2.0 Library Reference

> All properties are read/write unless otherwise stated.

Objects

Name	Description
Command	A Command object is a definition of a specific command that you intend to execute against a data source.
Connection	A Connection object represents an open connection to a data store.
Error	An Error object contains the details about data access errors pertaining to a single operation involving the provider.
Errors	The Errors collection contains all of the Error objects created in response to a single failure involving the provider.
Field	A Field object represents a column of data within a common data type.
Fields	A Fields collection contains all of the Field objects of a Recordset object.
Parameter	A Parameter object represents a parameter or argument associated with a Command object based on a parameterized query or stored procedure.
Parameters	A Parameters collection contains all the Parameter objects of a Command object.

Name	Description
Properties	A Properties collection contains all the Property objects for a specific instance of an object.
Property	A Property object represents a dynamic characteristic of an ADO object that is defined by the provider.
Recordset	A Recordset object represents the entire set of records from a base table or the results of an executed command. At any time, the Recordset object only refers to a single record within the set as the current record.

Command Object

Methods

Name	Returns	Description
Cancel		Cancels execution of a pending Execute or Open call.
CreateParameter	Parameter	Creates a new Parameter object.
Execute	Recordset	Executes the query, SQL statement, or stored procedure specified in the CommandText property.

Properties

Name	Returns	Description
ActiveConnection	Variant	Indicates to which Connection object the command currently belongs.
CommandText	String	Contains the text of a command to be issued against a data provider.
CommandTimeout	Long	Indicates how long to wait, in seconds, while executing a command before terminating the command and generating an error. Default is 30.
CommandType	CommandType Enum	Indicates the type of Command object.
Name	String	Indicates the name of the Command object.

Name	Returns	Description
Parameters	Parameters	Contains all of the **Parameter** objects for a **Command** object.
Prepared	Boolean	Indicates whether or not to save a compiled version of a command before execution.
Properties	Properties	Contains all of the **Property** objects for a **Command** object.
State	Long	Describes whether the **Command** object is open or closed. Read only.

Connection Object

Methods

Name	Returns	Description
BeginTrans	Integer	Begins a new transaction.
Cancel		Cancels the execution of a pending, asynchronous **Execute** or **Open** operation.
Close		Closes an open connection and any dependant objects.
CommitTrans		Saves any changes and ends the current transaction.
Execute	Recordset	Executes the query, SQL statement, stored procedure, or provider specific text.
Open		Opens a connection to a data source, so that commands can be executed against it.
OpenSchema	Recordset	Obtains database schema information from the provider.
RollbackTrans		Cancels any changes made during the current transaction and ends the transaction.

Properties

Name	Returns	Description
Attributes	Long	Indicates one or more characteristics of a **Connection** object. Default is 0.
CommandTimeout	Long	Indicates how long, in seconds, to wait while executing a command before terminating the command and generating an error. The default is 30.
ConnectionString	String	Contains the information used to establish a connection to a data source.
ConnectionTimeout	Long	Indicates how long, in seconds, to wait while establishing a connection before terminating the attempt and generating an error. Default is 15.
CursorLocation	CursorLocation Enum	Sets or returns the location of the cursor engine.
DefaultDatabase	String	Indicates the default database for a **Connection** object.
Errors	Errors	Contains all of the **Error** objects created in response to a single failure involving the provider.
IsolationLevel	IsolationLevel Enum	Indicates the level of transaction isolation for a **Connection** object. Write only.
Mode	ConnectMode Enum	Indicates the available permissions for modifying data in a **Connection**.
Properties	Properties	Contains all of the **Property** objects for a **Connection** object.
Provider	String	Indicates the name of the provider for a **Connection** object.
State	Long	Describes whether the **Connection** object is open or closed. Read only.
Version	String	Indicates the ADO version number. Read only.

Events

Name	Description
BeginTransComplete	Fired after a **BeginTrans** operation finishes executing.
CommitTransComplete	Fired after a **CommitTrans** operation finishes executing.
ConnectComplete	Fired after a connection starts.
Disconnect	Fired after a connection ends.
ExecuteComplete	Fired after a command has finished executing.
InfoMessage	Fired whenever a **ConnectionEvent** operation completes successfully and additional information is returned by the provider.
RollbackTransComplete	Fired after a **RollbackTrans** operation finished executing.
WillConnect	Fired before a connection starts.
WillExecute	Fired before a pending command executes on the connection.

Error Object

Properties

Name	Returns	Description
Description	String	A description string associated with the error. Read only.
HelpContext	Integer	Indicates the **ContextID** in the help file for the associated error. Read only.
HelpFile	String	Indicates the name of the help file. Read only.
NativeError	Long	Indicates the provider-specific error code for the associated error. Read only.
Number	Long	Indicates the number that uniquely identifies an **Error** object. Read only.

Name	Returns	Description
Source	String	Indicates the name of the object or application that originally generated the error. Read only.
SQLState	String	Indicates the SQL state for a given **Error** object. It is a five-character string that follows the ANSI SQL standard. Read only.

Errors Collection

Methods

Name	Returns	Description
Clear		Removes all of the **Error** objects from the **Errors** collection.
Refresh		Updates the **Error** objects with information from the provider.

Properties

Name	Returns	Description
Count	Long	Indicates the number of **Error** objects in the **Errors** collection. Read only.
Item	Error	Allows indexing into the **Errors** collection to reference a specific **Error** object. Read only.

Field Object

Methods

Name	Returns	Description
AppendChunk		Appends data to a large or binary **Field** object.
GetChunk	Variant	Returns all or a portion of the contents of a large or binary **Field** object.

Properties

Name	Returns	Description
ActualSize	Long	Indicates the actual length of a field's value. Read only.
Attributes	Long	Indicates one or more characteristics of a **Field** object.
DataFormat	Variant	Write only.
DefinedSize	Long	Indicates the defined size of the **Field** object. Write only.
Name	String	Indicates the name of the **Field** object.
NumericScale	Byte	Indicates the scale of numeric values for the **Field** object. Write only.
OriginalValue	Variant	Indicates the value of a **Field** object that existed in the record before any changes were made. Read only.
Precision	Byte	Indicates the degree of precision for numeric values in the **Field** object. Read only.
Properties	Properties	Contains all of the **Property** objects for a **Field** object.
Type	DataTypeEnum	Indicates the data type of the **Field** object.
UnderlyingValue	Variant	Indicates a **Field** object's current value in the database. Read only.
Value	Variant	Indicates the value assigned to the **Field** object.

247

Fields Collection

Methods

Name	Returns	Description
Append		Appends a **Field** object to the **Fields** collection.
Delete		Deletes a **Field** object from the **Fields** collection.
Refresh		Updates the **Field** objects in the **Fields** collection.

Properties

Name	Returns	Description
Count	Long	Indicates the number of **Field** objects in the **Fields** collection. Read only.
Item	Field	Allows indexing into the **Fields** collection to reference a specific **Field** object. Read only.

Parameter Object

Methods

Name	Returns	Description
AppendChunk		Appends data to a large or binary **Parameter** object.

Properties

Name	Returns	Description
`Attributes`	Long	Indicates one or more characteristics of a **Parameter** object.
`Direction`	Parameter Direction Enum	Indicates whether the **Parameter** object represents an input parameter, an output parameter, or both, or if the parameter is a return value from a stored procedure.
`Name`	String	Indicates the name of the **Parameter** object.
`NumericScale`	Byte	Indicates the scale of numeric values for the **Parameter** object.
`Precision`	Byte	Indicates the degree of precision for numeric values in the **Parameter** object.
`Properties`	Properties	Contains all of the **Property** objects for a **Parameter** object.
`Size`	Long	Indicates the maximum size, in bytes or characters, of a **Parameter** object.
`Type`	DataTypeEnum	Indicates the data type of the **Parameter** object.
`Value`	Variant	Indicates the value assigned to the **Parameter** object.

Parameters Collection

Methods

Name	Returns	Description
`Append`		Appends a **Parameter** object to the **Parameters** collection.
`Delete`		Deletes a **Parameter** object from the **Parameters** collection.
`Refresh`		Updates the **Parameter** objects in the **Parameters** collection.

Properties

Name	Returns	Description
Count	Long	Indicates the number of **Parameter** objects in the **Parameters** collection. Read only.
Item	Parameter	Allows indexing into the **Parameters** collection to reference a specific **Parameter** object. Read only.

Properties Collection

Methods

Name	Returns	Description
Refresh		Updates the **Property** objects in the **Properties** collection with the details from the provider.

Properties

Name	Returns	Description
Count	Long	Indicates the number of **Property** objects in the **Properties** collection. Read only.
Item	Property	Allows indexing into the **Properties** collection to reference a specific **Property** object. Read only.

Property Object

Properties

Name	Returns	Description
Attributes	Long	Indicates one or more characteristics of a **Property** object.
Name	String	Indicates the name of the **Property** object. Read only.
Type	DataTypeEnum	Indicates the data type of the **Property** object.
Value	Variant	Indicates the value assigned to the **Property** object.

Recordset Object

Methods

Name	Returns	Description
AddNew		Creates a new record for an updateable **Recordset** object.
Cancel		Cancels execution of a pending asynchronous **Open** operation.
CancelBatch		Cancels a pending batch update.
CancelUpdate		Cancels any changes made to the current record, or to a new record prior to calling the **Update** method.
Clone	Recordset	Creates a duplicate **Recordset** object from an existing **Recordset** object.
Close		Closes the **Recordset** object and any dependent objects.
CompareBookmarks	CompareEnum	Compares two bookmarks and returns an indication of the relative values.
Delete		Deletes the current record or group of records.

Name	Returns	Description
`Find`		Searches the `Recordset` for a record that matches the specified criteria.
`GetRows`	Variant	Retrieves multiple records of a `Recordset` object into an array.
`GetString`	String	Returns a `Recordset` as a string.
`Move`		Moves the position of the current record in a `Recordset`.
`MoveFirst`		Moves the position of the current record to the first record in the `Recordset`.
`MoveLast`		Moves the position of the current record to the last record in the `Recordset`.
`MoveNext`		Moves the position of the current record to the next record in the `Recordset`.
`MovePrevious`		Moves the position of the current record to the previous record in the `Recordset`.
`NextRecordset`	Recordset	Clears the current `Recordset` object and returns the next `Recordset` by advancing through a series of commands.
`Open`		Opens a `Recordset`.
`Requery`		Updates the data in a `Recordset` object by re-executing the query on which the object is based.
`Resync`		Refreshes the data in the current `Recordset` object from the underlying database.
`Save`		Saves the `Recordset` to a file.
`Supports`	Boolean	Determines whether a specified `Recordset` object supports particular functionality.
`Update`		Saves any changes made to the current `Recordset` object.
`UpdateBatch`		Writes all pending batch updates to disk.

Properties

Name	Returns	Description
AbsolutePage	PositionEnum	Specifies in which page the current record resides.
AbsolutePosition	PositionEnum	Specifies the ordinal position of a **Recordset** object's current record.
ActiveCommand	Object	Indicates the **Command** object that created the associated **Recordset** object. Read only.
ActiveConnection	Variant	Indicates to which **Connection** object the specified **Recordset** object currently belongs.
BOF	Boolean	Indicates whether the current record is before the first record in a **Recordset** object. Read only.
Bookmark	Variant	Returns a bookmark that uniquely identifies the current record in a **Recordset** object, or sets the current record to the record identified by a valid bookmark.
CacheSize	Long	Indicates the number of records from a **Recordset** object that are cached locally in memory.
CursorLocation	CursorLocation Enum	Sets or returns the location of the cursor engine.
CursorType	CursorType Enum	Indicates the type of cursor used in a **Recordset** object.
DataMember	String	Specifies the name of the data member to retrieve from the object referenced by the **DataSource** property. Write only.
DataSource	Object	Specifies an object containing data to be represented as a **Recordset** object. Write only.
EditMode	EditModeEnum	Indicates the editing status of the current record. Read only.
EOF	Boolean	Indicates whether the current record is after the last record in a **Recordset** object. Read only.
Fields	Fields	Contains all of the **Field** objects for the current **Recordset** object.
Filter	Variant	Indicates a filter for data in the **Recordset**.

Name	Returns	Description
LockType	LockTypeEnum	Indicates the type of locks placed on records during editing.
MarshalOptions	MarshalOptions Enum	Indicates which records are to be marshaled back to the server.
MaxRecords	Long	Indicates the maximum number of records to return to a **Recordset** object from a query. Default is zero (no limit).
PageCount	Long	Indicates how many pages of data the **Recordset** object contains. Read only.
PageSize	Long	Indicates how many records constitute one page in the Recordset.
Properties	Properties	Contains all of the **Property** objects for the current **Recordset** object.
RecordCount	Long	Indicates the current number of records in the **Recordset** object. Read only.
Sort	String	Specifies one or more field names the Recordset is sorted on, and the direction of the sort.
Source	String	Indicates the source for the data in a **Recordset** object.
State	Long	Indicates whether the recordset is open, closed, or whether it is executing an asynchronous operation. Read only.
Status	Integer	Indicates the status of the current record with respect to match updates or other bulk operations. Read only.
StayInSync	Boolean	Indicates, in a hierarchical **Recordset** object, whether the parent row should change when the set of underlying child records changes. Read only.

Events

Name	Description
EndOfRecordset	Fired when there is an attempt to move to a row past the end of the **Recordset**.
FetchComplete	Fired after all the records in an asynchronous operation have been retrieved into the **Recordset**.
FetchProgress	Fired periodically during a length asynchronous operation, to report how many rows have currently been retrieved.
FieldChangeComplete	Fired after the value of one or more **Field** objects has been changed.
MoveComplete	Fired after the current position in the **Recordset** changes.
RecordChangeComplete	Fired after one or more records change.
RecordsetChangeComplete	Fired after the **Recordset** has changed.
WillChangeField	Fired before a pending operation changes the value of one or more **Field** objects.
WillChangeRecord	Fired before one or more rows in the **Recordset** change.
WillChangeRecordset	Fired before a pending operation changes the **Recordset**.
WillMove	Fired before a pending operation changes the current position in the **Recordset**.

Method Calls Quick Reference

Command

Command.Cancel
Parameter = *Command*.CreateParameter(*Name As String, Type As DataTypeEnum, Direction As ParameterDirectionEnum, Size As Integer, [Value As Variant]*)
Recordset = *Command*.Execute(*RecordsAffected As Variant, Parameters As Variant, Options As Integer*)

Connection

Integer = *Connection*.BeginTrans
Connection.Cancel
Connection.Close
Connection.CommitTrans
Recordset = *Connection*.Execute(*CommandText As String, RecordsAffected As Variant, Options As Integer*)
Connection.Open(*ConnectionString As String, UserID As String, Password As String, Options As Integer*)
Recordset = *Connection*.OpenSchema(*Schema As SchemaEnum, [Restrictions As Variant], [SchemaID As Variant]*)
Connection.RollbackTrans

Errors

Errors.Clear
Errors.Refresh

Field

Field.AppendChunk(*Data As Variant*)
Variant = *Field*.GetChunk(*Length As Integer*)

Fields

Fields.Append(*Name As String, Type As DataTypeEnum, DefinedSize As Integer, Attrib As FieldAttributeEnum*)
Fields.Delete(*Index As Variant*)
Fields.Refresh

Parameter

Parameter.AppendChunk(*Val As Variant*)

Parameters

Parameters.Append(*Object As Object*)
Parameters.Delete(*Index As Variant*)
Parameters.Refresh

Properties

Properties.Refresh

Recordset

Recordset.AddNew(*[FieldList As Variant], [Values As Variant]*)
Recordset.Cancel
Recordset.CancelBatch(*AffectRecords As AffectEnum*)
Recordset.CancelUpdate
Recordset = *Recordset*.Clone(*LockType As LockTypeEnum*)
Recordset.Close
CompareEnum = *Recordset*.CompareBookmarks(*Bookmark1 As Variant, Bookmark2 As Variant*)
Recordset.Delete(*AffectRecords As AffectEnum*)
Recordset.Find(*Criteria As String, SkipRecords As Integer, SearchDirection As SearchDirectionEnum, [Start As Variant]*)
Variant = *Recordset*.GetRows(*Rows As Integer, [Start As Variant], [Fields As Variant]*)
String = *Recordset*.GetString(*StringFormat As StringFormatEnum, NumRows As Integer, ColumnDelimiter As String, RowDelimiter As String, NullExpr As String*)
Recordset.Move(*NumRecords As Integer, [Start As Variant]*)
Recordset.MoveFirst
Recordset.MoveLast
Recordset.MoveNext
Recordset.MovePrevious
Recordset = *Recordset*.NextRecordset(*[RecordsAffected As Variant]*)
Recordset.Open(*Source As Variant, ActiveConnection As Variant, CursorType As CursorTypeEnum, LockType As LockTypeEnum, Options As Integer*)
Recordset.Requery(*Options As Integer*)
Recordset.Resync(*AffectRecords As AffectEnum, ResyncValues As ResyncEnum*)
Recordset.Save(*FileName As String, PersistFormat As PersistFormatEnum*)
Boolean = *Recordset*.Supports(*CursorOptions As CursorOptionEnum*)
Recordset.Update(*[Fields As Variant], [Values As Variant]*)
Recordset.UpdateBatch(*AffectRecords As AffectEnum*)

RDS Object Summary

The Remote Data Service (RDS) provides a series of objects that can be used to access data remotely from a client over HTTP protocol. This section lists the properties, methods and events for two RDS controls—the **RDS/ADC Data Source Object** (DSO) and the **Tabular Data Control** (TDC). It also lists the properties, methods, events and constants for the `DataSpace` and `DataFactory` objects that are used by the RDS/ADC control.

> **All properties are read/write unless otherwise stated.**

The RDS Advanced Data Control (RDS/ADC)

The RDS/ADC Data Control is used on the client to provide Read/Write access to a data store or custom business object on the server. To instantiate the control in a Web page, an `<OBJECT>` tag is used:

```
<OBJECT CLASSID="clsid:BD96C556-65A3-11D0-983A-00C04FC29E33"
        ID="dsoBookList" HEIGHT=0 WIDTH=0>
  <PARAM NAME="Server" VALUE="http://www.yourserver.com">
  <PARAM NAME="Connect" VALUE="DSN=yourdsn;UID=anon;PWD=">
  <PARAM NAME="SQL" VALUE="SELECT * FROM BookList">
</OBJECT>
```

The `<PARAM>` elements are used to set the properties of the control at design time. They can be changed at run-time using script code. The following tables list the properties, methods and events for the control.

Properties

Name	Returns	Description
Connect	String	The data store connection string or DSN.
ExecuteOptions	Integer	Specifies if the control will execute asynchronously. The constant values are listed below.
FetchOptions	Integer	Specifies if the data will be fetched asynchronously. The constant values are listed below.
FilterColumn	String	Name of the column to filter on.
FilterCriterion	String	The criteria for the filter, can be <, <=, >, >=, =, or <>.
FilterValue	String	The value to match values in **FilterColumn** with when filtering.
Handler	String	Specifies the server-side security handler to use with the control if not the default.
InternetTimeout	Long	Indicates the timeout (in milliseconds) for the HTTP connection.
ReadyState	Integer	Indicates the state of the control as data is received. The constant values are listed below. Read only.
Recordset	Object	Provides a reference to the ADO recordset object in use by the control. Read only.
Server	String	Specifies the communication protocol and the address of the server to execute the query on.
SortColumn	String	Name of the column to sort on.
SortDirection	Boolean	The sort direction for the column. The default is ascending order (**True**). Use **False** for descending order.
SourceRecordset	Object	Can be used to bind the control to a different recordset object at run time. Write only.
SQL	String	The SQL statement used to extract the data from the data store.
URL	String	URL to the path of the file.

ExecuteOptions Property Values

Name	Value	Description
adcExecAsync	2	Default - the control returns immediately, allowing the user to work with the page while data is arriving.
adcExecSync	1	The client is suspended until the data has arrived.

FetchOptions Property Values

Name	Value	Description
adcFetchAsync	3	Default - data is fetched asynchronously while the client is executing.
adcFetchBackground	2	The first batch of data is fetched before the control returns execution to the client, then further batches are fetched as required.
adcFetchUpFront	1	All the data is fetched before the control returns execution to the client.

ReadyState Property Values

Name	Value	Description
adcReadyStateComplete	4	All the available data has arrived, or an error occurred preventing (more) data arriving.
adcReadyStateInteractive	3	Data is still arriving from the server.
adcReadyStateLoaded	2	The control is loaded and waiting to fetch data from the server.

Methods

Name	Description
Cancel	Cancels an asynchronous action such as fetching data.
CancelUpdate	Cancels all changes made to the source recordset.
CreateRecordset	Creates and returns an empty, disconnected recordset on the client.
MoveFirst	Moves to the first record in a displayed recordset.

Name	Description
MoveLast	Moves to the last record in a displayed recordset.
MoveNext	Moves to the next record in a displayed recordset.
MovePrevious	Moves to the previous record in a displayed recordset.
Refresh	Refreshes the client-side recordset from the data source.
Reset	Updates the local recordset to reflect current filter and sort criteria.
SubmitChanges	Sends changes to the client-side recordset back to the data store.

Syntax

datacontrol.Cancel
datacontrol.CancelUpdate
(Set) *object* = *datacontrol*.CreateRecordset(*varColumnInfos As Variant*)
datacontrol.Recordset.MoveFirst
datacontrol.Recordset.MoveLast
datacontrol.Recordset.MoveNext
datacontrol.Recordset.MovePrevious
datacontrol.Refresh
datacontrol.Reset(*re-filter As Integer*)
datacontrol.SubmitChanges

Events

Name	Description
onError	Occurs if an error prevents the data being fetched from the server, or a user action being carried out.
onReadyStateChange	Occurs when the value of the **ReadyState** property changes.

Syntax

onError(*StatusCode, Description, Source, CancelDisplay*)
where:
StatusCode is an integer containing the status code of the error.
Description is a string containing a description of the error.
Source is a string containing the query or command that caused the error.
CancelDisplay is a Boolean value that, if set to **True**, prevents an error dialog from appearing.

onReadyStateChange()

The Tabular Data Control

The Tabular Data Control (TDC) uses a formatted text file that is downloaded to the client and exposed there as an ADO recordset. The control cannot be used to update the server data store. To instantiate the control in a Web page, an `<OBJECT>` tag is used:

```
<OBJECT CLASSID="clsid:333C7BC4-460F-11D0-BC04-0080C7055A83"
        ID="dsoBookList" WIDTH=0 HEIGHT=0>
  <PARAM NAME="DataURL" VALUE="/data/booklist.txt">
  <PARAM NAME="FieldDelim" VALUE=";">
  <PARAM NAME="UseHeader" VALUE="true">
  <PARAM NAME="Sort" VALUE="tCategory; -dReleasedate">
  <PARAM NAME="Filter" VALUE="tCode=16-1*" >
  <PARAM NAME="EscapeChar" VALUE="\">
</OBJECT>
```

The `<PARAM>` elements are used to set the properties of the control at design time. They can be changed at run-time using script code. The following tables list the properties, methods and events for the control.

Properties

Name	Returns	Description
AppendData	Boolean	If **True**, specifies that the **Reset** method will attempt to append returned data to the existing recordset rather than replacing the recordset. Default value is **False**.
CaseSensitive	Boolean	Specifies whether string comparisons will be case sensitive. Default is **True**.
CharSet	String	Specifies the character set for the data. Default is **windows-1252** (Western).
DataURL	String	The URL or location of the source text data file.
EscapeChar	String	Single character string that is used to avoid the meaning of the other special characters specified by the **FieldDelim**, **RowDelim**, and **TextQualifier** properties.
FieldDelim	String	Specifies the character in the file that delimits each column (field). Default – if none specified – is a comma. Only a single character may be used.
Filter	String	Specifies the complete filter that will be applied to the data, such as "**Name=Jonson**". An asterisk acts as a wildcard for any set of characters.
FilterColumn	String	Name of the column to filter on. Not supported in all versions of the TDC.

Name	Returns	Description
FilterCriterion	String	The criteria for the filter, can be <, <=, >, >=, =, or <>. Not supported in all versions of the TDC.
FilterValue	String	The value to match values in **FilterColumn** with when filtering. Not supported in all versions of the TDC.
Language	String	Specifies the language of the data file. Default is **en-us** (US English).
ReadyState	Integer	Indicates the state of the control as data is received. The constant values are listed below.
RowDelim	String	Specifies the character in the file that delimits each row (record). Default if not specified is a carriage return. Only a single character may be used.
Sort	String	Specifies the sort order for the data, as a comma-delimited list of column names. Prefix column name with a minus sign (-) for descending order.
SortColumn	String	Name of the column to sort on. Not supported in all versions of the TDC.
SortAscending	Boolean	The sort direction for the column. The default is ascending order (**True**). Use **False** for descending order. Not supported in all versions of the TDC.
TextQualifier	String	The character in the data file used to enclose field values. Default is the double-quote (") character.
UseHeader	Boolean	If **True**, specifies that the first line of the data file is a set of column (field) names and (optionally) the field data type definitions.

ReadyState Property Values

Name	Value	Description
adcReadyStateComplete	4	All the available data has arrived, or an error occurred preventing (more) data arriving.
adcReadyStateInteractive	3	Data is still arriving from the server.
adcReadyStateLoaded	2	The control is loaded, and waiting to fetch data from the server.

Method

Name	Description
Reset	Updates the local recordset to reflect current filter and sort criteria.

Event

Name	Description
onReadyStateChange	Occurs when the value of the ReadyState property changes.

The RDS DataSpace Object

The **DataSpace** object is responsible for caching the recordset on the client, and connecting it to a data source control. To instantiate the object in a Web page, an **<OBJECT>** tag is used:

```
<OBJECT ID="dspDataSpace"
        CLASSID="CLSID:BD96C556-65A3-11D0-983A-00C04FC29E36">
</OBJECT>
```

A **DataSpace** object is also created automatically when a data source object (such as the RDS/ADC) is instantiated. The **DataSpace** object exposes one property and one method:

Property

Name	Returns	Description
InternetTimeout	Long	Indicates the timeout (in milliseconds) for the HTTP connection.

Method

Name	Description
CreateObject	Creates a data factory or custom object of type specified by a class string, at a location specified by the connection (address) parameter.

Syntax

> *variant* = *dataspace*.**CreateObject**(*bstrProgId* **As String**, *bstrConnection* **As String**)

For a connection over HTTP, the connection parameter is the URL of the server, while over DCOM the UNC machine name is used. When the **CreateObject** method is used to create in-process objects, the connection should be a null string.

The RDS DataFactory Object

The **DataFactory** object handles transport of the data from server to client and vice versa. It creates a stub and proxy that can communicate over HTTP. To instantiate the object, the **CreateObject** method of an existing **DataSpace** control is used. The class string for the **DataFactory** object is **RDSServer.DataFactory**, and the address of the server on which the object is to be created must also be provided:

```
<OBJECT ID="dspDataSpace"
        CLASSID="CLSID:BD96C556-65A3-11D0-983A-00C04FC29E36">
</OBJECT>
...
<SCRIPT LANGUAGE="JavaScript">
  <myDataFactory = dspDataSpace.CreateObject("RDSServer.DataFactory",
                                          "http://servername.com");
</SCRIPT>
```

A **DataFactory** object is also created automatically when a data source object (such as the RDS/ADC) is instantiated. The **DataFactory** object provides four methods:

Methods

Name	Returns	Description
ConvertToString	String	Converts a recordset into a MIME64-encoded string.
CreateRecordset	Object	Creates and returns an empty recordset.
Query	Object	Executes a valid SQL string query over a specified connection and returns an ADO recordset object.
SubmitChanges		Marshals the records and submits them to the server for updating the source data store.

Syntax

string = *datafactory*.**ConvertToString**(*recordset* **As Object**)

(**Set**) *recordset* = *datafactory*.**CreateRecordset**(*varColumnInfos As Variant*)

(**Set**) *recordset* = *datafactory*.**Query**(*bstrConnection* **As String,** *bstrQuery* **As String**)

datafactory.**SubmitChanges**(*bstrConnection* **As String,** *pRecordset* **As Object**)

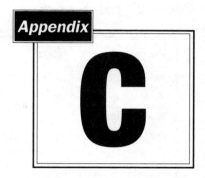

Properties Collection

Property Support

The following table shows a list of all OLEDB properties, and whether they are supported by the three main drivers: the Microsoft OLEDB driver for Jet, the Microsoft OLEDB driver for ODBC, and the Microsoft OLEDB driver for SQL Server. Since this list contains dynamic properties, not every property may show up under all circumstances. Other providers may also implement properties not listed in this table.

A tick indicates the property is supported, and a blank space indicates it is not supported. Note that support for recordset properties may depend upon the locking type, cursor type, and cursor location.

There are some properties that we have had to hazard a guess at for the description. This is because they are undocumented and we've been unable to accurately identify their usage. These are marked with a superscripted hash mark like this [#].

> Note. This list doesn't include the **I**property (such as IRowset, etc) properties. Although these are part of the collection they are not particularly useful for the ADO programmer.

Property	Used	ODBC	Jet	SQL
Access Order	Recordset	✓	✓	✓
Accessible Procedures	Connection	✓		
Accessible Tables	Connection	✓		
Active Sessions	Connection	✓	✓	✓
Active Statements	Connection	✓		
Append-Only Rowset	Recordset		✓	
Application Name	Connection			✓
Asynchable Abort	Connection	✓	✓	✓
Asynchable Commit	Connection	✓	✓	✓
Asynchronous Processing	Connection		✓	
Asynchronous Rowset Processing	Recordset		✓	
Auto Translate	Connection			✓
Autocommit Isolation Level	Connection		✓	✓
Autoincrement	Field		✓	
Auto Recalc	Recordset			✓
Batch Size	Recordset			✓
Background Thread Priority	Recordset			✓
BLOB accessibility on Forward-Only cursor	Recordset	✓		
Blocking Storage Objects	Recordset	✓	✓	✓
Bookmark Information	Recordset	✓		✓
Bookmark Type	Recordset	✓	✓	✓
Bookmarkable	Recordset	✓	✓	✓
Bookmarks Ordered	Recordset		✓	
Bulk Operations	Recordset			✓
Cache Authentication	Connection		✓	✓[1]
Cache Child Rows	Recordset			
Cache Deferred Columns	Recordset		✓	
Catalog Location	Connection	✓	✓	✓
Catalog Term	Connection	✓	✓	✓
Catalog Usage	Connection	✓		✓
Change Inserted Rows	Recordset	✓	✓	✓
Column Definition	Connection	✓	✓	✓
Column LCID	Field			
Column Privileges	Recordset	✓	✓	✓
Column Set Notification	Recordset	✓	✓	✓
Column Writable	Recordset		✓	

Property	Used	ODBC	Jet	SQL
Command Timeout	Recordset	✓2		✓
Concurrency control method	Recordset			✓
Connect Timeout	Connection	✓		✓
Connection Status	Connection	✓		✓
Current Catalog	Connection	✓	✓	✓
Current Language	Connection			✓
Cursor Engine Version	Recordset			✓
Data Source	Connection	✓	✓	✓
Data Source Name	Connection	✓	✓	✓
Data Source Object Threading Model	Connection	✓	✓	✓
DBMS Name	Connection	✓	✓	✓
DBMS Version	Connection	✓	✓	✓
Default	Field		✓	
Defer Column	Recordset		✓	✓
Delay Storage Object Updates	Recordset	✓	✓	✓
Description	Field		✓	
Driver Name	Connection	✓		
Driver ODBC Version	Connection	✓		
Driver Version	Connection	✓		
Enable Fastload	Connection			✓
Encrypt Password	Connection		✓	✓1
Extended Properties	Connection	✓	✓	✓1
Fastload Options	Recordset			✓
Fetch Backward	Recordset	✓	✓	✓
File Usage	Connection	✓		
Filter Operations	Recordset			
Find Operations	Recordset			
Fixed Length	Field		✓	
FOR BROWSE versioning columns	Recordset			✓
Force no command preparation when executing a parameterized command	Recordset	✓		
Force no command re-execution when failure to satisfy all required properties	Recordset	✓		
Force no parameter rebinding when executing a command	Recordset	✓		
Force SQL Server Firehose Mode cursor	Recordset	✓		
Generate a Rowset that can be marshalled	Recordset	✓		

Property	Used	ODBC	Jet	SQL
GROUP BY Support	Connection	✓	✓	✓
Heterogeneous Table Support	Connection	✓	✓	✓
Hold Rows	Recordset	✓	✓	✓
Identifier Case Sensitivity	Connection	✓	✓	✓
Immobile Rows	Recordset	✓	✓	✓
Include SQL_FLOAT, SQL_DOUBLE, and SQL_REAL in QBU where clauses	Recordset	✓		
Initial Catalog	Connection	✓		✓
Initial Fetch Size	Recordset			✓
Initial File Name	Connection			✓
Integrated Security	Connection		✓	✓[1]
Integrity Enhancement Facility	Connection	✓		
Isolation Levels	Connection	✓	✓	✓
Isolation Retention	Connection	✓	✓	✓
Jet OLEDB:3.5 Enable IRowsetIndex	Recordset		✓	
Jet OLEDB:Database Password	Connection		✓	
Jet OLEDB:Global Partial Bulk Ops	Connection		✓	
Jet OLEDB:ODBC Pass-Through Statement	Recordset		✓	
Jet OLEDB:Partial Bulk Ops	Recordset		✓	
Jet OLEDB:Pass Through Query Connect String	Recordset		✓	
Jet OLEDB:Registry Path	Connection		✓	
Jet OLEDB:System database	Connection		✓	
Like Escape Clause	Connection	✓		
Literal Bookmarks	Recordset	✓	✓	✓
Literal Row Identity	Recordset	✓	✓	✓
Locale Identifier	Connection	✓	✓	✓
Location	Connection	✓		✓
Lock Mode	Recordset		✓	✓
Log text and image writes	Connection			✓
Maintain Change Status	Recordset			✓
Maintains identity values supplied by the consumer	Recordset			✓
Maintains NULL for columns with a DEFAULT constraint	Recordset			✓
Mask Password	Connection		✓	✓[1]
Max Columns in Group By	Connection	✓		

Property	Used	ODBC	Jet	SQL
Max Columns in Index	Connection	✓		
Max Columns in Order By	Connection	✓		
Max Columns in Select	Connection	✓		
Max Columns in Table	Connection	✓		
Maximum BLOB Length	Connection			✓
Maximum Index Size	Connection	✓	✓	✓
Maximum Open Chapters	Connection			✓
Maximum Open Rows	Recordset	✓	✓	✓
Maximum OR Conditions	Connection			✓
Maximum Pending Rows	Recordset	✓	✓	✓
Maximum Row Size	Connection	✓	✓	✓
Maximum Row Size Includes BLOB	Connection	✓	✓	✓
Maximum Rows	Recordset	✓	✓	✓
Maximum Sort Columns	Connection			✓
Maximum Tables in SELECT	Connection	✓	✓	✓
Memory Usage	Recordset	✓		
Mode	Connection	✓	✓	✓
Multi-Table Update	Connection	✓	✓	✓
Multiple Connections	Connection			✓
Multiple Parameter Sets	Connection	✓	✓	✓
Multiple Results	Connection	✓	✓	✓
Multiple Storage Objects	Connection	✓	✓	✓
Network Address	Connection			✓
Network Library	Connection			✓
No temporary table created on FOR BROWSE	Connection			✓
Notification Granularity	Recordset	✓	✓	✓
Notification Phases	Recordset	✓	✓	✓
NULL Collation Order	Connection	✓	✓	✓
NULL Concatenation Behavior	Connection	✓	✓	✓
Nullable	Field		✓	
Numeric Functions	Connection	✓		
Objects Transacted	Recordset	✓	✓	✓
ODBC Concurrency Type	Recordset	✓		
ODBC Cursor Type	Recordset	✓		
OLE DB Services	Connection	✓		

Property	Used	ODBC	Jet	SQL
OLE DB Version	Connection	✓	✓	✓
OLE Object Support	Connection	✓	✓	✓
ORDER BY Columns in Select List	Connection	✓	✓	✓
Others' Changes Visible	Recordset	✓	✓	✓
Others' Inserts Visible	Recordset	✓²	✓	✓
Outer Join Capabilities	Connection	✓		
Outer Joins	Connection	✓		
Output Parameter Availability	Connection	✓	✓	✓
Own Changes Visible	Recordset	✓	✓	✓
Own Inserts Visible	Recordset	✓	✓	✓
Packet Size	Connection			✓
Pass By Ref Accessors	Connection	✓	✓	✓
Password	Connection	✓	✓	✓
Persist Encrypted	Connection		✓	✓
Persist Security Info	Connection	✓	✓	✓
Persistent ID Type	Connection	✓	✓	✓
Position on the last row after insert	Recordset	✓		
Prepare Abort Behavior	Connection	✓	✓	✓
Prepare Commit Behavior	Connection	✓	✓	✓
Preserve on Abort	Recordset	✓	✓	✓
Preserve on Commit	Recordset	✓	✓	✓
Primary Key	Field		✓	
Procedure Term	Connection	✓	✓	✓
Prompt	Connection	✓	✓	✓
Protection Level	Connection			
Provider Friendly Name	Connection	✓	✓	✓
Provider Name	Connection	✓	✓	✓
Provider Version	Connection	✓	✓	✓
Query Based Updates/Deletes/Inserts	Recordset	✓		
Quick Restart	Recordset	✓	✓	✓
Quoted Identifier Sensitivity	Connection	✓		✓
Read-Only Data Source	Connection	✓	✓	✓
Reentrant Events	Recordset	✓	✓	✓
Remove Deleted Rows	Recordset	✓	✓	✓
Report Multiple Changes	Recordset	✓	✓	✓
Return Pending Inserts	Recordset	✓	✓	✓

Property	Used	ODBC	Jet	SQL
Row Delete Notification	Recordset	✓	✓	✓
Row First Change Notification	Recordset	✓	✓	✓
Row Insert Notification	Recordset	✓	✓	✓
Row Privileges	Recordset	✓	✓	✓
Row Resynchronization Notification	Recordset	✓	✓	✓
Row Threading Model	Recordset	✓	✓	✓
Row Undo Change Notification	Recordset	✓	✓	✓
Row Undo Delete Notification	Recordset	✓	✓	✓
Row Undo Insert Notification	Recordset	✓	✓	✓
Row Update Notification	Recordset	✓	✓	✓
Rowset Conversions on Command	Connection	✓	✓	✓
Rowset Fetch Position Change Notification	Recordset	✓	✓	✓
Rowset Release Notification	Recordset	✓	✓	✓
Schema Term	Connection	✓	✓	✓
Schema Usage	Connection	✓	✓	✓
Scroll Backward	Recordset	✓	✓	✓
Server Cursor	Recordset	✓		✓
Server Data on Insert	Recordset			✓
Server Name	Connection	✓		✓
Skip Deleted Bookmarks	Recordset	✓	✓	✓
Sort on Index	Connection			✓
Special Characters	Connection	✓		
SQL Grammar Support	Connection	✓		
SQL Support	Connection	✓	✓	✓
SQLOLE execute a SET TEXTLENGTH	Connection			✓
Stored Procedures	Connection	✓		
String Functions	Connection	✓		
Strong Row Identity	Recordset	✓	✓	✓
Structured Storage	Connection	✓	✓	✓
Subquery Support	Connection	✓	✓	✓
System Functions	Connection	✓		
Table Term	Connection	✓	✓	✓
Time/Date Functions	Connection	✓		
Transaction DDL	Connection	✓	✓	✓
Unique	Field		✓	
Unique Rows	Recordset	✓		✓

Property	Used	ODBC	Jet	SQL
Updatability	Recordset	✓	✓	✓
Update Criteria	Recordset			✓
Update Operation	Recordset			✓
Use Bookmarks	Recordset	✓	✓	✓
Use Procedure for Prepare	Connection			✓
User Authentication mode	Connection			✓
User ID	Connection	✓	✓	✓
User Name	Connection	✓	✓	✓
Window Handle	Connection	✓	✓	✓
Workstation ID	Connection			✓

[1] This property is supported by the provider but is ignored

[2] This property is not supported by the Access ODBC Driver

Object Properties

This section details the properties by object type, including the enumerated values they support. These values are not included in the standard `adovbs.inc` include file (and are not automatically supplied when using Visual Basic), but can be found in `adoconvb.inc` and `adoconjs.inc` (for ASP, in VBScript and JScript format) and `adocon.bas` (for Visual Basic) from the supporting web site, `http://webdev.wrox.co.uk/books/1835`.

Connection Properties

Name	Description	DataType
Accessible Procedures	Identifies accessible procedures. Read-only.	Boolean
Accessible Tables	Identifies accessible tables. Read-only.	Boolean
Active Sessions	The maximum number of sessions that can exist at the same time. A value of 0 indicates no limit. Read-only.	Long
Active Statements	The maximum number of statements that can exist at the same time. Read-only.	Long
Application Name	Identifies the client application name. Read/Write.	String
Asynchable Abort	Whether transactions can be aborted asynchronously. Read-only.	Boolean

Name	Description	DataType
Asynchable Commit	Whether transactions can be committed asynchronously. Read-only.	Boolean
Asynchronous Processing	Specifies the asynchronous processing performed on the rowset. Read/Write.	DBPROPVAL_ ASYNCH
Auto Translate	Indicates whether OEM/ANSI character conversion is used. Read/Write.	Boolean
Autocommit Isolation Level	Identifies the transaction isolation level while in auto-commit mode. Read/Write.	DBPROPVAL_ OS
Cache Authentication	Whether or not the data source object can cache sensitive authentication information, such as passwords, in an internal cache. Read/Write.	Boolean
Catalog Location	The position of the catalog name in a table name in a text command. Returns 1 (DBPROPVAL_CL_START) if the catalog is at the start of the name (such as Access with \Temp\ Database.mdb), and 2 (DBPROPVAL_ CL_END) if the catalog is at the end of the name (such as Oracle with ADMIN.EMP@EMPDATA). Read/Write.	DBPROPVAL_ CL
Catalog Term	The name the data source uses for a catalog, eg, 'catalog', 'database', or 'database'. Read/Write.	String
Catalog Usage	Specifies how catalog names can be used in text commands. A combination of zero or more of DBPROPVAL_CU constants. Read/Write.	DBPROPVAL_ CU
Column Definition	Defines the valid clauses for the definition of a column. Read/Write.	DBPROPVAL_ CD
Connect Timeout	The amount of time, in seconds, to wait for the initialization to complete. Read/Write.	Long
Connection Status	The status of the current connection. Read-only.	DBPROPVAL_ CS
Current Catalog	The name of the current catalog. Read/Write.	String

Name	Description	DataType
Current Language	Identifies the language used for system messages selection and formatting. The language must be installed on the SQL Server or initialization of the data source fails. Read/Write.	Boolean
Data Source	The name of the database to connect to. Read/Write.	String
Data Source Name	The name of the data source. Read-only.	String
Data Source Object Threading Model	Specifies the threading models supported by the data source object. Read-only.	DBPROPVAL_RT
DBMS Name	The name of the product accessed by the provider. Read-only.	String
DBMS Version	The version of the product accessed by the provider. Read-only.	String
Driver Name	Identifies the ODBC Driver name. Read-only.	String
Driver ODBC Version	Identifies the ODBC Driver version. Read-only.	String
Driver Version	Identifies the Driver ODBC version. Read-only.	String
Encrypt Password	Whether the consumer required that the password be sent to the data source in an encrypted form. Read/Write.	Boolean
Extended Properties	Contains provider specific, extended connection information. Read/Write.	String
File Usage	Identifies the usage count of the ODBC driver. Read-only.	Long
GROUP BY Support	The relationship between the columns in a GROUP BY clause and the non-aggregated columns in the select list. Read-only.	DBPROPVAL_BG
Heterogeneous Table Support	Specifies whether the provider can join tables from different catalogs or providers. Read-only.	DBPROPVAL_HT
Identifier Case	How identifiers treat case sensitivity. Read-only.	DBPROPVAL_IC

Name	Description	DataType
Initial Catalog	The name of the initial, or default, catalog to use when connecting to the data source. If the provider supports changing the catalog for an initialized data source, a different catalog name can be specified in the **Current Catalog** property. Read/Write.	String
Integrated Security	Contains the name of the authentication service used by the server to identify the user. Read/Write.	String
Integrity Enhancement Facility	Indicates whether the data source supports the optional Integrity Enhancement Facility. Read-only.	Boolean
Isolation Levels	Identifies the supported transaction isolation levels. Read-only.	DBPROPVAL_TI
Isolation Retention	Identifies the supported transaction isolation retention levels. Read-only.	DBPROPVAL_TR
Jet OLEDB:Database Password	The database password. Read/Write.	String
Jet OLEDB:Global Partial Bulk Ops	Identifies whether Bulk operations are allowed with partial values. Read/Write.	Boolean
Jet OLEDB:Registry Path	The registry key that contains values for the Jet database engine. Read/Write.	String
Jet OLEDB:System database	The path and file name for the workgroup file. Read/Write.	String
Like Escape Clause	Identifies the LIKE escape clause. Read-only.	String
Locale Identifier	The locale ID of preference for the consumer. Read/Write.	Long
Location	The location of the data source to connect to. Typically this will be the server name. Read/Write.	String
Log text and image writes	Identifies whether writes to text and images fields are logged in the transaction log. Read/Write.	Boolean
Mask Password	The consumer requires that the password be sent to the data source in masked form. Read/Write.	Boolean
Max Columns in Group By	Identifies the maximum number of columns in a GROUP BY clause. Read-only.	Long

Name	Description	DataType
Max Columns in Index	Identifies the maximum number of columns in an index. Read-only.	Long
Max Columns in Order By	Identifies the maximum number of columns in an ORDER BY clause. Read-only.	Long
Max Columns in Select	Identifies the maximum number of columns in a SELECT statement. Read-only.	Long
Max Columns in Table	Identifies the maximum number of columns in a table. Read-only.	Long
Maximum BLOB Length	Identifies the maximum size of a BLOB field. Read-only.	Long
Maximum Index Size	The maximum number of bytes allowed in the combined columns of an index. This is 0 if there is no specified limit or the limit is unknown. Read-only.	Long
Maximum Open Chapters	The maximum number of chapters that can be open at any one time. If a chapter must be released before a new chapter can be opened the value is 1; if the provider does not support chapters the value is 0. Read-only.	Long
Maximum OR Conditions	The maximum number of disjunct conditions that can be supported in a view filter. Multiple conditions of a view filter are joined in a logical OR. Providers that do not support joining multiple conditions return a value of 1, and providers that do not support view filters return a value of 0. Read-only.	Long
Maximum Row Size	The maximum length of a single row in a table. This is 0 if there is no specified limit or the limit is unknown. Read-only.	Long
Maximum Row Size Includes BLOB	Identifies whether **Maximum Row Size** includes the length for BLOB data. Read-only.	Boolean
Maximum Sort Columns	The maximum number of columns that can be supported in a View Sort. This is 0 if there is no specified limit or the limit is unknown. Read-only.	Long

Name	Description	DataType
Maximum Tables in SELECT	The maximum number of tables allowed in the FROM clause of a SELECT statement. This is 0 if there is no specified limit or the limit is unknown. Read-only.	Long
Mode	Specifies the access permissions. Read/Write.	DB_MODE
Multi-Table Update	Identifies whether the provider can update rowsets derived from multiple tables. Read-only.	Boolean
Multiple Connections	Identifies whether the provider silently creates additional connections to support concurrent Command, Connection, or Recordset objects. This only applies to providers that have to spawn multiple connections, and not to providers that support multiple connections natively. Read/Write.	Boolean
Multiple Parameter Sets	Identifies whether the provider supports multiple parameter sets. Read-only.	Boolean
Multiple Results	Identifies whether the provider supports multiple results objects and what restrictions it places on those objects. Read-only.	DBPROPVAL_MR
Multiple Storage Objects	Identifies whether the provider supports multiple, open storage objects at the same time. Read-only.	Boolean
Network Address	Identifies the network address of the SQL Server. Read/Write.	String
Network Library	Identifies the name of the Net-Library (DLL) used to communicate with SQL Server. Read/Write.	String
NULL Collation Order	Identifies where NULLs are sorted in a list. Read-only.	DBPROPVAL_NC
NULL Concatenation Behavior	How the data source handles concatenation of NULL-valued character data type columns with non-NULL valued character data type columns. Read-only.	DBPROPVAL_CB
Numeric Functions	Identifies the numeric functions supported by the ODBC driver and data source. Read-only.	SQL_FN_NUM

281

Name	Description	DataType
OLE DB Services	Specifies the OLEDB services to enable. Read/Write.	DBPROPVAL_OS
OLE DB Version	Specifies the version of OLEDB supported by the provider. Read-only.	String
OLE Object Support	Specifies the way in which the provider supports access to BLOBs and OLE objects stored in columns. Read-only.	DBPROPVAL_OO
ORDER BY Columns in Select List	Identifies whether columns in an ORDER BY clause must be in the SELECT list. Read-only.	Boolean
Outer Join Capabilities	Identifies the outer join capabilities of the ODBC data source. Read-only.	SQL_OJ
Outer Joins	Identifies whether outer joins are supported or not. Read-only.	Boolean
Outer Join Capabilities	Identifies the outer join capabilities of the ODBC data source. Read-only.	SQL_OJ
Output Parameter Availability	Identifies the time at which output parameter values become available. Read-only.	DBPROPVAL_OA
Packet Size	Specifies the network packet size in bytes. It must be between 512 and 32767. The default is 4096. Read/Write.	Long
Pass By Ref Accessors	Whether the provider supports the DBACCESSOR_PASSBYREF flag. Read-only.	Boolean
Password	The password to be used to connect to the data source. Read/Write.	String
Persist Encrypted	Whether or not the consumer requires that the data source object persist sensitive authentication information, such as a password, in encrypted form. Read/Write.	Boolean
Persist Security Info	Whether or not the data source object is allowed to persist sensitive authentication information, such as a password, along with other authentication information. Read/Write.	Boolean
Persistent ID Type	Specifies the type of DBID that the provider uses when persisting DBIDs for tables, indexes and columns. Read-only.	DBPROPVAL_PT

Name	Description	DataType
Prepare Abort Behavior	Identifies how aborting a transaction affects prepared commands. Read-only.	DBPROPVAL_ CB
Prepare Commit Behavior	Identifies how committing a transaction affects prepared commands. Read-only.	DBPROPVAL_ CB
Procedure Term	Specifies the data source providers name for a procedure, eg, 'database procedure', 'stored procedure'. Read-only.	String
Prompt	Specifies whether to prompt the user during initialization. Read/Write.	DBPROMPT
Protection Level	The level of protection of data sent between client and server. This property applies only to network connections other than RPC. Read/Write.	DB_PROT_ LEVEL
Provider Friendly Name	The friendly name of the provider. Read-only.	String
Provider Name	The filename of the provider. Read-only.	String
Provider Version	The version of the provider. Read-only.	String
Quoted Identifier Sensitivity	Identifies how quoted identifiers treat case. Read-only.	DBPROPVAL_ IC
Read-Only Data Source	Whether or not the data source is read-only. Read-only.	Boolean
Reset Datasource	Specifies the data source state to reset. Write only.	DBPROPVAL_ RD
Rowset Conversions on Command	Identifies whether callers can enquire on a command and about conversions supported by the command. Read-only.	Boolean
Schema Term	The name the data source uses for a schema, eg, 'schema' or 'owner'. Read-only.	String
Schema Usage	Identifies how schema names can be used in commands. Read-only.	DBPROPVAL_ SU
Server Name	The name of the server. Read-only.	String
Sort on Index	Specifies whether the provider supports setting a sort order only for columns contained in an index. Read-only.	Boolean

Name	Description	DataType
Special Characters	Identifies the data store's special characters. Read-only.	String
SQL Grammar Support	Identifies the SQL grammar level supported by the ODBC driver. 0 represents no conformance, 1 indicates Level 1 conformance, and 2 represents Level 2 conformance. Read-only.	Long
SQL Support	Identifies the level of support for SQL. Read-only.	DBPROPVAL_SQL
SQLOLE execute a SET TEXTLENGTH	Identifies whether SQLOLE executes a SET TEXTLENGTH before accessing BLOB fields *. Read-only.	Boolean
Stored Procedures	Indicates whether stored procedures are available. Read-only.	Boolean
String Functions	Identifies the string functions supported by the ODBC driver and data source. Read-only.	SQL_FN_STR
Structured Storage	Identifies what interfaces the rowset supports on storage objects. Read-only.	DBPROPVAL_SS
Subquery Support	Identifies the predicates in text commands that support sub-queries. Read-only.	DBPROPVAL_SQ
System Functions	Identifies the system functions supported by the ODBC Driver and data source. Read-only.	SQL_FN_SYS
Table Term	The name the data source uses for a table, eg, 'table' or 'file'. Read-only.	String
Time/Date Functions	Identifies the time/date functions supported by the ODBC Driver and data source. Read-only.	SQL_SDF_CURRENT
Transaction DDL	Indicates whether Data Definition Language (DDL) statements are supported in transactions. Read-only.	DBPROPVAL_TC
Use Procedure for Prepare	Indicates whether SQL Server is to use temporary stored procedures for prepared statements. Read/Write.	SSPROPVAL_USEPROCFORPREP
User Authentication mode	Indicates whether Windows NT Authentication is used to access SQL Server. Read/Write.	Boolean
User ID	The User ID to be used when connecting to the data source. Read/Write.	String

Name	Description	DataType
User Name	The User Name used in a particular database. Read-only.	String
Window Handle	The window handle to be used if the data source object needs to prompt for additional information. Read/Write.	Long
Workstation ID	Identifies the workstation. Read/Write.	String

Recordset Properties

Name	Description	DataType
Access Order	Indicates the order in which columns must be accessed on the rowset. Read/Write.	DBPROPVAL_AO
Append Only Rowset	A rowset opened with this property will initially contain no rows. Read/Write.	Boolean
Asynchronous Rowset Processing	Identifies the asynchronous processing performed on the rowset. Read/Write.	DBPROPVAL_ASYNCH
Auto Recalc	For chaptered recordsets using COMPUTE, automatically recalculate the summary if the detail lines change #. Read/Write.	Integer
Batch Size	The number of rows in a batch. Read/Write.	Integer
Background Thread Priority	The priority of the background thread for asynchronous actions. Read/Write.	Integer
BLOB accessibility on Forward-Only cursor	Indicates whether or not BLOB columns can be accessed irrespective of their position in the column list. If **True** then the BLOB column can be accessed even if it is not the last column. If **False** then the BLOB column can only be accessed if it is the last BLOB column, and any non-BLOB columns after this column will not be accessible. Read/Write.	Boolean
Blocking Storage Objects	Indicates whether storage objects might prevent use of other methods on the rowset. Read/Write.	Boolean

285

Name	Description	DataType
Bookmark Information	Identifies additional information about bookmarks over the rowset. Read-only.	DBPROPVAL_ BI
Bookmark Type	Identifies the bookmark type supported by the rowset. Read/Write.	DBPROPVAL_ BMK
Bookmarkable	Indicates whether bookmarks are supported. Read-only.	Boolean
Bookmarks Ordered	Indicates whether boomarks can be compared to determine the relative position of their rows in the rowset. Read/Write.	Boolean
Bulk Operations	Identifies optimizations that a provider may take for updates to the rowset. Read-only.	DBPROPVAL_ BO
Cache Child Rows	Indicates whether child rows in a chaptered recordset are cached #. Read/Write.	Boolean
Cache Deferred Columns	Indicates whether the provider caches the value of a deferred column when the consumer first gets a value from that column. Read/Write.	Boolean
Change Inserted Rows	Indicates whether the consumer can delete or update newly inserted rows. An inserted row is assumed to be one that has been transmitted to the data source, as opposed to a pending insert row. Read/Write.	Boolean
Column Privileges	Indicates whether access rights are restricted on a column-by-column basis. Read-only.	Boolean
Column Set Notification	Indicates whether changing a column set is cancelable. Read-only.	DBPROPVAL_ NP
Column Writable	Indicates whether a particular column is writable. Read/Write.	Boolean
Command Timeout	The number of seconds to wait before a command times out. A value of 0 indicates an infinite timeout. Read/Write.	Long
Concurrency control method	Identifies the method used for concurrency control when using server based cursors. Read/Write.	SSPROPVAL_ CONCUR
Cursor Engine Version	Identifies the version of the cursor engine. Read-only.	String

286

Name	Description	DataType
Defer Column	Indicates whether the data in a column is not fetched until specifically requested. Read/Write.	Boolean
Delay Storage Object Updates	Indicates whether, when in delayed update mode, if storage objects are also used in delayed update mode. Read/Write.	Boolean
Fetch Backward	Indicates whether a rowset can fetch backwards. Read/Write.	Boolean
Filter Operations	Identifies which comparison operations are supported when using Filter on a particular column. Read-only.	DBPROPVAL_CO
Find Operations	Identifies which comparison operations are supported when using Find on a particular column. Read-only.	DBPROPVAL_CO
FOR BROWSE versioning columns	Indicates the rowset contains the primary key or a **timestamp** column. Only applicable with rowsets created with the SQL FOR BROWSE statement. Read/Write.	Boolean
Force no command preparation when executing a parameterized command	Identifies whether or not a temporary stored procedure is created for parameterized commands. [#]. Read/Write.	Boolean
Force no command reexecution when failure to satisfy all required properties	Identifies whether or not the command is reexecuted if the command properties are invalid. [#]. Read/Write.	Boolean
Force no parameter rebinding when executing a command	Identifies whether or not the command parameters are rebound every time the command is executed [#]. Read/Write.	Boolean
Force SQL Server Firehose Mode cursor	Identifies whether or not a forward-only, read-only cursor is always created [#]. Read/Write.	Boolean
Generate a Rowset that can be marshalled	Identifies whether or not the rowset that is to be created can be marshalled across process boundaries [#]. Read/Write.	Boolean

Name	Description	DataType
Hold Rows	Indicates whether the rowset allows the consumer to retrieve more rows or change the next fetch position whilst holding previously fetched rows with pending changes. Read/Write.	Boolean
Immobile Rows	Indicates whether the rowset will reorder insert or updated rows. Read/Write.	Boolean
Include SQL_FLOAT, SQL_DOUBLE, and SQL_REAL in QBU where clauses	When using a query-based update, setting this to **True** will include REAL, FLOAT and DOUBLE numeric types in the WHERE clause, otherwise they will be omitted. Read/Write.	Boolean
Initial Fetch Size	Identifies the initial size of the cache into which records are fetched *. Read/Write.	Long
Jet OLEDB:ODBC Pass-Through Statement	Identifies the statement used for a SQL Pass-through statement. Read/Write.	String
Jet OLEDB:Partial Bulk Ops	Indicates whether or not bulk operations will complete if some of the values fail *.	
Jet OLEDB:Pass Through Query Connect String	Identifies the Connect string for an ODBC pass through query. Read/Write.	String
Literal Bookmarks	Indicates whether bookmarks can be compared literally, ie, as a series of bytes. Read/Write.	Boolean
Literal Row Identity	Indicates whether the consumer can perform a binary comparison of two row handles to determine whether they point to the same row. Read-only.	Boolean
Lock Mode	Identifies the level of locking performed by the rowset. Read/Write.	DBPROPVAL_LM
Maximum BLOB Length	Identifies the maximum length of a BLOB field. Read-only.	Long
Maximum Open Rows	Specifies the maximum number of rows that can be active at the same time. Read/Write.	Long
Maximum Pending Rows	Specifies the maximum number of rows that can have pending changes at the same time. Read/Write.	Long

Name	Description	DataType
Maximum Rows	Specifies the maximum number of rows that can be returned in the rowset. This is 0 if there is no limit. Read/Write.	Long
Memory Usage	Estimates the amount of memory that can be used by the rowset. If set to 0 the amount is unlimited. If between 1 and 99 it specifies a percentage of the available virtual memory. If 100 or greater it specifies the number of kilobytes. Read/Write.	Long
Notification Granularity	Identifies when the consumer is notified for methods that operate on multiple rows. Read/Write.	DBPROPVAL_NT
Notification Phases	Identifies the notification phases supported by the provider. Read-only.	DBPROPVAL_NP
Objects Transacted	Indicates whether any object created on the specified column is transacted. Read/Write.	Boolean
ODBC Concurrency Type	Identifies the ODBC concurrency type. Read-only.	Integer
ODBC Cursor Type	Identifies the ODBC cursor type. Read-only.	Integer
Others' Changes Visible	Indicates whether the rowset can see updates and deletes made by someone other than the consumer of the rowset. Read/Write.	Boolean
Others' Inserts Visible	Indicates whether the rowset can see rows inserted by someone other than the consumer of the rowset. Read/Write.	Boolean
Own Changes Visible	Indicates whether the rowset can see its own updates and deletes. Read/Write.	Boolean
Own Inserts Visible	Indicates whether the rowset can see its own inserts. Read/Write.	Boolean
Position on the last row after insert	Identifies whether or not the cursor is placed on the last row after an insert #. Read-only.	Boolean
Preserve on Abort	Indicates whether, after aborting a transaction, the rowset remains active. Read/Write.	Boolean

Name	Description	DataType
Preserve on Commit	Indicates whether after committing a transaction the rowset remains active. Read/Write.	Boolean
Query Based Updates /Deletes/Inserts	Identifies whether or not queries can be used for updates, deletes, and inserts #. Read/Write.	Boolean
Quick Restart	Indicates whether RestartPosition is relatively quick to execute. Read/Write.	Boolean
Reentrant Events	Indicates whether the provider supports reentrancy during callbacks. Read-only.	Boolean
Remove Deleted Rows	Indicates whether the provider removes rows it detects as having been deleted from the rowset. Read/Write.	Boolean
Report Multiple Changes	Indicates whether an update or delete can affect multiple rows and the provider can detect that multiple rows have been updated or deleted. Read-only.	Boolean
Return Pending Inserts	Indicates whether methods that fetch rows can return pending insert rows. Read-only.	Boolean
Row Delete Notification	Indicates whether deleting a row is cancellable. Read-only.	DBPROPVAL_NP
Row First Change Notification	Indicates whether changing the first row is cancellable. Read-only.	DBPROPVAL_NP
Row Insert Notification	Indicates whether inserting a new row is cancellable. Read-only.	DBPROPVAL_NP
Row Privileges	Indicates whether access rights are restricted on a row-by-row basis. Read-only.	Boolean
Row Resynchronization Notification	Indicates whether resynchronizing a row is cancellable. Read-only.	DBPROPVAL_NP
Row Threading Model	Identifies the threading models supported by the rowset. Read/Write.	DBPROPVAL_RT
Row Undo Change Notification	Indicates whether undoing a change is cancellable. Read-only.	DBPROPVAL_NP
Row Undo Delete Notification	Indicates whether undoing a delete is cancellable. Read-only.	DBPROPVAL_NP

Name	Description	DataType
Row Undo Insert Notification	Indicates whether undoing an insert is cancellable. Read-only.	DBPROPVAL_ NP
Row Update Notification	Indicates whether updating a row is cancellable. Read-only.	DBPROPVAL_ NP
Rowset Fetch Position Change Notification	Indicates whether changing the fetch position is cancellable. Read-only.	DBPROPVAL_ NP
Rowset Release Notification	Indicates whether releasing a rowset is cancellable. Read-only.	DBPROPVAL_ NP
Scroll Backward	Indicates whether the rowset can scroll backward. Read/Write.	Boolean
Server Cursor	Indicates whether the cursor underlying the rowset (if any) must be materialized on the server. Read/Write.	Boolean
Server Data on Insert	Indicates whether, at the time an insert is transmitted to the server, the provider retrieves data from the server to update the local row cache. Read/Write.	Boolean
Skip Deleted Bookmarks	Indicates whether the rowset allows positioning to continue if a bookmark row was deleted. Read/Write.	Boolean
Strong Row Identity	Indicates whether the handles of newly inserted rows can be compared. Read-only.	Boolean
Unique Rows	Indicates whether each row is uniquely identified by its column values. Read/Write.	Boolean
Updatability	Identifies the supported methods for updating a rowset. Read/Write.	DBPROPVAL_ UP
Update Criteria	For chaptered recordsets, identifies the criteria used when performing a requery *. Read/Write.	String
Update Operation	For chaptered recordsets, identifies the operation to be performed with a requery. Read/Write.	String
Use Bookmarks	Indicates whether the rowset supports bookmarks. Read/Write.	Boolean

291

Field Properties

The field properties names are different from the other properties because they are less readable and appear more like the schema column names.

Name	Description	DataType
BASECATALOGNAME	The name of the catalog. Read-only.	String
BASECOLUMNNAME	The name of the column. Read-only.	String
BASESCHEMANAME	The name of the schema. Read-only.	String
BASETABLENAME	The table name. Read-only.	String
DATETIMEPRECISION	The number of digits in the fraction seconds portion if a datetime column. Read-only.	Long
ISAUTOINCREMENT	Identifies whether the column is an auto increment column, such as an Access Autonumber or a SQL Server IDENTITY column. Read-only.	Boolean
ISCASESENSITIVE	Identifies whether the contents of the column are case sensitive. Useful when searching. Read-only.	Boolean
ISSEARCHABLE	Identifies the searchability of the column. Read-only.	DB_ SEARCHABLE
OCTETLENGTH	The maximum column length in bytes, for character or binary data columns. Read-only.	Long
KEYCOLUMN	Identifies whether or not the column is a key column, used to uniquely identify the row. Read-only.	Boolean
RELATIONCONDITIONS	The conditions for relationships between chaptered recordsets. This is only available for client cursors. Read-only [#].	Binary
CALCULATIONINFO	The calculations for summary and grouped, chaptered recordets. This is only available for client cursors. Read-only [#].	Binary
OPTIMIZE	Identifies whether the column is indexed locally. This is only available for client cursors. Read/Write.	Boolean

Property Usage

Using the properties is quite simple, despite the fact that there are so many of them. You simply use the property name to index into the Properties collection. For example, to find out the name the provider gives to procedures you could do this:

```
Print oConn.Properties("Procedure Term")
```

For SQL Server this returns **stored procedure** and for Access this returns **STORED QUERY**.

You can enumerate all of the properties very simply:

```
For Each oProp In oConn.Properties
   Print oProp.Name
   Print oProp.Value
Next
```

This will print out the property name and value.

For those properties that return custom types, you need to identify whether these return a bitmask or a simple value. In its simplest forms, these properties will just return a single value. For example, to find out whether your provider supports output parameters on stored procedures you can query the **Output Parameter Availability** property. This is defined as returning values of type DBPROPVAL_OA, which are as follows:

Constant	Value
DBPROPVAL_OA_ATEXECUTE	2
DBPROPVAL_OA_ATROWRELEASE	4
DBPROPVAL_OA_NOTSUPPORTED	1

Examining this property when connected to SQL Server gives you a value of 4, indicating that output parameters are available when the recordset is closed. Access, on the other hand, returns a value of 1, indicating that output parameters are not supported.

For those properties that return bitmask, you'll need to use boolean logic to identify which values are set. For example, to query the provider and examine what features of SQL are supported, you would use the **SQL Support** property. For Access this returns **512**, which corresponds to **DBPROPVAL_SQL_SUBMINIMUM**, indicating that not even the ANSI SQL92 Entry level SQL facilities are provided. SQL Server on the other hand, returns **283**, but there isn't a single value for this, so it must be a combination of values.

This in fact corresponds to:

Constant	Value
DBPROPVAL_SQL_ESCAPECLAUSES	256
DBPROPVAL_SQL_ANSI92_ENTRY	16
DBPROPVAL_SQL_ANDI89_IEF	8
DBPROPVAL_SQL_CORE	2
DBPROPVAL_SQL_MINIMUM	1

You can check to see whether a specific value is set by ANDing the value. For example

```
lngSQLSupport = oConn.Properties("SQL Support")
If (lngSQLSupport AND DBPROPVAL_SQL_CORE) = DBPROPVAL_SQL_CORE Then
   core facilities are supported
End If
```

A full description of the constants is given in Appendix F.

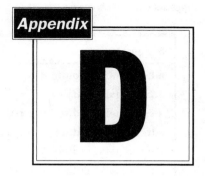

Schemas

There are two terms that are important when dealing with schemas:

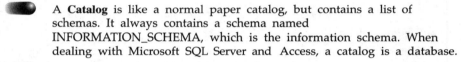 A **Catalog** is like a normal paper catalog, but contains a list of schemas. It always contains a schema named INFORMATION_SCHEMA, which is the information schema. When dealing with Microsoft SQL Server and Access, a catalog is a database.

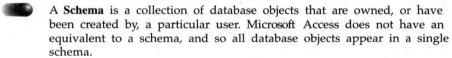 A **Schema** is a collection of database objects that are owned, or have been created by, a particular user. Microsoft Access does not have an equivalent to a schema, and so all database objects appear in a single schema.

This appendix details the schema objects that can be accessed using the **OpenSchema** method of the **Connection** object.

The table below shows the main providers and the list of schemas supported by them:

Schema	Jet	SQL	ODBC Jet	ODBC SQL
adSchemaAsserts				
adSchemaCatalogs		✓	✓	✓
adSchemaCharacterSets				
adSchemaCheckConstraints	✓			
adSchemaCollations				
adSchemaColumnPrivileges		✓		✓
adSchemaColumns	✓	✓	✓	✓
adSchemaColumnDomainUsage				
adSchemaConstraintColumnUsage	✓			
adSchemaConstraintTableUsage				
adSchemaForeignKeys				✓
adSchemaIndexes	✓	✓	✓	✓

Schema	Jet	SQL	ODBC Jet	ODBC SQL
adSchemaKeyColumnUsage	✓			
adSchemaPrimaryKeys	✓	✓		✓
adSchemaProcedureColumns			✓	
adSchemaProcedureParameters		✓	✓	✓
adSchemaProcedures	✓	✓	✓	✓
adSchemaProviderSpecific				
adSchemaProviderTypes	✓	✓	✓	✓
adSchemaReferentialContraints	✓			
adSchemaSchemata		✓		✓
adSchemaSQLLanguages				
adSchemaStatistics	✓	✓		
adSchemaTableConstraints	✓			
adSchemaTablePrivileges		✓		
adSchemaTables	✓	✓	✓	✓
adSchemaTranslations				
adSchemaUsagePrivileges				
adSchemaViewColumnUsage				
adSchemaViews	✓			
adSchemaViewTableUsage				

adSchemaAsserts

This identifies the assertions defined in the catalog.

Column name	Type	Description
CONSTRAINT_CATALOG	String	Catalog name, or Null if the provider does not support catalogs.
CONSTRAINT_SCHEMA	String	Schema name, or Null if the provider does not support schemas.
CONSTRAINT_NAME	String	Constraint name.
IS_DEFERRABLE	Boolean	**True** if the assertion is deferrable, **False** otherwise.
INITIALLY_DEFERRED	Boolean	**True** if the assertion is initially deferred, **False** otherwise.
DESCRIPTION	String	Description of the assertion.

adSchemaCatalogs

This defines the physical attributes of the catalogs of a database. When using SQL Server the catalogs are the databases within the Server, and for Access the catalogs contain the current database.

Column name	Type	Description
CATALOG_NAME	String	Catalog name.
DESCRIPTION	String	Catalog description.

adSchemaCharacterSets

This identifies the character sets supported by the catalog.

Column name	Type	Description
CHARACTER_SET_CATALOG	String	Catalog name, or Null if the provider does not support catalogs.
CHARACTER_SET_SCHEMA	String	Schema name, or Null if the provider does not support schemas.
CHARACTER_SET_NAME	String	Character set name.
FORM_OF_USE	String	Name of form-of-use of the character set.
NUMBER_OF_CHARACTERS	Big Integer	Number of characters in the character repertoire.
DEFAULT_COLLATE_CATALOG	String	Catalog name containing the default collation, or Null if the provider does not support catalogs or different collations.
DEFAULT_COLLATE_SCHEMA	String	Schema name containing the default collation, or Null if the provider does not support schemas or different collations.
DEFAULT_COLLATE_NAME	String	Default collation name, or Null if the provider does not support different collations.

adSchemaCheckConstraints

This identifies the check constraints available in the catalog. Check constraints identify the valid values allowed for columns.

Column name	Type	Description
CONSTRAINT_CATALOG	String	Catalog name, or Null if the provider does not support catalogs.
CONSTRAINT_SCHEMA	String	Schema name, or Null if the provider does not support schemas.
CONSTRAINT_NAME	String	Constraint name.
CHECK_CLAUSE	String	The WHERE clause specified in the CHECK constraint.
DESCRIPTION	String	Check constraint description.

adSchemaCollations

Collations identify how the catalog sorts data.

Column name	Type	Description
COLLATION_CATALOG	String	Catalog name, or Null if the provider does not support catalogs.
COLLATION_SCHEMA	String	Schema name, or Null if the provider does not support schemas.
COLLATION_NAME	String	Collation name.
CHARACTER_SET_CATALOG	String	Catalog name containing the character set on which the collation is defined, or Null if the provider does not support catalogs or different character sets.
CHARACTER_SET_SCHEMA	String	Schema name containing the character set on which the collation is defined, or Null if the provider does not support schema or different character sets.
CHARACTER_SET_NAME	String	Character set name on which the collation is defined, or Null if the provider does not support different character sets.

Column name	Type	Description
PAD_ATTRIBUTE	String	'NO PAD' if the collation being described has the NO PAD attribute, 'PAD SPACE' if the collation being described has the PAD SPACE attribute. This identifies whether variable length character columns are padded with spaces.

adSchemaColumnDomainUsage

This identifies the columns that use domains for integrity checking.

Column name	Type	Description
DOMAIN_CATALOG	String	Catalog name, or Null if the provider does not support catalogs.
DOMAIN_SCHEMA	String	Schema name, or Null if the provider does not support schemas.
DOMAIN_NAME	String	View name.
TABLE_CATALOG	String	Catalog name in which the table is defined, or Null if the provider does not support catalogs.
TABLE_SCHEMA	String	Unqualified schema name in which the table is defined, or Null if the provider does not support schemas.
TABLE_NAME	String	Table name.
COLUMN_NAME	String	Column name. This column, together with the COLUMN_GUID and COLUMN_PROPID columns, forms the column ID. One or more of these columns will be Null depending on which elements of the DBID structure the provider uses.
COLUMN_GUID	GUID	Column GUID.
COLUMN_PROPID	Long	Column property ID.

adSchemaColumnPrivileges

This identifies the privileges on table columns for a given user.

Column name	Type	Description
GRANTOR	String	User who granted the privileges on the table in TABLE_NAME.
GRANTEE	String	User name (or "PUBLIC") to whom the privilege has been granted.
TABLE_CATALOG	String	Catalog name in which the table is defined, or Null if the provider does not support catalogs.
TABLE_SCHEMA	String	Schema name in which the table is defined, or Null if the provider does not support schemas.
TABLE_NAME	String	Table name.
COLUMN_NAME	String	Column name.
COLUMN_GUID	GUID	Column GUID.
COLUMN_PROPID	Long	Column property ID.
PRIVILEGE_TYPE	String	Privilege type. One of the following: • SELECT • DELETE • INSERT • UPDATE • REFERENCES
IS_GRANTABLE	Boolean	**True** if the privilege being described was granted with the WITH GRANT OPTION clause, **False** if the privilege being described was not granted with the WITH GRANT OPTION clause.

adSchemaColumns

This identifies the columns of tables.

Column name	Type	Description
TABLE_CATALOG	String	Catalog name, or Null if the provider does not support catalogs.
TABLE_SCHEMA	Long	Schema name, or Null if the provider does not support schemas.
TABLE_NAME	String	Table name. This column cannot contain a Null.
COLUMN_NAME	String	The name of the column, or Null if this cannot be determined.
COLUMN_GUID	GUID	Column GUID, or Null for providers that do not use GUIDs to identify columns.
COLUMN_PROPID	Long	Column property ID, or Null for providers that do not associate PROPIDs with columns.
ORDINAL_POSITION	Long	The ordinal of the column, or Null if there is no stable ordinal value for the column. Columns are numbered starting from one.
COLUMN_HASDEFAULT	Boolean	**True** if column has a default value, **False** if the column does not have a default value or it is unknown whether the column has a default value.
COLUMN_DEFAULT	String	Default value of the column.
COLUMN_FLAGS	Long	A bitmask that describes column characteristics. The DBCOLUMNFLAGS enumerated type specifies the bits in the bitmask. The values for DBCOLUMNFLAGS can be found in Appendix F. This column cannot contain a Null value.
IS_NULLABLE	Boolean	**True** if the column might be nullable, **False** if the column is known not to be nullable.
DATA_TYPE	Integer	The column's data type. If the data type of the column varies from row to row, this must be a **Variant**. This column cannot contain Null. For a list of valid Types, see DataTypeEnum in Appendix F.

Column name	Type	Description
TYPE_GUID	GUID	The GUID of the column's data type. Providers that do not use GUIDs to identify data types should return Null in this column.
CHARACTER_MAXIMUM_ LENGTH	Long	The maximum possible length of a value in the column.
CHARACTER_OCTET_LENGTH		Long Maximum length in octets (bytes) of the column, if the type of the column is character or binary. A value of zero means the column has no maximum length. Null for all other types of columns.
NUMERIC_PRECISION	Integer	If the column's data type is numeric, this is the maximum precision of the column. The precision of columns with a data type of **Decimal** or **Numeric** depends on the definition of the column. If the column's data type is not numeric, this is Null.
NUMERIC_SCALE	Integer	If the column's Type is **Decimal** or **Numeric**, this is the number of digits to the right of the decimal point. Otherwise, this is Null.
DATETIME_PRECISION	Long	Datetime precision (number of digits in the fractional seconds portion) of the column if the column is a datetime or interval type. If the column's data type is not datetime, this is Null.
CHARACTER_SET_ CATALOG	String	Catalog name in which the character set is defined, or Null if the provider does not support catalogs or different character sets.
CHARACTER_SET_ SCHEMA	String	Schema name in which the character set is defined, or Null if the provider does not support schemas or different character sets.
CHARACTER_SET_NAME	String	Character set name, or Null if the provider does not support different character sets.
COLLATION_CATALOG	String	Catalog name in which the collation is defined, or Null if the provider does not support catalogs or different collations.

Column name	Type	Description
COLLATION_SCHEMA	String	Schema name in which the collation is defined, or Null if the provider does not support schemas or different collations.
COLLATION_NAME	String	Collation name, or Null if the provider does not support different collations.
DOMAIN_CATALOG	String	Catalog name in which the domain is defined, or Null if the provider does not support catalogs or domains.
DOMAIN_SCHEMA	String	Unqualified schema name in which the domain is defined, or Null if the provider does not support schemas or domains.
DOMAIN_NAME	String	Domain name, or Null if the provider does not support domains.
DESCRIPTION	String	Description of the column, or Null if there is no description associated with the column.

CHARACTER_MAXIMUM_LENGTH will vary depending upon the data type of the column:

For character, binary, or bit columns, this is one of the following:

- The maximum length of the column in characters, bytes, or bits, respectively, if one is defined. For example, a CHAR(5) column in a SQL table has a maximum length of five (5).
- The maximum length of the data type in characters, bytes, or bits, respectively, if the column does not have a defined length.
- Zero (0) if neither the column nor the data type has a defined maximum length.

It will be Null for all other types of columns.

adSchemaConstraintColumnUsage

This identifies the columns used for referential integrity constraints, unique constraints, check constraints, and assertions.

Column name	Type	Description
TABLE_CATALOG	String	Catalog name in which the table is defined, or Null if the provider does not support catalogs.
TABLE_SCHEMA	String	Schema name in which the table is defined, or Null if the provider does not support schemas.
TABLE_NAME	String	Table name.
COLUMN_NAME	String	Column name.
COLUMN_GUID	GUID	Column GUID.
COLUMN_PROPID	Long	Column property ID.
CONSTRAINT_CATALOG	String	Catalog name, or Null if the provider does not support catalogs.
CONSTRAINT_SCHEMA	String	Schema name, or Null if the provider does not support schemas.
CONSTRAINT_NAME	String	Constraint name.

adSchemaConstraintTableUsage

This identifies the tables used for referential integrity constraints, unique constraints, check constraints, and assertions.

Column name	Type	Description
TABLE_CATALOG	String	Catalog name in which the table is defined, or Null if the provider does not support catalogs.
TABLE_SCHEMA	String	Schema name in which the table is defined, or Null if the provider does not support schemas.
TABLE_NAME	String	Table name.
CONSTRAINT_CATALOG	String	Catalog name, or Null if the provider does not support catalogs.
CONSTRAINT_SCHEMA	String	Schema name, or Null if the provider does not support schemas.
CONSTRAINT_NAME	String	Constraint name.

adSchemaForeignKeys

This identifies the foreign key columns, as used in referential integrity checks.

Column name	Type	Description
PK_TABLE_CATALOG	String	Catalog name in which the primary key table is defined, or Null if the provider does not support catalogs.
PK_TABLE_SCHEMA	String	Schema name in which the primary key table is defined, or Null if the provider does not support schemas.
PK_TABLE_NAME	String	Primary key table name.
PK_COLUMN_NAME	String	Primary key column name.
PK_COLUMN_GUID	GUID	Primary key column GUID.
PK_COLUMN_PROPID	Long	Primary key column property ID.
FK_TABLE_CATALOG	String	Catalog name in which the foreign key table is defined, or Null if the provider does not support catalogs.
FK_TABLE_SCHEMA	String	Schema name in which the foreign key table is defined, or Null if the provider does not support schemas.
FK_TABLE_NAME	String	Foreign key table name.
FK_COLUMN_NAME	String	Foreign key column name.
FK_COLUMN_GUID	GUID	Foreign key column GUID.
FK_COLUMN_PROPID	Long	Foreign key column property ID.
ORDINAL	Long	The order of the column in the key. For example, a table might contain several foreign key references to another table. The ordinal starts over for each reference; for example, two references to a three-column key would return 1, 2, 3, 1, 2, 3.
UPDATE_RULE	String	The action if an UPDATE rule was specified. This will be Null only if the provider cannot determine the UPDATE_RULE. In most cases, this implies a default of NO ACTION.
DELETE_RULE	String	The action if a DELETE rule was specified. This will be Null if the provider cannot determine the DELETE_RULE. In most cases, this implies a default of NO ACTION.

Column name	Type	Description
FK_NAME	String	Foreign key name, or Null if the provider does not support named foreign key constraints.
PK_NAME	String	Primary key name, or Null if the provider does not support named primary key constraints.
DEFERRABILITY	Integer	Deferrability of the foreign key. Value is one of the following DBPROPVAL_DF types, as shown in Appendix F.

For UPDATE_RULE and DELETE_RULE, the value will be one of the following:

CASCADE   A referential action of CASCADE was specified.

SET NULL   A referential action of SET NULL was specified.

SET DEFAULT A referential action of SET DEFAULT was specified.

NO ACTION   A referential action of NO ACTION was specified.

adSchemaIndexes

Identifies the list of indexes in the catalog.

Column name	Type	Description
TABLE_CATALOG	String	Catalog name, or Null if the provider does not support catalogs.
TABLE_SCHEMA	String	Unqualified schema name, or Null if the provider does not support schemas.
TABLE_NAME	String	Table name.
INDEX_CATALOG	String	Catalog name, or Null if the provider does not support catalogs.
INDEX_SCHEMA	String	Schema name, or Null if the provider does not support schemas.
INDEX_NAME	String	Index name.
PRIMARY_KEY	Boolean	Whether the index represents the primary key on the table, or Null if this is not known.
UNIQUE	Boolean	Whether index keys must be unique. This will be **True** if the index keys must be unique, and **False** if duplicate keys are allowed.

308

Column name	Type	Description
CLUSTERED	Boolean	Whether an index is clustered.
INTEGRATED	Boolean	Whether the index is integrated (all base table columns are available from the index). This will be **True** if the index is integrated, and **False** if the index is not integrated. For clustered indexes, this value must always be **True**.
TYPE	Integer	The type of the index. One of the DBPROPVAL_IT constants as shown in Appendix F
FILL_FACTOR	Long	For a B+-tree index, this property represents the storage utilization factor of page nodes during the creation of the index.
INITIAL_SIZE	Long	The total amount of bytes allocated to this structure at creation time.
NULLS	Long	Whether null keys are allowed This will be one of the DBPROVAL_IN constants as shown in Appendix F.
SORT_BOOKMARKS	Boolean	How the index treats repeated keys. This will be **True** if the index sorts repeated keys by bookmark, and **False** if it doesn't.
AUTO_UPDATE	Boolean	Whether the index is maintained automatically when changes are made to the corresponding base table. This will be **True** if the index is automatically maintained, and **False** if it isn't.
NULL_COLLATION	Long	How Nulls are collated in the index. This will be one of the DBPROPVAL_NC constants as shown in Appendix F.
ORDINAL_POSITION	Long	Ordinal position of the column in the index, starting with one.
COLUMN_NAME	String	Column name.
COLUMN_GUID	GUID	Column GUID.
COLUMN_PROPID	Long	Column property ID.
COLLATION	Integer	Identifies the sort order, and will be one of the DB_COLLATION constants as shown in Appendix F.

Column name	Type	Description
CARDINALITY	Unsigned Big Integer	Number of unique values in the index.
PAGES	Long	Number of pages used to store the index.
FILTER_CONDITION	String	The WHERE clause identifying the filtering restriction.
INTEGRATED	Boolean	Whether the index is integrated, that is, all base table columns are available from the index. This will be **True** if the index is integrated, and **False** if it isn't. Clustered indexes always set this value to **True**.

adSchemaKeyColumnUsage

This identifies the key columns, and table names, in the catalog.

Column name	Type	Description
CONSTRAINT_CATALOG	String	Catalog name, or Null if the provider does not support catalogs.
CONSTRAINT_SCHEMA	String	Schema name, or Null if the provider does not support schemas.
CONSTRAINT_NAME	String	Constraint name.
TABLE_CATALOG	String	Catalog name in which the table containing the key column is defined, or Null if the provider does not support catalogs.
TABLE_SCHEMA	String	Schema name in which the table containing the key column is defined, or Null if the provider does not support schemas.
TABLE_NAME	String	Table name containing the key column.
COLUMN_NAME	String	Name of the column participating in the unique, primary, or foreign key.
COLUMN_GUID	GUID	Column GUID.
COLUMN_PROPID	Long	Column property ID.
ORDINAL_POSITION	Long	Ordinal position of the column in the constraint being described.

adSchemaPrimaryKeys

This identifies the primary keys, and table name, in the catalog.

Column name	Type	Description
PK_NAME	String	Primary key name, or Null if the provider does not support primary key constraints.
TABLE_CATALOG	String	Catalog name in which the table is defined, or Null if the provider does not support catalogs.
TABLE_SCHEMA	String	Schema name in which the table is defined, or Null if the provider does not support schemas.
TABLE_NAME	String	Table name.
COLUMN_NAME	String	Primary key column name.
COLUMN_GUID	GUID	Primary key column GUID.
COLUMN_PROPID	Long	Primary key column property ID.
ORDINAL	Long	The order of the column names (and GUIDs and property IDs) in the key.

adSchemaProcedureColumns

This identifies the columns used in procedures.

Column name	Type	Description
PROCEDURE_CATALOG	String	Catalog name, or Null if the provider does not support catalogs.
PROCEDURE_SCHEMA	String	Schema name, or Null if the provider does not support schemas.
PROCEDURE_NAME	String	Table name.
COLUMN_NAME	String	The name of the column, or Null if this cannot be determined. This might not be unique.
COLUMN_GUID	GUID	Column GUID.
COLUMN_PROPID	Long	Column property ID.
ROWSET_NUMBER	Long	Number of the rowset containing the column. This is greater than one only if the procedure returns multiple rowsets.

Column name	Type	Description
ORDINAL_POSITION	Long	The ordinal of the column. Columns are numbered starting from one, or Null if there is no stable ordinal value for the column.
IS_NULLABLE	Boolean	Will be **True** if the column might be nullable, or **False** if the column is known not to be nullable.
DATA_TYPE	Integer	The indicator of the column's data type. For a list of valid Types, DataTypeEnum in Appendix F.
TYPE_GUID	GUID	The GUID of the column's data type.
CHARACTER_MAXIMUM_LENGTH	Long	The maximum possible length of a value in the column.
CHARACTER_OCTET_LENGTH	Long	Maximum length in octets (bytes) of the column, if the type of the column is character or binary. A value of zero means the column has no maximum length. Null for all other types of columns.
NUMERIC_PRECISION	Integer	If the column's data type is numeric, this is the maximum precision of the column. If the column's data type is not numeric, this is Null.
NUMERIC_SCALE	Integer	If the column's Type is DBTYPE_DECIMAL or DBTYPE_NUMERIC, this is the number of digits to the right of the decimal point. Otherwise, this is Null.
DESCRIPTION	String	Column description

CHARACTER_MAXIMUM_LENGTH will vary depending upon the data type of the column:

For character, binary, or bit columns, this is one of the following:

- The maximum length of the column in characters, bytes, or bits, respectively, if one is defined. For example, a CHAR(5) column in a SQL table has a maximum length of five (5).
- The maximum length of the data type in characters, bytes, or bits, respectively, if the column does not have a defined length.
- Zero (0) if neither the column nor the data type has a defined maximum length.

It will be Null for all other types of columns.

adSchemaProcedureParameters

This identifies the parameters of stored procedures.

Column name	Type	Description
PROCEDURE_CATALOG	String	Catalog name, or Null if the provider does not support catalogs.
PROCEDURE_SCHEMA	String	Schema name, or Null if the provider does not support catalogs.
PROCEDURE_NAME	String	Procedure name.
PARAMETER_NAME	String	Parameter name, or Null if the parameter is not named.
ORDINAL_POSITION	Integer	If the parameter is an input, input/output, or output parameter, this is the one-based ordinal position of the parameter in the procedure call. If the parameter is the return value, this is zero.
PARAMETER_TYPE	Integer	The type (direction) of the parameter, which will be one of the DBPARAM_TYPE constants, as shown in Appendix F. If the provider cannot determine the parameter type, this is Null.
PARAMETER_HASDEFAULT	Boolean	**True** if the parameter has a default value, or **False** if it doesn't or the provider doesn't know whether it has a default value.
PARAMETER_DEFAULT	String	Default value of parameter. A default value of Null is a valid default.
IS_NULLABLE	Boolean	**True** if the parameter might be nullable, or **False** if the parameter is not nullable.
DATA_TYPE	Integer	The indicator of the parameter's data type. For a list of valid Types, see DataTypeEnum in Appendix F.
CHARACTER_MAXIMUM_ LENGTH	Long	The maximum possible length of a value in the parameter.
CHARACTER_OCTET_ LENGTH	Long	Maximum length in octets (bytes) of the parameter, if the type of the parameter is character or binary. A value of zero means the parameter has no maximum length. Null for all other types of parameters.

Column name	Type	Description
NUMERIC_PRECISION	Integer	If the column's data type is numeric, this is the maximum precision of the column. If the column's data type is not numeric, this is Null.
NUMERIC_SCALE	Integer	If the column's Type is DBTYPE_DECIMAL or DBTYPE_NUMERIC, this is the number of digits to the right of the decimal point. Otherwise, this is Null.
DESCRIPTION	String	Parameter description.
TYPE_NAME	String	Provider-specific data type name.
LOCAL_TYPE_NAME	String	Localized version of TYPE_NAME, or Null if the data provider does not support a localized name.

CHARACTER_MAXIMUM_LENGTH will vary depending upon the data type of the column:

For character, binary, or bit columns, this is one of the following:

- The maximum length of the column in characters, bytes, or bits, respectively, if one is defined. For example, a CHAR(5) column in a SQL table has a maximum length of five (5).
- The maximum length of the data type in characters, bytes, or bits, respectively, if the column does not have a defined length.
- Zero (0) if neither the column nor the data type has a defined maximum length.

It will be Null for all other types of columns.

adSchemaProcedures

This identifies the stored procedures or queries.

Column name	Type	Description
PROCEDURE_CATALOG	String	Catalog name, or Null if the provider does not support catalogs.
PROCEDURE_SCHEMA	String	Schema name, or Null if the provider does not support schemas.
PROCEDURE_NAME	String	Procedure name.
PROCEDURE_TYPE	Integer	Identifies whether there will be a return value or not, and will be one of the DB_PT constants as defined in Appendix F.

Column name	Type	Description
PROCEDURE_DEFINITION	String	Procedure definition.
DESCRIPTION	String	Procedures description.
DATE_CREATED	Date/Time	Date when the procedure was created or Null if the provider does not have this information.
DATE_MODIFIED	Date/Time	Date when the procedure definition was last modified or Null if the provider does not have this information.

adSchemaProviderSpecific

The contents returned by this setting are dependent upon the provider, and you should consult the provider-specific information for details regarding them.

adSchemaProviderTypes

This identifies the data types supported by the provider.

Column name	Type	Description
TYPE_NAME	String	Provider-specific data type name.
DATA_TYPE	Integer	The indicator of the data type.
COLUMN_SIZE	Long	The length of a non-numeric column or parameter refers to either the maximum or the defined length for this type by the provider. For character data, this is the maximum or defined length in characters. For datetime data types, this is the length of the String representation (assuming the maximum allowed precision of the fractional seconds component). If the data type is numeric, this is the upper bound on the maximum precision of the data type.
LITERAL_PREFIX	String	Character or characters used to prefix a literal of this type in a text command.
LITERAL_SUFFIX	String	Character or characters used to suffix a literal of this type in a text command.

Column name	Type	Description
CREATE_PARAMS	String	The creation parameters are specified by the consumer when creating a column of this data type. For example, the SQL data type DECIMAL needs a precision and a scale. In this case, the creation parameters might be the String "precision,scale". In a text command to create a DECIMAL column with a precision of 10 and a scale of 2, the value of the TYPE_NAME column might be DECIMAL() and the complete type specification would be DECIMAL(10,2).
IS_NULLABLE	Boolean	**True** if the data type is nullable, **False** if the data type is not nullable, and Null if it is not known whether the data type is nullable.
CASE_SENSITIVE	Boolean	**True** if the data type is a character type and is case sensitive, or **False** if the data type is not a character type or is not case sensitive.
SEARCHABLE	Long	Identifies whether the column can be used in WHERE clauses, and will be one of the DB_SEARCHABLE constants as shown in Appendix F.
UNSIGNED_ATTRIBUTE	Boolean	**True** if the data type is unsigned, **False** if the data type is signed, or Null if not applicable to data type.
FIXED_PREC_SCALE	Boolean	**True** if the data type has a fixed precision and scale, or **False** if the data type does not have a fixed precision and scale.
AUTO_UNIQUE_VALUE	Boolean	True if values of this type can be autoincrementing, or False if values of this type cannot be autoincrementing.
LOCAL_TYPE_NAME	String	Localized version of TYPE_NAME, or Null if a localized name is not supported by the data provider.
MINIMUM_SCALE	Integer	The minimum number of digits allowed to the right of the decimal point, for decimal and numeric data types. Otherwise, this is Null.

Column name	Type	Description
MAXIMUM_SCALE	Integer	The maximum number of digits allowed to the right of the decimal point, for a decimal and numeric data types. Otherwise, this is Null.
GUID	GUID	The GUID of the type. All types supported by a provider are described in a type library, so each type has a corresponding GUID.
TYPELIB	String	The type library containing the description of this type.
VERSION	String	The version of the type definition. Providers may wish to version type definitions. Different providers may use different version schemes, such as a timestamp or number (integer or float), or Null if not supported.
IS_LONG	Boolean	**True** if the data type is a BLOB that contains very long data; the definition of very long data is provider-specific, or **False** if the data type is a BLOB that does not contain very long data or is not a BLOB.
BEST_MATCH	Boolean	**True** if the data type is the best match between all data types in the data source and the OLEDB data type indicated by the value in the DATA_TYPE column, or **False** if the data type is not the best match.
IS_FIXEDLENGTH	Boolean	**True** if columns of this type created by the DDL will be of fixed length, or **False** if columns of this type created by the DDL will be of variable length. If the field is Null, it is not known whether the provider will map this field with a fixed or variable length.

adSchemaReferentialConstraints

This identifies the referential integrity constraints for the catalog.

Column name	Type	Description
CONSTRAINT_CATALOG	String	Catalog name, or Null if the provider does not support catalogs.
CONSTRAINT_SCHEMA	String	Schema name, or Null if the provider does not support schemas.
CONSTRAINT_NAME	String	Constraint name.
UNIQUE_CONSTRAINT_ CATALOG	String	Catalog name in which the unique or primary key constraint is defined, or Null if the provider does not support catalogs.
UNIQUE_CONSTRAINT_ SCHEMA	String	Unqualified schema name in which the unique or primary key constraint is defined, or Null if the provider does not support schemas.
UNIQUE_CONSTRAINT_ NAME	String	Unique or primary key constraint name.
MATCH_OPTION	String	The type of match that was specified.
UPDATE_RULE	String	The action if an UPDATE rule was specified. This will be Null only if the provider cannot determine the UPDATE_RULE. In most cases, this implies a default of NO ACTION.
DELETE_RULE	String	The action if a DELETE rule was specified. This will be Null if the provider cannot determine the DELETE_RULE. In most cases, this implies a default of NO ACTION.
DESCRIPTION	String	Human-readable description of the constraint.

For MATCH_OPTION, the values will be one of:

NONE   No match type was specified.
PARTIAL   A match type of PARTIAL was specified.
FULL   A match type of FULL was specified.

For UPDATE_RULE and DELETE_RULE, the value will be one of the following:

CASCADE   A referential action of CASCADE was specified.
SET NULL   A referential action of SET NULL was specified.
SET DEFAULT   A referential action of SET DEFAULT was specified.
NO ACTION   A referential action of NO ACTION was specified.

adSchemaSchemata

This identifies the schemas that are owned by a particular user.

Column name	Type	Description
CATALOG_NAME	String	Catalog name, or Null if the provider does not support catalogs.
SCHEMA_NAME	String	Unqualified schema name.
SCHEMA_OWNER	String	User that owns the schemas.
DEFAULT_CHARACTER_SET_CATALOG	String	Catalog name of the default character set for columns and domains in the schemas, or Null if the provider does not support catalogs or different character sets.
DEFAULT_CHARACTER_SET_SCHEMA	String	Unqualified schema name of the default character set for columns and domains in the schemas, or Null if the provider does not support different character sets.
DEFAULT_CHARACTER_SET_NAME	String	Default character set name, or Null if the provider does not support different character sets.

adSchemaSQLLanguages

This identifies the conformance levels and other options supported by the catalog.

Column name	Type	Description
SQL_LANGUAGE_SOURCE	String	Should be "ISO 9075" for standard SQL.
SQL_LANGUAGE_YEAR	String	Should be "1992" for ANSI SQL92-compliant SQL.
SQL_LANGUAGE_CONFORMANCE	String	The language conformance level.
SQL_LANGUAGE_INTEGRITY	String	This will be **Yes** if optional integrity feature is supported, or **No** if optional integrity feature is not supported.
SQL_LANGUAGE_IMPLEMENTATION	String	Null for "ISO 9075" implementation.

Column name	Type	Description
SQL_LANGUAGE_ BINDING_STYLE	String	"DIRECT" for C/C++ callable direct execution of SQL.
SQL_LANGUAGE_ PROGRAMMING_ LANGUAGE	String	Null.

SQL_LANGUAGE_CONFORMANCE will be one of the following values:

ENTRY	For entry level conformance
INTERMEDIATE	for intermediate conformance
FULL	for full conformance

adSchemaStatistics

This identifies the catalog statistics.

Column name	Type	Description
TABLE_CATALOG	String	Catalog name, or Null if the provider does not support catalogs.
TABLE_SCHEMA	String	Schema name, or Null if the provider does not support schemas.
TABLE_NAME	String	Table name.
CARDINALITY	Unsigned Big Integer	Cardinality (number of rows) of the table.

adSchemaTableConstraints

This identifies the referential table constraints.

Column name	Type	Description
CONSTRAINT_CATALOG	String	Catalog name, or Null if the provider does not support catalogs.
CONSTRAINT _SCHEMA	String	Schema name, or Null if the provider does not support schemas.
CONSTRAINT_NAME	String	Constraint name.
TABLE_CATALOG	String	Catalog name in which the table is defined, or Null if the provider does not support catalogs.

320

Column name	Type	Description
TABLE _SCHEMA	String	Unqualified schema name in which the table is defined, or Null if the provider does not support schemas.
TABLE_NAME	String	Table name.
CONSTRAINT_TYPE	String	The constraint type.
IS_DEFERRABLE	Boolean	**False** if the table constraint is not deferrable.
INITIALLY_DEFERRED	Boolean	**True** if the table constraint is initially deferred, or **False** if the table constraint is initially immediate.
DESCRIPTION	String	Column description

CONSTRAINT_TYPE will be one of the following values:

UNIQUE	for a unique constraint
PRIMARY KEY	for a primary key constraint
FOREIGN KEY	for a foreign key constraint
CHECK	for a check constraint

adSchemaTablePrivileges

This identifies the user privileges of tables.

Column name	Type	Description
GRANTOR	String	User who granted the privileges on the table in TABLE_NAME.
GRANTEE	String	User name (or "PUBLIC") to whom the privilege has been granted.
TABLE_CATALOG	String	Catalog name in which the table is defined, or Null if the provider does not support catalogs.
TABLE_SCHEMA	String	Unqualified schema name in which the table is defined, or Null if the provider does not support schemas.
TABLE_NAME	String	Table name.
PRIVILEGE_TYPE	String	Privilege type.
IS_GRANTABLE	Boolean	**False** if the privilege being described was granted with the WITH GRANT OPTION clause, or **True** if the privilege being described was not granted with the WITH GRANT OPTION clause.

PRIVILEGE_TYPE will be one of the following values:

SELECT	for SELECT privileges
DELETE	for DELETE privileges
INSERT	for INSERT privileges
UPDATE	for UPDATE privileges
REFERENCES	for REFERENCE privileges

adSchemaTables

This identifies the tables in a catalog.

Column name	Type	Description
TABLE_CATALOG	String	Catalog name, or Null if the provider does not support catalogs.
TABLE_SCHEMA	String	Schema name, or Null if the provider does not support schemas.
TABLE_NAME	String	Table name. This column cannot contain a Null.
TABLE_TYPE	String	Table type. This column cannot contain a Null.
TABLE_GUID	GUID	GUID that uniquely identifies the table. Providers that do not use GUIDs to identify tables should return Null in this column.
DESCRIPTION	String	Human-readable description of the table, or Null if there is no description associated with the column.
TABLE_PROPID	Long	Property ID of the table. Providers which do not use PROPIDs to identify columns should return Null in this column.
DATE_CREATED	Date/Time	Date when the table was created or Null if the provider does not have this information.
DATE_MODIFIED	Date/Time	Date when the table definition was last modified or Null if the provider does not have this information.

TABLE_TYPE will be one of the following, or a provider-specific value.

ALIAS	The table is an alias
TABLE	The table is a normal table
SYNONYM	The table is a synonym
SYSTEM TABLE	The table is a system table
VIEW	The table is a view

GLOBAL TEMPORARY	The table is a global, temporary table
LOCAL TEMPORARY	The table is a local, temporary table

Provider specific values should be defined in the provider documentation. For example, Access returns **PASS-THROUGH** for linked tables.

adSchemaTranslations

This identifies character translations that the catalog supports.

Column name	Type	Description
TRANSLATION_CATALOG	String	Catalog name, or Null if the provider does not support catalogs.
TRANSLATION_SCHEMA	String	Schema name, or Null if the provider does not support schemas.
TRANSLATION_NAME	String	Translation name.
SOURCE_CHARACTER_ SET_CATALOG	String	Catalog name containing the source character set on which the translation is defined, or Null if the provider does not support catalogs.
SOURCE_CHARACTER_ SET_SCHEMA	String	Unqualified schema name containing the source character set on which the translation is defined, or Null if the provider does not support schemas.
SOURCE_CHARACTER_ SET_NAME	String	Source character set name on which the translation is defined.
TARGET_CHARACTER_ SET_CATALOG	String	Catalog name containing the target character set on which the translation is defined, or Null if the provider does not support catalogs.
TARGET_CHARACTER_ SET_SCHEMA	String	Unqualified schema name containing the target character set on which the translation is defined, or Null if the provider does not support schemas.
TARGET_CHARACTER_ SET_NAME	String	Target character set name on which the translation is defined.

adSchemaUsagePrivileges

This identifies the usage privileges that are available to a user.

Column name	Type	Description
GRANTOR	String	User who granted the privileges on the object in OBJECT_NAME.
GRANTEE	String	User name (or "PUBLIC") to whom the privilege has been granted.
OBJECT_CATALOG	String	Catalog name in which the object is defined, or Null if the provider does not support catalogs.
OBJECT_SCHEMA	String	Unqualified schema name in which the object is defined, or Null if the provider does not support schemas.
OBJECT_NAME	String	Object name.
OBJECT_TYPE	String	Object type.
PRIVILEGE_TYPE	String	Privilege type.
IS_GRANTABLE	Boolean	**True** if the privilege being described was granted with the WITH GRANT OPTION clause, or **False** if the privilege being described was not granted with the WITH GRANT OPTION clause.

OBJECT_TYPE will be one of the following values:

DOMAIN	The object is a domain
CHARACTER SET	The object is a character set
COLLATION	The object is a collation
TRANSLATION	The object is a translation

adSchemaViewColumnUsage

This identifies the columns used in views.

Column name	Type	Description
VIEW_CATALOG	String	Catalog name, or Null if the provider does not support catalogs.
VIEW_SCHEMA	String	Schema name, or Null if the provider does not support schemas.
VIEW_NAME	String	View name.

Column name	Type	Description
TABLE_CATALOG	String	Catalog name in which the table is defined, or Null if the provider does not support catalogs.
TABLE_SCHEMA	String	Schema name in which the table is defined, or Null if the provider does not support schemas.
TABLE_NAME	String	Table name.
COLUMN_NAME	String	Column name.
COLUMN_GUID	GUID	Column GUID.
COLUMN_PROPID	Long	Column property ID.

adSchemaViewTableUsage

This identifies the tables used in views.

Column name	Type	Description
VIEW_CATALOG	String	Catalog name, or Null if the provider does not support catalogs.
VIEW_SCHEMA	String	Schema name, or Null if the provider does not support schemas.
VIEW_NAME	String	View name.
TABLE_CATALOG	String	Catalog name in which the table is defined, or Null if the provider does not support catalogs.
TABLE_SCHEMA	String	Schema name in which the table is defined, or Null if the provider does not support schemas.
TABLE_NAME	String	Table name.

adSchemaViews

This identifies the views in the catalog.

Column name	Type	Description
TABLE_CATALOG	String	Catalog name, or Null if the provider does not support catalogs.
TABLE_SCHEMA	String	Schema name, or Null if the provider does not support schemas.
TABLE_NAME	String	View name.

325

Column name	Type	Description
VIEW_DEFINITION	String	View definition. This is a query expression.
CHECK_OPTION	Boolean	**True** if local update checking only, or **False** for cascaded update checking (same as no CHECK OPTION specified on view definition).
IS_UPDATABLE	Boolean	**True** if the view is updateable, or **False** if the view is not updateable.
DESCRIPTION	String	View description.
DATE_CREATED	Date/ Time	Date when the view was created or Null if the provider does not have this information.
DATE_MODIFIED	Date/ Time	Date when the view definition was last modified or Null if the provider does not have this information.

Schema Usage

Using schemas is quite easy, since all you need to do is use the `OpenSchema` method of the connection object. For example, to list all of the tables on a particular connection:

```
Set objRec = objConn.OpenSchema (adSchemaTables)
While Not objRec.EOF
   Print objRec("TABLE_NAME")
   objRec.MoveNext
Wend
```

This simply opens a recordset on the tables schema and loops through it printing each table name. You can use the `TABLE_TYPE` column to check for system tables:

```
Set objRec = objConn.OpenSchema (adSchemaTables)
While Not objRec.EOF
   If objRec("TABLE_TYPE") <> "SYSTEM TABLE" Then
      Print objRec("TABLE_NAME")
   End If
   objRec.MoveNext
Wend
```

You can use the `Restrictions` argument of `OpenSchema` to only return certain rows. This argument accepts an array that matched the column names. For example, to find only the system tables:

```
Set objRec - objConn.OpenSchema (adSchemaTables, _
                     Array (Empty, Empty, Empty, "SYSTEM_TABLE"))
```

Since the type is the fourth column in the recordset, you need to specify empty values for the columns you wish to skip.

When connecting to Microsoft Access, there are some interesting things you should be aware of. If you wish to see the queries, then you might have to use both **adSchemaProcedures** and **adSchemaViews** depending upon the query type. Normal select queries appear as Views, whereas action queries (Update, Delete, etc) and CrossTab queries appear as procedures. This is only for the native Jet provider. For the ODBC provider, select and crosstab queries appear as tables with a table type of **VIEW**.

Appendix

E

Data Types

You might find the large array of data types supported by ADO confusing, especially since your language or database might not support them all. The following table details the **DataTypeEnum** constants and how they map to SQL and language data types.

A blank value indicates that the language does not natively support the data type, although there may be support in other libraries, or other data types might be used instead. For example, the **com.ms.wfc.data** import library for J++ has support for dates and timestamp types, amongst others, but these are not supported by J++ natively.

Constant	Access	SQL Server	Visual Basic	Visual C++	Visual J++
adBinary		binary, timestamp	Variant		
adBoolean	Yes/No	bit	Boolean	bool	boolean
adChar		char	String	char[]	String
adCurrency	Currency	money, smallmoney	Currency		
adDate	Date/Time[1]		Date		
adDBTimeStamp	Date/Time[2]	datetime, smalldatetime	Variant		
adDouble	Number (Double)	float	Double	double	double
adGUID	Number (Replication ID)[1]			char[]	String, char[]
adInteger	Number (Long Integer),	int, Identity Autonumber	Long	int	int
adLongVarBinary	OLE Object	image	Variant		
adLongVarChar	Memo, Hyperlink	text	String		
adNumeric		decimal, numeric			
adSingle	Number (Single)	real	Single	float	float
adSmallInt	Number (Integer)	smallint	Integer	short	short
adUnsignedTinyInt	Number (Byte)	tinyint	Byte	char	byte
adVarBinary	Number (Replication ID)[2]	varbinary		char[]	byte[]
adVarChar	Text	varchar	String	char[]	String, byte[]

[1] When using the OLEDB Provider for Jet
[2] When using the OLEDB Provider for ODBC

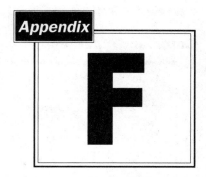

Appendix

F

Constants

Standard Constants

The following constants are predefined by ADO. For scripting languages these
are included in **adovbs.inc** or **adojava.inc**, which can be found in the
Program Files\Common Files\System\ado directory. For Visual Basic
these are automatically included when you reference the ADO library.

AffectEnum

Name	Value	Description
adAffectAll	3	Operation affects all records in the recordset.
adAffectAllChapters	4	Operation affects all child (chapter) records.
adAffectCurrent	1	Operation affects only the current record.
adAffectGroup	2	Operation affects records that satisfy the current **Filter** property.

BookmarkEnum

Name	Value	Description
adBookmarkCurrent	0	Default. Start at the current record.
adBookmarkFirst	1	Start at the first record.
adBookmarkLast	2	Start at the last record.

CommandTypeEnum

Name	Value	Description
adCmdFile	256	Indicates that the provider should evaluate **CommandText** as a previously persisted file.
adCmdStoredProc	4	Indicates that the provider should evaluate **CommandText** as a stored procedure.
adCmdTable	2	Indicates that the provider should generate a SQL query to return all rows from the table named in **CommandText**.
adCmdTableDirect	512	Indicates that the provider should return all rows from the table named in **CommandText**.
adCmdText	1	Indicates that the provider should evaluate **CommandText** as textual definition of a command, such as a SQL statement.
adCmdUnknown	8	Indicates that the type of command in **CommandText** unknown.

CompareEnum

Name	Value	Description
adCompareEqual	1	The bookmarks are equal.
adCompareGreaterThan	2	The first bookmark is after the second.
adCompareLessThan	0	The first bookmark is before the second.
adCompareNotComparable	4	The bookmarks cannot be compared.
adCompareNotEqual	3	The bookmarks are not equal and not ordered.

ConnectModeEnum

Name	Value	Description
adModeRead	1	Indicates read-only permissions.
adModeReadWrite	3	Indicates read/write permissions.
adModeShareDenyNone	16	Prevents others from opening connection with any permissions.
adModeShareDenyRead	4	Prevents others from opening connection with read permissions.
adModeShareDenyWrite	8	Prevents others from opening connection with write permissions.
adModeShareExclusive	12	Prevents others from opening connection.
adModeUnknown	0	Default. Indicates that the permissions have not yet been set or cannot be determined.
adModeWrite	2	Indicates write-only permissions.

ConnectOptionEnum

Name	Value	Description
adAsyncConnect	16	Open the connection asynchronously
adConnectUnspecified	-1	The connection mode is unspecified.

ConnectPromptEnum

Name	Value	Description
adPromptAlways	1	Always prompt for connection information.
adPromptComplete	2	Only prompt if not enough information was supplied.
adPromptCompleteRequired	3	Only prompt if not enough information was supplied, but disable any options not directly applicable to the connection.
adPromptNever	4	Default. Never prompt for connection information.

CursorLocationEnum

Name	Value	Description
adUseClient	3	Use client-side cursors supplied by the local cursor library.
adUseClientBatch	3	Use client-side cursors supplied by the local cursor library.
adUseNone	1	No cursor services are used.
adUseServer	2	Default. Uses data provider driver supplied cursors.

CursorOptionEnum

Name	Value	Description
adAddNew	16778240	You can use the **AddNew** method to add new records.
adApproxPosition	16384	You can read and set the **AbsolutePosition** and **AbsolutePage** properties.
adBookmark	8192	You can use the **Bookmark** property to access specific records.
adDelete	16779264	You can use the **Delete** method to delete records.
adFind	524288	You can use the **Find** method to find records.
adHoldRecords	256	You can retrieve more records or change the next retrieve position without committing all pending changes.
adMovePrevious	512	You can use the **ModeFirst**, **MovePrevious**, **Move** and **GetRows** methods.
adNotify	262144	The recordset supports Notifications.
adResync	131072	You can update the cursor with the data visible in the underlying database with the **Resync** method.
adUpdate	16809984	You can use the **Update** method to modify existing records.
adUpdateBatch	65536	You can use the **UpdateBatch** or **CancelBatch** methods to transfer changes to the provider in groups.

CursorTypeEnum

Name	Value	Description
adOpenDynamic	2	Opens a dynamic type cursor.
adOpenForwardOnly	0	Default. Opens a forward-only type cursor
adOpenKeyset	1	Opens a keyset type cursor.
adOpenStatic	3	Opens a static type cursor.
adOpenUnspecified	-1	Indicates as unspecified value for cursor type.

DataTypeEnum

Name	Value	Description
adBigInt	20	An 8-byte signed integer.
adBinary	128	A binary value.
adBoolean	11	A Boolean value.
adBSTR	8	A null-terminated character string.
adChapter	136	A chapter type, indicating a child recordset.
adChar	129	A String value.
adCurrency	6	A currency value. An 8-byte signed integer scaled by 10,000, with 4 digits to the right of the decimal point.
adDate	7	A Date value. A Double where the whole part is the number of days since December 30 1899, and the fractional part is a fraction of the day.
adDBDate	133	A date value (yyyymmdd).
adDBFileTime	137	A database file time.
adDBTime	134	A time value (hhmmss).
adDBTimeStamp	135	A date-time stamp (yyyymmddhhmmss plus a fraction in billionths).
adDecimal	14	An exact numeric value with fixed precision and scale.
adDouble	5	A double-precision floating point value.
adEmpty	0	No value was specified.

Name	Value	Description
adError	10	A 32-bit error code.
adFileTime	64	A DOS/Win32 file time. The number of 100 nanosecond intervals since Jan 1 1601.
adGUID	72	A globally unique identifier.
adIDispatch	9	A pointer to an **IDispatch** interface on an OLE object.
adInteger	3	A 4-byte signed integer.
adIUnknown	13	A pointer to an **IUnknown** interface on an OLE object.
adLongVarBinary	205	A long binary value.
adLongVarChar	201	A long String value.
adLongVarWChar	203	A long null-terminated string value.
adNumeric	131	An exact numeric value with a fixed precision and scale.
adPropVariant	138	A variant that is not equivalent to an Automation variant.
adSingle	4	A single-precision floating point value.
adSmallInt	2	A 2-byte signed integer.
adTinyInt	16	A 1-byte signed integer.
adUnsignedBigInt	21	An 8-byte unsigned integer.
adUnsignedInt	19	An 4-byte unsigned integer.
adUnsignedSmallInt	18	An 2-byte unsigned integer.
adUnsignedTinyInt	17	An 1-byte unsigned integer.
adUserDefined	132	A user-defined variable.
adVarBinary	204	A binary value.
adVarChar	200	A String value.
adVariant	12	An Automation Variant.
adVarNumeric	139	A variable width exact numeric, with a signed scale value.
adVarWChar	202	A null-terminated Unicode character string.
adWChar	130	A null-terminated Unicode character string.

EditModeEnum

Name	Value	Description
adEditAdd	2	Indicates that the AddNew method has been invoked and the current record in the buffer is a new record that hasn't been saved to the database.
adEditDelete	4	Indicates that the Delete method has been invoked.
adEditInProgress	1	Indicates that data in the current record has been modified but not saved.
adEditNone	0	Indicates that no editing is in progress.

ErrorValueEnum

Name	Value	Description
adErrBoundToCommand	3707	The application cannot change the ActiveConnection property of a Recordset object with a Command object as its source.
adErrDataConversion	3421	The application is using a value of the wrong type for the current application.
adErrFeatureNotAvailable	3251	The operation requested by the application is not supported by the provider.
adErrIllegalOperation	3219	The operation requested by the application is not allowed in this context.
adErrInTransaction	3246	The application cannot explicitly close a Connection object while in the middle of a transaction.
adErrInvalidArgument	3001	The application is using arguments that are the wrong type, are out of the acceptable range, or are in conflict with one another.
adErrInvalidConnection	3709	The application requested an operation on an object with a reference to a closed or invalid Connection object.

Name	Value	Description
`adErrInvalidParamInfo`	3708	The application has improperly defined a `Parameter` object.
`adErrItemNotFound`	3265	ADO could not find the object in the collection.
`adErrNoCurrentRecord`	3021	Either `BOF` or `EOF` is `True`, or the current record has been deleted. The operation requested by the application requires a current record.
`adErrNotExecuting`	3715	The operation is not executing.
`adErrNotReentrant`	3710	The operation is not reentrant.
`adErrObjectClosed`	3704	The operation requested by the application is not allowed if the object is closed.
`adErrObjectInCollection`	3367	Can't append. Object already in collection.
`adErrObjectNotSet`	3420	The object referenced by the application no longer points to a valid object.
`adErrObjectOpen`	3705	The operation requested by the application is not allowed if the object is open.
`adErrOperationCancelled`	3712	The operation was cancelled.
`adErrProviderNotFound`	3706	ADO could not find the specified provider.
`adErrStillConnecting`	3713	The operation is still connecting.
`adErrStillExecuting`	3711	The operation is still executing.
`adErrUnsafeOperation`	3716	The operation is unsafe under these circumstances.

EventReasonEnum

Name	Value	Description
`adRsnAddNew`	1	A new record is to be added.
`adRsnClose`	9	The object is being closed.
`adRsnDelete`	2	The record is being deleted.
`adRsnFirstChange`	11	The record has been changed for the first time.
`adRsnMove`	10	A `Move` has been invoked and the current record pointer is being moved.

Name	Value	Description
adRsnMoveFirst	12	A **MoveFirst** has been invoked and the current record pointer is being moved.
adRsnMoveLast	15	A **MoveLast** has been invoked and the current record pointer is being moved.
adRsnMoveNext	13	A **MoveNext** has been invoked and the current record pointer is being moved.
adRsnMovePrevious	14	A **MovePrevious** has been invoked and the current record pointer is being moved.
adRsnRequery	7	The recordset was requeried.
adRsnResynch	8	The recordset was resynchronized.
adRsnUndoAddNew	5	The addition of a new record has been cancelled.
adRsnUndoDelete	6	The deletion of a record has been cancelled.
adRsnUndoUpdate	4	The update of a record has been cancelled.
adRsnUpdate	3	The record is being updated.

EventStatusEnum

Name	Value	Description
adStatusCancel	4	Request cancellation of the operation that is about to occur.
adStatusCantDeny	3	A **Will** event cannot request cancellation of the operation about to occur.
adStatusErrorsOccurred	2	The operation completed unsuccessfully, or a **Will** event cancelled the operation.
adStatusOK	1	The operation completed successfully.
adStatusUnwantedEvent	5	Events for this operation are no longer required.

ExecuteOptionEnum

Name	Value	Description
adAsyncExecute	16	The operation is executed asynchronously.
adAsyncFetch	32	The records are fetched asynchronously.
adAsyncFetchNonBlocking	64	The records are fetched asynchronously without blocking subsequent operations.
adExecuteNoRecords	128	Indicates CommandText is a command or stored procedure that does not return rows. Always combined with adCmdText or adCmdStoreProc.

FieldAttributeEnum

Name	Value	Description
adFldCacheDeferred	4096	Indicates that the provider caches field values and that subsequent reads are done from the cache.
adFldFixed	16	Indicates that the field contains fixed-length data.
adFldIsNullable	32	Indicates that the field accepts Null values.
adFldKeyColumn	32768	The field is part of a key column.
adFldLong	128	Indicates that the field is a long binary field, and that the AppendChunk and GetChunk methods can be used.
adFldMayBeNull	64	Indicates that you can read Null values from the field.
adFldMayDefer	2	Indicates that the field is deferred, that is, the field values are not retrieved from the data source with the whole record, but only when you access them.
adFldNegativeScale	16384	The field has a negative scale.
adFldRowID	256	Indicates that the field some kind of record ID.
adFldRowVersion	512	Indicates that the field time or date stamp used to track updates.

Name	Value	Description
`adFldUnknownUpdatable`	8	Indicates that the provider cannot determine if you can write to the field.
`adFldUpdatable`	4	Indicates that you can write to the field.

FilterGroupEnum

Name	Value	Description
`adFilterAffectedRecords`	2	Allows you to view only records affected by the last Delete, **Resync**, **UpdateBatch**, or **CancelBatch** method.
`adFilterConflictingRecords`	5	Allows you to view the records that failed the last batch update attempt.
`adFilterFetchedRecords`	3	Allows you to view records in the current cache.
`adFilterNone`	0	Removes the current filter and restores all records to view.
`adFilterPendingRecords`	1	Allows you to view only the records that have changed but have not been sent to the server. Only applicable for batch update mode.
`adFilterPredicate`	4	Allows you to view records that failed the last batch update attempt.

GetRowsOptionEnum

Name	Value	Description
`adGetRowsRest`	-1	Retrieves the remainder of the rows in the recordset.

343

IsolationLevelEnum

Name	Value	Description
adXactAsyncPhaseOne	524288	Performs an asynchronous commit.
adXactBrowse	256	Indicates that from one transaction you can view uncommitted changes in other transactions.
adXactChaos	16	Default. Indicates that you cannot overwrite pending changes from more highly isolated transactions.
adXactCommitRetaining	131072	The provider will automatically start a new transaction after a **CommitTrans** method call.
adXactCursorStability	4096	Default. Indicates that from one transaction you can view changes in other transactions only after they have been committed.
adXactIsolated	1048576	Indicates that transactions are conducted in isolation of other transactions.
adXactReadCommitted	4096	Same as **adXactCursorStability**.
adXactReadUncommitted	256	Same as **adXactBrowse**.
adXactRepeatableRead	65536	Indicates that from one transaction you cannot see changes made in other transactions, but that requerying can bring new recordsets.
adXactSerializable	1048576	Same as **adXactIsolated**.
adXactSyncPhaseOne	1048576	Performs an synchronous commit.
adXactUnspecified	-1	Indicates that the provider is using a different **IsolationLevel** than specified, but that the level cannot be identified.

LockTypeEnum

Name	Value	Description
adLockBatchOptimistic	4	Optimistic batch updates.
adLockOptimistic	3	Optimistic locking, record by record. The provider locks records when **Update** is called.
adLockPessimistic	2	Pessimistic locking, record by record. The provider locks the record immediately upon editing.
adLockReadOnly	1	Default. Read only, data cannot be modified.
adLockUnspecified	-1	The clone is created with the same lock type as the original.

MarshalOptionsEnum

Name	Value	Description
adMarshalAll	0	Default. Indicates that all rows are returned to the server.
adMarshalModifiedOnly	1	Indicates that only modified rows are returned to the server.

ObjectStateEnum

Name	Value	Description
adStateClosed	0	Default. Indicates that the object is closed.
adStateConnecting	2	Indicates that the object is connecting.
adStateExecuting	4	Indicates that the object is executing a command.
adStateFetching	8	Indicates that the rows of the recordset are being fetched.
adStateOpen	1	Indicates that the object is open.

345

ParameterAttributesEnum

Name	Value	Description
adParamLong	128	Indicates that the parameter accepts long binary data.
adParamNullable	64	Indicates that the parameter accepts Null values.
adParamSigned	16	Default. Indicates that the parameter accepts signed values.

ParameterDirectionEnum

Name	Value	Description
adParamInput	1	Default. Indicates an input parameter.
adParamInputOutput	3	Indicates both an input and output parameter.
adParamOutput	2	Indicates an output parameter.
adParamReturnValue	4	Indicates a return value.
adParamUnknown	0	Indicates parameter direction is unknown.

PersistFormatEnum

Name	Value	Description
adPersistADTG	0	Default. Persist data in Advanced Data TableGram format.
adPersistXML	1	Persist data in XML format. This format is not supported in ADO 2.0 but will be supported in ADO 2.1, to be released with Internet Explorer 5.

PositionEnum

Name	Value	Description
adPosBOF	-2	The current record pointer is at BOF.
adPosEOF	-3	The current record pointer is at EOF.
adPosUnknown	-1	The Recordset is empty, the current position is unknown, or the provider does not support the AbsolutePage property.

PropertyAttributesEnum

Name	Value	Description
adPropNotSupported	0	Indicates that the property is not supported by the provider.
adPropOptional	2	Indicates that the user does not need to specify a value for this property before the data source is initialized.
adPropRead	512	Indicates that the user can read the property.
adPropRequired	1	Indicates that the user must specify a value for this property before the data source is initialized.
adPropWrite	1024	Indicates that the user can set the property.

RecordStatusEnum

Name	Value	Description
adRecCanceled	256	The record was not saved because the operation was cancelled.
adRecCantRelease	1024	The new record was not saved because of existing record locks.
adRecConcurrencyViolation	2048	The record was not saved because optimistic concurrency was in use.
adRecDBDeleted	262144	The record has already been deleted from the data source.
adRecDeleted	4	The record was deleted.

Name	Value	Description
adRecIntegrityViolation	4096	The record was not saved because the user violated integrity constraints.
adRecInvalid	16	The record was not saved because its bookmark is invalid.
adRecMaxChangesExceeded	8192	The record was not saved because there were too many pending changes.
adRecModified	2	The record was modified.
adRecMultipleChanges	64	The record was not saved because it would have affected multiple records.
adRecNew	1	The record is new.
adRecObjectOpen	16384	The record was not saved because of a conflict with an open storage object.
adRecOK	0	The record was successfully updated.
adRecOutOfMemory	32768	The record was not saved because the computer has run out of memory.
adRecPendingChanges	128	The record was not saved because it refers to a pending insert.
adRecPermissionDenied	65536	The record was not saved because the user has insufficient permissions.
adRecSchemaViolation	131072	The record was not saved because it violates the structure of the underlying database.
adRecUnmodified	8	The record was not modified.

ResyncEnum

Name	Value	Description
adResyncAllValues	2	Default. Data is overwritten and pending updates are cancelled.
adResyncUnderlyingValues	1	Data is not overwritten and pending updates are not cancelled.

SchemaEnum

Name	Value	Description
`adSchemaAsserts`	0	Request assert information.
`adSchemaCatalogs`	1	Request catalog information.
`adSchemaCharacterSets`	2	Request character set information.
`adSchemaCheckConstraints`	5	Request check constraint information.
`adSchemaCollations`	3	Request collation information.
`adSchemaColumnPrivileges`	13	Request column privilege information.
`adSchemaColumns`	4	Request column information.
`adSchemaColumnsDomainUsage`	11	Request column domain usage information.
`adSchemaConstraintColumnUsage`	6	Request column constraint usage information.
`adSchemaConstraintTableUsage`	7	Request table constraint usage information.
`adSchemaCubes`	32	For multi-dimensional data, view the Cubes schema.
`adSchemaDBInfoKeywords`	30	Request the keywords from the provider.
`adSchemaDBInfoLiterals`	31	Request the literals from the provider.
`adSchemaDimensions`	33	For multi-dimensional data, view the Dimensions schema.
`adSchemaForeignKeys`	27	Request foreign key information.
`adSchemaHierarchies`	34	For multi-dimensional data, view the Hierarchies schema.
`adSchemaIndexes`	12	Request index information.
`adSchemaKeyColumnUsage`	8	Request key column usage information.
`adSchemaLevels`	35	For multi-dimensional data, view the Levels schema.
`adSchemaMeasures`	36	For multi-dimensional data, view the Measures schema.
`adSchemaMembers`	38	For multi-dimensional data, view the Members schema.
`adSchemaPrimaryKeys`	28	Request primary key information.
`adSchemaProcedureColumns`	29	Request stored procedure column information.

Name	Value	Description
adSchemaProcedureParameters	26	Request stored procedure parameter information.
adSchemaProcedures	16	Request stored procedure information.
adSchemaProperties	37	For multi-dimensional data, view the Properties schema.
adSchemaProviderSpecific	-1	Request provider specific information.
adSchemaProviderTypes	22	Request provider type information.
adSchemaReferentialContraints	9	Request referential constraint information.
adSchemaSchemata	17	Request schema information.
adSchemaSQLLanguages	18	Request SQL language support information.
adSchemaStatistics	19	Request statistics information.
adSchemaTableConstraints	10	Request table constraint information.
adSchemaTablePrivileges	14	Request table privilege information.
adSchemaTables	20	Request information about the tables.
adSchemaTranslations	21	Request character set translation information.
adSchemaUsagePrivileges	15	Request user privilege information.
adSchemaViewColumnUsage	24	Request column usage in views information.
adSchemaViews	23	Request view information.
adSchemaViewTableUsage	25	Request table usage in views information.

SearchDirection

Name	Value	Description
adSearchBackward	-1	Search backward from the current record.
adSearchForward	1	Search forward from the current record.

SearchDirectionEnum

Name	Value	Description
adSearchBackward	-1	Search backward from the current record.
adSearchForward	1	Search forward from the current record.

StringFormatEnum

Name	Value	Description
adClipString	2	Rows are delimited by user defined values.

XactAttributeEnum

Name	Value	Description
adXactAbortRetaining	262144	The provider will automatically start a new transaction after a RollbackTrans method call.
adXactAsyncPhaseOne	524288	Perform an asynchronous commit.
adXactCommitRetaining	131072	The provider will automatically start a new transaction after a CommitTrans method call.
adXactSyncPhaseOne	1048576	Performs an synchronous commit.

Miscellaneous Constants

These values are not included in the standard **adovbs.inc** include file (and are not automatically supplied when using Visual Basic), but can be found in **adocon.inc** (for ASP) and **adocon.bas** (for Visual Basic) from the supporting web site, **http://webdev.wrox.co.uk/books/1835**.

Many of these may not be necessary to you as an ADO programmer, but they are included here for completeness, and are only really useful as bitmask values for entries in the Properties collection.

ADCPROP_UPDATECRITERIA_ENUM

Name	Value	Description
adCriteriaAllCols	1	Collisions should be detected if there is a change to any column.
adCriteriaKey	0	Collisions should be detected if there is a change to the key column.
adCriteriaTimeStamp	3	Collisions should be detected if a row has been accessed.
adCriteriaUpdCols	2	Collisions should be detected if there is a change to columns being updated.

DB_COLLATION

Name	Value	Description
DB_COLLATION_ASC	1	The sort sequence for the column is ascending.
DB_COLLATION_DESC	2	The sort sequence for the column is descending.

DB_IMP_LEVEL

Name	Value	Description
DB_IMP_LEVEL_ANONYMOUS	0	The client is anonymous to the server, and the server process cannot obtain identification information about the client and cannot impersonate the client.
DB_IMP_LEVEL_DELEGATE	3	The process can impersonate the client's security context while acting on behalf of the client. The server process can also make outgoing calls to other servers while acting on behalf of the client.
DB_IMP_LEVEL_IDENTIFY	1	The server can obtain the client's identity, and can impersonate the client for ACL checking, but cannot access system objects as the client.
DB_IMP_LEVEL_IMPERSONATE	2	The server process can impersonate the client's security context whilst acting on behalf of the client. This information is obtained upon connection and not on every call.

DB_MODE

Name	Value	Description
DB_MODE_READ	1	Read only.
DB_MODE_READWRITE	3	Read/Write (DB_MODE_READ + DB_MODE_WRITE).
DB_MODE_SHARE_DENY_NONE	16	Neither read nor write access can be denied to others.
DB_MODE_SHARE_DENY_READ	4	Prevents others from opening in read mode.
DB_MODE_SHARE_DENY_WRITE	8	Prevents others from opening in write mode.
DB_MODE_SHARE_EXCLUSIVE	12	Prevents others from opening in read/write mode (DB_MODE_SHARE_DENY_WRITE + DB_MODE_SHARE_DENY_WRITE).
DB_MODE_WRITE	2	Write only.

DB_PROT_LEVEL

Name	Value	Description
DB_PROT_LEVEL_CALL	2	Authenticates the source of the data at the beginning of each request from the client to the server.
DB_PROT_LEVEL_CONNECT	1	Authenticates only when the client establishes the connection with the server.
DB_PROT_LEVEL_NONE	0	Performs no authentication of data sent to the server.
DB_PROT_LEVEL_PKT	3	Authenticates that all data received is from the client.
DB_PROT_LEVEL_PKT_INTEGRITY	4	Authenticates that all data received is from the client and that it has not been changed in transit.
DB_PROT_LEVEL_PKT_PRIVACY	5	Authenticates that all data received is from the client, that it has not been changed in transit, and protects the privacy of the data by encrypting it.

DB_PT

Name	Value	Description
DB_PT_FUNCTION	3	Function; there is a returned value.
DB_PT_PROCEDURE	2	Procedure; there is no returned value.
DB_PT_UNKNOWN	1	It is not known whether there is a returned value.

DB_SEARCHABLE

Name	Value	Description
DB_ALL_EXCEPT_LIKE	3	The data type can be used in a WHERE clause with all comparison operators except LIKE.
DB_LIKE_ONLY	2	The data type can be used in a WHERE clause only with the LIKE predicate.
DB_SEARCHABLE	4	The data type can be used in a WHERE clause with any comparison operator.
DB_UNSEARCHABLE	1	The data type cannot be used in a WHERE clause.

DBCOLUMNDESCFLAG

Name	Value	Description
DBCOLUMNDESCFLAG_CLSID	8	The CLSID portion of the column description can be changed when altering the column.
DBCOLUMNDESCFLAG_COLSIZE	16	The column size portion of the column description can be changed when altering the column.
DBCOLUMNDESCFLAG_DBCID	32	The DBCID portion of the column description can be changed when altering the column.
DBCOLUMNDESCFLAG_ITYPEINFO	2	The type information portion of the column description can be changed when altering the column.
DBCOLUMNDESCFLAG_PRECISION	128	The precision portion of the column description can be changed when altering the column.

Name	Value	Description
DBCOLUMNDESCFLAG_ PROPERTIES	4	The property sets portion of the column description can be changed when altering the column.
DBCOLUMNDESCFLAG_SCALE	256	The numeric scale portion of the column description can be changed when altering the column.
DBCOLUMNDESCFLAG_TYPENAME	1	The type name portion of the column description can be changed when altering the column.
DBCOLUMNDESCFLAG_WTYPE	64	The data type portion of the column description can be changed when altering the column.

DBCOLUMNFLAGS

Name	Value	Description
DBCOLUMNFLAGS_ CACHEDEFERRED	4096	Indicates that the value of a deferred column is cached when it is first read.
DBCOLUMNFLAGS_ISCHAPTER	8192	The column contains a Chapter value.
DBCOLUMNFLAGS_ ISFIXEDLENGTH	16	All of the data in the column is of a fixed length.
DBCOLUMNFLAGS_ISLONG	128	The column contains a BLOB value that contains long data.
DBCOLUMNFLAGS_ISNULLABLE	32	The column can be set to NULL, or the provider cannot determine whether the column can be set to NULL.
DBCOLUMNFLAGS_ISROWID	256	The column contains a persistent row identifier.
DBCOLUMNFLAGS_ISROWVER	512	The column contains a timestamp or other row versioning data type.
DBCOLUMNFLAGS_MAYBENULL	64	NULLs can be got from the column.
DBCOLUMNFLAGS_MAYDEFER	2	The column is deferred.
DBCOLUMNFLAGS_WRITE	4	The column may be updated.
DBCOLUMNFLAGS_WRITEUNKNOWN	8	It is not know if the column can be updated.

DBPARAMTYPE

Name	Value	Description
DBPARAMTYPE_INPUT	1	The parameter is an input parameter.
DBPARAMTYPE_INPUTOUTPUT	2	The parameter is both an input and an output parameter.
DBPARAMTYPE_OUTPUT	3	The parameter is an output parameter.
DBPARAMTYPE_RETURNVALUE	4	The parameter is a return value.

DBPROMPT

Name	Value	Description
DBPROMPT_COMPLETE	2	Prompt the user only if more information is needed.
DBPROMPT_COMPLETEREQUIRED	3	Prompt the user only if more information is required. Do not allow the user to enter optional information.
DBPROMPT_NOPROMPT	4	Do not prompt the user.
DBPROMPT_PROMPT	1	Always prompt the user for initialization information.

DBPROPVAL_AO

Name	Value	Description
DBPROPVAL_AO_RANDOM	2	Columns can be accessed in any order.
DBPROPVAL_AO_SEQUENTIAL	0	All columns must be accessed in sequential order determined by the column ordinal.
DBPROPVAL_AO_ SEQUENTIALSTORAGEOBJECTS	1	Columns bound as storage objects can only be accessed in sequential order as determined by the column ordinal.

DBPROPVAL_ASYNCH

Name	Value	Description
DBPROPVAL_ASYNCH_ BACKGROUNDPOPULATION	8	The rowset is populated asynchronously in the background.
DBPROPVAL_ASYNCH_ INITIALIZE	1	Initialization is performed asynchronously.
DBPROPVAL_ASYNCH_ POPULATEONDEMAND	32	The consumer prefers to optimize for getting each individual request for data returned as quickly as possible.
DBPROPVAL_ASYNCH_ PREPOPULATE	16	The consumer prefers to optimize for retrieving all data when the row set is materialized.
DBPROPVAL_ASYNCH_ RANDOMPOPULATION	4	Rowset population is performed asynchronously in a random manner.
DBPROPVAL_ASYNCH_ SEQUENTIALPOPULATION	2	Rowset population is performed asynchronously in a sequential manner.

DBPROPVAL_BG

Name	Value	Description
DBPROPVAL_GB_COLLATE	16	A COLLATE clause can be specified at the end of each grouping column.
DBPROPVAL_GB_CONTAINS_ SELECT	4	The GROUP BY clause must contain all non-aggregated columns in the select list. It can contain columns that are not in the select list.
DBPROPVAL_GB_EQUALS_ SELECT	2	The GROUP BY clause must contain all non-aggregated columns in the select list. It cannot contain any other columns.
DBPROPVAL_GB_NO_RELATION	8	The columns in the GROUP BY clause and the select list are not related. The meaning on non-grouped, non-aggregated columns in the select list is data source dependent.
DBPROPVAL_GB_NOT_SUPPORTED	1	GROUP BY clauses are not supported.

DBPROPVAL_BI

Name	Value	Description
DBPROPVAL_BI_CROSSROWSET	1	Bookmark values are valid across all rowsets generated on this table.

DBPROPVAL_BMK

Name	Value	Description
DBPROPVAL_BMK_KEY	2	The bookmark type is key.
DBPROPVAL_BMK_NUMERIC	1	The bookmark type is numeric.

DBPROPVAL_BO

Name	Value	Description
DBPROPVAL_BO_NOINDEXUPDATE	1	The provider is not required to update indexes based on inserts or changes to the rowset. Any indexes need to be re-created following changes made through the rowset.
DBPROPVAL_BO_NOLOG	0	The provider is not required to log inserts or changes to the rowset.
DBPROPVAL_BO_REFINTEGRITY	2	Referential integrity constraints do not need to be checked or enforced for changes made through the rowset.

DBPROPVAL_CB

Name	Value	Description
DBPROPVAL_CB_NON_NULL	2	The result is the concatenation of the non-NULL valued column or columns.
DBPROPVAL_CB_NULL	1	The result is NULL valued.

DBPROPVAL_CB

Name	Value	Description
DBPROPVAL_CB_DELETE	1	Aborting a transaction deletes prepared commands.
DBPROPVAL_CB_PRESERVE	2	Aborting a transaction preserves prepared commands.

DBPROPVAL_CD

Name	Value	Description
DBPROPVAL_CD_NOTNULL	1	Columns can be created non-nullable.

DBPROPVAL_CL

Name	Value	Description
DBPROPVAL_CL_END	2	The catalog name appears at the end of the fully qualified name.
DBPROPVAL_CL_START	1	The catalog name appears at the start of the fully qualified name.

DBPROPVAL_CO

Name	Value	Description
DBPROPVAL_CO_BEGINSWITH	32	Provider supports the BEGINSWITH and NOTBEGINSWITH operators.
DBPROPVAL_CO_CASEINSENSITIVE	8	Provider supports the CASEINSENSITIVE operator.
DBPROPVAL_CO_CASESENSITIVE	4	Provider supports the CASESENSITIVE operator.
DBPROPVAL_CO_CONTAINS	16	Provider supports the CONTAINS and NOTCONTAINS operators.
DBPROPVAL_CO_EQUALITY	1	Provider supports the following operators: LT, LE, EQ, GE, GT, NE.
DBPROPVAL_CO_STRING	2	Provider supports the BEGINSWITH operator.

DBPROPVAL_CS

Name	Value	Description
DBPROPVAL_CS_ COMMUNICATIONFAILURE	2	The DSO is unable to communicate with the data store.
DBPROPVAL_CS_INITIALIZED	1	The DSO is in an initialized state and able to communicate with the data store.
DBPROPVAL_CS_UNINITIALIZED	0	The DSO is in an uninitialized state.

DBPROPVAL_CU

Name	Value	Description
DBPROPVAL_CU_DML_ STATEMENTS	1	Catalog names are supported in all Data Manipulation Language statements.
DBPROPVAL_CU_INDEX_ DEFINITION	4	Catalog names are supported in all index definition statements.
DBPROPVAL_CU_PRIVILEGE_ DEFINITION	8	Catalog names are supported in all privilege definition statements.
DBPROPVAL_CU_TABLE_ DEFINITION	2	Catalog names are supported in all table definition statements.

DBPROPVAL_DF

Name	Value	Description
DBPROPVAL_DF_INITIALLY_ DEFERRED	1	The foreign key is initially deferred.
DBPROPVAL_DF_INITIALLY_ IMMEDIATE	2	The foreign key is initially immediate.
DBPROPVAL_DF_NOT_ DEFERRABLE	3	The foreign key is not deferrable.

DBPROPVAL_DST

Name	Value	Description
DBPROPVAL_DST_MDP	2	The provider is a multidimensional provider.
DBPROPVAL_DST_TDP	1	The provider is a tabular data provider.
DBPROPVAL_DST_TDPANDMDP	3	The provider is both a TDP and a MD provider.

DBPROPVAL_HT

Name	Value	Description
DBPROPVAL_HT_DIFFERENT_ CATALOGS	1	The provider supports heterogeneous joins between catalogs.
DBPROPVAL_HT_DIFFERENT_ PROVIDERS	2	The provider supports heterogeneous joins between providers.

DBPROPVAL_IC

Name	Value	Description
DBPROPVAL_IC_LOWER	2	Identifiers in SQL are case insensitive and are stored in lower case in system catalog.
DBPROPVAL_IC_MIXED	8	Identifiers in SQL are case insensitive and are stored in mixed case in system catalog.
DBPROPVAL_IC_SENSITIVE	4	Identifiers in SQL are case sensitive and are stored in mixed case in system catalog.
DBPROPVAL_IC_UPPER	1	Identifiers in SQL are case insensitive and are stored in upper case in system catalog.

DBPROPVAL_IN

Name	Value	Description
DBPROPVAL_IN_DISALLOWNULL	1	The index does not allow entries where the key columns are NULL. An error will be generated if the consumer attempts to insert a NULL value into a key column.
DBPROPVAL_IN_IGNOREANYNULL	4	The index does not insert entries containing NULL keys.
DBPROPVAL_IN_IGNORENULL	2	The index does not insert entries where some column key has a NULL value.

DBPROPVAL_IT

Name	Value	Description
DBPROPVAL_IT_BTREE	1	The index is a B+ tree.
DBPROPVAL_IT_CONTENT	3	The index is a content index.
DBPROPVAL_IT_HASH	2	The index is a hash file using linear or extensible hashing.
DBPROPVAL_IT_OTHER	4	The index is some other type of index.

DBPROPVAL_LM

Name	Value	Description
DBPROPVAL_LM_INTENT	4	The provider uses the maximum level of locking to ensure that changes will not fail due to a concurrency violation.
DBPROPVAL_LM_NONE	1	The provider is not required to lock rows at any time to ensure successful updates.
DBPROPVAL_LM_READ	2	The provider uses the minimum level of locking to ensure that changes will not fail due to a concurrency violation.
DBPROPVAL_LM_SINGLEROW	2	The provider uses the minimum level of locking to ensure that changes will not fail due to a concurrency violation.

DBPROPVAL_MR

Name	Value	Description
DBPROPVAL_MR_CONCURRENT	2	More than one rowset create by the same multiple results object can exist concurrently.
DBPROPVAL_MR_NOTSUPPORTED	0	Multiple results objects are not supported.
DBPROPVAL_MR_SUPPORTED	1	The provider supports multiple results objects.

DBPROPVAL_NC

Name	Value	Description
DBPROPVAL_NC_END	1	NULLs are sorted at the end of the list, regardless of the sort order.
DBPROPVAL_NC_HIGH	2	NULLs are sorted at the high end of the list.
DBPROPVAL_NC_LOW	4	NULLs are sorted at the low end of the list.
DBPROPVAL_NC_START	8	NULLs are sorted at the start of the list, regardless of the sort order.

DBPROPVAL_NP

Name	Value	Description
DBPROPVAL_NP_ABOUTTODO	2	The consumer will be notified before an action (ie the Will event).
DBPROPVAL_NP_DIDEVENT	16	The consumer will be notified after an action (ie the Complete event).
DBPROPVAL_NP_FAILEDTODO	8	The consumer will be notified if an action failed (ie a Will or Complete event).
DBPROPVAL_NP_OKTODO	1	The consumer will be notified of events.
DBPROPVAL_NP_SYNCHAFTER	4	The consumer will be notified when the rowset is resynchronized.

DBPROPVAL_NT

Name	Value	Description
DBPROPVAL_NT_MULTIPLEROWS	2	For methods that operate on multiple rows, and generate multiphased notifications (events), then the provider calls **OnRowChange** once for all rows that succeed and once for all rows that fail.
DBPROPVAL_NT_SINGLEROW	1	For methods that operate on multiple rows, and generate multiphased notifications (events), then the provider calls **OnRowChange** separately for each phase for each row.

DBPROPVAL_OA

Name	Value	Description
DBPROPVAL_OA_ATEXECUTE	2	Output parameter data is available immediately after the **Command.Execute** returns.
DBPROPVAL_OA_ATROWRELEASE	4	Output parameter data is available when the rowset is release. For a single rowset operation this is when the rowset is completely released (closed) and for a multiple rowset operation this is when the next rowset if fetched. The consumer's bound memory is in an indeterminate state before the parameter data becomes available.
DBPROPVAL_OA_NOTSUPPORTED	1	Output parameters are not supported.

DBPROPVAL_OO

Name	Value	Description
DBPROPVAL_OO_BLOB	1	The provider supports access to BLOBs as structured storage objects.
DBPROPVAL_OO_IPERSIST	2	The provider supports access to OLE objects through OLE.

DBPROPVAL_OS

Name	Value	Description
DBPROPVAL_OS_ENABLEALL	-1	All services should be invoked. This is the default.
DBPROPVAL_OS_RESOURCEPOOLING	1	Resources should be pooled.
DBPROPVAL_OS_TXNENLISTMENT	2	Sessions in an MTS environment should automatically be enlisted in a global transaction where required.

DBPROPVAL_PT

Name	Value	Description
DBPROPVAL_PT_GUID	8	The GUID is used as the persistent ID type.
DBPROPVAL_PT_GUID_NAME	1	The GUID Name is used as the persistent ID type.
DBPROPVAL_PT_GUID_PROPID	2	The GUID Property ID is used as the persistent ID type.
DBPROPVAL_PT_NAME	4	The Name is used as the persistent ID type.
DBPROPVAL_PT_PGUID_NAME	32	The Property GUID name is used as the persistent ID type.
DBPROPVAL_PT_PGUID_PROPID	64	The Property GUID Property ID is used as the persistent ID type.
DBPROPVAL_PT_PROPID	16	The Property ID is used as the persistent ID type.

DBPROPVAL_RD

Name	Value	Description
DBPROPVAL_RD_RESETALL	-1	The provider should reset all state associated with the data source, with the exception that any open object is not released.

DBPROPVAL_RT

Name	Value	Description
DBPROPVAL_RT_APTMTTHREAD	2	The DSO is apartment threaded.
DBPROPVAL_RT_FREETHREAD	1	The DSO is free threaded.
DBPROPVAL_RT_SINGLETHREAD	4	The DSO is single threaded.

DBPROPVAL_SQ

Name	Value	Description
DBPROPVAL_SQ_COMPARISON	2	All predicates that support subqueries support comparison subqueries.
DBPROPVAL_SQ_CORRELATEDSUBQUERIES	1	All predicates that support subqueries support correlated subqueries.
DBPROPVAL_SQ_EXISTS	4	All predicates that support subqueries support EXISTS subqueries.
DBPROPVAL_SQ_IN	8	All predicates that support subqueries support IN subqueries.
DBPROPVAL_SQ_QUANTIFIED	16	All predicates that support subqueries support quantified subqueries.

DBPROPVAL_SQL

Name	Value	Description
DBPROPVAL_SQL_ANDI89_IEF	8	The provider supports the ANSI SQL89 IEF level.
DBPROPVAL_SQL_ANSI92_ENTRY	16	The provider supports the ANSI SQL92 Entry level.
DBPROPVAL_SQL_ANSI92_FULL	128	The provider supports the ANSI SQL92 Full level.
DBPROPVAL_SQL_ANSI92_INTERMEDIATE	64	The provider supports the ANSI SQL92 Intermediate level.
DBPROPVAL_SQL_CORE	2	The provider supports the ODBC 2.5 Core SQL level.
DBPROPVAL_SQL_ESCAPECLAUSES	256	The provider supports the ODBC escape clauses syntax.
DBPROPVAL_SQL_EXTENDED	4	The provider supports the ODBC 2.5 EXTENDED SQL level.

Name	Value	Description
DBPROPVAL_SQL_FIPS_ TRANSITIONAL	32	The provider supports the ANSI SQL92 Transitional level.
DBPROPVAL_SQL_MINIMUM	1	The provider supports the ODBC 2.5 EXTENDED SQL level.
DBPROPVAL_SQL_NONE	0	SQL is not supported.
DBPROPVAL_SQL_ODBC_CORE	2	The provider supports the ODBC 2.5 Core SQL level.
DBPROPVAL_SQL_ODBC_ EXTENDED	4	The provider supports the ODBC 2.5 EXTENDED SQL level.
DBPROPVAL_SQL_ODBC_MINIMUM	1	The provider supports the ODBC 2.5 EXTENDED SQL level.
DBPROPVAL_SQL_SUBMINIMUM	512	The provider supports the DBGUID_SQL dialect and parses the command text according to SQL rules, but does not support wither the minimum ODBC level nor the ANSI SQL92 Entry level.

DBPROPVAL_SS

Name	Value	Description
DBPROPVAL_SS_ILOCKBYTES	8	The provider supports IlockBytes.
DBPROPVAL_SS_ ISEQUENTIALSTREAM	1	The provider supports IsequentialStream.
DBPROPVAL_SS_ISTORAGE	4	The provider supports Istorage.
DBPROPVAL_SS_ISTREAM	2	The provider supports IStream.

DBPROPVAL_SU

Name	Value	Description
DBPROPVAL_SU_DML_ STATEMENTS	1	Schema names are supported in all Data Manipulation Language statements.
DBPROPVAL_SU_INDEX_ DEFINITION	4	Schema names are supported in all index definition statements.
DBPROPVAL_SU_PRIVILEGE_ DEFINITION	8	Schema names are supported in all privilege definition statements.
DBPROPVAL_SU_TABLE_ DEFINITION	2	Schema names are supported in all table definition statements.

DBPROPVAL_TC

Name	Value	Description
DBPROPVAL_TC_ALL	8	Transactions can contain DDL and DML statements in any order.
DBPROPVAL_TC_DDL_COMMIT	2	Transactions can contain DML statements. DDL statements within a transaction cause the transaction to be committed.
DBPROPVAL_TC_DDL_IGNORE	4	Transactions can only contain DML statements. DDL statements within a transaction are ignored.
DBPROPVAL_TC_DML	1	Transactions can only contain Data Manipulation (DML) statements. DDL statements within a transaction cause an error.
DBPROPVAL_TC_NONE	0	Transactions are not supported.

DBPROPVAL_TI

Name	Value	Description
DBPROPVAL_TI_BROWSE	256	Changes made by other transactions are visible before they are committed.
DBPROPVAL_TI_CHAOS	16	Transactions cannot overwrite pending changes from more highly isolated transactions. This is the default.
DBPROPVAL_TI_CURSORSTABILITY	4096	Changes made by other transactions are not visible until those transactions are committed.
DBPROPVAL_TI_ISOLATED	1048576	All concurrent transactions will interact only in ways that produce the same effect as if each transaction were entirely executed one after the other.
DBPROPVAL_TI_READCOMMITTED	4096	Changes made by other transactions are not visible until those transactions are committed.
DBPROPVAL_TI_READUNCOMMITTED	256	Changes made by other transactions are visible before they are committed.
DBPROPVAL_TI_REPEATABLEREAD	65536	Changes made by other transactions are not visible.

368

Name	Value	Description
DBPROPVAL_TI_SERIALIZABLE	1048576	All concurrent transactions will interact only in ways that produce the same effect as if each transaction were entirely executed one after the other.

DBPROPVAL_TR

Name	Value	Description
DBPROPVAL_TR_ABORT	16	The transaction preserves its isolation context (ie, it preserves its locks if that is how isolation is implemented) across the retaining abort.
DBPROPVAL_TR_ABORT_DC	8	The transaction may either preserve or dispose of isolation context across a retaining abort.
DBPROPVAL_TR_ABORT_NO	32	The transaction is explicitly not to preserve its isolation across a retaining abort.
DBPROPVAL_TR_BOTH	128	Isolation is preserved across both a retaining commit and a retaining abort.
DBPROPVAL_TR_COMMIT	2	The transaction preserves its isolation context (ie, it preserves its locks if that is how isolation is implemented) across the retaining commit.
DBPROPVAL_TR_COMMIT_DC	1	The transaction may either preserve or dispose of isolation context across a retaining commit.
DBPROPVAL_TR_COMMIT_NO	4	The transaction is explicitly not to preserve its isolation across a retaining commit.
DBPROPVAL_TR_DONTCARE	64	The transaction may either preserve or dispose of isolation context across a retaining commit or abort. This is the default.
DBPROPVAL_TR_NONE	256	Isolation is explicitly not to be retained across either a retaining commit or abort.
DBPROPVAL_TR_OPTIMISTIC	512	Optimistic concurrency control is to be used.

DBPROPVAL_UP

Name	Value	Description
DBPROPVAL_UP_CHANGE	1	Indicates that **SetData** is supported.
DBPROPVAL_UP_DELETE	2	Indicates that **DeleteRows** is supported.
DBPROPVAL_UP_INSERT	4	Indicates that **InsertRow** is supported.

MD_DIMTYPE

Name	Value	Description
MD_DIMTYPE_MEASURE	2	A measure dimension.
MD_DIMTYPE_OTHER	3	The dimension is neither a time nor a measure dimension.
MD_DIMTYPE_TIME	1	A time dimension.
MD_DIMTYPE_UNKNOWN	0	The provider is unable to classify the dimension.

SQL_FN_NUM

Name	Value	Description
SQL_FN_NUM_ABS	1	The **ABS** function is supported by the data source.
SQL_FN_NUM_ACOS	2	The **ACOS** function is supported by the data source.
SQL_FN_NUM_ASIN	4	The **ASIN** function is supported by the data source.
SQL_FN_NUM_ATAN	8	The **ATAN** function is supported by the data source.
SQL_FN_NUM_ATAN2	16	The **ATAN2** function is supported by the data source.
SQL_FN_NUM_CEILING	32	The **CEILING** function is supported by the data source.
SQL_FN_NUM_COS	64	The **COS** function is supported by the data source.
SQL_FN_NUM_COT	128	The **COT** function is supported by the data source.
SQL_FN_NUM_DEGREES	262144	The **DEGREES** function is supported by the data source.

Name	Value	Description
SQL_FN_NUM_EXP	256	The **EXP** function is supported by the data source.
SQL_FN_NUM_FLOOR	512	The **FLOOR** function is supported by the data source.
SQL_FN_NUM_LOG	1024	The **LOG** function is supported by the data source.
SQL_FN_NUM_LOG10	524288	The **LOG10** function is supported by the data source.
SQL_FN_NUM_MOD	2048	The **MOD** function is supported by the data source.
SQL_FN_NUM_PI	65536	The **PI** function is supported by the data source.
SQL_FN_NUM_POWER	1048576	The **POWER** function is supported by the data source.
SQL_FN_NUM_RADIANS	2097152	The **RADIANS** function is supported by the data source.
SQL_FN_NUM_RAND	131072	The **RAND** function is supported by the data source.
SQL_FN_NUM_ROUND	4194304	The **ROUND** function is supported by the data source.
SQL_FN_NUM_SIGN	4096	The **SIGN** function is supported by the data source.
SQL_FN_NUM_SIN	8192	The **SIN** function is supported by the data source.
SQL_FN_NUM_SQRT	10384	The **SQRT** function is supported by the data source.
SQL_FN_NUM_TAN	32768	The **TAN** function is supported by the data source.
SQL_FN_NUM_TRUNCATE	8388608	The **TRUNCATE** function is supported by the data source.

SQL_FN_STR

Name	Value	Description
SQL_FN_STR_ASCII	8192	The **ASCII** function is supported by the data source.
SQL_FN_STR_BIT_LENGTH	524288	The **BIT_LENGTH** function is supported by the data source.
SQL_FN_STR_CHAR	16384	The **CHAR** function is supported by the data source.

Name	Value	Description
`SQL_FN_STR_CHAR_LENGTH`	1048576	The `CHAR_LENGTH` function is supported by the data source.
`SQL_FN_STR_CHARACTER_LENGTH`	2097152	The `CHARACTER_LENGTH` function is supported by the data source.
`SQL_FN_STR_CONCAT`	1	The `CONCAT` function is supported by the data source.
`SQL_FN_STR_DIFFERENCE`	32768	The `DIFFERENCE` function is supported by the data source.
`SQL_FN_STR_INSERT`	2	The `INSERT` function is supported by the data source.
`SQL_FN_STR_LCASE`	64	The `LCASE` function is supported by the data source.
`SQL_FN_STR_LEFT`	4	The `LEFT` function is supported by the data source.
`SQL_FN_STR_LENGTH`	16	The `LENGTH` function is supported by the data source.
`SQL_FN_STR_LOCATE`	32	The `LOCATE` function is supported by the data source.
`SQL_FN_STR_LOCATE_2`	65536	The `LOCATE_2` function is supported by the data source.
`SQL_FN_STR_LTRIM`	8	The `LTRIM` function is supported by the data source.
`SQL_FN_STR_OCTET_LENGTH`	4194304	The `OCTET_LENGTH` function is supported by the data source.
`SQL_FN_STR_POSITION`	8388608	The `POSITION` function is supported by the data source.
`SQL_FN_STR_REPEAT`	128	The `REPEAT` function is supported by the data source.
`SQL_FN_STR_REPLACE`	256	The `REPLACE` function is supported by the data source.
`SQL_FN_STR_RIGHT`	512	The `RIGHT` function is supported by the data source.
`SQL_FN_STR_RTRIM`	1024	The `RTRIM` function is supported by the data source.
`SQL_FN_STR_SOUNDEX`	131072	The `SOUNDEX` function is supported by the data source.
`SQL_FN_STR_SPACE`	262144	The `SPACE` function is supported by the data source.
`SQL_FN_STR_SUBSTRING`	2048	The `SUBSTRING` function is supported by the data source.
`SQL_FN_STR_UCASE`	4096	The `UCASE` function is supported by the data source.

SQL_FN_SYS

Name	Value	Description
SQL_FN_SYS_DBNAME	2	The **DBNAME** system function is supported.
SQL_FN_SYS_IFNULL	4	The **IFNULL** system function is supported.
SQL_FN_SYS_USERNAME	1	The **USERNAME** system function is supported.

SQL_OJ

Name	Value	Description
SQL_OJ_ALL_COMPARISON_OPS	64	The comparison operator in the **ON** clause can be any of the ODBC comparison operators. If this is not set, only the equals (=) comparison operator can be used in an outer join.
SQL_OJ_FULL	4	Full outer joins are supported.
SQL_OJ_INNER	32	The inner table (the right table in a left outer join or the left table in a right outer join) can also be used in an inner join. This does not apply to full out joins, which do not have an inner table.
SQL_OJ_LEFT	1	Left outer joins are supported.
SQL_OJ_NESTED	8	Nested outer joins are supported.
SQL_OJ_NOT_ORDERED	16	The column names in the **ON** clause of the outer join do not have to be in the same order as their respective table names in the **OUTER JOIN** clause.
SQL_OJ_RIGHT	2	Right outer joins are supported.

SQL_SDF_CURRENT

Name	Value	Description
SQL_SDF_CURRENT_DATE	1	The **CURRENT_DATE** system function is supported.
SQL_SDF_CURRENT_TIME	2	The **CURRENT_TIME** system function is supported.
SQL_SDF_CURRENT_TIMESTAMP	4	The **CURRENT_TIMESTAMP** system function is supported.

SSPROP_CONCUR

Name	Value	Description
SSPROP_CONCUR_LOCK	4	Use row locking to prevent concurrent access.
SSPROP_CONCUR_READ_ONLY	8	The rowset is read-only. Full concurrency is supported.
SSPROP_CONCUR_ROWVER	1	Use row versioning to determining concurrent access violations. The SQL Table or tables must contain a **timestamp** column.
SSPROP_CONCUR_VALUES	2	Use the values in of columns in the rowset row.

SSPROPVAL_USEPROCFORPREP

Name	Value	Description
SSPROPVAL_USEPROCFORPREP_ OFF	0	A temporary stored procedure is not created when a command is prepared.
SSPROPVAL_USEPROCFORPREP_ ON	1	A temporary stored procedure is created when a command is prepared. Temporary stored procedures are dropped when the session is released.
SSPROPVAL_USEPROCFORPREP_ ON_DROP	2	A temporary stored procedure is created when a command is prepared. The procedure is dropped when the command is unprepared, or a new command text is set, or when all application references to the command are released.

374

RDS Constants

ADCExecuteOptionEnum

Name	Value	Description
adcExecAsync	2	The next **Refresh** of the recordset is executed asynchronously.
adcExecSync	1	The next **Refresh** of the recordset is executed synchronously.

ADCFetchOptionEnum

Name	Value	Description
adcFetchAsync	3	Records are fetched in the background and control is returned to the application immediately. Attempts to access a record not yet read will cause control to return immediately, and the nearest record to the sought record returned. This indicates that the end of the recordset has been reached, even though there may be more records.
adcFetchBackground	2	The first batch of records is read and control returns to the application. Access to records not in the first batch will cause a wait until the requested record is fetched.
adcFetchUpFront	1	The complete Recordset is fetched before control is returned to the application.

ADCReadyStateEnum

Name	Value	Description
adcReadyStateComplete	4	All rows have been fetched.
adcReadyStateInteractive	3	Rows are still being fetched, although some rows are available.
adcReadyStateLoaded	2	The recordset is not available for use as the rows are still being loaded.

375

ADO Error Numbers

The following lists the standard ADO errors and their descriptions:

Error Number	Description
-2147483647	Not implemented.
-2147483646	Ran out of memory.
-2147483645	One or more arguments are invalid.
-2147483644	No such interface supported.
-2147483643	Invalid pointer.
-2147483642	Invalid handle.
-2147483641	Operation aborted.
-2147483640	Unspecified error.
-2147483639	General access denied error.
-2147483638	The data necessary to complete this operation is not yet available.
-2147467263	Not implemented.
-2147467262	No such interface supported.
-2147467261	Invalid pointer.
-2147467260	Operation aborted.
-2147467259	Unspecified error.
-2147467258	Thread local storage failure.
-2147467257	Get shared memory allocator failure.
-2147467256	Get memory allocator failure.
-2147467255	Unable to initialize class cache.
-2147467254	Unable to initialize RPC services.
-2147467253	Cannot set thread local storage channel control.
-2147467252	Could not allocate thread local storage channel control.

Error Number	Description
-2147467251	The user supplied memory allocator is unacceptable.
-2147467250	The OLE service mutex already exists.
-2147467249	The OLE service file mapping already exists.
-2147467248	Unable to map view of file for OLE service.
-2147467247	Failure attempting to launch OLE service.
-2147467246	There was an attempt to call CoInitialize a second time while single threaded.
-2147467245	A Remote activation was necessary but was not allowed.
-2147467244	A Remote activation was necessary but the server name provided was invalid.
-2147467243	The class is configured to run as a security id different from the caller.
-2147467242	Use of OLE1 services requiring DDE windows is disabled.
-2147467241	A RunAs specification must be <domain name>\<user name> or simply <user name>.
-2147467240	The server process could not be started. The pathname may be incorrect.
-2147467239	The server process could not be started as the configured identity. The pathname may be incorrect or unavailable.
-2147467238	The server process could not be started because the configured identity is incorrect. Check the username and password.
-2147467237	The client is not allowed to launch this server.
-2147467236	The service providing this server could not be started.
-2147467235	This computer was unable to communicate with the computer providing the server.
-2147467234	The server did not respond after being launched.
-2147467233	The registration information for this server is inconsistent or incomplete.
-2147467232	The registration information for this interface is inconsistent or incomplete.
-2147467231	The operation attempted is not supported.
-2147418113	Catastrophic failure.
-2147024891	General access denied error.
-2147024890	Invalid handle.
-2147024882	Ran out of memory.
-2147024809	One or more arguments are invalid.

Listed below are the OLEDB errors, and whilst they might not be relevant for some of the ADO work, they are included for completeness:

Error Number	Description
-2147217920	Invalid accessor.
-2147217919	Creating another row would have exceeded the total number of active rows supported by the rowset.
-2147217918	Unable to write with a read-only accessor.
-2147217917	Given values violate the database schema.
-2147217916	Invalid row handle.
-2147217915	An object was open.
-2147217914	Invalid chapter.
-2147217913	A literal value in the command could not be converted to the correct type due to a reason other than data overflow.
-2147217912	Invalid binding info.
-2147217911	Permission denied.
-2147217910	Specified column does not contain bookmarks or chapters.
-2147217909	Some cost limits were rejected.
-2147217908	No command has been set for the command object.
-2147217907	Unable to find a query plan within the given cost limit.
-2147217906	Invalid bookmark.
-2147217905	Invalid lock mode.
-2147217904	No value given for one or more required parameters.
-2147217903	Invalid column ID.
-2147217902	Invalid ratio.
-2147217901	Invalid value.
-2147217900	The command contained one or more errors.
-2147217899	The executing command cannot be cancelled.
-2147217898	The provider does not support the specified dialect.
-2147217897	A data source with the specified name already exists.
-2147217896	The rowset was built over a live data feed and cannot be restarted.
-2147217895	No key matching the described characteristics could be found within the current range.
-2147217894	Ownership of this tree has been given to the provider.
-2147217893	The provider is unable to determine identity for newly inserted rows.
-2147217892	No non-zero weights specified for any goals supported, so goal was rejected; current goal was not changed.
-2147217891	Requested conversion is not supported.

Error Number	Description
-2147217890	lRowsOffset would position you past either end of the rowset, regardless of the cRows value specified; cRowsObtained is 0.
-2147217889	Information was requested for a query, and the query was not set.
-2147217888	Provider called a method from IrowsetNotify in the consumer and NT.
-2147217887	Errors occurred.
-2147217886	A non-NULL controlling IUnknown was specified and the object being created does not support aggregation.
-2147217885	A given HROW referred to a hard- or soft- deleted row.
-2147217884	The rowset does not support fetching backwards.
-2147217883	All HROWs must be released before new ones can be obtained.
-2147217882	One of the specified storage flags was not supported.
-2147217880	The specified status flag was neither DBCOLUMNSTATUS_OK nor DBCOLUMNSTATUS_ISNULL.
-2147217879	The rowset cannot scroll backwards.
-2147217878	Invalid region handle.
-2147217877	The specified set of rows was not contiguous to or overlapping the rows in the specified watch region.
-2147217876	A transition from ALL* to MOVE* or EXTEND* was specified.
-2147217875	The specified region is not a proper subregion of the region identified by the given watch region handle.
-2147217874	The provider does not support multi-statement commands.
-2147217873	A specified value violated the integrity constraints for a column or table.
-2147217872	The given type name was unrecognized.
-2147217871	Execution aborted because a resource limit has been reached; no results have been returned.
-2147217870	Cannot clone a command object whose command tree contains a rowset or rowsets.
-2147217869	Cannot represent the current tree as text.
-2147217868	The specified index already exists.
-2147217867	The specified index does not exist.
-2147217866	The specified index was in use.
-2147217865	The specified table does not exist.
-2147217864	The rowset was using optimistic concurrency and the value of a column has been changed since it was last read.

Error Number	Description
-2147217863	Errors were detected during the copy.
-2147217862	A specified precision was invalid.
-2147217861	A specified scale was invalid.
-2147217860	Invalid table ID.
-2147217859	A specified type was invalid.
-2147217858	A column ID occurred more than once in the specification.
-2147217857	The specified table already exists.
-2147217856	The specified table was in use.
-2147217855	The specified locale ID was not supported.
-2147217854	The specified record number is invalid.
-2147217853	Although the bookmark was validly formed, no row could be found to match it.
-2147217852	The value of a property was invalid.
-2147217851	The rowset was not chaptered.
-2147217850	Invalid accessor.
-2147217849	Invalid storage flags.
-2147217848	By-ref accessors are not supported by this provider.
-2147217847	Null accessors are not supported by this provider.
-2147217846	The command was not prepared.
-2147217845	The specified accessor was not a parameter accessor.
-2147217844	The given accessor was write-only.
-2147217843	Authentication failed.
-2147217842	The change was canceled during notification; no columns are changed.
-2147217841	The rowset was single-chaptered and the chapter was not released.
-2147217840	Invalid source handle.
-2147217839	The provider cannot derive parameter info and SetParameterInfo has not been called.
-2147217838	The data source object is already initialized.
-2147217837	The provider does not support this method.
-2147217836	The number of rows with pending changes has exceeded the set limit.
-2147217835	The specified column did not exist.
-2147217834	There are pending changes on a row with a reference count of zero.

Error Number	Description
-2147217833	A literal value in the command overflowed the range of the type of the associated column.
-2147217832	The supplied HRESULT was invalid.
-2147217831	The supplied LookupID was invalid.
-2147217830	The supplied DynamicErrorID was invalid.
-2147217829	Unable to get visible data for a newly inserted row that has not yet been updated.
-2147217828	Invalid conversion flag.
-2147217827	The given parameter name was unrecognized.
-2147217826	Multiple storage objects cannot be opened simultaneously.
265920	Fetching requested number of rows would have exceeded total number of active rows supported by the rowset.
265921	One or more column types are incompatible; conversion errors will occur during copying.
265922	Parameter type information has been overridden by caller.
265923	Skipped bookmark for deleted or non-member row.
265924	Errors found in validating tree.
265925	There are no more rowsets.
265926	Reached start or end of rowset or chapter.
265927	The provider re-executed the command.
265928	Variable data buffer full.
265929	There are no more results.
265930	Server cannot release or downgrade a lock until the end of the transaction.
265931	Specified weight was not supported or exceeded the supported limit and was set to 0 or the supported limit.
265933	Input dialect was ignored and text was returned in different dialect.
265934	Consumer is uninterested in receiving further notification calls for this phase.
265935	Consumer is uninterested in receiving further notification calls for this reason.
265937	In order to reposition to the start of the rowset, the provider had to re-execute the query; either the order of the columns changed or columns were added to or removed from the rowset.
265938	The method had some errors; errors have been returned in the error array.
265939	Invalid row handle.

Error Number	Description
265940	A given HROW referred to a hard-deleted row.
265941	The provider was unable to keep track of all the changes; the client must re-fetch the data associated with the watch region using another method.
265942	Execution stopped because a resource limit has been reached; results obtained so far have been returned but execution cannot be resumed.
265944	A lock was upgraded from the value specified.
265945	One or more properties were changed as allowed by provider.
265946	Errors occurred.
265947	A specified parameter was invalid.
265948	Updating this row caused more than one row to be updated in the data source.

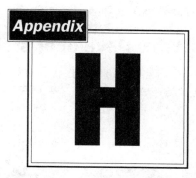

Support and Errata

One of the most irritating things about any programming book can be when you find that bit of code you've just spent an hour typing simply doesn't work. You check it a hundred times to see if you've set it up correctly and then you notice the spelling mistake in the variable name on the book page. Of course, you can blame the authors for not taking enough care and testing the code, the editors for not doing their job properly, or the proofreaders for not being eagle-eyed enough, but this doesn't get around the fact that mistakes do happen.

We try hard to ensure no mistakes sneak out into the real world, but we can't promise that this book is 100% error free. What we can do is offer the next best thing by providing you with immediate support and feedback from experts who have worked on the book and try to ensure that future editions eliminate these gremlins. The following section will take you step by step through the process of posting errata to our web site to get that help. The sections that follow, therefore, are:

- Wrox Developers Membership
- Finding a list of existing errata on the web site
- Adding your own errata to the existing list
- What happens to your errata once you've posted it (why doesn't it appear immediately?)

There is also a section covering how to e-mail a question for technical support. This comprises:

- What your e-mail should include
- What happens to your e-mail once it has been received by us

So that you only need view information relevant to yourself, we ask that you register as a Wrox Developer Member. This is a quick and easy process, that will save you time in the long-run. If you are already a member, just update membership to include this book.

Wrox Developer's Membership

To get your FREE Wrox Developer's Membership click on Membership in the navigation bar of our home site

www.wrox.com.

This is shown in the following screen shot:

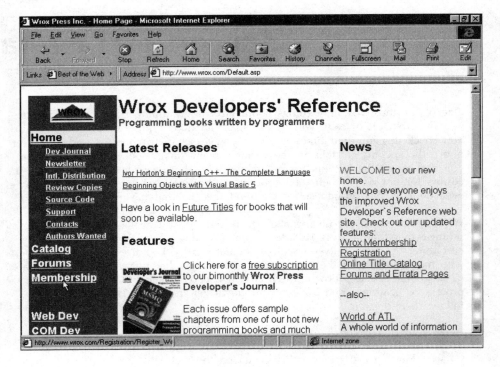

Then, on the next screen (not shown), click on **New User**. This will display a form. Fill in the details on the form and submit the details using the submit button at the bottom. Before you can say 'The best read books come in Wrox Red' you will get the following screen:

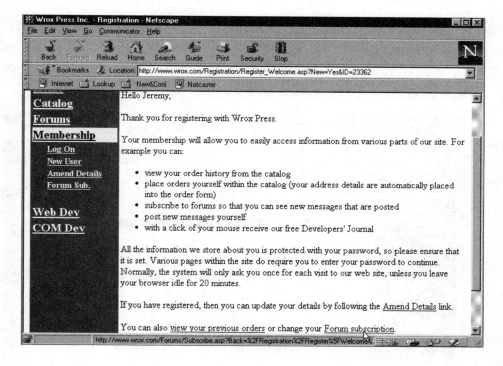

Finding Errata on the Web Site

Before you send in a query, you might be able to save time by finding the answer to your problem on our web site: `http:\\www.wrox.com`.

Each book we publish has its own page and its own errata sheet. You can get to any book's page by clicking on **support** from the left hand side navigation bar.

From this page you can locate any book's errata page on our site. Select your book from the pop-up menu and click on it.

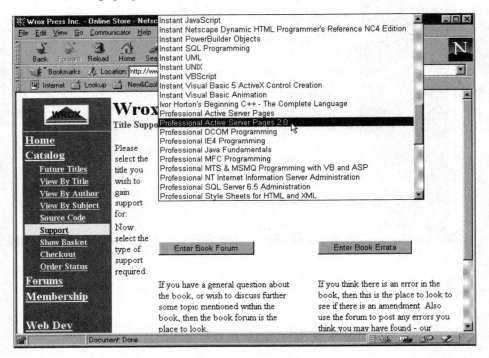

Then click on **Enter Book Errata**. This will take you to the errata page for the book. Select the criteria by which you want to view the errata, and click the apply criteria button. This will provide you with links to specific errata. For an initial search, you are advised to view the errata by page numbers. If you have looked for an error previously, then you may wish to limit your search using dates. We update these pages daily to ensure that you have the latest information on bugs and errors.

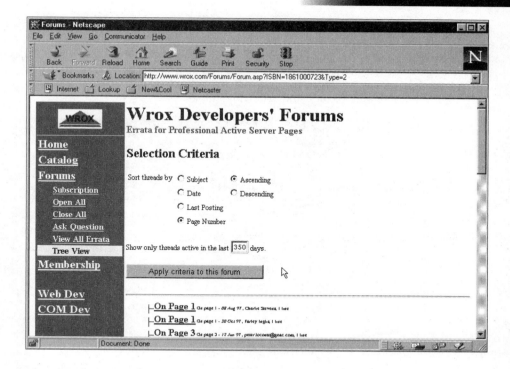

Adding Errata to the Sheet Yourself

It's always possible that you may find your error is not listed, in which case you can enter details of the fault yourself. It might be anything from a spelling mistake to a faulty piece of code in the book. Sometimes you'll find useful hints that aren't really errors on the listing. By entering errata you may save another reader hours of frustration, and of course, you will be helping us provide even higher quality information. We're very grateful for this sort of advice and feedback. You can enter errata using the 'ask a question' of our editors link at the bottom of the errata page. Click on this link and you will get a form on which to post your message.

Fill in the subject box, and then type your message in the space provided on the form. Once you have done this, click on the Post Now button at the bottom of the page. The message will be forwarded to our editors. They'll then test your submission and check that the error exists, and that the suggestions you make are valid. Then your submission, together with a solution, is posted on the site for public consumption. Obviously this stage of the process can take a day or two, but we will endeavor to get a fix up sooner than that.

E-mail Support

If you wish to directly query a problem in the book with an expert who knows the book in detail then e-mail **support@wrox.com**, with the title of the book and the last four numbers of the ISBN in the subject field of the e-mail. A typical e-mail should include the following things:

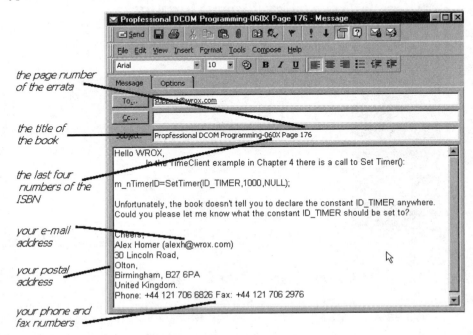

the page number of the errata

the title of the book

the last four numbers of the ISBN

your e-mail address

your postal address

your phone and fax numbers

We won't send you junk mail. We need the details to save your time and ours. If we need to replace a disk or CD we'll be able to get it to you straight away. When you send an e-mail it will go through the following chain of support.

Customer Support

Your message is delivered to one of our customer support staff who are the first people to read it. They have files on most frequently asked questions and will answer anything general immediately. They answer general questions about the book and the web site.

Editorial

Deeper queries are forwarded to the technical editor responsible for that book. They have experience with the programming language or particular product and are able to answer detailed technical questions on the subject. Once an issue has been resolved, the editor can post the errata to the web site.

The Authors

Finally, in the unlikely event that the editor can't answer your problem, s/he will forward the request to the author. We try to protect the author from any distractions from writing. However, we are quite happy to forward specific requests to them. All Wrox authors help with the support on their books. They'll mail the customer and the editor with their response, and again all readers should benefit.

What we can't answer

Obviously with an ever growing range of books and an ever-changing technology base, there is an increasing volume of data requiring support. While we endeavor to answer all questions about the book, we can't answer bugs in your own programs that you've adapted from our code. So, while you might have loved the help desk systems in our Active Server Pages book, don't expect too much sympathy if you cripple your company with a live adaptation you customized from Chapter 12. But do tell us if you're especially pleased with the routine you developed with our help.

How to tell us exactly what you think.

We understand that errors can destroy the enjoyment of a book and can cause many wasted and frustrated hours, so we seek to minimize the distress that they can cause.

You might just wish to tell us how much you liked or loathed the book in question. Or you might have ideas about how this whole process could be improved. In which case you should e-mail `feedback@wrox.com`. You'll always find a sympathetic ear, no matter what the problem is. Above all you should remember that we do care about what you have to say and we will do our utmost to act upon it.

ADO 2.0

Index

Symbols

B

M

N

O